'A journey to the end of the night for 20/21st century Germany. Meyer reworks Döblin and Céline into a modern epic prose film with endless tracking shots of the gash of urban life, bought flesh and the financial transaction (the business of sex); memory as unspooling corrupted tape; journeys as migrations, as random as history and its splittings. A shimmering cast threatens to fly from the page, leaving only a revenant's dream – sky, weather, lights-on-nobody-home, buried bodies, night rain. What new prose should be and rarely is; Meyer rewrites the rules to produce a great hallucinatory channel-surfer of a novel.'
— Chris Petit, author of *Robinson*

'This is a wonderfully insightful, frank, exciting and heart-breaking read. *Bricks and Mortar* is like diving into a Force 10 gale of reality, full of strange voices, terrible events and a vision of neoliberal capitalism that is chillingly accurate.'
— A. L. Kennedy, author of *Serious Sweet*

'The point of *Bricks and Mortar* is that nothing's "in stone": Clemens Meyer's novel reads like a shifty, corrupted collocation of .docs, lifted off the laptop of a master genre-ist and self-reviser. It's required reading for fans of the Great Wolfgangs (Hilbig and Koeppen), and anyone interested in casual gunplay, drug use, or sex.'
— Joshua Cohen, author of *Book of Numbers*

Praise for *All the Lights*

'His is a voice that demans attention, unafraid to do different, sometimes seemingly wrong-headed, things, confident in its ability to move, confront and engage his readers.'
— Stuart Evers, author of *Your Father Sends His Love*

Fitzcarraldo Editions

BRICKS AND MORTAR

CLEMENS MEYER

Translated by

KATY DERBYSHIRE

CONTENTS

EINS, ZWEI, DREI

I. (GIRL GIRL GIRL / WAITING FOR A STAR TO FALL)

When the evening comes I stand by the window. I push the slats of the blind apart with my fingers and look at the evening sky behind the buildings on the other side of the road. It's still getting dark early. The year's not even a month old and already it feels long and hard. Mind you, there's not much work at the moment. We all complain in January. I just want to catch one last sight of the sun and the last ray of light. I leave for work at eight in the morning; it's still not really light then. Everything's better in the summer. I bet everyone says that but on the other hand, in summer I think of holidays and I often don't feel like working. And I think things go best in the winter, if you leave January out of it. Mind you, lots of us probably see that differently. It's a shame the flat doesn't have a balcony. I could sit out there in the summer and sunbathe, better than the stupid tanning salon, and in winter I could stand out there before sunset and have a smoke and watch the sky, watch it turning red. I like to look at the moon on clear nights. It always reminds me of that song. My mother used to sing it to me before I went to sleep. 'The Moon Has Arisen'. When I hear it now, and that doesn't happen often, I don't know when I hear it at all, so... I can't really describe it. Sometimes I sing it in my head. Magda always used to say: 'I'm getting feelings,' when she meant she was feeling sad. But it's rubbish actually, that thing about the seasons. Summer or winter, autumn or spring, the phone always rings. Just not that much in January. When I was a child I used to think, when I was very little though, that there was a fifth season. And once I asked my mother if the

11

year starts on the first of January every year and if New Year's Eve is always one day before that. And if it ever snows in June. She laughed and hugged me – that's why I haven't forgotten it. Just like the song. I've often thought about the white mist in the song, before I go to sleep. When I have a child one day I'll sing them a different song. One that's not so sad. I'm more of a cheerful person. 'Alert and lively,' they wrote in my school report. They always had these assessments by the teachers. And Magda always used to say: 'Don't get so hyper, girl, you're as fluttery as a bird.' She'd say so many funny things, and sometimes they were fitting and sometimes they weren't at all, and I miss that. She's in Hannover now. She sends me cards sometimes and she always remembers my birthday. She always used to say letters and cards are more personal than text messages. She sends me these really cheesy postcards, puppies, giant hearts, roses with glitter on, and sometimes cards with music. I still write her emails and texts though. My mother's the only one I send postcards to. The last one on New Year's Eve. That was for Christmas too. We don't see much of each other any more but my New Year's resolution is to go and visit her more often. Because she doesn't like coming here to me, to the city.

The winter's cold this year, colder than it's been for ages. And I could hardly get to work in December, I had to leave the car at home. The whole city was buried in snow and the snowploughs could hardly keep up. I dread to think of my gas bill because I usually leave the heating on all day at home so it's nice and warm when I get back from work. I often slept here in December, and I even stay the odd night now. Because I don't want to go out in the snow. I used to go sledging every day when it snowed, when I was little. And sometimes my mother put me on the sledge and pulled me along when we went shopping. That was back in Jena. We have big hills there for sledging and skiing. I've never been into skiing though. I was really crap at it. My friends used to laugh at me, all the girls, and the boys even more. But I was good at sledging. I used to go hurtling down the steepest slopes, and even the boys had respect. It's actually a good thing that the winters are getting so cold again. It's the climate. But it could all be different next year. When I have a child I want to put it on a sledge and pull it along when we go shopping. I don't really mind if it's a boy or a girl. Mind you, maybe I'd like a girl better. I think you'll be able to choose, in the future. Decide for yourself if you have a boy or a girl. Maybe there'll be a pill you can take. But that's probably a long way off. Mind you, some things suddenly go really quickly, what with technology and progress. And it's rubbish, actually. It'd probably all turn out the same, compared to now. I know I wanted to have a boy, before I left Jena. That was back with Bert. I can't understand why I left him now. I thought, I have to get out of here, God knows why they call the place Jena Paradise, but he wanted to stay there, he had it all planned out. Because his father had this chemist's and he studied pharmacy especially. There's a lot of money in pharmacies. People are always getting sick. At every time of year. Especially now. And when they've invented those boy-or-girl pills they'll make even more money. They can even cure AIDS now, pretty much. I still don't like to think about it though. I've never met anyone with AIDS. People talk a lot of crap about it sometimes. We all go for our check-ups regularly. Even though we don't have to any more, not by law. It used to be different. But people think and talk a whole load of crap when it comes to that and when it comes to us. And I stand by the window and push the slats of the blind apart with my fingers and look out at the buildings on the other side of the road, with the sky turning red behind them now and the night coming up. Four thirty and the phone's only rung four times, and the door only twice. For me, I mean.

Because Jenny's been here since twelve and she stays till twelve. Twelve hours, that'd be too much for me. Ten hours is the longest I do. After that things start getting too hard on me. That makes me laugh, it could be one of Magda's. Although it's a bit of a stupid joke, not funny at all when I think about it. But now I'm getting feelings, thinking about her. Yeah, yeah, getting too hard on me. Don't go getting sentimental now. Because we were pretty close really, and everything came easier, work and everything. It's OK with Jenny. She only comes four times a week but she works Saturdays and Sundays and that's when I'm off. My weekend's really sacred to me. Like my arse. (That again!) Now I can light one up at last. I make sure I don't smoke too much, you know. One cigarette an hour. Or I try, at least. The most I get through is fifteen a day, and that's alright, I reckon. Jenny smokes like a chimney and she's constantly spraying her air freshener around. Spring Lavender fragrance. I can't stand it. We don't do a lot of talking. Sometimes we sit together in the lounge when we're waiting. I'd say we get along as colleagues. She's a totally different type to me. Three stone more than me, I bet, heading for motherly territory, but there's enough men into that, believe it or not. And I wouldn't say she isn't pretty. No, Jenny's pretty alright. In the face, and I don't mean that in a bad way. She's just womanly, and I mean that as a compliment. And we get on well enough, each to his own, that's what I say. Clients only have a good time if they feel like

14

a guest. I haven't seen Magda for a long time, and I often wonder how things are going for her in Hannover. It's calm there, the Godfather and the Angels have everything under control. And the girls have plenty of trade, I've heard. You hear all sorts of things, since the Angels have been here too. I don't have anything to do with them though. I just hear a lot of things. I've been with the boss's firm for eight years now. I always say 'boss' and 'firm'. Or sometimes I say 'the Old Man', because that's what some people call him. Out of respect. I think he gets on fine with them, with the Angels, I mean, because the guy who's top Angel here used to be a friend of his, they say, or at least they used to get on OK, divided the city up between them, but I don't know exactly. There's girls who know a hundred per cent what's up, who get all the gossip, although it's usually less then fifty, per cent I mean, of the truth, but when I get home from work and sit by the radiator I don't want to hear any more about all that shit.

I read somewhere the other day that the lawyer of the Godfather from Hannover city –apparently he's the big boss of all the Angels – that he's also Schröder's lawyer, the ex-chancellor. I'd like a lawyer like that myself. And what does it matter if he works for the Angels? Everybody's just doing business. Or they all want to, at least. Russian deals, Gazprom, girls and stocks and shares. The big money. Now I'm thinking too much about it again, but that's the way it is at work, when I'm waiting. And watching the day disappear. And the lights of the cars and the street lamps between the slats of the blind. Chasing across the walls, together with the shadows. It makes me go all funny, I get feelings and I zip my Adidas jacket up to my neck. I'm really fond of this jacket. I've had it for years now, I bought it back in Berlin.

It's got red stripes on the sleeves and you don't get them very often. I voted for Schröder in '98. That was my first election. That was back in Jena too. I need to put some moisturiser on my legs. The air's too dry. The radiator's turned up to five. And minus ten outside. At least. I'm getting dandruff again as well. Haven't had it for ages. But I use this natural shampoo, with nettles, that gets rid of it. It's better for my hair. All the chemical stuff is too aggressive for me. I tried it for a while, Head 'n' Shoulders and all that, but that made it even worse. That stuff stings my pussy like fire. Not that I rubbed Head 'n' Shoulders in down there, I don't have dandruff there, mind you, there's girls who have permanent dry skin down there, but it gets everywhere when you rinse it off in the shower. Showering and dry skin is a problem any-way, because you take so many showers. And with your pussy, because you're always shaving. But that's just part of the job. I got the natural shampoo from Jenny. She has these creams as well that she recommended for dry skin. There's this natural store at the station, I go there a lot now. It's really better for me, although I wouldn't buy perfume and deodorant there, mind you. I keep on going to the Douglas store for that. Even though they use embryos. *Come in and find out.* Pretty stupid slogan.

I need another cigarette now. Number eight today, I've been counting. I'm really trying to cut down. But I can't manage to stop altogether. All the girls I know from work smoke. Well, ninety. Per cent, I mean. Sometimes I think about why that is. When I'm waiting, when I'm standing by the window, even when I'm *right in the middle of it.* 'Girl, you're a fucking liar and a lying fucker,' Magda would say now, not that funny really either but we still laugh at that kind of crap, but really, what can you do when the stupid thoughts go dancing round your head like it's Mardi Gras up there. We don't really have a proper carnival here, not like other places, although a few idiots hold their little parades. But it's better and cheaper than coke or speed or that fibreglass mix. Crystal. Crystal meth. Smoking, I mean. Cheaper. But it's no good anyway, because it eats you up in the long run. Coke, I mean. C, and whatever. I tried it all, back in Berlin. Pretty dumb. Come in and find out. It wasn't all bad though. I can't be doing with all that victim crap. Because it was a great time, a wild time. Oh, the poor girl! That all fits in with their image. Their tabloid image. What I always say is: Oh, the poor guys. I do understand it, though, to be honest. That they come to me. And it's fine that way. And now it's Mardi Gras in my head again. Real carnival parades. Because I've been waiting for two hours and keep staring at the telephone, when I'm not standing by the window that is. It's pitch black outside now. Magda and I, we only used to have one phone. It worked fine. We were more than colleagues. Now I sometimes hear Jenny's mobile in the other room. She can tell it's January too, I think. Everyone can tell the difference. Not just us girls. My favourite taxi driver always says, actually he's only said it two or three times: 'January's hibernation time. Taxis, DAX, nocturnal services.' 'Nocturnal services' means me. Even though most of my work is during the day. He doesn't mean it in a bad way. Because no one has any money in the New Year, he says. He's a lovely guy. Used to work at a big printing press here in the city before the Wall, before '89. Talks about it a lot. In his mid-fifties. Married for almost thirty years. And two children. Always talks a lot. That's fine. I like listening. Although I'm not so sure about the DAX. I've never been into it and I never will. I know a few girls who swore by it. Three or four girls,

17

they bought and sold and gambled on stocks and shares like there was no tomorrow. A right little share club. But that was an exception. I wasn't in on it because I always say, after work I don't want to hear anything more about work. Mind you, it's not that easy, of course. It was different with Magda but I'm trying to give it up, all this talking about her and thinking about her. Because it is how it is now, and that's fine, because, and this is what my mother used to say when things weren't going well and she was sad about something: 'Things are just the way things are now, aren't they.'

But they're really pissed off now, I think, those girls I know who put their money on the DAX. How much, I don't know. There's no insurance that pays anything back. I don't know anything about it anyway. I play the lottery. As dumb as that sounds. Not long ago this guy I know won over thirty thousand. He's just a friend of a friend of a friend. Or maybe a friend of a friend. But he's not a guest. Through Mandy – she works at Hans's place. And she knows the guy who won all the money. Used an abbreviated combination. Five numbers. I saw him one time at Hans's dive of a place. Mind you, 'dive' is unfair. It's a nice clean place he's got there. Small but perfectly formed. Really clean. All the fixtures and fittings, I mean. Not exactly the dog's bollocks (Magda!), but I've only ever heard good things about it. Percentage-wise. Even though I say I want to be left in peace after work it always still comes to me. The gossip, I mean. Because of course I can't just say: *I'm off then*. I read that guy Kerkeling's book where he goes on a pilgrimage. Pretty funny. But I couldn't be dealing with all that walking. Santiago de Compostela. Finding yourself or God or the world or whatever it was he found. Sounds like compost. And of course I can say that. That I'm off.

Just like anyone, any tenant can hand in the notice on their flat. The phone rings in the other room. It's quiet in here and I turn on the radio.

I'm going to call my daughter Sabine. It's totally crazy, but I'd like to be called Sabine too. Because I really like the name. Strange working thoughts. Mardi Gras again. And I only mean my work name, my stage name. If I hadn't called myself Babsi, stage name I mean, I'd be Sabine now... Because I used to work with a Sabine and we got on quite well, not all that long ago. Not as well as me and Magda back in the day – she was almost like a sister to me, was Magda. The one I think of so often. The one I started off with. Snow White and Rose Red. She didn't used to shave her pussy, Sabine I mean, she didn't even have a landing strip. I've got a lot of respect for that. Honest to God, I like it. Why don't any of the guests like it any more? Eighties style. But smooth and blank puts money in the bank. She was doing well though, put it in her ads especially. If everyone's suddenly shaved then you can make good money out of short black pubes. She had long black hair, on her head of course, and now she's doing art, under her real name, hasn't been part of the firm for almost two years now. Photos and media stuff. And drawing as well. A lot of people here in the city do art. Artists, you know. People who are good at it. Or studied it. When I think that I used to be a student. Technical college. The Old Man collects pictures, I heard. But only big ones, the kind that cost a lot and make money. My feet are sticking to the floor. I should have wiped up that Coke earlier on. My second guest knocked over the bottle on the coffee table. I lie down on the bed. Still smells of work, even though I put a new cover on it earlier. The first guy was crap, the second one was OK. If I don't shave my pubes they come out blonde. I'm a natural blonde. I've always wanted dark hair, that's why I dye it sometimes. Is it OK to dye down there? Then maybe I would leave a landing strip. Mind you, they say it's not healthy, dyeing, maybe that's what's behind my dandruff that's come back, if I don't use that nettle stuff every day. I turn on the TV, still on mute. I turned it down earlier when my second guest came. The radio's on really quietly in the background. Sometimes when someone young comes along, some guy who's not bad looking either, I wonder – actually I only used to wonder right at the beginning – if he has a girlfriend and just needs a bit of a change, or if she's not good enough at blow jobs or never gives him one at all or whatever, or if it's because he really can't get himself a fuck. There's plenty of shy guys out there. But actually I don't give a shit. It's fifty-fifty with me, I mean between arseholes and bigmouths and the shy ones. But I can't say exactly, because the shy ones are sometimes just as crap, even though I do prefer the quiet ones – let Mummy deal with it. Then I can do the conducting myself and they don't ram me to a pulp. But fifty-fifty's not right anyway because there are all sorts of other kinds and that messes up the percentages. Sometimes I think about writing a list, a kind of types table.

Six o'clock, the news. The first guest was crap. The second one was OK. That's how you have to look at it, otherwise you go crazy. Or I do, anyway. The best hits of the eighties. I like eighties music. I was born in '79 and my music's more from the nineties, techno, Scooter, Hyper-Hyper, me and my mother went to Berlin in '95 for the Rolling Stones, Voodoo Lounge tour, no one from my techno gang was allowed to know, but my first school disco was in '88, just before the Wall fell. They played all the hits there. You know, that Opus song 'Live is life'. Falco, 'Rock me Amadeus'. Who was that other one, was it Trio or Peter Schilling? Da Da Da.

The phone rings. I don't love you you don't love me. Yeees? Hm. Yees. Of course. Right away. Rotkäppchenweg 12. Bose. Yes, like the hi-fi company. Hmmm. Yes. Can't wait. See you in a mo. Da Da Da.

It's five fifty-five. The city and the world. Get the news five minutes earlier. I must have drifted off for a bit. I'm always tired at the moment. Must be the weather. It's always the weather. Like so many things. The minute I close my eyes I start dreaming. Rotkäppchenweg: Red Riding Hood Way. There is such a road here, down in the south of the city, there's a whole corner made up of fairy tales, where the roads are named after them. The Brothers Grimm. My mother used to read me them sometimes. Not often. But I do remember a couple of them. I don't mean the usual ones that everyone knows. The ones the roads in the south of the city are named after. Sleeping Beauty Road. Frog Prince Way. Snow White Crescent. Cinderella Road. Snow White and Rose Red. I know that from Sabine, she used to live there, grew up round there, she told me. And went to school there too, in the Eastern Zone days – she's two or three years older than me. But the school wasn't called 'Rumpelstiltskin Secondary' or anything like that. I remember those fairy tales really well, like the song 'The Moon Has Arisen', and it really is up high above the houses over there, small in the cold clear night, and I go over to the coffee table and sit on one of the two seats because I don't feel like sitting on the bed right now. The blind's still moving and making noises against the window. 'Iron Hans' was one of the fairy tales. And there was 'Mother Trudy'. And 'The Fisherman and His Wife', I remember that one too. 'Manntje, Manntje, Timpe Te / Flounder, flounder, in

21

the sea / My wife, my wife Ilsebill / Wants not, wants not, what I will.' Or something like that. Grandma and Grandpa came from the coast. Bad Doberan. And my mother speaks the local dialect from up there when she wants. We often used to visit when I was little. What does *manntje* mean, Grandma? And what's a *timpe*? Grandma and Grandpa gave me the book of fairy tales when I turned eight. It was green and it had strange pictures in it, sometimes they scared me. I don't know where it is now. Mum still lives in the same flat in Jena and my old room's still the same. It's probably on the shelves there somewhere. I keep meaning to go and visit more often. The first guy spent a lot of money today and I'm glad of it. Good money for January, anyway. And he wasn't such an idiot really, could have done with cutting his fingernails, that's all, and cleaning them in the first place. If you ask me there's nothing worse than men with real dirt under their nails. Sure I say, 'Go and give your hands a bit of a wash,' but I can hardly hand him a trowel. There's worse, of course. Cheese, for example. Beauty's only foreskin-deep, Magda used to say. Sabine was a strange one, she never complained. I really did like her a lot but she was definitely a strange one.

I have a kind of scale, dirty nails and bad breath right at the top, but there's no difference in the end. Not much. And there's another scale just for breath. And then when they pant at you, you have to turn away carefully, your head I mean, so it doesn't look rude. I always have a bottle of mouthwash in the bathroom but it's unusual for anyone to use it, actually they never do. Or it's unusual, anyway. Of course if they want to stay for an hour, and even if they don't, I say they're welcome to take a shower beforehand. Or in fact I tell them to. And I say it in a charming way so that they actually do. Pop in the shower

22

and freshen up for me, honey, so I can lick you all over. Not all the girls are as tactful as me, I know that for a fact. Maybe they are at the moment, because of January. The Great Depression. But with me the January rules apply all year round. That's a bit bitchy, though, 'Anything they can do, I can do better,' and all that. I know that. Every girl has her own way of working. I'm the best, I'm the hottest, well, me too, I'll look you in the eye... but make sure you take a shower beforehand. Most girls know exactly how to do it. Because satisfied customers come back. It's as easy as that sometimes. Or as difficult. Depends how you look at it. That's something my friend Sabine said, I can't remember her proper name right now, even though we all use our real names with each other, Jenny's really called Jenny, she only calls herself Lola in her ad. It's stupid if you ask me because no one's going to believe it, but she says she's a big fan of Franka Potente, the actress. Takes all sorts. *Run Jenny Run*. Katrin, that's her name, Sabine's I mean. I keep meaning to find that art magazine, I must have it here somewhere, that's got something about her in it. Sabine is much nicer than Katrin, the name I mean because they're both the same person, and she told me one time she wanted to get her name changed, make an application for a new ID card, a stage name if you like, that was before she went into photos and videos and drawing, but even back then she always used to say, 'Profession: love artist.' I liked that. I'm much more pragmatic about it, like most of us girls. But making money's an art too. ('*Pragmatic*? *Quasi* if you like? Should have finished that degree, girl!' Magda in conversation with me, Lilli, February 2003.) It did get on my nerves a bit, that she always acted like she was way older than me, Magda I mean, big, big sister, even though she was only three and a half years ahead of me, although we were almost the same age in our ad back then. *Hello? Hello? Germany's biggest DIY store!* I hate that stupid ad. I wouldn't be caught dead in that DIY store. It was Sabine, I got muddled up there, she was actually one or two years younger than me, almost the same age I mean.

And when Mum used to read to me, it was pretty often actually, she only ever read the fairy tales no one knew. Or the fisherman and his wife. She enjoyed that, reading in her old dialect, even though I didn't understand most of it, but it sounded really lovely. This really strange melody. And Mum's voice was different then. Like she was a child again herself. I think Grandma used to read to her a lot, up in Bad Doberan. Molly goes chugging almost right past the house where my grandparents live, where Mum grew up. Molly's a little steam train, narrow-gauge railway, goes to the coast, all the way to the sea. I'd hide under the covers when she read 'Mother Trudy'. And then Molly would come rattling past Grandma and Grandpa's house with a big loud whistle, we usually went up there for Christmas, and sometimes we'd all go on a ride on Molly through the snow-covered fields, all the way up to the sea. And then I had that lovely green book in Jena and Mum used to read out of it, it wasn't very often, I remember 'Mother Trudy' very well, and I'd always hear the screams of that little steam engine. And I'd be lying under the big cover in the cold room in Bad Doberan, Mum always slept next to me but she'd stay up for a long time with Grandma and Grandpa before she came in. The last trains passed some time after eight but I was only eight myself and even younger, and then there was always that *choohooo choohooo*, I remember slipping under the cover in the dark in the big cold bed, and once I cried so loud that they all came running in the room. Mum, Grandma, Grandpa. *Eins, zwei, drei.*

Once I told the boss for a joke that he should open up a *franchise* (Magda: 'Hello! *Hello?*') down in that fairy tale corner. Because it was bound to be a hit. If he had apartments there. Red Riding Hood Way. Frog Prince Way. And the girls out of the Arabian Nights. He just laughed. He's like Rumpelstiltskin, in a way. But he's OK really. Otherwise I wouldn't have been working here for eight years. Although I do sometimes think about moving to Hannover. Lower Saxon City is on the up, since the Angels and the Godfather have had everything under control there. That's what I've heard.

She really was a bit of a women's libber, Sabine the artist, whatever that means. Nothing, really. And it doesn't go with the job that well. Depends how you look at it though, because actually it does, of course. Because we do raise the proportion of women in power and we do give the men a good fleecing. Well, a bit of both. I'm a bit confused now.

Sabine Sabine. Like the song. Like back at the school disco. Da Da Da. When I think of how us kids, us girls and boys, how we darted around the dance floor Sabine used to say you shouldn't say 'man' so often, as in 'mankind'. At work and after work. Because we had enough to do with men in the first place. True enough. But 'womankind'? Or 'humankind'? Sounds stupid. Totally eighties. Purple dungarees. It's nonsense really. She really was strange, Sabine was. Words don't change the facts. And the facts aren't that bad, if you ask me. And if she hadn't earned so much money she wouldn't be able to do her art now, because she saved up a pretty penny. I think so, anyway. But she never minced words, she was always on the ball, always aggressive and never lost for words and at the same time she had this dark silence in her eyes, it's hard to explain right now, but I think the guests used to like that about her. And her little bush. The last tango But sometimes I think she planned it all exactly, when she went and showed photos and pictures from work, guests, other girls, looking out of the window, drawings between two guests, what she scribbled down when one had left and before the next one came. Caused a big fuss. From the girls, from the guests, from the Old Man. Got everyone wound up. But I thought it was good.

And just before I nod off, because the flicker of the TV pictures makes me tired and the eighties aren't that great right now on the radio, the phone rings.

Yeees? I've never understood why Mum used to read me things like 'Mother Trudy' when she did read to me now and then. If it was my daughter it would be more like 'The Frog Prince' or 'The Hare and the Wolf', no, that's that Russian cartoon *Nu pogodi!* Wait until I get my hands on you! I'm still grateful for that moon song to this day. Yes, Babsi. Hmmm. Yes. Of course. Hotel? That's more expensive though... And where is it? Yes. Yes, of course. Just give me your room number and I'll call you straight back. Yees. Hold on a sec... Yes, now. Two four six. Thirty seconds. Be right back.

Just turned the radio down quickly. Best hits of the eighties. I love George Michael. And there was something on TV about Sexy Cora. Silence. And the telephone rings. And it rings in Jenny's room too. The doorbell rang earlier as well and I popped out into the hallway, and Jenny had already arranged her tits and was standing by the intercom and nodded at me and said 'Yes, come on up, I'm waiting for you,' because regulars often just come by without calling beforehand and it

26

could just as well be for me, but she says 'Holger' and grins and opens the door, and I hear him panting up the stairs, even though he's in his prime. But they all say that when they're just over fifty. He's been to me before as well but Jenny's more his type, I have to admit. So it's back into my room, Jenny's got it under control.

And I stand by the window and I don't know if it's good the way it is right now. House and hotel visits are on my set card, internet and newspaper ads, H & H, but I don't like leaving the nest. Especially not in January. Minus ten. And I've got him on the line. Sounds friendly, at least. I only ever do it with a number I can call back. Otherwise you're asking for trouble. Like with those pizza deliveries no one ever ordered. But I know the hotel numbers, I've done the odd visit there over the past few years. I wonder what he's doing in town, there's no trade fair on right now. Down on the icy street some idiot loses control of his car and slides almost like in slow motion and ends up facing the parked cars and touches them silently as they block his path. I have another look while I'm getting dressed, and there they are standing on the pavement and gesticulating. How fast the owner of that parked car found his way out into the cold. My car, my house, my rage. Maybe he was standing by the window like me. Like me.

And I get dressed, choose my clothes. Tight jeans, black top, the glittery jacket over that and then my coat. And then I have to get undressed again because I have to change my little sponge, it's always a big fuss, a special sponge that goes right up, pretty far inside, because of my period, started today, great timing, girls use them in pornos as well, they work fine just as long as no one comes along with a 12-inch ruler. And then the phone rings. But not in my room, at the firm, and Gerd picks

27

up, the baby face, used to be Alex, the baby face who's with the Angels now, and I tell him where I have to go and I say I'll call once I get back, and yes, I'll text him when I get there and everything's OK. I don't like going out to work. Don't like leaving the nest. Doesn't matter if it's winter or summer. I always try to persuade the house visits to come here instead. I mean, why do I pay rent every day if I'm going to be wandering around outside. OK, it's all money and they're all clients who call again if they're satisfied. If they like me. And they like what I offer them. I look at myself in the mirror, standing in the bathroom listening to Holger fucking Jenny. Or Jenny fucking Holger. I've had a few good times in hotels. When the guys splashed out on champers, wanted to spend half the night with me for loads of money. I'm almost an escort, times like that. There was always plenty of work when the car show was on. It was rush hour all week long. Sometimes I even worked on the weekend. There wasn't so much going on last year or the year before; I read in the paper they hold their sex parties elsewhere now. *Sex in the city, sex on the beach.* Portugal, South America, Budapest. It's all true what they say in the papers, they had no inhibitions, there were some real dirty bastards, but if you were lucky you'd end up in some little guy's room, this one guy was kind of cute, 2007, I remember him well, which is surprising after all the years and all the guests, before and after, but actually it makes no difference if it's a salesman or the boss, as long as they're paying they think they're getting the dirty bastard service. The polite ones, the nice ones are a rare commodity on the big cold market. That makes me laugh and I look at myself in the mirror, look at my white teeth and I'm *ready to go-ho.* Just got them bleached the other week.

2 8

And the telephone rings but I'm on my way to the night shift. Just before seven. The city and the world. The taxi's waiting downstairs. My favourite driver. The engine running. Police on the other side of the road. They send out a whole task force just for a couple of scratches in Germany. I went to Belgrade one time and no one there cares if you get a few dents. He opens the door for me, a real gentleman, runs all the way around the car for me, takes half a bow and moves his hand in mid-air in a broad sweep, 'Your car, madame,' and closes the door carefully once I'm on the back seat. He's always making jokes like that and I feel good when he drives me.

'I was pleased as punch when your number came up on my screen. Haven't seen you for ages. How's the big life?'

'Feels small,' I say. And he doesn't say anything because he notices I need a couple of seconds' peace. Notices I'm switching into Audrey Hepburn mode, or Sharon Stone if you like, but I prefer dark hair to my natural blonde, that's why I dye it sometimes, and Sharon Stone is too cool for me right now in winter. Julia Roberts. Let the comedy begin. And I close my eyes. I see and I feel the light flowing. 'Turn the radio on, please.'

'Will do.'

There's some techno track on, hard bass but not too fast, and he looks for a new station until I say, 'Do me a favour and turn it off again, will you?'

'Anything for you.'

And we drive slowly through the big white city. The main roads are cleared of snow, the digital thermometer says minus twelve. Hardly any traffic, and there are only a few people out on the pavements as well.

Seven ten. When can you get here? Seven thirty. Good. I'm only working till ten though. Three hours? Yes. Ten thirty. Sure. Room 405? No? Sorry, say it again. Yes. See you soon.

She sees the hotel from a long way off. One of the tallest buildings in the city. A grey and white monolith. A couple of bare trees around it. Steam rising from the gratings and manhole covers. Planes flashing in the sky and tracing lines through the frost. Windows bright, windows dark. At Christmas they try to occupy the rooms so that the shape of a Christmas tree appears on the main façade. There's still a fragment of it visible. Sleighs on the drive. The horses' breath steams and climbs the façade. A bearded man in a fur coat is standing outside the large revolving door, slowly beating a brightly coloured drum hung on a strap around his neck. Boom. Boom. Boom.

We're making slow progress. Ahead of us, one of those huge snow-clearers. Next to us on the pavement, steam comes out of a grille directly by the kerbstone. Another red light. My favourite driver swears quietly at the traffic lights. I can still see his eyes in the rear-view mirror. I don't feel like comedy today. I've done it like that sometimes, witty remarks, fast pace, like Julia Roberts in *Pretty Woman*. My favourite driver plays along and we squabble back and forth, punch-lines flying. I say 'How do you do?' as I pass the reception desk and toss the boys a wink... Must be the weather. Like every woman in every job, I have the odd bad day. As I said. Three hours. It's going to be a long time. But it's four hundred and fifty euros. I charge a hundred and fifty an hour for hotel visits. There's other people dream of hourly rates like that. When I think of what my favourite driver earns. I mean, it's probably not bad, there's people doing a lot worse nowadays. Long-term unemployed and that. And that's why I didn't vote for Schröder in 2005. If he's only half as OK as number two this afternoon, what time was it then anyway? With number one I really wanted to go back to blow jobs with a condom, like we did until three years ago, but you can't get away with that nowadays, not since the other girls have started offering it more and more, *bareback*, but only BJ, not FS, and the guests all started insisting on it, but condoms do taste like shit and as long as they give it a wash beforehand... So that's why I send them all for a shower, and if I had my way I'd check whether they push their foreskin back properly, they ought to make circumcision compulsory, we hardly have any Jews here, at any rate I always have a whole batch of Listerine and all that ready and waiting. Of course I still often do blow jobs with a condom. Usually I just tongue it a bit and a lot of them get off really quickly anyway, and then I put it on and make them come or I wait until they've calmed down a bit if they want to put it inside me. But I have had BBBJ in my ad for four years now, and normally you can't catch anything from it, you'd have to have a pretty big gaping wound in your mouth and him one on his cock, and cum never passes between my lips anyway. COB, cum on body, OK.

If this year goes well I'll have saved up a nice sum. Most girls can't keep hold of it, like guys with their cum – money I mean. Gucci here, Prada there. Sure I treat myself now and then, what do you think? (Wink, wink! Smile to camera, and my little winter comedy's rolling after all, oh well, it'll be a nice little hotel job, the perfect end to the working day, and a gentleman with champagne and hopefully not one of those monster dicks, mind you, who knows, wink, wink!) When I go out after work now and then I do wear nice things, why earn all this money otherwise? But putting something by is just as important. That's what I say to every girl who wants to get into the business. If you don't watch out, one day you'll be left with all your money down the drain. Times get harder and you can work and work until you go grey and your tits go wrinkly to get out of that misery again. That won't happen to me. I've got plans.

And here we are cruising along the big main road to the centre. The city seems to be glowing pale blue, snow on the rooftops, and there's the big hotel already. Twenty-seven floors and a few more on top. We stop at another crossroads, that's the road down to the zoo, I went there a couple of times with my mother when I was little, we came especially from Jena because it's such a big famous zoo, it was in the summer holidays, I remember it pretty well, I had this holiday pass that got you in almost everywhere for free and the summer holidays lasted two months back then, it was a really long time, I wonder what the animals do in this cold? But the zoo's totally different now to those days when the big beasts paced to and fro in the old cages, in summer and winter, I felt sorry for them when I was little, I know that, or maybe I only feel sorry for them now when I remember them, but the monkeys in the old monkey house must have had it good, the way they played around and ate bananas and put their hands on the glass. And now they're all in huge open-air enclosures, lions, tigers, monkeys, not all in together of course, there'd be no end to the killing, and the different kinds of monkeys have their own enclosures too, it's a really gigantic zoo, almost like a small town, and I should go there again, when I've got a daughter I'll take her to the zoo really often and show her all the animals, I always thought the

32

fish were really boring when I was little, mind you they had the most gorgeous colours. I only know the new zoo, the way it is now I mean because it's the same zoo of course, but it's still really different, I only know it from that TV show *Tiger and Monkey*. All us girls watch it. We know every animal. By name. And we think this or that keeper is good. Or hot. I only watch it now and then when I'm flicking through the channels. I pay and get out of the car. 'Take care of yourself.'

'Thanks. See you soon.' And I wave and watch him driving away. It's freezing cold, I adjust my scarf, cream cashmere, feels good on my skin. I scurry through the big revolving door. Through the other doors, left and right, people drag huge wheeled cases, the porters hold the doors open, taxis pull up and drive off again, I put my little bag over my shoulder, one hand on the strap, then I scurry past the reception desk and through the big lobby. A fountain babbles. There was a pond with fish in at the zoo that was full of coins. To the left of the lifts is the bar, I sat there one time, had a date with a client, at first I thought he wasn't coming, even though I'd called him back in his room, but if he says 'down at the bar' I can hardly go up and knock, and I've had it all before, standing outside a door, hotel or house, and no one opens up. Because they suddenly got scared or jerked off or whatever. I don't like doing house visits much and it's pretty unusual anyway for anyone to ask. Because a lot of them have a wife at home. But I've been in some flats, I wanted to run right out again, just keep on running. You'd think they'd be embarrassed. I'd be embarrassed. And I wouldn't go and invite someone round. Hotels are different. There are three of us in the lift. I press twenty-five. A young man and a woman, they must be together. Reminds me of my last boyfriend.

And I instantly get feelings. Because I went to a nice hotel with him as well. Even though it's a year and a half ago now. No time for that kind of thing now. And up we go. The little blue numbers above the door flicker, we stop at fifteen, my ear pops, an old geezer gets in, looks tired, tired eyes, old little face, I'm thirty-one now, most people think mid-twenties, that's what it says in the paper, that's what it says on my set card, I've got plans, one more winter, one more summer, I'm a professional, as cool as Sharon Stone with dyed black hair, we're the top league, we fleece the men for all their fuck-bucks (shut it, Magda! Wink, wink!), and up we go, the old man gets out at eighteen – ding! Make it snappy, granddad, I gotta go to the honeymoon suite! The other two probably want to go up to twenty-seven, there's a bar up there above the city skyline, I've never been there, but today when I stow the cash in my cleavage, it goes in my purse of course, today I'll drink a margarita up there at the bar, with a view of the city. I get out at twenty-five, give the couple a quick nod before the door closes. I see the room numbers. I walk the long corridor. A woman comes towards me, looks like a chambermaid, white apron. 'Good evening,' I say. *Once upon a time there was a little girl who was strong willed and forward*. I always wondered what that was. Forward. When I was little. When my mother read me 'Mother Trudy'. And how Mother Trudy turns the girl into a block of wood in the end and throws her on the fire and warms herself. Who comes up with something like that? And who reads something like that aloud? Sometimes I think maybe I read it myself in the green book, and because my mother did read me a couple of fairy tales Mardi Gras in my brain, memories in winter, 2011. It's long enough ago. I stop outside the door. I wait for a moment, silent. Music from inside. I smile. Put my hand on the door. Feel strong. Right, let's go.

II. (STREET OF DREAMS / HOHER SCHUH, SCHLANKES BEIN)

Colours flicker through the city, construction machines on torn-up streets, summer lightning far up in the north, three zeppelins circling above the buildings. 'Get your dirty tongue out of my mouth! And don't you start with your *He said she said he did she did*. I said I don't...' Silent people pushing life and night and day ahead of them, 'Six hundred and fifty-five thousand inhabitants is no big deal for a city, not global level, but we're expanding! A million's our target!' (I said silent!)

Green lights, trams screeching on the bends, passenger trains on bridges, embankments, in tunnels, stations, articulated buses winding through the traffic, number 60, every ten minutes, 76, 69, red for stop, on the goods ring the passenger trains meet the freight trains, several levels, a stone viaduct behind the sports pitch, allotments smoking, eastern outskirts, barbecue season, western outskirts, badamm, badamm, badamm, 'The trains clatter differently nowadays, it sounds different to the old days,' says an old man to his wife next to him on the balcony..., grey houses up above the tracks, the trains drive through canyons, suburban trains, rust-brown wagons, dilapidated freight stations, the big lakes on the edge of the city slowly evaporating, on the bottom the old digging machines, remains of brown coal in their shovels. The restaurant on the pier full of diners, staring at the water and waiting *When's the rain coming, we're waiting for rain, take a day off and go to the seaside... on ninety-two point three...* And the sun migrates quickly.

'That was because the factories made so much noise, pounding away all day long,' says the old man under the

35

sunshade, fixed to the wall with wire to guard against the storms, because they say there's a storm coming soon, ah, ah, ah, someone humping loudly, open window to the backyard, women's voices, tachometer, 'I need a taxi, right now!' the summer air conducts the sounds, electro-sound, 'that was because...'

Pssht goes the beer, bottle-top with Wernesgrüner emblem, everything glinting in the sun, all in a circle, metal, trams screech on the bends, thousands of workers flood into the factories, out of the factories, while the old man drinks with his eyes closed, 1964, solar eclipse 1999, 'and because they're all closed now, closed down and... ahhh, my God, that's good, there's no more pounding from the factories, it sounds different now, and freight trains are rare now too, only rare and empty, if at all.' What kind of rubbish is he talking, thinks the woman, thirty years it's been, if there's anything pounding it's in his head, let's hope he's not going senile on me, and she goes inside where the kitchen clock ticks. *The hottest summer since 2003...* badadadamm... *buy... ninety-two point*, a cop asleep over the newspaper, down outside the house, Plain-Clothes Cop 1, Golf Mark 2, head on his chest, Bild on the steering wheel, small ads next to the local sports section, most of them do BBBJ now, they say there's a new delivery due on Bones Square round the corner, the fixers have melted away at thirty-eight degrees and crystal rules the city, Cop 2 drinks Coke Zero and skims the ads, what do they mean by FF? Ping – a bottle-top on the bonnet, too lazy to get out, radio blaring, what the hell is COB? 'Hey, listen, you must know what COB means, and FF, do you hear me, COB!'

'Leave me in peace with your HB – F6, I know what that is.' He wipes the drool off his chin – I must have nodded off. We used to get the day off in heat like this.

'Even I know that. F6 cigarettes, because of the F6, the long-distance road, because that's where the tobacco factory was in Dresden so they named the cigarettes after it.'

'Yeah, yeah. Look at Mastermind over here. Dresden here, Dresden there, Chemnitz isn't anywhere.' He strokes his bald head. 'A cold beer, a nice cold beer.' He gets out of the car and looks up along the façade. Sees a multi-coloured sunshade protruding over the edge of the third-floor balcony. He runs a hand over the bonnet, feels the tiny scratch made by the bottle-top. He looks over at the taxi stand. The one-storey shack with the takeaway place has been empty for a couple of days. It ought to be a real money-spinner in the summer. In this heat it doesn't bother him that he's given up smoking. No appetite for it. All this ozone weighs heavy on the heart. He sees a woman running across the road, straight to the first taxi in the line of seven or eight cars. He counts. There are seven. He looks at his watch. Three o'clock on the nose. She gets in. At the back. Tall blonde. Very tall. High heels. Very high. Nice tits. Very nice. Look like they've been fixed. And off they go.

'Get the barbecue out.'

'You don't want to light the barbecue in this heat! It'll only smoke out the flat again.'

'We can go down in the yard, there's more shade down there.'

'I'm not taking one more step today.'

The taxi comes back. Joins the back of the queue. Doesn't time fly. And the sun migrates. He watches the two cops still standing in the sun over there in front of the house. No trees, no shade, and the sun migrates quickly.

'What's keeping the bastard?'

'Get back in the car. You're standing there like a farmer at the shooting range.'

'As if our Kai would notice. I heard the fair's on again. I'd like to go along with my daughter.'

'You're in the know! Don't you drive past it every day?'

'No. When I drive I always take the 7 past the racecourse.'

'The 6.'

'You know the one about the 7?'

'No.'

'There you go then.'

'Come on.'

'No.' He gets back into the car, leaving the door open. He leans down to his backpack and takes out a bottle of water.

'Give us a Coke,' says Cop 2 to Cop 1.

'Please!'

'Please.'

'Coke Zero?'

'Can you see any other Coke?'

'How can you drink that stuff, it's toxic.'

'Thank you, comrade. Toxic? Who told you that shit?'

'What do you think's in there? It's the same as light cigarettes.'

'It's not light, though, it's Zero.'

'Even worse. Artificial sugars. Toxic chemicals. I knew this guy, he smoked R1, only ever R1'

'Steffen from the black block?'

'Steffen from the hooligans department.'

'I'm not gonna get cancer from Coke Zero.'

'That'd make a good advert.'

They sit and watch it turning three thirty on the

block. A bottle-top falls on the asphalt next to the Golf Mark 2. Underarm, third floor. They don't notice though because they're watching the takeaway on the other side of the road, the one that's been closed for a few days. No one knows why. And now people come and shake at the door. And the two cops have an eye on the little station a short way down the road. See people coming out of the underpass, going into the underpass. Cop 1 turns the radio on, Cop 2 switches it off. Cop 1 on again. Cop 2 turns the volume down. Cop 1 up a bit more. The classical station is on, who tuned that in, mind you it's quite good sometimes, for relaxing, for keeping calm when there's some arsehole to pick up, someone they know won't open the door. Someone whose place they'll have to kick in so he comes quietly. Gotta be careful with raids. Because you can always end up with the wrong guy. Because there's always the odd bastard with a good lawyer. Or connections. Even though it's hard to imagine. It's pretty rare. Cop 1 keeps on turning the dial. Mega hits of the eighties. Most dirty bastards don't do anything if they happen to slip and fall once the door's finally open. Live is life. They're really still playing this shit. And they turn the dial of the old radio and slap each others' hands, and the zeppelins with the big advertising slogans on board turn away to land somewhere outside the city because the lightning's coming closer.

'This dirty bastard, you see, he always comes to this takeaway. He's got no fixed abode where we can pick him up. So we obs him here. He knows exactly how to play the game. As dumb as that sounds. Because back there, you see that collapsed wall, yeah, on the grass behind the takeaway shack, that belongs to the little ruin, former Reichsbahn, now Deutsche Bahn. Heim ins Reich. Our Kai. The crystal boy. But there's no takers, either way. No one wants to buy, no one wants to invest. Falling down. So he comes here, our boy, as nervous as the cartoon man in the HB ad, remember that one? F6. And he has his depot back there. That's where he gets his skag. A zombie. Take my word for it. The hotter it gets, the thinner the guy gets. Kai. He'll soon be in his wooden box, our Kai, remember that one? Kai the zombie. And he knows his stuff and he likes to sing. Otherwise we'll pick him up and lock him up. And there's no skag there. And no crystal neither. Mind you, you can get anything inside, if you know how. But things are tight right now anyway. You could say you can get more inside now, right at this moment, than outside. It's sold out everywhere. But not the end-of-summer sale. Just like with coke and the other shit. And we get leaned on from above because the zombies are picking off the old and the weak, mug-a-granny season, because the prices are going up. So we're supposed to clean up. Not just at the bottom – at the top as well. That's not our job right now. We're just the raid team. Reel the bastards in. The ones that got away. But seeing as most zombies have previous, we co-ordinate with D23. Drugs department. Pick one up and put a bit of pressure on and pass on the info. And then we get the info if some big stag's standing around waiting to get shot. Otherwise we sweep everything under the carpet, but right now it's a special situation because the zombies are going for anyone with a bit of spare change in their pocket, even running into baker's shops with guns and knives, and it's time for the mire to be... you get my drift? Hot and dry. Which doesn't make any difference because it's all great for the press and the politicians, we've got the skag and the coke and we're stamping out the scene, absolute rubbish of course, but then you just get more and more zombies on the lookout

for a score and a dollar. And we have to sweep them up
and all. And on the other side the Turks and the Arabs
are going crazy and pushing into town and onto the
market. Only the Vietcong in Chinatown do their own
thing. Pretty complicated, huh? Yeah. What do they call
it? A win-win situation. Or something like that. You get
my meaning? All for all, like the musketeers.'

And the taxis swarm out. Four o'clock. The city simmering. All windows open. If only the rain would come.
Fuck those few flashes of lightning. Too many people
on bikes now. Bad for business. And atmospheric disruptions pop on the radio and in your ears. Back to the
future. The mounted police comb through the parks.
The derelict houses shot demolition-ready by the cowboys of the black squadron. Only dirty bastards and
small fry inside. The legends and rumours circle like
a tornado from the central station through the whole
town. *Coke knows no season Summer time is Pepsi time.* By
the lakes outside of town, they're packed in like sar-
dines. Summer 2009. If the clocks are right. And shots
get fired at night, who needs that crap, they'll ruin the
market for all of us. Chaos is the beginning of the end.
('Rubbish! There's always people who profit from chaos.
It's all about the new order.')

And the driver drives through the shade of the old
streetwalkers' lane, where he used to bring clients back
in the day, years ago now. Drives on along 'Pretty
Peepers Alley', caravans on either side, long rows, few
lights, people, women, cars backfiring or shots firing,
year 1 after the Wall, year 2 after the Wall, here are the
pimps of the old republic waiting to get chucked out of the
new republic by the new guard of Eastern Zone brawlers
just getting organized, wind in their hair, bottle-blond,
short back and sides, skinheads, leather coats, Davidoffs

in leather cases, snow-camo bombers in the light of the street lamps, every second lamp broken back in the day, he drives on to the Fort because the man in the back of the cab wants sex on a shoestring, the football squads are taking everything in hand bit by bit, they're the best organized and the hardest hitters, back in the day, year 1, year 2, year 3, but the man in the back of the cab doesn't know that because the driver's drifting through the decades before this time, when the foreign investors want to take over the market. Alongside the road is the railway line. And industrial estates where there were ruins back in the day. Who even remembers the jokes about the wobbling caravans? Where they ripped you off and left your nads full but your wallet empty. Where territories were carved out and fought over. East versus West. East versus East. And the raiding squads raided. A woman (19) stands by the kerb and swears under her breath. *Dirty buggers! Poor buggers?* No. How the years fly. And in 2009 road-workers find curlers, hundreds of fossilized cigarette butts and condoms in a dried-up arm of the sewers. She's forty-two now and working at a coffee stall at the central station. And the taxi accelerates to 88 miles an hour. Because the rear lights of the Fort are visible behind the houses. He used to get his red-light dollar. The cum cumshaw. You bring us punters, you get paid. The houses used to outdo one another. Those times are long gone now. And back again along Pretty Peepers Alley. Nothing but a crumpled *Bild* on the back seat. He'd tried to tempt him with a couple of addresses, could have called Babsi, Lilli that is, any time, he told him to take a look at the small ads instead, but the guy was after small-change sex, he wanted to go to the Fort. And that's where it's cheapest, of course. Behind the turnstile. And is it safe there now, he asked, because the

42

newspapers, and the war and the city. Sure, everything's fine and dandy here! Fine and dandy, safe as houses! He didn't know for sure, a hundred per cent that is, what do you know a hundred per cent these days when they're all losing it in this bloody heat, when the clubs and the disco doors are getting attacked, when this poor fucker he knew, he'd even driven him a couple of times, to Babsi as well, got left to die on the kerb. Poor fucker, at the wrong time in a place without time. Like back in the day ten years ago, he thinks, boom, boom, and he accelerates his Mercedes on the 7, or actually the 6, the city highway, to 88 miles an hour. But the ghosts are back in town. And that makes him laugh. And he feels and he sees the lights flying past him.

Torn up streets with construction machines. Someone swears because his rubber soles are melting. The mounted police cause a traffic jam. The parks in the city centre are swept empty. The musketeers in the centre carry machine guns. The central station lies still and radiates the warmth of the day. The sky clouds over above the city. Then it looks as though someone's burrowing in the clouds. At the zoo, not far from the central station, a giraffe turns white overnight, and on the zoo show on TV they talk about a snow giraffe, it's to do with the atmosphere and the pressure, just like a man can go grey from one day to the next. The water in the canals doesn't move and starts to stink. For days now. And the trains go once an hour until eleven at night. Frankfurt am Main, Berlin, Hannover. And a man runs across the station concourse, up the big staircase to the platforms, two steps at a time, two men now running, a woman pushes her pram cautiously past them, clack, clack, down the stairs into the concourse of marble and glass, why doesn't she take the lift? Pigeons scatter up and out, and outside: thousands of tired pigeons on parched grass; one man to Berlin, one man to Hannover City. No rush, there's still ten minutes and fifteen minutes to go. The hire cars are waiting at the stations. Take the train, first class. Because it's less conspicuous. Could have taken the car... pro and contra, over and over. But the cops are getting annoying. Traffic jam caused by the mounted police. Who only caught small fry, but that's not what this is about. The cops are stopping everyone at the moment, anyone in a bigger vehicle, should have hired a Smart, but deals have to be done, offers made, and atmospheric disruptions pop on the radio and in their ears. Back in time at 88 miles an hour. The platforms surprisingly empty, summer-time, holiday season. Everyone's flown the nest.

Three streets away, you can't see the central station because the hotel's cube is in the way, that's where families walk to the zoo in the daytime, and not just families because the zoo's the most popular thing in the city, it's down to that show, *Tiger Tiger* and the polar giraffe, at any rate round there is the bookies where it's all about horses, where the Yugos & Co. don't have a stake because football makes the most turnover and profit, if you leave the slot machines out of it. There's a good few operators between Germany and Babylon and the horses are something for small-change gamblers, which isn't quite true though. The driver nods, now lined up over in the east of the city behind three other taxis at his regular spot, he knows the big horse betters he used to drive to the racetrack back in the day, year 1, year 2, year 3, when there were still so many races, never mind back in the Zone, but in those days he was still working at the big printing press, now embedded between the centre's new buildings, vacant and decaying, it hurts his soul every time he drives past, 140 km/h, what rubbish, he only accelerates like that on the motorway when he drives someone to the airport. The centre of the city glows blue and pink when evening falls. The sun stands the lowest in the rich southern suburbs. There, towards the gangway to the zoo, to the animals, that's where they're running now, the master thieves. But in the other direction, away from the zoo. Past the hotel's grey concrete, the windowed façade now twinkling red in the evening, the last of the sun, the lights of the city, a woman (30) stands at the pane, pressing both hands against the glass as she's fucked from behind by a guy with his shirt still on and his socks, and she doesn't know what to think about that, isn't it rude not to take your socks off for sex, but she can look down at the city, twenty-fifth floor, that's some view, the sunset makes her a bit sad, and she feels the guy doing his business inside her.

And there they are, out of breath already at the crossroads. The master thieves. Straight across the road, between the cars. Money fluttering out of their pockets. It was all a few days or weeks ago. Turks? No. Zombies. And the money comes fluttering out of their pockets and plastic bags. The biggest break-in of the year. All planned and timed down to the second. Into the bookies, alarm gun in, alarm gun out, shout it all about, mask slipped, face dripping with sweat under the wool at thirty-three degrees in the shade, money in the plastic bags, it's only two thousand six hundred, no one's going to be a hero for that because the gun looks real and the guys totally lose it when they don't have no stuff, no fix, no crystal. The old geezers sitting there on their stools, at their tables, while the races from overseas and England flicker across the screen. Watching the starting gates open in Belmont Park, New York, boom, and the horses galloping along the track. And the slips flutter in the wind, and the old geezers complain when the cops come along because they want to go on gambling.

And the professionals of the last days and weeks flee together on foot and by bike, a breathless marathon across the city, *three hold-ups in one weekend*, the man from Ghana lurches bleeding from the neck along the big road in the east where the Turks and the Arabs have their territories, *elderly tourist from Switzerland brutally attacked*, who would even think a black man would have enough money to rob? A black man from Switzerland? But times are bad, ten or fifteen years ago only a couple of skinheads would have jumped him at most, now it's all against anyone and best off with knives, the musketeers meet at the zoo, the jackpots shrink smaller and smaller in summer '09.

'We need cake for tomorrow.'

'I'm fine right here. It's not tomorrow yet.'

'You lazy bugger, get in here off that balcony.'

'Hold your horses. It's better than the telly out here.'

Because the two cops have finally grabbed the zombie and are dragging him across the grass, the eight (8) of the handcuffs clicks around his wrists, take him away, 'Head down, you idiot!' and read him the house rules in HQ2. 'If you sing us a nice song, my dear Kai, you'll be free by the morning!'

The moon has arisen. And is shimmering through the glass of the station concourse. It's not quite dark yet, the days often stretching out to midnight and almost touching hands in the morning. Winters '09, '10, '11 will be hard and dark, thirty-two rough sleepers freeze to death all in all. Five of them on their way home. One too many down the pub. There's no closing time in this city. The discos, brothels and clubs getting set for the night. In the apartments, the shifts are gradually coming to an end. 'Home time at last, you coming to the fair?' Not many women work after midnight, high heels clattering in the stairwell. 'No, not tonight, I'm off to get a massage.' 'Take care of yourself.' 'You too.' After eight the doors are guarded, the security men pool their knowledge – you've got to know your enemy. And Hans instructs his staff at his little club too; the discos are just the beginning. What did someone say to him that time? 'The pie's big enough, but if you're dead...' No, that wasn't it. It's years ago now. He can feel he's getting old. Something's got to happen, and soon. Two men at the coffee stall right in front of the platforms. On the left the train to Berlin, on the right the train to Hannover. Just popped in to WC White, who've expanded from Switzerland all the way to Germany, 50 cents a piss. 'A euro for a shite, showers 2.50'. Fifteen minutes to go. As though the planet were turning backwards.

'It's always nice and cool at WC White.'

'They're making more money than we are right now.'

'Mhm. Great concept, you have to give them that.'

'I like the shithouse cubicles. Always clean. And sealed in with not a crack. Nice and private.'

'We should take over *that* place.'

'Then we could retire.'

'People will always shit.'

'People will always shag.'

'But no one gives them any stress.'

'What if I open up budget public toilets here, Mister Piss?'

'You wouldn't get a licence. And even if you did, what would you offer? WC White is too good. Pricey but good!'

'Then I'll offer flat-rate shitting.'

'You do know all this flat-rate fucking is only going to ruin the market and the prices in the long run.'

'They should go public, do an IPO. WC White, I mean.'

'So should we.'

'When's the Old Man joining us?'

'Hannover, Berlin. In that order. On Monday, I think.'

'Monday's a good day for doing business.'

'It's about time something happened.'

'About time. The discos are just the beginning.'

And the driver's another one now, and he feels and he sees the lights racing past him, then he slams on the brakes. The radio broadcasts the speed traps and he leaves the city highway, drives behind a rubbish truck for a while then turns off, catches sight of the old, empty warehouses by the canal dock, behind them the sky turning scarlet, turns off again, hears the storm thundering far away, the woman already standing outside, smoking. She throws the cigarette away and gets in the car. And off they go. The cops next to him at the red light. Golf Mark 2. Budget cuts, or what? A haggard face on the back seat, shaggy hair, yellow eyes, 'Head down, you idiot,' he hears the screams and the shouts from the rollercoaster. In bright Chinatown, the big halls at the other end of town, the cops raid the last depots, crystal in exchange for stolen goods, hi-tech, handbags, money and bread from the baker's shop, car tyres, car radios, whatever the zombies can get hold of on their paths through the night, a ride through the Olympic rings, upside down, right side up, a famous roller coaster from Munich, he sees the woman in the rear-view mirror, dark hair with blonde streaks, now she's humming a tune that he knows, a nice song that his mother often sang when he was little. Just before midnight there's a fireworks display, between big wheel and rollercoaster, she wonders whether she'll be able to see it later, high above the city, the cops seize eleven tons of pyrotechnics in Chinatown, amber lights, green lights. They drive and she holds her hand out in the wind, all the windows down. 'Would you turn on the radio, please?'

'Anything for you.' Something touches her hand, small and wet like a snowflake.

III. (BOOM BOOM / BUMM BUMM)
You're flat on your back on the street. And you thought the nineties were over.

And they nearly are over, you wonder for a moment what year is it exactly, you know it, you do know it, all year long you've been getting up and going to sleep, getting up and going to sleep and running your business and there wasn't much sleep... but you can't put your finger on it, you feel your head on the asphalt, as if it had sprung a leak when it hit the ground, is it raining? You're flat on your back between the cars and you can see the tyres and the wheels, the light refracts and bounces off from an alloy wheel right in front of you, street lamps, headlamps, night, and you try to make out your face, 1999.

No, nothing's over. The violent days were long, but long ago as well, almost not true any more, the years of calm, your head on the asphalt, the city's quiet on a Sunday and the rain is red, the car is red, right next to you. You came alone, even though everyone said, 'Don't go on your own!' but you had to go alone, the nineties are almost over, all we want is to do business, you went to sleep for a bit and got up and it was almost evening by then. You had time to drink a coffee and stand outside in the dark garden for a while, it's getting dark early again now, you wanted to walk down to the lake but the phone rang. No, it didn't ring, you'd put it on silent and you saw it flashing through the window of the veranda. The display flashed and flashed in the charger like a miniature lighthouse. No, you hear it ringing, you never put it on silent, that must have been somewhere else, you've got a whole house full of telephones and none of them is on silent, the phone in your jacket pocket buzzes. You turn onto your side and try to reach into your pocket. It's hard, although your arms are fine. The phone buzzes and buzzes and you feel your heart beating, and then it stops and you take a deep breath and breathe out, take a deep breath, breathe out the fear, no one else is coming now, no, no one else is coming, he was alone, just like you, and you saw him walk away, he just turned around and left. Did he say anything? What did he say to you beforehand? You can't put your finger on it. 'This is from...' No, no names, never names, you might as well start with that now, they'll ask you, good thing they still can ask you, but they can ask you till their fucking tongues dry out, you breathe out the fear and look at your legs, which you can't feel any more. Edo, you bastard, I'm gonna... No, stop it, the nineties are... But you know you have to do something, you know you have to do it, all over again, and you thought... You thought too much, much too much and too little, you went alone. Never go alone, always take a man with you, always keep a man close. Watch your back, but he didn't come from behind, he came right at you, we want to do business, that's all there is to it, all we want is to do business. Edo, you bastard... Did he give you the name, did he send regards? You can't put your finger on it, you'll find out, you'll find out more than that, but how long can you stay lying here? If only the rain would stop, the nights are getting cool now but it's not raining, is it?

Now you've got your phone out of your pocket, your hands are trembling, it's pathetic, did you take something before you left to keep you calm or perk you up? No, you never take anything, hardly ever, not when you want to talk business. Just a little chat on a Sunday in the quiet city, and then you drop the phone when you switch it to vibrate, you bend over and pick it up, wipe it down, and there he is coming towards you, what a stupid place to meet, you can just see the old stadium's dark towers a couple of hundred yards away, now the parked cars block your view, the battery leaps out, and now you feel the pain in your knee and further up your other leg, no, you didn't take anything, adrenaline, your heart's pumping the stuff around your system, you're getting tired but you have to stay perked up, you mustn't fall asleep, and you're tired, so tired, don't sleep, you know that, not until they come for you, if only the right people come for you, but no, he was alone and he's gone, and you breathe out the fear and see the SIM card from your phone next to the battery on the asphalt. You see the tiny golden metal plates on the card. And something else flashes, something else golden, on the ground as well, a few yards away. A coin, you think, it looks like the pendant from a necklace, a talisman, the guardian angel of businessmen, Saint Michael, and you touch your chest, you're so glad you can stroke your chest, you're so glad that you've got tears in your eyes, your hands are trembling on you, and you're weeping, it's pathetic... If they saw you like this, and you reach for your chain, it used to be a little golden boxing glove, back when you were still fighting, kick-boxing, it's a few years back now, you were a real ace back then, they called you AK-47, like the machine gun, Arnold Kraushaar, they called you Arnie Short & Curlies at school, what with Kraushaar kind of sounding like 'pubes' – but you knew how to show them what for even then and you chased them right across the whole schoolyard, no more Arnie Short & Curlies, AK 47, you were pretty good at boxing too, even back at school, you even did a few amateur fights, kick-boxing wasn't around till after the Wall, after '89, the legs, the feet, the kicks, you were better at that than just with your fists, you trained every day, you wiped out the best lads in the ring with your kicks, you look at your legs, your pale trousers are black.

How long have you been lying here now? It can only be minutes, you know that. Time goes out of joint when you've got adrenaline in your system.

A taxi drives past, you want to call attention to yourself, you wave, but you're flat on your back right next to the cars and he can't see you. Pull yourself together! You try to get up, try to pull yourself up on the car with both arms, try to grab the door handle, grab it, boy, where's your strength, for fuck's sake, but your arms are weak and soft, rubber, you think, only with a rubber, girls, how often do I have to tell you that, they can put as much money down as they like, what use is it to you if you get yourselves the clap and the fucking plague, have you never heard of AIDS, Jesus, how stupid can you get! It doesn't matter if he's a regular, you get it? Jesus, girl, I'm only thinking of *you* here! You know you have to wait, breathe deeply, keep breathing deeply, if only you could feel your legs, you have to wait until your strength comes back, you want to shout... Help! Someone call the cops, but what use are the cops to you, what you need is a doctor, right now. How stupid can you get, in the middle of the night, like in some cheap gangster movie, you've got careless, the years of calm have made you careless, why didn't you listen to Alex, 'I'll come with you,' he kept saying on the phone, only an hour ago, out in the garden. 'No,' you said and you looked out at the lake behind the trees, your best man, you smile, you remember Alex putting on one of his shows in the ring last week, 'Cover up, Alexander!' you wanted to call out, but you bit your tongue because you know how he likes putting on a show in the ring, seen too many Muhammad Ali videos, or what was that boxer called again, the one he admires so much, a black American, they call him 'the King', Jackson... Jones, Jones Junior or something like that, he dangles his arms, Alex says, makes a fool of his opponents, sticks out his chin only to pull it back at the last moment when the punch comes, but Alexander the Great is no king, more like a duke or something like that, because he takes a lot of punches, staggers around uncovered in front of his opponent, and you're not sure if that's part of Alexander's show or if he's just about to go K.O., but then in the third and final round he did knock him over, he really let loose towards the end as usual, 'second wind', he always says, '*le deuxième souffle*', he's always showing off, that nutter, just because he speaks a bit of French, and you're still smiling and wishing he was here, and your face is all stiff, you must look terrible, but no one can see you, why aren't there any fucking pedestrians at this time of night, no one out any more, what kind of a crappy city is this, maybe it's the rain, they'd rather stay warm and dry, Sunday evening in front of the TV... Don't go crazy on me now, it's not raining, it's not raining at all, it hasn't rained all week, though the sky was dark today, clouds gathered by noon, for fuck's sake, what's happened to your nose, your sixth, seventh, eighth sense, without that you wouldn't be where you are now... On the street, you think, in the dirt, and you laugh, and your teeth are chattering on you, you've got the shivers, and you know that's not a good sign.

You were always the gangster as a kid, the Red Indian, the pirate, and you're flat on your back on the grass behind the house and looking up at the sky and you hear the others yelling, hear the caps firing, bang! bang! bang! and you think maybe dying might be easy. You always wondered if there are people who don't die, demigods like you'd read about, you used to read a lot back then but you've forgotten so much now, you were a better reader than most of your friends even in the first year, Heracles, but didn't he bite the dust in the end, after all his trials? And Thor, he was the Norseman with the magical hammer, wasn't he, a god? A demigod? Or just a man after all...? Didn't they have to keep eating the fruits from that tree so that they lived for all time? Did you really believe that when you were a kid? Once, you went to the Botanical Gardens and looked at the exotic plants and trees, just before they closed for the day, you took your little backpack along especially, camping knapsack it was called, was it red or blue? Everyone had one of those backpacks, one of those camping knapsacks, they only came in two colours, and on school trips and outings there were the reds and the blues. You probably had red, you think, what a joke, fate, destiny, sometimes you believe in that kind of thing, even though you've given up on the gods.

You stuffed your backpack, how old were you then, nine, ten? You tore off figs, prickly pears, pomegranates, guavas and whatever they were all called, trampled across the barriers into the beds, the branches and leaves in your face, that looks good, and that! And those rock-hard bulbs with a foreign name you couldn't even read properly... And then the fear.

The janitor or some kind of guard spoke to you as you wanted to leave, 'I have to give a presentation in Biology, exotic plants, bromeliads,' you said, you'd read it in an encyclopaedia, how crazy that the word comes to you now. You stuttered, and that burning and stinging down your body, all the way down to your balls, you'll never forget that because it kept coming back later, decades later, decades... How long that sounds, it's almost thirty years ago now, and back then you didn't have the strength to find it stimulating, to let it goad you on... 'You'll have to come earlier then,' the guy said, an old man, the guardian of the trees of life. 'You'll have to come earlier, that's when our students are here, they can tell you lots of useful things to make sure your presentation's really good.' The old man won't stop talking, and he's standing right up in front of you, and behind you the leaves and the branches, and he spits as he talks and has such bad breath you feel like turning away, and you feel the fruits and bulbs against your back through the fabric. The old man strokes your hair, his fingers as hard and calloused as the long tubers you felt and then tore off just before. 'Come after school tomorrow, when's your presentation... our students will be here then...' You never went back to the Botanical Gardens, and the old man's fingers were still on your head long after you got home.

In your bedroom, you chopped up your booty with your penknife. It took such a long time and the blade was far too blunt. You went into the kitchen and fetched a large breadknife, the very sharp one, and then you bolted it all down you, because you wanted to live as long as Thor and Heracles. You shat and heaved it all out, the gods couldn't have done better, even the next day, so bad you couldn't go to school, and once you were better your mother gave you a beating, she never did that, and with a slipper, and she cried and she bawled: 'Don't you ever scare me like that again, boy!'

You're flat on your back and you hear the caps firing, bang! bang! bang! And you look up at the sky, the stars... Alex'll end up breaking rocks if it goes badly, the asphalt's cold underneath you, it was so good lying on the grass back then, will the lawyers be able to help him? Your lawyers are the best in the city, and not only in the city, how often have they got you out of a fix, how often have they got your people out of trouble and your girls, Beatriz not long ago, when that girl was hanging up half-dead in Lady Kira's wardrobe, but Alex had to go and cock things up again, you've always told him: 'If you're not careful they'll take you away, and I need you here.'

And this time it's going to be hard to get him out of trouble, you know that, even if he refuses to realize it. Maybe that's why you didn't want him to come with you tonight, and once you're back on your feet you'll make sure he doesn't have to spend too long away. He's no king in the boxing ring but he's pretty good, no, you haven't been seeing stars, the clouds are still drifting across the night sky, and even if they weren't there you never see stars here, not even out at your place by the lake do you see the stars the way you see them in the countryside, in the mountains, when it all gets too much for you in the city. He's no king in the boxing ring, although he's pretty good, a count, perhaps, but on the streets... Like you used to be... How often have you told him recently: 'The best way to win a fight is to avoid it.' You'd never have said something like that, in the old days... AK 47. What days they were. Is this what you get in return for all the violence, the destiny you sometimes still believe in? Rubbish, no! You wouldn't be where you are now without all that, without the fights, without your fists, forget the street and the dirt you're lying in right now, you're at the top, you hear, at the top! And you want to get even further and higher, and that's why you have to get out of here and hit back and smooth everything out! And you shout and you're surprised at how high and thin your voice sounds. Forget your pride and scream! Scream for help. And then you try and put your phone back together but the fucking battery's slid under the car. Why did you leave your other phone at home? You'd never have gone out into the night with only one phone in the old days... But in the old days a mobile phone was the size of a brick, you should have smashed a brick on his skull, over and over, until he lay on the ground in the dirt, and the asphalt would have gone dark underneath him, and you'd have taken the brick with you and thrown it in the river over there from the bridge.

Someone must be able to hear you, you're shouting so loudly, maybe someone's already called the cops long ago, back when it happened, it was certainly loud enough. And you remember you're wearing a watch, you raise your arm slightly so your sleeve slips down, and you look at your Breitling & Söhne, you used to have a Rolex in the old days, you've only been lying here ten minutes at most and you're not surprised, because you know that time... As if the fruits from back then were still taking effect, differently than you thought... You burst into the bar, Alex and the others alongside you, no cap guns now, and you beat and you punch, with fists and baseball bats, and the crashing and the splintering and the screaming, men leaping aside and getting caught anyway, men ducking and hiding under tables and getting caught anyway, the bigmouth who tries to run up the stairs and gets caught anyway, and then you feel the old man's hands again, brushing so slowly over your head.

A child died, over there by the bridge, a few weeks ago. You read about it in the paper. A children's rowing club, they got too close to the weir in their boats, and two boats got caught in the current and went over the little waterfall. They managed to rescue the other kids from the two boats. One child's still in a coma. The boy didn't turn up for days. Miles and miles away. The current. You were over at the tram depot that day, keeping an eye on the girls. And you wondered what the helicopter was doing by the river. It circled over the bridge for a while before it landed. You stood by the window, the girls behind you, and the shrill screeches of the trams, and your sixth, seventh, eighth sense told you that where it was landing, there was death. And now you're not far from there... Your boy must never go rowing on the river. You're glad he's not in the city right now. You sent him away to a school elsewhere.

You watch the crowds drifting. You feel cool air blowing over from the river. You see the old stadium's dark towers. A car drives slowly along the opposite lane. It drives on towards the traffic lights, flashing amber.

The only way to win a fight is to avoid it. It was the Bielefelder who told you that back then. But that's rubbish, Bielefelder! you think. Now you can see it's rubbish, Bielefelder. But if Alex had listened to him he wouldn't be breaking rocks in his chain gang right now. You're dizzy, and all you can feel is your head and you move it to and fro on the tarmac. You hear sirens. They're coming, you think, they're coming at last.

The Bielefelder wanted to open up a big place here

back then, early nineties, an Eros centre, fifty rooms
or more, and his people did it in the end. You used to
get together a lot at that time. You and your people
took over a few things back then. Up and up and ever
onwards, Thor with his hammer, you wanted to do business, good business, and you invested in it. Invested fists
and cash and a lot more besides. He was a good man,
the Bielefelder. Old school, like they used to say over in
the West, back then. But he got pulled into the war, here
in the city where no one knew the old school and the
Bielefelder back then.

Your friend Hans the Hatchet, hadn't he started out as
a slaughterer or a butcher or something? He used to say:
'The pig's been slaughtered, and now everyone wants his
few pounds of flesh!'

He came to you, the Bielefelder, because he knew
he had to make a deal with your crew. Didn't he really
impress you back then? A tall guy, grey hair, the best
threads, and broad shoulders underneath the best
threads, Davidoff Filters, and he had a slight limp, but
with dignity, and a stick to go with it, with a silver knob,
a lion's head, the lion and the man both at least sixty.
He knew how to get you on his side. Promised you good
money if you didn't disrupt his business, and your people could take care of security, and if you know someone
who wants to put a roof over his girls' heads, first choice,
if you want, and his good name, good contacts, and a few
people with money behind him... Old school, and you
started realizing what that means.

And now you lick your tongue over your lips, your
tongue that's numb now, and you feel the cold sweat
wetting your face, so that's the rain, the clouds up there
are perfectly calm, and you wonder why the guy didn't
wipe you out, and you hear the sirens right nearby. And

then you crawl a few yards, more like inches, and bang! bang! bang! you're back on the grass behind the house, how soft it is, and you tell yourself that dying's just a load of shit, and you look up at the sky, with the sun and the stars and no moon and the planets, your grandfather once showed you Mars glowing reddish somewhere just above the horizon... And black all of a sudden, so black that fear rips your balls apart.

A thin tube in your arm. Two ambulance men. Then a sheet. The sirens distant, as if a second ambulance were driving alongside them, wailing. The vehicle swerves. Screeching brakes? The ambulance men busy doing something. You're still here. Back again. Then dark again. The sirens now loud, now quiet. You're still here. Not under the sheet, please. Not over my head, please. You don't want to go under the sheet and you try to shake yourself, the sheet slips off, you raise your head a little and see your legs, your trousers are cut open, you see your flesh, dark red and white and in shreds and nearly black. Where did it start? Your eyelids flicker, the light like a stroboscope. Up on the coast. You wish you were by the seaside. That bar. What was it called again... The name of a bird. Pelican... A white swan on the sign above the door. Goldpussy. And all the cash she raked in. That really impressed you. Goldpussy and the others, and all working for themselves, the biggest hook-up bar in the GDR, seamen from all over the world and dollars like it was LA. A place like this, and a percentage for me, one day. You hear Goldpussy laughing, and she disappears with three small Filipinos. Short time, that's what they called it, three in a row for a hundred dollars, that was worth two thousand marks at the black-market exchange rate, standing up and not even a bed, what a business, you thought, and you drank your beer, Goldpussy, Suitcase Grip and the others, and you'll give them beds one day, Mr Manager. You sit at the bar and laugh and believe in destiny. They say something to you, touch your shoulders and press you back gently onto the stretcher as the ambulance speeds on, and you toss to and fro, you have to understand it all, the sheet, and then you start to calm down, why should they put the sheet over your head? All down your body to your balls, you feel how fast the ambulance is speeding. Everything's wet, and they're busy doing something, and you want to say something but your mouth is so dry you can't say anything. Water, you want to say. Water. You wish you were by the seaside.

The blood, what did all the blood remind you of? You've seen plenty of blood, especially in the early nineties. You wonder if the Bielefelder's ever bumped anyone off, he's been in the business forty years, he was in Hamburg for a while, he said. Violence is bad for business, he used to say, but there's something in his eyes, and your sixth, seventh sense... You had to start by building up your business, and the blood, you know it was all necessary... You weren't where you are now. You raise your hands a little, hold them to the light of the ceiling lamp, it's good, you think, that the light's on all night. You're still weak; you've lost a lot of what you're thinking about the whole time. It was a good thing they didn't come for you any later. You've only spoken to Alex on the phone briefly, no visitors allowed yet. 'Those fucking Yugos!' What did he say? Didn't Claudia call? And your son? The tablets and the stuff dripping into your arm are confusing you, you slept for over twenty hours, you feel the punctures in your arms from the transfusions. They've given you plenty, new stuff, unused, and it'll make you strong. Did Alex name names, do they know if Edo sent him? You try to piece it all together in your head but you still can't put your finger on it properly, you know you need time, and then you'll find the answers. That guy, the father of the girl back then, he threatened to kill you, even though you had nothing to do with all that. No, you'd never get involved in disgusting shit like... But that idiot went to where you were. To the top. But you're not quite there yet – maybe this'll be the last step, a sign from destiny, which you still believe in sometimes. Why did he wait so long? It must have been '93. And he came four years later. No, you had nothing to do with it. But you knew about it, everybody knew about it. And then he showed up and came to you, because he thought... What did he think, that idiot? 'If you had your dirty fingers mixed up in it I'll kill you!' They dragged him outside, a short man, five foot three, an ex-jockey, an ex-drinker, as you found out later. 'You hear me, pimp! I'll kill you!' 'Shall we...' 'No. Let him go. If he comes back again, don't let him in. No more than that. Just don't let him in.' You heard him yelling as they dragged him out. 'I'll kill you! I'll knife you!'

You asked around. You found out where his daughter was. She was eighteen then, so fourteen in 1993, and everyone knew about it. About her and the others.

You're cold and you put your hands underneath the sheet. You could have smashed the place to pieces, like you smashed other places up. Did you want to get hold of the papers even then? Public prosecutors, judges and cops and rich bastards who were into little girls. You drove around the streets on your own in the evening, asked a few other girls about her. Most of them didn't know you. You had nothing to do with that shit. Drug victims. Junkies. You don't work with girls like that. The Bielefelder was right about that, 'Drugged-up girls mess up your business.' A bit of coke or whatever never did anyone any harm, in moderation, in moderation... But that... You felt sick when you saw all that messed-up flesh. Dark red and white and in shreds and nearly black.

And then she was standing on a corner, right outside a flower shop that sold drinks, and newspapers as well, the girls you'd asked about her wanted to push their way into your BMW, rubbed up against the door, leaned over the bonnet, and you could have heaved, although if it weren't for the needle you could give them a room in one of your properties, rehab for whores, that might be an idea, but if they didn't have their addictions they'd probably be doing something else, selling flowers and beer and newspapers, what a combination! And most of them had the clap or syphilis or maybe even AIDS, they don't use condoms, otherwise all the dirty buggers driving past slowly in their cars, their eyes as big as five-mark coins, would come to your girls.

You spotted her right away, your seventh, eighth sense... Looks a bit like her father, and you'll never forget his face screaming like that. And then she's sitting next to you, just as small and thin as her father, short, messy hair, spots on her forehead and on her face, encrusted with make-up, a miniskirt the length of a belt, a T-shirt you can see her scant breasts and nipples through, as if she were still thirteen, like back then, but you didn't know her or the others, you had nothing to do with it, and she tells you all the things she does, and for how much, and it's really not much, and you wonder if she did the same when she was thirteen or if she was clean then when those dirty bastards fucked her, you remember you could get hold of heroin on every street corner in '92, you wonder whether the papers and the videos were worth you keeping your mouth shut back then, wonder whether maybe everything might have turned out the way it is now either way, but you know the whole thing back then must have broken her. She fumbles at you and you say, 'Stop it,' and you give her money and tell her to go, and you know what she'll do with the cash, and you think you'll have to come back but perhaps you won't come back. You watch her trotting down the street, past the shop, towards the station. You gave her a hell of a lot of money, how amazed she looked, her eyes as big as... but dull and red. Perhaps she'll be clever and jump on some train, there are night trains to Paris and Copenhagen, but you know better, at the station, at night.

You've got a private room and everything's white and clean, an art print on the wall, flowers, and you remember the beeping of the emergency room, intensive care, the same quiet, even beeping from all the beds, now and then and then a groan, snoring loud, snoring low. The council of nine, you think, the knights of the round table, you think, as you're already half-asleep, and elsewhere, you're gone and back again, gone and back again, the council of nine is meeting again soon, and by then you'll have to be fit and show them you can smooth it all out, alone if need be, you and Alex and your people. A beeping sound, drawn out and never-ending, and you touch your chest and feel the even thudding and hear the even beeping, the long tone turns into a whistling, a shrill whistling in one of your ears, you're almost deaf in the other since a kick in the ring ruptured your ear drum, and then the gun that the guy who can hardly walk now fired next to your ear, the knights of the round table, you loved reading that as a kid, King Arthur and Perceval, who went looking for the Holy Grail until he went crazy, Sir Galahad and his friends, and you hear the doctors' feet clattering while you're still half-elsewhere, the pages rustling, the swords clashing, and you at the head of the table in a golden helmet, but how does that work with a round table, you hear coughing, a dull expulsion of air that sounds almost like a roar, life, someone here wants to live, and then you hear the gurgling inhalation of air. The doctors and nurses speak quietly to each other, the even beeping around you, and your good old sense can't tell you if that was death or if this is still life.

Your eyelids flicker, the light like a stroboscope, and you see shadows around your bed. What's the time? You feel for your Breitling but it's gone. Your legs are stiff as if made of wood, you turn your head and see the print of flowers like a dark splash of paint on the opposite wall. You wish it were daytime, but then the sunlight would spill into the room.

You open your eyes and you're not alone. There's a woman sitting there, on the chair by the wall, right under the flower print. She's black, her skin, and black curly hair and a pale pink dress. You don't understand right away because it's not possible. You work with a couple of African women, it used to be the Vietnamese to begin with and now it's the Africans, but why has this woman of all people come to visit you? And didn't they tell you, no visitors for one or two days? But maybe she sneaked in unnoticed. There's always one man in a car down outside the entrance, Alex took care of that, and the cops are keeping an eye out too. But only the best girls work for you. You get yourself half-upright, turn around to her. She's sitting there, looking at you and not moving. Her face as if cut from black rock. 'Arnie,' she says, and her lips barely move. 'Mary,' you say, and she goes on speaking, and that sounds strange in this little room, which still seemed so large not long ago.

Something's not right, you think, what's she doing here?
And what she says is wrong. You want to turn away, and
now the sheet over your face might be a good thing, but
she's here. And when you thought of all the blood at
some point, just now or yesterday or hours ago, she was
here then too. 'We did everything we could back then,'
you say. And it's true, even. You got hold of him, a few
weeks later, and if the cops hadn't stuck their oar in he'd
be flat on his back somewhere outside of the city by now,
and in a few years the grass would grow especially green
there... (No, that was just your first flush of anger back
then, she was one of your girls, on your premises, and
your shoulders and your neck and your chest ached as
if you'd been pumping iron, all night long and all day
long, but you'd probably only have broken a few of his
bones.) 'He loved me,' she says.

'Maybe,' you say and you try to stay cool, but the
blood and black Mary creep into your head, there's a
plaster on your forehead, on the spot where you hit the
street, days ago, hours ago, at some point. The guy was
young, in his early twenties or so, nineteen, as you later
found out. 'You should have come sooner,' she says, and
you don't understand that and you don't want to understand it, because *she's* the one who's come. The sheet
underneath you is wet. 'You shouldn't be here,' you say.
And the shadows you saw through your eyelids not long
ago are back again, and you shake your head because
there's a hand in your hair, she's standing by your bed
now, and you pull the sheet up under your nose and feel
your warm breath on your face. The way she's looking at you, you can't stand it, there's suddenly so much
you can't stand, and the room's full of people now, their
breathing, their sounds, their smells, they're muttering
and whispering. 'I'm flat on my back outside the city,'

you hear, and you know where she is, in the mire, but you only know it vaguely, you've got nothing else to do with it. 'And my work, at the court, how's it going without me?' You hear it and you pull the sheet up to the plaster on your forehead. Because you know if you get up and limp across the room between them all and open the table drawer, there's a tiny person flat on their back in there, laughing broadly at you. Leave me alone, you think, and perhaps you whisper it too, go away, Mary, you brought all this with you!

You stand in front of her and look at the huge wound in her neck, like a black grin from ear to ear. 'There's this guy, Arnie, he keeps coming back, he scares me.'

'A regular, girl, you treat him right, make eyes at him, and if there's any problems just call me.'

Your phone rings. You look in your pockets, no ringing, just buzzing and vibrating, you've put it on silent. It falls down, the battery leaps out, where's the SIM card? And you roll onto your side. There's something flashing and glinting next to you. You reach for it. A bullet casing. The sirens go quiet. The ground underneath you is wet. You turn again. Over there a traffic light is flashing, amber. Cool air from the river. You tremble. The old stadium's towers. So dark.

THE LONG NIGHT OF THE RIDER

They tell stories about the short man. They say he never sleeps. And they say he's searching. Has been for years. Every night. They say he used to be a famous rider. A horses man. Before he started drinking. Some say he used to drink when things were going well too. Others say they've seen him riding the horses. When they were little. The short man is looking for his child, they say. His daughter. And they say he doesn't drink any more because his liver's kaput. Others say he's started again. And he's getting shorter and thinner by the day because the booze is eating him up. And he once won the big derby, in the eighties, when they were little. They don't know for sure though. Most of them are too young, can't have seen him when they were little, in the nineties, because by then he wasn't riding any more. Only now, during the nights. 'I saw him once.'

'Oh, you saw him?'

'Yeah.'

'Where was that then?'

'It must have been a few years ago, 2003, 2004...'

'Long enough ago... but not that long. And you haven't seen him since?'

'But I hear him sometimes. Behind the station, in the station.'

'Hear him? You're not back on the coke are you, or smoking the ice? Crystal?'

'Course not, you know that. I wouldn't be here otherwise, would I?'

'Yeah, yeah. Nothing wrong with a little snifter in your own home, it's your free time, but if you really want to make some cash over the years, drink carrot juice, vitamins A, C and E. But rocks, crystals... worse than any snifter they are, that ice burns you out.'

'I know, I know. That's a long time ago, Arnold.'

'Yeah, yeah, it's always a long time ago. And then you still go telling me about hooves, hoof sounds in the night.'

'Sorry, Arnold, I shouldn't have started on it.'

'All right, all right. We all have the odd bad dream.'

'I'm really grateful to you for the...'

'Do me a favour'

'Yeah?'

'If you want to work, work. And pay the rent. And you do pay your rent. And if you don't want to work any more, let me know. Just tell me. If you can't do it any more. And if you need a holiday...'

'I don't need a holiday. And I've been clean for five years now.'

'You know I hate all that drugs shit.'

'I know. That's why...'

'And it's not just because of the cops or the health office or because of some stupid fucking licences...'

'No, I'

'Shut up a minute. Let the Old Man do a bit of talking'

'You're not old, Arnold.'

'Yeah, yeah. Course not. You know when you start thinking about everything in the autumn?'

'I don't know. Yeah.'

'I don't mean that October autumn, Indian summer like the Yanks say...'

'I've never heard that.'

'When everything's bright and golden. And when you think summer's come back again.'

'You've got such a way with words. I've always liked that.'

'Keep away from that guy. Don't even think about

him. He's crazy. And he goes looking for ghosts where there aren't any. Never have been. He's looking for his own ghosts but he's years too late.'

'People say you...'

'Who says that? Who says what?'

'That house back then, was it '93?'

'How old were you then, baby?'

'I don't know. Pretty young'

'It makes me angry. It makes me sad. That people would tell you something like that'

'No, Arnie, listen, it's just, it's just because it was in the paper again the other day'

'Shut up for a minute, baby, shut up for a minute. And never start on it again. A friend of mine always says, Coppenrath & Wiese.'

'The cakes?'

'Not the bloody cakes. The people you know just as well. The ones who think they're better. The ones whose eyebrows twitch when they see us or hear about us. Just shut up a minute, baby! They think it's all the same. That quiz show guy Günther Jauch, *Who Wants To Be A Millionaire*. They think scum's red. And they hear something and read something and think, that guy, that one, he's one of them, that woman, she's one of them... and they think it's all the same, it's all the same. And they don't know nothing, nothing at all. And they come to you and come to the girls and talk crap and think...'

'Think they're better than us? Sorry. I didn't mean to upset you, but it's just because for years the short guy has been... All right, I'll shut up.'

'Oh, come on, girl, not like that. Don't be like that. Don't start apologizing for anything. Not to me, not to them. It's nothing to do with you, it's nothing to do with *any* of you. It was that piece of scum. *The guy*. Not the little girl. An ex-boxer, classic case. Less than scum. *That guy*. '93. Business was different then than now. The scum's gone now. We made sure of that, we got rid of the scum. None of it, no, none of it is in my pockets. And that man's riding... Oh, what am I saying, now I'm talking just as much crap as you... That guy, short and sly as he is, he's digging in the dirt and he thinks, he thinks there's some of that dirt in my pockets. In my house, in my head, autumn or winter, or somewhere else.'

'I know, Arnie, I know you...'

'You don't know nothing. Nothing at all. I spoke to him a couple of times, the rider... before...'

BOOM, BOOM. (The ground-floor flat trembles, the water in the whirlpool quivers, tiny waves on the surface although there's no one in there any more and no bubbles, no millions of bubbles tickling naked torsos. Home time, almost twelve.)

'Aren't they crazy, Arnie? With their tunnel?'

'Yeah, yeah, yeah, they're crazy all right. You're so right, girl, you're absolutely right, baby. Go on home now. What a crazy gang in this crazy city.' The stick he leaned against the table falls over as she gets up and leaves the room. The ground quakes and vibrates beneath his feet. He didn't know they went on drilling at night. He rarely takes the stick out with him but when winter's coming he can feel his leg getting stiff. He meant to go back to the station but it's too late now. Get a bit of shopping, there's a good wine and whisky shop there. The girls go home or lie down to sleep wherever they are. Home time. Business only goes on after midnight in a handful of apartments. Phones are switched off, automatic messages switched on. 'Hello, this is Sissy, you can enjoy my wide range of services again from nine to...' He'd better tell Frank to empty the jacuzzi and

71

clean it. The club's open a few more hours. Time to go back to the office. Time to go to sleep. He has to make a call, tell them to look in at the club again, call Alex, is it still Alex after all these years? Sometimes he can barely remember. When the ground vibrates. The sounds of the night. The screeching of trams and passenger trains that he knows from his childhood. He rubs his left leg, feels his kneecap hard through the fabric.

He drinks his coffee at the little coffee place right by the platforms. Opposite the platforms. He likes this upper level of the station, so close to the trains. It was only there, at the little coffee place, that he learned to love the taste of a good americano. Didn't know what it was to begin with. Americano. American coffee, or what? 'Is it sweet?' he asked when he first read it above the counter. 'No, it's not sweet.' Espresso topped up with boiling water. He likes all the coffee variations, now that he's given up drinking. He can drink americanos by the bucket without his ticker flipping out. It's because there's so much boiling water in them. He'd never heard of it before, topping up espresso with boiling water. Espresso only came after the Wall fell. *Expresso*, because it's quick to drink. Easy on the stomach. Easy on the heart. And let's not even mention the liver and the spleen.

Before the coffee place opened up by the platforms a few years ago, he used to go to the bakeries downstairs. The coffee was cheaper down there, still is. He wonders what year they completely rebuilt the station. He remembers the old dark hole of a place. The black sarcophagus. Before they dug everything up and renovated. He used to go to the bars then and drink. The bars in the station. One was down in the tunnel between the two concourses, one was up by the platforms. He

remembers the dirty arched glass roof, above both concourses and above the platforms. Now light shines and
falls through the glass, the sun, stars, planes; back in the
day, years ago, the little glass squares were black with
dirt. The fluttering of the pigeons, he can still hear it
and see it. And he hears the clatter and clanging from
the platforms and the tracks, the sounds of the trains,
the rails, the journey, the sounds that disappeared as
the light fell through the glass. Old station. New station.
Where did all the pigeons end up? The construction pits
come and go and the years don't matter to him. When
night comes.

Since he gave up drinking he's drunk coffee and
smoked. Back when he used to drink he drank coffee
and smoked as well. But not nearly as much as now.
Not as much coffee, at least. He already used to smoke
like a chimney back then. But differently. When he was
still riding it was because of his weight. And because
of the drinking. Which was also partly because of his
weight. Because he always had to smoke after a couple
of schnapps. Not that he'd always had weight problems,
those started when forty came into view. Just before the
Wall fell. And the drinking was just an excuse for it. His
weight. That's how he sees it when he looks back now.
But the schnapps always used to burn out his appetite
and his hunger. And gave him courage when his best
years were over. They didn't have coke yet then. But
they had pharmacists and vets with enough pills and
potions, powders and injections. They all take coke now,
the top jockeys and the mid-level jockeys. He thinks.
But he doesn't know for sure. They caught Starke at it
the other day or the other year, in Hong Kong, what a
great man, what a rider, but the hunger and the weight
and the courage can really get you down. When there's

so much money at stake. Not like back in the day, it was peanuts then. Peanuts. His problem was that he didn't speak English, otherwise he'd definitely have found something somewhere after the Wall fell. He thinks of that too while he puts his hands around the big cardboard cup of americano. And feels the night above the glass roof and behind the exits. The side exits. West and east. Through which a hot wind sometimes blows, making some nights warmer than the days.

He pulls the collars of his trench coat together. He knows he smells, not badly but a little at least, he and his trench coat. He hasn't had a shower in a long time, feels his greasy hair although it still looks fine, shiny and silver, when he combs it, and he knows that the fabric, his old trench coat, is no longer clean. He bought it in West Berlin, '89. How long ago that is now, so long ago it's almost not true... Coffee stains. Food stains. Tiny holes burnt by cigarettes. But it's night and behind him, on the west side, is the black hole. And on the other side, in the east, the street with the drugs. Two black holes – shouldn't they cancel each other out? Cocaine keeps him awake, now and then, when he needs it. He bought a gun as well but he threw it away, even though it... That must have been in the old deutschmark days, he's not sure any more. These are the years and the nights. And the coffee and the fags and the coke. That he snorts so rarely. Because he used to have a gun before. And he has to keep away from the coke as well because he never wants to drink again.

When he was standing by the water, the wild lights of the fairground at his back, he threw the gun in the river. Rollercoaster, big wheel, lights on the water. The screams of the merrymakers ringing through the air. His first one. A Makarov. From a Russian he knew from betting. Who was actually a Yugo, as he found out later. But he spoke perfect Russian. And had the best contacts to the Russians, who started flogging their guns and everything else, '90, before they disappeared bit by bit from the city.

Hand grenades and anti-tank grenades were cheaper than you'd think. It would probably have been tricky to buy a tank. He used to imagine that sometimes. He'd been a tank driver on his national service. Because he was so short. Some of his colleagues at the horses were so short they'd been decommissioned. Good for a desk job, at least. He'd have liked to have a tank, in '93. Or an anti-tank grenade. Drive the tank into the court and flatten all those bastards. Break through walls and negotiations, into the courtroom where that bastard M. was grinning to himself, along with the judge and the public prosecutor, and then kept on grinning when he got not even four years. There would have been collateral damage, sure. But there was collateral damage before and no one cared. He was still a heavy drinker in those days. And he's glad he never got his hands on a tank. Not even an anti-tank grenade. Two or three times he'd had a chance to get hold of heavy artillery. There was this Czech guy later on who offered him a Bren. When he'd started to get off the drink. 'What the hell is that?'

'Good MG. Heavy MG. Breaks holes in brick walls like fist.'

If he'd known where the bastard lived he'd have bought the Bren, he still had a bit set aside, his inheritance from his mother, and he'd have gone and pulverized him and his house as well.

Because he couldn't get it out of his head that the bastard lived in a nice little medium-sized house. Incredible. That was when he had a relapse. You're not allowed to take anything, not even coke, when you're clean. But the coke's only once a month, about that at the most, when he can't stop running round the streets, ringing at doors, calling the numbers, when he looks the girls in the face, looks really closely because he doesn't know what she looks like now.

He even went to Berlin when he got a tip-off. Because the Czech guy he knew from before had a listen out for him. He never found out where the bastard disappeared to.

He heard this, he heard that, heard the bastard M. did this and that when he got out of jail, didn't he have a building firm...? But that must have been in the phase when he was sleeping so deeply, so deeply...

And in Berlin he went up and down a good few streets, looked into a good few clubs. Because he doesn't even know if she works outside or in an apartment. Or in a club. Or maybe not at all any more. But he's met a couple of girls over the years who knew her. He's collected information over the years. When he was sitting with the women in the rooms, sometimes he even thought it might be good if she had working conditions like they did. And all he wants is to see her again. And he knows the working conditions don't change anything. Because he didn't look after her in '93, because he didn't protect her in '93, because he didn't go running into that third-floor hell with an anti-tank grenade in '93. And because she had no choice. And because she was still a child. He held the gun to his head, often enough. That time when the fairground at his back cast flickering lights on the water, as well. But he can't just disappear like that. Clack, clop, clack. Hooves clatter in the big empty station concourse, almost twelve already. No more trains to Berlin. Why don't they just extend the tunnel vibrating under his feet all the way to the capital city? *Build a sub-way, build a subway, from St Pauli to...*

They stood by the synagogue. They stand by the station. Most of them are younger than she is now. The Czech guy told him to look in Charlottenburg and he meant Kurfürstendamm, isn't that Schöneberg? Zoo Station, all near there at least, then there's Kurfürstenstraße, somewhere round there was an old geezer who had a young girl from the East, she might be the one, I'm happy to pass on the info, you scratch my back... and so on, and him running around Berlin-Mitte now as well is to do with other information that he's collected and still collects in all the years. *Berlin, Berlin, we're going to Berlin...*

He passes people, weekend people, tourist people, the pubs are open and shining out onto the streets, he sees women and girls against the walls, on the kerbs, on traffic islands. He looks into the young faces, a few old faces in amongst them, their bodies squeezed into tubes and husks, swaying in the summer wind, or is it autumn already, a golden October, Indian summer as the Yanks say, he has a photo of her in his wallet, no, he took it out of there long ago and put it in the chest pocket of his denim shirt, as always, he got the photo laminated in a stationery store in Berlin, because they didn't do that in his stationery shop and he didn't know it was even possible before he saw the ad in the window of the stationer's in Berlin. Where he's now stumbling between Mitte and Kurfürstendamm. The Reichstag dome vanishes and shines in the sunlight. He doesn't know his way around this city, between the years. He used to go to Hoppegarten a lot, those long afternoons for the riders, sometimes his wife would come with him, and her in the buggy, a brightly coloured blanket to keep off the wind if it was autumn, and it was often autumn because that's the season when the races turn magic, when the sun's low in the sky, he feels the soft ground beneath the hooves, sees the colours of the flowers and the woods from the corner of his eye, like wet fields, hears the dull drum of the hooves, lies and nestles and stretches out on the warm body, the big warm body, his body lying long over the saddle, over the neck, the whip between his fingers, the leather straps between his fingers, as he intuitively counts the whip strokes on the straight, the curt commands, he's flying, they're flying, while he directs them to the outside, there's the gap, the free space, the lane, brief seconds of decision, the ground churned up by the hooves of the previous races that afternoon, on the outside lane, that's where you'll win, you know that and feel it and see it, that you only have two or three opponents, riders, horses to outrun, outfly... And you think (afterwards?) that they're both standing there by the fence and firing you on, that dark scent of earth and grass and animals, bodies merging, he's wet and covered in dirt after the race, they gallop to an end, after the finishing line, slowing down, around the bend, past the grandstand, and he doesn't know for sure whether he came in first, second or maybe only third, the horse, its name now long forgotten, stretches out, elongates its neck, because he stretches with it and directs it with hands and straps, stretches its long body to the finishing line, across the invisible line on which time stands still for an instant, but he feels and sees out of the corner of his eye that two other bodies stretch alongside him, the colours like a wet field.

And he sits exhausted in front of the monitor, in front of one of the TV sets in the big, small room, light flickering, people flickering beside him, no windows, he drinks no-alcohol beer and a coffee, smokes, coughs, sees the other monitors out of the corner of his eye, dust particles and tiny missiles, football, Bundesliga, English league, Italian league, dog races, horses, and he doesn't know whether he's in Mitte, on Kurfürstendamm or in his city, in the East. At some point, the air smells of earth and smoke, two guys with ski masks and guns come along. He's almost certain they're not real guns, though. He used to have real guns to wipe the bastard out. And then, because he hasn't drunk for a while and has kept his hands off the coke as well, because he can't sleep with it either, he understands a few things. Understands that *something* was messed up, is messed up, in his head, while he lay long and stretched out, in the station concourse, in the darkness of the East and West exits, in the streets he wandered, under the glass roof.

He gives instructions to load the barrel. Stifling air in this bloody tank. He feels the humming of the enormous engine in his body, in his head. The missile clatters into the barrel, someone loads the grenades while he operates the control panels. The gun turret turns and jabs through the years. He hears his footsteps in the station concourse. No pigeons scatter.

'Take a good look at her, then you might recognize her.'

'What, how am I supposed to recognize anything in this photo?'

'Come on, take a look, it's a good photo. If you get it laminated it can last for ever.'

'I don't know, I don't know, I'd rather go now.'

'No. Fuck, you can't go! I've paid you for an hour, I want you to take a good look, take a really close look!'

'There's a bit of a reflection...'

'No, no. There's no reflection. You just have to tip it

against the light, look. Have a look, that's the face, that's her face...'

'You said yourself it's an old picture...'

'Don't talk to me about time, girl, you don't know about time. What's going to change, with that nose, no one can say... You can't tell me that nose looks any different now!'

'Come on, have a bit of a feel, have a feel of my tits, they look different now...'

'They're not fixed, don't lie to me, they're not fixed, you can't tell me they're fixed! Just take a look at the nose, look at the nose!'

'You don't know nothing about my tits, nothing at all. You think you know something because you're paying. Then go ahead and fuck me at least, you stupid arsehole. And don't put my tits down.'

'Your tits are fine, your tits are wonderful. You've got beautiful breasts, beautiful breasts...'

His trench coat smells of horses because it's raining outside. He threw it on the table. The room's so small. How can they make a getaway on foot, he thinks, the notes fluttering across the road, fluttering over the crossroads while they make their getaway across the crossroads on foot, running towards the city centre. One of the guns was a toy, the other a gas pistol, probably converted. That was in summer, that hot summer, everyone sweating, not just the ones running. Notes sticking to the road. Ski masks sticking to skin. He sweats under the leather, feels the whip at his back. And asks and asks but doesn't get an answer. 'Haven't you had enough yet, you dirty bastard?'

'Get your hands off me, you piece of shit, I'm not gay.' Kurfürstendamm or Mitte or his city? 'I've always wanted to get them done, please don't tell anyone my tits are shit, I'm getting them fixed soon... I've got someone in Poland, Doc Poland's fixing my tits...'

'Your breasts are lovely, stop it... they're... they're fine the way they are!'

'You have to fuck me, otherwise it's not right.'

'Stop it, leave me... You said you might know that nose.'

Is it fog or is he tired? The air is humid, as if there were a river behind the buildings.

'I want them to be big and I want everyone to love them. Everyone to love me.'

He sees the girl standing at the takeaway. Sexy Cora's tits swell up in his worst dreams. He dreams about them by day when he's sitting on the tram, when he's sitting on the train, when he's sitting in the launderette and staring at the round window, his old trench coat swirling and whirling in the foamy water behind it. How beautiful it looks. 'I've got a dick as well. Do you want to stroke my little dick? Make it nice and hard and then I'll fuck you!'

'Leave me alone, you leather beast, and tell me if you...'

Who was it who told him she was on Kurfürstendamm? In the capital city where he only knows the Hoppegarten racetrack. He was in West Berlin in '89 and bought the trench coat. He thinks it was at KaDeWe, the Department Store of the West, but he's not sure of that. His career was just over then, a break, he thought at the time, and at some point he was sitting on a train toilet with a bag of beer cans, hip flasks in his pockets, while they squeezed between and on top of each other out in the corridors and the compartments, on the train heading West. The three of them went to the station together, to that cave of blackened granite, dark dirty glass roof, pigeons scattering, crowds of people on the platforms, trains clanging and rumbling, and they lost sight of each other. He sees *her* still holding her mother's hand and stumbles onto the train. And he wasn't the only one in the toilet. Three of them were squatting there between and on top of each other, good thing he's so short, a rider, ex-jockey, and then they want some of his beer! Hands off! But just a sip... The door's open and the bodies snake in, and hands reach in for him and he feels his old scars, falls and fractures, on the toilet bowl. Sweating. And half-naked.

What does he want with the trannies? What have the trannies got to tell him? He's looking for his girl. But he doesn't know where he is. And he doesn't know where she is. She holds onto her mother, clings to her mother's leg, her mother waves, and *she* waves, and he twists and turns between the bodies and can't even jump, the short man, the rider, the ex, and he's so drunk at KaDeWe that he spends it all on a trench coat. Welcome money. Savings. And he tries to remember it. And now he knows he was standing by the cases for the jewellery and diamonds. What a hard and cold and beautiful glittering.

Because there's something wrong. With the years, after all the years. Because '93's turning into '98. Because the one bastard's turning into the other bastard. But far up above them, above the two bastards, the condemned man, *him*, the one he has to wipe out, but only once he's found *her*; far up above, in his head, his brain, which is swelling up like Sexy Cora's tits, is *him*, the man with the plan, the man with the money, *Skag knows no season, summer time is crystal time*, the man who has the information he needs, '93, '98, and who might be able to tell him where exactly in the calendar he is now, 2001 or 2010, and whether the bloody Mayans weren't right after all. Because the air's felt dark and humid for years now, like a wet field in autumn.

'It's bollocks. Who needs this shit?'

'Wait, wait a mo, I'll turn it down, there's something wrong with the sound system. No one can stand it. It must be the... It sounds like a horde of...'

'What do *you* say, Hans, what do *you* say to this shit?'

'We ought to pay our Serbian friends a visit... Maybe we ought to give him...'

'And then? He did it to me personally. Me personally. He pissed on *my* foot!'

'Did he? Did he? Yes, he did.'

'Weren't you going to turn that thing off? Are we at the racetrack here?'

'Ellen! Ellen, go round and just pull the plug... No one can stand it!'

'That's better. The agreements, the agreements are clear! No one can come along and says: this is my business now!'

'You're right, sure. His business is no business.'

'Yeah. Yeah. Everyone knows everything runs smoothly for me. Everything runs by the rules. The AK rules. Everyone knows that. And that's why they come to me. Room, rent, cash, protection. I don't need anyone creaming cash off my girls.'

'You said it, you said it! Room, rent, cash, paperwork, protection. It's all neat and tidy.'

'We mustn't lose our heads. That only leads to chaos. And chaos, you know...'

'Is no good for business. Only for the one causing the chaos. Deliberately. I learned that from you.'

'I haven't told anyone else – that I've gone back to school. Used to be different. Learn, learn, and once again learn, as dumb as it sounds.'

'Lenin?'

'Could be. I don't care if it was Karl Marx. We're not

a trade union and we're not going to give some sponger an easy ride.'

'We can't afford it, can we?'

'It's not our money. We get daily rents. But it's the principle as well. Jenny comes along, Moni comes along, and they say there's this guy... There's this wanker creaming cash off us.'

'If you look at it like that we could, I mean *you* could just ignore it...'

'No, of course I couldn't.'

'Of course not.'

'The *rent business model* only works one way and it doesn't work this way! Then you get some guy coming along and saying these are *my* girls, I'm taking fifty per cent or whatever off your girls. It causes stress in the works. That's not Karl Marx, it's not Erhard or Keynes and it's not Lenin either, it's bollocks, it's out of date!'

The ground vibrates. The windows rattle. Sounds on the street, sounds they don't know. ('One thing you mustn't forget, Arnold, these guys aren't quite kosher, they come here from their war... They've got their finger on the trigger and they want to do business.')

They carry the short man so his feet don't touch the ground. They chuck him out again because the boss tells them to leave him alone every time. 'He talks, he talks too much.'

'Let him talk. We've got other things to worry about. Or do you think there's anything in it?'

'In what? Course not.'

'In a few months we'll be in the middle of 2000. If the computers hold out. We'll hold out. We need peace, the markets need peace... We won't let any old wankers come messing up our business.'

'We're going where we're going?'

'Far and high.'

He's been watching this takeaway for days now.

2010. He feels old, feels tired. Been looking for years. Keep on keeping on, rider. Someone showed him a photo. A young woman. He's not sure, because of the nose. Is that the little bump just before the tip, the tip of her nose, that little bump in the middle of her nose? She'd be thirty-one by now. He's in Berlin and watching the takeaway. He saw her there the night before. Didn't have the courage to go in, though. Because he thinks it's not her. Because he thinks it's her. He's standing by a construction fence on the other side of the road. He sees the man behind the counter. He can smell the sausages and chips. Does the guy there have something to do with it? The girls who work on the street here often take a break at his place. Drink a coffee. Eat a sandwich or a sausage. Sometimes he thinks she's dead. Sometimes he imagines she took a train to Paris one day; she always wanted to go to France when she was little, ever since he told her about the Grand Prix de l'Arc de Triomphe, where the best horses and riders in the world line up and fly towards the million-bucks prize money. When the Wall came down she wouldn't stop talking about Paris and France. She was only ten then and he was still a drunk. The takeaway's open around the clock.

The night before, once she was gone again, vanished in the darkness, miniskirt, much too tight and short, what with the nights getting so cold in October already. But it's June and it's raining. Been raining for two days. Was raining in his city when he got on the train to Berlin.

His daughter wasn't wearing a miniskirt; she wore black trousers and a blouse. He wandered along Kurfürstendamm a few months ago because he'd got a tip that there was a young girl from the East, from his city even... 'But she's not that young any more.'

'Well, she might be thirty, what do I know, could be the one you're looking for.'

He knows he's wasting his money. They bring him tip-offs and he pays for them. He knows he'll soon be broke. Maybe he can sell the gun. He's already sold an original Emil Volkers he'd got from some old gambler, almost fifteen years ago. It was a nice picture. Two horses, one brown and one white, galloping with their riders between green hills. Sometimes he still dreams of that picture. He's sitting on an old pony and trying to follow the horses. The riders turn around and laugh. His modest inheritance from his mother's almost used up. He doesn't know how the divorce stands and who he still owes money for it. He calls his ex-wife every week to ask about his daughter. She doesn't know anything. Or she doesn't say anything. Only ever wants money. He lives in a friend's flat, the friend died a few years ago. Stomach perforation. Ex-jockey. Sometimes he thinks he'll have to shoot her, kill her. Because she let it all happen. Because she didn't look after her when he couldn't look after her. He's felt the gun on *his* head too, as though a stranger were pressing it against his skull. When he wanted to throw it in the river, the lights of the fairground at his back. 'She's not in business any more,' the guy told him at the other takeaway, the one near Kurfürstenstraße where the station forecourt and the street corners smelt of piss, so bad he could hardly stand it. But Kurfürstenstraße and Kurfürstendamm are a good way apart, aren't they? Aren't they? Frankfurt am Main, near the station, where has he got those city maps, scan the streets, scan the people, scan the skin, Turks, no, Lebanese in Mercedes Benz limos cruise around.

'Used to be here all the time, out in all weathers, very

popular. Lot of them came because of her. She fucked herself famous, pretty much. Fucked around, get it, come on, a laugh won't hurt you. Because the girls from the East are a better lay, that's what they say, eh mate? And because she used to do everything. Top service. She was working for Kurti, in case the name says anything to you.'

He wished he could shoot him, kill him, not Kurti, whose name meant nothing to him, though he'd kill him too if it was really all true what the guy told him. It was him he wanted to blow away, that bigmouth, that sausage-eater with ketchup drying in the corners of his mouth. Who stared after every girl and every young thin lad. Miniskirt, tight trousers, short sweaters, rain-wet hair, Beate Uhse Sex Centre, wanking cabins, football pubs, grey low prefab blocks, drugstores, confused tramps with stiff jeans, shop windows covered in fly posters, blue neon letters, kebab shops, takeaways, betting shops, taxis to Tegel, Flughafenstraße, rubbish bins, rubbish bags, city tours, millions of fag ends next to the kerb, small feet, big shoes, sports, varicose veins, a woman with a moustache, hip flasks, tranny with a bulge in his trousers, blue-and-white-striped shopping bags, Schultheißeck Bar, Kindl Jubilee Pilsner, fifty years and not a day... Newsagent, miniskirt, leather skin, video cabins, Müller milkshakes, cars by the kerb-stone, engines running, on the streets at night, World Time Clock, Mitte, Zoo, girls, fabric balls, paper balls, cheap rum, travel agency, basement with subway exit, 'Where's the ball gone, where's the ball?' Neutrinos in the light of the street lamps, girls, boys, old women, 'Everything must go!' Eighties, nineties, greatest hits, regards from the pub, light in the night, light in the morning, August, old cop car, cheap hairdresser, the broken tower of a church behind the buildings, sunsets, sunrises, haircut. 'I come from a village,' he says. (Much later he finds out the girl he thought was his daughter came from a village.)

He rides around the tall dark church, again and again. Then he sits down on a bench. Because he's dizzy. Ring a ring o' roses. Not much light, between the benches, between the trees. The dark church. The north of the city. Where he's been looking for her for years. Where he looked for her before he went up to the sea, Rostock, all the way east to the city on the border. All the way to Berlin, where they're building up the Reichstag out of glass and steel and concrete, to pass new laws for the whores. Clop, clack, clop. He rides through his memories while he watches the archway of the old vacant school standing black a way away from the church. Where the girls sometimes stand. Not till years later, in the year 2525, did he work out how it all came together; in his city, behind the station, by the church in the north, he thought he understood, he thought he saw structures, lines of power and money, the street and the politicians, the Bosses' Buddy and vice versa. CLOP, CLOP, CLOP, the drumming of the dates, numbers, voices confuses him because every hoof-beat brings something new, CLOP, CLOP, the wild hordes like the Mongols of yore, concentrate, little old man, you have to keep an eye on the church gate.

There's not any one family in Berlin who says what's what / Each of the families named here plays a certain role in the city's criminal structures / And if you're inexperienced and you start trouble with one of the families you can get in trouble / But there's not one boss in this city, and the structures are constantly changing / Even Winne on Oranienburger had to learn that the hard way / And the two MC groupings are involved as well

/ But they're under even worse observation by the authorities than the Arab families / And they're all not that clever / 3 of the Abou-Chackers are behind bars right now / One's constantly driving without a licence and had an arrest warrant out on him, one organized the poker robbery and is waiting for his sentence (really, it was such an amateur job), the other just got arrested for influencing a witness / I met the head of the El or Al-Zein family myself in detention / He wouldn't be broken for years, and then he did give in / Now he's lost most of his power / But back to the subject: with the aforementioned families you can easily get on the wrong side of someone but they're actually all harmless compared to other countries / And if you go looking for trouble you can find it with the Albanians as well, they go fishing in other waters and don't get in the way of the Arab families / I'm just a normal lad with a former criminal past, and I've paid for that past / But Berlin's a multicultural city and you just have to get used to it as a Berliner / The police gave up long ago / They're always trying out some new operation or other, but the police have no power at all in Berlin. Stop.

He's sitting in the underground station, sitting perfectly still on the bench, feeling the sun and the day that the people carry past him, the trains coming in and bringing the winds from the tunnels along with them. He laughs. A newspaper on his knees. No one's taking that away from him. But he sits perfectly still. He remembers that grey horse whose leg broke during the race, and as he went down, tried to roll off the back of the tumbling, stumbling grey horse, and when he lay on the grass right then, the wet green, he sees it limping on, far behind the other horses galloping towards the finishing line, sees the front right leg, only held together by skin beneath the joint, dangling to and fro. Where on earth are you going to?

And they can't deport the families any more / But no one

89

with any guts has to be scared of the families / None of them are bulletproof. Anyone can get their hands on a weapon nowadays, if you really want to / The Germans are just usually a bit cleverer than that and don't want to end up in jail / You could say that was a weakness / But there are enough Germans who could certainly stand up to the Arabs, one on one. Stop.

And he sees them in the shadows, sees them as if through two tiny spider's webs covering his pupils, Iris I, Iris II, girls, two of them, young and thin, later a car stops, he grips the gun that he didn't throw in the river, what does he care about the capital, it's winter there now, he's wearing two sweaters one over the other underneath his trench coat and he wonders how the two girls can dress so thinly in this cold and why they're not sitting in an apartment, but he hasn't met wrecks like them in the apartments, and he hopes and he prays to somewhere up in the colder layers of air where the birds and the water freeze that she's sitting in an apartment, that she's in the warm, better dead than on the street, he sometimes thinks, he stands up and goes to the car, the old church at his back, he's in his city, he knows that for sure, takes his flashlight out of his trench coat, sees the punter jump with shock, about to close the door of his car, probably thinks it's a gun, one of those long silencer guns, plop, plop, he switches on the Maglite and shines it right in the girls' faces, done too much much too young, he sees and he hears the car driving away, sees them looking at him with big wide eyes, staring into the beam of his Maglite, white faces, no sun beds, spots on their foreheads, hardly made up, they turn away, probably thinking about whether to just run off, vanish in the darkness, run away from this short, exhausted man who can't possibly be a cop, and then when they realize that, not a cop, just him on his own with his big long Maglite, they start shouting at him: 'Stupid wanker, scaring off our customers, gay bastard,' he's noticed the girls in the apartments prefer the word 'guests', 'customers and custom are for butchers,' a kind middle-aged whore once told him, one he went to see a few years ago, his daughter's picture as an excuse for an escape from loneliness, she came from Poland, born there at least, he read about her on the internet, it was that Jerry, that legend, that jizzkid, boy oh boy, that Jerry knows a lot about the trade, and he was sitting there, sitting on the edge of the Polish woman's bed like a stupid schoolboy, and her telling him she's got cancer, cancer on the inside, and then he thought he understood why she offered Greek so openly in her ad, or she told him that as well because she had cancer anyway, *allegedly*, because he doesn't believe everything they tell him any more, not for a long time, inside, at the front, FS, and she gave him, after Greek, she pretty much made him and then later she gave him a little bag of peanuts in chocolate coating, Polish chocolate-coated peanuts with a Polish name on the packet, which still crackles now in his coat pocket, they were good, and the woman complained the whole time, where she was from, where she... was from and where she'd been. Told him she didn't – somewhere on the border, border town, border river – didn't see daylight for months in this one house, longer, much longer. And then later she told him, that same evening, that same night, that hour, those fifty minutes, 'No, no, I've still got ten,' passed by as if they were east of... Eden City, the city of oblivion. (That was a book he read in the eighties, something utopian, later they would call it 'science fiction'.) Time, time, forget, ride through the scum, but she was such a nice kind woman that he wanted to lie down next to her and sleep. Sleep.

And he really did sleep. Fell asleep next to her. The dried jizz on his trench coat from Berlin, from the capital city. He'd only taken it to the cleaner's a few days before.

'There's something left in your coat pocket.'

'I emptied them all out.' That was in the good days when he still had a dry cleaning card, when he used to take his shirts and sweaters to this dry cleaner's. It was a chain, they had a few branches around town and one was right next to the place he was living at the time. 'You've still got something in your coat pocket.'

And he reaches into the coat, rummages in the pockets, finds a bag, half empty, of chocolate-covered peanuts. He used to get his dry cleaning done cheaper with the card, a bonus card. Bonus Cum Card. A stamp for every fuck. Boom, boom, boom. It shakes him through and through. He heard they used to use explosives to dig up ground they wanted to cultivate. That kind of thing was normal in those days.

The almost empty peanut bag crackles in his coat pocket when he walks the streets of the capital and the streets of the city. *I fell into a delirium of fear. Dreamed everything empty.*

He remembers the containers outside Rostock. That container brothel outside Rostock. How did he get there, and wasn't it the middle of the nineties, or '96 or '97? Just before all the killing started over there. *Who rides so late to find his child*. He thinks there must be something wrong with time. When he caught the bastard here in the city, that must have been '99, a year before the zeroes kicked off the chaos that's still going on now, why didn't they blow him away for good, there was a rumour going round for a while that... And why is the bastard still driving the streets today, no projectile in his flesh any more, information makes you just as guilty, documents and photos make a person just as guilty, even though enough people told him the bastard had nothing to do with it and that using information can't be a death sentence, especially since no one knows if he even has the information.

But the short man in the trench coat, in the now grubby trench coat, knows the bastard's rise wouldn't have been possible without information, without photos and documents. He thinks he knows. On his paths between the streets and the years and the cities. He's looking for his daughter, who must be in one of the photos that bastard must have. There are others in the photo. He received information on where the man who was there is, the gentleman with the little girls, M. For whom the word bastard isn't enough. For whom no words go far enough. Whom he hates so much more than the man who used information and photos to... finance his rise. Debts. He'll never find him, the man with the young bodies. Whenever he seems to get close enough he disappears, as if he kept crawling through trap doors in the asphalt into escape tunnels. Is the man with the information, *the big landlord*, protecting him, digging the tunnels for him? Mind you, he's met men and women over the years, they told him very different things, that the landlord would only dig *one* hole for that bastard M., with a stone on top, and then they said: *That is that*, as though it were the only truth. But he has to forget him, has to forget them all, Eden City, has to find his child. Finds other things. Other people. Stands at the takeaway, near to that one street in West Berlin, wipes spilled ketchup off his coat, he'll have to buy a new one soon before this one turns to rags, the coat billows in the wind when he rides, like he used to ride in the old days, without fear, with fear, who rides so late through night and light, so often he's been to this street in the east of the capital that was never his capital, strolled along this curved, narrow street, although he'd never say 'strolled', past the girls who come in the evenings, sun and wind and snow out of the gratings, how young they are, the old ones are mostly over in the West, weathered women, their stomachs bloated beneath the thin fabrics, *up and down the city road, that's the way the money goes,* when the stallions come, the whore's parade, *the great race, it's post-time,* in the evenings when the cash-desks close, the rattle and rustle of the notes in the machines, the slots pay out; and he strolls past the faces, oh, you blonde Barbies, with soft gentle faces, in the evening light, in the morning light, *Ken can,* hears voices, 'We have to get rid of the net, we have to sabotage it at least,' he doesn't understand, 'or they'll end up only ever fucking on the net,' just looking, faces, hair, fabrics, skin.

'Hey, honey, you lonely?'

'Hey, lonely, wanna taste my honey?' No, he's never heard that but he could have done. A hotel round the corner from there, he hears the muezzin calling from the synagogue, great merciful God, high up in the city's domes, dommes, dames, *some other place* and *some other time,* not many cars on the streets, 'Take a good look at her, look at the photo, and please, tell me...' until the guys came and carried him away. Not even all that unfriendly. Angels. Patches or logos on their leather jackets. Winged skulls, high above the city. He can even understand it. Tourists and villagers stroll along this curved street; he gets in the way. The young ladies made a complaint. He can understand that. He wipes the ketchup off his coat with a paper napkin. He had a portion of chips. And a small coffee to wash them down. The man behind the takeaway counter has a big red swollen nose. His face is red too, his skin looks unhealthy. It's probably down to... the short man thinks and pockets the paper napkin, the empty chocolate nut packet cracking in his coat, it's probably down to the grease on the air, fumes from the frying, that he breathes in every day. A friend of his opened up a takeaway, just after the Wall fell, back in the city he's going back to soon, he opened up a chip shop and made a lot of money, back in the day after the Wall fell. That friend, he remembers it now, before he talks to the girl, finally, that friend who used to work in the stables like he did asked him if he wanted to come in on his chips business. The chips market was on the up and up in those days, no Ronald McDonald in sight and no Burger King, and a chip shop in the right place was a real hen that laid golden eggs, or better a golden girl, but he was at the end of his glorious career. Memories of his few wins, more and more remembered wins over the years, and his daughter, his little girl, far away. So far away, and once he noticed it she was even further.

And so on. His liver hurt, his heart hurt.

It was on a very warm day. The pollen flickered through the air of that warm day. Once upon a time, you could soon say, right? Where are you going? 'If you love someone, set them free. If they come back they're yours – forever.'

It was on a very warm day. The pollen flickered through the air. Once, she couldn't stop laughing. Down in the underground station. Because she read *this* in a newspaper: *Big excitement over small traffic sign. Two police officers took down a traffic sign in W., thinking it was a fake. A check proved that the sign is genuine. The police officers had to put it up again!*

Then there's more and more yearning. Berlin at last!

And the day was very warm, and the pollen flickered...
A-tissue, a-tissue, stroke the trembling flanks. Dogs
don't sweat; horses do.

'I've been off the game a long time now.'

'Do you remember her?'

'You seem to be a nice guy but I can't help you.'

'You're a pretty girl. And I thought...'

'Sorry. You know what *I* thought?'

'No.'

'An old client coming back to me. Or even worse'

'What would be worse?'

'You know. Someone's asking after me. I've been off
the game a long time now. I go and visit my kid every
week. Every weekend.'

He holds the gun to her head but it's not her. And she
doesn't know anything. What a warm day, and how the
pollen flickers.

'What do you mean by that thing, your so-called life's
motto? ...Forever.'

'I don't know what you mean. And you know what
scared me the most?'

'When you saw me?'

'He's your age.'

'How do you know how old I am, you little bitch?'

'You're a nice guy. No one's taken me out for a meal
in a long time.'

'We couldn't exactly talk at that dirty takeaway.'

'They do good chips, little man.'

'I'm five foot five!'

I used to be a gardener. I love flowers. There's a lot
of nature in our village. I did go to the city you told me
about, one time. But by then I'd been here for a while.
No one's taken me out for such a fine meal in a long time.
My grandma used to take me to the village pub. 'When

96

you were little.'

'When I was little.'

'And I thought I'd found you.'

Tulips were my favourite flowers. I had a good friend and then she left, went to the city you told me about, the one I was in for a while. She wanted to get out of this giant city, this city of giants, and earn proper money there in peace. 'You must have made good money too. Show me your nose.'

'Coming on me costs extra. And don't touch my face.' And it was such a warm day that I put my short skirt on again. The flowery dress. I gotta go there, I'll be free there.

It's seventy-five miles to Berlin. I like being a gardener. And I wanted to go back to it, the gardening, but we'll see. I wasn't bad at school either. And my apprenticeship was easy enough. Because I liked being... What a warm day. I've never had a problem with pollen. Otherwise I couldn't have done it. The plants, the trees, the flowers and me.

'Did he have other girls?'

'He didn't have me, little man.'

'Take a good look at her. You can't have been the only one.'

'I'm off the game now. I don't want to hear about it any more.'

'There's no need to be scared of me. Why am I buying you wine if you're not going to tell me anything, you bitch.'

'I've got a kid now, lives with my nan.'

'When you were little.'

Party in the capital city. I worked hard to buy all I wanted. I was a kiosk girl. I was a takeaway girl with flowers in my head. I was Julia Roberts with a flat stomach.

'You're scared he'll come back, aren't you?'

'I'm not scared. Not of anyone, not any more.'

'If she was with him I can kill him for you.'

'You're sick.'

'Have another glass of bubbly with me and think about it.'

'Where did you get the money? He even bought me champagne.'

You need much more money when you've got a kid. My nan always took care. But I went to visit them as often as I could.

'I used to have a child as well.'

'I can't help you, little man. Where did you get all this money from?'

I never took anything when I was pregnant. I never took anything. Only sometimes, at night, when we were on the road. Here and there. But not much. No, it was a boy. I'm glad of that, when I think about it, I'm kind of glad of it. No, I won't tell you his name, I won't say. Because he's my kid and it's private and no one here in this world is allowed to know about him. And then I was only ever tired all the time. And all I wanted was to sit or lie down, no, not lie down actually, but maybe just for me all alone, I always wanted to sit down or lean against something because I was so tired. He said it would pass and he'd take care of the kid with me, the boy, once we had enough money together.

'If it was my kid I'd never have left you alone. You and your boy.'

Sometimes I even thought, when I was high, that it was a girl. Because in the old days I always used to imagine having a girl, because flowers and plants, they're not for boys. He used to give me flowers in the beginning.

No. That's not true. I'm just thinking that up because it would have been nice.

'Don't lie to me, for God's sake.'

I can't help you. Maybe I really did see her, maybe I even... and talked to her. But you have to understand, I'm all empty, all tired. I never get any peace because he's looking for me. That's what they say round here.

'I thought you were off the game, girl?'

'I am. But once you know people round here...'

And I sometimes come by here on my way home from work at Karstadt, I've got a proper job again now in a department store, even though I'm scared he'll be waiting for me here. He's fifty-six. And he was so good to me in the beginning.

'Don't talk it up, for God's sake, here, have another glass. And you really never got your nose done? Don't lie to me, you only come here to get hold of a bit of skag now and then. Don't lie to me, you...'

I'll be out of here in a few weeks. I'm going to move back to my nan's place and then I'm going to try and find work somewhere near where I'm from. There's nature and tourism there, I can go back to gardening...'

'There's nothing there! You'll never make it there! Just forests and idiots. How are you ever going to... Don't lie to yourself, girl.'

'You're a good man. No one's listened to me for a long time.'

And I've got a friend in the city where you're from, little man. I've been thinking I might be able to go there. She works in an apartment, earns really good money, but I don't want anything to do with that any more.

'You're a beautiful girl. Someone ought to take care of you, you're something really special.'

When he wakes up he's back in the container brothel

in the port town. He doesn't know what time of his search he's in now. Plush over the metal walls. Bluish light. Maybe ultraviolet. A red heart, also plush. He's lying on the big bed. His daughter is naked on top of him. Her teeth glow in her open mouth. She's had her nose fixed but he still recognizes her. When he wakes up she's gone. He blinks, not immediately knowing where he is. He lurches along a long twilit corridor, water dripping down the walls. Ahead of him and behind him he hears footsteps, or is it an echo of his own? He recognizes the rusty iron doors in the walls on either side. The walls, the ceiling, the floor, the doors vibrate, a rumble somewhere above the rock, or is it the roar of a giant drill eating its way through the ground, hollowing out the city, Project City Tunnel, why not all the way to Berlin, what a whore's pipeline that would be, 'No!' he calls out over and over, and at last he hears his voice in the dying roar of the drills, the trains, 'These aren't my thoughts, there are strangers in my head,' and when he jerks open one of the rusty doors it opens with a never-ending screech, with a terrible scream in the old hinges, and he sees his daughter, strapped down to a hospital bed, naked, legs thrust apart, she's shiny, her body's shining, he stands in the door, sees the long line of men next to the bed, ejaculating on her, rubbing their stiff dicks on her, other men shove him aside, shove their way into the room from the corridor, shove their way into her from all sides, no, he doesn't recognize her, refuses to recognize her and walks on, everything getting smaller, like the shrinking picture on an old TV screen, spaces, rooms behind iron doors, water dripping down the walls, and he wipes his cool, wet forehead.

His head rests next to the wine bottle. He had two dreams, which he remembers even though he can only have been out a short while. Empty plates, empty glasses, empty chair. Paris, France. He dreamed he was holding money in his hands, lots of notes. In some room, in some dark corridor, more like twilit. The gun somewhere heavy in his coat. A girl in a small bed in the shadows. 'Gimme the bloody money, you bitch. And don't lie to me, don't say you don't know her.' Everything is blurred, bad reception on an old black-and-white TV, as though he had tiny spider's webs over his pupils. The church, the dark street behind the station. He hears the long drawn-out train signals during the night. He'll have to keep going. He doesn't see the construction lights, the ambulances, because that's later, but not much later. Capital city. Eden City Two. He pays the bill, moving to her chair; it's still warm. Pollen floating above the pavement and the asphalt. She could have been her, and he wouldn't have noticed. Shots? He didn't hear any. He disappears in the other direction, the second dream still in his head, on his retinas. Even though it's night-time there's a ring of bodies around the takeaway. Around the cops, around the ambulances, around her. They'll catch the grim old man later. Two holes in her flowery dress. They're moving in closer and closer. If they could stand on top of the domes and the towers...

'I'm telling you, I even saw him...'

'Don't tell stories, girl. You get a good night's sleep for a change. And do something to get rid of your bad dreams.'

'Yeah, you're right. Goodnight.'

'Don't run away, I'll give you a lift home.'

'But my car's out the front.'

'Leave it where it is, I can see you've had too much bubbly.'

'Prosecco, Arnie, we always drink prosecco now.'

Clop, clop, clop. A huge, never-ending concourse beneath the arches of steel and glass. The pigeons scatter. Slowly, because it's time to sleep.

IN THE YEAR 2525

I.
Pimp? No, no.

II.
A year has 365 days, ladies and gentlemen, and let's assume a 5000-euro turnover per day. Plus x. Just an estimate. More precisely: if at least two adult service providers work in each of approx. fifty apartments. So a hundred ASPs. And that would be approx. one seventh of all the ASPs officially registered in the city, according to the stats we have. Each of these hundred pays 80 euros daily rent. In euros: 8000. Turnover. That makes: 2,920,000 per year (in words: two million nine hundred and twenty thousand). Euro. Turnover. Roughly. Whereby, as we know, it's often a significantly larger sum, as Company X is currently expanding. We have to be aware of what these figures mean in terms of tax income. Plus the taxable intake from the service providers themselves! Just make a rough estimate *for the fun of it* up to the year 2025. Ladies and gentlemen. Now just internally, between us, but across the board of authorities, for the benefit of the nation, the federal state and the city: The rouble's got to keep rolling in!
(Inland Revenue I, Section B2, Room 001)

III.
In the old days I'd have said, no doubt at the right volume and you'd have pissed your pants and all: Are you taking the piss, you arsehole? Or maybe a bit more polite, because *official* or *unofficial*, that is the question: You

dickhead, are you trying to take the mickey? Think about it, when was the last time anyone called you a dickhead, if that's ever happened. I've never used the word cunt as a swear-word, I have far too much respect for women for that. But back to the subject: You have no idea, no idea at all. I can tell you something, I can tell you a whole lot about pimps, while we're on the subject... I can tell you a lot, but me, my line of work, or let's say: what I do, my job, my profession? No. And what's this supposed to be in the first place? Some kind of committee for investigating un-American, I mean *immoral* behaviour? McCarthy's whorehunt, red light in the year zero? Oh, you're surprised at that, Mr Kraushaar's an educated man! Come on, as if your posse could ever impress me, you know the Olsen Gang, the Danish film trio with their genius criminal coups, of course you know the Olsen Gang, but on the other hand I don't know anything about you, where you're from, because the Olsen Gang's more of an East German thing, at any rate we only ever laughed at the cops once we'd seen the Olsen Gang, at the cinema and later. Even though I get on fine with the cops in my city. Almost all of them. A good relationship, I'd say. Even better with the judiciary. Politics. And I've seen some very different types, *the firm*, if you know what I mean. Stasi. But that sounds like something out of a science fiction film now, *Blade Runner* or whatever, totalitarian states of the future like in *Judge Dredd*, do you know that one, with Stallone. State Security, Big Mother, robot pimps, replicants, will we soon be dreaming of electric women?

As a child I sometimes dreamed I'd been abducted by aliens. No, not because of *E.T.* It must have been the early eighties when they showed *E.T.* in the Zone, and I was twenty-something then, so let's say it was ten years before that.

Early seventies. Some film or other must have given me the idea, mind you, I read a lot in those days, utopian literature we called it, I didn't hear the term 'science fiction' for a long time. There were plenty of classics, East German literature, the Russians, just take Stanisław Lem, *Solaris*, star diaries, he was Polish if I remember rightly. That impressed me, really impressed me, much more than those Norse sagas I was into before that, Thor, Odin and whatever their names were, my grandfather gave me a book for Christmas in the early seventies, an old book with illustrations, Thor swinging his hammer Mjölnir, the great serpent at Ragnarök, Búri the Producer, the Nornir were even before the gods, *ørlög*, fate, the eternal world order over the gods and men, Odin, who ordered the stars in the sky, towards Ginnungagap, the cold void, night and moon, *Urdhr* – the past, *Verdhandi* – the present, *Skuld* – the future, *Wild roared the waters as the flood did rise, | The waves boomed out in the trembling blaze, | Then down crashed the All, | A giant, magnificent, flaming ball*, yeah, truckloads of pathos, and how come I still know all this stuff by heart, you ask? Because the words and numbers rattle through my synapses, year after year, and there can be millions of them, but *Solaris* or that other one by the two Russians, *Roadside Picnic*, that's the one! I always thought, before I die, one day, the way you think as a child, so before I die I want to meet one of those alien beings, the giant flaming All, I'd like to be absorbed into that vastness one day. That ocean in *Solaris*, that intelligent ocean, I always wanted to get in there as a child, dive in, because I thought that was where eternity was and you'd get absorbed into it. So I imagined the aliens coming to get me... I really tried to make it happen in my dreams at night, and sometimes it worked out and then I was far out in space with them, in the All.

What I mean to say is, even if you might not get it right now, I've been used to seeing things with a certain overview from an early age. From above, because if you don't have an overview you'll never last long in our trade. But of course that's not specific wisdom for our industry, it's not wisdom at all, it's just that I've done a lot of thinking about standpoints. Where do I stand and where do I want to go, and from where do I have the best view? Of my stuff and others'. And that was another reason I went to uni in the early, or more mid-, nineties. '94? '96? Something's not right, I should know the year instantly; I always have numbers and dates and sums and years at my fingertips. Rattling synapses.

You might call it paradox. The thing about uni and the numbers, but I'm an entrepreneur! Everyone knows I used to go to the football, third half if you get my drift, our crew was there from right after the Wall fell. I never saw that as a contradiction. Coppenrath & Wiese never understood that. That's what I call the... how shall I put it, 'decent citizens'? So Coppenrath & Wiese, like the cakes, I got it from this dumb pimp who tried his luck here in the early nineties. A real storybook pimp, he was. *Early nineties*, like I said before. Well, if you look at it one way I'm a decent citizen too, a respectable citizen, as they say. I've got my own company. Construction and letting. Actually I wanted to go into advertising and logistics as well, what did I do all those years of... well, it wasn't that long either... studying for? It was on the side as well, evening classes, university of applied sciences it's called. I had to get my higher education entrance qualification first to get in. Almost thirty I was then. Because in the old days I... because it wasn't easy to get into an ESS in the old days, Extended Secondary School. That's how it worked in the Zone. You had to play by the rules. I'd say I've always been an individualist. Everyman's friend is everyman's fool.

All those early retirees, I won't say anything against OAPs and real early retirees, my father's taking early retirement soon, a rentier, he calls himself, although that's not the right word. For the early retirees, and you know I mean all age groups, Coppenrath & Wiese, I always was and always will be a pimp. The red-light man. The whoremonger. What's that all about? Letting. I'm in the letting industry. I have two successful companies. I'm investing in my own fitness studio. Businessman. Manager. Yes. But a pimp? A whoremonger? Who pockets girls' hard-earned cash? Who makes girls work for him? Disgusting. No, then you don't understand anything, nothing at all about the business. About the scene. Or you can say 'milieu' if you insist, like the academics do. Am I in the dock? No. Where am I? Where am I. Where. I. Sometimes I wake up at night and then I'm shocked at the dark. That deep darkness you sometimes come round to in the night. Then I touch myself. No, not like *that*, for God's sake. Touch my arm with my fingertips, press my fingertips into my skin so I can feel I'm still here.

All those French sociologists talk about the 'prostitution milieu'. What's that supposed to be, I ask you? The pussy possesses a warm and moist milieu. That's what it says in the books, school books, biology books. Vagina. Vulva. Warm and moist, that's true enough. It's all about pussy, someone... who said that? Was it that Japanese guy, it's all about sushi, the one who used to come to Hans's club? That's what popped into my mind, what with milieu. Fanny. Not a bad word either. Cunt, well.

107

No, not really. We had that before. Respect. Pussy. Hm. Hm. We didn't use to say that in 1999, it wasn't a common word over here, although it was in some pornos. A couple of the girls who work for me, or who work in my apartments, they... damn, I've lost my thread, what was I... pornos, pretty good business, I thought long and hard about it and never minded if the girls... tough business but good business. There's always a future, always. VHS, DVD, internet.

There's almost no pimps left in the city, if you want to know. You never know if one or other of the girls takes her money home to her husband, or never exactly. And I don't want to rule it out a hundred per cent that a couple of my foreign girls might have a... let's say an agency behind them that... let's say *earns through them*. But I've got no financial interest in my girls, I only call them 'my girls' because they rent their working space from me, I can't emphasize that often enough, that I have no interest in them being under pressure, in dodgy deals happening, in mental pressure and coercion going on because then, and every good manager and landlord in our industry knows this, business gets worse, not the other way around. I'd have to take steps. A hundred times, no, a thousand times and more I've said it, over and over: 'People will always want sex,' yes, that too, as simple as it sounds, that's the way it is but I have to watch out, a bit too much confusion, I wanted to say something else entirely, we don't need chaos, it's bad for business, do excuse me, my leg...

Why am I telling you all this anyway? Oh yeah, I forgot, the big clean-out... the Messrs Clean want to know if we're doing dirty business... but why, for God's sake, is it so pitch dark outside then – I can see the window – and the sky as full of lights as a planetarium?

The newly founded enterprise will only prove a success if the objective business environment presents a solid foundation. The market environment and location and financing issues should be thoroughly examined.

Are you trying to test me? First semester stuff. Of course. Solid. What else? People will always want sex. People will go on having sex the day after 9/11, OK, it's 1999 right now but that's not too far off to talk about, and you made the rules and put me in this... what is it anyway? A space capsule? Interrogation room between the stars? And if you blew up Cologne cathedral, the next day the girls' phones and doorbells would be ringing so hard they'd have to work overtime. Yeah, yeah, the market environment. Do you know the formula for taxis and whores? The golden ratio for the golden pussy ration. *Capitalist production can by no means content itself with the quantity of disposable labour power...* What's that doing here, this isn't the right place for that. We'll put that further back. Or further down.

You lot don't get anything, you don't understand anything:

One whore and one taxi for every thousand inhabitants. So for seven hundred thousand that makes seven hundred. Give or take. With three million you get to three thousand. So there ought to be about three thousand five hundred whores earning money in Berlin. There's more. I know that for a fact. If I cover half of this city, provide apartments and clubs for two hundred and fifty women, I have to watch out of course that more doesn't come from somewhere else. I remain constant. Solid foundation. Which doesn't mean I'm not investing and expanding at a moderate pace. But the competition? So a situation analysis? Information on the market situation, on customer and competition structure, on the existing supply range. *But the value of a commodity represents human labour in the abstract, the expenditure of human labour in general. ... On the one hand all labour is, speaking physiologically, an expenditure of human labour power, and in its character of identical abstract human labour, it creates and forms the value of commodities. On the other hand, all labour is the expenditure of human labour power in a special form and with a definite aim, and in this, its character of concrete useful labour, it produces use values.*

Oh yeah, use values, we analysed that in the early nineties, mid-nineties. When the Gucci stores all shut up shop again. Back to the West. The foreigners didn't get their feet far enough in through the door either, and then BANG, door slammed, feet OUCH. Edo? I don't know any Edo. My leg? What about it? They put something in my tea, that's why I'm talking and talking, and the night flying by outside. *Here comes the sun, here comes the sun, little darling*

Shit, the Beatles! So it is mental pressure after all. Speaking physiologically. Of course. We profit from it. Pressure. Drive. Safe as the Bank of England. One of my drivers always used to say his father knew the Beatles personally. Star Club, Hamburg. He was a seaman, my driver's father. I never thought it was all that spectacular. If he'd met them himself, OK. But Frankie was only forty-something, fifty maybe but probably not, when he used to drive the girls. No idea where he is now, some people say he won the lottery, others say he had cancer, brain tumour, nasty, he was a really nice guy. Frankie goes to Hollywood. Maybe. I'm tired. I don't know what I'm doing here. I can't sleep, though. What do they call that loop you get caught up in – a Lipsius strip? No. I'm in a cold tunnel, between the years and the stars, and the universe flying by outside.

IV.

('I mean, I'm not stupid, I did go to school for ten years and I've done a bit of reading, always have, even though my father was just a decent working man in our steel town, but those Roman numerals, those Roman X, V and so on, one to three are perfectly OK, but after that I always have to think about it, what is it, minus 1, plus 1, V as in four or five, and from ten on it gets really stupid, OK, it doesn't usually go that far... but still, we're in Germany here and I reckon we should use German letters, numbers I mean, yeah, yeah, I know, Latin, no, or Arabic or whatever they're called... Oh, Jesus.'

Hans Pieszek in conversation with Arnold Kraushaar, February 1998)

In the evenings he studied. Sat in his office not far from home, books and papers spread out on the desk. The telephone always nearby. He'd got one of those huge Loewe mobile phones way back in 1992, though he hardly used it. The city wasn't as big as Berlin or Hamburg and everyone knew how to get hold of him in an emergency. A bottle of red wine or cognac (Hans sometimes brought him a good bottle from the wholesaler's), coffee and a few fags, now and then a little nose of speed but not too much, and he'd often sit like that with his books and his papers until the morning. If you wanted more than the whoremongers and the shady characters and the bigmouths with their big watches who one fine day ended up taking their watches to the pawn shop or their coked-up noses back to the gutter, if you wanted more you had to do more. Finishing off his school qualifications went quickly enough... but the degree was harder than he'd thought. Of course he learned something about the markets and how money comes and goes, about tax models and analyses of diverse market situations. He couldn't have known that the Prostitution Act would make a lot of things easier in 2002. The money's the drug. He hardly touches coke now. He sits in the big white room, his books and papers spread out, listens to the lecturer, watches the girls in front of him, early twenties at most. The money's the drug. For ninety per cent of the women working in his apartments. Most people work for cash and not because it's fun. A few of the women working in his apartments tried out the porn industry before as well, and what he hears is... tougher work or at least just as tough. He thought about investing in that branch of the industry for a while, he'd met the Porn Pope back then, just after the Wall fell, who sold his stuff in this gigantic hall, his people did the security. The guy made tens of thousands on one weekend. What was it he said? People will always want... No, it was different: shares in shagging are always going up! *The value of a commodity is equal to the value of the constant capital contained in it, plus the value of the variable capital reproduced in it, plus...*

Before he went to his evening classes to get his higher education entry qualification, he'd always check on the club and the girls, instruct his people, that's a year or two ago now but times change quickly in his business, the cash flows and flows and that's why he needs solid foundations. Chaos is an enemy for business and only benefits the person wanting to take over. *Straight to the point. Thank you, Mr Kraushaar.* (He knew all that before, at least in his belly and his fists, he plumbed the depths of chaos in the years after the Wall fell, but now it's all been constantly on his mind, since he's been sitting and studying through the nights. He understands things differently now, compares the events and memories with the laws and theories from the books and the seminars, tries to understand the secret of the market, and it's the same market everywhere, he's understanding and seeing that more and more clearly, be it sex, sweatpants or millions made by Deutsche Bank, Ackermann-style.) He laughs, pours a dash of cognac in his coffee and looks out of his office windows into the night. He sees the lights of the street behind the trading estate fence, headlights dazzling, rear lights vanishing in the dark, some of them no doubt driving to his clubs, to his apartments.

The lecturer gestures at the board with a pointer. 'Growth Strategies.' Yes, that interests Arnold Kraushaar. He listens and stops watching the two girls diagonally in front of him. One of them he'd call 'hot', which is different to 'pretty' or 'beautiful'. The sex bomb type. Blonde, young, big tits but not too big. Fifty apartments, he thinks, that ought to be doable in this city over the next few years, he knows the golden formula and he knows his goal. Fifty per cent. And then the next stage. He's young. He has good people. And a vision. And he puts the money in the bank, fifty per cent of it, and invests the rest, roughly, because: *Bank capital consists of 1) cash money, gold or notes; 2) securities. The latter can be subdivided into two parts: commercial paper or bills of exchange, which run for a period, become due from time to time, and whose discounting constitutes the essential business of the banker; and public securities, such as government bonds, treasury notes, stocks of all kinds, in short, interest-bearing paper which is however significantly different from bills of exchange. Mortgages may also be included here. The capital composed of these tangible component parts can again be divided into the banker's invested capital and into deposits, which constitute his banking capital, or borrowed capital.*

The lecturer points the rod at 'Specializers' and starts talking. And Arnold Kraushaar listens carefully and

113

stops watching the two girls diagonally in front of him. He doesn't need to approach girls. On the scale he's working on at the moment he can find plenty, enough of them come to him, a lot of them want to earn money in his apartments. He's currently building up a reputation, and that's priceless and can't be done through advertising. *Word of mouth.* When they say, 'With Arnie, with AK, everything's fair. And if there's any trouble he's right there.' Priceless. *The general value form, which represents all products of labour as mere congelations of undifferentiated human labour, shows by its very structure that it is the social résumé of the world of commodities.*

But he's much more interested in the girl next to the girl with the big tits. He's not so interested in blondes, not for private purposes. He doesn't think hair colour's the main thing anyway. But there still have to be enough blondes at any one time. Because there are men who are only into blondes. It's always in and out of fashion. Depending on whether there's a blonde woman in the headlines, a hit actress in the movies or some idiotic bird who gets her tits out on prime-time TV. That one in front of him's more the cute mousey type, or better cute brunette. A nice dark brown. Almost black. He likes women with glasses but the ones she's wearing are far too big. Maybe that's a sign of intellectualism, though. Or a leap into the fashions of the future. There's a whole league of women wearing big black glasses. Now and tomorrow. That's not so much his area. But that girl would get the guys, she'd drive men crazy, have them taking money out of their pockets without even thinking about it, more than the sex bomb next to her. Arnold Kraushaar knows that much. *These companies operate in narrow market segments and offer high-value goods at good value for money, tailored to specific customer needs.*

He likes the lecturer, a West German, around fifty; he knows what he's talking about. Seven years since the Wall fell and six since unification, there are still plenty of idiots running around town with no idea of how to play the game. Getting ripped off by the privatization arseholes and real-estate wankers.

She's pretty flat-chested, droopy shoulders, hair a bit too short as well. If her hair were a bit longer she'd look a bit like Adrian out of *Rocky*, when she was still a real cutie. He was always into Adrian. He's seen it really often, when a girl came by wanting to rent a room from him, a really pretty one, a real bombshell, and she'd often bring along a little cutie who'd also like to... but only together and best of all in the same apartment. *Cost leaders produce large amounts of products. The focus is therefore on the efficiency principle. Accordingly, one manager at the highest management level must take intensive responsibility for this particular area. Production and operating processes must be organized as strictly as possible.* Because they need security and safety to begin with. And a cutie, a mousey one, a little grey mumsy type, she gives the pretty one, the sex bomb, the feeling that the men are, that they're all drooling over... and that she's the more desirable one, and all that psychological crap. And the mousey one feels good with her pretty, clever friend, because the friend knows all about men. But what usually happens is that the men end up queueing up for the little mousey one, the one sitting diagonally in front of him and polishing her round glasses. The one turning round and giving him a quick smile, uncertain, that's how it seems to Arnold, and then turning back to the lecturer, her glasses back in place, and Arnold thinks she'd be a real hit. He's into Adrian. Because men, and he's sure of this even though he hasn't been in the business as long as the Bielefelder, for example, who doesn't seem to come from Bielefeld after all, because men, guests, clients, feel more confident with a cute little ordinary mousey girl who'd never get wolf-whistled at on the street. 'This concerns the cost leaders' growth strategies,' says the old lecturer and taps the pointer against the board. He gazes at the class over the top of his glasses, and for some reason Arnold likes the old man. The glasses he wears are pretty fashionable, even, he's got style, this old West German, he'd like to know what brought him to the city, Strenesse or Porsche, the Bielefelder sometimes wears a similar pair, bloody expensive. But the pie's big enough at the moment. Even though the Bielefelder, who doesn't even come from Bielefeld, is always warning him that times and the market are changing for the worse. 'The day will come, and we have to be prepared.' *Capitalist production can by no means content itself with the quantity of disposable labour power which the natural increase of population yields. It requires for its free play an industrial reserve army independent of these natural limits.* Cost leaders. Growth strategies. Reserve army.

He's seen plenty of price wars in the few years since the Wall. People ruining each other. And why should he discuss prices with the girls, they do all of that themselves, even if he tries it the pussy network is permanently active and almost impossible to control; they know how to make a living so that he can make his. He has a couple of confidantes among the girls whom he meets now and then so they can keep him up to date on what's new, who's having what problems, who wants to move on to a different city and what the customers are saying about the competition.

He sits in his office, head bent over his books, then

116

he looks up at the window, sees his reflection there, pale against the night, fractured by the lights of the cars, headlights, rear lights, the trading estate is dark, shadows, buildings, fences, and somewhere between the Z Haulage trucks he sees a guard's flashlight. He looks at his watch, Breitling & Söhne. It's not one of his people. He stands up, goes to the window, leans his forehead against the glass for a moment and sees the glass fogging up in front of his mouth, then he pulls down the blind. A feeling of fear. So much out there. Too much out there. Inside. *The pie's big enough, and if you're dead you can't eat any of it.*

He's right about that, the good man, Arnold thinks, but the market is calm and constant at the moment, the days of shots fired on Pretty Peepers Alley seem to be over, he knew early on that the future's not on the street but in real estate, and he flicks through his papers while the lecturer goes on talking and explaining, the Bielefelder's seen a lot and he has vision, ideas, influence, has his ears to the ground everywhere, Frankfurt am Main in the West, Frankfurt an der Oder in the East, he knows people in real estate, knows how to bring them round or get them on his side. He provides good information so that we can protect and stock his Fort. You have to stay in the background, Arnold Kraushaar thinks, and suddenly he fancies the brunette diagonally in front of him, the inconspicuous, untouchable cutie in the specs, but he doesn't fancy stress at home, Claudia finds everything out and if it's got nothing to do with business she can kick up a real fuss, no, for God's sake, he doesn't need that. He's got enough stress with all the studying and the business, and his son... *yeah, yeah, of course, our son, Claudia, our son.* Is he a good father? Sometimes he wonders about that but he'll take care of him, take more care of him, in a few years when Stefan's seven or eight, once he's settled at school, that's when he'll need me the most and I'll be there then. And I'm still here now, he thinks and wonders whether he's an 'Innovation Champion'. In every free moment, if he ever gets a free moment, he takes care of his son. Because if it was any different Claudia would kick up a huge fuss, and she's good at that, but she gives him the time he needs. And if there's one thing Arnold Kraushaar, a.k.a. AK 47, knows, then it's how to deal with women. (Yes, of course, it's not a laughing matter! Who's that laughing? The Old Man, young AK, reaches for his stick. He's in on the deal. The Angels are flying.)

Companies of this type are characterized by activities in a narrow marker segment with innovative products and wide-ranging service. The old man, the lecturer at the front there, keeps them on their toes. Innovation Champion. What an incredibly dumb phrase. And narrow market segment, not so much. *The total process presents itself as the unity of the processes of production and circulation. The process of production becomes the mediator of the process of circulation and vice versa...* But they'll have to offer something more in the next few years; up till now a quick fuck and a quick blow job were what most people wanted. Maybe from 2000 on it'll go best for the ones who do blow jobs without a condom. That's different right now. If they ask him to, he puts it in the ads for them. Bareback blow job. 'Innovative' and 'service', he thinks. Greek active/ Greek passive, anal in both directions, the classic man shafts woman, or woman with strap-on shafts man, that's big on the horizon, and he'll make sure a couple of the girls he rents rooms to always have it on offer... S&M, GS, all getting big now, scat as well, all that dirty stuff, never mind *people will always want sex.* The year 2000's

118

still a long way off. But he's got big plans, service and in-novation, sex temples, internet, gangbang specials, the time will come when he'll have to invest, cash has to flow to get cash flowing. He almost laughs out loud because it all seems so simple. *In that case, the market-value, or social value, of the mass of commodities – the necessary labour-time contained in them – is determined by the value of the prepon-derant mean mass.*

Sometimes Arnold Kraushaar gets the feeling every-one stares at him in the seminars, or when he arrives and leaves. What he'd like to say then is, 'What you looking at, arsehole?' The girls can stare as much as they like, that's fine. Most of his classmates know who he is. He's one of the oldest in the courses and seminars, Business Administration; what will the others do next, with their degrees in hand? Climb the career ladder? They all want that, somehow, at some point. He's not that interested in the degree certificate, although it'll look good on his CV and for all the real estate guys, the banks, the cops, the judiciary, who can make life difficult for him. He feels his hand going up. Hey, he's gone and put his hand up again and wants to answer and say what he knows and thinks about market mechanisms and chances at market leadership. But his voice is suddenly too high and frag-ile, as if his voice were breaking, and he hears himself saying, fast and breathless and without pausing, almost, 'If there are alien life forms, do they have socialism on their planets as well? Perhaps there are other systems we know nothing about, creatures without sexes. Because they're not human beings. And what if they come to earth one day, maybe in fifty years or a hundred years, and they want to show us they live better than we do if they don't even need socialism, what if they want to meld us into one, men and women into one being that can live

119

forever?'

He feels himself not looking at the teacher as he asks his question that isn't a question, biology lesson, but at Katrin, who sits two rows in front of him. Right next to the wall. He can see the left half of her face; sometimes she leans her head against the wallpaper, over the bricks and mortar. He knows left is left for her because she has a tiny birthmark there. On her cheekbone, just below her eye. He knows about cheekbones from the school boxing club. The head guard protects the cheekbone. The tiny birthmark is perfectly flat, otherwise it'd be a mole or a liver spot. Do liver spots come from your liver? He knows what a liver punch is. He's twelve years old. He touched her birthmark once. Carefully, with his fingertips. Behind the houses, by the canal. He looks at her, hears the others laughing, hears the teacher laughing too, 'We'll talk about hermaphrodites another time,' feels himself blushing, and imagines himself socking the teacher a liver punch. Later, he tells Katrin about his dreams and she asks him if he means sex. But he's talking about the year 2525 and how the earth will be covered by a huge ocean that consists of a kind of organic plasma, in which all life forms meld into a single one. She chucks a stone in the canal, its water dirty and foul-smelling, but they've got used to it; they sit here almost every afternoon.

And I think we just imagine that we're here, says Arnold. How old do you have to be to have sex, says Katrin, but he looks past her into the night. Sees the lights of the cars behind the fence. Puts out his cigarette. He hardly smokes any more; he's giving it up. Sometimes he tells the girls they shouldn't smoke so much. Some of them are chain smokers and their curtains and beds and clothes stink to high heaven. He gets

120

everything washed and changed regularly. Mountains of laundry. He's got a good deal with a laundry. If he didn't take care of it... some of the girls are extremely hygienic, most of them are, but he has to take care of the bedding, the towels and all the textiles, or one of his people does, or else the flats would go to pot. The laundry man's coming, the laundry man's coming, washing everything out at ninety degrees! Taxes, laundry, advertising, studying, his son, Claudia, the construction company, the gaming arcades, the gym, the ladies, the investments, the contracts, paperwork, arrangements... He lights another one, stands up and goes over to the window. He leans his head against the glass, the cigarette in the corner of his mouth. He blows the smoke against the glass and then he pulls down the blind, over the mirror. He turns around, dropping the cigarette.

What the hell are you doing here?

V.
The 2002 Prostitution Act has changed things, as I'm sure you all know. Fundamentally. Let's take the aforementioned sales and income tax of the aforementioned approx. 100 adult service providers, each of whom makes an average monthly turnover of approx. 6000 to 9000 euros. Of course, the total turnover declared is actually a much lower sum; there's no need to mention the actual taxable income and I'm sure that won't surprise you, ladies and gentlemen... Could I have a glass of water, please! We're trying out a flat daily tax rate of 25 euros... Thank you. Ah... a flat-rate of 25 euros tax per day to counteract that effect. If we work on the basis of estimates, approx. 400,000 women are working across Germany, whereby insiders refer to well over half a

million and some sources even approach a million. Turnover: 9.125 billion euros. As you can see, we're dealing with sums and figures that we have to get under our control, that has to be our objective. If the state can't take over the monopoly for legal, organizational and moral reasons, then, ladies and gentlemen, our directive can only be: the syndicates must continue to exist, but we have to take our share!

(Inland Revenue I, Section B2, Room 001)

VI.
Sex.
Business. Sometimes I think it's one and the same thing. Constellations, the Plough, Ursa Major. A funny thing. Venus, Mars, the rings of Saturn, the universe doesn't give a shit, there's no sex going on out there, nowhere, cold and empty, the black hole of Cygnus X-1, so far away and yet here among us, here among us... You spend half your life thinking of nothing else, seventy-five per cent, probably more. And that's to do with the cold and emptiness out there, that's what I think anyway. Cygnus X-1, six million years old, seven billion ways to die, man, woman, doesn't make any difference. 6,070 light years away... There's a certain pressure involved in the whole thing, masculinity-wise, purely physical I mean, *the material gathers in a flat accretion disc*, and that means mental pressure as well, naturally. Us poor men. If it was different, I mean if women had the same physical and mental pressure, I'd have another twenty or thirty apartments (these are just figures, though, theoretical expansions) with guys in them, rent-a-studs. Heteros of course. I've got nothing against gays but the homos find their fucks of their own accord. And women

do too. Saloon-bar psychology? Evolution. Darwin. Biology lessons. Business Administration. It'll be that way in 2121 and it was that way when Jesus was born... No, I'm not a religious man. I was socialized in socialism. You wouldn't believe how much fucking went on there. Fucking and humping. Which is pretty much the same, right? But no whores. No business. Only on the margins.

Just a bit of trade-fair sex, a couple of pub pimps in Berlin, and there was this one bar up in Rostock. Why bother? People married young, people started humping young, then you married someone else, and then a quick one here and a quick one there... There weren't any pornos either, officially; I do think it's all connected. That business is booming now, I mean, because of the pornos, sex, there's sex everywhere. So it's 1999. It's good for me, of course. What with it not being available for free on the net and the sex meet-ups on the net not yet being free and without financial interests... paedophile shit hidden in a lot of forums as well, I'm in favour of the death sentence, I am, even though I've read my Kant like the best of them. The net will abolish itself in the year 2322. The other day, Jesus, it was the other day, someone wanted to trick me into taking an eighteen-year-old. I'd rented two new units at a good price and I could still use one or two extra girls. And he said he had this girl, she needed a room urgently, a job, a bit of money, she's good, she's pretty, she's already had a go and so on. Sure, I say, how old is she? Twenty-two? Fine, fine. Even with nineteen or twenty-year-olds I can get a hell of a lot of... trouble, you know, because the stupid law doesn't define coercion properly until 2002.

Penalties shall also be imposed on anyone who prompts a person under twenty-one years of age to take up or continue prostitution or the other sexual acts detailed in section 1.

Of course there are still eighteen-year-olds working in my places. Legal age of consent and that's it! I've never prompted a woman to do anything. Not by force. Why bother? All I do is rent out. There are armies of girls who want to earn big money with me, do business. They prompt themselves of their own accord. That's it! That's what the Coppenrath & Wieses can't get into their heads. Put an ad in the paper: escorts wanted for exclusive nightclub. Your phone won't stop ringing – all night long, in the day, all the time. Go ahead, ask! Ask the girls. Take a walk around, Commander, beam yourself down and ask them. And take *that* away, for God's sake, it's too bright, far too bright!

Two women. Two-bedroom apartment. Magda from Cottbus and Lilli from Jena. Ads in three newspapers. Stage names: Anna (24) & Babsi (23). Two sweet country girls. 9 a.m. – 11 p.m. BBBJ, FS, cuddles, COB, dildo play, hot shower fun, GS, multiple relaxation. Tel: 0173XXXXXX. And the phone rings again. They're both sitting in the living room, which is the waiting room. Reception room sounds better. They laugh at that, and the phone rings. Magda, Anna that is, picks up. Yeees? Yes. Lovely. Anna and Babsi. I'm Anna. Mmmh. We're waiting for you. It's number 72, Bauhausstraße. Looking forward to seeing you! It says 'Engel' on the doorbell. See you in a mo.

They've fitted out the flat with basic stuff. Ikea furniture. A sofa and coffee table in the reception room. Where they're both waiting. Simple double beds in each bedroom. The blinds are down. Red light bulbs in all the lamps. Ikea rugs. Lava lamps on the windowsills. One in Anna's room and one in Babsi's room. Dimmed light's always important, makes a lot of things go unnoticed. Makes everything a bit more relaxed, automatically. They've both worked in the business before and they know how things work best. Magda in a big brothel in Cottbus but that was too much stress after a couple of months, the Polish girls were more aggressive about getting the clients and there was something she didn't like about the atmosphere in the place. Lilli went to college in Jena but she dropped out, didn't know what to do for a while, split up with her fiancé and then went to Berlin and worked as a trade-fair hostess and waitress, and that was where she met Magda. And now the apartment in the big city that's not quite as big as Berlin, and the phone rings, and business hasn't been going badly, for three weeks now. *How long are we going to stick at it? As long as it works!* Rents are low here, no comparison to Berlin. Never mind Munich. Or Hamburg. And Frankfurt am Main. And the world ends in Frankfurt an der Oder. And the phone rings. And then the doorbell rings. *Who's going?* Magda's had three guests already today, so Lilli goes. That's what they've agreed. They always work together, not in shifts like other girls. And agreed is agreed. The pie's big enough. Home-baked apple pie. Magda wonders whether she ought to put Greek in her ad, or maybe that would be unfair to Lilli, they'd have to talk it over anyway though, Lilli wouldn't do it, Magda knows that, she's done it a few times herself but never with guests, but when she flicks through the ads in the papers she sees it's on offer more and more, must be something to do with the new millennium that's been going on for two years. She remembers the freaks and crazies who said the world was going to end when the year 2000 came. Where was she on the big night, the turn of the millennium that was only real and proper a year later, somehow, because the numbers work differently than you think, there was some kind of complication like that, she tries to remember. And Magda knows her freaks and crazies, and she sees Lilli taking off her Adidas jacket and walking to the door with her breasts bared. The doorbell's rung twice more by now. Someone's in a bit of a hurry. They talked it over for a long time before they decided on BBBJ, bareback blow job. *I mean there's no point if one of us does it and the other doesn't.* But even in 2002 that's still something special, BBBJ, although it's making the rounds, and if one girl does it then the customers – the guests, we're not at the market here, although some guests are pretty odd customers, not 'pretty' or 'decent-looking' in other words, they're the worst, see above, freaks and crazies, and Magda hears Lilli buzzing him in after breathing 'Yes, this is Babsi' over the intercom, totally pointless if you ask Magda, but she just wants to make it clear who's upstairs at the door. Sometimes they both sit in the lounge (that sounds the best: loouuuunge – like looovely) and have a bit of a chat with the guest, ask if he'd like a coffee or a glass of water, there's always coffee waiting on the hotplate in the machine, sometimes Magda thinks more guests go into Lilli's room with her then, she's kind of better at talking, she did go to college, but then she adds up and realizes it's sometimes that way and sometimes the other way and now they've been discussing for a few days if they should put *hot 3somes* in their next ad, because there's some guys who have asked and they didn't say no, because he wanted to pay five hundred for an hour, and who cares, and anyway it's usually better to stroke each other than the guests doing it, most of them have no fine motor skills anyway, it's just a show, and most of the time they're busy with the guy but they're not quite sure yet, but there must be five hundred work-ing girls in the city, you have to offer something out of the ordinary what with all the competition, and some-times after work they lie down close and stroke each other, no music, no TV, just the humming of the fridge from the kitchen, but that's something different, they'd never give that away and sell it and it's nothing to do with lesbians, even though they've kissed as well.

Magda sees Babsi, whose name is actually Lilli, walk-ing backwards to the couch, step by step. A bald-headed man strides into their lounge. He's wearing an open black leather coat, both hands in his coat pockets. He stands still, looks around. Takes a few steps; it looks to them like he drags one leg slightly; turns around, looks at the doors to their rooms, nods, slowly takes his left hand out of his pocket and strokes his chin. He's not clean-shaven and his stubble shimmers silver, as if he were already going grey. He's maybe early to mid-for-ties but he could be older, deep lines on his forehead and next to the corners of his mouth. He's not particularly tall, slim.

Sit down, he says to Lilli. She sits down. His eyes are empty. She can't think of any other word for it. Blue. Empty. As if he were somewhere far away. As if it's cold there. He walks over to the seat on the other side of the coffee table, picks up a copy of a women's magazine and puts it on the table next to the ashtray and the cigarette packs, the telephone and the plastic flower vase, and then he sits down. Slowly. He lays out the sides of his coat over the arms of the chair, pulling the black leather smooth, looks around again, nods.

– You're doing good business.

– It's going OK.

Lilli looks at Magda, Magda looks at Lilli.

– How long have you been in town?
– Three weeks.
– How long do you want to stay?
Lilli shrugs. Magda shrugs.
– Where are you from?
– Berlin, says Lilli.
– Cottbus, says Magda.
– I was born here. Berlin's a big city.

The phone on the table rings. The display lights up. The main raises one hand. He shows them two fingers, forefinger and middle finger, like the victory sign.

– There are two options.

They don't answer, looking at each other. Magda reaches for the cigarettes on the table and takes one out of the pack. The phone's stopped ringing. She takes the lighter and smokes.

– You give up this flat. I'll give you a new one. Everything in there. Everything you need. I'll take care of your ads. I'll take care of Inland Revenue. Health Office. Laundry. Contracts. Paperwork. My people. You pay a daily rent. A hundred. You. And you. Like everyone else. You stay free. You can earn as much as you like. You can do what you like. Five days, six days, full time. Eight hours, ten hours, twelve hours. Duo or shifts. Your decision, I just have to know.

They look at each other. Past him. When did Lilli put her Adidas jacket back on? Ash drops from Magda's cigarette onto the rug and she rubs it in with the golden tip of her shoe. She's wearing black Versace high heels. Peep-toe pumps. With the famous golden strip around the tip. She bought them in Berlin. Almost five hundred euros. Sometimes guests want her to keep them on while they're fucking. They're her favourite shoes. She never used to wear them for work to begin with. But now

Versace gives her a good feeling. She's got the shoes on, she's the lady. *Kiss my Versace, honey!* And she wants to buy new shoes. For her free time.

– The landlord... she says and puts out her cigarette.

– I'll take care of that.

He gets up. Walks to the window. Pushes the slats of the blind apart with his fingers.

– It's nothing personal. What am I supposed to do? It's you two today. In a week it'll be four other girls. I've got apartments. Or you can work in a club if you want.

– We want to be together... says Lilli.

– Fine, fine. No problem. However you like. I'm not saying tomorrow. I'm not saying the day after tomorrow. I'll take care of everything. I could say: from today, or retroactively, you pay your daily rent to me. You and you.

– We...

– No. No. Out there...

He taps a finger against the window.

– The plague's out there. And cholera. And scum walk the streets like they're the new aristocracy of our contaminated times. The phone rings. And then the doorbell rings. And the grim reaper's on his way to you.

– We...

– Yes. We...

He turns around to them. The blind moves, rattles against the windowpane. It's snowing outside but they can't see that.

– You?

He points at Lilli.

– Lilli.

– And you?

– Magda.

– Babsi and Anna.

He smiles. His eyes are on them and elsewhere. Blue. Empty.

– Times have changed. The laws have changed. But there are rules. And my company offers what you can't do on your own. Security. You're clever women. You haven't got some sponger at home on the sofa making you work your pussies sore for him! Tough but fair. Tough but fair. There are others in this city. They'd like to be sitting on this sofa, or on another one, and turning over every cent the two of you make here. Business is going well, am I right?

They nod. Look at each other. Look at the rug.

– Nice shoes. Versace?

She nods.

– My wife wears them too. Different model. They have the best design. Almost like out of the future.

He smiles and strokes his chin.

– Of course you can always stay living here. It's none of my business. Maybe you have another flat for living in. That's none of my business. You can live there, later, when I tell you where. Work, sleep, however you want. Every girl does it differently. Some only go home for the weekends. Some work weekends. I just have to know. For the ads, for the paperwork.

He goes back to the armchair and sits down.

– I'll keep them off your back. You get it?

They look at each other. Lilli has her arms crossed in front of her chest, her hands touching her shoulders. Her hands gripping her shoulders.

– Do you understand?

They nod.

– Yes, says Magda, it sounds fair.

Lilli gives her a careful nudge, just a brief touch of the leg with the tip of her shoe, but she says it again:

– Yes.

– You don't have to do anything. You can go back home whenever you like. Cottbus. Berlin. Hawaii. The road to the stars... But you're clever girls. You're smart. Clever & Smart, but not like the idiots in the comic. You know that comic? *Clever & Smart*? And you want to earn money. In my rooms you can earn money without any cops, any bloody Yugos or Russians or perverts going for your knickers or your wallets. Or anything else you don't want. You work for your own accounts in my rooms. That's my proposal; you know what I mean.

And they know what he means. It's a Thursday. He's coming back on Monday. He's left his card, he's left an address, he's left a phone number for a girl who works with him, 'in my rooms,' as he says; they can call her. Lilli stands by the windows, sees him walking along the pavement to a BMW parked outside the building, sees the other man in the car, sitting in the passenger seat, sees the man in the leather coat getting in the car, feels Magda standing behind her. Feels her breath on the back of her neck, smells the cigarettes on her breath, *you smoke too much*, doesn't know if things are fine the way they are, Magda's often told her how things can go in the adult services business, told her that in Cottbus and other places they just got the competition out of town, *one way or another*, you're always pissing someone off, the other girls bite and the managers want to manage. But here in this little metropolis of citizens and traders the market has calmed down over the last few years, and Magda had told her about a friend of hers who'd been working for herself in a little apartment in Munich for years. And if it works in Munich...

They watch the car drive off. The snow falls and melts on the window. He switches on the windscreen wipers.

Have I gone soft? he thinks and he sees his face in the rearview mirror, it's nearly Christmas, but... but... that's not right. February 2003. Lights dazzle him. Alex, he says and turns to his passenger, to his young soldier and companion and chief of security, Alexander the Great, tell me honestly...

Yes, says Alex, you know me. So honest it hurts.

The question is... have I changed a lot in the past few years, or even months?

You're dead, boss. That's your problem.

You bloody joker! You dickhead! And as they start to laugh a light dazzles from somewhere, and as he's still trying to think whether snowflakes are always as long and golden as bullet cases and it must be down to the strange changes of the light in the winter... Touch me, Alex, just touch me, put your hand on my shoulder so I know I'm still here.

VII.
We've never got this far before.

And you'd prepared a talk. 'Irrational Purchasing.'

As if everything weren't irrational. That's the thing. With or without bricks and mortar, with or without stones and rocks. (What rocks? How do you know about the rocks?) Or cocks.

Hard rock. Hard cocks. Who killed Cock Robin?

The Angels are coming to town. No. That's later. In the year...

You're standing at the front of the class. *Katrin was my first love, if you like*.

Oh sure. That was bound to come at some point. The love thing. That's always to blame for everything.

Nonsense. Irrational. Like purchasing. Not biology.

132

Business Administration. So you've gone back to school.

There's no killing the past, is there? Or the future, either. Irrational. Not past, not begun.

HEY, THAT'S ENOUGH OF THAT NOW. All this chewing over and over bollocks... Chewing over bollocks? BLS? Ball-licking and sucking. They have excellent service, they do. Wrote this guy on the net. A regular. Jerry 1. Whores platform. Internet. We didn't know anything about that yet in the nineties.

So you'd prepared a talk. The day before.

No. Long in advance. Bullshit. BS. There's the plague out there and cholera. Those dirty bastards really get girls to shit down their throats. BS. Brown shower. Or on their heads. Or they want to watch it coming out. Out of their arseholes. Makes me sick even thinking of it. Hearts like diamonds, the girls have got. *They* wouldn't think of such a thing. Coppenrath & Wiese. Clever & Smart. It's them. Walking round the streets and fattening up their perversions. At home as well, of course. Pornos and whatever, it must come from somewhere. No one knows why. Babsi was telling me...

Lilli?

Yep. She said this one guy came and wanted her to piss in her peep-toe pumps so he could drink it out of them, or lick it up really because they're open at the front, it all runs out. But I think she had a different name. And if someone says: a hundred extra. Or two hundred, what do I know. OK, Versace. And you can clean the shoes again. Dettol. They ought to sponsor my company. But if you see and hear all this over the years, years, years, you can't help thinking...

If only the Mayas had been right with their prophecy for 2012?

No. No. No. Hearts like diamonds. And sometimes

when I wake up at night I touch myself, pinch myself, press my fingers against my ribs, because I'm scared I'm not here any more.

So you're standing at the front of the class.

Over and over again.

Can you still speak any Russian?

Doesn't matter. I can still understand it pretty well.

Good for business?

Good for business. And what can I say, I've never been a great talker. Oh... we all hated bloody Russian. Then the Russkis left, and then suddenly they're back again. Gorbachev's birthmark, sign on his forehead, plague and cholera. You sound tired.

I am tired, for God's sake. And while we're on the subject of Russians, we took care of that lady who was running a place with her daughter right near me, where I've got my own units. That's in a couple of years, from '99 on. We made sure they arrested those two bitches...

Aha. You're an informer now, are you?

Are you taking the mickey, Commander? Are you taking...

The piss? We've had that already. Let's put it down to your good connections...

The sarcasm, the never-ending condemnation. *They* had girls there, the devil knows how they got them over here...

You know how it works...

And again. And again and again. Of course I know. You just have to turn on the TV and you know. Let's not even talk about the net, later on I mean. Would your lot have been glad if the Russians and the Yugos had taken everything over? And imported girls from the meat markets in Kosovo? Of course I know, but I try to stay clean. Relatively. And let's think a bit further... I mean

Ackermann, that big money-monger...

WE'LL LEAVE HIM OUT OF IT. (What's this? You trying to shut me up, where the stars burn out by Cygnus X-1? Where they send in the bailiffs to seize people's bedrooms while they're asleep? Where they bet on the systems burning in the interstellar storm? And act like they're better than the ones betting at a monitor for small money or big money, on the horses, yes, I used to have a few arcades once, that's how it started, if I was a different man I'd bet on the big collapse, oh no, not the Greeks, Greek's always a hit on the other side of the flush, we bet on life, at least on life, the banks are selling packages of American insurance policies now, the idea is for the policyholders to die young because then the gold starts flowing... At least we're dealing in flesh and in life... Yeah. Yeah.

I've voted CDU and FDP, for years. The conservatives and the liberals. Because of taxes and small businessmen. And because the lefties have shit for brains, reds and red-light don't go well together, but...

WE'LL LEAVE THEM OUT OF IT.

So you're standing in front of the class. If only the light weren't so bright. The best deals are done in back rooms and in the dark.

A platitude. As common as muck. A common muck market.

Yeah, yeah. Willy, give us a wave!

We're amazed. So far away. And didn't they say: Willy, come to the window?

Erfurt. 1970. I was eight years old at the time. West Germany's Chancellor Willy Brandt on a visit to the East. And believe it or not, my old mother and me hopped on the train and high-tailed it to Erfurt. She wanted to be there. My dad had no time. Always working. That's

135

the free world up there – that's what she whispered in my ear.

Really?

She did. Really quietly. And it wasn't all that easy, just a quick pop over to Erfurt. We had to change trains and it took ages. Three hours, it must have been. And then comes Stoph, chairman of the Council of Ministers, one of our lot, comes out on the balcony, and his name was Willy as well, or Willi. Give Willy five, we used to say. Later. Katrin. Hm.

Wanking?

What else? But they wanted to see Brandt. And I thought, when he was standing up there in that hotel, it was right by the station, I tell you I've got such a good memory it's heading for 3-D, and I thought, they're going to blow him away, like Kennedy.

Like they did with you?

WE'LL LEAVE THAT OUT OF IT.

Touché.

No. No. No. If only the light weren't... It's dark here. And cold.

2003. That will be or was a bloody cold winter. January. February. March. 3-D cold. Hard. Hearts like diamonds. For the third time.

We never auctioned any girl off. Every girl got her chance. Every girl made her living so I could make my living. Fairness comes first.

Can I ask them? Can I ask every one of them? Can I beam myself down, Captain my Captain?

Because of Willy Schneider. That's why. No one can tell me that wasn't planned. That was the only reason for Willy. My BS.

Your own personal bullshit, eh? Brown shower. The man with the plan.

You see, we understand each other. And my wife, Versace...

Peep-toe pumps?

No. Python ankle boots. Peep-toe ankle boots. Bloody expensive.

But the best design?

You can say that again. They were a good present. A birthday shopping tour. Shoes from the future.

And now back again. A short talk. But nice and slowly. There's many a man's lost his lunch between sound and light.

You don't say. Suddenly everyone wants to be a cosmonaut, ever since *Alfons Zitterbacke*.

Alfons who? I thought since Gagarin or Sigmund Jähn?

Yeah. Them too. But Zitterbacke... that's another one of those Olsen Gang things from the Zone. I thought the information was flowing. As long as the cash is flowing.

WE'LL LEAVE THAT OUT OF IT.

You're running out of jokers, AK.

I've never needed them. Not even for the whore question for half a million.

You can find it all on the net nowadays. Vicky P. Dia.

We haven't got that far yet. No, we're not that far yet. 1999. (That clever hippy pimp in Hamburg told me later. Further education. Middle English *hore*. Latin *carus*, he says, dear. That's what I've said all along. Not cunts. Hearts like...)

And you're standing at the front of the class, and the old man's sitting in the front row and fiddling with his stylish glasses, and they're all looking at you.

And you feel that you're all alone here and far away, and you think of Alfons Zitterbacke, one of your childhood heroes, and how he wanted to be a cosmonaut once in one of those stories and switched to food in tubes, and seeing as you couldn't just get hold of cosmonaut food in the Zone and probably not in Moscow or Silicon Valley either, he started eating mustard and toothpaste until he lost his lunch, and you can't help laughing, and then you start off, your pad of notes in front of you. And you talk about Willy Schneider, his theses, and about the powerful instrument of discounting and you're surprised, there's still space somewhere in the back of your head, that you're standing there in your shirtsleeves, a white shirt from Hugo Boss, yes I'm the Boss, when it must be the tough winter of '02-03 or whenever out there, because your feet, especially one of them, are still so cold and clammy from the snow on the streets and pavements, you always park your BMW a little walk away, not that you've got anything to hide but safe is safe and you need the fresh air when you walk to the university of applied sciences, where you enrolled and applied at some point over the years, and you speak loudly and clearly about colour strategies and the influence of colours on the purchasing moment and the purchasing decision and about the advertising effect of colours and about market research that tries to capture the irrational along with the rational, and about Professor Willy Schneider, who you really talked to on the telephone about his theses, a fine, clever man, in your opinion, further education, further education, but there's more at stake here. And you look out of the window and see the snow falling and speak his words aloud, and the sound of your voice confuses you because you want to sound confident and deep and knowledgeable and manly, *red price signs make consumers, or potential consumers, think the product is cheap; however,* but that's not true and it's part of the... and the thing with Schneider (why are so many clever people called Schneider, like the real estate man with the big plan, the one who trusted in *chaos* and knew very well there are Coppenraths & Wieses all the way up to the highest of echelons?) and his so-called rewards centre in the consumer's brain... You have to take a deep breath and look at your notes and keywords and you see the old man's nods of acknowledgement... and your big fat slab of brain ('Nothing more than a slab of intestine-like strands of grey flesh!' Hans Pieszek, the ex-butcher, on 22/10/1999, in conversation with Arnold Kraushaar) compares and contrasts everything to your business, like on the evenings and in the nights when you were studying and preparing for your big day.

And constriction scares people. Says Willy. And the consumer's uncertainty is the enemy of consumption. *All three circuits have the following in common: The self-expansion of value is the determining purpose, as the compelling motive.* And they're all staring at you, and the old man nodding like a nodding dog. And you explain the principle of 'open space' and rooms and corridors and that the whole damn economy's running 'counter-clockwise'. The corporations have to slow the customer's speed.

You're squatting over the toilet bowl, losing your lunch. The party's over. How did your friend Willy wave to you on the telephone, while you were watching the girls outside the window and Alex, who runs the place while you're studying, and the construction machines out back in the yard, and how are you going to co-ordinate it all? *The consumer's rationality has been seriously overestimated in the past.*

BS. GS. Greek, active/passive. S&M. BLS. BBBJ. COB. COF. HJ. AP. FS. TS. H&H (ball-licking and sucking, bareback blow job, come on body, come on face, hand job, anal penetration, facesitting, transsexual, house and hotel). The bigger the shopping trolley, the more we think: I must have forgotten something, for God's sake! If only that huge mobile phone, '96 vintage, wouldn't ring so loudly.

But he knows the number; it's Internal Revenue calling. How did you manage to invest so much at that point? We can't find any data on that amount of money coming in. Straight to the point and hard-kicking and always ready to take an opportunity, like Olaf Marschall, FC Lok's striker hero. Except that traitor moved to Dynamo later on. But I've had enough of all that Zone crap. So long ago. So far away. Orion. Rings of Saturn. X-1. APF. FJ. DP. (Armpit fuck. Foot job. Double penetration.)

But believe me, Mr Kraushaar, researchers have now found, and this is what I think too, that consumers – we, that is – are controlled by our hormones and drives.

Isn't that wonderful? Katrin wants him to bring wine, but she's only, they're only fourteen. And the water in the canal is covered in foam. How dirty. Ice flowers on the glass. Alex slams on the brakes but he's driving himself, or is it a driving lesson? His head thuds against the steering wheel. He looks pale and white in the rearview mirror, as if bled dry. Put snow chains on, Alex. Snow chains? Are we on a tour of the Alps or what? Who cares about Coppenrath & Wiese.

Wrong. Absolutely wrong. *They're* our best customers.

VIII.

('...and from ten on it gets totally crazy, but OK, we don't usually get that far!')

('The whole bloody economy's running counter-clockwise. People just like going clockwise.')

('One cut and they're bled dry. Down into the gutter.

By the pint. The smell. You never forget it.')

And as he's not a religious man and thinks anyway that the Muslims all over the world want to mess up his business, even though he knows, because that clever hippy pimp in Hamburg told him about the houris and the harems and so on... but you have to watch out because from 2525 at the latest the world rules will be made by the halal slaughterers in Mecca and the syndicates and firms will have to pay a hell of a lot for a bit of peace from the crescent moon, until at some point the sun implodes...

Katrin, why am I sweating so much in the middle of winter?

You're kicking the bucket in your coma. Leather coat. The cash goes on flowing. Our son's too young. Or he was. No heir to your flesh. We've arranged things since you've been gone.

Alex? No? The Man behind the Mirrors? He's still small fry. The Yugos? They'll always stay on the streets. The Bielefelder?

Who wants to be a millionaire?

No. No. That conman who's always acting like butter wouldn't melt? Talking about his Fort? The one who's been doing business for a hundred years in Hamburg, Berlin and Frankfurt am Main and God knows where, that's what he's always saying with his smart phrases, and investing money and he knows every politician and every pimp between France and Poland? Like he's the bloody Highlander. If we hadn't let him buy his way in here, let him do his deals and open up his place and knock back the bubbly with the politicians while we backed up his arse, that man from the West... The representative of an oh-so-powerful syndicate. Him? Have you ever been to his Fort? That place that's getting more and more run down every day? Where the little Vietcong babes milk the customers with their hands between their legs, like their pussies are nailed up? They're bound to come back, the dear guests who are nothing but customers in his place. Conveyor-belt principle. And where the German girls cost more than the foreigners? Where they don't even have beer at the bar because he hasn't got a licence? Coffee and non-alcoholic Becks. No bubbly, no champers, no cognac VSOP, and the guests have to go through a turnstile. A meat supermarket, West-German style. Innovation? Visions? Rotten meat, more like. It's all just legend. I don't know anything. No big deeds, no heroic myths on board the Spaceship Ragnarök. Maybe in another universe. Parallel, you know.

Let me out, Alex, stop here. I need some fresh air. Just a quick breath.

He looks at the sky and the snow falls cool on his face.

He opens his mouth. Feels salt on his lips. Hears music from the car, the door still open. Alex messing around with the radio. Golden Oldies FM. He has to get things straight in his head. Lights dazzle him. He lurches against the wall. Ahead of him, a little way along the road is the railway line that cuts the area in two, and an iron bridge. A train lumbers along the tracks. He can't see it yet. The sun low behind the buildings. Morning or evening. He looks over at the car. He sees a bald man in a black coat adjusting the rearview mirror with both hands. When he looks at the sky he knows... Stars. Diamonds. Astronauts. And him somewhere in between, and now neither here nor there, in a tiny room made of shining chrome.

IX.

('But through eternal night the twinkling of starlight. So very far away, maybe it's yesterday.'

'You write that, Hans?'

'No. Found it on the internet, lyrics, USA.'

'Nice one.')

('How did Arnold Kraushaar get so far in the early and mid-nineties?'

'With his fists. With his fighting fists.' Mallorcan Frank, ex-employee, in an interview, May 2018, Mallorca.)

Rubbish. Absolute rubbish. Can you lot hear me? I don't even know this Frank guy! And I've never been to Mallorca. Ibiza. Dominican Republic. I don't holiday with the plebs.

X.

('Hey, Arnold, have you got legal insurance?'

'Yeah. Advocaat.'

'Devil's advocaat?'

'Exactly. I recommend it to everyone!' Arnold Kraushaar in conversation with Hans Pieszek, August 1997.)

Actually I wanted to say something here about the Aldi principle and how they spy on and regulate their employees, and the Ackermann principle and that if there's been an obituary... and that the accusation of exorbitant rents against AK wouldn't be legally tenable, because the things, is that how you say it? the benefits, that's it, which he offers, and that the security issue, when it comes to the women I mean... and that it's a good thing he kept the market in German hands for such a long time... and that when the Angels came later, because the Turks and the Yugos... and that if you compare the markets now, and by that I mean a kind of morality comparison, it comes out either way to the detriment of... In the year 2525.

– MANDY, THE BED IS BREAKING!
– NO, MISTER, IT'S NOT THE BED, IT IS
A BAND FROM MY HEART, WHICH WAS
PUT THERE IN MY GREAT PAIN.

I'm not that into sex. Never have been. I guess I must have always got the wrong kind of guys, thinking back. Only once – I was eighteen and he was always very gentle with me, but it didn't last long.

The guy's twisting away at my nipples. And I'm acting like it turns me on, all his fumbling about. I'm pretty good at teenage giggling, like in films, they're always showing films on TV where American teens do this exact same stupid giggling, you can practise it, you can learn how to do it, the guests are into it, most of them, in Japan giggling means masturbating, someone told me that once and it's true, I looked on the internet and I didn't find anything at first but then at the library there was this book about geishas, the Japanese love maids, I haven't masturbated for ages, maybe there's something wrong with me? But I'm fine more or less, I'm happy enough, if you can say that, and I moan and wriggle a bit underneath him so he gets down to business at last. I could just lie there and blink at the lamp and wait until he's finished tweaking and twisting. But I've seen him downstairs a couple of times, he's a regular, he was really throwing his money around, used to go up with Steffi but she's not here any more, she's working in a little apartment now and I envy her the peace and quiet she has there, now and then. All the bubbly down at the bar, and always the same brand, I can't stand the sight of it by now, and when I'm not working I never drink sparkling wine any more, not even on New Year's Eve. Champers, yeah, but that's a pretty rare occasion, it's expensive isn't it, but it is something special. I'm almost always alone on New Year's Eve anyway, watching films at home or reading my books, eating a pizza and drinking a glass of wine. I'm not that into New Year's Eve. Celebrating on demand? No thanks.

0.2-litre mini-bottle of Red Riding Hood brand sparkling wine for thirty euros, and we're sitting at the bar, the stereo's tootling out the eighties from A to Z yet again, thanks for that, Hans! And he drinks G&T, you sweet Red Riding Hood, he whispers later up in my room, wetting my ear so I wash it and wash it out once he's gone because I don't want anyone's spit in there, otherwise it is the way it is, but in my ear? No thanks, it gets my whole shell-like burning. And he drinks G&T and smokes and offers me one, and I say, 'No thanks,' his pack is on the bar and then I do take one out and smile at him. I don't smoke much but that doesn't make much difference, passive and active, and the whole crew smoke like a chimney, and the boss smokes and most of the guests and all. As if all the new smoking laws had nothing to do with us, in the market I mean, at the club, sometimes I remember what it was like when I used to be able to smoke on the train, because I had to go to Berlin sometimes, and I'd just stand up in the buffet car, it's not far, and I'd drink coffee and smoke a cigarette, no one was bothered that all the kids had to walk through, it must have been 2006 or 2005, that's when I started smoking again you see, but I'd quit for almost two years before that. 2006 I made a packet thanks to the World Cup. And I had to start smoking again what with all that stress.

Yes, thanks, lovely, no, Steffi's not here today, yes, I mean Silvana, yes. And yes, no, I don't know Switzerland, I've never... and what he says about my bob, how my... no, I've never heard it, Austria? No, not been there either, it's very nice, but... he says he's always noticed me, what a funny word, 'bob', you don't hear that very often nowadays... but at least you're nice, and I put my hand on your knee, sure we can go upstairs in a mo, and I cross my legs almost as slickly as Sharon Stone in that film. It's just the little gestures and I don't go all out like some of the other girls, you wouldn't believe the shows they put on, I'm more the reserved type, but some guests really like that, and the slick leg-crossing like... sometimes I wish I could be that seductive, in the way that... I just don't have it in me, all I've practised is the stupid giggling, but a bit of quiet's a good thing now and then... And if he doesn't come up with me? Oh well, someone else will come along, the night's still young, and Steffi, Silvana, is a totally different type to me, maybe he wants to test the waters first, check out who's here today, and she's got much bigger breasts as well, mind you, plenty of men like my little handful, nice and firm, yeah, I think it comes from all the swimming. I really like swimming, sometimes I go straight from work because I can't sleep right away, or I wake up again after two or three hours, early in the morning the swimming pool's nice and empty, and I swim my lengths all on my own.

You're very beautiful, you're very sweet. Thanks, that's kind of you. Bubbly, bubbly, Red Riding Hood brand night after night, oh Grandmother... Yes, my child? And of course we tip the half of it away or only sip at it, but it all tots up...

He doesn't know that, never heard that word, he's not from round here, 'tot up' I mean, well it means something like... but he's already moved onto my breasts and is twisting and tweaking at them. I know Silvana's really noisy and all that and I'm trying to do what he likes because then he might come back again – he said he often comes to town.

And we're sitting down by the bar, still and again and over and over, and Beatriz is already perched on the other side of him and waiting for him to get bored of me, and I drink and laugh and tip my head and put a lot of effort in now, the only way I can, but Beatriz has real fire, the Latina type, no wonder what with coming from Bolivia, must be in her mid-forties by now but doesn't really look it, honest to God, I mean if I still look as good as her when I'm forty, and she's got two kids and all, she talks about them sometimes, the boy's sixteen now, I wonder what she tells him, maybe I'll have two kids as well when I'm forty one day, oh, well, one would be good enough, a little girl (did he really just whisper 'You sweet little cunt' in my ear, sometimes I think the bubbly's making me crazy, and he's thrusting and thrusting and still isn't done) or a boy, a little boy, but I have a really nasty dream, I have it often funnily enough and I can't find out why that is, I dream someone comes into the house where I live, a man comes, and he's naked and covered in hair, almost like fur, and he takes my child away... it's a girl, my child in the dream.

Beatriz will do almost anything and once he knows that he's bound to go up with her, she used to work as a domme for a while, even worked for Lady K., I think, she was famous all round town but she's in jail now, for something that happened in her studio, and I've heard Beatriz was in prison for a little while and all because of that thing... lost your way in the dark woods... and then I wake up and want to go swimming, want to float on the lukewarm water and then the only place I go is the bathtub because I'm so tired, and I stare at the ceiling and think about whether to buy the Mini with the Union Jack on the roof now or wait till next year – it's a gorgeous motor but the salesman can't keep it back for me for long.

And he's lying on top of me again and fumbling and tweaking at my nipples, he brought his G&T up with him, and my head's spinning from the three mini-bottles down at the bar, even though I only drank maybe half of them at most, but he looked at me so funny, I thought as I just kept on sipping at my drink, some girls like a drink and there are days when I don't mind a drop either, but then I'd rather just have a plain glass of wine. I've made a nice bit of money today with the mini-bottles so I won't complain, because this one guy sat at the bar with me earlier and bought me one, but then he went up to a room with Anette, she's a bit chubbier, there's nothing you can do about that, but sometimes I do feel a bit empty then, all alone, it's stupid, I know, it's not so much because of the money, no, the next guest is bound to come along, and I wouldn't say I'm depressed either at him taking a ride on Anette, no, it's just this short moment of loneliness. Hard to explain, and then it's over. Five mini-bottles if I'm counting right, that's earned me a nice bit of money, I get a percentage, and the night's still young. Sometimes on bad days there's hardly anything left over, even though Hans only takes his fee when I go up to a room, and depending on how long the guests pay for, Model M/L he calls it sometimes, don't know what that's supposed to mean, so neither of us makes any money if I don't have a guest who comes upstairs with me. At the 'Penthouse Deluxe' in Berlin where I worked for a little while the boss used to take fifty per cent. That's a pretty big cut if you ask me, what with us doing most of the work.

149

You see, you do like me now, and I did notice how you kept looking over at Beatriz, right over my shoulder. You're still holding onto my breasts while you slide your face down me. Oh, I know, Steffi used to say sometimes how much you like going down. And you do it with feeling, she said, not hard and firm like planing down wood, she said, because there are guys who suck and press away at you like... but you know, I'm not that into it, never was, OK, it shouldn't pinch, and even though I'm moaning now it's more of a quiet squeak because men like that, I chirp like a little bird. And you try to find my clit, to hit it exactly in rhythm with your tongue, but all there is is something like a very quiet, distant throb inside me somewhere, not unpleasant, not pleasant, that's the way it is, and I chirp like a... we've had that already. And suddenly I'm tired.

Oh, Beatriz, what would you have wanted from Beatriz, and I only do the usual, which is plenty anyway, and because I have to get that right as well, only what I tell them, what I say beforehand, usually up in the room I mean, if they don't start asking down at the bar, but usually we only talk properly up in the room and talk about, what do you want, well, sometimes downstairs already, it always depends if they have the guts, I very rarely let anyone kiss me, on the mouth I mean, and I very rarely open my mouth for them, almost never actually, but... I can actually deal with it happening sometimes, it's funny because most girls say, no, never. Like Steffi. Silvana. Never. She always said, to me I mean, that she wouldn't give that away.

Beatriz, why's she going round my head again, I wish I knew. We always have a laugh when she talks about her time working for the dominatrix, and she must have worked other places and often as an active dominatrix and in studios and that, before the bad thing or after, because none of us seem to know exactly when it was. And I mean, what with us laughing with her, and her sitting in our midst like an old show mistress, a lady show master who knows *all the tricks in the book*, I mean that makes all the bitching behind her back really bad. Pretty shitty. Yeah.

Because we have to laugh. You wouldn't believe it. She had this one client who wanted to be her dog, he wanted that and it was all he'd ever wished for and he paid a whole lot of money for it, she says, and I believe her right off, because we've all had the odd guest or client who we've had to turn down or send away because it's not in your repertoire, scat and all that, so anyway she takes him for a walk, on a proper lead with a collar, and him just in a T-shirt and shorts because that's how he wanted her to take him out, take him for walkies... we couldn't stop laughing at that... and this one time she went out with him because she needed cigarettes, and she went to an off-licence, or no, I think it was one of those corner shops we used to have in the Zone, neighbourhood shops they were called, the kind where all the old folks go because it's just round the corner and they know everyone there, the women behind the till and the other old folks who go there as well, and she ties him up outside, to a drainpipe, I think, one of those pipes anyway, and before that he followed her along the road on all fours. And when she ties him up and goes in the shop he starts yowling and whimpering, you wouldn't believe it. And when she comes back out again the dog man jumps up at her, almost screaming, like howling with joy, you know, licking her shoes, licking her legs, can't get a hold of himself. I reckon if someone like that came here, if someone wanted to make like a dog here, Hans would grab him by the collar and throw him out on the street. Mind you... if the guest's paying... But we haven't got an S&M room here. Maybe we'll get one, one day.

Olaf was his name, when I was eighteen, the one who was so gentle and kind to me, I'd never had that before and I was heartbroken once he was gone. And then he came back, two years later. And he was actually, if I think back, he was actually the only one I felt anything with. Pretty crap. Pretty funny. But it is how it is. Or was. I've just always had the wrong guys. Sometimes I think there must be something wrong with me. But I look and I don't find anything, and it's not always kitchen-sink psychology. I mean, I'm doing fine. And I've got plenty of time for myself. After work.

He slides up me again, his tongue must have got tired. And I see that he's almost hard. This is going to be easy. Sometimes I have to jerk away at them like crazy, so much my arm almost breaks off, because they've drunk too much. Or if I have to suck them off for hours, I've only got a small mouth, then I get this cracking sound when I massage my cheeks and jawbones and open and close my little mouth. That's what it feels like to me, anyway. Unrelaxed, unfitting and unappreciated. *Oh, Little Red Riding Hood... Yes, Grandmother? Why've you got such a wonky mouth, my dear?* Oh no, I don't need any more bubbly, no thanks. Will I suck it for you? Of course I will. Where do you think you are, honey? I don't say the last bit because he knows perfectly well where he is. Plus dreams. Plus illusions. So I smile and put a condom on him. Some girls can do that with their mouths; I'd like to try that out one time.

The guests are really into that, I've heard. Doesn't matter really. It's always been fine the usual way. Yeah.

He's getting really hard now. And while we're sitting

downstairs at the bar, still and before and then later and over and over, and the eighties are tootling through the air, I watch you. The way you are a bit unsettled after all. Just a little bit. We've both got our routine. It's all fine.

After work I go home, close the front door and count my money. Virtually, I mean. It always goes straight into my account. Most of it. A lot of it in cash, instead. I've known Hans a long time; we always find a way. Because of the taxes. The other day the Job Centre sent along a team, they really did. Vice, you know, the cops from the Vice Squad, like in the movies, they don't actually come any more. It's all above board here. But the Job Centre inspectors, they're the worst, they want papers, they check everything. I don't have a problem with it. They just want to see that no one's claiming and working. You know, benefits and the club. Benefit fraud? No. That would be stupid of me. I earn enough. Even after tax. And I've got private health insurance, Continentale. I'm not plugging them though. They're just one company out of many. I never want to get sick. Never have been much so far. Lucky for me. And I'm not quite... I mean, I'm well away from thirty. Twenty-five, twenty-six, twenty-four, twenty-seven; it goes so quickly. No one has to know. I still look happy enough in the mirror.

Are there some waiting for Prince Charming, or whatever you want to call someone like that? Could be. I don't think so, though. I can't imagine it, even though there's probably a tiny niche in your brain that's always open for that kind of crap.

He gets really hard when I've got him in my mouth, yeah, yeah, with a nice condom over him, I'm old-school about that, although I do give him a quick suck without one, just quickly, but then I put the thing over him, with both hands, nice and carefully, maybe he's disappointed

153

that I don't go on without a condom because I did it without for a moment, but he's still off and away, in and away, in my mouth, and I see his Adam's apple bobbing up and down, his moaning a slight gurgle. I can't say which of the girls, apart from Beatriz but a lot of that's just talk, does blow jobs without a condom, I mean bareback to completion.

Good night, Prince Charming, lie back and relax.

What's that supposed to mean about my hair? I'm not a boy, not a Bob. We used to have a budgie, wasn't he called Bobby? Me and my sister. Or was he called Rudi? I'd have to think about it, then I'd definitely remember. All I know is that she stepped on him, by accident. We cried like crazy and blood came out of his beak until he was dead at last.

I try to get him in nice and deep. It goes quicker then. There's a real art to deep throating. I can't imagine it. And I don't think Miss I Can Do Anything B. can do it either. No, really I don't. Switch off her gagging reflex, I mean. Hello – how's that supposed to work? No. You hear it and read it everywhere, that it's on girls' set cards here and there. Whores-dot-net. Jerry's radio station. And so on. I'm tired and I feel like watching films or reading my books at home.

And the other day I watched this film with the girls before work, this old movie from the eighties or even the seventies it was, I think, about girls who have their clit, we call it the tickler in German, stupid word really, they have their clitoris at the back of their, what do you call it, at the back of their throat. And they can only come if the guys go in really deep, yeah, it was funny actually. We did laugh. Because then they saw atomic rockets when they came... in their throats, of course. Yeah, throat orgasms. What a load of crap. But still it was better than,

154

mind you not really because this one was hilarious, this other ancient porno where this guy finds a bottle with a genie in it, and he has to make his wishes come true, the genie does. You know the way. And his first wish is women, obviously. Beautiful, willing women, obviously. Big breasts and so on, obviously. But after a while that's not enough for him, what an idiot, so he wants a second dick, a guy with two dicks, what a nightmare, we all said so. And Hans was nagging because we had to start work in a minute. But he was busy because the wholesaler was delivering the bubbly and so on. Red Riding Hood, no thanks. And he almost broke the lot of it, almost dropped it, and a couple of mini-bottles did end up on the floor, he was so shocked, because we were more yelling than laughing. Because Mister Magic Wand's second stiff dick was on his forehead. He looked like a unicorn. It looked really realistic, in the film I mean, not just like a strap-on round his head.

Steffi was still there when we used to watch all that crap on the TV above the bar. It's a shame she's working somewhere else now. I used to have one for the road with her sometimes. A Campari or a Southern Comfort or a Pernod, to take away the taste of bloody bubbly. And the rubber. You do take the ones that taste better, or at least don't feel like a big rubber finger from a glove.

I think she, Steffi I mean, liked bubbly and champers and all that kind of thing, liked drinking it. Sometimes she took me to the Star Club, it's not called that but we always called it the Star Club, a few of the girls used to meet there after work or on the weekend. Hans went there sometimes as well and the Old Man and a few of the security people or guys who had little clubs or a couple of apartments. They were real parties back then, with coke and that, but I didn't go there with her much,

I'd often rather stay at home or go swimming.

Come on, you really turn me on, put it in me. I turn my head a bit while he lies down on me, while we're sitting downstairs at the bar, I turn my head a bit and smile the way I always smile, he's getting heavy on top of me, I say: Come on, baby, let me ride you. I see the clock on the bedside table, just under twenty-five minutes for the second round, I hear the music dull and quiet from downstairs, see the red blinds, can you see the stars, is it a clear night, will there be rain by the morning? What must it be like to work in an apartment, like Steffi does now? I've been at Hans's club for two years, before that I spent six months in W. outside M. I started back in this little brothel outside J., the mountains nearby, and sometimes I'd go hiking, I miss that sometimes, even though I do a lot of swimming and sometimes go for a walk, but the city's so flat, you have to go a long way before you get to the mountains, yeah.

And then you must be on your own all the time. I mean when there're no guests there. And how many guests have to come so you can put aside a bit of money, make proper money, if it costs a hundred a day in rent when you rent one of the Old Man's apartments, so I've heard... but OK, I suppose it's all-inclusive and I could put everything else in my own purse, and the guests wouldn't be drunk or half-cut so often... Steffi was pretty clever, yes, she was, and she'll have had some kind of plan when she left here and moved to an apartment. Hans wasn't happy about her wanting to leave because she got on well with him, more than well, if you get my meaning, the bed's creaky again today, as I move faster and faster on top of him, ride him to the finishing line, mind you, better slow down, there's still twenty minutes to go, not that he wants to have another try and manages

156

it and all, although I can't hardly imagine that because he's not twenty any more, *I'm not that into... do you hear!* and actually I like being on my, I'm often alone, but if I was on my own at work as well most of the time... and he shoots his load. I feel him pumping, feel his sweat. And he leans over to me, puts his hand on mine for a moment, my hand resting on the bar by the ashtray, and then he buys me a drink. Hey, Red Riding Hood. Thank you.

And I'd like to go back to working days. Sit on the train after work in the evening and go home with the other home-goers after their shift... in the morning we're silent, in the evening we talk and we whisper because we're looking forward to getting home, the whole carriage is looking forward to getting home, after work. And then I could go out at night again, maybe go to the cinema for a change, visit friends, but thinking about it most of them have left town and the others live in my hometown, I'm not from here, and the girls from work... well, I don't want to hang out with them all the time, even though we did use to do stuff together sometimes, but most of them only ended up hanging out at the Star Club anyway.

Round the corner from where Steffi's working in the apartment there's a fun fair that's always there. I've never been to her place, I mean her workplace, but I know more or less where it is. We used to go there as kids. Me, my mum and my sister. The ghost train, how we screamed in there sometimes. We were always crazy about the fun fair, especially the ghost train. Even though it wasn't actually scary. And there was this little railway line as well, run by this old couple, she'd sell the tickets and he was the conductor, and on either side of the track there were all these wooden figures and buildings, knights and wizards and castles and witches' huts,

a little fairyland, we went rattling round and round that
track, and sometimes it seemed like hours and hours
and even longer, and I could go there with Steffi one
time, maybe not on the fairyland railway, that's probably not even there any more, but on the rollercoasters
and the really fast rides, sometimes I've walked past or
gone past it on the train and heard the popping of the air
rifles, maybe you couldn't actually hear it in real life but
I heard it all right because I'm really good at shooting
air rifles, and I thought for a long time about just going
in there, drifting around from stall to stall, from ride to
ride, and just going ahead and shooting myself the biggest bear or whatever they have there. But I would have
felt stupid, lugging some huge pink teddy bear halfway
across town; mind you, maybe that would have been
nice, in a way.

And Steffi, she'd be amazed, her jaw would drop...
with me winning us teddy after teddy and sangria and
felt-tip pens and ashtrays, Olaf taught me back in the
day. No, my father taught me. In the small town where
I'm from there's an observatory, for looking at the stars.
We went there with school and me and Olaf went there
too. We did a lot of stuff together, even though it didn't
last long. Dad taught me it, how to shoot an air rifle. In
the really old days when I was little, before the Wall
fell, he used to go out hunting with people from politics
and that, he sometimes told us, but not so much later.
But he didn't have a proper rifle any more, only the air
rifle. It looked good, shiny wood like precious timber,
the butt of the rifle. We often practised shooting in the
garden. My sister wasn't as good as me. I think she's got
the rifle now. She took most of Dad's things to her place
when he died. I don't like thinking about it. I'd like to
go and visit her one time. It's not so easy now though,

since Mum's known. Mum, I say, I only dance there. My sister's moved back in with her since she lost her job. She could start here, any time. But no... I'm getting tired now. Sitting at the bar and waiting for a guest who's nice and goes upstairs with me for an hour. Or two or three quickies. There's always a last rush after midnight.

My phone's been ringing the whole time and I didn't answer; I knew the number. I still write to Mum a lot. It's her birthday in July. I work in a bar, Mum, I've even done a cocktail course. Why I can't tell her, I don't know... I'm twenty-six and it was my decision. And the way they looked at me once they knew. Like I had some disease, like I was sick. Because someone saw it on the internet, because someone recognized me, one of Mum's stupid friends. I'd like to go back to the observatory one time. They let us look through the big telescope. Planets and stars. If you look at the sun through it you go blind.

Sometimes I envy Steffi because she's not in contact with her family any more. Doesn't want anything more to do with them. I hope and I think Mum can accept that I do what I do, because I can decide for myself. Any time.

And I can understand Steffi not having contact or wanting it any more. Her parents went to the West, buggered off when she was really little. And she had to go into a home for a while, some kind of home, and then to a foster family. She ran away from them a few times, she told me when we were having one of our rare drinks for the road, the ones I like remembering so much. The woman was old enough to be her grandmother. Which would have been OK, she said, but apparently she was a really awful old bitch. A real old hag, apparently. So she emptied out the larder, put it all in her backpack, everything that fitted in her little blue camping knapsack, and ran away. And seeing as it wasn't that easy to run away in the GDR, I mean it's not that easy even now to hide out somewhere at the age of nine, but there's Zoo Station and all that, no, Mum, that's not nothing to do with my work, nothing at all.

Run, girl, and hide in the woods...

I can hardly remember anything from the East, I was only little when the Wall came down, five years old, but my father used to talk about it a lot. He had plenty of time, he was usually at home, taught me how to shoot an air rifle.

He's getting faster and faster, come on, come on, shoot it, shoot it, yeah, yeah, yeah! They usually come faster if you fire them on. Might become a regular. He looks happy and satisfied. Regulars are really important. Makes things much easier. If they're halfway nice and especially well turned out and clean. I've got this one regular, I find him really unpleasant. He asks me every time if I won't give him a blow job without a condom. Come back in five years' time, maybe I'll have to... no, I don't have to do anything, but maybe by then I really will do it or I'll have taken my retirement. Nice little house. I'd have to look for someone nice, someone with money who gives me my space. We can have sex, that's fine, because I'm not bothered about sex... Steffi always liked sex. A lot of it. From an early age. For me it's more like all... sounds stupid, maybe, but... mechanical, and then professional, so it doesn't bother me. Normal, I'd say. In my childhood... I was always a late one. My sister, she's a year and a half younger than me, she was masturbating when I was still... oh, what do I know. Maybe I'm missing out and maybe it'll come to me later in life. I doubt it though. Because I have had more sex than most people, just for business I mean. Stroking, cuddling, yeah. I like all that, yes. Like with Olaf. Back in the day.

It's not like I don't think of it, sometimes.

The hairy guy sometimes asks if I can come and visit him at home, he says he'd be happy to pay a lot more. Says he's got a house, a villa, on the edge of town. Yeah right, and I bet he's got a basement out there and all. He went up with Beatriz a couple of times and she told us he's a switcher. I'd never heard of that. She said he wants to get penetrated hard with a dildo and he likes to ram her in the bum as well and yells insults at her while he's at it. Crazy. Makes me shiver.

I haven't stolen the slightest thing from you! What? No, nothing, it's nearly home-time. Sometimes I think this place is haunted. Spooks in the red-light district. What was that film called again, that GDR children's film? *Spooks under the Big Wheel? Spooks in the Highrise?* Or were there two films, two different films? I saw them on TV later, after the Wall I mean, they show a lot of those old things on the Zone channels, but they're really good, no, really. Helped me to understand my father. That he was so... sad would be the wrong word... after the Wall, when the Wall fell. I was only very little. It's not long till Christmas. Red candles arching in the windows. Rubbish, you're talking crap, girl, it's still three months to go. Sometimes I think this place is haunted. Like a big old castle. The way B. always talked about that studio, I imagined it like a castle. At least like a big old villa. Where they almost killed that girl, that woman, that sub. The one they were training as a maid there, they hung her up in the wardrobe. Bristling with needles. And stuff like that. And then things kind of got out of control, apparently. In this film there was one guy who could put his head through walls, and one time he came up out of the plughole in the sink, and the kids kept on whacking him over the head with a frying pan. He was something

161

like a ghost, him and his wife, who was a ghost as well, obviously, and they had to do good deeds in this GDR high-rise block because they'd killed a policeman a hundred years ago or longer, he'd found out about them because they were robbers. They had an inn and they robbed the guests there and then killed them too. And didn't they hang them up in the wardrobe as well first, but maybe I'm getting muddled up. In my head, in my head. Knock, knock in my head. No, of course not.

And then I could share an apartment with Steffi, if I think about it. He's finished. Lying next to me.

You have a nice rest, you deserve it, you've been working really hard.

And then we could go to the cinema sometimes, after work, the two of us. What was that film we saw with all the girls back then? Most of them have moved on since then. Sometimes they come back and then it's all, hey, you're back again! There's a lot of coming and going. Travelling people. But I've kind of found my place here. Sitting at the bar, drifting on the stream of the music, the lights, the voices, the door opens, guests, customers, guests, Hans had to put in a new ventilation system not long ago because of the smoking laws, it's much better now and I've really promised myself to give up altogether, but I'm still young and I can take anything. The smoke and the night and the bubbly, it gets you down in the long run. No need to tell me that. But I like the night.

Yes. It makes us kind of on the other side. Sounds funny, I know. We're something special. Night workers. We're allied to the silence. Sometimes I think we're all sleepwalkers. Even though there's always a lot of action here.

Hold the condom nice and tight, we don't want to get uptight, do we? Hold on, I'll put it straight in the kitchen roll.

It was Hans wanted me to call myself Mandy. I didn't like it to begin with but I got used to it. I was like Mandy, he sometimes said to begin with. Quite often actually. Because there was a Mandy working in his club before, years ago. I think he was in love with her. That's what I imagine sometimes, anyway. And then I think I'd like to be in love again. Then maybe everything would be different. Fun and sex and rock 'n' roll. But I think those days are over. Even though I'm still young. Where I'm from there's this guy Max, he was a virgin until last year. In his late twenties, just imagine it. Mind you, I can. Imagine it, I mean. And now he's got married. I haven't been there since then. And when I was there at his wedding for a bit I didn't see my mother, either. Because she didn't want to. Life goes on, somehow. Easy money, I often tell myself. The guy's sitting on the edge of the bed, getting dressed. His back's wet with sweat. Who else earns a hundred and twenty an hour? Ten minutes left on the clock. Now he's talking. Says his name's Holger. Offers me a cigarette. Thanks. He gives me a light and I hand him his half-full G&T. He drinks and smokes and says this and that.

While I switch off for a moment and sink inside myself and gather my strength, little mental break... and a pretty girl like you... Oh, no. Stop it, will you, please. Don't start on that one, don't tell me I could be doing better. I do it because I want to, do you get that?

And downstairs at the bar and upstairs in the room, bar, room, *the greatest hits of the 80s*, Hans, the really good gel's run out! Red Riding Hood, no, Grandmother... Maike turned up here the other day, *Hans, I think the bed's broken again*, worked here for a couple of weeks. There were English guys here the other week, and Japanese.

163

I think my English is still quite good. She's a friend of Olaf's, Maike is. Or she used to be, anyway. I'm over him now, have been for ages. In theory. It's such a long time ago now. Maike's alright. Showed me everything at the 'Deluxe' back then, explained it all.

And morning comes again. And morning comes again. And later, in the warm water of the swimming pool, I turn onto my back, just lie there without sinking, float and drift and feel a great calm inside of me, as I look through the arched glass roof at the clouded, dull sky. Then it goes blue, I'm reflected in the sky and I see myself floating and drifting. How good it feels.

AMALGAM

The flic, le cop, the captain, the eternal gripper, the bloodhound, the old detective floats in the heart of the seas as they clear out the mires outside the big city, draining them and making them *urban* (as once the farmers made the land *arable*, his grandfathers once loosened the ground, the hard earth with the aid of explosives), creating new building land because the city's pushing its way out there, the suburbs expanding, honeycombs of detached houses, estates, interrupted by the low cubes of wholesalers, supermarkets, DIY superstores, he remembers as he slowly emerges from the dream he always dreams, the dream of a never-ending stretch of water, no ship, no land, only the occasional fish, a whale, something *big* at least, diving up from the depths, the *blue*, the *black*, he remembers and feels the tingling in his hands numb from sleep.

When they find the bodies, in the ground, in the mire, he rolls off the big fat woman he's struggling with, as if he wanted to punish himself because it doesn't seem to be a punishment for her, but who knows, she's hiding inside her incredible flesh. He surfaces from the depths, a thousand metres.

High blood pressure. Stabbing pains in his head. He feels his blood vessels and his brain behind the vitreous humour of his eyes, pressure behind the choroid, behind the retina where everything's reflected, where the blind spot is. Dots, lines, ellipses flicker around the room before him. He needs to take a tablet. Must be from the bubbly.

He'd sunk into his dream, deep into the blue, the dark blue black. Sometimes he sees ruins there, walls, the ground folded into wrinkles, these remainders of cities

or whatever they may be are half submerged in the rug-
ged, wrinkled ground, temples perhaps, he sometimes
thinks after waking; he's fifty-six, been in the city for
seventeen years and having the dream ever since. He's
often thought of getting sent elsewhere, posted back to
Cologne, maybe to the Federal Criminal Police, back to
the Federal Intelligence Service where he once squatted
in the cellars as a young man and researched, photos,
material, flesh, or he could take retirement and move to
the coast somewhere. The sea air would do him good. He
has a little hut, a *datscha*, as they say *here* and *there*, near
the border town, on the border river, up in the northeast. Bought it cheap ten years ago. A long way from
here. In the no man's land between Poland and Germany.
He's got a little motorboat there that lives in a tiny shed
in the winter, his boathouse, for years he's been promis-
ing himself to take a trip up to the estuary, to the lagoon,
the great branched basin from which three narrow arms
flow into the sea. He struggles for air, like every time
he wakes from this dream of the depths. His phone on
the bedside table. Next to the torn condom packets. He
hears her in the bathroom, hears the shower running.
She doesn't have a lot of clients, he knows that, so her
skin's not dry as parchment, not like the girls who take
a shower after every guest, though usually they only
do that at the beginning, when they're new. With her,
he thinks, it's a sign that she's feeling good, that she's
in a good mood. Because she's singing as well. It must
be the bubbly. But she always drinks it. Even the first
time, how long ago is that now? She opened the door in
a dressing gown, or was it a silk petticoat? Or whatever
it's called, and a glass of bubbly in one hand, laughing
so her tits and her hips shook like jelly: 'Hello gorgeous,
come on in, the sun's coming up!' And it really was in the

morning, but a winter morning, the sun a pale, ragged yellow stain behind the fog and certainly not visible to her, on the ground floor, blinds down; the only daylight comes in through the kitchen window, a tiny backyard that he sees through the door left ajar as he walks past.

He's still got a headache and he feels the stumbling beat of his heart. He doesn't know who works here after her when she leaves at four in the afternoon, or if someone else comes along after twelve already. He sees the two calls on his phone, sees he must have picked up the first one. A tiny envelope flashes and he opens the text message, reads the directions. 'Waterworld,' she says suddenly and sits down next to him. Water drips from her hair onto his legs and his belly.

'What?' He straightens up and she massages his balls, strokes her fingers through his grey pubes. 'Don't.' He pushes her hand away. 'I'm not twenty-five any more.'

'Oh, my dear, I'll get it up for you in a jiffy.'

'I've got to go.'

He's very sparing with the Viagra, a quarter of a pill, half a pill, never more than that, but he still feels it and he sits up again. It's not sensible to drink on top of it. He'll have to take blockers, later, to bring his system down a bit. He's dizzy but the headache's going away now. His blood's falling.

'You know, that Kevin Costner film where they're on the sea the whole time, always on the water, and in the end he gets webbed feet. Skin grows in between his toes.'

'And what's that got to do with me?'

'Because of your bad dream, I mean.'

'What do you know about my dream? How do you know what I dream about?' He wants to push her hand away but she's already squatting down in front of him.

'Because you told me about it, my dear!'

167

He has a brief view of the metallic, dully gleaming, blackish silver of her fillings as she opens her mouth and starts sucking his half-stiff penis. 'You're the only one,' she mumbles, and his cock bounces out of her mouth with a *plop*, 'the only one I do without a condom, my sunshine.' He knows she's lying. He's seen her ad, *untranslated French, French both ways*. He remembers her smell the first time she lay naked before him. And he remembers his shock when she opened the door. Wineglass in hand. Eight thirty in the morning. 'Ohhh, the sun's coming up, come in, my dear!' He didn't have a type of woman he felt most comfortable with, a favourite type. Blonde, dark, slim, plump, big tits, small tits, long legs, big arse... But he'd never shagged such a fat woman. And he hadn't reckoned on coming up against a nineteen-stone woman; he'd envisaged something else under 'womanly', as it said in her ad. He liked that old-fashioned word, 'humping'. Or was it her who'd used it? 'Come on, give me a real hard humping!' Why on earth did he keep going back to her after that first time? 'Where's your cat got to?' he asked when she was in the bathroom. He heard her spitting his cum in the sink and washing out her mouth and gargling. Her ad didn't say anything about *swallowing*. And probably she wasn't lying when she said he was the only one she did it for. It's good to stay on a cop's good side. His phone rang, not a tune, just a kind of scale; he couldn't remember programming it that way. He grabs her by the shoulders when he comes. Claws his fingers into her flesh. Sees red stars because his head's almost bursting. He coughs; there's a tickle in his throat. How old must she be? Hard to guess. Early thirties, late thirties. Maybe older. No, more likely younger. 'What cat?' She pokes her head into the room, a toothbrush in the corner of her mouth. Foam on her chin. He runs his fingers along her cellulite, along the stretch marks on her thighs, while she moves in front of him on the big bed. 'I haven't got a cat, and certainly not here, my dear! The only cat round here's down here!' She laughs and sways her hips and pulls her labia apart with both hands, pushing the waves of her belly aside. Give me pink. Then she pops back into the bathroom. He picks up his underpants from the chair, then his trousers. He searches his jacket pockets for the blockers. He needs something to rinse them down with but he doesn't want any more bubbly. He wants to bring her champagne; he's been meaning to do it for a while now. For more than a year now. But it's always Red Riding Hood Medium Dry. Then he does take a sip from his glass and chokes down the tablet. Sits on the bed again and leans against the wall. It only takes seconds for him to feel his heart beating more calmly. The calm spreading through his whole body. 'I'm going out for coffee with my mum later. I'm knocking off early today.'

'Good thing too.' He could swear he'd seen a cat prowling around here to begin with. Maybe the cat's in the locked room. The flat has two small rooms and the door to one of them is always locked when he comes by in the morning. He doesn't know who rents her the apartment; he's never asked. The Old Man, probably. The man in the shadows, the man behind the mirror, only has a few apartments with women in them. He has his women in his clubs. But a lot of things can change, from one day to the next, and the cop, the eternal detective, the captain, isn't sure he's up to date. He hasn't been to clubs or brothels since Cologne. Maybe she works here alone for herself. He ought to know that, after all the months, years. There aren't a lot of women in town working for themselves. Or in their own apartments, really. Not paying daily rent. He knows that.

Waterworld. He's never heard of it. He doesn't know much about films. Can't even remember when he last went to the cinema. Cologne? No, that's too long ago.

He thought he'd never told anyone about drowning in that dark sea, in and on and under that blue-black surface. She hums and sings a tune while getting dressed outside. He runs his tongue along the stretch marks on her thighs. Or what he thinks are growth scars, the snow-white traces on her flesh. He almost choked the first time he went down on her. His tongue started burning, she was so moist, so wet and so acidic. 'Oh, my dear, the sun's coming up.' The antiseptic soap dispenser on the side of the washbasin. The broad field of her short stubble on his face. Now *her* phone rings, somewhere in the corridor. Later he stops at a petrol station and drinks a can of Coke. It's stupid, he thinks, to think about who likes *that kind of thing*. Who likes her. Who goes to her apart from him. To begin with he sometimes felt like turning around, going back down the couple of steps to the front door of the building from the raised ground floor and disappearing. Back to the police station. Back to work. But there was something in her voice, in her, about her, the way she spoke to him with a laugh in her voice, her chubby round face, her huge, pendulous breasts. Which he's licking and kissing. Bubbly in the morning, policeman's warning. It was the only ad that said *8.00*. Most of the girls start work at nine or ten. The air and the city cold, the stains of the sun behind the buildings, piles of dirty snow by the sides of the road. His car parked two streets away. Like it is now. He's paid for three hours, as usual, and he'd like to stay. He feels the blocker calming him down. Winning the battle against the pink pill, the half a pill he took after getting up, from the small leather pouch he used to keep his cigarettes in, a present from... *Oh my lover*, is that music coming from the kitchen? A howling hit of a tune. They'll call back in a minute. Seventeen years ago, and even fifteen years ago, he could have said he'd taken a wrong turning, in the tangled veins of the streets and narrow roads, traffic jams, building sites, because the city moved and still is moving. Back then he once took a trip on a zeppelin and admired the gleaming railway tracks, branching off a thousand times over, straight as a die or in wild, harmonious curves, arches and ellipses. That was that incredibly hot summer and the centre of the city glowed blue and red in the twilight hours, seen from such a height. As if it were a different city and not the one they'd taken off from. He saw the movements and the tangling together of the buildings and streets and suburbs. The station, its temple-like dome, the lower tracks like canyons, which the goods trains and passenger trains took slowly, the raised railway embankments, bridges and brick viaducts, saw the thin flags of smoke rising out of and above the allotment gardens, barbecues, bonfires, sat in the long, narrow car beneath the bloated body of the zeppelins and thought that he... 'My sunshine, your telephone!'

He's fully dressed by now, her sitting beside him and smoothing the fabric and telling him about going for coffee with her mum. He rejected the call and put the phone in his inside pocket. Three bodies in the mire. In the swamp. Out in the woods. They're picking them up now. More of a copse really. He'll stop on the way and drink a can of Coke. Maybe take another half a blocker. He's careful with that stuff. 'We're going out to the lakes. There's a really nice restaurant by the pier, right by the pier. It was Mum's birthday yesterday.'

171

'What lakes?'

'The great lakes, my dear. You ought to go out there, get a bit of colour in your cheeks!'

'The Great Lakes are in America.' But he knew which lakes she meant, outside the city where they'd once dug up the ground, huge diggers burrowing for brown coal, lignite. He'd seen the open pits when he came to the city seventeen years ago, on the southern edge, right behind the houses of the suburbs, giant pits where the diggers were dismantled, the flooding soon to begin, and now, after all the years, it had come into fashion to buy a yacht or a boat for sailing the lakes and the canals. From a distance they looked like a bay, like a bodden or a lagoon, as though you'd passed through strange portals from the flat, riverless city to the coast.

'Have a good one, Starsky!'

'Have fun with your mum.'

He'd like to ask her how old she is. Mid-thirties, that had been his guess from the beginning. But he knew it was easy to guess wrong, like with the dead. He remembers them getting called in to an old woman in Cologne, she was sitting behind the main station with a side view of the cathedral, in a little nook between the wall and the pavement, and she was nineteen, they found out later, but her skin was furrowed like a field and grey-blonde hair like straw. She'd just died, not an overdose, her body full of poisons, she'd sat down in that nook that was so tiny they'd had to lever her out of it. He shakes his head, locates himself in the apartment again, the street, the city, *Win a thousand euros, only on ninety-two point three, it's gonna be a golden Monday*, the radio whispers hoarsely from the kitchen, the door ajar as usual, a quick peep into the room, a little light falling on the table by the window.

'What have they got for me, I wonder,' he thinks, feeling tired after the hours spent with her, the blocker's working fine this morning, and she puts her hand on his shoulder before he opens the door and leaves. 'Come back soon, Starsky, and take care of yourself.'

'You too.'

In the early eighties he did a short stretch working for a kind of film consulting company for the Sunday night crime shows, *Let's be having you, young man*, to make the murders and the detective work more realistic. He didn't think much of the realistic ones. Corpses at the station, robbery with murder among drinkers, drugs, domestic strife, who cared about all that? He preferred the dramas, the dramatic soap opera ones, Schimanski's fists, cognac and cigarettes for Detective Haferkamp, it's a long time ago but he can still remember watching that series in amazement in the early seventies, what was it called, *The Old Man*, no, *The Inspector*, amazed at the countless glasses of wine, beer, brandy, schnapps, whisky that the detectives consumed, always a cigarette between their lips, Munich, city of vice, classier than Cologne, he remembers the little blue booklet that did the rounds at the academy, *The Munich Billeting Guide for Erotically Inclined Visitors*, he approaches the junction for the motorway to the capital; the motorway to the south, heading for Munich, crosses the city's ragged edges at the other end of town; black capital letters SALON WHORES, HOSTESSES AND OTHER SOLOISTS OF THE HORIZONTAL TRADE on a pale-blue background, almost turquoise, although he's not quite sure what he thinks is turquoise really is turquoise, colour theory, a slim blonde lady next to the letters, back, legs, arse, one breast just visible, the tip of a breast next to her outstretched arm. He can remember the headings of the chapters introducing the girls, a telephone number at the end. 'Michaela's chest's excellent' or 'Michaela's breasts are excellent', 'the young pussy cat', 'Cleopatra in Schwabylon', that makes him laugh and he brakes although he would have made it across on the amber light, but he's in no rush to get out to where the bodies must be, where they're waiting for him and the machinery's beginning to take its course, cars, experts, lots and lots of police tape, never mind just putting the flashing light up on the roof. He moves slowly in the stream of vehicles, multi-lane traffic, the bustle of the suburbs that will soon reach into the neighbouring town, DIY stores between them, fields, the airport that squats on the field at night like a glowing UFO, he changes gear and drives slowly into the green, a rubbish truck in the lane next to him, is that because the needle in his head is skipping like on a scratched old record? Blocker, Viagra, bubbly. The black lady in the rubbish... Stuffed into a grey metal skip. How the hell did the boy manage to drag her down there? In broad daylight. They put out a reward back then, the Old Man and the others, the boys from the round table, and the rubbish man found her. Her window was at the back of the building. She was alone at the time. No, there was another girl in the next room. But working, and not quietly either.

Then he threw her out the window, that was what the forensic medicine report found, numerous broken bones, she must have still had some life in her so not even post mortem, but her brain was already dead apparently or already falling asleep, not a needle skipping back and forth, but who knows exactly, Africa, money, luck, love, the boy suddenly putting his hands around your throat, you die and you fly, not for long, not far because it's only the second floor, then he leaves perfectly calm,

174

closes the window first, walks round to the side street and stuffs her in the skip. How old was he? Twenty-one? Twenty-two? And her? He forgot her name long ago. But not her face or her eyes. Red from burst blood vessels. Sexual offences legislation at the academy. The right to sexual self-determination. Punishment norms for behaviour with a sexual component. What they call the optic radiation brings the last images from the retina along the optic chiasm to her brain, *Because I love you so much, Mary*, there it is again, her name, he's driving, hasn't switched on the navigation system, doesn't want any strange voices in his car, he knows he'll get *there*, feels and hears his phone ringing and vibrating in his jacket pocket, he knows they're waiting for him, the living and the dead, doesn't yet know one of the dead is nearly naked, and it's the first time, will be the first time that he sees bodies preserved in the mire. Or semi-preserved. The man will be missing a leg, something he won't understand for a long time. Removed cleanly with a meat cleaver, a butcher's saw, practised, smooth. But why? Post mortem, they'll be able to tell him with certainty later. Cause of death: six shots to the upper body, large-bore firearm. He sees that straight away. Three bodies in one small mire. One of them though, a woman's body, has been resting there longer than the other two. It's a good hiding place actually, a good location. Even though the bodies and the evidence don't decompose quickly; the worms stay away. Mires and swamps are deep. No one swims in them, no one fishes in them, no one drives a boat through the thick marshy water. In the olden days people were scared will-o-the-wisps would lure them in. Apparitions were seen. Yet still they drained mires, for agriculture, fields for planting. That's all long over now, though, and who was to know the city

175

would push its way out there so quickly and pick the dead out of the mud? He's standing at the petrol station, by his car, drinking a can of Coke, rinsing his mouth and gargling to get rid of the taste of *her*. 'Five minutes,' he'd said on the phone, not waiting to hear who it was. He worked at his own pace and they knew that. The last images are going through his mind again, the boy in the room. His hectic red face. The dark skin that arouses him. The breasts, the *pink*. He's been going to her for weeks. Murder for love, so to speak. It didn't take long for them to catch him, plenty of witnesses, the other girl shagging in the room next door while the blood vessels burst in the black woman's eyes, fingerprints, a phone number in a notebook, a card that plays a tune, I'm singing in the rain, when you open it. Murder for love, if you like. Jealousy. No fulfilment. Thoughts and ideas of love and fulfilment that didn't correspond to reality. A stupid stallion. A poor girl. And as he stands before the three bodies lying in a kind of casing made of planks, a provisional jetty leading to them, construction machines, shovels, digger arms as if frozen mid-motion, it seems to him as though days, months had passed between his Coke stop at the petrol station and his arrival at the site. A copse. A swamp, a network of several small mires. Only a dirt track leading to it from the country road. To this offshoot of the heath further northeast, touching the suburbs here and there, the outer reaches of the two towns almost become one; am I the only person who sees that? That the markets and marketplaces are becoming more and more linked, steel and concrete town halls, the meat markets expanding, the bricks and mortar, sticks and stones, the rock growing, in a red-lit circle where everything's linked, the rubbish truck, the fat woman, the Coke, the Viagras, the blockers, uppers and downers, lost cats, the right to sexual self-determination, scraps of memory like old police badges, the Angels on their motorbikes, peat mosses, flyovers, sixty-six municipal brothels in 1865, trade chronicles, he burrows in the old files, real estate on silver strings leading all the way to Italy, and the fall of the real-estate boss Silvio Lübbke, three bullets, boom, boom, Dead Peepers Alley, houses for pocket money, clues, clues, the country air so clean and pure, soon they'll be building here but we'll stop the diggers, the question is, who brings three bodies out to this mire, this swamped puddle, where everyone knows they won't decompose, when you can dig holes in the sandy ground of the heath or drive out to forest lakes like the 'Blue Eye', and there must be anglers there who discover the remotest of lakes, the woods arching around the north-eastern belt of the suburbs and incorporated villages to the south, all of it flat as a pancake.

He puts on the rubber boots given to him by a young policewoman he doesn't know, huge yellow things probably left over from the Zone, and slaps uncertainly in the far-too-big boots along the wooden jetty, a few planks nailed together. The diggers came across the bodies early in the morning, the water had been pumped off in the previous days, all that was left was black-brown, gloopy mud and peat mosses, ancient, fossilized branches, green and white at their tips, protruding from the water surface, green islands of duckweed everywhere, that's what it's called, that's what they called it as children when they went paddling in the forest lakes, and then his colleagues took over the close work, securing the evidence, the forensic team is on site, scene of the crime, scene of the discovery, leg hacked off. He squats down on the jetty, leans forward, looks into the wood-encased square, *looks about right*, he thinks, three in one coffin, two women, one at a clear distance from the other two bodies, there's only this one spot on the banks where he's standing now, where they've laid out the jetty, where you can get rid of something in this mire, this swamp – what's the difference? Do we have to consult biologists, marsh experts? He assumes the water that's been removed was once a pond, a puddle of water that began to go marshy over the years or the centuries, turned into mire, the ground here is sandy and clayey, he knows that from other investigations in the surrounding countryside, these aren't the first bodies to be put to rest outside the city, buried, submerged. He remembers the old farmer, can't have been far away from here, who drowned his wife in a fit of rage, in an argument, who pressed her head into the rain barrel where they later found the woman's silver necklace, on the bottom of the barrel, and he lugged her out to the heath and tried to bury her, but then he came to them of his own accord not much later, so many of them turn themselves in, stumbling to and fro between their nightmares.

He sees the long, narrow concrete parts with small holes beneath the two bodies lying together, the bodies fastened onto them, bases for building-site fences, he thinks, pretty heavy. Pretty heavy for one man. But possible. Might not even have been necessary. But the puddles on the surface made him, her, uncertain. Did he know this swamp? The one body, the woman on her own, has been here longer than the other two. It looks that way, at least. The skin more leathery. Dark. The face reddish brown. The body shrivelled. The high-heeled shoes on the feet look huge. The other woman is barefoot. He climbs down to them, carefully. His yellow boots slurp into the ground. He sinks almost up to the shaft. Then he sees the mud-smeared plank, several

178

planks alongside each other, and he steps onto them. He can hardly get the boots out of the sucking ground. His colleagues must have stood here to cautiously uncover the three, the three question marks. Plastic crates and two zinc bathtubs full of mud and earth and peat mosses standing on the bank. To be sieved through later, in search of the gold or at least the gold dust of evidence. The leg's disappeared. Or is it somewhere else in the mud? Chucked in afterwards by the removal man, weighed down or not weighed down. A mire never gives up its secrets. Your own weight pulls you down into the depths. The woman on her own is not weighed down. At least not visibly. They told him she'd got caught on the digger's shovel as it dug its way into the half-drained swamp from the bank. An early-morning shock. The guy tipped the shovel, as if on impulse – get back! – and the body slid back to the others. He puts on rubber gloves. No smell of old corpses, of liquefying bodies, that odour he's smelled so often. He always has a little tin of tiger balm in his pocket to rub under his nostrils. It's good for headaches as well. Or if you catch a cold. A classic. He touches the woman's face, she's lying on her side, curled up next to the man. Like wood, like leather, the lines on her forehead still discernable, lips slightly parted. Her teeth black. But perhaps that's just the mire, got into her mouth. Again he touches her face with his fingertips, surprised at how soft and elastic her skin feels. He feels and hears himself humming a tune. *Oh my lover.* The three of them are so well preserved that this part of the mire must have been fairly dry. Later the mire expert confirms that, the man who holds a presentation at the police station on 'bog bodies and conservation in marshlands', from the special commission on bog corpses. They all learn a lot. A little baffled, he squats on the planks between the bodies, still leaning over the woman. He can't make out how she died. Her neck seems slightly deformed but her whole body is bent, as though the chemical and biological processes in the airtight space had removed all hold from her bones... No posture, at any rate.

Only now does he see that she's naked. What he took for a dress is dried mud. Plant particles. If she got caught on the prongs of the digger then she must have been lying differently before, but it seems to him that she's been lying on her side like this for years. One hand, one arm resting on her stomach, beneath her breasts, as if she wanted to protect herself, and now he sees something on her leather décolleté that could be a hole, a bullet wound, a stabbing injury, but that's up to others to find out, forensic medicine. He lifts her body briefly. What happens to the flesh of the dead once they disappear in these muddy depths? Later he plays back his words on his Dictaphone. And hears the birds chirruping in the background. And is rather muddled, because he recorded the mire expert's presentation later. Not all of it, but lots of parts; he pressed record whenever it seemed interesting.

There's a man with one leg missing. Fastened to a small concrete base. The left leg has been removed directly below the hip. The preservation has begun here, too. His skin colour remains in places. Brown, dark brown. Streaked with white and yellow. The other woman, the one further away, is very dark, very black. No pale skin. More like bitumen. This skin too feels very soft to the touch, almost elastic. Pressing my fingers in. (...) Yeah, fine, I'm looking, throw it down, where else!

Large holes in the man's chest. Clearly visible. Bullet holes. Looks like a large calibre. Large areas of clothing shredded, some bullet holes the size of a fist. Both bodies have the same concrete bases attached. Looks like washing line. Washing lines. To attach them. Directly below the rump. What I notice is... as if the woman, and this is clearly a younger woman than the other one, as if she wants to crawl away from him, from the man with the large holes in his chest, both bodies lying on their backs but she's turning away or attempting to. Bending away from him on her base. Not that she was still alive. Possible. If it is possible. Maybe the digger. That separated the bodies.

The naked woman presumably dumped here previously and clearly separately. Approximately a metre and a half between *couple* and *woman*. Possibly a coincidence. No. Connections are always possible. The site. Not a coincidence. Impossible. The naked woman has red, visibly red high heels on her feet. The other woman has clothes but no shoes. Barefoot. (...) Yeah, yeah, alright, give me a bit of time, will you. I need files, on all missing women over the past twenty years. (Laughter.) Looks like a clean cut. Look for the leg, try and find us the leg, please.

Forensic medicine says the cut is similar to cuts used in a slaughterhouse. For chopping up cows, for example. Clean, a clean cut. Day three.

The peat mosses present in the mire give marshes a strongly acidic milieu.

Peat moss is essentially responsible for these extreme living conditions in raised bogs. And in low mires and fenlands.

Fuck you, bugger off home. I listen to my tape. Over and over. I've got hours on the machine. It's not tape. If I rewind far enough I'm in Cologne. I'm with the woman I often go to. The body's usually found accidentally. It'll

181

soon be summer again. Autumn again.

There's a lead on the woman. The woman with no clothes. She was strangled and stabbed. Her boyfriend, her ex-boyfriend, identified her. Thanks to the marsh mosses! A former legal secretary at the justice department, Bärbel Kahn. Went missing 1997. Her car full of blood, front seats smeared with blood, we found it outside a DIY store down in the south of the city. Near the great lakes. Which were still half-flooded open pits at the time. Why wasn't she deposited there? Only her fingerprints in the car. Her fingers are so well preserved that we could make a comparison. Not a hundred per cent. But there's a high probability that they're the fingers of the legal secretary Bärbel Kahn.

Huge swamps, deep mires, impenetrable jungle, gigantic trees that grew several hundred yards up to the sky. Between them ferns as tall as houses, blades of grass, growths and shrubs...

What's this rubbish got to do with the specifics of marsh corpses? But the man, the expert, went back to the beginning. Took the long view. Huge mires, rotted forests in the layers beneath us. Overtime. Presentations. Forensic medicine. Files. Papers. Data and flesh.

This mire is like the whale in the old folk tale that spits out three little people. Rubbish. (Laughter.) I have to pay a visit to Eliot Ness, the guy they put out to pasture. Information. They want to put the Bärbel Kahn case in the relationship category. Murder out of jealousy. But who? Her ex-boyfriend? No way. He said she was onto something. Onto something big. Real estate. Old news by now. You slept too long in the dark, dark mire, legal secretary Bärbel Kahn. 1997. A different millennium.

The man's been identified. A little lowlife. Drugs. Street prostitution. The main suspect in the professor murder, years ago now. Got acquitted though. Never particularly popular. Probably involved in the *Columbus Butterfly* case as well. On the margins. Never proved. When the meat-market bosses went clean, washed their hands, when the great peace began, peace for business's sake, he was out of the game quick. I think he must have got on the wrong side of someone with his dirty little deals. The large calibre looks like someone was mighty angry. Who kills someone with a Czechoslovakian-English machine gun? An execution. A puzzle. The girl died of heart failure. Meds. Drugs. She must have looked as black on the inside as the outside. She did as well. It's going to be difficult to find the killers in all this chaos at the moment. The killers. I'm still assuming it's not just one killer. Not just because of the years between them. Eliot Ness thinks the man with the shredded chest knew too much. The same as Bärbel. But Eliot Ness has been saying that ever since I've known him. Secrets. Too much knowledge. Someone gets dangerous for somebody. Through knowledge. Through too much knowledge. Bygone dirty laundry. Secrets. Incriminating material. He can only keep on top because... He only disappeared because... We're not in Hollywood, that's what I say to Eliot Ness. But he holds his peace and goes on drilling deeper into the past two decades. Even though they put him out to pasture.

The girl in the mire was certainly a whore, albeit in a whole different branch of the industry to his fat whore, a whole different set-up, poisons and pavements, not comparable to his fat lady and her cosy waiting in the warm. They still haven't managed to identify her, no fingerprints, no previous, no file that matches her case, no missing person in the past years who fits the bill, she could be from elsewhere, hepatitis C, nasty, and he'd driven around the station, the central station that glows in different, softer colours in the autumn light, like the leaves on the trees, ochre, red and brown, but in the nights when winter's drawing in, when your breath starts to steam, the monolith turns black. Seen from above, a silver network of veins leading to the dark clump of the heart. Did the girl work there? Work's the wrong word, maybe. His cheerful chubby one, his favourite whore – she works. Sensibly. Protected. Halfway protected, at least. Insured. Registered. Hygienic. That's what he thinks while he drifts, eyes half-closed, through the streets in his car. But what does he even know about her, he wonders. He doesn't even understand why he stays with her. A constant guest. He's been with a lot of them over the years, the decades, experienced the changing customs and morals as a client, experienced the change here in the city, tried to make sure... what, actually? To make sure he only goes where it's hygienic, where the shadows aren't visible? Driving through red, green, amber. The flashing of the traffic lights. The angle of the falling light almost horizontal by now. Slowly fading to red and reddish.

'Bogs form above all in flat landscapes with sandy or clayey ground through a rise in the water table...' Yes, for God's sake, he'd had enough of the bloody expert. What was the point of it? Of course he knew it sometimes made sense to approach things via a diversion or via the *source* of things, but what did all this jargon have to do with their bodies? Except that they found out how years and centuries remained preserved in the layers, came about, shifted... He was the only one in the team who tuned in to the mire presentation for a while, on his Dictaphone as well, because he hoped it would get his thoughts on the matter moving. But he deleted almost all of it before he went to see Eliot Ness. 'When the Saale Ice Age withdrew from the Schlieben Basin it had formed twelve thousand years ago, it left behind an extended swamp and mire landscape. But most areas were drained and made productive over the past five hundred years in particular.'

He shakes the voices out of his head. He sees the small glass dome of the small sandstone-coloured station, the neighbouring station in the neighbouring town that's gradually becoming a suburb, next to the flyover he's driving along. The tangled web of tracks that catches the last light. A dark shade of silver. Who cuts off a man's leg after he's killed him, almost shreds his chest with a huge antique gun, then submerges him together with a woman, a young woman between twenty-five and thirty, who's already dead, died, kicked the bucket from her years of poisons, when the heart suddenly stands still, strapped to concrete blocks with washing lines, because they both apparently belonged together, even though she was still trying to turn away from him in death, which he could well understand if things were the way he thought they were.

They knew now where he'd dossed down. Where he'd lived, which dosshouse he'd lived in. Behind the central station. And that the girl was there with him. The young woman.

We're living in the century of poisons, he thought and then he thinks that we're well into a new century, millennium, so it depends how you see it... A little bedsit that someone had emptied out before the landlord came to check when the rent didn't get paid. A guy who rented out flats and rooms to builders. Not only to builders, of course. They'd worked on him for a long time. Hadn't found much out though. Of course not. A year, said forensic medicine. There were two Bosnians living there now. Worked on building sites. Even had contracts. But even if they'd been working cash in hand that wouldn't have interested them. They'd still taken the place apart. Fitted furniture. Floorboards. Wallpaper. Nooks and crannies. Nothing. Of course not. The killer, or a second or third man, presumably tried to divide up the body at first. To dump the parts separately. Not here though, there was no blood anywhere. But then decided against it for some reason. Because the swamp suddenly popped into their, his mind. Why? Because he, they, had already dumped legal secretary Bärbel Kahn there in 1997? Or because they knew about it? But then it would be stupid to take the bodies there. Or were they certain that only coming, future Ice Ages or Heat Ages would roll over the blackened bodies and perhaps bring them to the surface one day? Or on the contrary, they'd layer them further and further, deeper and deeper into the ground.

The thing with the real estate tsar, said Eliot Ness. What real estate tsar? The one who rebuilt the city's old trading houses and arcades with big loans? Who lost a fortune through speculation? The one loved by the big banks and the politicians great and small? All over the country. Whose empire of loans and property collapsed when the city began to shine again? So many years ago. Mind you, it's not that many years, let's say *a few*. Four or five years before the new millennium. Back in the day. He sees the German flag up on the roof of the old building right behind the neighbouring town's station, fluttering and snapping in the wind, though of course he can't hear the fabric snapping from inside his car.

Chaos is coming. It's only a matter of time. Or it's already here. Here too. The tracks now only glinting dull in the light of the October sun, almost disappeared. A red sickle behind the buildings, only visible if you look down the side streets and alleys, between the buildings. Moon, sun. Black, red and gold. He knows the woman in that building. The woman they call the 'boss lady'. Although she's only the boss to a certain extent. Funny that the flag's in motion like that, he thinks. When there's hardly any wind when he winds down the window. How glad he is that he gave up smoking years ago. And got a grip on his drinking too. If you can get a grip on some-thing like that. He winds down the window. Maybe they've installed a wind machine up on the roof, behind the flag. It was a bit of a coup back then, when the boss lady got hold of the flag at auction. Original Bundestag. Original Reichstag. He remembers the whores' proces-sion, not even all that long ago, when they had the flag with them, the roof empty that day, Berlin, Berlin, we're going to Berlin! All the whores outside the Reichstag, outside the Bundestag, how he laughed when he saw it on TV, and how they both laughed, the chubby girl who'd have liked to go along but then kept out of it in the end, though she thought it was a good thing they were kicking up a stink, demanding their rights. Placards and banners, the whores' chorus and in amongst them the flag, flying here again now to show that business is still booming, that the women count on each other, even though that's just another utopia in a way. But a nice one. That's at least half-true, come halfway true. With that march on Berlin.

'Aside from that, the decomposition level is extremely low and the water table is higher within the mire than in the surrounding area. Raised bogs usually contain small elevations and water-filled hollows, and small lakes referred to as bog ponds.'

He shakes his head to silence the voices. He presses

187

and beeps his way through the files on his Dictaphone. He's deleted a lot but he's still got it at home on his computer. Not at the police station. Has Eliot Ness got him crazy already? He finds files he doesn't even know. He finds data and facts he doesn't even know. He's afraid to look but he does it anyway. Closes and opens. Maybe delete everything. Somewhere near here is where they'll shoot at the head of the Outsiders crew. BOOM, BOOM. The guys who keep people off the Old Man of the Mountain's back, that's what Eliot Ness calls the rent tsar Kraushaar. A business matter. Business for this business. Trade. What's that got to do with his bodies? He called Moon-Eye in Berlin the other day to make a date to get hold of some information. But Moon-Eye cancelled.

He knows he's overstepping boundaries. He doesn't want to end up like Eliot Ness. That business isn't in his department. All he wants is to put ticks after his three bodies. BOOM, BOOM. A blood-smeared car. More or less. He feels dizzy. Not long ago he had a drink here, at the bar in Madame Gourdan's house. Because he knows the boss lady. New boys on the door. Outsiders crew. He's still got his old badge from Cologne, just as a souvenir. A lucky charm. What's going to happen when the big families from Berlin close in on this place? The Los Locos syndicate is already here. What's that got to do with his mire-tanned bodies? He ought to get out of here. He feels his badge attached to a chain in the inside pocket of his jacket. 'Look after yourself, Starsky.'

He knows he'll soon be unable to keep track of the chaos. It's none of his beeswax either, really. Eliot Ness is waiting for him.

How proud the boss lady was of that flag she got at auction. How she presented it along with the girls, to the press, to the clients. But to the press first of all, because the guests only came back once the press had left. The naked young arses next to black, red and gold. Tits on the left of it, tits on the right of it. And then the incensed citizens in Berlin and here. The German flag flying on the roof of a brothel, Sodom and Gomorra.

A wonderful woman, the boss lady. A woman who knows exactly how to arrange herself. The right people on the door. The right *crew* on her side. Press coverage for fair business, hygiene and so on. PR. Nice clean bar. Nice clean taxpayer. He thinks his little corpse, the woman whose heart stopped, would be better off here, would have been better off than with that bastard who only gave her the poisons she needed. Or in one of the Old Man of the Mountain's apartments or in that little place where he had a drink with a Japanese guy once. Over in the town centre. Where he's heading again now.

He laughs when he hears the news. Info Radio. They report an explosion, not far from the site where they found the bodies. Where the officers dig something out from under the rubble, later on. A chemicals fire. With nothing, but nothing at all to do with his case.

And he thinks it must be a barrage of fire to distract attention. Some other business of no interest to either him or Eliot Ness, whom he's not even allowed to contact. Some little meth lab. Some little farmhouse where the Czechs are in on the game. Expansion of the crystal border in the mountains, which aren't all that far away. The way they encode it on the radio makes him laugh. It's almost night by now. BOOM, BOOM. The projectiles from a Bren. Czech-English make. Brno and Enfield. Hence the name. A light machine gun. Could be a coincidence.

Two meth cooks burned to death in the inferno. One

189

woman. One man. Seven or eight miles from the mire. Could be a coincidence.

Dictaphone: day twenty. 'You haven't been here for a long time, Starsky.'

He rings Eliot Ness's doorbell. A cop put on ice in his study, a chaos of pinboards. Photos, sheets full of notes, court files, newspaper articles, voices, words, images. They're almost the same age. But they don't talk about that. Former chief investigator, Organized Crime. Detective Inspector. DI OC. 'I don't see anything,' says the man in the middle of his pinboards. They have a cognac each. 'How's work?' asks DI Ness.

'We're stuck.'

'Everything's stuck,' says Ness. 'Heard about the fire-works display in the meth kitchen?'

'I heard, yes.'

'The crystal border's closing in,' says Ness, 'the front line is right here now.'

'Is it?'

'My dear man, my dear man, it's all connected, the cronies are in charge, you must be familiar enough with that from Cologne.'

And when Eliot Ness says his 'my dear man, my dear man' in the local accent he thinks, the old cop thinks of the 'my sunshine, my gorgeous sunshine' that his chubby girl always calls to him across the never-ending boundary of her threshold. 'Come on in, the sun's coming up.' He oversteps that boundary, goes to her and *sends his kite flying*, a song he sometimes hears on the radio when she has the oldies channel on in the kitchen, a song she tells him about, a song from her youth although she can't be that old yet, but an oldie, an oldie from the East, an evergreen. He's often thought, these past few weeks and months, that he likes her. His big fat woman with her wonderful stupid phrases. 'Step inside, my gallant knight,' which boundaries shall he overstep, he thinks, the dead are with me and the ground's opening up in very different places.

He sits, and that's just one form of remembering, at the bar of the flagged building, drinks a beer because one beer's always fine, then drinks another while they enter, one after another, while he talks to the boss lady. This and that, the things going on, the things he's heard, how are the ladies, so and so and this and that, all nice and casual because he's not asking questions as a cop. Because he's learnt in all the years that you get more answers if you don't ask questions. 'Shit,' says Eliot Ness, 'you have to dig deep.' The Outsiders crew; he hardly heard their motorbikes coming, their 'mopeds' as they call them, and he knows not even half of them even have mopeds, Eliot Ness confirms later that they're the vanguard for the Old Man of the Mountain but that that too is crumbling. That they're close to the Angels. But that's crumbling too. None of his beeswax though. As he drinks his golden Radeberger beer.

And in march the seven, eight, nine men to the boss lady, and the flag flutters in the wind on the roof. Hearts like diamonds. Where's he heard that before? And people say they can smell a cop a mile off. They even shook his hand when they came in, seeing he was having a confidential with the boss lady. *It's the taking part that counts.* The girls take their positions, it's nearly time, it's nearly evening. The boss lady says, 'Excuse me a mo,' and goes to one of the tables with the men, in the shadow, in the half-darkness, and the girls sit next to him at the bar. Leather jackets. T-shirts. Big buggers. *Outsiders*-branded, inscribed. On T-shirts, jackets, skin.

191

He sips at his beer and one of the women goes behind the bar. Standing in. He puts money down on the bar and buys a round. A young woman next to him. Dark hair. You could be my daughter, he thinks. You could be my father, she thinks. And doesn't think it, of course. Because she's seen the old cop here before. Because she knows he only buys rounds. Because the boss lady told her he only buys rounds. But she told him to be nice to him anyway. *Nice*. How nice? She knows he'll soon be gone; now that the evening's darkening to night he's only disturbing things.

He tries to remember the name of the flower that grows on the edge of the mire. Five red petals coming out of a calyx, yellowish, a calyx like a little vase. Now he realizes that countless flowers are blossoming and fading around the edge of the mire they excavated, even though it's autumn now, but perhaps time runs slightly behind in the seclusion and twilight of the little woods outside the city. He thinks. Is it a maiden pink? He sees the policewoman whose name he doesn't know on the other side of the mire's hollow, bending down and picking a couple of flowers. He doesn't know exactly how long he's been squatting by the bodies, how many minutes or hours; it's twilight already, he sees the evening sun between the branches and leaves of the trees, they probably let more light through at the beginning of autumn and that's why the flowers are still blossoming here. He thinks. And because of the nutrients in the soil. 'Maiden pinks,' he hears his colleague calling from over there. Maybe she just says it to herself. His left leg has gone to sleep. It's the right leg the man is missing. Someone wanted to divide him up but then gave up on it. He thinks. 'Marsh Helleborine,' he hears his colleague, 'Eyebright.'

Who are you, girl? And why are you still crawling away from this one-legged man in death? I wonder what they want to build here. Will build here. The dead disappear and the houses and plots grow. Were there settlers here once before? The remains of their houses and bodies in the layers beneath him. And perhaps another mire and another three bodies. And perhaps the traces of a man who once stood there on the edge and stared at the dark surface of the swamp. The red lights of the wind turbines vanish in the night, flash up again, there and elsewhere, different intervals, a flashing and extinguishing, glowing and extinguishing, that he can barely tear his eyes away from. And off he goes. His Dictaphone whispers ahead of him on the dashboard, the voices mixing with the quiet music of a local radio station, he hears dates and days, mire stories, Eliot Ness. 'Autumn crocus,' how did his colleague's voice get on the tape? 'Leg apparently severed with some kind of butcher's saw,' someone talks about gigantic ferns, dead trees and layers upon layers, dry and moist. He hears the fat lady's sighs, when did I last go to see her? *Take some leave and go to the seaside*, what kind of nonsense is that, it's autumn and the season's long over. Turned cool as well. 'Globeflower.' Another woman's voice; one he doesn't know. He's got a couple of days' leave at the beginning of November. Maybe then he'll head up to the lagoon at last. And on to the sea, downstream along the River Oder. *On ninety-two point three... Have you ever wondered who's got the Valachi papers... What papers...? Why he took such a sudden rise and owns and rents out the best real estate...? When it's Christmas... The guy's a free man again even though I got him sent down. Only three and a half years... It's Piemont cherry time again... A ritual submersion of corpses in the mire... The Outsiders have got the Old Man's back... Autumn crocuses.*

They're sitting in Eliot Ness's conservatory. It's dark outside, the night falls fast. The last time he was here, on a Sunday afternoon, the sun was shining outside as if it were still summer, but the light was golden and heavy. Ness smokes. They talk about beta-blockers for a while. Ness's wife has been living in Berlin for a few years now. Couldn't take it, seems like. Ness lives in a small block on the southern edge of the town. Far away from the mire where they'll soon be laying foundations. The place where they found the bodies wasn't the crime scene and the investors want to make some progress before winter. They drink cognac, as always when he visits Ness. The lucid moments are getting fewer and farther between for the former head of the Organized Crime department. He hasn't visited him all that often over the past few years. He's thought about it. Three or four times. But twice in the past few weeks. He has to watch out not to get lost in Eliot Ness's web. He's got three corpses. And no killers. They talk a while about 1990. And '89. Where they were, what they were doing. What they wanted. Later. The great lakes can't be far away. Few lights in the houses around them. The conservatory is the only place in the flat that's free from chaos. Not that Ness would call it chaos. His web of documents, scraps of paper, newspaper articles, copies of files, names and ciphers, linked by arrows. Strewn with notes. The old cop doesn't want his three bodies to belong to that web. But he knows that at least the legal secretary Bärbel Kahn does.

'She was on the track of the big Monopoly players.'

'That little secretary? Are you sure? She had no influence at all.'

'She had material. If you've got material you've got influence. Whether you want it or not. You're dangerous and you're in danger. Whether you want that or not.'

'And what did she want?'

'Maybe she didn't want anything. Maybe she just stumbled across it all. Saw too much, heard too much. And collected it all up. Maybe she wanted to turn her knowledge into money. Or maybe she was just disgusted. By the whole thing.'

He wants to ask Eliot Ness again what exactly *the whole thing* is. But he knows that then the chaos will spill over into the quiet, cool conservatory. For years now, Ness has been researching and digging and burrowing just for himself: files, dates, money, names, connections, transfers.

'Another cognac among colleagues?'

'I'd be delighted, Mr Ness.'

Eliot Ness gets up and goes over to the old-fashioned bar trolley by the glass wall. Two of the large windows are open at the top and it seems to him he can hear the trees rustling outside. A garden with various different trees, apple trees, some of them old and crippled, and a large horse chestnut around which the apple trees are planted, almost in a circle, the horse chestnut in the middle like the mother tree. Or father. When his mother died in 1990 he was still smoking. It's hard not to smoke when your relatives leave you. Ness agrees with him on that. Behind them on the wall, on either side of the door, are two pictures behind glass, graphics or something, he doesn't know much about art. The old cop has his Dictaphone in his jacket pocket. 'Go ahead and take your coat off.'

'Thanks, but I feel better with my jacket on.' What a stupid thing to say, he thinks.

'Let's go in the conservatory then.'

And that's where they are now. The Dictaphone is off. Why should he bother recording; his memory's still fine.

Ness brings the two cognac glasses over to the rattan chairs and the small table. Puts them on the marble top. Doesn't really go together, this furniture, thinks the old cop. 'Did you go to her place?'

'Bärbel Kahn? I went to see her old boyfriend. He doesn't know anything.'

'He's not saying anything. I know.' Ness takes a seat. He's smoking again. Prince of Denmark. 'No additives, pure tobacco,' as Ness once told him.

'Ever heard of the 'Outsiders', Mr Ness?'

'Mhm.' Ness nods. Swirls his cognac around the glass. They're almost bizarrely large, these bulbous cognac glasses, the old cop's never seen such huge ones.

'Everything's in flux. But they'll disappear from town in time as well. What's going to happen with the Angels, that's what you have to ask yourself.'

'And the Old Man?'

'Of the Mountain...' Ness laughs. 'Maybe he'll disappear too.'

'Just like that?'

'No. He's been where he is for too long for that.' On his shoulder shines Bärbel Kahn's blonde hair. She looks good for forty-eight. That's a good age to look good. 'I told you about the Valachi papers, didn't I. How do you think the man got where he is today? Where he's been all these years.'

'With his fighting fists?' The old cop grins, imitating the locals' intonation.

'That too, my friend, that too. At least in the beginning. But you don't get hold of the silver strings just like that.'

'You mean...'

'He knows. And he's got material. You remember that

bad case, '93. The house. The apartment. And then in winter everything went belly up.'

'The Old Man had nothing to do with that, as far as I know. No, he definitely didn't have anything to do with it.'

'Right, Mr Barrister. But other people did. The Princes of Denmark. Not real royals but far up the ladder. And welcome guests in that dark house.'

'And my case...' He instantly regrets going too fast. He drinks a sip of cognac from the huge glass, breathes in the scent, old, dark and heavy.

'Has nothing to do with it, in principle.' They gaze at the window in silence, looking at their pale reflections apparently merging with the outlines of the trees and the garden. The only light is from a small standard lamp next to them. VSOP – Very Superior Old Pale.

Ness taps the small bronze statue on the table. 'It's a puma. I bought it in America. It's by a famous artist, a sculptor and painter, his horses and cowboys and animals are unique. There's even one of his pieces in the Oval Office.'

'Now you sound like the Old Man of the Mountain yourself, or the princes with the silver strings...'

'If I was Machiavelli I wouldn't be sitting here. And drinking cognac with you. And talking about the dead.'

And the dead flat on their backs in Forensic Medicine, the outdated coroner's department, lying in metal drawers, their decay setting in via the oxygen that barely got close to them in their years of peace in the mire, inexorable decay, they keep halfway in the cold until their funerals but the hours in the open air have taken a lot out of them. *Oh, lie down, tired limbs, and rest.* But it's the skins, the layers of skin in their eyes that interest him. The last glances. Just one glance at those last glances.

Sometimes he thinks he's dreaming, thinks he's sleeping and bolts upright, gasping for air.

He's still sinking in the water, in the depths, but it's different now. In the rubble and remains of temples or concrete constructions, he can't quite tell, he sees people. His head tosses and turns on the pillow, what's that flashing light? Position lights from submarines? When he wakes up she's sitting naked beside him, leans over him and he feels her breasts on his belly, on his chest, and he feels better, he breathes and breathes, relieved, even though she rolls all her flesh onto him and embraces him.

'But the other two...'

'Aren't of any interest.'

'Not of any interest... too young for you?'

'What does that mean, my dear man, too young? How long?'

'About a year or so.'

'Then they ought to be fresh, like a piece of Saxon layer cake thrown into a bucket of tar. You could still eat it after a year. If you cleaned it.'

'Layer cake, Mr Ness?'

'You're not telling me you haven't come across our local speciality after all your years over here?'

'I know quark pancakes.' Is that the moon behind the trees?

'And Dresden layer cake, I was over in Dresden when they shot the man from the Nazi cell.'

'I heard about that. Wasn't that '93 as well?'

'An eventful year. Eventful years. They came from all directions. The caravans, A Thousand and One Nights.'

'But...'

'Your case, I know. A wonderful confectionary from Bohemia. Originally. August the Strong imported it.

But you didn't come for a history lesson.'

'If history takes us to where we find the answers...'

'We're seeking them, to and fro. Round and round in circles. Wait...' Eliot Ness puts his glass down and goes to the door.

And then they're sitting again, two plates alongside their cognac glasses, two cake forks alongside the plates, yellow-and-white layer cake on the plates, large slices, fresh. The old cop spent almost fifteen minutes alone in the conservatory, thinking. The dead and the mire. The killers he'd never get his hands on. How could he? The bullets from the Bren ought to lead back to the Bren. Going backwards or *flying* backwards, right into the explosion. Not one Bren in the whole of the city. The trail leads to the Czech Republic? But that case doesn't seem to interest Eliot Ness all that much. Bärbel Kahn, she's the one he's interested in.

He remembers that Eliot Ness even suspected links to the old 'Cinema' case, no, not just suspected them, exposed them, because the same mechanisms were in place in the city down on the River Elbe, 'Who reaps the benefit when they wipe each other out?' He knew too little about it himself and he didn't believe in all Eliot Ness's links. Two small-time pimps from somewhere in the Ruhr Valley shoot some Nazi colleague out of the picture because he gets in the way of their business; there can be no whores and no whore administrators in the New Germany. What a stupid idea. Because the Thousand-Year Reich of a thousand and one nights is the most powerful of all. And the Nazi comrade came from the Ruhr Valley himself. To do some agitating here. Ironic, you could say. But the Nazis' attempts soon came to a stop. Ruhr Valley pimps gone, Nazis gone. ('Well, not gone, but at least they're not disrupting the market any more.') The market too large, the market too new, too much to be gained for too many, the brakes pulled on the Nazis from inside. The market too large, the market too new, not yet structured. He remembers the burnt-out bar where a punter burned to death. Might even have been that same year. First half of the nineties. He was curled up at the bottom of the stairs. Suffocated. Collateral damage. The 'Hotel Bar' case. Because the girls used to sit there and the competition didn't like that. He'd communicated with his colleagues in the city down on the Elbe at the time. If only he could finally get some information from his sources on who's sold or bought an old Bren in the past few years... Down the Elbe, up the Oder, down the Elbe. The rivers all lead into *the whole thing*, says Eliot Ness.

And then they eat their cake by night like two old ladies. And he's still not quite straight on what *the whole thing* is supposed to be. Though he does know, approximately. He can place one of the bodies. But the other two? His other two sheep? Sure, there are plenty of new cases by now. And no one's interested in these old stories. Two of which were only a year ago. He'd never have thought they were so fresh when he squatted next to them in the mire. The mire expert explained it precisely, said there were pockets of oxygen or something like that. All on tape, all on tape.

The man with a leg missing, a small-time dirty rag dropped by the big guys. Worked on doors in the nineties. Tied up in the shots at that punk. BOOM, BOOM. It wasn't his case but he remembers it well. Round and round in circles, round and round in circles... if only the circle would close up! The dirty rag's father-in-law, the professor, they got him banged up nice and proper back then. It was his gun, hunting rifle, and his car, a

Mercedes, a huge limo that the punk had stolen. At least that was what the father-in-law thought – fatal mistake. And the dirty rag and the dirty rag's friends set out with the professor to fetch the car back. A shot went off along the way. 'Dirty rags,' that was what they used to call the small-fry in Cologne. Small fish in a big pond. Not a good word for them. It reminds him of that TV series. St Pauli, Hamburg. The folklore of the good cops and the golden-hearted whores. All my whores. *Small Fish, Big Sharks*. All a load of rubbish. Business, like anywhere else. And they don't know if he worked the door in the dark house. Maybe on the margins, like he was always on the margins, Mr Dirty Rag.

'How do you like it, my dear man?'

'It's nice, very nice. I think I have actually tried this cake before, in all the years I've been here. It's cool and creamy at the same time.'

'I couldn't have said it better myself. It's the layers and the quark in the dough that make Dresden layer cake so special. And as you can see and taste, here in this city too.'

Not waiting for an answer, he goes on: 'There's another variety of Dresden layer cake. Freiberg layer cake. That kind, my dear friend, is far flatter and contains, sadly, sadly, no quark. But it's also very tasty. Have you ever been to Freiberg?'

'If you mean the Freiberg with the Mountain Academy, no.'

'Hm, hm.'

Then they lean back in their rattan chairs and stare through the mirror into the darkness of the garden.

'If you know who'd profit from your death, then as now...'

'That ought to be a whole lot of people, if what you

say is true.'

'You have doubts.'

'If I didn't have doubts I wouldn't be here.'

'You won't find a killer because there isn't one.'

'For all three?'

'Of course there's the man with the weapon, the man with the gun, the man with the dagger...'

'And the man with the Bren.'

'And the man with the Bren, if you like. Yes, perhaps. Do you remember the Bricks and Mortar Man, Mr Lübbke, the administrator of the houses and plots?'

'The department head of real estate and property declarations? Of course. I was on that case. Miss Kahn, yes. We'd got that far already.'

'Miss Kahn, of course. We'd got that far already. You know it all yourself.'

'If I knew it all I wouldn't be here.'

'Take your time, slowly, slowly. Will you have another, my dear colleague?'

'I'd be delighted, Mr Ness.'

BOOM, BOOM. The last glance. The Bricks and Mortar Man. The one they shot at four times. Shut your mouth, Lübbke! The one who's still alive. Far away now. And in a very different place. Organized Crime took over the case back then. There were others in on it. The feds, the Federal Crime Police, the State Crime Police. A long time ago. 'And who turned a blind eye? Who knew the shots would fall and let the others go ahead? AK and the others...' The web closes in on him. He knows his body is still asleep. Apnoea. He has it now and then. He hears himself gasping for air, over and over. The silver string between the real estate and those who invest. Those who want real estate. Those the department head gets in the way of. Past tense. A long time

202

ago. Eliot Ness is right. There is no killer. The business has gone independent. He doesn't want to know about it. Not any more. The Valachi papers. What a crock of shit. Legends and fairy tales. 'Of course there's the man with the dagger, the man with the gun...' Yes, but where, where is he, for God's sake? They caught the Bricks and Mortar Man killers. That was his case as well. Everyone knew there was more behind it than those four little nigger boys, who were maybe supposed to just fire a few warning shots, maybe in the leg but maybe in the head. People are always getting warned. They keep their mouths shut. That was a Czech gun as well. Just a few calibres smaller. The crystal border. He wants it all to be coincidence, he wants to sleep, sleep... Wherever he is, wherever he's flat on his back right now. Sleep until it's all over.

All three of them must have looked in too deep. Like Eliot Ness, whom they put out to pasture. And his little crew are flat on their backs in the narrow metal fridges at Forensic Medicine. Miss Kahn back then, the other two not all that long ago. What brought them there, that is. He's not sure with the two. That couple in death, strapped to the concrete bases, her crawling away from him. Even in the dark mire. The only one they know nothing about. They've made a picture of her, based on the fragments of her face. And handed it out everywhere. Behind the station, to the poisoned young whores on the pavements. *Mirror, mirror, on the wall...* It's possible someone gave her the toxins on purpose. Anything's possible. Her picture's attached to his fridge. Short dark hair. Thin top lip, full bottom lip. Why are you sulking at me, girl?

The boyfriend seemed glad when Bärbel turned up again. After all these years. 'I knew she was dead.'

They didn't find any papers, haven't found any. No evidence of her alleged discoveries, investigations into the real-estate Monopoly players. He bolts upright, gasping for air. His eyes accustom themselves to the dark. A bed. His bed? He smells the fresh scent of sheets. Someone's lying next to him. He touches and feels, skin like leather, smooth and rough, and when he turns around it's the mire girl lying next to him and smiling at him with a cleft in her wrinkled brown face.

Her last glance: the room she lived in with him. Small and dirty. No, not actually all that dirty. A bed, a table. Bottles on the table, sparse light through the net curtains at the window. Outside, not far away, is the central station; she doesn't see that. She can tell she's dying, hears footsteps on the staircase, looks at the two bottles on the table, the light refracting in them; it's these occurrences of the light that capture her attention while she drifts away. Is it the sun or a street lamp of the lights of a car or a neon ad? She sat herself down on the floor, leaning against the wall, a few hours ago. She took a few tablets and everything else that was left. She's been high for weeks and her heart won't play along any more. Her last glance. That glinting on the bottles by the window, far less spectacular in reality. The image on the layers of skin in her eyeball.

Doctor Death is leaving him alone for a while now. That's their deal. In return he goes out to the mountains some weekends, towards the crystal border where Doctor Death has a weekend plot, a *datscha* as they call them here. The doctor lost his driving licence, years ago, but they say he's dried up now. Sometimes the old cop spends hours with his dead. Not this time, though; he's already spent a lot of time with them in the mire. Too much time. There are only two of them left now.

Legal secretary Bärbel Kahn has been under the earth
for a few days now. Or back under it. He went to her
funeral. Her mother was there. Her old partner with
his wife. Her son from an early marriage. Apart from
that, only cemetery staff. And the old cop standing
in the background, not wanting to get too close to the
small group, to those who had come. They were more
shocked that she's turned up again than anything else,
he thought. Missing for more than ten years, they try to
forget it somehow, at some point, and then suddenly they
dig up the ground outside the city, on the edge of the city,
between the towns, dig up the earth, the mire, drain it for
construction, how ironic, seeing as Ness said she must
have got on the track of the dirty real estate deals back
then, and then, years of quiet, years in which the seeking
and questioning gradually turned into forgetting: Hello!
I'm back. *I never really went away, I was just hiding.* At
least now they know she's dead. No more unnecessary
daydreaming. He walks between rows of gravestones, on
the narrow pathways that are supposed to take him back
to the main path, at least to one of the main paths, and
he looks across hundreds and thousands of graves and
stones, like a miniature city, he thinks. Trees between
them, benches between them, wide and narrow pathways
between; he loses his bearings. He can't remember ever
being in this giant cemetery before. He turns around
and recognizes Eliot Ness standing on the margins, but
directly next to the group of relatives and officials, and
watching them lower the small coffin. Her mother didn't
want her cremated. He wonders for a moment whether
to go back again. He hadn't planned to disappear before
she disappeared. He'd even brought along a little bunch
of flowers, but then he'd put them on another grave on
his way when he made out the small procession from a

distance. It was a dried-up, overgrown grave that could do with a few flowers; he only saw the name out of the corner of his eye.

What does Ness want here? he thinks. To take his leave from the big cases? Because there are no solutions left? Because the silver strings lead all the way to the top, wherever that may be? The bottom. The top. Eliot Ness kept on talking, more and more names, dates, procedures and numbers and figures came pouring out of his unceasingly opening and closing mouth towards him, wove around him like a web, around them both, around everything, because it was about everything, as Eliot Ness kept on saying, the world, the cartels, the crises, oh no, not crises; a war, for more than twenty years now. A war in which everything overlaps and shifts, the alloys of power and money.

The old cop thinks of Eliot Ness and his grand speeches, Ness grabbing him by the shoulder when he started drifting off, too much cognac, too much time, grabbed him by the shoulder, showed him file after file with his face contorted, explaining now in a whisper and now in a shout who had hindered his investigations and when, back then. Or was he whispering all along? In the conservatory's quiet night. The two forts. The town hall, which the locals call 'the fort', and the big brothel, the Fort, the house near Pretty Peepers Alley, motorway entrance, motorway exit. It's not going well there, he's heard. All the years of wear and tear. Forget the forts, forget the provinces, whispers Eliot Ness. The boundaries have been overstepped in the past. The old cop's had enough. Too much theory. Too much conspiracy. Even if Ness is right about it all, his dead are still left without killers.

He sits on the stool, looking at the rows of empty or

occupied refrigerator drawers. The light of the neon strips is beginning to hurt his eyes and he takes his sunglasses out of their case and puts them on. He doesn't quite know why and he doesn't think about it later either, but then he stood up from the stool, pulled his man out of the cold and examined his hands again, very closely. Because it's all been done already. Prints, fibres, DNA. Nothing. No clawing at the killer's body. How could he, with that huge gun? That veritably ripped his ribcage to shreds. Even a single shot would have been fatal. Someone must have been mighty angry at him. He has to take off the sunglasses to really understand what he sees. Has to put them on again to really understand what he sees.

And he's sinking again. Sinking into the dark blue depths. Bolts upright. Heart of the sea, or what? Two suns above the water, or is one of them the moon?

Later he thinks it was probably her *moon face* as she leaned over him, as he was gasping for air.

Later he tells her about his grandfather, and *he* learned it from *his* father, so his own great-grandfather, she laughs and they're drinking bubbly, which makes his heart race despite the blockers he takes, he tells her about his grandfather who had a piece of land not far from Cologne, you could see the cathedral when you climbed up the village church tower, and there, on his land, he loosened the earth with the aid of explosives. No, she says, I don't believe you.

But it's true, that's how they used to do it. A hundred years or so ago, everyone did it.

You're not that old.

'Our farmland, as we all know, is not dead earth.'

On the ground he sees the moving layer of graves,

the rising and falling away of the hills across which the endless field of stones extends. But it's only water that's moving.

Before he wakes up he sees the altar-like gravestone with the figure, the statue. A bearded, grim, rutted man of stone or bronze, he can't tell precisely, holding up a globe. Large wings going down to the ground grow out of his back. Someone's standing in front of the figure, in front of the grave, which must have been erected for an important man, standing there as bubbles escape from his mouth. Could it be himself? No. He knows the man. The Old Man or the Man behind the Mirrors? He's tried before to recognize these temple-like constructions. *Explore this city that you do not know*. But every time he rose gurgling, gasping for air, up out of the dream.

Amalgam, the fluttering and snapping of the flag in the wind on the whorehouse, the Outsiders, the Angels, 'the Turkish fright' they say in the brothels, discos, whorehouses and they defend the market, the borders remain in place; *crystal*, the cop thinks at first when he holds the tiny shimmering stone between forefinger and thumb, it's cold because it's been in the cold with the one-legged man, seemed almost grown into his skin, his hand, dead layers, last images, four shots at the real-estate man, the Lord of the Bricks and Mortar, back then, stab wounds in the legal secretary's neck and chest after she'd been choked and almost strangled, flashing wind turbines, zeppelins above the city, mail from Berlin, reinforcements from Hannover, population figures constantly rising, *Have a good life, Starsky*, drives by night, Organized Crime, OC, OK, KO, great big Mercedes limos full of Turks and Yugos cruising the city as if this here was Kurfürstenstraße or fucking Berlin, flaneurs, the press forgets the bodies in the mire, the old cop

208

reads the whores' ads on the back pages of the *Bild*, are they getting more or less? All online? The two corpses are cremated and no one comes, he lies flat on his back with his fat lady and smells her sweat and her juices, he drinks G&T with the boss lady and the *pretty peepers* before they start their shifts, 'I wanted to be sexually active,' Eliot Ness arranges his strings, which suddenly turn into ropes, nooses, snakes as fat as an arm, '...when the excess water had flowed off from the Elbe glacial valley, the remains of organic substances gradually settled on the ground of the remaining lake over centuries and millennia,' the tannoy announcements drift beneath the large steel arches and echo away, in the Dead Railwayman the skat cards show *à grand ouvert*, why all the laughing over and over...? Someone might steal it if they're passing through, a whore's childhood memories on the tram-ride to work, of that lost boy Timm Thaler, the silver strings branch together with the silvery shining rails, who'll fall? And who's behind the mirrors? Trains arrive and trains depart, and his fat lady's laughter scratches his ears, that hoarse scratchy laugh, 'Come on, one more glass of bubbly, my sunshine!' Red Riding Hood, Red Riding Hood, only ever Red Riding Hood, 'The sun's coming up!' Capital crimes, criminal offences against sexual self-determination, missing persons department, gang crimes (narcotics, gambling, organized crime, counterfeiting crimes), the old cop, *le Bulle*, remembers his time at the academy, remembers his grandfather visiting him once, not long before he died, his hands calloused, an old earth worker who still loosened the ground with the aid of explosives the way he'd once learned it, a little booklet about this almost forgotten procedure was always on his desk in the farmhouse, next to the pipe stand and the hand-carved wooden box full of seashells, which he always used to say were from their honeymoon, Deauville, France, he talked about that all the way to the end, never saw more of the world than that. He wasn't much interested in it either, seeing the world, the old cop whom his wife used to call 'Captain' for a joke, and he thinks of the lagoon up in the northeast, thinks of his next holiday, drives through the city by night, which starts at four or five o'clock in the late autumn, early winter, the compound eyes of a dying hoverfly see the image of the room in countless fragments, 'Greed, of course that as well or mostly greed, or a... let's call it... an unsophisticated need for freedom, yes, yes, that's how it was, I thought I had to get sexually active,' voices, voices, he remembers the hours he spent squatting in the mire and listening to the semi-mummified bodies of the dead, the hours when he dreamed of removing the skin from their eyes to cast a glance at their last glances, miniature images, lights under an electron microscope, the past permeating everything, but what's this? When he suddenly wakes up somewhere or at some time in this circle, wakes up from sleep and the dream that she, his fat lady, called 'in the heart of the seas' in a sudden attack of feeling, he's not susceptible to kitsch, '...several narrow and remote streets, such as Zimmerstraße, Kupfergässchen and Sporergässchen for more sophisticated tastes, Ulrichsgasse for soldiers and workers, have a wealth of such houses, from where harlots in fantastic costumes called to him outside every, I say every house on those streets and encouraged him to enter,' he listens to his tapes and thinks about the new case, body parts in the river, a young man at the very top of the list, *Murder on Computer Game High?* Killer and killed, 'The quiet in the city is misleading,' says an inside informer about the motorized syndicates, what quiet? he thinks, but of course it is quiet, he thinks later as he drives past the airport that glows in the night like a huge UFO in the fields... but we've had that already, it's the natural way of things he thinks, and looks forward to his G&T at Madame Gourdan's, the boss lady of the fluttering flag, he has the feeling he never meets any normal people any more apart from her and the others, no one he can talk to.

And when he removes the tiny diamond from the cut skin of the hand of his one-legged dead man, who must have pressed it so hard at the moment of his death that it pushed through the layers of skin deep into his flesh, he holds it up to the light of the neon strips, almost dazzled by the miniscule, beautiful refractions and rays, *like the compound eyes of a hoverfly*, and he knows he's finally found a lead. But it's night outside and he takes a mahogany boat downstream along the border river to the lagoon.

And when she's sleeping next to him, snoring because it's a hard job in those morning hours and the bubbly and her circulation and all the damn fucking collide with each other, he puts the tiny diamond between her huge tits, his sperm still splashed over them, 'Shoot it, my dear, yes, yees, shoot that load, my sunshine, come all over me, you horny dog!' and watches while in the city and in the ever enlarging circle nothing happens for seconds, he holds his breath and watches the stone moving to the restless beat of her heart.

ETERNITY TWO

HELLO THERE, FANS,

Hello, hello, hello! And a wonderful evening, a deep gentle night to all of you listening in live to Jerry's Cherry Pie Show! Put your headphones on, turn your speakers down and send your wives to your cold marital beds, or turn the speakers up if you're all on your own-some. Jerry will bring the city of the night to your hearts and your members, and we'll give the whores our roses, applause, applause, thirty minutes straight to the webs of cavaliers and seekers, Wanderer's Night Schlong.

There are rumours going round, pretty nasty rumours, that I'm no longer among you, no longer on hand and eternally randy, and I'm shocked, deeply shocked, dear fans, that people are saying Ever-Ready Jerry can't go cherry-testing for you any more. For you, for us and for himself, let that be known! One moment please...

Anja P., born in Weißenfels in 1988, left school in 1994, trained as an office clerk in Magdeburg from 2004 to 2007, occasional escort jobs in 2006 and 2007, extended visits to Berlin, moved to ... in 2009, officially resident there, working in an apartment on G.-Straße from 2009, visiting hours Monday to Friday, 10 a.m. to 8 p.m.

Oh no, Jerry's red hot and good to trot! Life's flagpole is stiff and straight, and the girls blow my flag deep into the wind! It's getting your Jerry, Ever-Ready Jerry, all sentimental. No big flutter, the Dead Railwayman's still riding those rails of desire. Desire, desire, desire and now and then Great Balls of Fire, because not all the cherries can give Ever-Ready Jerry the big kick... to his COCK... because your upstanding Jerry gets it up

212

honestly or he doesn't get down to it at all, you crusaders of the night, you travelling men, listen up and listen in and chip in, to the tips, Jerry's top tips for hours of fun... or maybe just minutes, because there's nothing wrong with a quickie now and then!

I've read and heard all the whispers on the web, in our little worldwide community, how the big question right now is about the Puszta pussies and whether I can give you premium assurance cover on the matter. And good old Jerry can.

The Hungarian wave is still rolling in, like back in '89 when hundreds of thousands streamed towards Buda and Pest in trains and cars because the gates to the West were opening there, but now there's a crisis in Hungary, the state's just scraping this side of bankruptcy, say the papers and the people, the summer's hot, the autumn's hot, and if the girls stay here then the winter will be hot, hot, hot and all... Sweat, sweat, sweat, or my name's not Ever-Ready Jerry.

But more on that later, fans, because in the past few weeks and months your Jerry's been out testing so hard the rubber started smoking, or you might even say: melting and burning up on the hot skin and in the hot heroines! With Supersexy Ariella from Lake Balaton for instance, you'll find her as ever on whores dot net or on the hottest page of our red-topped newspaper, right after the sports pages, or on the pages of sex dot dot dot net as in fishnets, you know what I mean, city names are like adult games, but you know either way what dot dot dot your Jerry is talking and writing about in the big, big city, online radio, sex on the city beach, yeah, yeah, yeah.

'Supersexy body' says the supersexy lady's ad, or the ad placed by our legendary manager of desire, and for a hundred an hour or a hundred and fifty if you want her to call on you in your love nest, all you'll want to do is plant your sex, your supersex, in her gorgeous sculpted body. Oh yeah baby! And that's what she's got, although I'm sceptical about the eight and a half stone on her set card on whores dot net. Add another stone or so, and once you've filled your rubber johnny, or splashed your load on her – oops – tits, it'll soon add up to eleven. But she's not a fat lady, just a red-hot arse and super tits. Thumbs up. Thumbs in. Chocks up and away. Her German's not bad at all, fucking, blow jobs, passive golden showers, passive rim jobs, I've read that in a few ads now, it's turning into a trend, and that rosette's a tasty sight, YEAH, YEAH, YEAH. And her accent: cream of the cream, it'll get all your juices flowing when this little sweetie gets it on.

And because someone asked here, I'm afraid you can't take the back door into her house, but she'll gladly give you a good going over in that department if you want, and likes oiling her little fist for a round of passive FF.

Mannie-Fox from Geithain wrote to me yesterday and said he spurted ten yards with her little fist up his arse. Yes, fans, we're loved for our openness, all official and up-front. Open words, open orifices.

Zsuzsa F., born in Budapest in 1991, father officer, mother interpreter for English and German, lost training placement in 2008 during the state crisis, 2008 Budapest party scene, 2009 trip to Prague with two girlfriends, active in table dance bars, service assistant in a casino, contacts with Zoltan M.'s placement agency, from 2009 initial activities in the sexual services sector in an apartment on K.-Straße in Dresden.

But there's anxiety simmering in our still hot late

summer, what's up, what's going on, can we still get a good fuck in peace? Exotic women, velvet-skinned, black-skinned, Turkish delights, Suzy Wongs, we love all that, and good old home cooking too and dirty little German girls and a spot of Russian *War and Piece* when those sweet bodies start contorting, but the main thing is there's plenty of choice and the market sucks us dry and the prices stay the same as they were, let's stick to the good old days, eh? But everything's getting more expensive and the politicians say our pensions are safe in their hands. And that scares your Jerry, your Ever-Ready Jerry. If Aladdin and the Forty Bandits take over here, in our ... dot dot dot big city. Locos from all over the place. Scum from the capital. But our city's had enough of scum. We're liberal and politically correct. And because we revere open words here like we do open orifices: Send 'em back, with a good, hard smack.

We're right behind our almost legendary manager of desire on this one, our Old Man of the Mountain. I remember how they almost wiped him out over ten years ago, and he stood right back up and gave the Yugos and the Turks (did someone say Turkish face mask?) a good oiling and shoved them back through their keyhole, if you know what I mean. Nothing but bare bones left over. That's what you hear, beneath the streets, in the salons.

But everyday politics and the decline of German morals are outside our remit, you're listening to Jerry's Cherry Pie Show, Jerry on the pull. All I'll say is, no need to be scared, the shots have been fired, the smoke's cleared, the *situation's* almost calm now. Help's approaching from the capital and from Hannover City, the market will soon be regulated again, and then we can go out wandering undisturbed again, wandering through the night, boom, boom without the BOOM, BOOM, Girl

Girl Girl, waiting for a star to fall.

And back to our Balaton Girl, our Puszta pussy. The romantic souls among you will get your heart's content with candles and wax play, I haven't tried it out myself yet, good old Jerry's more into the good old in-and-out. The good old Hokey Pokey, that's what it's all about.

But what a beauty, let me tell you, listen up 'cause the clock's struck twelve. You'd think Ariella had gills, taking that eel so deep in her mermaid mouth and sucking you to semenless sleep. No actual throat action, though. But almost, you could say, on a good day.

If you want to get even deeper into pussymouthing around there are better places to go, and more on that later, deep throat fans, but I can't stop praising and raising foxy Ariella, 'cause she kisses too and shows you what your cock tastes like, 'cause she'll blow you without a translator, of course, but she doesn't want a load shot in her sweet mouth. And I'd almost believe her and our legendary manager of the red-lit pussycats, the tycoon of the baboons – sorry, sir! – that she's twenty-four, 'cause her skin and the round curves between her arse and her pussy, between her thighs and her hips, are so silky and smooth and soft that I feel like dialling her number right here and now. Eighteen to mid-twenties. And she's not in any hurry and you won't be under any stress, oh guest, oh generous friend of desire, if you pay for the full hour, 'cause she's gentle and hot, just the way we like it and need it, a cigarette, a coffee, a few close words in her bed... perfect for all aficionados... Heh heh... Old Jerry's getting poetic just thinking about Ariella's hot breath. Once you've tasted her pussy, seen that foxy lady holding her butt cheeks apart while you fuck her... Heh heh, this one looks like she's getting job satisfaction, Jerry's very special cherry bomb with cream on top for tonight, another oasis on our wanderings through the apartments and streets of the night.

And her Hungarian countrywoman Aruscha will suck your dicks way down in her throat, bareback if you like (although only for oral, not for full service, of course), that's what I wanted to tell you before! When I was in their apartment in dot dot dot with our lovely Ariella, Aruscha was in the room right next door, a Hungarian double-A, sadly no anal with either of them but still a double wham bam, but make it quick, fans, because I hear Aruscha, a blonde bombshell but I can't tell if it's natural, the deep throat artiste, is looking to move on soon. I tested them both out but there's no splashing down Aruscha's throat, she's a great gargler when she swallows your eel but she can tell perfectly when your juice is on the brink, or on the slow rise up from your balls, she's a priceless lullaby in an evening dress, although she charges a ton and a half for an hour all-inclusive but that does include coming on her sweet, round little face. Hot, hot, hot to trot.

Someone wrote to me the other day to ask what 'Jerry's Cherry Pie' is all about, the name of the show.

Must have been a young fucker, a young night wanderer, if he's never heard of that song, 'Cherry Pie', bit of a rock classic, maybe you can pick it up in record stores or maybe it's not on the market any more. One thing that's definitely still on the market, and almost a classic herself, is Moni, Moni the Milf in house number 23, in the south of the city where the sun always shines, although there aren't too many model apartments waiting for our visits down there. The former master butcher has his club nearby, although he doesn't like to hear he's a master butcher and a former one at that... and I've been praising his club for years now as an old-school oasis, we might get back to that later if we have enough time, if we have enough listeners, but this is modern theatre I'm doing here and I don't have to worry about time or listeners; small but perfectly formed, his place is, and think a little big and XXX-better than the big fort at the other end of town, which I hear is almost bankrupt, that's what wagging tongues are saying on the street, but I digress, fans, last time we heard from each other was eight and a half weeks ago, that was my last time on air, and that's a bloody long time, so it's easy to get carried away in conversation, huh?

But we want to spread tips to the masses, to all you un-tiring shaggers and carpetbaggers, all of us keeping the only true people's economy running, keeping it coming. The big tit. No money in the world will buy you a bet-ter fuck than money can buy. HEHHH, APPLAUSE, APPLAUSE. That's what I think sometimes. In the background you can hear another golden oldie, another classic, 'In the year 2525', let's just let that run on for a bit and listen and feel and remember that we live in anxious times, but your Jerry gives you security, gives you con-stants, HEH, HEH, HEH, better if it was Constance, I used to know a girl named Constance, WOW, WOW, WOW, let me tell you, she was a constant as well, that was just after the Wall on the legendary Caravan Alley, we spent a good few nights rocking those pussy wagons, any questions?

And if you think back to those years between time and stream, between bricks and mortar, between rock and hard place, there's no way back and that's a good thing too, even though things are hotting up again now; there weren't any apartments or luxury girls back then, or as good as none.

218

Zofia G., born in H. village near the Hungarian-Croatian border in 1988, worked on parents' farm after completing school, placed in Germany via an agency, presumably Zoltan M., active in erotic shows and strip bars from 2009, active in apartment prostitution in various German towns since 2010, together with a former classmate from H. village, most recently in XXX, sends money to her family at regular intervals.

From there to here, the present without a past, we're wandering like the ancient philosophers.

God is dead. Sex lives. Long may it reign. Moni the Milf is very much a milf. You can do anything you like with her. Everything your brains desire. A three-hole pony. An old hussy. But I don't mean to be rude, not at all. Because, and here it comes: I love these old leathery lovers. Even her voice gets me going like a Roman candle. Her body's as taut as an old saddle. Or her bodice, at least. A babe of the century, at least half a century. That lad who wrote to me the other day about what my 'Cherry Pie' was all about, I recommended her to him right away, cross my heart, because – (pun alert) – the best way to learn to ride is on an old mare. That's not an issue for us experienced punters, but good old Jerry likes to help wherever he can. I haven't got an answer from him yet, he's probably passed out somewhere with his balls drained dry, 'cause an hour with Moni means lust and pain and madness and your brain bursts and bubbles away somewhere in her orifices.

'Behold, thou art fair, my love; behold, thou art fair; thou hast doves' eyes within thy locks: thy hair is as a flock of goats, that appear from mount Gilead. Thy teeth are like a flock of sheep that are even shorn, which came up from the washing; whereof every one bear twins, and none is barren among them. Thy lips are like a thread of

219

scarlet, and thy speech is comely: thy temples are like a piece of a pomegranate within thy locks.

Thy neck is like the tower of David builded for an armoury, whereon there hang a thousand bucklers, all shields of mighty men. Thy two breasts are like two young roes that are twins, which feed among the lilies. Until the day break, and the shadows flee away, I will get me to the mountain of myrrh, and to the hill of frankincense. Thou art all fair, my love; there is no spot in thee.'

The song of good old Salomon.

I always tell the truth, fans, and I have to say that at Moni's place at XXX, where Moni lives when she's turning tricks for cash, it's a whole apartment building as you know or you're just finding out right now, and there are other girls there too, as I talked about nine and a half weeks ago, if you recall, so anyway this house, to be perfectly honest, could be a bit nicer, they could wipe all the dust off the windowsills, for example, that'd be a good start. More dead flies on those windowsills than in a garibaldi biscuit. Our revered manager of the night doesn't have his finger in this pie, as far as I know, 'cause in his places, in his oases of willingness and availability, things are a good bit cleaner, as far as I can tell. Eden City.

That's not to say that Moni's place and number 23 are dirty, because we can have our way there like dirty dogs, especially with... YES, GENTLEMEN.

She'll do pretty much everything. Z to A. From zipless to analingus. HEY, you guys out there, is it summer right now, is it autumn, or is it snowing in the big, big city?

A face like a grandma, a body like grandma's great-granddaughter. HEYYY, that's got you listening, huh? Prick up your ears, prick up your pricks. That's

220

the sexy discrepancy. And I don't mean to be rude, maybe 'grandma' wasn't too pretty, but what a fine kitty! Loose? No. Tight. My God, but she's tight. GIRL GIRL GIRL, she's got cheeky short blonde hair, maybe a bit wrinkled in the face, but she'll blow, she'll swallow, she'll pull out all the stops and put in all the plugs for you, for us, an unbeatable hundred an hour and no extra costs for Greek or the famous throat fuck, it's all part of the service once she's got the cash in her pocket.

PRAISE BE TO HER, you'll find her on whores dot net and on the XXX website. And if there was a talent contest to see which girl's the nicest fuck and which girl never watches the clock for the paid-for hour, that dark blue, thrilling, midnight hour, then there's one sexy senior winner at number 23 and far beyond. And here comes our song... LIKE A VIRGIN... OOOH... VERY FIRST TIME... LIKE A VIR-HIR-HIR-GIN. There are a few of us, I know, who prefer a turn on a young body. And sometimes I'm just the same, just thinking of our Puszta nymphs, those greedy girls in their mid-twenties, and I've always got a few tips up my sleeve all the way down to eighteen, for where to find young blood – eat fresh, pay less, as they say.

Willy, my buck, shoot out your horn.

MY DEAR FANS. Jerry's still online after all this time. Coming out of the big city to the cold, cold beds. Out of the hot, hot beds into the empty city. Are you still there, are you still with me? But I see the mails and messages are still coming in on my hot, hot line. Someone writes that I've got no style and I'm a slur on all hobbyists and so on... Everything A-OK with you? What with me bowing down to the ladies of the night, to the wonderful nymphs du prairie (as they were called in the Wild

West, where they invented the term 'red-light district', and don't say I never teach you anything, will you?).

Anja N., born in the industrial town of D., Ukraine, in 1991, broke off apprenticeship as an industrial mechanic, 2009 employed according to own statements as hotel staff member in W., Germany, 2010 active as sex worker in XXX night club in F., according to own statements misled about precise nature of the work, contact with the Hydra sex workers' organization, brief return to D. in early 2011, active in XXX club in Berlin since late 2011.

What do we know about our women anyway...? One kind or the other. We saddle them up, our sweet little ponies. We've talked about three of them. Independent and open-minded. Our Solomon Songs. Yea, though I walk through the valley of the shadow... I will fear no evil... no semenless days. Our rod and our staff... they penetrate deep.

HOUSE AND HOTEL. CODENAME CARMEN. It's not long ago at all I was at her place. The problem with Carmen was that she didn't want to leave her place. And her back was covered in scars. She had something cut out or lasered on her back. And I tell her: Hotel please. But she goes: No, sorry, no can do right now, come to such and such a place instead. So I jump in a taxi. Spent ages looking for the entrance. Like that old basement with the young, young girls, back in the day. My God, was she sexy, was she pretty, clean-shaven kitty, DO YOU LIKE MY LITTLE CLEAN-SHAVEN FANNY? Could have been my daughter, age-wise. A great little girl. The only problem was, she didn't want to do an hour. Even though an hour... She only wanted Pay As You Earn, a hundred a pop, but I have to say, her mind wasn't on the job, not properly. Even though I offered her two hundred and fifty for an hour, she wanted everything quid pro quo, no all-inclusive. Wash your hands if you want to finger me – I already have! I don't like all that this costs this and that costs that, it's old-school, hardly any of the girls are like that now, the market... But her pussy tasted of piss, I'll never forget that. I LOST ALL MY GLADNESS.

Peggy D., born in Plauen / Vogtland in 1971, trained as a secretary, several further education courses up to 1989, from 1987 to 1989 shorthand typist for Interdruck in Moscow, fluent Russian speaker, married since 1993, daughter born 1993, opened office supplies shop in XXX together with husband Ulf D. in 1995, insolvency 1996, active in apartment prostitution for XXX's company since 1998.

The one woman over in the amalgam of the city, the neighbouring town, the suburb... I can't say it here, but I almost fell in love with her. ARE WE OFFLINE RIGHT NOW? Our respected man, our manager of the vented, I mean prevented prostheses ('cause we all know what happened in '99, that dark, dark year), our king of the lets, is there and renting out apartments; I saw him limping to his Mercedes. I saw his boys, his army keeping business calm there, and while I gave her a nice shiny pearl necklace she praised him. To the skies. 'He's a real good guy!' And the working conditions. PRAISE BE TO HIM: *submissive lady, horny and devoted.* Now, I don't know whether she works for *him* or the other man in the shadows, although he only administers the brothels and clubs, but who cares, they're both upright businessmen. If you ask me, gentlemen.

And here we are again. HELLO, FANS. I was never really gone. I'M RIGHT BACK HERE, TO BRING YOU CHEER.

And you're expecting tips from me. I'm right with you. There's a sour taste of piss on my tongue. So horny. We wander among the hundreds of harlots, we test them out, we try them out, we're glad to give them our money. We're back online. And off we go, and up we go, ringing at those doorbells. Apartments, little brothels, nice clubs, wonderful women. Six to seven hundred in our city, and rising, always in parallel with the population figures... Now don't you all start complaining, the emails have started coming in already, an endless stream of flatulence telling me to get to the point because we've got a surprise guest coming up tonight, but first: my section 'Scat – where's it at?' is no longer, I've axed it, no more brown showers for lonely hours round here, if you get my meaning, fans. I've always tried to imagine what's so sexy-hexy about shit hitting a face or a man's horny-taut skin... but no, let me tell you, I'm a selfish bugger, even though I do get that the joys of a nice amber shower are nothing to be sniffed at, so I've got a wee tip for you on that front. Tip top topping! There's this Nicole, a never-tiring nympho, you'll find her number on my page, and here's her address right now because there's nothing like a nudge to get you pressing her buttons. The Iron Castle, that wonderful whorehouse in the south of our City of Eden, and I mean that as a compliment to the working girls, our women who devote themselves to the hardcore denizens, number X, XXXX Straße, ring the bell downstairs, the choice awaits you inside, hot wet Nicole was on the second floor the other day, where she'll gladly part her legs and squat above you – champagne weather – in the cool white bathtub and her hot

224

yellow juice will come... and now my poetry's at an end... pissing all over you, hot and randy and sexy as hell. If that's what you want. Back when I was married it was important to take a shower afterwards. Oh, how important. 'Cause don't forget, female noses are suspicious. Where were we, we've lost the thread. The thread of juice running out of the prize-worthy sweet cunt-mouth of N. N.... Take a look at my site, the section with loveable oral providers will get your mouth watering just reading it... I'll have to have a look myself soon who's offering that wonderful juicing service, 'cause there aren't many out there... as you can see, there's something for every man out there. But now back to rock-hard reporting, back to the rock-hard educational work, WE WANT THE FACTS, not just the contacts and the contractors! *J'accuse*, I accuse, with the lead piping in the ballroom: that gossip factory worker who accuses the Old Man of the Mountain, our entrepreneur of desire, the landlord of paradise, of importing women, of coercing women or co-operating with the importers and coercers, and then this accuser even mentions names in the wilds of the web. Seems legally dubious to me, but let's let the facts speak for themselves, the protocol of shame here unabridged on my page, just a click away, and right here and now your Jerry will read out a few parts of it live and with notes, and good old Jerry can assure you everything is legal and kosher in the rooms of our land-lord king! And it's the hot, hot Puszta girls, our sweet hungry Hungarians, who are supposed to be working by force! And the concerned citizen names more than one of them by name, we heard about them earlier on, reviewed just like a good book, and I'll quote in a min-ute from the protocol of the elder, or more likely the younger, and if you want to know and read everything, the great whore conspiracy or exploitation, then don't click between the legs of the cute girl at the very top of my page – that's where you'll find numbers and addresses and ratings – click on the little hydra head with snakes curled around it at the bottom, and before our surprise guest gets a say I'll just read a few extracts, no comment:

'The eastern European women have to work seventeen to eighteen hours a day in the apartments; it's like third-world exploitation. They're not allowed free time of their own, they're not allowed to leave the apartment alone, are held there by force. The middlemen send the girls from one city to the next around Germany and Europe so that they can't forge contacts to other girls outside the apartments.

'The pimps use violence when the women don't meet their demands. They have to provide extra services without protection. The punishments when the women don't provide these services are so severe that they are forced to do everything the clients and pimps demand of them. They have to pay much higher daily rents for the apartments than the German women and hand over almost all their income to the middlemen. I have strong indications that the authorities profit from this system of coercion and do not take steps against these crimes for that reason.'

So far, so bad, fans. And the lines are buzzing and the data's flashing through the net, and I, your Jerry, your Ever-Ready Jerry, am flowing through the voices and the pages and gliding through the tangle of silver strings, and the telephone's ringing and I'm looking forward to my surprise guest, the man who once found his way back from the underworld like Orpheus, back to the light, back to the light.

But before we let the big man have his say, here comes

a pre-recorded comment from a love artiste, a sex worker I've visited several times myself and praised to high
heaven in one of my recent shows, but who now – sadly,
sadly – works in another profession. And who wanted to
make a clear statement on these accusations against her
former boss and landlord. Roll tape:

'I don't know what kind of a scene is being made here
about BEEP. I rented apartments from him at fair prices
for years. I've worked with Hungarians and women from
all over the world, and it was usually a good working
relationship. I've never heard or experienced anything
like the accusations of beatings and forced prostitution.
BEEP is a decent person, always there for his girls. I really value him in this industry. And I can't relate to all
the negative statements, all these accusations, I can only
say the opposite. He's a fair person and a great man.'

The man with the BEEP will tell us in just a moment
what's going on with all the accusations or lies, oh, beg
your pardon – but everyone's presumed innocent until
proven guilty and there's more than twelve angry men
out there, and the defence instinct is a powerful thing
when someone wants to paint us punters and night wanderers as beneficiaries of misery and force – so he'll
clear us up on what this whole scatstorm is about.

But first this, which was pre-recorded as well, fans, so
here you go:

'My dear Jerry, how nice that I get my say on your
show, that's not exactly common practice these days.
Kisses for that, my good man. But next time don't go
broadcasting so much horny smut on the airwaves,
you're driving my guests round the bend. Oh well, my
good man, you do know how to get business booming! So
as you know, I'm a good German woman in the prime of
my life, and I've been renting an apartment from BEEP

for several years and I'd never want any other landlord, can't imagine a better place to work than in his property. What that XXX writes is all untruths and by no means facts. None of it is thought through or fully researched! That good man needs a few things explaining to him! And I've often, in my professional experience if you like, I've often picked up on a young foreign woman playing a guest for sympathy, because there are plenty of guests who fall for it and give the girls money or whatever else, it's pretty clever of the girls, although I think it's not worth it in the long run – but that guy's obviously fallen for it hook, line and sinker. And before he goes round libelling people, which might even be a crime in itself but I'm not an expert, he ought to have got some more information from the right places. I won't deny there's plenty of stress and problems in the trade, envy, bullying, if you know what I mean, but I've always tried to work fair and clean, and all I can say is that BEEP also works fair and clean.'

Thanks for the compliments and the criticism, my dear, and now it's time, ladies and gentlemen, fans out there, all you night watchers and night wankers, live on Jerry's Cherry Pie Show, we'll have to change the name any day now, it's blow time, just send me your wishes and ideas. But now you've waited long enough and I'll open up the line for one of our most respected citizens. I sometimes get a bit disrespectful and call him the 'Old Man of the Mountain' but only to express my admiration. For legal reasons and less legal reasons he'd prefer to remain anonymous today, in formal terms, as he told me earlier. I have to admit I'm a tiny bit nervous.

AHEM HEM

'So, welcome to the show and thank you for coming to state your position on the accusations.'

'Good evening, everyone. You call them "accusations", do you?'

'Well...'

'Let me start by telling you that you're taking a big step towards educating people with your "little show", as you call it, I mean by taking a relaxed and open approach to the issue of sex work, sexual services and especially the sex workers themselves, even though you do occasionally overdo the puns and end up in a kind of ironic, I think, sexual frenzy...'

'Well, good old Jerry does tip over the edge every now and then, I have to admit.'

'It's all about give and take, just like in other businesses, my dear Jerry – you don't mind me calling you Jerry, do you...?'

'Of course not!'

'You took my side from the beginning, if I can judge from the last few minutes, although they seemed like hours, to be frank.'

'I just couldn't imagine anything else, you see, having frequented most of your properties.'

'I appreciate that, my dear Jerry, I really do, but I'm not always sure you get the full view of things, your role is that of the guest, the ever-glowing client...'

'Oh yeah, Jerry gets it glowing, now and then at least. But that's why I'm glad I can talk to you about the facts.'

'Facts, Jerry. That's exactly what it's all about. Far too few of our fellow citizens know the facts. They look out into the night and think they see cesspools...'

'Me? No, I...'

'Not you, my dear Jerry. Our fellow citizens, Jerry.'

'You've chosen to take an unusual step by facing up to

our admittedly small listener community.'

'Don't say "face up", my dear Jerry. That sounds too much like I'm in the stocks. You have respect for our work, that's what I appreciate about you. And by that I mean the work of the women without whom I'd be nothing, and I mean that "nothing" just the way I say it, and my work, my company's work.'

'Thank you, thank you. And I have no intention of putting you in the stocks, Mr... What shall I call you for our little chat... Mr Orpheus?'

'Typical Jerry!' (LAUGHS)

'Jerry's Cherry Pie Show.' (LAUGHS)

'Well, why not? As you like it. I do know what you're referring to, of course, and that's exactly what I meant when I said you don't always have a clear view of the facts, the things...'

'I do my best, Mr Orpheus.'

'The French version would be Orphée.'

'Pardon...?'

'No, forget it. You're right, my dear Jerry – we want to be transparent. Transparency has become increasingly important to me over the past few years. You introduced me as a respected citizen. In actual fact, though, the situation is slightly different. What does the general public know about me? They certainly don't know that I make sizeable donations to various organizations, including the sex workers' organization Hydra, but I don't want to shout about it...'

'The upright moral citizens would probably say you want to salve your guilty conscience.'

'Guilty conscience? One of the ladies said it very well earlier: we try to be fair. And we are. Give and take. When it comes to the absurd assertion that some of the women in my properties are working fifteen or sixteen hours in a row, anyone can see from the set cards that that's not the case, of course not. Most properties have at least two ladies working in them, who co-ordinate their working hours with each other, and they're rarely more than nine hours. And taking a walk, taking a break, popping out to the shops; I'm a landlord, Jerry, not a jailer. You just go ahead and ask, Jerry, if you have any questions on that subject.'

'Fans, you're listening to Jerry's Cherry Pie Show, the show for friends and guests of whores. As usual there are plenty of puns on the tip of my tongue, but this is a serious matter we're talking about. So, my dear Mr Orpheus, the author of these... let's say "indictments"... talks or rather writes about forced prostitution in your properties, talks or rather writes about coercion, exploitation, organizations in the background, Hungarian pimps, alliances that you, Mr Orpheus, are supposed to have with the authorities, in other words the town hall and the police force. Goes on to write about instructions for services enforced upon the women, referring to the Hungarian sex workers to whom I admittedly gave the ironic promotional name of Puszta pussies in my recent shows, which was by no means intended disrespectfully, but was only meant to take account for the greedy, but by all means respectful viewpoint of the clients...'

'Jerry, Jerry, you're making matters worse. There's no need for you to defend your choice of words. Although I'll admit I find them rather extreme...'

'So you're a loyal listener to my little show?'

'I wouldn't put it quite like that. But what are we talking about? Of course I'm familiar with these things, of course I try to understand how the guests tick. The worst kind are the ones who bottle everything up, who can't express their desire and their sexuality. So I'd much rather we laughed together about Puszta pussies, amber showers, about the diversions of the sexual alphabet, the sins great and small, and what's a sin anyway? You clients can talk away as long as you don't lose respect. Now your little show, my dear Jerry, is sometimes right on the borderline. But if you want to come and enjoy yourselves with respect, then come. And then talk the way you talk. I haven't once heard you use the word 'hooker'. Because that's the thing.'

'That's the thing.'

'Yes, Jerry. You know our set cards, our ads. If we get you clients turned on then we're doing it right. You dwell in the apparent world we create for you. Keep on believing. And take a shower beforehand. The ladies will do their business and still keep up appearances.'

'Let's hear a round of applause far above the city roofs, a roar of applause for our cherished Mr Orpheus, for our cherished cherry ladies, to whom we devote our hard-ons, whom we cherish more than our own wives, well, sometimes anyway, a round of applause that drowns out the droning of the planes flying low over the suburbs, ladies and gentlemen, live from Eden City'

'Jerry the Entertainer. I think you've lost the thread.'

'Return to Go. This person's accusations. The floor's all yours, Mr Orpheus. We've got plenty of time, centuries of time.'

'What else is there to say? Alliances with the police and the authorities? Every one of the ladies working in my properties is registered and the authorities are aware of every one of my apartments. I pay my taxes, the ladies pay their taxes, that's the only pact going on. And when it comes to the great self-righteous chief prosecutor shooting venom at me from the cover of the net... but never mind... I've already pressed charges for libel and defamation of character.'

'I had an anonymous female caller before the show who told me this man had fallen in love with one of the women who work in your properties...'

'I don't want to confirm or deny that here. The fact is, it does happen occasionally that a client falls in love with a sex worker and feels compelled to get her out of the trade, even if the woman in question might not even see herself as a victim but just goes about her work of her own volition. It can go as far as stalking. I know that many of my tenants, especially those from eastern Europe, have invested their money in businesses or property, usually in their home countries. I could give you plenty of examples of ladies from Hungary, the Czech Republic or Russia who gave up sex work long ago, returned home after a few years.'

'Oh, yes. And how we miss them.'

'And with regard to the ominous large organization that allegedly smuggles the girls over here, all I can say is that my business motto is: from free entrepreneur to free entrepreneur.'

'And can you rule it out that there's someone, whatever you want to call it, some organization, pimp ring or whatever, operating in the background?'

'You're the one calling me Orpheus.'

'Mr Orpheus.'

'And we both know exactly why.'

'Mhm. Everyone knows.'

'No. Not one of you knows anything. You're all feeding off legends. At that time, I ran up against an organization. Full-frontal. It was over a Bulgarian girl, who wanted to work for me in peace. Marshall Tito's boys didn't like the idea.'

'Marshall Tito?'

'Did I just hear a lighter clicking, my dear Jerry?'

'You did.'

'Filter?'

'Yes.'

'Fire accelerants.'

'Pardon...?'

'Cigarette paper contains fire accelerants. There are specially declared cigarettes, they ought to be available everywhere by now, you used to only get them from tobacconists, without burning agents. I'd advise you against those burning agents.'

'Are you a smoker?'

'Gave it up, my dear Jerry. And that's why my leg aches these days when the weather changes.'

'Both legs?'

'That's what the legends say. And since then I've been allergic to organizations that put pressure on the women I work with. I don't need fire accelerants. But when I have to, I lower my head and take a full-frontal charge.'

'I see.'

'Of course transparency's important. But we don't do all our business in the bright light of day. We are who we are.'

'And who are you?' AHEM HEM.

'How's the schedule looking?'

'This is modern theatre, Mr Orpheus, we've got all night.'

'Ask me a few specific questions.'

'Rents.'

'That's not a question. But I know what you're getting at. I'm sure you'll understand I can't give you a detailed answer, but in terms of turnover and profits all my information is available. This person, who's under investigation for several charges, gave some figures in his ridiculous article. I could of course tell you and your listeners a few rough numbers in return, but I'm sure you'll understand I can't go into detail. The rent the ladies pay for their respective properties is composed of several factors. The newspaper ad, for instance, costs more than thirty euros per day, plus internet advertising, also a share of the basic rent, then the daily tax rate, and on top of that pro rata personnel costs, and that's not all. My tenants know exactly what they're paying for: security, spotless cleanliness...'

'And we, the never-tiring stream of punters, we pay for the third S...'

'Sex. I just want to explain how the money's distributed, and I also offer certain reserves, in case anyone wants them, and we mustn't forget, my dear Jerry, that the properties are handed over to my tenants in a ready-to-use state. I'm always there for the girls, my company's clean. Go ahead and call the cops, my company is clean.'

'This person, as you call him, the author of this indictment, claims the police are covering up forced prostitution in your properties, which...'

'...is ridiculous, I hope you were going to say.'

'Something along those lines. I mean, we're not in a banana republic here.'

'You said it, my dear Jerry. My activities are fully within the bounds of our capitalist state. They used to try and tell us the two were incompatible.'

'Long time ago – *The Internationale will win our human rights.*'

'Long time ago, Jerry. *The earth belongs to us, the workers. How many on our flesh have fattened.* Of course human trafficking happens, forced prostitution and so on. An outgrowth of the system. Which we never wanted here in our city, which we never wanted to profit from. No social market economy. Slaveholders. And ultimately, my dear Jerry, we're all slaves to the system in one way or another.'

'So you can guarantee that there are no forced prostitutes working in your properties, there's no organization in the background that you might not know about...'

'Yes. I can only repeat that I was intervening on behalf of a girl that year when the shots were fired. Marshall Tito's men regarded her as their property. Long time ago. Every one of the women working in my properties has her own history, her own story. After all these years, I understand how people's minds work. I can tell when something's fishy. And in purely pragmatic terms – why should I invite problems into my properties when a simple newspaper small ad is enough, I've got no shortage of tenants, voluntary tenants who are responsible for themselves. Of course there'll be the odd one where a certain material poverty plays a role. Debt. A large family. Don't want to claim benefits. If that's what you call coercion, my dear Jerry, then I'm guilty. Then we're all guilty. In all parts of our society. Every woman has her own story. That, my dear Jerry, is what people have to learn, have to tolerate and not tar everyone with the same lead brush.'

'Lead brush?'

'Just a saying.'

'You mentioned the shots in the past, Mr Orpheus. But we've all been particularly worried in the past few months as well. Outside investors were threatening hostile takeovers. The Angels came to the city... How's the situation right now?'

'It's stable. I can't say anything detailed about the current situation, as I'm sure you'll understand.'

'Mr Orpheus, thank you very much for the interview.

I have one last question...'

'Yes?'

A stream of light, a stream of voices, faces, women, silvery smiles, coppery hair, wires, circuit boards, streets... Am I still online? Jerry? Hello? Are you still there? Don't turn around and never look in the mirror. Hello? Hello? It's cold.

He pushes the paper plate with the half-eaten cheese roll aside, wipes his fingers on the paper napkin, then screws it up and puts it on the plate. He pulls up the collar of his coat, adjusts his scarf. Cold for November. He throws the half-empty coffee cup in the bin next to the table but leaves the paper plate where it is, picks up his leather case, puts the newspaper in his coat pocket and crosses the concourse towards the platforms. He has to look for the right platform first, through the tunnel on the left. His breath comes out in clouds. A young woman is trying to lug a pram up the staircase.

Clack. Clack. One step at a time. 'Wait a minute...'

'Thank you. The lift's broken.'

He reaches a hand out for the rod between the wheels. He can't see the child in the pram, thickly swaddled and hidden between covers and cushions. Once they get up to the platform it starts crying. The woman thanks him again and he says, 'No problem.' He wonders where she might be from. Didn't sound like the East, from her accent. More like Hannover. The train isn't here yet and he takes his cigarette case out of his inside pocket. He has to unbutton his coat, feeling the autumn wind cold on his neck and chest. He's got Davidoff Filters in his leather cigarette case; they're the most elegant-looking. Long and white with a little gold band before the long white filter. And it's appearances that count on this trip, as they usually do, and he's thought about that often enough. He takes one glove off to smoke. His silver lighter feels cool on his palm. Twenty years ago he'd have put on a hat. Borsalino or something posh along those lines. No one wears hats these days, especially not in the trade, and especially not in the East.

He thought over and over whether to take the car. But his registration plates would have attracted attention, no matter whether he took the Bielefeld-registered Benz or the Audi from the city. And they suggested on the phone that they ought to take things slowly, said they had a driver anyway, the Colonel can guarantee everything but better to be safe than sorry what with the border so nearby, and so on. And he'd parked his car, the Audi, at a friend's place in Neukölln. Took a taxi to Ostbahnhof, which they're now calling Berlin Main Station. He thought briefly of having the taxi drive him all the way to the border town. But sometimes it's good to approach things slowly. He hadn't been in Berlin for a while, the last time was 1988, eight years ago, and no one thought the country behind the Wall would collapse a year later, as quickly and suddenly as a toy fort. The city is different now, feels different to then. But he's never liked Berlin. 'How's business going?' he asked his acquaintance.

'Oh, these aren't easy times, you know. The Russians, the Yugos, the Lebanese. Is there any room left for us? The old deals don't count any more. But we get by. There's enough pie to...'

'There is, there is. Still is.'

'And you? Gone East, I heard?'

'That too. You know me.'

'Come, let's drink to that.'

'Whisky at lunchtime. Nothing's changed here.' And they sat there in the dark bar in Charlottenburg and drank Johnnie Walker Black Label and talked about the old days, which got better with every glass, just as they got younger while the cleaning lady washed away the traces of the night behind them.

He watches the woman with the pram, standing a

few yards away from him, smoking as well. He doesn't approve of that. Mothers shouldn't smoke. He's old fashioned about that, or new fashioned, depends which way you see it. But who knows, maybe she only smokes two or three a day because she can't quite manage to give up, and that would be OK. The girls in the East smoke like chimneys, more than the ones on the other side, where he's from. He sometimes thinks. Seems that way to him. Could be wrong though. Because they all used to smoke in the old republic; politicians, prostitutes, actors, housewives. Once, not all that long ago, he slapped the cigarette out of a whore's hand, she was six or seven months gone. An ex-whore, in other words. She didn't work for him any more. Only up to the fourth month. Although there are clients into that kind of thing. Word soon gets round when a pregnant girl's working. And then the clients come and they all want a go. *Shoot their load on the big round belly.* But not at his place. She did go on working, though, he found out later. So not an ex-. First freelance and then somewhere else. *Pregnant and horny.* He slapped her once or twice round the face. Because of the cigarette. Because of the baby. The rest of it was none of his business. But she's sitting there in his lounge because she's got papers to pick up from him or some other mess to clear up, needs a stamp and a signature and who knows what, and smoking one after another, with a belly up to her chin. Stupid cow.

He throws his cigarette on the tracks. He exhales the last puff of smoke, watching the woman with the pram; there's not much else to see on the platform. Just a few people clustered by the timetables and benches. It's dark between the iron arches, the afternoon light can barely penetrate the dirty glass roof. He glances at his Breitling, spots the woman pushing back her sleeve almost simultaneously and then leaning out over the edge of the platform and looking in both directions. She sees him, flicks away her cigarette and smiles. Come off it, girl, he thinks, I'm old enough to be your father. He's not into young blood any more. A woman has to be somewhere between thirty, thirty-five and forty to get him interested. There are exceptions, of course. His common-law wife is forty-five and huddled in his residence near Osnabrück. No children, no wife. That's been his maxim for almost... thirty years? He lights up another. Even though he wants to slow down with the smoking. They announce the train's arrival at last. Almost on time.

Where's she going? Definitely not from the East. He's got enough experience to tell now. Not that it matters. He has to concentrate. He'll need a clear head in two hours' time. He hasn't got much luggage with him; he reckons on one or two days. He thought about taking some artillery along. The border's a dark place, wild lands, mist above the river and deep woods on the other side, primitive locals, even seven years after the Wall. But you have to reckon on getting checked. He did used to have a gun possession card and a gun licence, he'd got it issued in Osnabrück in the early eighties, he had good connections to politics and the authorities, he was often in Hamburg, on business, and things started getting pretty hot there in the mid-eighties, dark days, dark nights, mist coming off the sea. Though it was nothing compared to the craziness that seemed to sweep through the cities in the early nineties, like an epidemic of greed and violence, but what can you know, 1996, even though he thought he had a feel for the times and the people. He doesn't even know if the licence for his gun is still valid. He throws his cigarette on the tracks, sees the train still a little way off, tracks and buildings and the sky getting greyer and greyer. Maybe it's another train, for another platform. He sees the cigarette end smouldering between the sleepers. But he wants to cut down on the smoking anyway. His eighth today; he's started counting. He can still feel the six whiskies he drank with his acquaintance Moon-Eye. Actually he's almost a friend. A good one in fact, thinking about it. Six whiskies, six Davidoff Filters. He shakes himself, shuts his eyes for a moment, sees the lights of the train through his closed eyelids, pulling in from the dark afternoon to the gloomy platform with screeches and hisses, hears the voice from the tannoy again, strangely distorted, barely comprehensible, and his friend's eyes shimmer in the dark of the bar, which won't open up again until the evening.

He'd never had much to do with him but now he it feels like they're oddly close, he wants to ask his advice about his big trip, but doesn't in the end. Sometimes he wonders why he didn't move to Berlin, why he's never had anything going on in Berlin, nothing big anyway – but it just wasn't his city. Munich, Neuss, Bielefeld, the Ruhr Valley, Hamburg, that's where he feels safe. Usually. And now in the city in the East as well, his new branch office, his annexe for the past few years. But Berlin, such a big, ragged city, which now seemed even bigger and even more ragged...

'Moon-Eye,' he said, 'we're living in strange times.'

'The times are always strange, either way. You know, it's only my old lady calls me that now.'

'Sometimes I think we should all just pack our bags and bugger off to South America.'

'And surrender everything to the Mongolian hordes?'

'You're right, Moon-Eye. What would the ladies be without us...?'

'Nothing, my friend, nothing. They'd be weeping. And the cops as well. And Inland Revenue.'

He gets a flash of dizziness as he boards the train. Just for a second, or even less, something inside him cuts out, in his head, as if the system were briefly interrupted, a black, no, a white space, a fraction of a second of nothingness. Then he's back, clutching the handrail next to the door, feeling someone behind him, feeling that someone touch him briefly before he gets into the carriage. He jerks the sliding door open and sits down on the first vacant seat. The case parked between his feet. His heart beating normally. Everything's fine. Boom. Boom. Boom. The platform is empty, the window dirty. A few figures walk past him. Then the train sets into motion. Jolts. Halts for a moment. Rolls on again. He takes the newspaper out of his coat pocket and puts it on the little table beneath the window.

It occurs to him that he bought a first-class ticket. Later, when the conductor points it out, he says, 'I'm fine sitting here.' It sounds funny, he realizes, but the conductor nods and walks on. He doesn't feel like getting up. He's a little tired. They're moving through rain; he sees the forests blurred, villages. The train makes a lot of stops. Stopped a lot in Berlin as well. Lots of building sites there. Huge cranes behind the buildings. Construction ditches by the side of the roads. Half-finished castles of glass. He could have invested in construction companies, he thinks, if he'd been stupid. Better in building land, but that could have gone wrong as well, a million today, a hundred thousand tomorrow. They were building like crazy in the city in the East as well, in his new annexe. The grey there was gradually disappearing, still. The banks were handing out loans like sweeties. But when the air came hissing like a huge fart out of the big real-estate godfather who'd bought up half the city – what a stink that was! – when the banks dropped him all the way down to jail, he was glad he hadn't invested in a construction company in the city in the East or a piece of real estate in the bright lights of the city centre. He knew things would work out that way. The quicksand principle. Dominoes toppling. And he invested early enough in the right properties, and the prices and the price slump in the city centre regulated the market the way he needed. On the edge of town. Construction land. Motorway access roads. The Fort. A big deal. Cost energy and time and money. He got loans as well. He has a good reputation. Did some building with his people in Bielefeld, even invested in Neuss years and decades ago, has shares and percentages in Frankfurt am Main and elsewhere, not bad ones either. And with your own construction company you always have to make sure you get the right contracts and deal with the right people. That would have been doable. With or without a godfather. The new land is big enough. But ultimately it's just peanuts. It's just that desire for something solid that everyone has sometimes, everyone who feels the endless flow of the money and the market almost painfully after all the years. Digger daydreams. Like he used to build little houses in the woods with his brother, out of wood and rocks and clay. He's often thought about that and remembered it. But he's the man with the plan. The man who contracts out the contracts. The man with the good nose for business, who looks after the money and invests it. His brother's. His people's. The company in the background. The silent partners. His firm. The red-light-sector share. And now the border.

'It pays to be big.' He'd said that himself. 'The bigger the company, the better the profits. Think big, as our friends from the finance world say.'

That must have been two or three years ago now. He always has that kind of patter going, to impress people. He was the man with the plan. The man from the West. Not one of those small-time pimps, the street investors who got fished one by one out of the big goldfish bowl of the Emerging East, where even the godfathers could drown.

'I'll take a look at it. Might turn out well. Might get big. Looks that way at the moment. The timing's good. The right people. The right information. A lot of money in it. Needs a lot more money put in.' And now he's on the way, on the trip. He wanted to do it himself, like in the old days.

You have to find something, in the dark, on the margins, and then light the lights there so it shines all the way to the centre like a giant Christmas tree! His partner in the city in the East knows that. His partner has his own construction company. Among other things. His partner listens to him. Invests in property. Among other things. A young man with a vision. With plans. A man who believes in the red-light-sector share. Thirty-three years old. Or thirty-four? Doesn't make any difference, not the exact age. And a man on his way up. Willing to learn. *Learn, learn, and once again learn.* (They both laugh because that was Lenin. And they raise their glasses and forge their pact. Up in that hotel, the bar on the twenty-seventh floor.) A man who forges and extends contacts. Manages information. Has a monopoly on model apartments, or is on his way to one. A man who reminds him of his own youth. Even though his was different. Of his own path. His own energy and drive. Initiative. The will to build something up, create something big, in a market now surviving only on its myths, that could suddenly be formed here

245

in the East after the big zero hour. And the boy was in on it. He'd started with a couple of amusement arcades, so they said. Invested money in apartments. Knew from the very beginning that there was only small change to be made on the street. (And they look out over the evening city and dream of the red-light-sector share, the serious market in bodies. And the old Bielefelder forgets for a moment that he had plans far beyond this collaboration, that the lad was just the means... and the city, his annexe in the East, glitters darkly in the evening light like a heap of brightly coloured marbles.)

Forests, fields, villages. Dilapidated farmhouses and farmyards in the rain. And the evening sets in fast. Never mind South America. What does it have to offer him? He has a little house near Osnabrück where his wife sits it out, the woman who's not really his wife. She's only ever said something once, about getting married. He's surprised she doesn't put the screws on him, after all the years. Or didn't. Because she comes from a very middle-class family. Small town. Almost a village. And her parents didn't think much of him. Even though he had a *von* in his name. But what difference does that make? And he'd changed his name, years ago now. Told her one time though. He couldn't keep up the legends anyway. They used to call him 'the Count' in the seventies. He went drinking with ministers, with and without *von* in the name, because it's only about money anyway, and shook the big bankers' hands, cut ribbons and held topping-out ceremonies with press and celebs. Whorehouses, sauna clubs, model apartments, call the girls! And he's met the biggest bourgeois types in the trade, knickknacks in their cabinets and white three-piece suites and child seats in the car. He hates that family shit. His partner in the city in the East is starting something up. Starting a family as well. Doing it right. But what difference does that make?

He built the house at the end of the eighties, when he met her. She was still a teacher then. Primary school. Bit of a caring one. Studying sociology at night school. Even that made her exotic in that small-town dump. It seems ugly to him now, left over from another time, long ago. The house. Flat roof. Little garden. All white. Out there, one of those dilapidated farmyards, that's what he ought to buy. For his retirement. And do it up. Digger daydreams. Somewhere to retire to. With or without her. He's not bothered. It's a bloody long time to go. You can always find someone. Cold heart. But he needs the business. The city. The cities. The Fort. The clubs. The women. The money. The market strategies. The competition. The speculation. The investments. The information. The players. The *flow*. The glances into the future. And the looks back. His brother is as cool as a cucumber (now) and makes good money in Bielefeld. Growing up together near Stuttgart. He's often thought of those days recently. He was eight years older than his brother, sent to boarding school. And then later, when their old man was finally broke, they moved to the Ruhr Valley. Had a little haulage firm. That grey air. He's often thought of it recently. The years don't make much different after all the years. And they do make more and more of a difference. He realizes the famous coin (shield?) is three-dimensional, four- or five-dimensional, with so many sides, parallel possibilities. Tails, heads, eagles, lions, doves, copper, silver. Arrows. Looking forward, looking back. And never forget left and right, the flanks. *Yes sir, Herr von Clausewitz!* Just like the days and nights are always touching at one point and everything is constantly flowing apart and yet together. He laughs out loud in the empty carriage. That made an impression. With the Zone molls and their men. They know nothing or little about him in the city in the East. Legends. That's important. And it's a good thing too. He's the man with the plan. The Bielefelder. The Count. Six whiskies with Moon-Eye. And he always fills the glasses to the brim. Friedrich von Pfeil. His father. 'Arrow', it means. And his great-great-great-great grandfather, a military man knighted by Frederick the Second. Some lieutenant general in Breslau. Every firstborn male descendant of the family has to be called Friedrich, what a load of bollocks, but that's what it says in the family register from 1792. Their old man told them that a hundred times over. Von Pfeil. Picked up a little country estate in Baden-Württemberg around 1900. Via connections. Had to get out of Prussia; too much whoring around. Grandfather shot to pieces in WW1. And his father, always stuck to the rear echelons in WW2, thrashed the economic miracle into them. A von Pfeil is always on top, in the finest society. The old country house by the forest, the local kids throwing apples and stones at the windows at night. Snowballs in winter. And singing. *You are Prussians, dirty rotten Prussians...* Mother buggered off when they were little. London or Paris. The old man wouldn't talk about it. *You sleep under the bridge or at the railway mission.* And the little houses he built in the woods with his brother – the bastards smashed them up every time. The old man wouldn't talk about it. Boarding school, law degree. Dropped out. High-tailed it to London. Count von Pfeil. Took the family fortune to Munich. Took the old man to the cleaners when he sold the land. Sex industry in the age of the economic miracle. Swinging sixties. Rooms by the hour in Munich. *Shag subscription: 20% off.* Three of his girls were in the 1974 red-light district guide. *The*

Munich Billeting Guide for Erotically Inclined Visitors. Their old man went gradually down the pan in the Ruhr Valley. And his brother ran the haulage company. Drove one of the lorries himself for a while, on the road, to get away from the old man and his stories and dreams until they buried him in a miners' graveyard, and the von Pfeils always the first in line (last of the line now, what with his brother not having children either, as far as he knows), Friedrich, Bismarck, loyal to the Kaiser, and took tea with Stauffenberg like all the good military men, and always believed in the Other Germany. So the thing with the hookers was a 'big deal', as they said in London. Swinging. In Munich, he let his blond hair grow down to his shoulders. The Count and his girls.

'Eisenhüttenstadt', he reads on a sign on a road alongside the tracks. The train moves slowly along the embankment. It leans so far to one side in the drawn-out curve that his newspaper falls to the floor. He can't tell how far away the town is, in the rain. Which then stops, ten minutes later. Isn't that where that elephant was from? The thug who took over that little club a few years ago? The one who's satisfied with what he's got. The master butcher. The football hooligan by way of Berlin. The man who'll spend his whole life stinking of the streets that spat him out? One of those foot soldiers he impressed with his words and his reputation and his suits. The ones who lose their temper at the drop of a hat. Always shouting about something. Can't look even two or three years ahead. A gigantic smelting works, chimneys, pipes, iron towers, in the middle of the fields outside the town. A huge building complex, clouds drifting above it, and the chimneys spewing flames to the sky. Small trains on small tracks, open wagons filled with glowing red steel.

He must have dropped off. He wakes with a start, the unfolded newspaper falling off his knees. Wasn't it on the floor just a moment ago? 9.11.1996. 'Government Relocation: Golden Bridges to Berlin'. Saturday. He looks at his watch. They ought to be there any minute. He mustn't forget to check the lottery numbers. It's a quirk he has. Buys a ticket every Saturday. Eight numbers. Full system. With a couple of million, he could buy the brewery over in Baden-Württemberg. Without making a loss. The woods are almost deforested. It's dark outside. Goes quickly in autumn. He sees his face in the glass. Diagonally opposite, a fat little man in a hat. He sees him in the glass as well. He looks like he's asleep, his head on his chest, hands clutched across his belly. His own face haggard and white. Grey hair. What do his eyes say? Blue. Cold. He likes that. No more information. He's the Highlander on his journey through time. The woman he never misses far away. None of anyone's business. He'll have to sort it out soon. Sees it differently, one day yes and one day no. The Fort and the shares at the other ends of the world. Somewhere over the rainbow. Is that a river where the lights are reflecting? And a road alongside the river. Otherwise nothing but fields. Or meadows. Or steppes. Tannoy voices. I've always come up with stories, if I had to. I'm the man without a past. Only the money and the influence tell the important stories, the right stories. I've come from far away (in German terms at least), and we want... what do we actually want on the border? Business, my old friend, we want to do business. And keep your eyes clear like two moons in winter, but always make sure... I know, I know.

He takes his glasses case out of his coat pocket as they pull in, a small station, a roof over the platforms, end of the line. Graduated tint. Darker at the top, lighter at the bottom. He's short-sighted. Minus one point eight. One point nine on the left. Minus. Some kind of cylinder as well. A special measurement. His eyes are getting worse and more and more light-sensitive. Years of working nights. Living underground. Says his doctor. Slightly tinted. Good for the eyes. Says his doctor. Because they kept getting infections. Went red. Like conjunctivitis. But it's light sensitivity. His eyes well protected behind the pale blue of the tint. Before he disembarks he wakes the fat man with the hat. 'End of the line, mate!'

'Who? What? Are we in Poland already? Thanks, mate!' The fat man yells at him as if he'd just woken from a bad dream. He adjusts his scarf and glasses, picks up his leather case and steps down to the platform. He had the glasses made in the city a year and a half ago, at Fielmann Opticians. Porsche brand.

He's directly beneath a lamp and the glasses do him good. No one on the platform. They know when he's arriving. A couple of platforms, a roof extending half-way along them, the wind buffeting his hair. Not much light. Litter under the benches. Further forward along the train, the woman with the pram is being picked up. A big guy in a cop's uniform. Or a border guard. He can't quite make it out at a distance. Arrival. Nothing's private any more. What a shabby station, he thinks. Like in a village. You can tell the Russians and the Poles aren't far away. A dirty dark red engine with no carriages attached is stationary on the other side of the platform. A man in blue overalls leans out of the engine window, smoking.

He walks towards the stairs, taking his cigarette case out of his coat pocket; only three left behind the elastic band. He's got two packs of Davidoff in his case, though. Ahead of him, a yellow timetable behind glass.

251

Formerly behind glass. The glass shattered, the timetable scribbled on, empty beer cans and cigarette ends on the broad base of the display case. Shards crunch beneath his shoes. He wants to check his return journey but then he gives up. Night encircles the tracks. He walks up the stairs, his cigarette at chest height. He's in a dark tunnel that stinks of piss. Next to the staircases, display cases with yellow timetables. With glass. Without glass. He's in the Gütersloh tunnel. He's in the Neuss tunnel. Iserlohn. The stench of piss. The crunch of glass. The rubbish bins wonky in their anchoring. Grey mist floats through these stations. He knows that smell. He feels like the years are flowing together again, yellow timetables, dirty engines, empty beer cans, travelling by night. He laughs, and his laugh echoes in the border town's piss tunnel. No, he just smiles, it's someone else's laughter, drunk laughter, and then he sees the fat man from the train passing him.

They're waiting in the station concourse. It's seven on the dot. Feels like midnight to him, though. A newsagent's stall that sells beer and spirits and cigarettes and everything else you might need as well. Couple of guys loitering around. Old, young. Drinking Holsten Pilsner out of cans. A night on the town, Saturday. He hears his own footsteps. Clack. Clack. Clack. He loves that sound. Wore the shoes with the high heels. The beer drinkers follow his progress. Like a cave, this concourse is. They're waiting by the double door. The tall one in the dark coat must be the Colonel. The other guy's wearing a plainclothes-policeman jacket, a Magnum moustache, Ruhr Valley-style, polo neck beneath an open jacket, holding a rolled up umbrella with a hooked handle beside his leg like a shotgun. He walks up to them. Stops right in front of them and says, 'Good evening. How's the Emerging East?'

The tall one laughs and says, 'Brought along a case of used notes to buy up our local industry, have you?'

They grip hands. The Count feels sweat. Could be rain, though. 'Welcome to the city of humanists.'

Magnum only nods at first and then reaches out a hand. 'Had a good trip?' the Colonel asks. He must be around fifty. Short grey hair, clean-shaven. Windsor knot on a mauve collar, purple tie. The Count smiles and says, 'I don't travel by rail very often. But we don't want to promote car exports here in your town. You seem to have everything under control, just not in the car park.' They walk outside. Three taxis right outside the door. The drivers are smoking underneath the station awning. Drizzle. 'Our Polish friends don't take anything we pay duties on, if you get my meaning. There's a reason for everything. Anonymous, anonymous, if you get my meaning. No new registration plates in the game. Too much traffic at the border. They're all here. Russians, Federal Criminal Police, Federal Intelligence Service, Poles, Ruhr Valley pimps, crazy ex-Yugos, real-estate syndicates.'

The Count nods. Squat little buildings around the station forecourt. No signs, no architecture of a city, a medium-sized town. He looks around, storing up his impressions before he speaks.

'We do understand. But in future, my partners and I can't come on the regional railway. And we've got nothing to hide.'

'In future,' says the Colonel as they walk to the car park, where a Russian Volga is waiting, long and black and shining wet in the light of a street lamp, '*we'll* make the future. And all perfectly legal.'

And later, fully dressed on the bed at his hotel, he

253

doesn't know quite how to categorize things. Reception will call him at three in the morning, wake him up if he's asleep. He has a date with the Colonel, he wants them to watch the Mike Tyson fight on Premiere TV. He's not all that keen on boxing. But that doesn't matter. He met the Count von Homburg a couple of times, must be twenty-five years ago now. Drank gin and tonic with him at the 'Ritze'. Where the whole world and the pimps and the boxers and the drinkers and everyone rubbed shoulders. The man was a celebrity back then. Not a particularly good boxer and not a count either, but still got in the ring with the world's best. He had a lot of respect for that. That Argentinian, what was his name... Oscar Fuerteventura or something like that, he'd fought Ali and Frazier before him, was the one to finally beat the Count von Homburg's blue blood out of him.

No, *Prince* von Homburg he was called. Prince Wilhelm von Homburg. A kind of stage name. He used to swagger down the Reeperbahn in Hamburg in a fur coat and hat and a cigar in one hand. The Count and the Prince; but he was only a newcomer from Munich. They never talked much. He asked him a lot about Munich, he remembers that. Did he know such and such. Later they got him for pimping and drugs and involvement with organized crime – he'd done business with the Angels in Hamburg. 'Anyone who wants to make money is organized.' He laughs – another of his wisdoms – and picks up the cigarette case from the bedside table, but it's empty. He turns cautiously onto his side and gets up. Sometimes his back hurts after long days and long nights. He's got a good physiotherapist in Frankfurt am Main but he doesn't make it to see him all that often, even though he goes to Frankfurt almost every week. Only takes him four hours in the Audi. Even though the motorways in the East are crap. He gets his back into shape again nicely. He's always amazed at the crunching and grinding of his joints and bones. He feels completely stupid lying on his front over the inflatable ball, beforehand, and doing all the exercises.

He goes over to his suitcase, still upright by the door. Takes out his coat and hangs it up in the wardrobe. His scarf is damp and he shakes it, strokes it smooth and lays it over a hanger. The hotel's pretty good, right next door to the town hall. The town seemed very small to him when the Volga took them first to a restaurant and then to the hotel. He can't get the thing with the bats out of his head. What was that all about?

'And do you know what I meant earlier, the city of the humanists?'

'Henry Maske?'

'A boxing fan! Of course. And actually, our good old Henry is part of the whole thing. The big picture. But...'

'But?'

'How do you like my Volga, by the way?'

'Nice car. Don't see a lot of them. Well looked after.'

'It is, isn't it? I used to dream of a Chevrolet back in the East. No chance of that.'

'And I always thought the Stasi was number three. After the CIA and the KGB.'

'We were, we were. But a Chevy in the East? Even Honecker only drove a Volvo. And I'm not Erich Mielke. But this Volga... I got it directly from Moscow in '85. KGB issue. Not a scratch on it. Looks a lot like a Chevy. For me – and I'm not telling you this because I miss communism – the Volga is one of the best cars of the twentieth century.'

'The age of the humanists.'

He rummages in his case. Puts the ironed and folded

shirts fresh from the laundry on the table. He has a branch of the Röver chain in the city of his annexe and he's more than happy with it. The old East German ladies working there know how to wash, iron and fold a shirt. And they know they have to smell good. Not too noticeably, not of some bloody fabric conditioner or perfume. Just fresh. There's a science to it, you have to feel good in a smooth, fresh, soft shirt. He's got a shirt card for fifty marks. They have three branches in the city and more outlets in the smaller neighbouring towns and in Dresden on the Elbe. Washing, ironing, sewing, keys cut. They make good money. He likes the company. He used to know a man in Neuss who put all his money into a laundry service when things went downhill with the girls and the competition put him on spin cycle. In Düsseldorf. Not a bad idea. One of the market leaders by now.

He takes the two packs of Davidoff Filters, puts one back in the case and opens the other one. Pulls twelve cigarettes out, one by one, his hand calm, that's good, he likes the look of that, and puts them behind the elastic band of his leather cigarette case. One by one. On his way back to the bed – he needs peace and quiet and time to think – he spots his little shortwave radio between his sponge bag and the pile of underpants and vests. He bends over the case again and then he lies down on the bed, the cigarette case by his pillow, the radio on the bedside table, and then he has to get up again because his lighter's still in his coat pocket. Takes a look at the minibar while he's at it. The whisky with Moon-Eye's evaporated now and he only had a Campari before dinner and a glass of Chianti to wash down the meal in the Italian restaurant. And that's evaporated as well, out by the bats.

He doesn't fancy beer. Even though it's Holsten. If it was DAB, the Dortmund Joint Stock Brewery that flooded the whole of the East to begin with and took it over with its joint stock, he might have had one. Because it's from where he's from. Which isn't really where he's from. Cold Chianti's not really necessary either. Mind you, it can't be much worse than the one at the restaurant. Jim Beam? No. That stuff's undrinkable. Jägermeister? He's hated it since he was seventeen. Too sweet. Although they say there are herbs in it that make you aggressive. If you drink it for too long. Goldkrone. That'll do the trick. Had a job getting used to it in the city in the East, at first. 'How about a cognac?' people asked in all seriousness now and then, pretty often in fact, and then came out with this crap. But he quite likes it by now. At least doesn't burn too much. Thirty-two per cent. Helps him think. About the bats as well. He squats in the light of the fridge, unscrews the two 4-cl bottles and pours the liquid in a glass. Closes the fridge, goes over to the bed.

He smokes, the ashtray resting on his chest and moving when he breathes in deeply or expels the smoke. Magnum didn't say a word while they were eating, tomato sauce in his moustache. The Colonel ordered pizza without asking him. Three different kinds. Frutti di mare. Quattro formaggi. Salami. One bottle of Chianti, one bottle of San Pellegrino. And a glass of Coke for himself. Magnum goes for Fanta.

He likes pizza but he'd rather have had pasta, although he's not sure they'd have served up anything decent in this place. There are one or two good Italian places in his annexe in the East now. They say the godfathers have a share in them, but that's what they say about every Eyetie place. Money laundering. But that's no reason to open a restaurant at the other end of the world. And because the godfathers are greedy for East German real estate. They would have gone belly-up in the East German sea when the giant fart made its waves. They're sitting on their comfy backsides in Munich and the Ruhr Valley, he knows that. And maybe in Berlin. The Pizzas like investing wherever there's money to make and money to launder. Quattro Formaggi. But that doesn't touch on his business.

'And how do you say it?' The Colonel fills their glasses and orders another bottle. The Count knows exactly how much the stuff costs wholesale. It's so cheap that not every wholesaler even stocks it.

'Pizze. Get it? Pizze! Due Pizze, por favor! Not pizzas! Pizze!' He links his thumb and forefinger in a circle in mid-air.

Hold your breath, thinks the Count, you just hold your breath and eat your shit. He's hungry too, though, but he sticks to the four cheeses; the salami looks pre-sliced and he doesn't like the look of the seafood either. But he's their guest and the formaggi's not bad. The two of them eat like pigs. There isn't even antipasti on the table, just a breadbasket.

'We had a guy from the Red Brigades here at the end of the seventies. It wasn't just the Red Army Faction we got over. My God, the poor man suffered. 'Cause there weren't any Italian restaurants in the Zone. None! Nulle Pizze!' He laughs and Magnum joins in, a long thread of cheese stretched between his teeth and the piece of pizza he's holding up, tearing as he laughs. The plainclothes jacket is on the chair next to him, a mobile telephone in one of the breast pockets, one of those huge things with a long aerial that look like a walkie-talkie. He didn't notice it earlier, even though he gave them both a close inspection on his way across the station concourse.

He puts his glasses on the bedside table next to the ashtray; he's put out the cigarette. The last time he was with his wife in Osnabrück was two months ago, in the house. It was still summer. She does a lot of voluntary work with children. Still works part-time at the school. She's getting thin and her hair's going grey. He's surprised she stays with him.

He picks up the shortwave radio. He always has it with him when he's travelling. He doesn't want to watch TV alone in a hotel. He dials through the whistling and white noise and the words and the music until he finds WDR, West German Radio. A lot of Polish and Russian in between. Sounds like Polish and Russian to him, anyway.

'Goodness, Harald, that's pretty tough stuff!'

Domian, it sounds like that gay lad Domian, he can tell his voice straight away. Who's he got calling in? He thinks about looking for another station but WDR reminds him of his youth, his brother, the haulage firm, the miners' graveyard where his father's buried.

'It's been a bit of a cosy show,' says Domian. What was the guy's real name? Is that his surname or a stage name like *Domenica*, the Whore of Whores? He met her once in Hamburg. He's never been interested in this psychological phone-in crap.

'The two or three callers who voiced criticism,' says the man somewhere on the telephone – his voice sounds familiar – 'they're right as well, of course. And I was almost sorry you cut off the young man who said I was an arsehole, 'cause he's not wrong about that on all points.'

'Really?' Domian laughs. 'What points is he right about?'

'I can understand these people who, er, er, let's say, call up and say: I don't like that "Gaywatch" you do and that, I can understand it that some people feel a bit like their toes are being trodden on.'

'Yes.'

'Yes.' Now the Count knows who it is calling that gay lad Domian, it's that chat show host, Schmidt, Harald Schmidt, he's seen him a couple of times on that hidden camera show he used to present, must have been a few years ago, and now he's got his own late-night programme on one of the private channels, the girls are always talking about it but he's never seen it. He liked that *Candid Camera* show, and *You Bet* as well, that was when Frank Elsner still did it, in the seventies and eighties, in Munich with his girls, champers and wheat beer and chicken, they were always good Saturday nights. This Schmidt, he thinks, seems to be on his way up if people are getting pissed off with him.

'... Do know any gays and lesbians?' It's always the gays and lesbians with Domian, he thinks. He picks up his glass; a brief whistling sound when he touches the radio, white noise.

'No, of course not. But I suspect a lot of people I know are gay and are, er, hiding it from me, and if I creep after them at night, through the bars and around the parks and so on, at that moment when I found out they were gays, er, of course I'd say: Wow, you're gay. And then of course I'd use it on my show the next day, guess who's gay?'

'Yes.' That makes the Count laugh. And he's glad he always has his shortwave radio with him. He takes another cigarette, and the bats and the Colonel and his partner in the city – he called him earlier on to give him the latest details, he was sitting with his books again, for

260

his training, or is it even a degree? – it's all suddenly far away. He laughs and drops ash on his chest. He blows it away.

No traces on his white shirt. The fifteenth today, although he's trying not to smoke so much.

'Of course I know some gays. And I know a lot of gays, er, who don't have any problem with my sense of humour, you know?'

'There are plenty of gays working in this industry.'

'I couldn't say. But I hear there are occasionally homosexuals in the entertainment industry.' The Count remembers a businessman in Munich, it must have been in the early seventies, he wanted to organize the gay callboys and rent boys in a club, rooms by the hour with a bar, if you like, it was all going to run in his wife's name, nice place, very discreet, it's got potential, he said, pots of money, 'cause there's plenty of gays who'd come and pay, he said, 'cause you should see all the grubby nooks and crannies where they have to go to get a shafting, he wanted the Count to come in on the investment, but he didn't want anything to do with it. There's no doing business with shirtlifters. They work on their own account and there are plenty of bars in the gay quarter where they can meet. No one had ever tried out a big professional faggot brothel, or at least he'd never heard of anyone. Now and then there were attempts to make money, to cream off some money, but no one actually wanted anything to do with it. The rules are different, different circles. Nothing came out of that project either. His father, and it surprises him thinking about it, always spoke politely and with respect of the gays, a few gay aristocrats they were distantly related to, or at least the Count always thought they were gay when he was a child, at least they were *different*, he could understand

261

that at that age, a few of them would sometimes visit his father in his country house by the woods in Baden-Württemberg. Real has-beens, no home to go to, no families left, no money, maybe *that* was what they had in common, and then they'd sit together and drink wine and smoke (he was always impressed by the long cigarette holders, mother of pearl or carved wood) and talk about the old days, before the war.

'The humanists, my friend, the humanists. The Humboldts were at home here. Ulrich von Hutten. Martin Opitz, if the names tell you anything, but you're an educated man, I hear. Thomas Müntzer, although he wanted to spread humanism and progress with the sword. Yes, and of course our human boxers Henry Maske and Axel Schulz as well.'

'Thanks for the tour of the town. I'm impressed. And we're the heirs to the tradition?'

'Sure, sure. Maybe people won't be talking about us a hundred years from now. But who knows? The border has laws of its own. And we're raising standards and public hygiene and profits.' The Colonel raises his glass. 'To the future. To business. To our future. To our business. To the humanists and the sword. May it stay in its sheath!'

They drink. The waiter clears away the plates and the leftovers.

'I think,' says the Colonel and wipes his lips and looks at the red wine stains on the napkin, 'I think *now* we have a bit of time for a *real* tour of the town.'

The telephone rings. He jumps. Puts out his cigarette in the ashtray, knocking over the radio. He gets to the phone on the third ring and picks up the receiver. 'Yes?' Just a click, no one on the line, a crackling sound, then the engaged tone; he hangs up. He looks at his watch. Not nearly three. Should he call reception and ask whether they dialled his number or if they noted the caller's number? No need to get worked up. He needs peace and quiet. On his way back to the bed, the radio crackling and the voices of Domian and Schmidt only vaguely audible, the phone rings again. He waits. He plans to pick it up on the fifth ring but then it stops. He goes over to the window, pushes the net curtains aside and looks down at the square. The tall town hall opposite rears its head out of the darkness, Gothic arches above large round windows, above them more miniature towers and steeples, an ambulance in the shadow of the entrance portal, as though someone had parked it there and forgotten about it, or the emergency's taking its time. He hasn't yet placed this town on the border in his head; when they drove along the streets in the Volga earlier he saw white and grey tower blocks behind the crooked old houses, a strange jumble against the evening sky, which is clearing now, stars, the clouds floating towards the river that must be somewhere out behind the buildings. Later he sees the arches of a bridge, lights and houses on the other side, another town or part of this one; that must be Poland. A line of trucks on the hard shoulder of the wide road leading to the bridge, the images glide slowly past him, dark trucks, barely any of the cabs lit up, shadows flitting between the long tall vehicles and trailers, are they women? Then he sees precisely, as though the picture were standing still for an instant, a woman, white skin, *white skin under short fabric*, clambering into a truck, one foot still on the asphalt, her hand on the handle of the open door, swinging herself in, vanishing into the cab, the trucks parked in close succession, a twisting grey snake in the night, endless, he can't see the border, the serpent's head; they turn off, a park alongside the road, like a wood, fenced in, figures leaning against the fence, women? Women again? But he can't make them out, too many shadows, perhaps just rough sleepers, night wanderers, the station's always nearby in this small, medium-sized town, the Colonel driving quickly and taking the curves fast, the figures standing apparently motionless there by the fence and under the trees. In the days that follow he sees almost only young and very young girls on the streets, the border town's meat market.

'Kai, 32, asks, er, the Samantha Fox thing, was that staged?'

'No.'

'No? It was spontaneous...?'

'It was spontaneous, she just challenged me directly, I got the feeling she might have been a bit angry afterwards, and... by the time I went to grab her other tit she was gone.'

Domian laughs. The Count is standing in the hotel room, flicking through his calendar. He's got an appointment with his tax advisor on Tuesday, his lawyer from Frankfurt is coming to the city in the East especially; he has to be back in time for that. But he should have got things sorted here by Sunday or Monday at the latest, got the necessary information, made the decision, bought the property; the Colonel has already hinted several times that other interest groups were interested and in the starting blocks, but what else is he going to say to get the deal kick-started; the Count has his information, the project is still fresh, everything has to be thought over, he'll trust his nose and his guts and his knowledge and his strategy... He doesn't take a Valium, no beta-blockers, even though he wants to sleep, shut the system down into the dark to wake from a dreamless sleep, to wake from blackness and take an analytical approach... the way he's always done. But there was something else. Right, that bloody Tyson. You have to roar with the lions when it comes down to it. The telephone rings. He walks back to the radio.

'Of course your viewers get the impression you have no respect for anything or anyone. So, er, what do you respect?'

'...That's hard to say off the cuff, what I respect. I mean, er... I'm not, I don't actually know, to be honest. I mean, if we come up with a joke on a certain subject, we just make it...'

'D'you know this one? What do you call a Pole with no arms?'

'I don't know, what do you call a Pole with no arms?'

'Trustworthy.'

They're standing outside a dilapidated building with a wire fence around it. The brick entrance is in the darkness, three holes where windows once were, no street lamps to be seen. The arcs of the headlamps hitting the wall a few feet above the ground. 'And you've brought me here to tell Polish jokes?'

'No, no, no. Patience, my friend, patience.' The Colonel is standing behind the open door of his Volga, leaning on the car's roof. 'This here is unique. You'll never see anything like it. Just like our just cause, socialism, was unique. Joking, just kidding! But this here outlasts eras and systems. And just like our future brothel's going to be unique, eh? Eh?'

'We shall see.'

Birds. Some of them are circling directly above the arcs of the car headlamps. And he realizes they're bats. They're coming out of the empty windows. They're circling above the flat roof. More and more of them, as if

265

they'd scared them into flight. He can see the ones cir- ·
cling above and in the light quite clearly, their wings
translucent, almost transparent. He remembers having
seen a few bats as a child, between the woods and the
house, in the evenings when they'd sit outside, but he's
never seen these little creatures so close up and precise.
He can make out their thin arms and tiny hands, the
wings spanned across them.

'Now's the time when they come out to go hunting.'
The Colonel stares at the house, leaning on the roof of
the car, Magnum still smoking on the back seat. 'Now's
the hour of the bats.' The Count is standing on the other
side of the car. He nods and says, 'Impressive. Really.'
He takes out his cigarette case and lights one up.

'It is, yes, isn't it? We're exactly in the restricted zone,
right on the border. Forty or fifty yards. Behind the
fence. Construction freeze. Absolute no-building area.
Supposed to be an official nature reserve soon. But I tell
you, when I want to relax, when I want to come down
because everything's making me sick, the border, the
grime, the deals, the hookers, well, you know. Then I
get in my Volga and come here.' He knocks on the roof
of the car. He doesn't smoke, thinks the Count; sensible
man. 'Come on, out you get, come and tell our visitor a
bit about the bats!'

The Count looks at his watch. White noise on the radio, Polish voices, the reception wavering. Two o'clock.
'Don't forget, at three. I want to introduce you to a few
people.' He needs a coffee. He switches off the radio,
goes over to the telephone and calls the desk. Five minutes later there's a knock at the door. A young blonde
woman holding a tray with a pot of coffee and a cup.
On the saucer, a pale biscuit and a dark biscuit and two
portions of creamer. He takes the tray and says, 'Thank

you. That was quick.'

'You're very welcome,' she says with a slight accent. He gives her a five-mark note. 'Thanks very much,' she says with half a curtsey. He closes the door, puts the tray on the table. 'If you need anything, a girl or two girls or anything else, just say the word.'

'No, thanks. I'm here on business.'

'Well, well, a wise man.'

He drinks his coffee, black. Goes over everything in his head again, contracts, lawyer, percentages, maximum investment sum. If it hadn't been for those bloody bats that fascinated him so much. 'A whiskered bat, up there, right in the middle of the window, can you see it?'

'Upside down.'

'Yes, right, it's hanging put for a moment. Unusual. There's these small ones and the big Brandt's bats. Pretty rare. You see the long pointed ears? Can't tell from here if it's a small one or the large kind. My bet's a Brandt's bat. Hard to tell apart. Whiskered bats usually hunt down by the river.'

'A bat expert, a real bat expert!'

'I used to be in forestry. And that one, that one circling right above us, oops, gone again, that was... look, there it is again, and another one! And another one.'

'They're bloody big! Almost the size of a bird!'

'Yeah, those are some of the largest. The name says it all. Greater mouse-eared bat. They're the most common here.'

'This is the most exclusive bat hotel in all of Germany,' says the Colonel.

'I see. Yes, I see.'

He reaches for the coffee, paces the room with the cup. 2.30 a.m. He goes over to his case and takes the folder out of the inside pocket. Removes the map from the folder and goes to the table. He puts the cup on the tray and pushes it aside, unfolds the map and spreads it out on the table. Five places are marked on it, five red crosses. Three of them with question marks because they're rather far out of town. But that's not necessarily a disadvantage. The town will grow, that much can be assumed. EU funding, the new capital not far away, cross-border traffic, companies settling and others already showing interest. The population drop since the Wall fell will soon reach thirty per cent. He places the lists of pros and cons on top of the map, flicks through his documents and notes. The federal government will be investing, a showcase town with good neighbourly relations to Poland. The foreign ministry will be getting buildings here. The gateway to the East. The Yanks want to invest, and the Japanese. Almost twenty per cent unemployment. The objective, already begun: to smash the currently existing sex market. Concentration on one property. Two properties maximum. Exclusivity in all of Brandenburg state. Intercity link to Berlin at the planning stage. Possibly also via Schwerin to Hamburg.

It could be throwing money down the drain or it could be a deal with a future. On the other side of the border there are girls working in every town, every village. Clubs, sex shops, brothels, streetwalkers, caravans, private apartments, Polish pimps, Russian syndicates. The tourists come by the busload and hump their way through a whole weekend for a hundred marks. Cigarettes and booze for a third, if not less.

The factor is the cop. The cop he'll be meeting later. The Colonel has a link to the properties, old contacts, old boys' networks, new money. It has to be a clear strategy: this side of the border, it's us. Only us. The other side of the border is the cesspool. Polish politicians want to tighten up the law. A plus. Get the best hookers over to Germany, that's where the good money's to be made. Infiltration of the border market. Push the Polish border business back into Poland. A club such as doesn't exist yet on either side of the border, never has existed.

'Trade?' there's a crackle on the line. 'You've been in the business long enough. You know those Polish girls are crazy for our hard cash. Da, da, da! And we're employment agency number one in Brandenburg! We rent and let! The cesspool is on the other side of the border.' He's sitting in his Fort, in the city in the East, and he doesn't know what to make of the Colonel. When he calls his brother later, all he says is, 'Keep your hands out of that. One Eastern annexe is enough.'

It's perfectly legal, little brother, all perfectly legal. When the cards get reshuffled you need a good hand. Naive? We're not naive. It'll be a good clean deal because this is the future. They're still beating each others' brains out now but everything will be different in a few years' time. Once the chaos is over the money will flow. And the profits will be biggest where everything is clean. Mind you, you never know when it comes to cleanliness. You know that yourself. It's a tough business and we're not exactly Samaritans. There's no need to lie to ourselves on that one. You know very well I agree with you, *when everyone's happy the money rolls in*. In the end. But it's about business first and foremost. Only business. For the time being. The information's too good, the contacts are too good. The assurances seem to be serious. The cop. The Colonel. The Russians are keeping out of it. The competition's under control. The politicians are interested in thinning out the trade and trading in the thick of things. Clean taxpayers' money. The laws will be changing in a couple of years. The liberalization of the sex market is coming up. The right people are on our side.

'Too shadowy. Keep your hands off it.'

'I've been in the business for thirty years.'

'That's different. What do we know about the Russians? Ex-KGB, powerful syndicates, they're shipping the women all over the place. From all over the place. Kosovo. The Baltic. Commodity futures, you know. The markets are getting overrun. We never wanted anything to do with all that. You keep away from the border.'

'We have to take a look. We have to weigh up the opportunities. They're looking for outside people, investments from clean investors. It's all about percentages. The risk isn't too high. I got the contact and the information from an old Russian, I've known him for nearly twenty years! Nothing's set in stone. Why shouldn't we take a look if the firm can make money out of it?'

'Then take a look. You've usually got a good feel for things.'

He hasn't spoken to his brother for years now. The kid's settled down, so it seems. And he'd hoped he'd come in on it with him. Wanted to put out feelers on the telephone and then go over and see him. Bielefeld. Where he hasn't been for years either. He should have gone to see him in the first place. He never trusts the phone lines. Voices turn to data and waves and float through the offices and switching stations, distributors, get split into nanoparticles, electrical impulses in the air, hisses and crackles, lightning flashes through the sky of voices; you can call yourself up if the planets are in the exact same position as years previously. They usually only talk in codes, about cars and commodities and deals in stocks and shares, substances, raw materials, options, East, West, South, North, from the borders into the land and back. Europe's going to change, believe you me. The whole market's going to change. Poland's not lost yet. He's sitting on a train and sleeping and dreaming of the woods behind the house, the two of them building little houses there out of wood and rocks and clay. Bats upside down in the trees.

'I've told you before to stop your bloody smoking. Can't you get that in your head? And are you planning to keep on fucking away here until the baby comes, or what? Don't you set foot in my place ever again, you stupid cow! Go down the dole, for fuck's sake, if you're broke!'

The concrete blocks are almost vacant. Only a handful of windows are lit up. The buildings are scheduled for demolition in 2003, like almost all the tower blocks in the border town. The three of them are in the lift. Magnum is now wearing a blue bomber jacket and a white shirt and really looks a bit like a forester. The ceiling light flickers. The Count puts on his tinted glasses. They're in one of the two tall, narrow blocks he noticed earlier on, on the way to the bats or on the way back, he's not sure now. They get out on the fourteenth floor. They walk down a long corridor, the Colonel in the lead. The doors on either side are made of brown wood, splintered in many places, scratched, words and letters, the small round spyholes at head height looking dull and clouded over, the doorbells next to the doors small grey buttons on the grey-white wall, name signs left over by some of the doors, Schmidt, Lorkowsky, Janka, Meier, A. Weiß, G. Barth, the Colonel stops outside a door at the end of the corridor. The Count hears quiet music from inside.

The Colonel rings the bell, pressing the button several times. Perhaps a code but he already rang the intercom downstairs, and only once.

Magnum announced they were coming from the car, on his brick phone. 'It's me. Five minutes.'

The door opens. A man in a black suit jacket with a grey polo neck underneath it. Good quality that doesn't match his face. The Colonel nods at him, they shake hands, and the guy waves them all in, closing the door behind them. The Colonel leads them straight into a room. The Count hardly has time to glance around the hall, coat rail with one or two jackets on it, that must be the bathroom over there, three more doors, the one to the kitchen ajar and the Count sees a man in a green bomber jacket sitting on a stool directly behind the crack of the door. A milking stool, he has time to think; he didn't expect that kind of furniture here. And he thinks that bomber jackets seem to be some kind of East German thing. Although they're gradually disappearing from the trade in the city in the East where he has his annexe.

The room's not particularly large, just the usual size of a living room in a flat. A bar on one wall. Four bar stools in front of it. A young woman behind the bar, a shelf of bottles, a large fridge. A few tea lights on the counter, a few tea lights on the tables, low coffee tables in front of upholstered seats. A large TV directly in front of the windows.

Premiere is on, the pre-match reports, is that Axel Schulz? He counts five men on the sofas and seats. And two women. One of the men gets up and comes towards them. He has shoulder-length hair and a short, stubby, piggy nose. Wearing a loose black Hugo Boss shirt. 'Mario,' he says and holds out his hand. 'We spoke on the phone.'

272

The Count looks around and nods and says, 'Nice cosy place you've got here.'

'It's just for relaxing after hours. Watch a bit of boxing, drink a few beers, few nice drinks, meet friends. Welcome to the border.' The Count makes out the remains of acne scars or pockmarks on his face. 'Good that you're here. We've got a lot to talk about. Heidi, get us four beers, will you!' Then he turns back to him and says quietly, 'Only German girls here, a bit different, our German embassy if you like.'

'I'd rather have a cognac or a whisky.'

'How about a G&T? Heidi, get us four G&Ts, will you!'

The Colonel pushes the bar stools aside and stands next to them at the bar. 'I've already told you about our Mario. We've got everything under control along the border, haven't we?' He puts his arm around Pig Nose's shoulder. His shadow, Magnum, goes over to an armchair and sits down. 'We could have met at my place,' says Pig Nose, 'really nice place, nice club, you'll have heard of it I bet, but it's too busy right now over the weekend. And wait till you see the view from up here. The only place you'll get a better view is from the old Oder Tower. And we couldn't get in there, I'm afraid.'

'We don't have to,' says the Colonel. 'Much too large a property, total money pit, but the other four towers... well, you'll see it all tomorrow.'

'2 p.m., that's our viewing appointment!' Mario laughs and spreads out the four bottles of beer and four gin and tonics, which the girl seems to have made in record time.

'I've seen quite a lot today already.' The Count takes a glass for himself, the ice cubes clinking. 'Nice little town.'

The twitch at the corner of the mouth, that twitch

over and over again, the twitch in the corner of the lieutenant's mouth when he joins their little group later on.
He feels his own mouth twitching in imitation even
years later, on the left, where the heart is, when he thinks
back to all this, and sometimes just of its own accord. He
sees cigarette smoke and dust in the light of the big TV
screen. As though the guy had had a slight stroke, he
thinks, because one half of his face is oddly stiff behind
and next to that twitch, as if frozen in place, only the corner of his mouth moving: 'Everyone believes in Tyson.
The bookies are hardly taking any more bets on him.
But I tell you, I'll tell you with the experience and the
feel for people I've built up, I don't mean to sound cocky,
over all the years, here and on the other side of the border and far away in the good old USSR...'

What the hell was this cop doing, thinks the Count,
over in Russia? But he's heard plenty from his contacts
in Berlin, Hamburg and Frankfurt am Main. About the
elite troop from Unit 1 that allegedly co-operated with
the KGB. Rumours. Legends.

'And you know, there's one factor, an important factor... I don't know if you're as interested in boxing as I
am...'

'Yes. I'm quite interested. I used to know Prince von
Homburg and Jürgen Blin, who had a bout against Ali...
but that was a long time ago.'

'Blin? Homburg? You'll have to tell me about them
later. All in good time. What I'm getting at is, Henry
told me a couple of days ago, last Thursday it was, or not
last week but the Thursday before that, I invited him to
dinner after his training session but he has to watch the
calories, so Henry said he thinks old Holyfield has the
right tactics, the right strategy and the heart to break the
will, the machine in front of him, you see, 'cause that's

what it's all about...'

'It's about a lot of things.'

'...prison, you know, and I know all about that, it goes deeper, much deeper than you think, it's a toxin that'll always be in his veins, poisoning his blood and his heart and his whole body and his tiny brain and everything around him and all...'

'A toxin, you say. So how long was Tyson... I remember he went down at the beginning of the nineties...'

'Three years. And that's the whole point. The factor. All the crap about jail making you tougher and all that – it makes you weak. I don't want to step on your toes, but I do know...'

'You know *what*?'

'Well, you're a man of the old school, serious, a businessman, an investor, that's why we're meeting here, and even if you...'

'Let's skip all that. Old school... what's that supposed to mean? It's nothing but stories and legends. You seem to have done your research.'

'Likewise. Information's everything. Even though I have different reasons to your business partners. What I'm interested in is transparency. Regulation. Cleanliness. I want a clean, regulated, serious market.'

'Sounds like good reasons. But I'm sure that's not all there is to it.'

'Both of us bear a certain risk. In the old days we'd have called it "operative information procurement."'

'I've got nothing to do with *that*. I represent interests. And it's not just my decision to take.'

'And I've got nothing to do with that. You know, it's a good beginning to a good business deal if we speak openly.' They drink their gin and tonics as the ring announcer pronounces the fight about to begin any

275

moment. *Ladies and Gentlemen, live from Las Vegas it's sssss-howtime!* 'If you want to put a bet on Tyson, I'm up for it. Here and now.'

'No. I believe in Holyfield's chances.'

He looks at the screen. He can hardly tell the fighters apart. Saw Tyson fighting once in the eighties but those were different times. They stand facing each other, dark statues, their faces motionless. Thousands of camera flashes all around them. Sweat runs down their faces in curved tracks. The droplets shimmer in the air when they're released from the skin, tiny projectiles of salt on their way through space, the seconds ticking by when they hit the floor of the ring, in Las Vegas the coins come clinking out of the one-armed bandits in slow motion. *Let's get it on.*

'Holyfield. Old school. You're a wise man. An old-school boxer, as the Yanks say. Of course, anything can happen in a match like this.'

'There's always a certain risk.'

'But there are insurance policies. That's why we're sitting here. Have you enjoyed the view yet?'

'I've seen all sorts of things today, yes.'

'Don't let looks deceive you. Times are going to change. Not today, sure, and maybe not tomorrow. But faster than some people here think.'

'That's our assumption. Otherwise I wouldn't be here.'

'In a couple of years we'll be the showcase town on the border. The outer fortifications of Berlin. The German-Polish annexe of politics and finance. The foreign office will have departments here. Not at the end of Europe. At the beginning. In the middle.'

The Count is smoking too much. He watches the room through his tinted glasses, which filter the light.

276

People moving behind the cigarette smoke. The pre-match reports on TV. Sound turned off. You can see the fighters sitting in their dressing rooms. The ring is empty. He hears quiet music, lets his eyes roam the walls in search of the speakers. A small mirror ball revolving directly above the bar scatters brightly coloured stars and dots on the woman's skin, in his hands holding the cigarettes by turn, left, right, flashing light on the glasses and bottles. Mario, the man with the brothel in town and the man with the brothels and shares along the border, is next to him at the bar, looking into the colours reflected on the Count's lenses and then speaking quietly directly into his ear. 'When the cop comes later, don't let him deceive you. He thinks he's playing the cards, but we're the ones dealing them out.' There's a paper napkin in front of him, and Mario writes a word on it with a ballpoint pen. A vertical line, then a series of mainly squat letters, then another line to finish off. Informant. He scrunches up the napkin and puts it in his trouser pocket. 'I need a piss. And then this'll go down the toilet. Just so you know I'm being open with you. This is a big deal. And don't let him deceive you; he's not just a talker. Why do you think the competition's disappearing round here? And I'm here. It all goes together; you won't get an insurance policy like this anywhere else.'

'I don't know if my partners will like that napkin.'

'Don't forget: *We're* your partners. And the cop's our man.'

'Don't get me wrong – everything from today and tomorrow that...'

'We know you're a discreet and honest man, we know you always do your deals nice and clean. And what does it matter what I say to you... Heidi! Make us another two G&Ts, will you!'

'What do you think, who's going to win tonight?'

'It's a sure thing.' Mario takes the gin and tonic – the girl has made it in record time again – and hands him the glass. The ice cubes clink and the Count feels his hand growing cold.

The bodies are leaning on each other. Swaying forward, swaying back. The heads meld together, the legs and the rump bending into one another like liquid plastic, the gum shield red and blue in a single huge mouth, the punches droning through the room, tearing the bodies apart again, round three, round four, back then in the different time Tyson was faster than light; now his fists bore through the glass and into the room as if in slow motion. The room is crowded now, every sofa and every armchair occupied, men and a few women standing between the seats and tables. Half-naked ring girls come in from the corridor and squeeze through the boxing fans with their cards, past the bodies, the cop sitting on a chair against the wall, all alone. His twitching, right in front of the wallpaper. Never mind *German embassy*, thinks the Count, a couple of exotic types have turned up after all. Romanians, Russians, as far as he can tell. No one takes any notice of the cop. And after the seventh round he's suddenly vanished, a white mark on the wallpaper. *What's up, Cop?*

He can still hear music from somewhere in the flat, strange music, singing, sounds like folk songs, must be coming from one of the other rooms. Fairly quiet. He recognizes two or three ponces immediately as ponces – one of them is wearing a gold chain with gold letters spelling out PIMP. ('Ponce in tracksuit with gold chain, *The Pimp on the Border*, scene 5, take 1!') The Count folds his hands together. Small sparkly stones on the letters. Las Vegas. ('Laugh track whenever the guy comes into shot!') Just like he recognizes the Russians and Romanians. Two or three suits are there too, relaxed with their ties loosened, Windsor knots, the girls sitting or standing beside them, some with long fluffy bunny ears, Playboy bunnies, finance, he'd say, or more likely local politicians. Or pimps. Or whatever the hell else. His instinct is gone and all he can feel is that he's dizzy. Nonsense, it's tiredness from the journey or the fatigue blockers or whatever. He wouldn't have let the pimps and Romanians and Russians in. And the girls shouldn't be wearing bunny ears.

The girls form a human chain to the bar to transport beer and drinks to the boxing fans. The mix doesn't suit him. The light confuses him. Too many voices tonight. Not serious. He knows this mix very well, though. From the city in the East and from the old days. You're being over-cautious, he thinks, they seem to have everything under control. You have to howl with the wolves... Jesus, what bollocks. Quiet music, the boxing match in full throes.

'You look thoughtful, partner.' The Colonel suddenly standing next to him; he was gone for quite a while.

'The partner's wondering who the partners are.' He drinks and puts his glass down on the bar.

'I've got two thousand on Tyson. *Mr* Partner! What do you reckon?'

'Round eight. It's not looking good for him. But maybe he's saving his energy.'

'And a thousand on Holyfield. At ten to one odds.'

'That means...'

'That means, if Tyson wins like we all thought...'

'I didn't think that.'

'You're a wise man, judging by the state of play so far.'

'Intuition.'

279

'Did you make a bet?'

'I don't bet. Not on sport.'

'Sensible. Too risky, right?'

'That's not it. It's a principle.'

'A man needs his principles.'

'Says John Wayne?'

'...so if Tyson wins, and it doesn't look like he will right now, I'll get back the three thousand I invested. Placed the bet in Moscow, private bookmaker, the only ones who'd pay me three for two, must have had a feel for it and wanted to get the Tyson betters in.'

'Looks like they managed it. But maybe he's saving his energy.'

'I'd bet with you right here at this bar that he doesn't come back up. If you were a betting man.'

'Looks that way. And if Holyfield wins...'

'I bet on him here. Good old Germany. Bet here. Twelve to one. That'd be twelve tons. I could have got better odds, wasn't keeping my eyes out. But the bet's still on.'

'Twelve thousand. Bet both ways. No risk. But no win if the favourite makes it through.'

Mario has run up to the screen, shoving the people and the bunnies aside, and now he's yelling, 'Knock him out, knock him over! Time to eat him up, Mike!'

But Mike seems to have left his hunger in jail. He's taking more punches with every round, and everyone in the room with money and hopes invested in Iron Mike gets quieter and quieter, and in the tenth round he's on the ropes, his body encircled by a strange light ('There it is again, bloody hell!'), Holyfield's hands sinking into it like into liquid plasma, and the fight's over. An unspectacular ending. And out the show! The plasma freezes as the body falls. Falls. Falls. Loops of light. Cut.

'Look at our Mario, take a look at him! Our clean-shaving, all-smiling lad. Don't let appearances deceive you, he's a good businessman, usually has the right nose for things, even if it is a bit flattened, for who to bet on and who not to, but you and me and the inspector...' when he says 'inspector', almost whispers it, the Colonel laughs, 'he knows times are going to change...'

'Mario?'

'Mario. He controls the market this side of the border. He thinks he controls it, but without the inspector and without my properties, without the old contacts, he'd be... He's willing to share. Sell shares, and our big new thing, it's his thing too, can be his thing, for the time being, if you get my drift...'

'I think I do.'

The Count drinks and smokes Davidoff Filters, watching the naked people in the bare room and thinking of his information. The KGB, the border, the money, the women, the traders and how to get a foot in the door without dipping it in the cesspool. He wants to ask what role the Russians will play in future and whether the Romanians want to play big like in the 1994 World Cup, when that little Maradona of the Carpathians Gheorghe Hagi... But this isn't the right time, and he knows these questions and answers wouldn't clear things up, wouldn't make them clearer. What are all these characters doing here if the cop's aiming for a clean, regulated, serious market? And what's the cop doing here if the Romanians and Russians and the dodgy pimps – there aren't many of them, he has to admit that – are watching Premiere with them? In a great big show. Bunnies and gold. In this ugly flat above the rooftops. But he knows too that it's better to bring people together, the last players, to keep an eye on them, and then to sift them out, if need be, no big deal in itself. The ring girls have gone. Poker or Old Maid.

He's down by the river, looking up at the thin white tower block. The one he was inside before. And standing by the window and looking out at the land and the river and the land behind the river. Long after the fight, which he wasn't really interested in. Because he saw other things on the screen. And then outside the window in the night as it was turning into morning. A tower, swathed in scaffolding. Workers. Machines. Himself in a yellow helmet, construction plans in his hands. The factor is the cop. The insurance policy. The man who's clearing the market. Closing down the competition. Two rooms were locked in the flat. He tries to make out where he was standing by the window, before. On the other side he sees the pale pink morning behind the woods. He ordered a taxi at the hotel and got it to bring him here. The car is parked a good way away, up on the embankment. Fifty marks on the dashboard. Unit 1. He's heard of it before. They came past the snack bar earlier, in the taxi, 'Peace Border Snack Bar', a little low building, a wooden shack that was still open. A little bridge led across a ditch to the hut, in front of it a slate sign, a kind of blackboard, with the prices on it. He bought himself a small bottle of Goldkrone, there wasn't much choice. An old woman, a grandma, sat there on a chair behind the counter and looked up in surprise when he entered the room.

He looks out at the water flowing dark to the coast. To the lagoon, the bay from which three arms lead to the sea. A couple of nutria scurry along the river bank, not far from him. Vanish somewhere above the water; that must be where their dens are. Magnum from forestry – he hasn't seen him since he got to the flat – could probably tell him a thing or two about these beaver-like

282

animals. Thirteen years later he'll be sitting in a restaurant in the city in the East and eating nutria cordon bleu. Nutria farms spring up around the city. He doesn't like the taste of the meat, a little like chicken but with a slightly stringent, bitter note to it. He only eats half of his dish. His stick with the heavy silver knob, which he leaned against the table, tips over and lands on the floor with a bang. He looks at the woman sitting opposite him, moving an empty wine glass to and fro on the table. It's the first time she's visited him here.

As he opens the door to the room he knocks something over. A chair, as he sees later. Who puts a chair so close to the door? A woman is squatting on a plastic sheet, three men standing in front of her, wanking. They're wearing black balaclavas. The woman has her hands behind her back, handcuffed. There's a tap on his shoulder. The man from the door. The other three take no notice of him and go on wanking. Plastic sheets on the floor, two mattresses, the clothes next to the knocked-over chair. The man shoves him silently aside and closes the door. 'Private,' he says. Music from the other room.

He goes for a walk along the canal with his wife. Ice floes on the water. The coldest winter for years. The airport closed, trains cancelled. She's wearing the Russian fur hat he gave her years ago. Mink. The old run-down harbour warehouses rise up before them in the twilight like towers. The days are short. He wants to tell her about his dream. Nutria meat between his teeth. A club, a brothel on several floors, like the Pascha in Cologne, right by the canal. He'd close down the Fort for it. With a roof terrace. With several bars. Whirlpools. But the warehouses are too dilapidated, no one wants to invest, the city's too small and business isn't going so well any more. Hostile takeovers on the horizon.

He lies on the bed and waits for the phone to ring. He pours a little Goldkrone in his coffee. Between the net curtains, he sees the town hall's entrance portal, a grey morning, clouds, he sees raindrops on the glass. The plans and documents are next to him on the big double bed. The viewing appointment is set. Four old water towers. A small house in the centre. But it's the towers that fascinate him, and they're going to convert one of them. Equity and loans. He can offer up to five hundred thousand. AK and his own people. He has a dream of a club on the border. A little way outside of this strange town. A round old tower with lots of rooms. Bars, whirlpools. Exclusive. And a wonderful view. Unique in the region. Girls from Poland, girls from Germany. Black girls and Russian girls. BBWs and slim models. Girlfriend sex and S&M. And the Intercity to Berlin once an hour and via Schwerin all the way to Hamburg. Local politicians support the project, the authorities are on board, taxpayers' money flowing in both directions, and the inspector from Unit 1 keeping the competition off their backs. Europa City. Everything's going to change. He switches on his little shortwave radio. Domian and Harald Schmidt. He laughs – what a joker, that Schmidt. No respect for anybody.

'Turn-off porn. That'd be an idea, right? You've given me an idea for a big gap in the market. I'll start producing turn-off pornos with me as the star. So if anyone's too randy or feels like he's too hot under the collar, he can just put on a porno with me in it and fall asleep nice and calm, no need for medication.'

He sits down on the grass of the embankment. He can hardly move his left leg any more. No blood. Just a swelling as big as a fist. There's something broken in his knee, he can tell. He always has a few painkillers on him. For his back. Valium as well. And beta-blockers to bring him down. So he can sleep without dreaming, dive into the black and emerge again before he takes an analytical approach to things like he's always done. Beside him is the walking stick he bought off the old lady for a hundred marks in the little shack, 'Peace Border Snack Bar'.

Between the forests, like a broad swathe, he sees the lights of the town on the other side of the border. They vanish slowly in the pale early daylight. It's been a long time since he watched a sunrise out in nature. Mist between the trees and above the river. He hears the birds, quiet from far off. His passport is in his inside pocket. When did he last leave the country? 'Sometimes I think we should pack our bags and bugger off to South America.'

'What do you want in South America, they'd kidnap you and cut our your guts in the jungle.'

'Moon-Eye, we're living in strange...'

'Time to change the record.'

About to stand up and limp back to the taxi, the walking stick in his hand, he hears music. Singing. Faint echoes. He's taken too many tablets. And then he sees the ship. It's heading downstream, coming slowly around the bend in the river. Still half concealed by the morning haze. Some kind of cruise ship. A paddle wheeler with a low, wide chimney emitting a smell of diesel, a trail of smoke mingling with the mist, two decks, both empty. 'I love to go a-wandering...' He thinks it must be on tape. Or on a record. It sounds like a gramophone. Scratchy, underlain with crackling. Horribly distorted. He can make out the large speakers on the top deck, or are they square black crates? Even the birds are drowned out. And then the second boat. A few yards behind. A small police boat. It's snaking across the water in curves, as if it wanted to keep its distance, an escort. '...I love to wander by the stream...' He slips, climbing up the embankment. He's not sure, as he crawls further up to a small tree, the crutch in his right hand, whether the music isn't coming out of the grey funnel-shaped loudspeaker on the police boat. The verses mix, the scraps of song disappearing into the woods and coming back to him. 'High overhead, the skylarks wing / They never rest at home.' Now he sees his wife on the upper deck of the cruise steamer. She pulls the collars of her coat together and leans against the railing. Is there a glass there balanced on the slim metal rail? She takes a couple of steps and bends out far over the prow, like a figurehead, and her coat flutters in the wind. And her hair. ('What colour? What does the colour matter, Messieurs! If I say 'une blonde' nobody would believe me anyway! But she really was wearing a fur coat, open at the front. Her blonde pubes curled in the wind, she really looked a lot like the wonderful Kerri Kendall.' 'Kerri Kendall?' 'Playmate of the Month, September 1990, you philistines!') Figures behind the portholes. Bodies. Hands. Faces pressed against the round glass panes, distorted like in a house of mirrors. The ship cruises towards the sea. To the lagoon. He's never been to the Baltic.

He hears the engine chugging. CHUG, CHUG, CHUG, CHUG, CHUG. Getting quieter. He can still see the diesel, thin, trembling lines in the fog, still smells the diesel. Sees the paddle wheel in the foamy water long after the big ship and the police boat are out of sight. And fading away, but still here where he's squatting: 'I wave my hat to all I meet / And they wave back to me / And blackbirds call so loud and sweet / From ev'ry green wood tree.'

He walks down the stairs, his glasses slipping on his sweat-damp nose; he took the lift down to the seventh floor and then got out. Now he hears footsteps in the stairwell, further up; he walks faster, takes off his glasses and puts them in his pocket, and then he trips. He hears footsteps below too as he falls, many of them. Very many. Trampling, voices. At least make an effort to be quiet, for fuck's sake! He tries to hold onto the banister. His knee crashes onto the concrete steps. Once, twice. He wants to roll off somehow but his leg twists wrong. A flash of black but he doesn't scream. *I'm too old for this shit!* The heel of his left shoe has broken off. He's on the fifth floor. He limps to a flat. Pushes the door open with his shoulder; it's hanging wonky in the hinges. Bites into his hand because he has the feeling his kneecap is fucked. Pulls the door closed behind him and squats down on the floor. Waits five minutes. Hears sirens. Hears the raiding squad in the building. Then crawls along the hall to the living room. Sees the Colonel down outside the building as he leans both elbows and his upper body on the windowsill. There's someone behind him. Two girls. They sit down on the floor now, next to each other, backs against the wall. 'It's OK,' he says, 'everything's OK.' He sees the patrol cars down outside the building. For a moment it seems as if the Colonel looked up at him, nodded at him, as they put him in the car with his hands behind his back.

They pick up the inspector at home. At the same time. Must have missed him by a matter of minutes. He was sat in front of the TV watching the match; he'd taped it. That's what the Count reads in the paper two days later.

Next to the window is a small shelf unit. A couple of porcelain figurines. Photos, black and white. A party, it looks like, in a village somewhere. People sitting around a big table outdoors, men, women, a grandma in a head-scarf, a farmhouse in the background, a pump, washing on a line, all the people holding big beer glasses up to the camera and laughing. He takes a cigarette out of his case and then passes it over to the girls. He sees them putting Mario in a car in the dawn light. Who'll take over the brothels now? Everything seemed well organized, well planned. The contacts were right. (He couldn't have known that the public prosecutor had been investigating the inspector, his informant Mario and the Colonel for months.) 'Want some advice?' says the man in the bomber jacket, coming out of the kitchen with a cup of coffee. The deal's off. He knows that right away, his instinct tells him so. Russian accent. Could be Polish though. What does he know? 'Go. Five minutes. The deal's off.' He drinks and laughs, throws the newspaper on the bed next to him. The nurse brings his pills. Later he calls his lawyer, his tax adviser and his partner. *Informant to the informant. Brandenburg Criminal Investigations Office launched major operation. Further suspects held in custody. Brothel owner M. (42), arrested on the same date, allegedly a paid informant for the inspector... CIO investigators faced the question of 'who was actually whose informant'... Investigators also broke up an international ring of people-smugglers that had been active for years... The successful police officer gone bad was not only an informant to the brothel mafia... The GDR police service's Unit 1 operated like the Stasi, responsible for... The brothel manager rewarded the lawman's favours with... Numerous further arrests.* Did the guys in the other room at least get to finish their wanking session?

He takes a taxi all the way to Berlin. They take care of his leg at the Charité hospital. He has to get back to the city as soon as possible – business goes on. He spent over an hour in the empty flat with the girls. 'This town is a dump,' he says. 'If you want to earn good money, I've got a place down in the Southeast. You're welcome any time. Only have to pay for your room. Or would you rather go to Berlin?'

They whisper between themselves. The blonde seems to be from Poland. Or Russia. What does he know? Later he finds a pack of playing cards on the shelf by his shoulder. His knee's killing him.

They play Old Maid for his last cigarettes. She comes from Lithuania, speaks Russian and a little German. Jana comes from some village nearby. In the taxi to Berlin, they sit on the back seat and stroke the shiny fur of the Russian hat the Colonel gave him only the night before.

'You've brought visitors along?' says Moon-Eye in the afternoon, *smog in Berlin, what a din*. He's sitting at the bar on his own, listening to oldies and reading the paper. Only glances up.

'You take care of the girls, I've got an appointment at the Charité.'

'Industrial injury or did you have a bad dream?'

'Just a scratch. If it spreads to the brain I'll give Domian a call.'

'The gay voice of the Rhineland. Have a drink first. And then you're better off at the Urban Hospital, it's just round the corner. Those East German doctors'll only mess you up.'

'They already have. I'll be back soon.'

'Before the next blue moon... How's business?'

'Going on. As usual. What do *you* think?'

'I've given up that thinking stuff. And as I go, I love to sing, my knapsack on my back.'

'What?'

'Oh, never mind. You get your arse over to matron.'

289

'Yeah, will do.' He closes his eyes and sees: loops of light. Bodies like liquid plasma. Flashing stones. Las Vegas.

THE CONFERENCE OF THE WHORES

My dear colleagues, my dear fellow campaigners, my dear friends, I'd like to welcome you once again! I'm incredibly proud, *proud to the bottom of my heart*, as the speaker before me said, that so many of you have made it here today! I am a whore, and I'm standing proud! (...) Thank you, thanks very much.

Three years since the Prostitution Act. I remember well how many of us believed back then – now we've finally found our place in society. Now we can exercise elementary rights, the time of semi-legality in which we all had to act, work and live is over now.

Let me quote once more from the Act, my dear colleagues, my dear fellow campaigners:

'Should sexual acts have been performed in return for a previously agreed payment, this agreement forms the basis of a legally effective claim. The same applies if an individual, particularly within an employment relationship, is on standby for a specific time period to provide such acts in return for a previously agreed payment.'

As you all know, the criminal code was also amended at the same time, to establish that the creation of an appropriate working environment is not a punishable crime, provided – and this is a point I'm sure we'll have to discuss here over the coming days – no exploitation of the sex worker takes place.

Where do we stand today, three years after the Prostitution Act came into force? How many of you, of us, have employment contracts? Are we also automatically exempt from the accusation of indecent behaviour? Are we limited in performing our work by the continuing existence of restricted areas? Why are there no standardized regulations by the authorities, or no standardized interpretation of the existing legislation, when it comes to registering workplaces and developing employment contracts?

I'd like to take this opportunity to welcome the operators of brothels here today, or as they put it so nicely, brothel-like workplaces. Sadly, only a few brothel operators are taking part in our conference, but I'm looking forward to our discussions with those of you who have come, and to your suggestions and reports.

I'd like to remind you that the service sector union ver.di prepared a model employment contract back in 2002, granting sex workers a wide range of rights as is standard in other employment relationships. We have to ask ourselves, we sex workers and the workplace operators, why there have been so few, no, too few changes and improvements in our working conditions and our work since the Prostitution Act came into force. At the same time, and above all, I'd like to ask the members of the ruling and opposition parties present here today, and again I have to say, sadly, that only very few politicians have come along, but I'd like to ask you to devote intensive attention to all these questions and to take them back to your parliamentary groups. You're welcome to put your hands up and have your say after each of the speakers! We're all needed, we all have to stand together and talk openly with one another, we're here to change elementary things, to solve problems that have been going on for decades! We have to finally put an end to the double morals when it comes to sex work! We need workable regulations, so as to be able to act, live and – yes – work on the labour market and ultimately in society as responsible, insured, registered but free employees or freelancers, exercising and abiding by our rights!

I know many of my colleagues prefer to work free-lance. And there can be no objection to that in any way! The path to self-employment has often been the first step. But were there to be an adequate alternative in a regulated employment relationship, including a basic wage... a minimum wage, as has been discussed on many occasions with a variety of model suggestions... But, my dear friends, how is that to take place? I'm asking that honestly, I'm asking you, and above all I'm asking the brothel operators who are present with us today.

At least when it comes to the workers behind the bar and the dancers and artistes, we've made some progress. And we ought to go on working on this area, keep on keeping on.

Let me say perfectly openly and honestly that I myself would like to go on working as a self-employed sex worker, as a self-employed service provider, like I've always done. Like most of you, I'm sure, like most of us.

Since 2002 I've been in possession of what's known as a contract for services. My boss is a fan of the new legal certainty, which gives her at least a certain protection from police raids. My contract for services clearly regulates my status as a self-employed service provider, obliging me to pay taxes on my income of my own accord.

I have a private health insurance policy. I know many of you are insured under a different profession. One of the things I had to provide was what they called a drugs screening. Plus an examination report from my GP. I took that step deliberately. And we should all take that step deliberately and consciously!

Migrant sex workers, however, face further difficulties, but they should be surmountable once all the necessary documents are presented. That's the law, that's de jure – if I can put it like that – these are our rights, we're entitled to them! But I know from talking to many colleagues that things often turn out differently in practice. That there are good reasons why people give other descriptions of their work for their insurance policies. I hope we can speak openly in the discussion in a moment about all the difficulties and all the obstacles!

We want to develop the Prostitution Act further – it was a major step in the right direction but our goal is that there should be no stigmatization, no denigration of our hard work from any direction! When I hear, for example, that the Act only benefits the brothel operators, then that's something we have to discuss at our conference.

The last thing I want to say, and I have to admit that since I started preparing for my speech here I've been shitting myself for days, as we say round our way, because I've never done this in front of so many people: I'm really looking forward to listening to my colleagues speaking in a moment. I'm looking forward to my Greek colleague – a Greek sex worker loses her licence when she gets married, at least that's what I read in our brochure – bloody hell, what year are we living in? And I'm looking forward to my English colleague, who'll tell us about the Anti-Social Behaviour Orders that penalize her and restrict her work, and to our French colleague, who is still at risk of ending up in prison. We're really international here, and I believe we do all have to come together if we're going to keep on talking about Europe. I can only talk about our situation here in Germany and the way I perceive it. And what we have to improve.

What we definitely need is an issue of guidelines on implementing the Prostitution Act. How do we secure our pensions? We're all thinking about it. And how can we make sure we don't end up getting lumped together with those women who are done injustices? I know that force and coercion are a big issue, in politics, in the media, in society. And I know, and we all know, that these things go on. Forced prostitution is a crime. But what I want is for us not to be tarred with the same brush. What I want is a trade union. What I want is for Hydra to carry on working autonomously. What I want is for us to continue our dialogue, together. What I want is for us to keep meeting regularly, at conferences, in discussion groups, at demonstrations. And there are lots of other things I want.

But first of all I want all of you and all of us to have a good, productive conference, with results that help us go further. Thank you very much.

(Day 1, 18 March 2005)

LIGHTS IN THE CATHEDRAL

The music's barely audible down here. Like a faint rumble behind the walls, above the walls.

Sometimes he thinks he knows the times when the trains clatter along the nearby tracks. But especially at night, there doesn't seem to be any regularity to them. He sits up in his office and listens out for them. 11.30 p.m., 1.40 a.m., nothing for hours, and the next day it's completely different. The passenger line runs around the area, the goods line runs beneath the buildings, underneath the streets. Now in autumn there's often mist above the tracks, gathered in the cutting in the cool damp nights. Bushes grow there; the old sidings that once led to factories now end at wastelands, backyards, vanish into the earth, wooden sleepers rotting away. And in the summers the steel contorts in the heat, there's a flickering above the old goods ring as though it were all asphalted over. He's heard they want to shut the line down in the next few years. The old galvanising works is long gone, since the early nineties. Only the admin building left standing, some West German bought it cheap, payola, set up a club in there and then sold it again. Nigh on twenty years ago.

Where was he from? And what was his name again? Hagen? Siegen? Hildesheim? Towns he only passed through for the first time a few years ago. Ugly concrete, low-rise centres, dirty streets, stations like dark caves, stinking tunnels between the platforms like thirty years ago in Bitterfeld or Frankfurt an der Oder in the Zone, the drawn-out glow of the amusement arcades, takeaways, off-licences, brothels which he sometimes saw from his car, sometimes from train windows; he wanted to explore the country, took time off, the club was fine without him for a few days, he wouldn't call it leave. Dortmund; he wanted to stand in the Westphalia Stadium once in his life and then he did, felt like a stranger in amid the seventy or eighty thousand, he can't remember the game. Hagen W. from Hagen? Siegfried Augentaler? He could check in his files, there are copies in the safe, and a bottle of Springer Urvater the previous owner left him. Three quarters full. All these years he's been meaning to drink it on a special occasion. Then he forgets again. He found a little silver-coloured stainless steel casket in the safe as well. But there was only a mirror in the lid when he opened it up. And a note. 'Must write to Laura.' He wanted to throw them away, the note and the box, but they're still in the safe next to the bottle, up in the office. Hans makes a mental note to look up the man's name and where he was from. His memory often deceives him. He's getting old. A lot of things are like yesterday. A lot of things are far away. He stopped in Hildesheim once. Three or four years ago. When he felt the need to get out of town in a rush. He came out of the pub they call the Dead Railwayman in the central station early one evening, the one next to the staircase to the platforms, and got on a train. Ended up in Hannover, night-time by that point, not far from the Steintor quarter, but what did he want there? That was before the Angels came to the city. *Been there for years. Always have been. No.*

Took a stroll around town. No. He got on a train. And got out again in Hildesheim. Was that the end of the line? Possibly. He'd called his club from Hannover. Called his man on the door, and then called Alex as well. Yeah, yeah, the pact. We raised our glasses and forged the pact, for everlasting peace in the brothels, on the streets. So many years ago. Just had to get away for a bit, be back tomorrow or the day after. Yeah. Yeah. Call if anything's up. Called Mandy, Mandy 2.

He retched. Stumbled against the tiled wall. Heard himself retching in that tiled shithouse in Hildesheim station.

He'd never met him, the big guy from Hannover. The Godfather. The Chancellor of the Angels. (The big guy's lawyer really did work in the same chambers as the eternal ex-chancellor and lawyer Gerhard Schröder – Hanoverian connections.) He was just a little brothel owner (Brothel? No, are you taking the piss?) with a little club. Hans's Night Club. That wasn't the name. 'The Dead Railwayman.' No. 'The Pretty Peepers.' Yeah, that was more like it. 'The Paradise.' That was what the unknown man whose name and memories were in the safe and in the little casket had called it back in the day. 'Moulin Rouge'. Like in Paris? No. He pondered on the train, thought about it. Everything was already staked out, had a name already, no point in renaming the place. Why bother? The place was running fine. Had its ups and downs. 'The Diamond Heart.' What bollocks.

And he looks out at the evening, out at the dusk, dark grey, grey scraps of cloud, landscapes in front, outlines of woods, houses and lights moving on the streets, disappearing; soon all he'll see is his reflection. He drinks his wine, he drinks his coffee, he asks the man who comes down the aisles of the carriages with a little trolley for a coffee, thinks about how he looked for the name of his club back in the day, and in Hildesheim he puts fifty cents in the slot next to the door, the disabled shithouse is closed, they're usually the cleanest, he thinks, his club isn't suitable for wheelchairs yet but in all the years there's only been three or four wheelchair users come in there, like that one time, he even came with his carer or male nurse or whatever he was, and they lifted him in, him and Martin and the friend of the wheelchair guy, he started complaining because the chair was all wonky and almost tipped over, told them about all the official bodies that could intervene and make trouble, but instead of chucking him out, the management reserves the right, they opened up a bottle of Extra Dry while his boy, the cripple, you're not supposed to say that nowadays without the PC brigade coming down like a ton of bricks... but he meant well, anyway he was already at the bar, bit low down, what can you do, and all the girls flitting around him, where else is he going to get so much attention from the ladies, and Hans was back in his office and laughing and giving the girls instructions while the carer or the friend of the wheelchair guy was still complaining out front, but he soon shut up, he had both their wallets to take care of and he drank the best whisky at the bar, to start with... they were satisfied customers. Yeah. No two ways about it. They both got a good fuck out of it. The cripple and his boy. The carer and his boy. Three girls carried him up to a room, the cripple.

And Hans puts a coin in the coin slot of the station toilet in Hildesheim and leans into the buzz of the door (*Please push immediately, or insertion invalid!*), stands in the tiled room of the little white toilet temple, all empty, not a soul, not a sound, absolute silence, then he hears a drop of water hitting a water surface, somewhere, hears the neon lights humming above him on the ceiling, goes over to the two cubicles, opens the door of the first one, looks at the round shit-stained white of a toilet bowl, stumbles back retching, opens the second door, sees the same explosion of excrement in the bowl, even on the walls, brown spatters, runs retching, almost yelling, back to the platform and takes a deep breath.

Saliva running down his chin.

'I've never seen such a disgusting shit-covered shit-house in all my life. Unbelievable. Just unbelievable.'

The music's barely audible down here. A quiet rumble. Perhaps it's the trains. Midnight, 3 a.m., 11.30 p.m. Behind the walls, above the walls.

'What do I care about your bloody shithouse?'

He takes a seat. The table, made for him by an old welder friend a few years ago, is covered in a cashmere tablecloth. 'If you go to my shithouse, upstairs I mean... that's a whole different matter. Cleanliness, you know. You've got to feel comfortable, guests have to feel comfortable. It starts with the shithouse. And I spend a good bit of money on it. There's nothing like a good toilet brigade. If you gotta go...'

'Are you trying to get rid of me?'

'No. I just want to tell you something. Or haven't you got time? Are you in a rush?' He puts his right hand on the table. His welder friend made the shelves on the walls as well. Steel and wood. Simple, functional. At first he was planning to get the whole room panelled, like a gentleman's club.

'You know why I'm here.'

'Too soon, much too soon. Timing, you know, timing is everything, always is.'

'You can spare me your games, Mr Pieszeck.'

'Games? It's no game. Let's get straight to the point then.'

'You're not exactly cautious.'

'And you must be cleverer than I thought, a real Mr Kray.'

'What?

'Just kidding, no need to be scared.'

'Scared? Why should I be scared? I'm here to do

business with you. We could...'

'Come to an agreement. That's what you mean.'

'Yes.'

'And you're right. Take a seat.' He reaches for one of the chairs, pushes it over to him. Welded steel tubes with thin metal sheets as seats. Red velvet cushions on top. That's the only kind of furniture he has down here. All from his old welder friend; it was a good commission for him. He'd been unemployed for years. The man sits down. The two neon lights on the ceiling illuminate their bodies.

'Do you know where we are?'

'In your club.'

'Underneath it. In the catacombs of the old factory.'

'The galvanizing works? That was the partner brigade to my old school, 1984.'

'Tell me what you know.'

He doesn't know nothing, you stupid arsehole. He's bluffing. He just wants something. Hans pulls up a third chair. *I'd rather stand.*

'I know enough. You could say, when it comes to this matter: everything. And I'm not a greedy man. I just want to get out of here. Out of the city.'

'South America or Mallorca? You should have come alone.'

'I am alone.'

The cellars of the old galvanizing works branch out beneath the buildings, only the admin wing left standing, linked with the cellars of the other long-vanished factories in the area. In some of the corridors the plaster flutters off the walls when a goods train passes a few yards above. In some of the corridors iron doors rust away, numbered, stairs leading to deeper basement storeys. Sometimes he shone a torch down one of the

301

staircases, went down a few steps, directed the ray of his long Maglite torch at the floor, let it wander until it was lost in the dark, the ray of his flashlight not touching walls, an enormous room. Puddles flashed in the light, and when the ray crossed a grey squeaking tangle he legged it back up.

'He'll lick me out for hours on end and then he smokes a fag and buggers off. He's a right dirty bastard. I mean, what do I care? But he had a ring on his finger, no skin off my nose but I do imagine him going straight to his wife and kissing her. I mean, he was up to his chin inside of me, slobbered all over the bed. But he probably never kisses his wife. When I kiss my Marco, after work I mean, when I get home, I've always given my mouth a right good clean beforehand... and I always use a condom anyway, most girls do blow jobs without now... that's the new era. I mean, I'm not that old yet, and most people think I'm younger than forty-five anyway... but it can happen overnight, you just get over the hill and you can't do it any more, mind you I'm doing well at the moment and my Marco's there for me too, we're saving and saving, and I'm working like buggery, and he's working like buggery...'

The air conditioning's on full blow, the former admin building of the galvanizing works sweating, particles of zinc and chrome seeping out of the walls, floating months later between the mists, autumn, summer, November, July, only a few freight trains still clatter along the goods ring, G&T's back in nowadays, gin and tonic – the old Count always insists on spelling it out – he's lost a lot on the stock markets, rumours, Hans is sitting in his office, wants to stop smoking but lights another one, his father slowly dying up in the steel town where he came from many years ago, his father showed him a glowing blue picture, that's what death looks like, Hans waits, looks at his watch, Glashütte, used to belong to Erich Honecker, rubies on the inside, in the casing, rumours, someone knows too much, he thinks of the castle on the water in the woods far outside of the city, on the heath, a pond covered in water lilies, the moat behind the grounds, the water still and dark, what does this man want from me, he thinks, listening to the music outside, inside, voices, laughter, later he'll put the Hits of the Eighties on again, *an unprecedented fear*, he turns around, he's alone in the room, looks at his watch again, then at his mobile phone, the red landline telephone is right in front of him, hardly any calls on the landline now, he'll be able to cancel it soon, but an office number's an office number, he uses Skype to communicate with his friend in Tokyo, the diamond trader, changing accounts and usually in code, and he doesn't communicate at all with the Lebanese twin brothers from Berlin, they wait until he gets in touch, he's sweating, the air conditioning keeps the working rooms upstairs nice and cool, it all costs a packet, the darkness in the corners of the room, filing cabinets, shelves, a safe, he moves the adjustable head of the desk lamp, his laptop closed, Alex taught him how to use it a few years ago, not all that difficult, Windows, Excel, Apple, he hated the net to begin with, took the mickey, but he still had ads placed, got websites set up, before he started doing his own business by mail or online banking, reading the visitors' book, he doesn't quite trust the system and he does important transfers at the terminal in the post office bank in the city centre, his tax advisor will be calling again soon, he wants to go down to his cool cathedral beneath the bricks and mortar, beneath the rock, beneath the floor, the cellar beneath the cellar, secret passages like in a fort, but it's brightly lit is his little cathedral, his hobby room hardly anyone knows about, he told the Count once that he wanted to build something down there, 'What, down there?' 'Just a hobby cellar,' 'For a spot of carpentry to calm the nerves, or what? I used to have an electric railway as a child, my brother and I, a lovely old Märklin set, probably worth a bit of money now,' 'Make a nice gift for your children,' silence, the building sweating, the air conditioning on, the electricity meter rotating, Hans sweating, the Job Centre came round the other day to check the girls aren't claiming benefits, competencies have changed, the cops have left him in peace for years now because he keeps the place clean, because AK is on good terms with the cops, the authorities and the city, the cops have always known who works at his place, his books are balanced, everyone profits from the good order in the system, he needs to get more exercise, he's put on nearly a stone, if not more, touching the antiques calms his mind, taking care of them, placing them on the shelves on velvet cushions, *only a crazy person would collect these old things like artefacts*, 'Don't you get fresh!' there's a knock at the door, 'Yes?' Mandy puts her head round it, 'Yes?' 'Can you come for a minute, please?' 'Yes,' he takes his jacket off the back of the chair and then drinks a sambuca with Mandy at the bar, with three coffee beans, Mandy 2, he sometimes thinks of Mandy 1, where she might be now, he didn't say a word back when she left, *Where are you going?* be right back, Klaus perched on his stool by the door, nods at him, Hans watches the smoke rising to the ceiling, the guests chatting to the girls, smoking, drinking, ordering bubbly for the girls, and they smoke too, almost all of them, the ventilation system cost a fortune, not quite, fuck all that non-smoking crap, even though he wants to give it up himself, he lights the sambuca, moves the glass with the blue flame to and fro in front of his face, feels his fingers getting warm, knows he has to blow out the flame before the glass shatters or his skin melts, he sees thin dark streaks sinking in the clear spirits from the roasting beans, don't come in the front door, he told him on the phone, Mandy leans forwards and blows out the flame, 'Are you asleep, my fearless iron Hans?'

'What?'

He whisks away the towel from the cashmere table-cloth. 'What's that supposed to be?'

'Money. You've got eyes in your head.'

'How much?'

'You can count. Go ahead.'

'You don't get me, do you?'

'Twenty thousand.'

'I didn't come to count to twenty thousand.'

'There isn't any more.'

'I want to see the rocks.'

'Coke? Crack? Crystal? You're not at your bloody dealer's place here.'

'I want to see the rocks.'

'And what are you hoping to get out of it?'

'That's up to you, Hans.'

'There's no point discussing it. You know it's impossible.'

'Seeing as I'm the only person who knows the circumstances... Nothing's impossible.'

'We can throw everything at the wall, and nothing will come out of it, nothing at all.'

And forge bands around your heart and watch it beat inside of you.

'What?'

The stairs creaking. Couples going upstairs. Hands

and arms around hips. Small hands on legs, on bellies. Arms in arms. Some strangely separated, as though the gent would like to keep up appearances while people can still see him, only to let it all hang out in the room behind closed doors. And outside, the city moving. Big Klaus sliding to and fro on his stool. Gets up now and then. Looks through the spyhole when the bell rings. Not a loud ring; we don't want to disturb the guests. Hans looks into the blue flame of his Sambuca before he drinks it. The upper layers of the three coffee beans are beginning to seethe in the heat, forming miniscule bubbles, secreting dark streaks that sink slowly down the glass. We've got to keep a cheerful face on. He feels the agitated beat of his heart. Puts the warm empty glass on the counter. 'You're saying you only ordered three mini bottles, not four?'

'Right! Two ladies, three bottles.'

'Two ladies, four bottles. But...'

'No, I...'

'You're our guest. What we say is: excuse us. Be our guest. I see you're drinking gin and tonic. Good choice. Sapphire? Allow us to get you one on the house. Mandy!' He waves, raises his arm, Mandy nods, he takes two or three steps over to the bar stool where Caro's sitting, whispers in her ear for her to just wait a moment in the seats in the front corner, make herself comfortable, 'I'll bring you a coffee or a sambuca if you like, in a minute,' because he sees that Gabriella, the sweet Hungarian girl sitting on the left of the cheapskate, is the lady he likes, 'Make yourself at home at our club, and please excuse the inconvenience. Three proseccos. It really shouldn't happen, but you know how it is... and if there's anything you want, if you've got any questions, just let our Mandy here know, we're always here for our guests!' Mandy 2

306

puts a gin and tonic next to the guest's almost empty gin and tonic. Hans hears the bell that no one else hears. Looks over at Big Klaus, who gets up and pushes aside the velvet curtain to look through the spyhole. In his office, he has his little monitor on the table next to the desk. Camera above the door. That's new too. Relatively. How long ago it is that Steffen sometimes used to do the door here. AK's man. His best man, that was what people said back then. Hans paid fair for AK's brigade. You could talk to Steffen, he used to have good chats with him after they shut up shop for the night, over a glass of wine at the bar or at... what was the name of that twenty-three-hours pub again? Football, philosophy, life and war and meaning and all that. Even though he'd always start in on his Japan crap sooner or later. Or was it China? Far East on the Eastside. He disappeared, wanted to climb the career ladder with the Angels, long before he, Hans, met his Japanese friend and started using Skype... 'What bloody fucking net? Is that where we'll be trapped in 2020, or what? You two have watched too many science fiction films, Steffen, Arnold. You're crazy, *Bild*, the Red-Light Guidebook, we're already in the future!'

Hans is holding the photo, trying to remember what the guy used to look like, he must have seen him before nigh on twenty years ago, in the early, mid-nineties. Street pimp? Security? They called it something else back then. Was he from the football brigade? He only knew about the shit he got caught up in back in the day, in the mid-nineties. He'd only called in information on him very cautiously so as not to attract attention. He had to deal with this thing calmly. But how? Where did that arsehole get his information from? A call five days ago, in the afternoon. Here in the office. Unknown number on the display. 'The philosopher's stones are glittering.'

'What?'

'There's a letter in your post with a number and a time. Call from a phone box.'

'Who is this? What do you want?'

'Travel money. Times two.'

Hans had looked through his post immediately. Inland Revenue, Friends of the SPD, Deutsche Bahn Bonus Programme, brochures from Remy Martin and Red Riding Hood, tax advisor, another one from Inland Revenue, lawyer 2, invoices from Herrmann's off licence, which he still did business with now and then for old times' sake, although he usually just drove to the wholesalers, post from the commercial waste collection people, the gas and electricity works, the newsletter from the local church, which he got once a month since he'd put a couple of notes in the linen donations bag for the half-senile old biddy who'd come round collecting well after midnight, pretty strange working hours, it was a sudden attack of generosity, two doctors' bills, he had private health insurance, actually they ought to pay him a commission for all the girls he'd brought to the insurance company over the past few years, based in Dortmund, a letter from the Job Centre, probably about the recent visits they'd paid, their inspectors, the competencies had changed all over again, a thick A5 envelope from the whores' trade union, that was what he called them although they had another name, and somewhere in the middle of this pile in his club's mail box an envelope, no stamp, no sender, 'To Mr Pieszeck' it said in childish handwriting, a mix of block capitals and joined-up letters. He had put it aside and sorted the other letters, opening some of them. He'd been wanting to get a secretary for years, his own Miss Moneypenny to take care of all this crap, but what would that cost him, for fuck's sake, with everything already costing him an arm and a leg. Yes. 'Tomorrow, Tuesday, 4.30 p.m.'

He'd immediately found out what number it was. A phone box at the central station, up by the platforms. The guy didn't seem to be too bright. He'd thought about going there at the allotted time. But it was very busy there at 4.30, a lot of coming and going, the long-distance trains once an hour, the regional railway transporting the commuters to their villages, the cash desks in the shops on the lower floors of the central station doing big business at that time of day. Always police around, station security, video surveillance everywhere... he could have approached this stranger who'd talked about the philosopher's stones he claimed were glittering so brightly, could have spoken to him without danger. But he didn't know exactly what and exactly who was behind it all. What was going on, for fuck's sake, what was going on...? Someone knew, but what exactly? And who exactly? Was it a coincidence that the Turkish and Arab attacks had been... but he had his insurance policy from Berlin. He was the man with the route to Japan. He'd broker the stones to Japan.

He had called one of the students who took care of his website. That didn't seem much of a risk. And as he was strolling to a phone box outside the supermarket at the bus station, his student assistant was standing in front of the café near the old station waiting room, which was a newsagent's now, keeping his eye on the call box with the number from the letter. 'A hundred. Just a few photos. I bet you've got a good camera with a good zoom on it.'

'Hello?'

'Hans Pieszeck?'

'Who else?' The guy, as yet anonymous, had clearly

watched too many films. What a load of bollocks. Play along for the time being.

'Just so we understand each other, I'm not on my own.'

'And?'

'I think you know what it's about.'

'Hm. You tell me.'

'It glitters so bright, so bright...'

'You ought to make yourself clearer or I'll hang up.'

'No, Hans Pieszeck. You won't do that.'

Hans heard the tannoy in the background. Crackling and buzzing on the line, coins clinking; the guy must be putting more money in. Voices, more loudspeaker announcements, women's voices apparently chatting right next to the phone, then getting quieter. Platforms and trains beside and behind the man talking about the glittering stones.

'The question is, what will you do?'

'The question is, Hans Pieszeck: what's it worth to you?'

'I'm a worker, I've been doing hard graft for my money for years. And glittering, believe me, where's the glamour in my trade? If you're looking for a job, come see me. Introduce yourself. You know where to find me... Wait, hold on a mo.' Hans put a two-euro coin in the slot. A few yards behind him, the supermarket door opened and closed for the steady stream of shoppers, loaded down, stocking up their supplies after work and coming out with large quantities. He heard the clatter of shopping trolleys extracted empty from the three-lane shelter and pushed empty back into the three-lane shelter. Lit up a quick fag. 'Where were we?'

'Your mind's not on it, my dear Hans.'

'I don't think we know each other well enough for first-name terms.'

'I know what you've got.'

'You're scared my phone might be tapped, that's what this movie set-up's for.'

'No. You're clean. Everyone knows that. But we're cautious. Make me an offer.'

'One you can't refuse? I was being honest a minute ago.'

'I used to know someone, he always said: hearts like diamonds.'

'How can I make you an offer if you start out saying times two?'

'That was just the general direction. I think I know how much is on the table.'

'You think, Anonymous. How are we ever to come together if you do so much thinking?'

'Hans, Hans. Mr Pieszeck. I've heard you pay a lot of money in Berlin for information. The authorities, the lookouts. I've heard there are plenty of zeros involved. And I'm coming to you with far less zeros. It'll all be just between the two of us. Purity, Hans. You know that old band, Karat.'

'Spare us the East German rock anthems. You don't know what you're letting yourself in for. And I don't mean me.'

'And that's why my demand... don't get me wrong... it's a moderate demand. I don't want to get in the way of your business. But you mustn't forget me, so I forget you.'

Hans turned around, the receiver still pressed close to his ear. He wasn't dizzy, no, nothing like that. His head was perfectly clear, he felt the autumn air, took a deep breath and smelled that cool, moist autumn air, looked into the yellow light of the opening and closing supermarket entrance, ran his free hand over the metal of the payphone, flicked away his cigarette, burned down to the filter, watched a car with Berlin registration plates driving into the car park, pulled his jacket collar together while he held the receiver between his cheek and his shoulder, he'd put on weight, he wasn't happy about it, the suit jacket barely fitted any more, he fingered a cigarette out of his case, dark brown leather, Mandy had given it to him back in the day, years ago, and felt the voice vibrating on his chest because the receiver had slipped down.

'Hans?'

'Yes.'

'We ought to talk about the details.'

'We ought to.'

'How does tomorrow sound to you?'

'No. In three days. I need some time, I think you'll understand.'

'Sixteen tons. A thousand and one nights. And hundreds and thousands.'

'Talk straight! How much?'

'A hundred thousand.'

'Come to my back door. Midnight.'

'And remember, what I know, someone else knows.'

Hans looked at the photos on his desk in front of him. His student assistant had done a good job. He was always reliable and up-to-date with the website as well. The women came and went. Not much continuity these days.

What was this arsehole doing back in town? He'd soon found out who he was. He'd contacted his man at the cop shop. Had a Berlin address until two and a half years ago. Presumably active in the grime round the back of the central station. Crystal and skag and broken young bodies. The cop also had an address for him with an accommodation agency. That had cost money too. Went fairly quickly though. Had to – he didn't have much time. Three days. Which had cost even more. It was only a couple of clicks on a computer but the cop wanted to get his share. 'I'm not the electoral register. And he's still registered in Berlin, anyway.' But the man was reliable and kept his mouth shut, his pension was at stake, so it wouldn't make waves on the dark pre-winter lake.

Three days. He'd been surprised that idiot had gone for it on the phone. He'd cancelled his appointment with his urologist. It wasn't acute anyway. He'd gone to the gym, AK's fitness club, over in the northeast of the city, and tried to drop a few pounds. They trained in a cage there now, at the back. Free fighting. He'd gone to the punching bag like he used to. And he had the feeling he'd got slower. His left arm dangled, and when he put his all in he heard and he felt his elbow cracking. It was autumn, and everything smelled of goodbyes.

He could hardly train or work in peace; the attacks by the Turks and Arabs were the hot topic, of course. The doors of the discos were no longer safe, Los Locos Ltd. were making their presence felt in the city, the security crews were getting attacked, the apartments weren't safe any more, the big takeover was on the horizon, they were already at the bar in the Wöhler Brothers' strip club, AK & Co. were negotiating, the man behind the mirrors was channelling the light and directing the rays on to Hannover, *is a pact a pact?* Yeah, yeah, I'm in, I'm in on it, of course. We need peace and quiet. Business. Free ticket from Berlin. The Lebanese twin brothers had offered him a certain security, via middlemen. It seemed they had connections to the Los Locos boys in the city. He was to keep calm and not fight on the frontlines. It wasn't that simple.

He spread the photos out like a fan. Pushed the ash-tray to the edge of the table.

In the old days he would have taken a different tone with that stupid cheapskate at the bar. Fuck one glass of bubbly or prosecco. It was a matter of principle. It was about business. He had to be there for both, for the women and the guests. The days when the girls liked to pull a fast one were over, long gone. He'd always said what was the main thing in the training sessions he ran with Beatriz. Money, of course. That was only one part of it though. Making people feel at ease. Creating regulars. Comfort factors. Forget the peanuts. Do we want to be high class? Yes, we do.

We have the best drinks and the best girls. He'd even sent Mandy 2 and two others who seemed reliable to him, who wanted to keep working for him, on a cock-tail course. Even though he only offered long drinks and two or three cocktails. Caipirinha and Mojito and Cuba Libre. The rum and Coke days were over. He'd even offered them employment contracts. But the girls preferred to work freelance. No one wants a 400-euro contract plus extra in the rooms, either, they'd rather freelance, and sure, there's plenty of cash in hand. Until recently he'd had an employee behind the bar, a great girl, but she went to Munich, said she'd got an offer from some classy joint. Letters from the Job Centre. Every hour they spent in the rooms was noted down on his books, although the extras up there were their business. But whoever did the bar got a kind of wage. He was in the process of bankrupting himself. Thanks to the 2002 law. But he wanted to move with the times and once the starting difficulties were overcome, once his *small but perfectly formed* club found its feet again in the stream of the times and the money... bugger that Bielefeld Count and his Austrian business partners, those two were always preaching you had to be big, think big and the RED-LIGHT-SECTOR share or something like that...

And he offset or paid for the stripping classes for the pole behind the bar as well. He'd even had these two student girls for a while who only wanted to dance, but now they go up to the rooms as well. The cash is just too tempting, it's always that way.

What was this arsehole doing back in town? The guy, that dirty rag, almost went behind bars for that professor back then, did time on remand, *ship ahoy*, because he was married to his daughter or together with her at least and originally confessed to the shots from the hunting rifle. Some dumb kid bled to death in the dirt back then, even though he hadn't even stolen the professor's car in the first place. Boom, boom.

Old stories. What was true? After all these years. Stories and legends that didn't interest him; he had work to do, he had to take care of his business, his staff and the girls. 'Once the door's closed it's all about money, that's all, I mean, obviously. We bitch and chat away down at the bar, just the way you do talk, *Sex and the City*, right, and this girl and that girl's doing bareback now, blow-outs, ha ha, right, and this girl and that girl... it's just chatting, and it does us good in a way, we have a lot of laughs, that's all part of it in a way!'

'Once the door's closed it's all about money.'

'Everything all right, Hans?'

'Yeah, yeah, Mandy. Just talking to myself.'

The cellar underneath the cellar. In one of the corners is a table with a wooden top, where the rails of an electric railway run between tiny stations and mountainsides. And the artefacts, the antiques, rest on velvet on the shelves.

315

'Put that thing away. What's that crap about?'

'Yeah, yeah, sure. You love the double barrels.'

'If they're loaded with diamonds.'

'It's not as simple as you seem to think.' Hans puts the rare hybrid creature of revolver, brass knuckles and knife back on the shelf. He runs a hand over his face, smells the oil, smells the grease. It's a good smell. He takes care of the artefacts, the antiques, oils them regularly. 'It's from the Dutch army. Late nineteenth, early twentieth century. A bastard. Practically unusable. It'd rip your fist off if you fired it. Because there's no barrel. Large calibre. Nine point five. Custom made. It's such a freak show, doesn't even make sense in close combat. The knife's like a mini-bayonet. The grip's a knuckle-duster. The blade's only fixed with a single screw. The trigger doesn't have a guard. Officers used to carry them.' He reaches back into the shelf, inserts his fingers into the brass knuckles of the grip. 'One of the curiosities in my little collection.'

'Is it worth something, at least?'

'Oh, yes. It is. Two or three thousand. I can do you a pick 'n' mix bag. Put this 1892 Schönberger on top for example.'

'What?'

Hans walks over to another shelf. 'A self-loading pistol, Bauhaus style although it's from much earlier, with a beautifully designed slim barrel. See that ring on the butt? You can hang it on your key ring, this one.'

'Get off my back with this crap.'

'What's up? Haven't we got all the time in the world? The paper's over there. Our pretty coloured pictures. You can take it.'

'Can I offer you something else?'

'Excuse me. Aren't I a terrible host? We have to have

a drink together, to business and to silence. They're almost all display models here. They don't shoot. I've got a gun possession licence but the firing pins have been removed. On most of them. Springer Urvater, old as the hills, that's the right tipple for you and me.'

Hans twists the lid off the bottle, the one he took out of the safe that afternoon. He goes over to the table in the corner with the large wooden top, where he sets up his electric railway. He takes the one glass balanced between the rails and the mountains and the houses, and goes back over to the little desk where the bundles of cash are spread out, the other glass between them. He fills both glasses. The arsehole takes one and looks around the room. 'Nice place you've got here.'

'Yes, nice and quiet.'

'A real hobby cellar.'

'You mean because of my electric railway? I never had one as a child. Always wanted one. But my father was a simple man, a simple steel worker. There weren't any train sets for Christmas.'

'Railways, weapons, diamonds... You lead a fulfilled life, Hans.'

'You could put it like that. Bourgeois values and Jules Verne's visions.'

'What?'

'Old weapons, the nineteenth century. The eighteenth century. And then technological progress. First duels, then mass murder. *Facing the Flag*. I read that as a kid. It's always fascinated me.'

He takes a shiny dark wood box off the shelf, opens the lid and tips the box so that the arsehole can see the two long-barrelled flintlock pistols in their velvet-lined compartments. 'Got these at auction last year. The miraculous perfection of outmoded technology. The powder pans have rainproof closing mechanisms. A wonder of fine mechanics from old Master Prochaska in Bohemia.'

'The Czechs. Weapons and crystal. You should be running a museum, Hans.'

'I should be living on an island in the middle of the sea, where nobody bothers me.'

He puts the box back and raises his glass. They're facing each other between the shelves where the weapons rest on velvet, where small cardboard boxes are kept full of train set parts, a few books, wooden boxes in which Hans keeps some of his larger exhibits. The arsehole raises his glass too and they drink.

'The rocks, I want to see the rocks,' says the arsehole, drinks another sip, 'Go on, give me one of the rocks.'

'No can do. They don't belong to me. I'm just storing them.'

'You tell me how badly business is going, you tell me about your troubles, and you don't want to bugger off with the stuff?'

'Take your hood off!'

'What?'

'Take your stupid hood off so I can see your face properly.'

'What's all this crap about?'

'Please.'

The man puts his glass aside, puts both hands up to the hood of his white tracksuit jacket and pulls it back. Hans stares into his furrowed face.

'You look fucked. That's why you're talking so much crap. They'd just wipe you out.'

The man sits down on the chair. Puts his hands on the money. 'I want a hundred thousand.'

'I can't give you a hundred thousand. Tax back

payments, business expenses, alimony, extra charges, it's all killing me, who do you think I am, for fuck's sake? This isn't the fucking Pascha, this isn't Cologne. I can give you what I've got here. And I've got no guarantee you won't run around talking. You don't know what you're letting yourself in for, kid.'

'Show me the rocks. If you don't show me the rocks I'm leaving. And if I don't leave...'

'Yeah, yeah, your other man. I know. And what do you expect to get out of it? Enlightenment? The source of eternal youth?'

'Show me the rocks. I want to see them.'

Hans is in his office. Music echoing, voices, laughter, a busy night tonight, the girls going up the stairs to the rooms with the guests or into the two mirrored rooms behind the bar where the showers must have been before. Hans found plans in the safe years ago, the floor plans for the admin building of the old galvanizing works, along with the little jewellery box and the bottle of Springer Urvater. Voices, laughter, now and then someone knocks at the door and he says, 'Yes, come in,' and then he says, 'Later, later, not now, I have to go out for a bit.' He doesn't know how long he's been sitting here now. The bottle in front of him. In the corner, the black-and-white glow of the monitor showing the entrance area. Slowly, very slowly he moves his arm until the sleeve of his jacket slides back and he can see his Glashütte. Past one.

He doesn't know what to do with the body. The man's down there between the shelves. His shoulder hurts. He doesn't know how he got the Bren out of the box. *A little tour of the exhibition.* What should he do with the man now? His contact at the cop shop won't tell that he asked after him if they start looking for him. If anyone does start looking for him. But the link is there. The student. The cop. He'd have to get rid of all of them. But the cop's just small fry, waiting for retirement and cashing in. And someone else is waiting. He has to find out where. He has to go down there and search his pockets. He's lost too much time already. Nothing must go wrong now. He remembers he does have an address, remembers the cop got him that address. He gets up. Then he sits back down again. The bottle in front of him is almost empty. He remembers the man drank a lot. Filled up his glass several times. He didn't have to talk him into drinking like he'd planned. What had he planned at all for the evening? He doesn't know any more. Gets up and then sits back down again. Was it a coincidence that a freight train came clattering along the tracks just as he took the huge Bren out of the box? But the walls are thick. The music echoes across the bricks and mortar, through the rock and stones. And the explosions weren't as loud as he'd imagined they would be. But actually he hadn't imagined anything.

'We have to be cold and clear-headed now,' he said, and then he turned to the black-and-white picture on the monitor, two men outside his front door, one pressing the bell. Two coats, and the one ringing the bell was wearing a woolly hat. The nights were getting chilly. He saw the two of them complaining, laughing, putting their hands in their coat pockets and taking them out again, turning to each other, laughing. Klaus saw them on the monitor in the niche by the door, then probably saw them through the spyhole, pressed the buzzer and let them in. Come on in, friends. His second man was sick. He'd probably called in sick because everything was blowing up in the city at the moment. They hadn't come to his place yet. He had an insurance policy but you could never be sure. Too many interests in the game. Interests who knew nothing about the rocks. Which was a good thing. Two or three days ago he'd seen an Audi with Berlin registration plates over in the car park. There was a meeting with AK and the others lined up any day now. He had to check his calendar. Was it a coincidence that the man, the arsehole, turned up now and wanted money, maybe a couple of stones? But the man was a fool who knew nothing, knew little. But where did he know it from? He didn't know any more. Didn't know nothing.

Hans saw the walls disappearing, saw them turning transparent as glass, a big glass cell, saw the ladies stepping out of the mirrors, saw red mist drifting through the rooms of his club, saw himself down in the cellar, taking the big bulky Bren out of its crate.

'Working in a nightclub is pretty hard work. Yeah. Of course it's relaxed and laid-back as well. I used to be in a brothel before and, no, that was too much like, how can I put it, a conveyor belt. You just sit there and wait, sit outside your door, we had these bar stools kind of thing, and then you'd often only get short tricks, mostly blow jobs, and then they'd always try to bargain with you, which I can't stand at all, it's the biggest crap of all, a lot of arseholes, a lot of foreigners, not that I mind foreigners, but the kind of guys who can't get it cheap enough, enough to make you puke, but you block it... or I just block it all out, ignore it. And it's a whole different system here. Hm. I prefer it to the brothel, definitely, for me, other girls probably see it differently. It all... everything has its pros and cons. You have to... I mean I always have to watch out, what with the drinking and that, to make sure you don't get fucked up by all that, but when I think about it, this here seems to be the better working situation. The boss is OK. And I wouldn't exactly say boss, I'm freelance... H., he's... I feel good working here for now. Sure, there are things where I say, where I'd say, hey listen, there's this thing... And I get the feeling he listens. Working in an apartment is always another option, I think. Maybe in the future sometime.'

Hans leans over the man. The white hoodie vanishing into the holes in his chest, the fabric folding into the body. It's not white any more either. The Bren is on the table, in between the train tracks, a couple of the green hundred-euro notes curled up into tubes by the heat of the barrel and the chambers. Did he really want to offer him that twenty thousand?

Could he have walked out if he'd taken the cash? Where had the man got his information? And where should he take the body? He'd heard about the man at the crematorium but that wasn't safe. Possibly just a legend. *Bren Mark 1, Product of Czechoslovakia.* He threw the separate parts in different canals, later, the waterways slicing up the west of the city between the old disappeared or converted factories. There was also an Enfield Bren almost identical to his type of Bren. Only the fold-out bipod was constructed slightly differently, apparently. He could have checked in his books. He'd bought the giant gun four years ago from a Czech. The guy had been all over the Balkans in the nineties, selling old Russian goods and leftover stock from the Czechoslovakian army to the crazies in the wars there. So they said. Never been used, allegedly. Complete with a charger clip. Most of his pieces were absolutely harmless. An old Nagant revolver with a shorter grip and a shorter barrel. He'd read a lot about it as a child. *How the Steel Was Tempered, The Dagger,* the Reds and the Whites used the legendary Nagant revolver, or that was what made it legendary. White Guards, Red Guards. He went to the shelves, stepping around the body, and rested his hand on the cool Nagant. He'd never tried it out. The chambers had been loaded since he'd bought it. A few of his pieces had no firing pin, couldn't be fired and had no ammunition either. The Ruger Blackhawk, for example. He takes a few steps. Rests his hand on the metal. From 1955. Magnum calibre. The barrel's empty though. An homage to the old Western revolvers coming back into fashion all of a sudden through the movies. In America. For a few years now he's been trying to get hold of a Winchester, like Wyatt Earp, like Butch Cassidy. He turns around, looks at the body flat on its back between the shelves, shakes his head, moves his shoulders, doesn't know what day and what time it is now. Moves his arm very slowly until he can see his Glashütte. Past one.

The upper body is completely twisted, like an S. The legs stretched straight backwards, the arms flung out on either side. The lower back, the rump flat on the floor, the upper body like a human spiral. The bloody holes in the chest. He doesn't know how many shots hit him. 'You bloody idiot.'

He takes a few steps back to the shelf with the Nagant revolver and picks it up off the velvet. He still knows how much he spent on all the velvet backings. Little canvas sacks next to each weapon, little boxes he had made, big wooden crates for the larger weapons, the carbines, the machine guns – he doesn't have many. He takes the revolver, aims it at the body and fires. He has to pull the trigger with all his might. Feels the mechanical procedures inside the small machine. Feels the cylinder, the drum, pressing against the barrel at the front before the pin hits the bullet. Only a small, tiny detonation. A

PAFF, barely audible. He sees the bullet hit the floor, right next to the man's head, and he ducks because he's scared of the ricochet, but nothing bounces back from the floor, hammers into his flesh, enters his body with a whistle. The Nagant is quiet, just like he read years ago. The cylinder closes up to the barrel as it fires. The NKVD, the bloody Reds' secret service, used this same gun with silencers. Executions. Silent killings. Because the Belgians who constructed this over-constructed shooting iron wanted to create a one-of-a-kind revolver. A gun that kept its detonations inside its metal casing. Because the cylinder and barrel form a single unit through the mechanism. The only revolver for which a silencer made sense.

Hans puts the barrel against his forehead. No one would hear him down here. On the first shot, he had gripped his right lower arm with his left fist. The shot still went wrong. It wasn't the first one that evening. He feels the cool muzzle on his temple, shifts it and feels it on his forehead.

The phone had rung and rung while he was up in the office. He pulls the trigger and watches the bottle of Springer burst. He flings the Nagant against the shelves. Grabs the man by the shoulders, moves the body to and fro. How heavy he is. Surprisingly little blood on the floor. He has to get a tarpaulin; hasn't he got plastic sheets in the storeroom? Then he remembers the small linen bag the man held in his hand, one small canary-yellow diamond and one boron-blue on the floor by the man's outstretched hand, and he picks them up. Clenches his fist and feels the sharp, cool edges of the pea-sized brilliant cut, feels the tiny flat surface on the upper side, feels the rays of the minimum thirty-two facets in the top section and the minimum twenty-four facets in the lower section pressing through skin and bone. He squats on the floor while the building's in motion.

'My first contact was when I was eighteen. It was on the Black Sea, that's where I was from. All I wanted was to leave home, all I wanted was to go somewhere I'd have opportunities. Somewhere I could earn proper money. My brother-in-law's sister asked me. That was in V., and it was mostly tourists there. It went OK. Yes. Sex was sex, you know, I've never thought much about it. It went pretty well, because I knew my brother-in-law's sister, because it was a good contact. Boris is his name. I had my routine there, OK, *budyet*, *budyet*, and I made good money. It was always OK, only the Brits were bad, sometimes, they were... they were annoying. But it was a really good place there in V. And especially in the season, I earned so much, I thought at the time it was really good money. It was a lot. I always worked for myself there. I spoke quite good German from school and I was always really good at it and it got even better with the German tourists. I had friends there as well, girls I knew from before, could be they had someone because there was someone behind them who controlled it all. I always worked for myself though. And I knew early on I'd soon be going abroad. Then I came to Germany with my friend L. We did it together. We flew on a plane. She knew who had the right contacts for our work permits. And then we had Germans in the family, yeah really. We've settled down here in the city now... it's home now, I'd say. I want to say. We speak Russian when we meet up, of course we do. The Black Sea, sometimes I think of it. Of course I do. But I feel like a German now. That's a good thing.'

He holds the leg in his hand. The bone makes things difficult. He puts it down carefully on the model railway table, which he's covered with a plastic sheet. The body is on another sheet. He fetched a large steak knife out of the storeroom, he's got all sorts of tools in there, the knife was there when he took the place over at the end of '92, with other kitchen stuff, knives, crates of crockery, the guy from the Ruhr Valley must have had big plans, maybe he wanted to open up a restaurant somewhere or put a kitchen into the club, the first sex nightclub with hot meals, but there must be somewhere else already doing that, not a bad idea, Hans had thought at the time, he remembered it when he fetched the knife. It's not easy to cut off a leg. His father used to do his own slaughtering and he wanted Hans to do an apprenticeship as a slaughterer, but then he started as a gardener to piss off his old man.

He turns away and vomits. 'For fuck's sake, you bloody arsehole. Hans the Hatchet. Yeah, yeah. Forget it.' He cuts off the leg below the hip joint, using the giant knife and a hammer.

He takes a deep breath, picks up the Springer and drinks a gulp out of the bottle, rinses his mouth and spits the liquor on the floor. He sits down next to the man by the wall and stretches out his legs, three legs side by side now. He makes sure he doesn't put his feet on the plastic sheet. 'Was I supposed to go telling people I was a gardener and not a slaughterer? What do you think, mate? They'd only have taken the piss. Hans the Hatchet, he can fix it. That's not bad at all. But Hans the Gardener? Nah. And I bet there were always a few were scared of me chopping them up. Like you, now.'

He lights a cigarette. He's put the Bren back in the crate. He feels sick and he feels light. Absolutely empty. As though his body were an elongated balloon, all he can feel is his head and his brain. 'It's your own fault.

You stupid arsehole. I can only pay for my own ticket. You can't just come here and fuck everything up for me. What did you think was going to happen? You come here and you want to fuck everything up for me. You know what's always been the most important for me? My peace and quiet. I just wanted to run my club in peace. Everything's going to change here soon anyway. And now I want to earn my retirement fund and you come here and fuck everything up for me.' The man's eyes are wide, his eyeballs twisted so that only the whites and a tiny slice of the pupils are visible; he's looking inside his own head. His mouth is slightly open, as though he wanted to say something. He touches the face with his fingertips, slowly stroking its stubble, puts his hand on the man's hair. 'You and me. We messed up.'

He gets up, throws his cigarette away, stumbles against the wall, steps in his vomit, thin and yellow, he hasn't eaten since the afternoon. He leans against the wall and then sits down again. 'Sorry I have to chop you up but I have to get you out of here somehow. I don't think I can take your head off.' He laughs and feels the saliva rising again. He takes a deep breath in and out again, looking into the light of the neon tubes on the ceiling. If he turns his head a little he can see the foot, lying with the toes down on his model railway table. He stands up, takes the cloth he'd stashed the money under, and wraps the leg up in it. It feels cold. Under the plastic sheet, he sees the train tracks as if through frosted glass, the little green hills, the houses and stations. He takes the wrapped-up leg carefully in both hands, goes to the steel door leading to the deeper cellars and catacombs, undoes the big iron bolt and opens the door, the leg jammed under one arm. He goes back again to fetch his Maglite. He takes a slow walk along the dark corridor, absolutely empty, the

327

beam of the torch ahead of him on the floor.

When he comes back without the leg it seems as if the man has moved slightly, crawled a foot or two towards the steel door as though he wanted to follow his leg. The torso has slipped off the plastic sheet, which is now suddenly crumpled like an unmade bed, and he sees the blood on the stone floor underneath the sheet, dark stains. He bolts the door again, locking it as well. He has to drag the body to the back exit; he'll park his car right outside. The man's blood-stained trousers are on the model railway table, where the leg was not long ago. Hans puts his hands in the pockets and finds a necklace with a white and black stone on it, a small piece of rock with a hole worn into it by the sea.

He puts it in his pocket. Squatting next to the man to search his hoodie, he sees that the white, slightly too large underpants are wet at the front. He tries not to look at the black and red stump of leg. The rats will eat his leg. And the bone? But who's going to find it down there? He'd thought about dragging the whole man out there. But that would start to smell. The stench of decay must be a horrible thing. And he wasn't sure whether tramps didn't bed down in the tangled corridors and cellars now and then, perhaps in the winter. What had be been thinking when he cut off the leg, when he wanted to dismember the whole body? Disposing of him piece by piece? He'd seen this film once where they'd got rid of a whole body, taken it apart and gutted it. Squeezed the intestines down the sewers, chopped everything up smaller and smaller, squeezed it into the sewers. It might even have been a mistake just to leave the leg here. But it was too late. The traces were there. The hoodie pockets are empty. He remembers the man's coat is still up in the office. He goes to the other, smaller door, opens it... and as he steps through the third door, above the little metal staircase, into Storeroom 2 where he keeps the cleaning fluids and scrubbers and brooms and boxes of toilet blocks and piles of bog paper, he instantly hears the music again, thinks he can hear the voices and footsteps again, the girls laughing, the banknotes crackling, the glasses clinking. He closes the third, inconspicuous door behind him, has to bend down because the entrance and exit is so low, sometimes he thinks everyone knows the *down there* is down there, the place he discovered in 1994, and everyone knows what he gets up to down there, but all he does is model-making, looking after his collection, sits there in peace a long while after closing time, listens to the silence, drinks a cognac while he works on his trains or takes care of his collection and admires it. Railways and weapons, the story of modern times. He goes into the office, which has direct access to the bar room. He sees the coat – Drykorn as he later notices, a pretty good brand, you could call a make of schnapps that too – hanging neat and tidy over the back of a chair. *For beautiful people.* Two glasses still on the desk. Hadn't he offered him the Springer downstairs? It's hard to piece together the events of the past hour and a half.

He takes the coat and goes through the pockets, side pockets, inside pockets. Finds a form from a letting agency. A key ring with three big keys and two smaller ones; one of them looks like it belongs to a bike lock. Finds taxi receipts, one from today. Hasn't the arsehole even got a car? In a small inside pocket, one he didn't feel straight away when he patted down the fabric, he finds a small purse. Baby-pink leather. *Are you taking the piss?* He sits down, pushes the two empty glasses around the table. An ID card with a photo of a different man.

A man with the same name his contact at the cop shop gave him.

Issued over ten years ago. The photo clearly even older. Gelled-back hair. All the man down there has left is short grey stubble. Hans adds up the numbers. He's seven years older. But this guy's bloody shot to fuck. *Spare us the puns, arsehole.*

'What?'

He goes over to Big Klaus and tells him he has to pop out but he'll be back by closing time. 'Call me if anything happens.' Seven or eight guests at the bar. He knows two of them; they've been here often. Considering the city's blowing up some nights, it's all going pretty well. But there's a trade fair on right now – plumbing equipment? He can't remember, although he always knows when which trade fair is on. Mandy's mixing drinks. He'll have to go through the applications soon; he needs a proper bar woman. The girls take turns but he needs them for the rooms. The student temping for him called in sick. Bloody chaos. He goes to the bar for a moment but then he remembers he has to drive.

'Everything alright, Mandy?'

'Everything's fine, Hans.' He needs a proper barwoman, for fuck's sake, as soon as possible. Mandy ought to be sitting with the guests. A nice milf would be best, reliable, experienced. No going to the rooms. The five girls have got enough on their hands. Ordering prosecco or Red Riding Hood. Sitting between the guests, leaning to the left, leaning to the right. He can't stand the little cans of prosecco but they're all the rage. 'Give me a small Johnnie Black.'

'With pleasure, Hans.' He feels like he's inside that stupid computer game he sometimes plays on his laptop in the office. Red-Light Sector Manager. Some cheap crap he got for Christmas from AK a year or two back. Plus a bottle of Johnnie Black. Better than nothing. He almost never manages to manage the chaos in the game. Either he gets the wrong girls together, too old or too cheap, or he forgets the cleaning ladies, or he saves money on the door staff – even though he's been doing fine in real life for all these years now. Then another time he spends all his money on exclusive fittings for the rooms.

And when someone's having sex in the rooms all you see is a big red pulsating heart, and that annoys him. Ten years ago, could be longer actually, he had the idea – he remembers the stupid early-morning bullshitting in the twenty-three-hour bar that probably doesn't even exist any more, but he's not sure, he hasn't been there for years – he had the idea for this game, for a game where you have to run a brothel, a bar, a nightclub. But the others had just laughed. It consoles him though that the inventor of this cheap crap version certainly won't have made a fortune out of it. And he wastes the money, the virtual money, on fitting out the rooms, buys the best drinks for the bar, employs a professional barwoman and then saves too much on the cleaning crew, for fuck's sake, two old ladies for the cleaning must be enough, and then he forgets to call the other girls who want to work for him in time because he doesn't notice in time that some of them are off sick or suddenly don't feel like it any more, because he, the manager with the mouse, isn't sharing the clients out properly or not coordinating the bonus points and the strip shows well enough, it's a much bigger place than his, and then he suddenly has problems with his taxes even though he always clicks on Call Lawyer in the menu, and his club on the laptop descends into utter chaos every time and then goes bust. *You can all of you kiss my arse.*

The voices, the women, the guests. The little Russian girl is upstairs again. She's got real talent, she can magic up a drink out of every guest's heart, or wherever else they come from. And take every man upstairs, whether he wants to or not. Business is going well. He pushes the empty glass towards Mandy 2, who's been watching him for a few minutes now, smoking a cigarette, 'See you later,' 'See you later, Hans.'

He turns off before the junction. The side road is empty and he parks right on the corner. Turns the key, rests his head on the steering wheel and then leans back. He fetched two bed sheets out of Storeroom 1 but now he's annoyed because what use are they anyway? Even more stuff for him to get rid of. He'll have to scrub the floor of his little cathedral with cleaner's solvent, have to see what he's got for his cleaning crew in Storeroom 2. When he went for a piss he saw the paper was nearly running out. He ought to call, not that they suddenly have none left. He's worrying about all this crap although he's got the man in the boot of his car. *It's not crap. Shut the fuck up, will you.* He hears the rumble of planes, far above the dark houses. The post office has its own flight gates at the big airport outside the city, where the planes take off and land even at night.

He hasn't fallen asleep, he's just staring at the night and the walls. The morning leans in slowly over the buildings. No pale stripe yet, no dark blue yet, the black of the night slowly blending into it at the edges, but he can tell he hasn't much time left in darkness. He opens the window, the cool air touches his face, and he throws his cigarette end on the pavement and turns the key. He doesn't close the window as he drives.

Through the opened blinds he sees the first pink behind the buildings, behind the central station, the big grey sarcophagus. Perhaps he's wrong though; a neon ad is reflected in the glass, the light sliced into pieces by the slats of the blind. He's sitting by the dead girl. He thinks of how he pressed the revolver to his forehead a few hours ago. Four in the morning. Four thirty-something. He hears the trains rumbling along the tracks towards the central station or away from it. He picks up the body, lifts it and feels her small breasts against his chest. She's wearing only a T-shirt. His shirt gets wet; it must be her saliva. He's put on leather gloves. A small, light girl. He's already got her halfway over his shoulder. He stumbles back. The girl on the floor again. He puts his hand on her face. Squats down in front of her. She's still warm, or is it his hand? The glove from his right hand is on the floor between her legs. He's so tired he could fall asleep on her dead body. *Oh, my Sleeping Beauty.*

He searches the dump of a flat. The glove back on now. The two tiny rooms. The bathroom. Was she turning tricks for that arsehole? He finds a bag of crystal. Another one of H. He chucks them both down the toilet and flushes. He lifts her up. How light she is. *Weary now, I go to rest.*

He drapes her arm around his shoulder, puts his own arm under her armpit and lugs her to the door.

He takes the key with him. Puts it in his coat pocket with the guy's mobile phone. It was turned off. He doesn't find another phone in the flat. He knows who rents the place out. He'll clear everything out. Just a few clothes in the wardrobe. A bed, a table, two chairs. A camping stove in the kitchen. With a gas bottle. Couple of empty cartons, milk, wine, juice, half a loaf of bread. Butter, gone yellow already. Maybe he should leave the girl here. Put her into bed. Cover her over. Her eyes open suddenly, he puts his hands in their leather gloves around her neck, then he picks up a pillow, presses it against her face, leans on the cushion, but he doesn't feel any movement. A holdall full of dirty washing next to the bed.

He's driving. Broad, snow-covered fields on either side. He shakes his head. I must have nodded off for a moment. The streets are empty. The lights of the airport. He turns off. He feels the city behind him. The sky's getting lighter. A dark blue on the horizon. He looks in the rear-view mirror, has the feeling he's driving backwards, goes down to third gear and doesn't know why, he sees the Bren's explosions in his rear-view mirror, he goes back up to fourth, a dark red glow ahead of him, a dark red glow behind him, he puts the radio on, he's been talking for a few minutes and he doesn't know what he's saying, 'Oh yes, oh yes, everything's taking it's course, comrades, march so boldly in step,' he shakes himself, smokes, adverts, he turns the radio dial, music, voices, Info Radio, around the clock, *on ninety-two point ba-da-da-dum, buy...* winter's on its way, what can he do, he has to go to Berlin, he has to get out of here, in the long term, comrades march on t'wards the light, the bloody alimony's wiping him out, hardly anyone knows I've got a daughter, a man has to dream, doesn't he? We are the brave mire soldiers, we march into the mire with our spades, we march into the mire as night fades.

They're whispering in the boot behind him. He stopped briefly at the building site. We need ballast. He found the washing line in the flat. I've got a plan! *I love it when a plan comes together.* Don't start in with that A-Team crap. No one remembers that crap nowadays. I used to watch it when I was young. You're not that old. You're not that young. You look tired, girl. We'll wash your hair one last time, we'll put your little head in the shower, nice and careful. So soft. Where do the traces lead? The traces lead back. No, that's crap. We're going where we're going. You look tired, arsehole. And they're whispering in the boot, and he's talking and talking. You have to keep on functioning. Keep on keeping on. That much is for sure. Your pensions are safe. *Weary now, I go to rest, close my eyes in slumber blest. Father, may thy watchful eye, guard the bed in which I lie.*

And then there's suddenly a silence and a coolness, inside him, behind him, ahead of him, and he opens the side window, breathes the cool morning air, his breath steaming, he looks into the dawn behind the woods and he knows, suddenly, that everything's going to be fine.

MY HUCKLEBERRY FRIEND

I.

I haven't got a car. I take the tram every morning and I have to change once. I've often thought about getting my driving licence. But I'm fifty-three now and to be honest I don't know if I'd manage it. I could kind of imagine it, me learning to drive, but my husband didn't use to have a driving licence either, it wasn't unusual in the GDR not to have a car. Or having to wait forever and a day for the car to come. My husband, my ex-husband I mean, he got his driving licence in the mid-nineties – we were still married then. Sometimes I think it was because he was out and about in the car so much, and that was because of his new job, out of town and long trips and all, it was because of that it all went belly up or started to go belly up, but there were other reasons too, so many other things came into it, the way it always or usually is, and we'd been married nearly twenty-five years and all, met, got together, got married, had kids, that's the way it was back then.

That's the kind of thing I think about when I get on the tram in the morning to go to work. All the girls I know from work have a car. They can't even imagine me riding around for almost an hour, or three quarters of an hour, depending, halfway across town. But it's much cheaper either way, they have to admit that, especially now that petrol's going up and up. And I'm trying to save up. Every now and then I take the train to my sister's place, she lives just outside Meißen, and there's this village there, just after Leisnig, with all these little houses, and some of them look empty, right on the edge of the woods, and I always imagine buying a place there one day, because it's not that expensive there, I made

336

enquiries one time, I mean, as a summer house or a retirement home, sounds stupid I suppose because I don't
feel that old yet, but you always have to think of these
things, at my age, although I do think I've got a good few
years to go, four or five at least, well, I do know I'll need
a car then, so I'll need my driving licence, so I can get
over there and get out of there again when I want to. We
used to have a garden once, more a weekend allotment it
was, a *dacha* as we call it round here, just outside of town
and right close to where we used to live at the time, with
a brick hut and almost four hundred square metres of
land and nice hedges all the way round the outside so
you had a bit of peace and quiet, that was the most important thing for me, but then we sold it right after the
divorce came through. That annoys me sometimes now
because it was very nice there, really it was, but our boy
wasn't interested either, wanted to go abroad even then,
Copenhagen, that's where he works now, so the money
was more important at the time.

I have to go and visit him again in Denmark, I think of
that a lot when I'm on the tram on my way to work in the
morning. I want to see the girls again, my granddaughters. And my boy as well, of course. But that's not always
that easy because of the thing with Henry, he's my boyfriend and we want to get married because we've been
together for six years now, and the chemistry's not quite
right between Henry and my granddaughters. 'You go
on your own,' he says every time, and he's got a kid as
well from his ex, so it actually works quite well for both
of us that we've both got our own thing, our own family stuff, and my boy's a bit more relaxed about it all now
as well, but for the girls their real granddad's their real
granddad. My two granddaughters. They're nine now.
My Henry's not a granddad yet, he's eight years younger

337

than me, and his son... sometimes I think he's gay but he can't get up the courage to say so, because he's the real fragile type, I like him a lot and he likes me, I think. It's fine that it's all kind of patchwork, like they say nowadays, it doesn't bother me. Henry's got a daughter as well but they've pretty much lost contact. That's a shame if you ask me, but I can understand it in a way because she's from before his first and so far only marriage, and the mother lives in Berlin, and apparently it just happened back then, as it does now and then, and the girl's really close to her new dad. Actually I don't talk about any of this to anyone, it's a private matter, although I get on alright with most of the girls, but they're all much younger than me, spring chickens, and sometimes they really do cluck-cluck in your ears, sometimes they really do tell all plus a bit of imagination, if you're not careful, so I think: Ohhh no, that's enough for now, and I can't talk about family problems with them anyway, patchwork, age and all that, they're too green behind the ears and I don't want to either. Because it's a private matter. The only one about my age is Birgit. Around fifty, I mean. But she's from the West. And she's very self-contained, very quiet and withdrawn. A bit jaded, I reckon, but who isn't in our job? A whole lot of us, I think sometimes, when I'm pretty much happy with everything. Sometimes I imagine it, the two of us, me and Birgit I mean, and how we'd laugh if I showed her my maze of a family tree, over coffee or something, and me getting all muddled up with the kids and the grandchildren and Henry's kids. Because it's really kind of funny. And because it could all be a lot worse and everyone could be uptight about it all, oh no, I'm glad it all works more or less. 'And you really think he's gay, ah, that's sweet of you to worry about him like that,' she says. When I imagine it. Even though we never talk in real life. And when I talk to my other friends, the other women, I leave out the other side. I leave out a lot. It's a bit stupid sometimes. Because they never really understand.

But if there's one thing I'm good at it's putting myself in other people's shoes, if you like. Because I've always worked with people, even back in the day when I was a hairdresser. Birgit's always joking about that, when I imagine us sitting together after work, over a coffee and a glass of wine, and then I can't help laughing, sometimes right in the middle of my work, me on top, they like that when the mature lady goes cowgirl. 'Fifty per cent of whores are former hairdressers.'

No, that's rubbish of course, 'Fifty per cent of hairdressers turn into whores,' she says then, but that's just a stupid joke, like I said. Actually I did an apprenticeship in a galvanizing factory, Galvanotechnik, we did tin plating and metal plating, but it turned out I have a bit of an asthma problem, which I didn't even know before, so then I had to leave. That was all back in the GDR. Birgit doesn't know anything about all that, or I shouldn't think she does because she's from the West. And I don't even know if she'd even be interested in all my stuff. She's almost a bit exotic, what with coming from the West, round here I mean. I don't know any other girls here from the West. I mean, I don't know that many other girls anyway, but I do know a few.

After the Wall, so almost up to the end of the nineties, from about '94 on, I was a carer for old folks. Suddenly there were hairdressers coming out of the woodwork and I wanted to try something new. That's pretty much it. I liked it, it was a good job. And I learned a lot, for later as well, for now I mean.

Changing nappies and that, the sore places, turning

their bodies, listening. Smells, peeling skin. Drips and drops. Talking. Dry flesh. Sore flesh. Being considerate. Being strict now and then. Yellowed toenails. Dying. Listening. Sometimes I talk about it with my Henry. We didn't used to know each other then. He likes listening when I talk. Sometimes. Because he's got so many things of his own to talk about when we see each other in the evenings, after a long, long day. And because I ask him, 'How was your day, old man?' That's what I call him, usually, for a while I used to call him 'boy,' that was mostly back when I was learning English, I mean freshening up my English at evening classes. I used to go straight from work. That's a while ago now though, it was before the new law. Because I had more money back then, of course. Evening classes, language classes, language-learning trips. Because you could do more cash in hand, but I'd better just shut up about that. And now it's not just because of the new law that things aren't going so well. I mean, it's still going well enough, otherwise I'd be thinking about what else to do if it wasn't working at all, but luckily it's still going alright. With my Henry as well. Because it's not like we don't have much sex. No, no, it's pretty much the opposite. My Henry's always been a brothel-goer, always has been. Because otherwise we'd never have met, would we? It wasn't at a brothel, though, of course not. I'm saying that specially, because it does happen. But as far as I can tell that's the exception that proves the rule. It was an over-40s party where I met him. And I'll tell you, I was shitting myself about giving him the whole truth, as they say. And then it turns out he's an old hand, an old punter if you like, who always used to go and visit the girls, in the brothels and in the apartments.

I miss the old trams. Those pale yellow, square

carriages. After the Wall a few of those vintage versions still used to run for a few years, as far as I can remember. They used to have this one round headlamp at the front, it looked really mysterious at night, especially in the winter. When I was a kid. And the rumbling and the screeching on the bends. And sometimes the electricity flashed and crackled between the overhead cable and the pickup, blue flashes. You had to whack the punchers really hard, the things to punch your ticket. There'd be a real bang. And you'd always get a different pattern of holes in the card. It was card, wasn't it, back then? Like the train tickets for the slow train to the countryside. When we went off to the villages. People's faces are so grey in the mornings. The man in front of me has his newspaper spread out like a sail. I read over his shoulder for a bit, to begin with. It says something about the Angels. And about the man who got shot dead by accident. I think I knew him. Not sure, though. I think he came to visit me one time. What would people think if they knew...? But really it's a good solid job. Since the new law came in the Old Man, my boss I mean, pays a flat twenty-five euros a day to the authorities, in tax I mean. Sometimes I try and work out how much pension I'll get. The morning plays in my head and muddles everything together. I'm tired today. That's unusual because I've always been an early riser. The early bird... 'dies in a storm,' this one girl used to say... could it be it's starting already, the memory loss, because I always used to remember names. She was only with me in the flat for a little while, though. She was a student. That's what she said, anyway. And that's what it said in the ad, in fact. Because the boss said people are into that kind of thing, the guests get really into it if they read 'young student', and because he thought we'd make a good combination,

341

I suppose. Like mother and daughter, that kind of thing. Now we're sometimes a real OAPs' home. When Birgit's there with me. And that girl really did use to bring books with her and revise, or read them and make notes and so on, sometimes with a laptop. She was doing law, she said. When we used to get talking now and then, when there wasn't much custom, I remember it well, that January dip two years ago, she used to tell me she wanted to be a lawyer. That's crazy if you ask me. You always think they come from rich families. But that girl was from some village and if it ever gets out she can shut up shop, she might as well just give it all up if a guest recognizes her. Just imagine, you're in court and there's some prosecutor or judge who was a real dirty bastard, and you got him really worked up so he'd keep coming back and paying, it'd be embarrassing for the both of you, but she wanted to go to the West then anyway, to a big city, maybe Berlin, or in Munich or Hamburg where you can start all over again, they're far enough away from here. She always used to drink that milky coffee. Latte macchiato. Same thing, if you ask me. She always used to bring, when she came, mostly afternoons she worked, but not every day, she only did every day in the holidays, she arranged it like that with the Old Man, so she'd always turn up with a big cardboard cup, that foam was pretty good, I have to admit, but I'm more your filter coffee kind of girl. I drink much too much of it and recently I've been getting heartburn so I take this stomach gel. Not on prescription. I've got private health insurance so I always try to do as little as possible on prescription and with a doctor and all that, because then your rates go up, but I've got something back every year so far, touch wood. Because I don't want to get sick, I mean who does, but it's always bad for us because no one pays your wages when you're ill. You end up sitting at home and not earning anything. Or lying in hospital, if the worst comes to the worst. As far as the insurance is concerned I'm a self-employed masseuse and osteopath. And that's pretty much what I do, not much difference all in all, most of our *kleeche*. Hardly any of the girls knows that word nowadays, and Birgit certainly doesn't. *Kleeche*. It's a Saxon word, that's what it is. It means hard work. My forehead leans against the window for a moment, but it's dirty and that's no good for your skin. I have to really watch out, I do a lot for my skin, I like to spend a lot of money on it... I bet I'd make a good sales girl for cosmetics.

When I told Henry the other day that I'm thinking about offering light domination stuff, I mean that I want to... I mean, I can't just start from scratch as a dominatrix, you can't just jump in at the deep end, but the idea that it might be something I could do, professionally I mean, I'd had it for a while. I've already met up with Feliz one time, she used to be called Beatriz, and she gave me a kind of crash course, I mean I shouldn't think I'll ever be a real Lady L. 'Light domination,' it should say in my ad, I'll tell the Old Man that soon, and then I'll see how it goes. 'From Benefits to Dominatrix' it said in the paper the other day. That was on the tram as well. This girl really did get a grant to register a freelance business. Massage. Seems to be a real trend. Seeing as we're just passing Inland Revenue. Used to be the Russians in there. Huge army barracks. When the tanks came out of there we'd stand on the pavement and stare. That was something. They must have been going to practice or manoeuvres or something. And I remember when there was a fire over in the old tram depot. That must have been in the early seventies. The fire went on all night. And we stood by the windows and watched the flickering of the flames. You could see it for miles around, it was incredible. I come down to earth, and I'm almost at the park. No, I'm not, not yet. The big square block of the hotel, the big grey and white thing rears up alongside us. I must have nodded off just before the Inland Revenue. Over in the hotel, in the bar, it was exclusive, you could only pay with West German currency there if I remember rightly, my friend Mia used to work in the hotel when there was a trade fair on. I always used to call her Pia for some reason. She got good hard currency for it back then, sometimes even dollars, she used to tell me. Over a few glasses of bubbly, she always used to have the really good stuff, Mumm and Söhnlein and all the brands, so I'd always think, wow, she must be rolling in it, and then she starts telling me, once we'd got through two bottles, and to start with I couldn't believe it, never mind good little Pia-Mia, because that's how she came across sometimes, she was actually a real sly one, the way you think sometimes. I mean I'd always heard there were girls that used to go there when there was a trade fair on. The ones who were into that kind of thing. I mean, it must have been exciting at the time, and you can't compare it to how we work now. Twice a year, two or three nights' work in a row, and it wasn't exactly hard graft, not the way Mia told me anyway. I wouldn't have gone for it back then, though. I mean of course you think about it and that, but it was in the eighties, and me still happy as Larry with my husband, not that that always had anything to do with it. Pia was too. As far as I remember. Married, kid at school. One of the two was her real name, and the other one I just gave her as a joke, can't remember how I came up with it. Wasn't there an actress, Pia Cramling? Mia Farrow? She just wanted to find out what it was like. I always used to wonder how

344

much her husband must have known, later. I mean, all that money, all that lovely hard currency, she can't have hidden it or spent it all on herself. And there must have been some girls who hoped they'd find their rich West German prince to fetch them over the Wall. Or to come back for the next trade fair. And then she'd wrap him round her little finger. It does happen now and then, that you really like someone. Now and then. That fire took days to go out, I can't get it out of my mind now. The stink of it, for days. There was a lot of rubber and plastic and oil. Funny, me thinking of it today, remembering it right now, when I've been coming past the old tram depot for years now. They built it all up again pretty quickly afterwards.

I'd better not nod off again or I'll end up at the terminal loop out at Bürgerruhe. Is the Bürgerruhe restaurant still there, I wonder? Went for the odd meal there with my first husband. We'd usually get the tram there. Past Pretty Peepers Alley where the caravans used to be. No, I wouldn't have done that. Not in one of those mouldy caravans. Someone says that's where the Old Man started off. But I can't imagine that and you know how much crap people talk. It's already half seven now. Nearly. I start at nine. But I like to get there an hour early. Drink a coffee. Make a pot to start off with. Open the window. Air the apartment. The smells of the last day, the last night. Sometimes I meet someone on the stairs. I think they know pretty well what goes on in our place. Some of them, at least. They all say hello nice and friendly but that's normal anyway. I've heard other stories, though. I've been in the same building from the beginning so I don't know what it's like in other places. The boss knows where he can have what kind of apartment. Over in the west of the city he owns whole buildings. That's what

I've heard, anyway. We're passing the museum. We often used to go there with school, class trips, to the museum. Ethnology. We'd stand in front of the cabinets of artefacts, pots, shards, amulets. One time we went in a yurt, a kind of tent it was, from Mongolia. When we passed the zoo earlier I thought I'd like to go there for a coffee with Birgit, but that would be too intimate, you go there with children or your family. Maybe the vintage teahouse in the Game Park. If it's still there. I have to ask my Henry one time if it's still there, my old man. All I need now is to start calling him 'daddy'. Can't stand that. That's what my mum used to call my dad. 'Daddy, can you come here please!' Oh boy, I'm drifting off again... But sometimes there's something in the air, there's... I don't want to say 'vibrations', but it feels like you've already been... how can I put it... kind of like a déjà vu. You know what, I think I'd better get off two stops early and walk the rest. I need to get some chewing gum anyway. Fresh air.

II.
Two individual pots of coffee. Two pieces of apple cake. For a while they studied the menu in silence.

She'd never thought she'd ever go for a coffee with her. She's always been strict about that. You've always been strict about that. Private is private, and work stays at work. She's a totally typical East German from the deepest darkest Zone you think, and you laugh.

Nice, though. She joins in with your laughing, even though she doesn't know what you're laughing at. The café here's very nice too. Very classy. Old furniture. Stucco ceilings. Little round tables. Pale wood panelling. Like a coffeehouse. Vienna.

Two glasses of liqueur. They raise their glasses, not touching them together. Chin chin, Susanne. Chin chin, Birgit. It's good to be sitting here without having to say much. A little cup of coffee, a little glass of liqueur. Pear. It's more of a brandy. Williams pear? Nearly Christmas again? Yes, we often drink it where I'm from. The Palatinate. No, not Bavaria. They talk differently in Bavaria. You think you'll soon be leaving the city. More coffee? Yes, why not. Cake? One more slice. But cheese-cake this time. It's good coffee.

Latte macchiato? No, thanks. I was in Saarbrücken when the Wall came down. Saarland, yes. That's where Lafontaine's from, yes. She voted for Lafontaine. No, really? Blossoming landscapes, that ridiculous prom-ise from Kohl was a step too far. Oh, right. Ungrateful, she thinks. And then you think she's actually very nice. You didn't trust Kohl either, back then. Didn't trust Lafontaine either but you had other reasons for that. She wanted to stab him, back then, that crazy woman, you know. Yes, of course I remember.

We aren't half beating around the bush, just to avoid the unpleasant conversation topics. No, it's really very nice here. Yes, the city too. You can tell straight off that she's only been doing it ten years at most. Which is a lot, of course. You could tell her how you first worked in a big brothel in Essen. But you both want to drink cof-fee and forget the rest of the world. An afternoon, late summer, early autumn. The leaves on the trees gold-en and bright. And the sun low in the clear sky, early on. Few clouds. People bustling through the streets. Slowly though. Not like on a high-summer high or in the Christmas rush. Yes, Christmas will soon be round again. You could swear she has kids. One kid at least. You hold your cup, your arm bent, looking very serious.

A migratory rat, you think, you've always been a migratory rat. Saarbrücken, Essen. No, Essen – Saarbrücken – Munich –Hannover – Cologne – Düsseldorf.

Have you ever been to Vienna, she wants to know.

Why Vienna?

Oh, just. Just because... it's closer from...

You've been to Vienna. Of course you have. And it's not closer at all. Quite the opposite. On holiday, years ago. You were twenty-two at the time. It's almost thirty years ago now. You went on your own, because you wanted to. No one's ever left you. Because you never gave anyone a chance to. Migratory rats, that's not your phrase. An old woman said it to you, years ago. She wasn't all that old at all. Looked old though. In the ladies, you stand in front of the mirror and see once again that you don't look that old yet, not as old as you ought to look. Because you let everything bounce off. You notice your memories often start with 'years ago'. If you were to write them down. Which you've often thought of doing. Yes, years ago already. The café sounds from behind you as the door to the ladies opens. Oh, it's you. No, another woman. Brief glances, brief smiles. Your hair's fine.

How did you get onto Vienna before?

Just did.

Have you ever been there then?

No.

No?

Yes. My boyfriend always wants to go to Vienna. We've been to the Alps a few times though... Another liqueur?

Oh, yes. Do you like pear?

The pear kind's very nice.

They make it themselves where I come from. In the

villages. Almost every farmer has his own little distillery going on. Pear, apple, quince. The priest always made the best schnapps.

Are you in the church?

Are you?

No. Not many churchgoers here in the Zone. Zone... You laugh. They laugh. We laugh.

But you've got plenty of lovely churches here in the city.

Yes, that's true.

I noticed from the very beginning.

Have you been

You've always been here, right?

Right. You can tell from my accent, I guess.

A little bit.

They order two glasses of pear brandy from a lady in black and white, who presses an empty tray to her chest and then puts the empty glasses on the empty tray. And the cake plates. On the street outside the window, people are strolling around town. Gliding slowly past the display windows. When she stood in front of the mirror she suddenly saw her work equipment, on a shelf beneath the mirror and around the edge of the sink. Sprays, creams, gel, the dispensers, the brushes, the mouthwash, the kitchen paper holder on the wall. She hears voices from the other side. Essen – Hannover – Düsseldorf. The mirror's surface ripples like water. The air flickers. She takes a step back. Back at the table again, she knows that distance will always stay her first rule. On this side and on the other.

She could say: distance, but friendly and nice at the same time. Human. Professional. Being a professional had always meant a lot to her. It would be going too far to say it made her proud. Mirror, mirror on the wall, who's the most professional of them all...

They drink water, sparkling, out of little bottles and little glasses, to go with their pear brandies.

They sip, look around, put their glasses back down. Less movement on the street outside the window now. A lovely afternoon. Almost evening now.

Good to have the afternoon off.

Good we've got the afternoon off.

I feel like never getting up again.

I like the way the music's not too loud here.

A waltz. Is that what made you think of Vienna?

A waltz, yes. Did you ever take dancing lessons?

I went to dance classes. Before my communion... after my communion.

Communi-what?

All you know is communism.

You laugh and then freeze back up. Distance. Then you relax again. Good to have the afternoon off.

Socialism, she says. It'll all be forgotten, only a few years on.

If a few means fifty. It won't go that quickly.

Fifty... sometimes I don't know if that's a lot or a few. Years...

Years. You really should go to Vienna some time. The two of you. You really should go together.

Do you go away sometimes? I mean, a really long way. Or to...

She falls silent suddenly. They're both silent. A quiet waltz in the background. The murmuring guests.

I like the way it's so quiet here. You hear yourself saying. And you see yourself drinking. And you see the two of you quietly smiling. I danced a waltz in Vienna once. But that's really years ago. The poor boy. *Rosenkavalier*.

You look at her but she doesn't seem to understand.

Or she's submerged in her own memories. *Rosenkavalier,* what nonsense. Goodbye, dear old distance. The mirror is everywhere. But stop thinking about it, don't get yourself wound up, relax. Only the occasional person walking past outside the window. The murmuring behind her grows denser. Glasses clink.

If you really can't dance...

No, I can't dance.

Then...

I mean, I can dance kind of, I've always liked disco dancing, back in the day I mean... but not your classic dances. Waltzes. No, really. No, I can't.

She smiles and cups her chin in her hands. Moves the glasses accidentally. You sip the remains from your glass, feeling the pear brandy on your upper lip, feeling the tiny hairs stroke as you run your forefinger across your upper lip. You run a razor along your upper lip now and then, very carefully, when you're doing your legs, but you like the peach fuzz, it's so fine that no one sees it, it only gets darker when you haven't been over it with the razor for a while. It's only been since you turned forty, and that's nearly ten years now... and back to the years again. Hobblety jig, hobblety jig, like in the fairy story where all the animals are sick and old and hobble around, hobblety jig, hobblety jig, but the two of you are in fine health, luckily, right, and you look at her sitting there with her arms propped up and thinking, and you look at yourself in the eternal mirror, the liqueur, as she calls it, is a brandy from your faraway or not so near homeland, the pear makes your faces red, dyes your cheeks red, good job the two of you aren't sunbed women, don't get your skin simmered down to the bone, dark, the young whores' skin looks so dark these days that you can't help thinking of skin cancer... that you can't help thinking: no. Alright, now and then you do go under the sun lamp you've had at home for years, in your flat that is, but you take care with its rays, and only very rarely and only for a little while. An English rose tone, that's what you want. Where were we...? Once my working day's over it's all out of my mind. All of it. Right away. I can't say I ever suffer from it, and most of the time, most of the time I don't even think of it, don't think about it. That's what I tell myself. And that's it. The truth needs telling over and over. To yourself, you know. They're fantasy stories, just fantasy stories. I stand behind the mirror and I'll whip my clients if that's what's wanted. Leather and chains. It's worth the investment. Distance. Professionalism. Homeland? What can I say? Dancing?

Waltzing's not simple. But it's quite easy to learn.

Do you think I could, I mean, at my age...

It can't do any harm. Listen to how the music glides, how you... I'd say, yes you can.

You mean dancing classes, Mia?

Mia?

Shit, sorry!

Slipped a line?

Something like that.

But you must have had them in the East, something like dance classes.

Of course we did. But first of all we sang together, marched together, went to the Soviet friends together, collected articles for the class pin board together and did lots and lots of sport. Gymnastics, on the bar, on the floor.

Don't tell me you could do the splits?

I could. I could still manage it at seventeen, eighteen, nineteen. I used to play tennis, messed my knees up with it a bit. You don't believe me though.

What?

That I can do the splits.

Could! That's what you said.

And then she stands up all of a sudden, takes a few steps out behind the table, takes a few steps into the empty space, the floor space between the tables, grabs hold of her loose trousers with both hands, positions herself like a jumping jack and slides her legs slowly, very slowly apart along the wooden floor. And you think: No, girl, don't do it, we're both of us fifty, even though we don't look it.

But she slides her legs further and further apart, very slowly, the lady in black and white with the tray pressed against her chest looking wide-eyed first at her, at them, and then continuing on her way between the tables as she approaches the splits. But then she comes to a stop, and she jumps up and yells. 'Bloody hell, that bloody hurts!'

It sounds as shrill and as high and as low as it sounds when anyone tries to do the splits without warming up at the age of fifty. She hobbles to and fro a little, a waltz, a waltz in an endless loop, keeps gripping her thighs and contorting her pale – English rose! – face, and then she sits down.

You lean back, the glasses are empty, you feel the fruit brandy pulsating in your face, you bend over, lean back again, laughing in your mind, silent in your mind, you shake your head, and then you reach for her hands, which you can't get hold of quickly, and then you put your hands on her shoulders, bend forward again, and then your heads are so close, your hair so close that it's touching, and she puts her hands, still moaning quietly, on top of yours, and still silent, still without words, the two of you laugh.

353

III.

Kaput. I don't drink any more. Kaput. Only a little
bit. Haven't for years. Haven't for many years now.
My body and my head don't need it. I'm always on the
hop. Stop while the going is good. I don't know if my
mother's still there. Far away over there. In the palat-
able Palatinate. Maybe I admire her. The dancer, not
my mother. I'm doing fine. I've got my rules. At the
harbour, this ridiculous harbour of this ridiculous city
where I'm sitting now, lying, sitting, waiting, it's the last
stop. What should a girl regret when there's nothing to
regret? Only the others are kaput. That was the way in
Essen, that's the way here. They're mirrors in which I
dress. Which they slide off against. I've always admired
the ones who've kept their sense of humour, my colleagues, all my women. I can't do that. The boss, the Old
Man, he's OK. I've known much bigger arseholes. I used
to hate the East Germans, at least a little bit, in the old
days. When they all came over to us. When everyone
wanted to know what they're like in bed. Because there
were rumours going round about oh, how liberated they
all were. Because they didn't have any shops over there
for decades, for centuries it felt like, no proper establish-
ments when it came to the big golden fuck. And all the
lovely ladies came over to us in the West and made business difficult. But plenty of years have passed since then.
Now our paths are crossing again here. I'm not bitter.
I've still got a few good years ahead of me. But I want to
keep moving for those years. I've got a good contact in
Hannover, the big meat market where the Angels rule
the roost.

I see it all purely rationally. I milk and I milk and I
put away what I can. Even used to have funds and shares
but that's all kaput now. Who was to know Europe would

bleed dry? But I wasn't quite stupid, luckily. Luckily I wasn't quite stupid. I've got my account where it still goes in. And I kept a few of the funds and bonds and shares, because an excess of chaos at some point always leads back to order. And vice versa. We saw it happening. So I'm waiting and keeping hold of the rest.

Over there, when I look out of the window, are the old decrepit warehouses of the old harbour. And right behind them the woods set in. A canal leads far into the land. Lots of nice canals, new, almost like Amsterdam. I didn't even notice that the Angels have come here too and are doing business and making contracts. Because it has no effect on me. And I didn't find out until much later that this guy died a year ago, I probably even knew him, a guest, collateral damage. I've often sat in the middle of these kind of wars and earned my money. Essen – Hannover – Düsseldorf. It's not pretty but life goes on. Of course I don't want the Russians, the Yugos or the Arabs messing with our fair deals. There's still a club not far from me. The boss has a share in it, I hear. But I'm only staying a bit longer and then I'll be gone. Moving on. I've got a few years. I'm satisfied, all in all. And I always say: Once the long day's work is over I'll forget everything afterwards. Quickly. Immediately. I don't suffer in any way, and I don't think too much about those weird women who have no idea but are always trying to tell people what it's like. And so on.

Some of the young girls have a whole different approach. When it comes to profit. Make a quick buck and get out quick again. I don't need stupid comments. Not from anyone. When I close the door to my little flat I close the door on everything else, everything that happened at work that day. You can't afford illusions. Of course I have dreams. But I keep them to myself.

When I look out at the old harbour like this I remember there used to be a man here, so they say, a man who had a dream of upgrading the whole thing, buying it all up, they called him the Bielefelder, and some people called him the Count, why, I can't say, and he owns the Fort at the other end of town where I don't want to work because I was once in a similar place in Hannover. There are birds live up there under the eaves. I see them when they fly off. Who would have paid for the whole thing? I hear people down on the street. I wait. I count up my cash every day and think: Give me your money, you fools.

Only a while longer and then off to Hannover, and then I'll pack it in.

I'm the good old sexy mother in among the young things. I'll do bareback blow jobs, I'll swallow if the money's right, and I'll greet you in leather if that's what you want. My orifices are open for you. I'm not kaput. I'm waiting. I'll strap on a big fat cock if that's what you want, and you can fuck my tits as well. Your juice runs out of my hair, runs out of my mouth. You can take me up the arse, I'll take your balls in my mouth. You pay a hundred and twenty an hour, all-inclusive. And fifty for a quickie, me up against the wall. I'll be your mummy if that's what you want. I'll spit your juice out in your mouth if that's what you want. Slap me on the arse if you want. And I'll piss on you if that's what you want, in my bathtub. I don't do scat, you'll have to go to Janine at number 53 for that. You can stroke me as well. And you can kiss me. There's mouthwash in the bathroom. You can snuggle up to me because your mother was mean to you. You can punish me too, I'm slightly sub, if that's what you're into and you pay me for it.

Rimming's only passive with me. Active at number

53, that's rare, it's a goldmine, but other than that – feel free, feel free, as long as you pay in advance.

And I watch the money in my account, it's not a Swiss bank account but it's safe enough. I watch it growing. Watch enough other girls wasting it all.

I'm on the hop. And I'm dancing. Who'd have thought that? I was alone in Vienna back then. I'm glad I haven't got kids. What with everything kaput out there. Almost thirty years ago, in Vienna. I prefer not to talk. I've said much too much. But when I dance with her. That East German from the deepest darkest Zone. What with me living in the deepest darkest Zone for years now. I won't forget that. In the years I've got left. The good years. The hard-working years. Us dancing a waltz there and moving the tables out of the way. Me leading her. That incredible woman. Arms on shoulders. The café almost empty. Waltz after waltz, waltzes on an endless loop. The two of us dancing. And her saying to me how fabulous I am. That was better than Vienna. Where I stumbled round on my own, the mid-nineties it was, and I say, you have to follow my leg more with yours. And I say nothing after that, because she's already got how she has to move along with me. And she picks up pretty quickly how the two of us have to dance the waltz. That swing – it was almost like we were floating on air. No wonder people started staring.

And suddenly the music stopped. And they played one of those time-to-go tunes. Right when she almost had it. Right when she was ready to lead. And we danced a while longer in silence, in the empty café. It must have been ten minutes, from beginning to end. I bet they'd never seen that before, two fine ladies like us, mature ladies, fine ladies with their endless waltzing... and us floating around that baroque 1870s or whatever parlour.

And then the crooning from the speakers at the end. We were just short of kicking up a real fuss, the two of us. Just short of throwing glasses. Because our hair and our skin were touching. Because all we were doing was dancing. 'There's such a lot of world to see...'

And then we let go of each other. '... Moon River, and me.'

That's how I imagine it in my mind, looking out at the harbour. After the splits gone-wrong we said goodbye. It was very close, even without waltzing, even without my Huckleberry friend.

The doorbell rings. I get up. Here I am.

It was snowing again. Hans looked out of the window at the low, four-storey blocks stretching in a long concrete ribbon behind the hotel. Beyond the buildings he could see the snow-covered fields, a couple of isolated farms, and further back, barely recognizable in the murky afternoon haze and the driving snow, the woods he often ran in as a child.

He closed the curtains and looked for a minibar but didn't find one. Only a bottle of mineral water on the table next to the tiny TV.

He hung his black suit in the wardrobe. He was glad he'd got his driving licence back a week and a half ago – his good suit would have got unnecessarily crumpled in a travel bag. He probably would have taken a taxi, even though it was more than two hundred kilometres. He'd looked up on the internet how long it would have taken by train. More than three hours. His father hadn't ever had a car in his life. He'd always cycled to the works and taken the bus in the hard winters. Or he'd march straight across to the bridge, across other people's property, fields, building plots. They took the train when they went to Berlin or to visit relatives on the coast. Hans remembered those train trips decades gone, in another world, beneath another sky. Walking to the station, all lugging their suitcases, sometimes their father took the handcart along and stowed it with the stationmaster, whom he often played cards with. When Hans was very small he was allowed to sit on top of the cart, the big suitcases behind his back.

He put the bottle on the table and filled the glass. Johnnie Black. He'd sworn by it for nigh on twenty years now. 'It's drinkable,' the Count always used to say, 'it's drinkable.' He could still remember his first bottle, drunk in Berlin some time at the end of the eighties, a couple of glasses at least, and he remembered being surprised by the label: 'Black? But it's usually red.'

He downed the glass in one, tipped a little more in, drank more slowly. He pulled the curtains apart again, opened the window and lit a cigarette. Nigh on a year now he'd been trying to give it up. But he wouldn't get through the evening and the next day without smoking.

He stood by the window and smoked, a non-smoking room, and noticed that he couldn't see the fields behind the low concrete blocks only a few yards away from him, on the other side of the street. But a minute ago he'd been looking out on the endless white fields. Maybe that had been on the drive here, which had taken him past the snow-drenched plains, the windscreen wipers scraping across the glass, low voices on the radio, he didn't like music in the car so he usually listened to Deutschlandfunk where they talked almost uninterrupted, or it was other memories of other views where the river flowed too, bare trees in long rows, there must have been paths or roads there before, the snow driving faster, he felt the cold air, threw his cigarette butt outside and closed the window again.

He took his coat, wrapped his scarf around his neck, pulled on his leather gloves, put his hat in his coat pocket, drank down the glass and went to the door.

Even from a distance he saw that the road ahead of him rose and led across the first bridge, and then he knew he was heading the right way. He'd left the car in the hotel car park. He was glad to have his driving licence back at last. He'd had so much stress over the past six months. He'd handed hundreds of taxi receipts over to his tax

360

advisor because he couldn't always find someone to drive him around. He'd even got Mandy 2 to do it for a while but that was a bit embarrassing. Better Big Klaus, but even better a taxi.

They'd lived in the old town centre back in the day. It had only been a village to begin with. The centre of Steel Town was ahead of him, across the two bridges, between the arms of the canal. The river, which he hadn't seen yet that afternoon, was somewhere behind him on the edge of the old town, where they'd lived back in the day, not far from the river.

He wiped the snow off his head, put on his hat. Perhaps he should have taken the car after all. He was walking his father's route, but later, once everything was built over, he couldn't just walk straight across any more, walking the route he'd taken so often himself as a child and a young man. Over to the centre. But not for over twenty-five years now.

When the road divided he had considered for a moment which direction to take, had seen the bus passing, going a different way to the one he remembered, must be taking a detour past the new buildings on the far edge of the old town, the village they'd converted into a city sixty years ago, no, not converted it, they built a new city around it, but a mile or so on there were another two bridges that also led to the centre of Steel Town. Hans stomped on through the snow, the stream of cars beside him, saw the bus vanishing between the buildings.

He stood on the first bridge, looking down at the railway lines. Several tracks, freight cars on one side, a few of them open at the top, looking like huge mining drams and filling up with snow. The station must be somewhere back there. He could stroll from the hotel to the station in fifteen minutes, he guessed. Then he'd pass the cemetery and the old church. Perhaps that little pub was still there on the station road, the one where his father used to play cards.

He stood for ten minutes or longer until his feet got cold. No trains passed beneath him. He lit a cigarette, the lighter extinguishing two or three times in the driving snow, he turned to the street, looked at all the cars with their lights on already, it was getting dark now, the whole day had been murky and dark, and he too had switched on his headlights as he left the city, driving towards Steel Town in the morning.

On the other side of the bridge, on the footpath, he saw an old man and an old woman, huddled close together and stomping through the snow slightly bent. Hans leaned against the railings, felt the icy metal through the fabric of his coat, threw the half-smoked cigarette onto the tracks and walked on. It seemed to him that he heard a train but he didn't turn around again, looking at the tall warehouse building with the triangular top by the canal, below the second bridge that took the road over it. In the old days the tugs used to take the canal, which led past the warehouse almost directly to the works. Tug after tug, ship after ship moved along the dark water, the banks straightened and fortified, asphalt footpaths alongside the banks. As a child, he'd often stood down there or up here and watched the tugs and the ships. Ice floes on the dark water. It seemed far colder here than above the railway tracks.

Ice floes on the dark water. Behind the bend the lights and the buildings of the steelworks, the chimneys with their steam that seemed to swathe the buildings, the huge smelting furnace a black tower in the dusk. Hans spat in the canal, saw his father stabbing a long pole into the glowing red river pouring out of a kind of giant barrel,

362

the sparks flying, arcs of light surrounding the man that must be his father, Hans standing at the works gates, a bottle of beer pressed to his chest as he waited, feeling the bottle's cool surface, watching the grey tangle of rods, pipes, buildings, small towers, big towers, linked by conveyor belts, roads between them, tracks with waggons on them, people in work suits with dark faces, the air tasted of charcoal and salt

Hans walked on. The road led to a newly built area, grey and white tower blocks; they must be from the sixties or seventies, as far as he remembered. A Netto discount mart on one side of the road, on the other side the big red illuminated K of a Kaufland supermarket. He'd never understood why the big corporations had to compete face to face like that. AK had explained a few things about the discounters' competitive behaviour – he'd studied business administration.

Yeah, yeah, competition is good for business. If a club or a brothel opened up across the road from him he'd pull out all the stops, though. Mind you, that wasn't all that easy anyway, just going into the business in the city. On the other hand there were enough places where everything was concentrated in a tiny area, what with the restricted zone regulations... Load of crap! He took off his leather gloves, put them in his pockets, bent down and grabbed at the snow, made a snowball and threw it towards the tower blocks. Pale garden walls ran parallel to the front of the buildings, stone picket fences made of countless gaps and tiny windows. Hans ran for a moment, bent down again and launched a snowball at one of the walls, behind which there were snowed-in benches, two table-tennis tables made of concrete. He was holding a third snowball in his cold red hands when he saw two young lads approaching him, probably heading for one of the supermarkets, and he threw the lump of snow away, smiled as they eyed him in passing, a stocky middle-aged man – probably very old, to them – playing in the snow.

Straße der Republik crossed Karl-Marx-Straße, Stalinist fifties buildings on either side, a miniature version of Berlin's Stalinallee. The first time he went to Berlin with his father and sister, must have been in the late sixties, early seventies, they stood in amazement on the huge Soviet-style boulevard no longer named after Stalin. His father told them about the place and they felt, he and his sister, as though the steel town between river and canal were nothing but a village for dwarves. And his father told them about the Russians' even larger boulevards, the Soviet cities, and how the tiny people walked around in these huge spaces. *When the Steel Was Tempered*. What a book that was!

Hans stood on Lindenallee, which crossed Straße der Republik, remembering how it used to be called Leninallee, the steel town's shopping street. Evening had come quickly and Hans looked at the lights and the windows of the few stores, looked at the white cube of the vacant hotel on the other side of the road, the snow falling thicker now; he walked with his head lowered against the wind as it drove the snow into his face, past the shop windows, no one goes out in this weather, saw the blurred oval of the small theatre a little way ahead, the pillars outside the entrance, the semi-circular staircase. He saw that the programme was illuminated in a glass case right next to the stairs. A little later he found himself in a bakery, took off his hat, had to put on his reading glasses, ordered a coffee and a piece of poppy-seed cake. He only took off one glove while he leaned against a tall table, looking into the driving snow through the window. A few people came out of a shop on the other side of the road – did it say 'Bookshop' above the entrance? He felt his phone vibrate in the inside pocket of his coat, drank his coffee and waited for it to stop moving under the fabric. *In memory of the first activist, Comrade Adolf Hennecke, we are here today to honour the steel worker comrades who have rendered outstanding performance in over-fulfilling the three-year plan...*

He sat at the table in his hotel room, drank a glass of Johnnie Black, looked at the dark windows of the new buildings through the gap between the curtains, the light of a TV flickering in only one of them, his phone next to the bottle – his sister had called twice. He picked up the phone and typed a text message, letter by letter. He hated predictive text, couldn't use it. 'Will be at cemetery tomorrow 11 a.m. Best wishes, Hans'.

He saw it was almost twelve by now. She was probably asleep. But who can go to sleep early on an evening like this, a night like this? How long was it since he last saw her? Four or five years. No, longer. She hadn't been there the last time he'd visited his father in hospital, two weeks ago. She'd never been there when he visited. He'd chosen a hospital in Berlin, later a good hospice, wanted to pay for everything, but the old man had refused. *I'm dying here. At my own expense.* He didn't know he was up-river in the border town, in the old district hospital. And then he did remember. *Take me home, Hans.*

Two weeks ago, he couldn't speak to him any more. The old man lay in his bed like a piece of weathered wood, dying. Slowly.

'Why didn't you tell me sooner, Hanna?'

'He doesn't want to see you, Hans.'

'*You* don't want him to see me, is that it?'

'You were gone all these years.'

'Yes, I was.'

'You didn't give a shit about us.'

'I always thought about you... I always wanted to send you money, you know that.'

'We don't want your money, Hans.'

He filled the glass again. Opened the window at the top and smoked a cigarette as he drank. Fuck the non-smoking room. He'd put a small, round, travel ashtray next to the bottle, like a medallion that opened, Marilyn Monroe smiling on the lid. Mandy gave it to him years ago, Mandy 1. *The* Mandy, his Mandy. He'd never tried to find out where she was now.

'I'd always have come, you know that... I always wanted...'

'Have you never asked yourself why our father suffered so much all these years?'

'Yes, he's suffered in the past months, but that's nothing to do with me.'

'Have you never asked yourself what I'm supposed to tell my children?'

'Just tell them Uncle Hans is making money in the big city.'

A click on the line.

Hans turned on the TV, flicked through all the channels with the remote, stopping for a moment on a crime show repeat on a regional channel, two detectives from Munich, he liked them a lot, they'd gone grey over the years, both of them, they had no family either as far as he could tell but they didn't seem unhappy, as far as he could tell, Franz and Ivo, yes, he liked them, they gave off such a sense of calm, they were like an old married couple, the curly-locks and the long-nosed one, had he

366

seen this episode before? Ivo was striding through a dense forest. Oh, fuck it: he switched it off again.

He still had his coat on, felt the heavy damp fabric, he had his shoes on as well, saw the grubby prints on the floor. How long had he been sitting here, looking outside through the gap between the curtains? He must have kept opening the window – the room was cold. And the small, round ashtray studded with butts. He picked it up, went into the bathroom and tipped the butts and the ash down the toilet. He pressed the lid of the ashtray shut, heard the closing mechanism click, Marilyn Monroe smiling. He took a quick look in the mirror. Ran his hands through his short grey hair; he wanted to grow it. His father's hair had been quite long, over in the old district hospital. Thin and white, almost down to his shoulders. He had put his hand on his father's head for a moment, on that soft silky hair. And you always used to complain about my long hair, until I shaved it off and went to Berlin.

His lips had almost vanished, they'd taken his false teeth out. Where on earth were they? He couldn't find them anywhere, neither on the bedside table nor in the little cupboard. And the drawer was empty too. He had made sure he got a good room; his sister didn't know that or didn't mention it. On the phone. We've talked far too little all these years.

He stood by the mirror. Don't look at me like that. He saw that the cigarette butts were floating in the toilet and he flushed. Even after the short whirl of water, at least half of them were still in there. He held the tooth mug under the tap and turned it on until the cup overflowed, then drank. He took the half-full cup back to the table. Took off his coat and hung it on a hanger, over the door of the wardrobe. Mustn't put the damp coat in the wardrobe. Otherwise it'll smell musty in the morning.

Sitting back at the table, he noticed he was cold. The window was open at the top. He lit a cigarette. I know, Father, I ought to give it up.

How blue the picture was. Tomography or something like that. He'd spoken to the doctors on the phone, gone over to the border town, the former district hospital. Although his sister didn't want to know. She'd called him too late.

So this is what death looks like, he'd thought at the time. He stood with his cigarette by the window, open all the way now, the curtains pulled aside, he looked at that one window in the grey block opposite, the light of the TV still flickering there, and the longer he looked into that blue-and-white light... He threw the cigarette end down into the snow, leaned far out, felt the snowflakes on his face before jerking around and seeing the bed, the sheets rumpled, the pillow flattened, the cover screwed up against the wall, even though he hadn't lain down at all yet. Carefully, he shut the window and drew the curtains closed.

The earth pelted down on the coffin. *You mustn't get me burned.* His father had told him that twice. Upriver, in the border town, in the former district hospital.

He nodded, once, twice, felt the last crumbs of earth falling from his palm, glanced at the long lid of the coffin, only a few handfuls of earth on it, nodded again into the steaming of his breath, then turned away. Saw his sister's face, her standing a few feet aside from the grave with her two children. She was wearing a black fur hat, Russian style. It hadn't been snowing since the morning. He went over, stood next to her. While the other mourners stepped up to the grave he tried to look at her without anyone noticing. Her round, oval face. Like their mother. Dark blonde hair under the hat. And he didn't want to look at his mother's grave, directly next to the hole in the ground. He'd been sending flowers to her grave for nigh on twenty years now. Earlier on he'd seen the fir branches under the snow. How on earth had they dug a hole in this rock-hard earth? Probably with a little digger. The pastor stood bent over next to the long, slim hole. About twenty people had turned up. He didn't know most of them. Or not any more. He still had a couple of great-aunts and uncles here. He looked across the white graves, bare trees with thin, bare branches and snow-covered conifers between the graves. If he turned his head slightly he could see his sister, if he turned his head slightly he could see the chapel. How old were her children now? He tried to count. *Our Father, who art in heaven, hallowed be Thy name...* That had been earlier, still in his head. But Father hadn't even been a churchgoer. Their mother was. They often went to church together, Mum, him and his sister. They'd often met workmates of his father's, who'd send him their regards. After Mum died, seventy-one it was, they never went to church with their father. Only at Christmas. Because his sister had always made a fuss. At Christmas. He could see the church as well, the pointed red tower, far beyond the trees of the road outside the cemetery. The old town. The edge of town. The village.

He suddenly felt the cigarette in the corner of his mouth, coughed, threw it in the snow, saw and felt his sister looking at him. He turned to her and said quietly, 'Sorry,' saw her smile, put his hand on her shoulder, stepped closer to her and then put his arm around her shoulder, said again, 'Sorry,' and felt her leaning against him. He pressed her shoulder with his hand, felt himself

369

stumbling backwards, felt her holding him, reaching her hand past his chest and taking his free hand and holding it, and once he looked her in the eye she let go again.

The children stood silent next to them and looked at him like they didn't know he was their uncle. 'Go fuck yourselves.' He put on his gloves. He'd whispered it so quietly that no one could have heard it, as he was leaving. His hands in his coat pockets in their leather gloves, he walked past the grave to the gate.

He was in Liv's Flower Boutique on Bahnhofstraße, the smell of pine needles and earth, his hands laid on the sales counter. The woman came through the door between the shelves on the back wall, flowers, wreaths, fir branches, cacti, large plants with dark red blossoms in large pots, she was holding a few pieces of paper. 'It's all paid for, Mr Pieszeck.'

'I know. I just wanted to say thank you.'

'That's very nice of you. So you're the one who's been paying for the flowers and wreaths all these years, then.'

'Yes.'

'I've always wondered if you'd ever turn up. Would you like a receipt?'

'No. And now I have turned up.'

'And I'm the one who ought to be thanking you.'

'No need for that.' He shook his head. Still leaning on the table with the cash register on it.

'My sympathies, about your father.'

'Thank you.' He stood upright, put his hands in his coat pockets.

'It was for the best in the end.'

She stroked the collars of her blue work coat. Nodded. He looked at the lines next to the corners of her mouth. Now she smiled. 'Sometimes,' she said, 'sometimes it's...

a mercy at some point... I'm sorry.'

'No. There's no need to apologize. Liv. You are Liv, aren't you?'

'Yes,' she said.

He nodded. 'So you've always been here, have you, Liv?'

'Yes.'

'Then you knew my father?'

'Only by sight, Mr Pieszeck.'

'Hans.'

'Hans.' He looked at the lines by the corners of her mouth. Short black hair, slim face. Early forties, maybe. 'And you've always been here in this town?'

'Yes.'

'And you knew my father as well?'

'By sight, only by sight, Hans.'

'Do you know where he lived, down by the river?'

'No, not really.'

'That's where I grew up, I grew up there.'

'Then maybe we have seen each other before.'

'Where did you grow up, Liv? If you don't mind me asking.'

'On the other side.'

'By the works?'

'Do you know the little neighbourhood by the harbour?'

'Yes. Of course. My father was at the works.'

'My uncle was at the works, too.'

'I used to work as a gardener over in Village 3, years ago.'

'Schmidt's Gardening?'

'M-hm.'

'They've been closed a long time now.'

'I thought as much, Liv. Are you named after Liv

Ullmann?'

'The actress? No. My great-grandmother was called Liv. Her father, my great-great-grandfather, came from Sweden.'

'Sweden... So do you ever go over to Sweden? To visit relatives?'

'Oh, no.' She laughed. 'There's no connection any more.'

'It must be very cold there all the time,' said Hans, 'and the daylight is over by midday...'

'I don't think it's quite that bad.'

'So you have been there, then, Liv.'

'No, never.'

'I was just kidding. Don't take it the wrong way.'

'No, it's alright. Are you heading home now?'

'I'm on my way.' He nudged his travel bag with his foot.

'Oh, have you come by train?'

'No.' He laughed. 'I wish I had. I just had...' he bent down, undid the zip of his bag, 'I didn't know I was going to meet *you* here, I'd been imagining an old flower lady.' He put the bottle of wine down on the counter. 'And I did tell you I wanted to say thank you.'

'You shouldn't have.'

'Oh yes. Now I'd say I should have.'

'And that's why you go lugging your travel bag in here.'

'You know, Liv, I'm a bit of a strange person.'

'Yes. Yes, I think you are.'

Hans was sitting on the bed in his hotel room. He was still wearing his black suit. He wished he'd packed a pair of long johns. But he hadn't felt the cold at the graveyard. The TV was on, switched to mute. He reached across the sheets next to him, looking for the remote. His cigarette packet was next to him. He picked it up, held it towards the TV and pressed the letters, the plastic wrapping, the writing about death. 'Go on, turn off, you piece of crap.' He threw the cigarettes at the picture, at the screen, at the thick glass.

He had two nephews, Klaus and Manfred. Once, his sister had said on the phone that she was glad she didn't have daughters, otherwise they might end up working for him one day. For fuck's sake. *Go fuck yourselves.* There was some stupid talk show on. *And family?* While the idiots got stuck into each other without sound, a little boy with a brand new school satchel suddenly stepped on set, into the picture. Close-ups of faces, crying mothers, fathers with their hands in front of their faces. Pictures, pictures, writing. And Hans remembered when AK's son started school years ago. What was it like with AK's parents, how was the relationship between father and son, parents and child after all these years? 'And you get on well with them?'

'Of course, what do you mean?'

'Nothing. I'm just asking.'

'Everything's fine. Like if I worked in an office, like if I was a grocer. And I am in a way.'

'You are. And what did they used to do, for work I mean?'

'Curious Hans.'

'Sorry. Too much wine.'

'It's alright, my Hans the Hatchet.'

'Don't say that.'

'There you go. On a par.'

'On a par?'

'My parents, Hans. Perfectly normal. Like anywhere else. Nothing special. Well, in their way. Office jobs.

Their whole lives.'

'And no one's angry with you?'

'No. No one. Everything's fine.'

'Hmm.' And he remembered, as he flicked through the channels with his cigarette packet before he chucked it away, how he'd stood with his back to the party at the celebration for AK's son starting school, how many years ago was that now? Stood by the banks of the big lake, behind him the smell of a barbecue, the children's laughter, the relatives' voices, a perfectly bloody normal family party, a starting-school party with tables loaded with food and drink, punch in big glass bowls from which the ladies ladled, AK's mother, AK's father, remembered how they spoiled the boy, who had brought his friends, slightly older, and the neighbours' kids of the same age, along with their families, so that they could celebrate together, *The boy only starts school once*, just a few hard nuts in among the relatives, Arnold had been strict about the dress code, Alex mixing the punch after an old recipe from his foreign forefathers, that's what he said anyway, laughing, one of the W. brothers was there, had brought his son along, the W.s had invested in restaurants and the big strip club, were gradually getting out of the apartment business... Was Karate-Steffen still in town back then? Hans had stood by the lake, the open red wine bottle jammed under his arm, had looked over at the opposite bank in the evening haze, the hills blurred as if through a giant magnifying glass, he stood on the bank and watched the shining water surface turn pink under the big evening sky...

And he packed his things while the snow went on falling outside.

'And Hans doesn't have to go home?'

'Where do you think my home is?'

'In the big city.'

'Have you ever wanted to leave here, Liv?'

'No.'

'Because of your shop?'

'Where else would I go, Hans?'

They were in the Peking Restaurant on Bahnhofstraße, two or three hundred yards down from the station. He'd ordered sake and they were drinking hot sake, pouring the clear, steaming liquid out of the little jugs into even smaller cups.

'And you've really never come here before?'

'No.'

'And you've never drunk hot sake either?'

'No.'

'But your shop's just round the corner, Liv.'

'My shop's round the corner.'

'You're a bit of a strange woman, Liv.'

'Maybe I am.'

One of the waiters brought the starters, various dumplings, various rolls, spring, summer, vegetarian, and a bottle of white wine. 'Here you are,' he said, and poured their wine.

'Sake and white wine,' she smiled, and Hans looked at her, 'I wonder if that's a good idea.'

'Good idea, bad idea – I don't even know your surname,' said Hans.

'What does it matter?' she said and reached for a spring roll, and Hans took a starter too.

'Probably not at all,' he said, and ate and chewed and wiped his chin. 'Maybe I'd like to know more about you.'

'Curious Hans.'

'When did you leave?'

'Curious Liv.' He pushed his arm beneath her back, pushed and pushed, felt the sheet crumpling under his arm until she lifted her body slightly and he could push his hand through and put it on her shoulder and draw her head down onto his chest.

'You don't have to tell me anything, Hans. But you were suddenly here.'

'And you were suddenly here. I left in '84.'

'Thirty years ago.'

'Not quite.' He shifted onto his side and went to pull her up close but she was already there. 'Time flies,' she said, and he put both arms around her back. Pressed his head to her breasts. 'Yes, it does,' she said, pressing his forehead against her.

'And now you're in the big city.' He felt the vibration of her voice in her breasts, and deep inside her.

'I've got a bar,' said Hans, 'a cocktail bar.'

'Oh, so that's why you know so much.'

'What do you mean?'

'About drinks, Mr Rick.'

'Mr Rick?'

'*Casablanca*, Hans.'

'Long time ago, Miss Flowers.'

She ran her hand over his head. He took her hand and ran it over his stubbly face. 'All these years I haven't been here.' He turned on his back, looked at her bedroom ceiling, her hand still in his hair.

'You were waiting so you could meet me, huh?'

'If I'd known you were here I'd have come years ago.'

'And why did you leave?'

'Are you really asking that, Liv?'

'No, not really. I just want to know who my Hans is. Now, I mean.'

'Your Hans?'

'Sorry. I'm just so glad you're here.'

'No need to apologize, my Liv. I can't imagine anything better right now. Can't imagine anything better at all, at this moment. I'm probably talking rubbish again.'

'Are you married? Even if you are, it doesn't matter, I don't care. Sorry, but it doesn't matter to me, it's me who doesn't care.'

'No, I'm not.'

'Maybe you're a fabulous liar. I just want to be with you now.'

'And I want to be with you. That's not a lie. I'd tell you otherwise. And...'

'Shut up, Hans, and come here.'

He looks into the dark. It's his second strange dream. Since he's been sleeping at her place. He hasn't turned his phone on for three days. She wakes up next to him. 'What's up?'

'Nothing, nothing. Go back to sleep, Liv.'

'Did you have another bad dream?'

'What do you mean, another?'

'Oh, Hans.' He feels her hand on his chest. He's wearing her ex-husband's pyjamas. 'He never wore them – I was going to give him them for Christmas.'

'Pyjamas for Christmas?'

'They look good though.'

'Hmm, yes.'

He puts his hand on hers, feels the sweat on his forehead and chest. 'Don't you want to ask?'

'What d'you mean?'

'What I dreamed about.'

'You didn't want to tell me last time.'

'I went to the works. All alone. The whole town was

empty. It was snowing... Is it snowing outside, Liv?'

'I don't know.' He hears the duvet moving, her getting up, feels the cool of the air, he sees her standing by the curtains, she's wearing one of his vests, he can't remember when she put it on, wasn't she wearing a short nightshirt, but they spent all evening drinking wine and having sex. She was forty-four and hadn't slept with anyone for three years. She drew the curtains aside, the big white space of the garden behind her house, a few snowflakes spinning through the air, it had been stormy outside last night but now the wind seemed to have died down, she turned to him, 'Just a few crumbs,' he looked at her neck, saw her pointed, slightly pendulous breasts beneath his vest, she looked like a little girl standing there in the brightness of the snow, the curtains fell closed again and all he could see was the outlines of her body, and when she was lying beside him again he took her hand, surprised again at how rough and chapped her palms were, stroked her hard-working hand stabbed and roughened by the plants and thorns and needles in the long years, 'Your hands are so soft, Hans.'

'Ach, uninteresting hands, you've got beautiful hands, I like feeling them.'

'Oh, stop it,' he could feel her smiling, and he moved his hand in the dark air, stroked her face and her smiling mouth.

'And I walked through the snow, barefoot, but I wasn't cold, I was wearing short leather trousers, I think I wore trousers like that as a child but I wasn't a child in my dream. I walked across the two bridges, stopped a long time on the first one, and everything was in twilight, big steam engines on the tracks, and I walked on through the snow, and the canal was frozen over but under the ice was a strange dark red glow, and the snow fell, really,

378

really big flakes of snow, and they fell slowly, they float-
ed, they were like white butterflies.'

He was leaning on the wall now, the pillow shoved
behind his back, and she put her head on his shoulder.
'Like butterflies,' she said.

'And then I walked along the long streets, Lenin,
Republik, you know the ones, but they never ended, the
way it is in your dreams sometimes. Past the theatre, and
there were buildings there I'd never seen before. Big
grey towers. They went all the way up to the sky. And
the twilight, as if it came from a huge moon, but I didn't
see the moon, I read once that you can only see in black
and white in moonlight, if you're reading a newspaper
for example.'

'I don't think that's true.'

'We'll try it out when the moon shines again.'

'Yes, Hans, let's do that.'

'So I kept on walking, on and on through the snow.
And then I saw tracks, they were quite big so they
couldn't have been my own, me walking in a circle, you
know. And these tracks, they were huge. And more kind
of square, like someone had been walking in snowshoes.
So I followed them but then they stopped. And when I
look down at myself I see that I've got giant, hairy feet.'

'Well,' she laughed against his shoulder, 'you do have
at least size tens. And you have got hair on them.'

'No, not true. You can't imagine how big they were all
of a sudden, and it even seemed like they were getting
bigger and bigger. So then I started running. And that
was fine, the running. Not the way it is sometimes when
you can't move from the spot, no, I was almost flying,
made great big leaps, but kind of in slow motion as well.
And then I was at the works.'

'The steelworks.'

'Yes. But no, wait, before that I heard this dull hammering, more like a dull drum, a kind of drumming. Boom, boom, boom. Totally monotonous, and it came from somewhere in the distance. That was in the empty streets. And it could be it came from me, maybe it came from my giant strides, me putting my furry feet down on the ground. Boom, boom, boom. And I don't know exactly if I still heard it at the gate, at the works gate. And then I went in.'

'Did you meet your father?'

'Yes.' He felt that he was breathing heavily, that he was out of breath, he had to pull himself together to go on talking and she stroked his face again with her rough hand.

'He was standing there by the smelting furnace, wearing his rough leather apron and the face mask with the tinted glass at the front, and he took a run-off out of the furnace with the big long iron rod, and suddenly he threw it away and leaned forward, and the steel flowed over his hands, and the glowing red steel was everywhere. And then I called out. Dad, I called out, watch out, Dad, you're burning. But he didn't hear me. And I couldn't even hear myself. Fuck.'

'It's alright, Hans, everything's alright.' She kissed his neck and his chin and then his forehead.

'Yeah, yeah. It's fine. Everything's fine. The things you dream. And I called out and called out. But the stubborn old man with both hands in the burning stream of metal. Something was forming, something took shape. Figures, steel girders, I couldn't make it out. He stood there bent over, no gloves at all, and the funny thing was that the whole floor, everything was covered in gloves, covered in protective gloves. And I try to go to him. The hall is huge with a high dome, like a cathedral, yeah, and there's flickering and sparks flying, from the river of steel there in front of him coming out of the big high converting container, it wasn't the normal furnace, I knew that one, he'd showed me that one time, we even went there with school once. I can hardly piece it all together now. But I tripped up, kept tripping over all the bloody gloves. And then he turns round to me and takes off the mask, and his face is so white that I have to close my eyes for a moment in my dream, it's that dazzling, his white face. And his eyes are glowing red as though the steel had flowed into them, as though it was inside him, and then he says: 'I've been waiting for you so long.'

'Did you visit him often in hospital?'

'No, not often. We... we didn't get on that well. The last thing he said to me was that we shouldn't burn him. He said he didn't want his ashes in an urn.'

'But you didn't burn him, it wasn't a cremation.'

'No. We didn't. It wasn't. And he said something else as well.'

'In your dream?'

'Yes.'

'Can't you remember it?'

'No, wait... No.'

'Don't think about it, Hans. Forget your bad dream.'

'But I know it was important. I know he said something else important to me.'

'Was he angry with you for leaving, back in the day?'

'He never understood it. A bar. That wasn't an honest job for him. He came from a farming family and then he was a steelworker his whole life long. He said something, I know he did, I know he said something else.'

'Let's go back to sleep, Hans. Maybe it'll come to you in the morning.'

He runs both hands under the vest she's wearing, his

vest, puts his hands on her breasts, strokes them, pulls the vest up over her head, kisses her, strokes her pubes, sucks at her breast and pushes his fingers inside her, she whispers at his ear, pulls the covers aside, presses up to him, and he knows he has to forget the city and the stones and the dead, forever.

He's driving. The wide white fields on either side of the road. Forests. Villages. Little houses between the bare trees. Someone had to go and tell her, at some point. Bloody village, bloody Steel Town.

They're walking along the river. Ice floes on the water. He tells her about his daughter. Tells her his ex-wife doesn't want him to see her. Tells her about his grandfather, who used to be a farmer until the collective took his land away. She tells him about her ex-husband, who met another woman in Berlin when he went to work there.

He saw the baby clothes in the wardrobe and she told him about her miscarriage, years ago now. They stamp through the snow, he throws a snowball in the water, stays back a while and then throws a snowball at her. 'I want you to make me a cocktail, Hans,' she calls, 'something special just for me!'

'Sure, will do. Casablanca Liv. Rum and snow and fresh mint.'

He grabs a handful of snow, runs after her, hears her laughing and feels the snow melting in his hand.

THE COLUMBUS BUTTERFLY

Back story: Scrooge is sitting at his desk when his secretary comes in with important news. The notepad she's holding in one hand is blank, though. She takes a pencil and writes 'IMPORTANT NEWS' on the blank notepad. The writing's too big and crosses over the edges into the picture.

'A Mr Schmitz wishes to speak to you, Mr McDuck!' she says excitedly.

'Tell him to come in!'

And here he comes, in black and white. 'A wonderful good morning to you...'

The man has blond hair; she colours it blonde later. With a yellow pencil. I always used to colour in the black-and-white pages, sometimes still do. I bought a lot of Donald Duck pocket books at the flea market in the summer. For two marks or two fifty. Sometimes they cost three marks but that's too expensive for me. Some people give you a special price if you buy several at once. I like the ones with Donald stories best. Mickey's OK, and I like Goofy as well.

The first one today had grey hair. That goes quite well because I always imagine them in black and white. I imagine everything in black and white, actually. Later I do some drawing and colouring. I've been going to the flea market for two or three years now. I don't know exactly how long. Anyway, it was the first flea market where they had comics and videos. 'Stop! Spare yourself the effort! Application rejected!' Scrooge is strict and on form. Anyone could come along. They all want to talk him into something. Issue 86 is one of the last pocket books with a back story. I'm cold: I put on a bathrobe.

It's cold outside already. The year's almost over and then the real winter will come. But the winters here in the city can be quite mild. Because we're so low down.

Lowland bay, that's what they taught us back in History of the GDR. I hope next year will be a milder winter. It hasn't snowed at Christmas for a long time. I'm not quite sure though. Before the story starts off, you see Scrooge with two sacks of money. He swings them around and wobbles his hips. He stands there with his sacks, legs apart. Tina makes stupid jokes about Scrooge's sacks. She's always making stupid comments. That comes from her reading too many *Bravo* magazines, even though she's two years younger than me. She says, anyway. Daisy Duck in a bathrobe. We listen to a lot of music. Tina Turner, Michael Jackson, Modern Talking, I like George Michael best. Issue 86 is called 'Day in the Life of a Billionaire' and on the second and third pages Scrooge pulls a big iron platform up on a rope. The sacks are piled up on the platform. Sacks of money. Scrooge is standing on a pile of cash. All coins. Golden coins. I coloured in the coins. Not every one of them, obviously. Just the two or three falling down from the iron platform because one of the sacks must have a hole in.

I've always done a lot of drawing. Didn't matter what else was going on. It was like holding my ears and my eyes closed. I used to draw all over everything. Even my hands.

The first one today had grey hair and smelled good. To begin with. Then it stings in your nose and your eyes and all over. I started colouring some of the coins purple, on the black-and-white pages. He took the biro away from me because pencils don't draw on skin. Sometimes my sharpener goes missing and then I ask the others about my sharpener. I don't know where it always gets to. The other day I found it in a crack in the bed. Behind the pillow where the head always goes, my head always goes. Sometimes my head goes at the bottom though, where the feet usually go, the man's feet, depending, or I breathe into the bricks behind the wallpaper when I have to stand up. The place smells musty. The wallpaper smells musty. The bricks are damp, I think. We used to live in a musty building like this, in the old days. In a musty flat like this. Because it was right at the top of the building and the roof used to leak. When I was in the attic, drawing. And the rain was outside. And underneath me, underneath the floor I mean, was my room. I didn't have so many pocket books then. Issue 86 is my favourite Donald Duck pocket book because it was the first Donald Duck pocket book that belonged to me. My mum gave it to me. For Christmas. Or I think for my birthday. My birthday's in November, so just before Christmas. It must have snowed *once*. Because I remember we went sledging. But I was so little then that I can hardly remember when it was, exactly. It must have been on that little hill in those little woods. The woods seemed huge to me at the time but that's normal, Tina told me, it's like with dicks, only sometimes she says 'willies' and laughs, and that laughing scares me. And I don't scare easily. I went back to that hill again later, a year or two ago I mean, if I think carefully, and sometimes that's not easy, it was a year and a half ago. When I started going to the flea market. My watch is broken. He gave me a new one a couple of days ago. A quartz watch. I shouldn't do the strap up so tightly, he says, and he's right. I stabbed new holes into it, now he's taken the fork away from me, and sometimes my arm tingles. Because I strap it round me so tightly. He wants to take the watch away from me

385

then. And I promise, because I'm scared he'll take the watch away again, I promise I'll always wear it loose around my wrist. And sometimes I take it off because sometimes they say it bothers them, the watch. I hide it in the tank in the bathroom, the toilet tank I mean. It's waterproof. Says so on the back. I know the others are jealous of my watch. On the front of issue 86 Scrooge is showing his empty pockets. Turning them inside out, his coat pockets. There, I haven't got a watch any more! It's a frock-coat. That's what Scrooge says himself in some of the pocket books. And Scrooge hasn't got a watch either. He's probably too stingy. Scrooge looks all innocent with his big duck's eyes. They go all the way from his beak to his hat. It's a top hat. He wants us to believe he hasn't got a penny. But behind him, on the cover I mean, are piles of money. Coins. Gold coins. (Sometimes Scrooge has a pocket watch on a chain, I've just remembered.)

The watch I had before, before the quartz watch I mean, was a Ruhla. With a black cat between the numbers. A black cat's head with white eyes. It was a kiddies' watch, obviously, but I liked it. Mum's boyfriend gave it to me. Her boyfriend at the time. The eyes were made so they moved when you moved the watch. There were these tiny marbles in the white eyeholes. They moved and rolled around, and it looked really funny.

I wanted to sell the watch but I couldn't. Because there were new watches everywhere. Because no one wanted my Ruhla from the GDR. They still stole it though. On the very first night after I left home. Sometimes I imagine where that watch is right now. And who must have nicked it. I was staying with Tina. In this demolished building. But it wasn't actually demolished yet, it was just that the flats were almost all empty. That was

386

where the big factories are. They're empty too now. And the old harbour wasn't far away. I didn't even know we had a harbour here in the city. Because it's not my part of town. I'd never been here before. And I didn't even know the city was so big. It's like with dicks, Tina said. I didn't get it to begin with, where she got all that stuff about dicks. First I thought she meant clever dicks or something. What with her two years younger than me. She always says. She is, as well. At least one year. And she can wear make-up and do whatever she wants. But she's always saying things like 'A bit of cheek'll get you everywhere' or, 'Better a dick than on the streets.' I respect the way she says that. Because I couldn't do it. And it's because of her I'm here. But she can say what she likes – I hear her when she's crying.

And sometimes I think the watch belongs to a watch-lover now. Not that the watch-lover stole it. Because that was one of the girls or boys I was in that flat with. It's really crap when I get my period.

She reads the foreword. She knows it almost off by heart. And actually she does know it by heart, number three makes her eyes water because he's put on so much aftershave. She doesn't laugh at Tina's aftershave jokes. Or she only pretends to. Ha ha, *after* means anus in medical German. Aftershave – it's not that funny really. Because her anus stings. When she's on the toilet she opens the lid of the cistern and checks whether her watch is still there. It floats on top of the water.

'Dear young readers, when you get to my age someone might suggest that you write your memoirs – as has just happened to me. And if you're just as busy by then as your old friend Scrooge McDuck, you might be just as grateful for the help of a so-called ghost writer as I was. I have to admit, what came out in the end is worth reading. The young man certainly has talent... and imagination! You'll soon notice, of course, that none of the stories he wrote down are true – but they're extremely well invented. You'll be bound to agree when you read the following "almost true" episodes from my life.'

And it'll soon be over, I can hear and feel it by now, and I try not to go stiff as a board because then it's never over, and I imagine the cat in my old Ruhla watch, rolling its eyes. And the watch-collector wearing it all around the world. Africa or Buenos Aires. And maybe Paris – or London. Because that's not so far away. Because I've been there, or almost. London. Because my mother had booked the trip for the two of us. In the summer or the autumn of '90, as soon as we got the Deutschmark. But then Manfred turned up. And it was all over with London. I still said that I'd been, at school. To London. To the Tower. But I messed up. Talked too much crap. I wanted to show off. Said we'd been along the Thames in a motorboat. And I said the Tower was in the back garden of the Palace. And that the Queen went out for a walk there, sure, and that we got her autograph. And I said Michael Jackson played a concert there and they let us in because the Queen gave us special tickets... I couldn't stop telling stories, I got really out of breath in the playground. Because they were all standing around me. Because they all wanted to know what it was like in London. They never did otherwise. And none of them had ever been to London. Never. Only the one. Stephan. I imagined beating him up. Because when he was on his own I was stronger than *him*. I only notice how weak I am when they're on top of me. But I wouldn't think of launching a punch then.

Scrooge flips out pretty often. When it comes to his money, that's when. Then he shakes and shivers all over.

'I went and counted wrong again!' Tina and the other girls don't think it's funny, I don't get that. 'It's kids' stuff,' they say.

'Over again from the beginning! It's enough to drive you round the bend!' And then he rolls all over the coins, the ones I've coloured in all different colours. 'I just can't get that dream from last night off of my mind!' And Scrooge puts his hands behind his back and stands all unhappy in his Money Bin.

'There's a mistake,' says Tina. She's only wearing a T-shirt, pulled down over her thighs. Her third visitor just shaved her.

'What? Where's the mistake?'

'Not "off of". Off!' She puts her index finger on the speech bubble.

'You can say both. Otherwise they wouldn't have written it like that.'

'But you say "off my mind". Not "off of my mind". That's just wrong.'

'Yeah, but you say "out of my mind". It's the same as that.'

'It's still wrong though. It's bad grammar.'

'How do you know, you didn't even finish middle school!'

'Oh, and you did?'

'Yes, I did. I went to school for eight years.'

'You're lying!'

'No, I'm not!'

'So tell me what eight squared is, then.'

'Easy peasy, sixteen of course. Are you taking the mickey?'

'Sixteen? Maybe in your stupid comics, for your Uncle Scrooge McDumb maybe!'

'McDuck!'

'Why do you even read that rubbish when it's only black and white? It's a rip-off. And it's kids' stuff!'

'Half of it's in colour, clever dick. Better than your stupid Doctor Sommer and his problem page!'

'Ha, ha, Doctor Sommer's a woman. You didn't even know it was a woman!'

'Of course I knew! I don't need anyone to tell me about the birds and the bees though. You wait till you get your period.'

'I already have, ages ago. You don't know nothing. You still think the pill will make your tits grow!'

'Maybe yours still will, Little Miss No Arse and No Tits.'

Tina grabs at her, punches her on the shoulder and the chest and tugs at the bathrobe. They both fall off the sofa, Tina's T-shirt slips aside and she sees the red welts around her pussy as she tries to protect her face; the other two girls get up, walk over to the wall, both almost naked as well, and look down at the two girls rolling on the floor, biting and scratching. 'Stupid cow!'

'Little cunt!' Tina slaps her round the face and on the chest. Then she stops suddenly and rolls off her.

When he's gone again they sit side by side on the sofa as if nothing had happened. Tina's T-shirt is stretched out of shape now, almost down to her knees like a miniskirt. Like a dress. But also because she's always pulling on it. The bathrobe is gone and the other girl's wearing a T-shirt now too. Sitting there side by side in their white T-shirts, they almost look like sisters. One of them's slightly older. They shift closer together and their hands touch.

I don't understand why the flat's so small. There are four or five of us here. I mean, it doesn't have to be the Money Bin or Scrooge's villa, but this place is much too small to feel at home. How can the men feel good in this musty little flat? But there's some things I don't want to think about, can't either. And I don't want to. Where am I supposed to go when it's snowing outside? It's not snowing yet, although I don't often look out. It's Christmas soon. My birthday's been and gone. I know I can leave soon. I know he'll give me the money then, the money he's been putting aside for me. He'll only give it to me if I don't say anything, though. If I don't tell anyone. But who am I supposed to tell, who would I tell all this? She's ashamed. Sitting on the carpet, in the corner, colouring in. I don't like this part of town, don't like the neighbourhood. It's always dark here. 'It's no use! There's no point in me working today!' Scrooge looks tired and sad, trotting out of the Money Bin. And he is only a duck. Even though he was singing further up, in a dream bubble. That's like a speech bubble only with a picture in it. Sometimes I draw on the colour pages. Because I've coloured in all the black-and-white pages. Because Christmas has been and gone. There's a speech bubble floating above the dream bubble, the little duck's song, and this duck is really much smaller than Scrooge, who's sitting by the dream bubble and saying something too. I think he's a kid, in the dream bubble, where he's fishing and singing. 'Once I caught a fish alive... one, two, three four five...' Notes are fluttering around him. The fishing rod is a stick with a string on it.

I've got another pocket book with me. But that one's ripped, they ripped it when I wasn't paying attention one time. I don't know whether that was in the demolition building or here, though. All that's left is the back story and part of the beginning. All we got for Christmas was *Bravos*, a pile of *Bravos* and *Pop Rockys* and sweets. There was something about George Michael in one *Pop Rocky*.

I put that one aside straight away. Then we got to have a lie-in. I got a headache from the bubbly. I don't actually like alcohol. Even though I'm old enough to drink it in Germany. Last year on New Year's Eve, I was still fifteen then, I was allowed some too. But only half a glass. I was instantly tipsy and Mum laughed. We laughed a lot. All my Donald Duck pocket books are still at Mum's place. If Jochen hasn't chucked them out. I really don't look much older than Tina. Or she looks older than she is. I get the feeling she's getting thinner and thinner. Sometimes we sleep here and sometimes he takes us somewhere else. If we run away he'll find us. I'm not that fast. I'd be much faster if I was a boy. We ran away from home and now we want to run away again.

They run. They run through this dark, empty street. It's named after the federal state in the north where they'd love to go on holiday, by the seaside. Past old factories, even darker side streets, across railway tracks coming out of large factory gates and crossing the street. Next to them, below the street, passenger trains run as if along a canyon. Double-decker carriages, the people in the carriages staring up at them, moving their lips, opening their mouths, putting their hands on the glass like they're screaming. Or calling. They see the next station hundreds of yards away, a couple of hundred yards off, they can't really tell the distance. A small station on the edge of the city. Ahead of them. Once they're in the tunnel leading to the platforms they hear the rumble of the train above them. It rolls onwards without stopping, gets quieter, da-dum, da-dum, da... and the tunnel is dark and silent. Huge smileys on the walls grinning at them. Footsteps on the staircase, on the stairs. Ahead of them. Behind them. They hold hands, walk to the wall and press themselves up close to the bricks. But it's all just...

'Oh, for a country life! Outside, revelling in un-touched nature! Outside in the fresh air!'

Scrooge comes towards her. He's wearing a red night-shirt and a blue nightcap with a red bobble dangling behind his back, which bounces up and down with every step he takes. 'Not like in this grey concrete jungle!' He wobbles his hips, 'Hello, my dears!' and they see their faces in his huge duck's eyes, he swings his walking stick and the blue bobble on his red nightcap dances on his shoulders.

I get tired a lot. And I sleep a lot. Whenever I get a chance. Because I can hide, there. Because I don't want to dream and there's *nothing* there, if I don't dream. Two of the other girls used to be in a home. Uncle Scrooge is the only man I know, I mean the only one who has mon-ey, a lot of money, who doesn't want to fuck me. I wish I had an uncle like him. I've given up wishing for a father.

'Maybe one of them will take us with him. I bet one of them takes me away with him,' says Tina. She's got her period, she says, and she's feeling like shit.

'And then?'

'Maybe he'll adopt me.'

'After he's shagged you?'

'Why not? It has been known.' She tries to laugh. But she hardly laughs any more, not since New Year's Eve. She hid a little bottle of liqueur behind the radiator. On New Year's Eve the men we already knew came. Issue 86 has disappeared. No one knows anything about it. No one will admit to anything. If only I could pop home to get the other comics. On one of the stalls at the flea mar-ket where I bought the comics, the last time I was there was in summer, I think, or at the beginning of autumn because the trees had changed colour, were starting to

393

change colour, but autumn doesn't start until the end of September, on one of those stalls there was always this boy, he came along with the people who sold comics there. And videos as well. But I didn't have a video recorder so I never bought videos. Even though Jochen brought one with him when he moved in with us. But I wasn't allowed to use it, and even if I had been allowed to I didn't want to watch videos on his video recorder. Once he watched a porno with Mum. I came home from school early because I didn't want to go to sports and I crept in, that was before he and Mum took my key away from me. Actually it was just him who did it but if Mum doesn't do anything to help me then it's her fault too. That's what I think. I still only hate him, though, and not Mum. They didn't sell pornos at the stall. Although I did sometimes see men coming along and whispering to the people from the stall. And then they'd go over to the van where they kept all their stuff. Sometimes I got there so early in the morning I saw them setting up the stall. There was a tree right by the stall. They always set up in the same place. I used to squat down on the roots. And watched them setting up the stall. Really early in the morning. It was still dark. And the sun behind the old stadium. Sometimes even at five thirty. Once I walked around town all night long, kept hiding somewhere for a couple of hours, hardly got any sleep. And then I took the tram to the flea market. I never bought a ticket and they only caught me once. I think it's funny that anyone would want to be a fares inspector. There's a house near this one station where the punks live. I don't like the punks much because a lot of them stink. But when I think about it, they still smelled better than the men and their aftershave and their perfume. And they always let you sleep in their house. I knew exactly how to get in. Because they told me how. But I couldn't sleep properly in the dark rooms because they didn't have any electricity. Only candles. And tea lights. And they usually weren't in because they spent all night hanging around somewhere or other. Drinking and punk music and all that. Sometimes they'd come home then and I'd be sitting in the hallway. And they'd ask if I wanted something to drink. Or a joint. I don't like alcohol, I only used to take a sip now and then.

Further south there's this strange part of town. I used to go there a lot in the autumn. That's last year already, looking back from now. But I think and I count when I'm lying on the bed and waiting for them to finish. She always sees the big fan hanging on the wall above the bed, when she's underneath with her face up she sees it. Otherwise the wall and the bricks and the window and the windowsill with dead flies on it. Every page, every section of this fan, between the wooden spokes, is a page out of issue 86, the one that went missing. Colour and black and white. Later she has gaps in her memory and counts wrong and submerges herself in darkness when she sleeps.

That's where the joyriders hang out. There's some in my neighbourhood too but most of them have gone south to where the punks have their squats because they let them in. They're kids, just like me, just a bit older, if at all. I often used to meet them at night. There was even something about them in *Bravo*. Maybe one day there'll be something in *Bravo* about us. But they let me sleep there too. Later someone got shot there, but I had nothing to do with that. I can't know about that yet.

'What's that?'

'I'm shooting the cloud of gold into the stratosphere with anti-gravity rays! It's perfectly simple!'

And I take the tram all across town in the morning. I had a wash in one of their bars, in a pub the punks have over there. Because I want to be clean when I get to the flea market, where they're setting up their stall. I shoplifted a lipstick and something for my spots. I've never got caught. On the tram that time, I screamed and cried and said my mum got off too soon by accident. And I gave them the address of a friend from school. Because she wasn't a real friend at all. Because I want to look pretty when I get to the stall. They know me by now, I've bought so many comics there. I can't understand how anyone wants to be a fares inspector. But so many people are unemployed now, and if I had money, more money I mean, because I've still got a couple of notes hidden in my backpack, then I would buy a ticket. A monthly one would be best. I could use it to ride all around town. Through every neighbourhood. There and back. And even on the trains, if I buy the expensive kind, then you can lie down on the seats and sleep between the terminuses.

The joyriders in the south live in a back yard and a house. They hide the cars in the backyard, if they haven't joyridden them to death already. I think they're crazy. But they've always been OK to me, in the two or three nights I've slept at their place.

And I think they'll let me stay longer. And then I sit on the tree and watch the men working. Later I helped out sometimes and carried the crates of comics and videos to the trestle tables. Because the boy, his name was Robert, asked me. Asked me to help out. Because he's seen me there so often. And maybe he liked my shoplifted lipstick. It was my nicest one, if I think back, and sometimes that goes fine and sometimes it doesn't. My nicest one in the past few years. Him letting me carry the crates. And me wanting to. Because I could lend a hand.

Tina tells me about her father. She hasn't seen him for an eternity. 'Eternity? You're only thirteen!'

'Fourteen!'

'Was it your birthday?'

'No one cares anyway.'

'Yes, I do, I do. I want to know. I want to give you a present.'

'What present?'

'Wait and see, just wait!'

It's the time when they're naked. *He* is always there, almost always there, and introduces them to the men. Tina's father used to have some kind of job to do with horses. He drinks and that's why she doesn't see him any more. Because her mother doesn't want her to see him. Because he drinks, because he's sad. And gambles his money away. And Tina tells a lot of stories and she doesn't know which ones are true. And Tina doesn't either, she sometimes thinks. Like London, like the queen, but that's long ago now. Sometimes, when she's in the car with *him*, she really believes she went to London with her mother. Then she sees everything from above. As if from above. The Tower and the Thames and the flea market and herself and Tina and on the edges of the pictures the bill of the little duck, pecking into the picture. She's cold. She sees the pictures in issue 86 between the spokes of the fan on the wall. She starts counting. It doesn't matter any more what she thinks. She can go home in a couple of weeks. *He* says. She doesn't know what she'd want at home. She's sixteen, but actually fifteen, and she sees herself from above. Far away. Teeny tiny, she's sitting on the sofa and moving her head back and forth. Back and forth. A duck's bill pecking. She presses her legs together. To make sure she has a duck's bill *he* shaves her. And if *he* doesn't shave her, *they* shave her. She recognizes them by their aftershave and their perfume, not by their faces. Sometimes by their faces. But she doesn't want to look at them.

'Was it really your billday?'

'My what day?'

'Don't be stupid, your birthday!'

'Well, what do you think? You think I'm lying?'

'I never know with you, dear sister.'

'Don't you get mean with me... I've had enough of that today.'

'No, no. Wait a second.' And she runs into the bathroom. Reaches into the cistern and takes out the watch. Runs, naked, back into the room. The toilet water running over her hand. She sees the men talking in the hallway but she's soon back in the room with her naked friend. The watch is broken. She only notices later. When she sees the quartz watch on Tina's arm. As she pretends to hold onto the doorframe, doing a little dance there before she disappears into the bedroom. And there's the watch on her thin wrist. A few drawn-out seconds. TICK TOCK. And she sees that it's standing still, perhaps has been for days or weeks. Forget waterproof. But Tina doesn't say anything and doesn't complain and is happy about the watch on her birthday that isn't even her birthday.

'Oh my! What do my inflamed eyes see before me? The mountain is vanishing into thin air!' Be quiet, Scrooge.

They sit together against the wall, their legs entangled on the carpet. Then they put their heads together, feel their bare skin beneath the T-shirt, and the man on the camel says: 'Nothing but sand, as far as the eye can see!

398

Where on earth should I start looking?!'

The cat's eyes roll and wink, TICK TOCK, Tina sees the fan on the wall, TICK TOCK.

And I keep looking over at the boy. He's about the same age as me, or maybe seventeen.

I'm sitting on my tree again, him standing by the stalls, and I'm watching him serving customers, watching him write in a book, like a homework book, probably the issues and the volumes of the comics he's just sold. Have they got the *Columbus Butterfly* yet? Out of the comics from the GDR I like *Atze* and *Mosaik*. There weren't any others anyway, I don't think. The two mice in *Atze* were quite funny. Fix and Fax. Now there's Fix and Foxy but they're not mice, I'm not sure what kind of animals they're supposed to be. To begin with, *he* gave me something to drink and there was something in it. And I was like half asleep when he lay on top of me. I don't even like alcohol. I couldn't even scream. Tina drinks a mouthful of the liqueur she hid. But then she pours it away because she says it smells like the one man's aftershave. The one with the good suits and the expensive glasses. She's stopped making her stupid jokes about the word. Aftershave. Fix and Fax always used to speak in rhymes. They were written underneath the pictures. And everything that ever happened to them was in rhymes. I always used to wonder who came up with them. It must be difficult. I keep looking over, at you my imaginary lover. No, that doesn't quite work. I like your comic stall, because you were so handsome and tall. Or you are. That's a bit better. Because I can't look forward from then into the future. Funny. You're cute, actually. And one day he comes over to me and my tree and asks me if I want to have a lemonade with him. Sure, I say. He has brown hair, a bit long, a bit greasy. Even though I've dolled myself up especially for him. I ask him if they've got the *Columbus Butterfly*. No, he says, but maybe next time. And he says it costs more than the other Donald Duck pocket books. But he can probably get me a good deal. I ask him if the others at the stall are his parents. No, he says. We're at a food van and he gets me a portion of fries as well. I tell him they're called *pommes frites*, because they're from France. And I went to Paris with my mother. Really? Sure. Right after the D-Mark. Summer 1990. I eat the fries much too fast and I'm finished before him. Because I haven't eaten any proper food since yesterday. Because I'm saving my money for the pocket books. And I never want to go back home because of Jochen.

He's only wearing a T-shirt and he has pretty strong arms. That must be from carrying all the crates. His name's Robert. Didn't he have a different name? There was a Robert in my class as well, but he was awful. His kisses taste of *pommes frites*. I'm glad I'm not a virgin any more. I do read *Bravo* now and Doctor Sommer. Tina says we could write in about our sex experiences. She makes that face that scares me, and later I'm lying in the sun with Robert on the little hill outside the old stadium. Doesn't he have to go back, I ask him. But he says he can take a break now because most customers come in the morning and it's already afternoon now, and he doesn't have to get back until they take the stall down. They still tell him off though and the one man gives him a slap on his greasy hair. I ought to tell him to wash it more often. Even though it feels good when we're kissing. I washed my hair at the drop-in centre yesterday afternoon, and that was the last time I ate anything as well. It's strange in the city at night. Everything moving. And every dark street corner's alive. Tina tells me about the caravans but I've never heard of them. Her cousin's boyfriend has something to do with them. She doesn't know exactly. But he's really tall. She says. Must be six foot five or so. And much stronger than *him*. He looks after people, that's his job. And when he finds out we're here he'll definitely come.

Robert promises me the *Columbus Butterfly* when we're lying in the sun on the grass. I've even caught the sun on my face this afternoon. He wants to kiss me too often and I take out a tissue, put a bit of spit on it and wipe the ketchup off the corners of his mouth.

He lives in Karl-Marx-Stadt, it's called Chemnitz now, he tells me, two years it's been called that now, and he works in this junk shop where they sell comics and videos and records and furniture and all that kind of thing. He says he likes the Hulk comics best. I don't know them. He says, and I think he only says it so he can kiss me again, he says he likes Mickey as well though.

Mickey's crap, I say. And he kisses me anyway. And he says he'll try to ask if I can work on the stall as well, or maybe even in Karl-Marx-Stadt. I can't tell him yet that everything's awful. That I know issue 86, the one he sold me, almost off by heart. Because he says The Hulk's so strong. And because then he goes and says I'm almost as strong as The Hulk, who I don't even know, when I give him a bit of a slap on his greasy hair when he gets fresh. And I push him away, but just as a joke. And he tells me about The Hulk. I wasn't that interested though, at the time. Yawn. That superhero crap's boys' stuff. What I didn't know was that Mickey's included in the *Columbus Butterfly* too. Sometimes everything hurts and then all I want to do is scream, but I do it quietly because otherwise it hurts even more when *he* comes, and no one can see the dream bubbles and the speech bubbles.

The guests who come are almost always the same. Regular customers who frequent the girls. The girls don't know how much they cost because *he* takes the money. They have to be naked almost all the time. It looks strange from above. Four or five naked girls. In this room. In this flat. Snow falling outside. Winter '93.

I couldn't do it if I was myself all the time. They only had crap videos on the stall. Backstory: 'Hello friends! Just imagine, the other day the Beagle Boys... But wait, you'd better read it for yourselves. Here in this pocket book from the series "Walt Disney's Donald Duck" you can find out about the daring and dangerous adventures I've been through in the battle against the Beagle Brothers. Uncle Scrooge and Huey, Dewey and Louie are in the stories too, of course:

Uncle Scrooge and the Divining Weed
Donald Duck, Class Representative
Uncle Scrooge Doesn't Believe in Horoscopes
Donald and the Lie Detector
Scrooge and the Aurum Nigrum
Donald Duck and the Wild Greens
Donald in Search of Rare Earths

Enjoy all your exciting reading – with best wishes from

Donald!'

When we hear a ring we gather together. Telephone or doorbell. Then we know what's coming.

When the telephone rings *he* knows he'll soon have to shut up shop. Because people say so. They say he'll have to close the place down. But the cash flows and flows. The young cunts from the streets bring in as much money as he imagined. Just a couple more months and he can bugger off with the cash and invest it or blow it elsewhere. It's a matter of time. And the time's right, right now.

Because: chaos on the streets. He knows exactly where they hang out. He has his sources on the street, though they don't know what's going on. All he has to do is pick up the little cunts. What can he say – they're only hanging out on the filthy streets, anyway. He's got a friend with the cops, and that's the key factor. His contacts are beating a path to his door. The market's exploding in the city but he's an exceptional case. Nothing to do with the market itself. Just like they don't want anything to do with him. The *Bild* prints his small ad just like the other small ads. And the key factor is mouth-to-mouth propaganda. About the mouth-to-mouth treatment. That's why his apartment's a bestseller. And that's why the cash flows, so much that he's proud he can run the whole show. Proud he can pick up the little wrecked pussies from the streets. Who knows where they'd end up otherwise, anyway. And when he comes along they learn something useful. And when he shuts up shop they can go wherever they want!

Of course, he seized the opportunity. And no one can say otherwise! The people who come and pay good money, they'd be looking either way, whatever happened! So it's best if he takes care of the girls. And they're constantly telling stories and lies about how old they are. And when he shuts up shop and buggers off none of them will be any worse off than before. No way!

The thing is, he has to get out of here. Soon. Pocket the cash and bugger off. But the cash flows and flows. And his cop says everything's fine and dandy. Because he gets to shag for free. The cop. Because he likes shagging this one girl, the youngest, the most. He knows all about the dirty bastards who frequent his little cunts. There are a few people from the scene, which isn't his scene, who ask him what's going on at his place. The usual, he says, babes who look younger than they are. And stupid gossip, you know how it is. Lies. Slander.

And because he runs another apartment where the babes aren't quite as young, it all goes fine and dandy. And because the men like coming to his young cunts and can't get enough of coming to his young cunts. The men he knows all about, the men making laws and representing them and investing in this dark, chaotic city. Solicitors, judges, property sharks, ex-Stasi men, politicians. His insurance policies. Winter '93, and he lugs all the cash to the bank.

If I wasn't so nice to them it wouldn't work out. I don't just walk into some teenager's bedroom and say, 'Hey, girl, come with me!' They're at rock bottom. They got fucked over long before I met them. When I say 'gang-bang' they know exactly what I mean. And when they start in with their 'blow jobs' and 'anal' I'm even surprised myself. Surely everyone gets it nowadays, that it's all about money. I mean, we're not in the Zone now. And we're certainly not in the time after the Zone. There's enough opportunities for everyone. Don't nobody come accusing me of exploitation. That's not what it is. I've learned a few lessons and I'm certainly not a lamb, if anyone gets that. I stick my cock in the cunts so they know what's going on nowadays, how things work nowadays. Why be so down on me? They're shoplifting and hustling out on the streets, and I take care that it's a bit better organized. How do I know how old they are, 'cause they lie, they lie whenever they open their little cunt mouths. I've only ever hit anyone as an exception. And they love opening them, that's all I can say.

'Hmm... hmmmm... Where can he have got to?'

'Every one of you, off to look for Mr Gearloose! Off you go!'

'But I'm tired!'

'You're always tired when there's work to do!'

I can only go back. Because I can't do it any more. I've long since stopped counting.

He said if I let him touch me and if I touched him, I could go to Chemnitz with him. The boy from the flea market. I often think of my mum now. And I want the pills he gives us sometimes. *He*. And I want my comics, because I've only got half of one, the ripped one, with the back story and a few pages, not even up to the middle. And I even often think of Jochen, he only hit me now and then and actually all he ever did was tell me off.

Mum often thought about moving to the West, after '89. We only went to the West once, to Berlin. That was in December '89. I liked it there. All the shops and the big wide streets.

The bright lights in the early evenings on those big wide streets.

It was just before Christmas. It was snowing. So much mushy snow on the pavement. And my shoes were all wet and when we got back home, the train took all night, I caught a cold. Didn't have to go to school for five days. That was before Jochen. Mum made me tea and I stayed in bed all day long and watched TV. And I read my first Donald Duck pocket books, which I bought with my 100 DM welcome money in Berlin. Mum took half my welcome money. The old songs disappeared. We stopped singing them at school, from one day to the next. I used to sing a lot. In the Young Pioneers. I was in the Pioneer choir. That helped because I was only middling at the other subjects. I never want to be on the bottom again. I never want to lie down again. 'Our homeland is not just the streets and the houses, / Our homeland is all the trees in the wood. / Our homeland is all of the grass in the meadow...' that was a classic, although I wasn't good at learning the words. But I know almost all the Donald Duck pocket book off by heart, funny, I don't get it, I can't be that bad at learning words then. I just found it hard in front of the class. There was even this one girl, she wet herself in front of the whole class. Pitter, patter, and her trousers were wet. Pale trousers. Ugly pale GDR trousers, too short in the legs, I can't understand how people could wear them. Right round her pussy. A big stain. And it smelled. It's not true, none of it.

'And we love our homeland, our beautiful homeland, / And we protect it.' It's all muddled up, Robert, I like you too. I want to come with you. Tina only laughs now when I tell my nonsense stories. Because I've collected them all up, in a corner of my head. But that was OK, the thing with the welcome money, you can buy a whole lot for fifty marks. Mum cried when the Wall came down. Because she was really scared of what might come next. Because she used to be a typist for the Party. For this newspaper that belonged to the Party. I don't really understand it all properly. And I don't want to. And she bought us a hairdryer and a mixer for the kitchen and a little radio for the kitchen as well. They included the other fifty marks of my money. We already had a mixer and a hairdryer as well, actually, but the new ones were special. I used to make myself pudding in the mixer, those new packet mixes, light and creamy milk mixes. Chocolate. Vanilla. Whisked up with milk. I don't want him to sell the films, later. I'm scared they'll sell the films at the flea market. Or the photos. I know he's got a hidden camera. And I know I'm on film. And I'm scared Mum might see it one day. And then drink even more, out of worry. I don't want anyone to see it. Sometimes I think I can rewind everything and delete it. In my head.

When it's all over I want to go back to the flea market. But I don't know if it's there in the winter, it's snowing outside. I usually sleep sitting up, if I can. On an armchair or something. I never want to lie down again.

'Oh dear! That was the worst adventure in my whole life! But now I can say: All's well that ends well!'

(Future story: In March 1993, the apartment on Mecklenburger Straße is raided by the police. The operator, M., is later sentenced to just under three and a half years in prison. No details of the clients are released to the public. Alleged videos and photos never emerge.)

TOKYO, YEAR ZERO

I. THE TEMPLE
Where are you?

Look up. But the sky above you is grey, a big grey orifice, and your face gets wet. Snowflakes melting on your coat.

You stumble and lean on your stick. You feel the smooth wood on your hand as it clutches the knob.

You're on the pavement of a wide street, people walking past you as it goes on snowing. It looks like they're wearing masks, white masks made of snow, but the lights are dazzling, a bright glow, flickering strange neon symbols you can't decipher, can't understand, have never seen before. Orange, red, pink, pale blue, green, purple, all around you, night-time rainbows above bright suns, you close your eyes for a moment and seek darkness and seek silence, how did you get to this city you don't know? How long have you been wandering this endless city?

You want to go down a narrow alleyway but the lights and the colours reaching out from there are even brighter and more radiant than those you're now standing between and you're moving your head and twisting your body and still leaning on the stick. Tall buildings, rectangles with colourful tendrils growing out from them, signs and symbols glowing bright on the vines. You lean against a wall and look at the knob of the stick. A dragon's head, you think. Or the head of a demon. A man gave you this stick, handed it to you, it was resting on both the man's open hands as he passed it to you. His torso bent slightly forward. That was... hours, days, weeks ago?

'It will not only help you walking. This is an old symbol and it will protect you in our world.'

People walking ahead of you, an unorganized flow in all directions, cars on the street moving very slowly, you see countless black limousines melding into one dark ribbon in the midst of the radiant cubes and towers, and you look at this big slow movement of black vehicles, look at the bright tendrils growing out of the façades and apparently moving too, seeming to grow, upwards and sideways and diagonally, along the façades, large characters that are a mystery to you. No one takes any notice of you leaning there against the wall, holding the stick in both hands, touching the head of the dragon, the head of the demon, as though you were blind. You're among strangers. Strange faces. White masks, as if made of snow.

You search your pockets and find a small appointment diary, from the health insurance company, 1999, all the days and months crossed out, scribbled over. You find a plane ticket but you can't remember getting off a plane, getting on a plane. 11/2/2000, you manage to read before it drops out of your hand, no, a hand came out of the stream of people ahead of you, getting denser and denser, and grabbed at it, and it disappeared. You close your eyes and see them waving at you. You're in a train carriage, your head leaned against the window, your forehead pressed against the cold glass, watching the bus driving below the train track. Children raise their hands, laughing, uniforms, school bags, the yellow bus turns off, disappears between low, narrow grey blocks, and you watch them waving around the corner. Then suddenly a forest, the trees like big ferns touching the window where your head is resting. A stick leant between your legs. It touches your knee and knocks at your knee whenever the train goes into a curve, and you run your hands over your healed wounds and have the feeling there are still two holes underneath the fabric of your trouser legs, holes you can stick your fingers in. And the forest comes towards you, and the forest moves away from you, and cuttings between the trees with low little houses in them, with curved roofs.

The snow drifts begin. Where are you? Where are you going? Open your eyes. A dark river beneath the train and beneath you. Small ice floes on the water. The way the sounds change when you cross over the bridge. Didn't you see mountains, hours, days ago? When the man gave you the stick. When the man led you to the shore of the sea. Low, curved hills.

Or were they the brown roofs of the houses?

The man speaks to you. You're sitting in a room made of paper. You're at the other end of the world. 'Sekai, do,' says the man, and you drink something out of a small bowl, something that seeps warm into your painful legs, relieving the coldness and the feeling they're someone else's legs, 'Indeed, it is difficult to understand.' Yes, you understand that and want to speak and you open your mouth and feel that you're drinking while you want to speak, and you sink back onto the bench, 'to understand the world as it is...' The man speaks slowly and rolls his Rs, looking at the low table with the jugs and bowls, grey hair flopping over his forehead.

'The world,' you want to say, because you understand, you think you understand, and your chest gets wet and the bowl slips empty to the floor, and you move your legs aside and move your arm and move your hand so that he leaves, 'Who are you?'

'Although it seems true, it is not, and although it seems false, it is not.'

You're sitting in a room. The key with the big plastic tag on the table in front of you. Two other keys alongside

410

it. Silver tags with spherical ends, like miniature clubs. A chip card in a cardboard slipcase. A number on it. You look out of the window.

A park opposite. Snow on the trees, towers behind the park, behind the trees, far away or very close by, the distances change, tower blocks connected by bridges, corridors of glass. A temple-like low building with a curved roof among the white and the green of the park, for the trees aren't bare, winter in this city, but days, you remember them now, that smelled of spring, the air suddenly mild and the sky clear, no grey any more from which the snow fell wet on your face, but then another icy gust of wind that grabbed you on your paths through the night, on your way along the neon alleys, along the river, across empty parks like small woods, where are you going? And what are you looking for?

The window is open; you don't know how long you've been sitting here. You stare at the yellow light reaching you from the door of the temple. You take the lift to the twenty-seventh floor, a little old woman next to you. You lie on the bed, covered by your coat, and the yellow light of the temple reaches in through the curtains. Isn't there a man sitting there at the table? At the one you were just sitting at, or at some point? You look up at the ceiling so you don't see him any more. But you do see him and you know him. And you know that he shouldn't be here.

'Don't worry, I came alone.'

Later, you flee from that voice. You're standing in a hall, in an enormous room, pachinko, pachinko, the drone of loudspeaker announcements, you're looking at the faces of the men, the gamblers, sitting in their endless rows of space seats and looking into the depths of the mirrors, in which silver balls run through a labyrinth of steel pins, alleys, traps and channels, on rotating plates, and new labyrinths of thousands of steel pins come about, dense jungles of nails, you've never seen a game like this, you walk along the rows of sleeping gamblers, you walk along the streets of your city, stand before the machines of your first arcade, insert a coin to test it out, hear the rattle in the machine's slot, feel the gamblers' money rotating in your machines, two arcades in the west of the city, *you must explore this city that you know already*, onward and ever onward, *there is no way back*, you see yourself as a young man (.........................

....

....) 'No need to run away, I just wanted to see how you're doing,' (.....

....

.....), onward and ever onward, and you stumble out of the enormous room, how long were you wandering lost in the labyrinth of machines? Fleeing that voice, 'Now we've both got nice holes in our body, haven't we?' 'I've got nothing to do with your holes, Bricks and Mortar Man,' 'Oh, how nice that someone still remembers that stupid name they gave me. But the big properties were free for you too once I was gone, weren't they?' 'You're not here, you're not dead,' and then everything fell silent, everything fell silent, the tangle of melodies, the clinks of the coins, the speaker announcements, the rattle of the balls, and the gamblers in their space seats turned to the aisle and looked at you. Silver eyes, as though there were coins laid over them. 'No, I'm not dead. Almost dying is sometimes not a stroke of luck. But you have to admit that you knew back then...'

'I didn't know anything. Go away and leave me alone, Bricks and Mortar Man.'

'And the real estate was free when I nearly died. When your great rise began.'

The alleys crossed and branched off and got lost in the dark, only to flare up again, bar after bar, hotels, strip bars, karaoke bars, love hotels, massage, blow job salons, manga tanga, garishly lit glass fronts, the windows elsewhere glowed dark red, you recognize the English words in among the many symbols, walls of glass, schoolgirls in uniform in the window, tiny women crowding a dark side alley, the glowing tips of their cigarettes, let there be light, you're on the inside of the great machine, and onward, ever onward you walk and you don't know where to, and you don't know why, the Bricks and Mortar Man has gone, the voice brought no other voice along from *there*, men in suits talk at you in English, you know they're touts but you don't want to enter the buildings, you don't want to go to the bars, and then you are in a bar, at a table, a woman in only her underpants dancing awkwardly at a pole on a platform, you look at the shabby wallpaper, a fan pattern, and the music reaches into you louder and louder, takes away the fear that someone who shouldn't be there or can't be there will sit behind you or next to you again, the woman in panties dances, another woman sits next to you and talks to you, you try to understand, try to remember your paths over the past few days or weeks, you see the stick leaning on the table that's supposed to protect you, that's what the man told you, and before that or after that you sat in a tub of hot water, it smells of sulphur, and you put your hand in the water, on your leg, and you feel your other hand on your other leg, you breathe onto the water surface, and you see the little waves in front of your face, in front of your breath, between the steam, a semi-dark room, but when you lean your head back you see the clear night sky above you and the stars, *This is Hakone, Greyhair-San, where the hot water comes from the heart of the earth and goes into your mind and goes into your body*, 'My name is Kraushaar,' you say, and the young woman smiles and sips at her drink. There's a glass in front of you, too, and you want to take a drink, feel the ice cubes cold on your lips, the glass seems to be empty, just ice cubes, you make out a bar counter behind the woman at the pole dancing awkwardly to the music, 'Mimi,' says the woman sitting in front of you at the table, a tea light, 'you American?'

You don't know what to say and you nod and look over her shoulders at the other tables, most of them empty, candles in glasses, only one man by the woman at the pole, a man in a dark suit looking at you over bare shoulders, but he's alone at a table, a slim white back moving as though this woman, leaning over to him and not there, were talking animatedly to the man in the dark suit. The man turns around to you and then looks back at the dancer.

The small breasts at the pole. Wallpaper with a fan pattern, a narrow room, a narrow corridor, but when you lean your head back you see the clear night sky and the stars. 'Where is Hakone?' you ask, and she smiles, streets and alleys and people and snowflakes drifting between the buildings, the façades, who's dancing over there, and who's sitting alone? And snowflakes touch your eyes.

'You Hakone-San?'

'Hakone, hot fountain, near the coast.'

'You want *hako*? In Haikyo?'

'Tokyo?'

'Hai!'

'Hello.'

'You want *amai*, girl, *ima*, you *onaka*?'

You don't understand, and your legs are cold and

stiff, and you move your legs under the table and see her shaking her head and then nodding and raising her empty glass. She has blonde hair. She's wearing a brown suit. 'Don't worry, I've come alone. It's lonely in the mire.' Darkness. You feel your chin touching your shirt. Sounds. The clinking of glasses, ice cubes, the girl's voice like a silver string in the midst of the ever louder music, 'You want good meal?' 'Nein,' you say, 'No,' you say, 'Sayonara,' you say as you get up, some time later, a bundle of money on the table, your money, and as you turn around, outside in the garish fog that opens up before you and reaches into your body and your eyes from all directions, the girl is standing behind you, holding steaming plates of noodles in both hands, so close to your face that you breathe into the steam and make out big chunks of meat between the white strings, you feel sick, a man next to you, yellow suit, someone singing loud and off-tune behind the half-open door, a small man was standing on the platform, his shirt un-buttoned, his glasses misted over, a microphone in his hand, the dancer naked on his chair, at his table. 'Where you go?' and you shove aside the girl and the man in the yellow suit and walk between them back through the door, the door you just passed through onto the street, hear the plate smashing on the pavement, walk past the singing man, the woman dancing again behind him, still dancing and holding the pole with both hands as though she'd collapse onto the ground otherwise, the man in the dark suit who was just singing a moment ago has gone, you pick up your stick, which you almost forgot, your legs are cold and numb, and you limp outside, *love hotel*, someone whispers in your ear, or did you just read the English words on your paths through the light of this night? The man in the black suit walks alongside you and puts his hand on your shoulder.

'Welcome to Hakone, Mr Kraushaar. *Willkommen.* You good friend of... *mein guter Freund Hans.* I don't speak German, just a little. I am very sorry. Good friend of Hans is good friend of mine. Welcome to Hakone. *Willkommen*, Kraushaar-San. We will do all the best for you, so you can rest. And you will forget all the hard times and all your troubles. It is a great honour for us to have you here. You can stay as long as you want. Please be my guest, my houses are yours, sit down and feel comfort, Mr Kraushaar.'

II. SNOWLAND

You enter the temple courtyard through the red-brown wooden gate in the low wall surrounding it. It has stopped snowing. On the way, you walked along the banks of a river. Abandoned ships you took for junks swayed in their moorings. Large seagulls perched on the rotting cabin structures with brightly coloured lanterns strung between them. The wind blew cold in your face and under your coat. A narrow path directly by the water, above it the streets and the buildings. Now no one comes towards you, you hear no cars on the streets above you. You walk across a big wooden bridge, look down at the dark water. The river disappears between the buildings.

You're standing at a crossroads and you see a giant golden Rolex advert; its light would have dazzled you only days ago. It's just after eleven on your Rolex – haven't you adjusted it yet since you've been in this country, on this island at the other end of the world? Silver trees on a boulevard. Ten thousand lamps between the bare branches. You try to remember Christmas, New Year's

416

Eve, but there's nothing. And you unfasten your Rolex, throw the watch in a beggar's paper cup as he squats beneath one of the silver trees, all alone on this big empty boulevard. There's a clink and a rattle as the watch hits the coins and you hear the beggar, a haggard man with a haggard brown face, grey hair flopping over his face, calling something to you as you walk on. 'Stay, my friend, I'm all alone here!' The illuminated sign of a strip bar, but you're not interested. You're looking for the temple whose yellow light reached into the room you were lying in. *Gentlemen's Club – Live Nudes – Topless*. You're no longer or not yet in that neon district where tens of thousands of women and thousands of touts and tens of thousands of clubs and bars and salons and basements and first floors full of women wait in manga uniforms, in school uniforms, in smart suits, half-naked, in the light and the dark and fan out, bodies and bricks creeping towards you, and the tracks rattle between the signs, *just a short rest for once, just a short lie down*, what time might it be, and you cross over the road, walking slowly towards the '24-Hours Pet Shop'. No cars. This part of the city seems abandoned. You turn around, the high windows of the gentlemen's club on the first floor, a small staircase leading to a small door, a pale blue illumination, you're not sitting at the bar, you don't see the girls, who all look very Japanese, dancing naked, with gas masks on their faces, in glass cages (. . . . .), *a Ming vase is a Ming vase*, you used to joke, Vietcong Town, but now only a handful of Asian women work in your properties (. . . . .), you're not sure whether this information suddenly popping up is correct. Darkness. You're lying on your back. It's cold. Snow or ice cover you. A sound like someone opening a large drawer. You're flat on your back. Someone leans over you and touches your eyes with silver tweezers. 'Let me see your last images, big man.'

Like an explosion, it reaches in through the layers of your eyes, and you duck, flinch, standing in the endless stream of vehicles, in the middle of the wide street, walking towards the trees with the lamps and stopping in front of the 24-Hours Pet Shop. Cages are piled up inside the shop. Stacked in the shop window. You make out rabbits and small dogs behind the bars. You see birds and glass boxes with strange reptiles inside them. And a man in a white coat bustles to and fro between the cages and boxes. High cages holding large parrots. Low glass boxes holding rats or mice. A young girl comes out of the door, wearing a gas mask, its trunk with the protective filter touching a white rabbit she clutches to her chest. The dark eyes of a small dog being dragged along by a man on a lead studded with glittering stones, presumably bought along with the dog in the shop. The dog splays its front legs against the stone of the pavement. You squat down and reach out your hand.

The dog licks a little snow from your cold, clammy fingers. And you push your hand beneath its body. Feel it quaking and trembling, and you see the little puddle on the stone. The short tail clamped between its hind legs. All you understand when the man shouts at you is the word '*gaijin*'. And he's not actually shouting at you. He's speaking loudly and firmly in a deep voice. He leans over and reaches for the small dog, what breed it is you can't tell. The lead gets tangled around the dog's front legs, and now the man, like the woman before with the very big long rabbit, presses it to his chest. He's wearing a jacket with the logo of some kind of sports team. Where is your stick? It's on the pavement next to you. When you pick it up you see it's got wet. The dog's piss drips from the wood.

The dog looks at you. Its eyes wide. It's sitting on a stone plinth. In the courtyard of the temple. You stand by the plinth, see the front teeth bared. Snow on the dog's head like white hair. Is it laughing or howling at the sky, full of rage? The sturdy torso rests on broad paws. You're alone in the temple courtyard. Yellow lanterns lit inside the temple, a small staircase leading up to it. Wooden pillars in the portal, behind it a room, more slim pillars, walls made of wood and paper, far back you make out the large lanterns. It seems far away to you. Go in. Just rest for a moment. It's afternoon. The dusk already resting on the treetops.

Didn't you go to a temple courtyard in Hakone, that strange place they sent you to from your city, inside a temple even? With the man whose guest you were. Who made you tea in centuries-old vessels, poured the tea into smaller vessels that were only slightly younger. Who explained the ceremonies to you, but your body and your brain were too weak to take it all in. A never-ending cycle of bowing. And when you left the chopsticks in the rice the circle fell silent. Men in dark kimonos. That's what you'd call their robes. The men lowered their heads. And the shadow of your chopsticks on the paper wall. Like the thin, bone ears of a rabbit skeleton. What nonsense.

'Shin-de-iru.'

'Put this down, Greyhair-San.'

'My name is Kraushaar.'

'Put this down, please. This means death. The sign of death.' And his chopsticks stabbed out of the rice like two fingers. And when he tried to take hold of them he couldn't manage it. His hands felt all the strength seeping out of them. The men who were invited to the meal, in their dark kimonos, kept their heads lowered, didn't move, only the man who gave you the stick later or earlier spoke to you quietly, his head lowered as well.

'This is the shadow of death. You must put it down please.'

'Kage,' you hear a sonorous voice from the depths of the room.

A fat man dressed in white robes walks to and fro on the temple's terrace, in steady haste, bowing repeatedly towards the temple and then disappearing inside. You stride slowly past the dog, then you see another dog, another stone statue on the gate on the other side of the courtyard. That one too is baring his teeth, but he doesn't look as angry as his brother on the opposite gate. The noise of the city is inaudible here. You feel how cold it's got again, put your hands in your coat pockets, feel something moving there in among your keys, a tiny silver ball falls onto the stone floor and stops in the small strip of snow in front of the staircase leading to the main building, to the sacred shrine, you don't know much about these things, didn't you have a friend, an employee, your third man, who knew about these things? Far East, Buddha, Kung Fu and Confucius. Steffen, you remember now. Fragments in your head. Karate-Steffen from... what was the name of the place, and what are you doing in the courtyard of this temple? Was it *Kleinmutzschen*? Far away from *everything*. And you want to pick up the silver ball, you reach into the snow at the foot of the staircase, you can't find the ball but what do you want it for anyway? It must be from that strange 'pachinko' game, with a rattle the ball falls and runs through the channels and alleys between the steel pins, changes direction, rotates back, disappears into a slot. When did the Yugos come along, you think suddenly

420

and you put your hands in the snow. A war here, a war there. You stand up and wipe your hands over your face, your palms wet and cold. You feel your stubble and you wonder when you last shaved. How long have you been in this city? And why is it winter here, when in your city, so far away, on another sphere of the world, it's winter as well? And you're standing between the two dogs on the stone plinths, two or three snowflakes moving very slowly before your face as though floating, as though the seconds passed more slowly in the courtyard of the temple, you close your eyes again, and again you see a flash and two silver projectiles disappearing somewhere in the darkness, you cross the empty courtyard very slowly, your eyes still closed, you hear your footsteps, the temple behind you, the temple ahead of you, what does it matter, you think, whether the past is correct, what was once true, and whether your paths will end here...? The yellow light from inside the temple. Evening has come and you're still here. On the cold stone of the courtyard. You hair is damp, your breath steaming white in the dusk.

Like a manger with a roof, the small water basin in the shade of the temple building. The water is coated in a layer of ice. A wooden ladle on a string. You reach for the ladle, feel how dry your mouth is, can't remember when you last drank anything. Then you see the dark green, almost black body of a frog, as big as a fist, underneath the thin ice. It floats motionlessly in the water, its limbs splayed away from its body.

III. KABUKICHŌ
You raise your head. You're at the counter in a very narrow bar. Shiny green tiles on the wall next to you. The

421

bar top is made of polished wood. In front of you is a full glass. The narrow room is only a few yards long, like a tiny tunnel.

You see a woman in front of the shelves, which hold countless bottles. She seems to be oblivious to you. Her black hair is up and she's wearing a traditional blue robe. You've seen these kind of robes before, some time in the past few days. Your legs and your feet hurt, you must have been walking a lot. Around Hakone, wherever that strange place might be, only a few images and memories in your head, the sea, low, curved ridges of hills, and around this city, Tokyo, however you may have got here, a long train journey, how did you get from the house with the paper walls to the station, you remember a snow-capped mountaintop you saw out of the train window. When was that? No station in your ragged memories. Your hair is damp. You stroke your smooth, cold face, feel a small scabbed cut below your cheekbone. You turn around and hardly recognize the stick leaning against the wall in the shadow behind you. Matte yellow light above the bar and the woman by the shelves. You reach for the glass, the ice cubes clink quietly. As you lift it to your mouth you realize it's empty. 'Konnichiwa,' you say to the woman and you remember the man in Hakone tried to teach you a few scraps of Japanese. The man who gave you the stick now standing in the shadows. The stick with the dragon's head. Or was it the head of a demon, a dog-like gargoyle...? You don't want to turn around again. 'Konnichiwa,' you say, the man who took you to the hot sulphur springs. The man they sent you to, a long flight, a long corridor, along the borders into space.

It's only now that you hear the quiet music. Some Japanese tear-jerker, a woman singing laments to a piano. 'And my tears, pearls on a winter's day...' You look up. Is the woman humming it, exactly to the tune of the quiet music, or is it somewhere inside your head, some pop tune you heard somewhere sometime? You're afraid the voices are coming back. The woman turns to you. She has pushed the lapels of her blue robe apart so that you can see her breasts. One breast – the left one? – is brown, almost black, and with a shock you make out the giant birthmark covering almost her entire breast, extending up to her collarbone. The woman hums something again, leans forward, reaches under the counter and then she's holding a tiny pair of nail scissors.

You want to say something but she bends over again, spreads out a newspaper on the counter, places one hand beneath the breast with the dark brown birth mark, leans her upper body far enough over that her breast is directly above the newspaper, feels it with her hand and cuts off a few stray hairs growing out of the birthmark. You see them falling slowly and barely visibly onto the paper, disappearing between the black symbols.

'What are you doing?' you want to say and you can almost touch her shoulder, her breast, without reaching your arm out far, that's how small and narrow the room of the bar is, that's how close you are to her.

You hear the quiet snip of the scissors between the songs that all sound the same. You button your coat and stand up. You want to put a banknote down on the bar, you feel your wallet in your inside pocket, but then you don't bother. The woman is still taking no notice of you, seems undisturbed by your presence. *You're not even here.* You want to leave and you turn to the wall but you can't see a door in the shiny green tiles. A sound on the other side of the tunnel. Again, you turn around. The woman runs both hands across the newspaper, a tiny pile of

423

black hair. You can't help looking at the birthmark. You make out the dark nipple in the middle of the stain. A man standing at the other end of the bar. You walk towards him, he walks past you. Your shoulder touches his shoulder. A rustle of paper. You hear him saying something to her. You grip the handle of the small, dark wooden door he must have used to come in. *Where are you? You want to go home.* As you turn around, holding the handle, the door half open, you see the man in the pale suit, who reminds you of the man in Hakone, who reminds you of some other man, you see him grabbing her breast with both hands and leaning over the bar to her, laughing.

Later, when you're in the car and looking out through the tinted windows at the streets of glass and light, your hand is warm and moist because the knob of your stick is warm and moist. *'Willkommen in Kabukich,'* says the old woman sitting opposite you and holding a glass in which the ice cubes clink quietly. She speaks German with a dark accent. In a wooden minibar next to her and in front of you there are bottles and glasses. 'Welcome to Tokyo. Help yourself, Kraushaar-San.' She gestures at the bar shelf, showing you the palms of her hands. Small hands. She's wearing an unbuttoned grey coat over a dark suit. Her hair is almost white. She touches your knee. No, it's just the car braking and she bends towards you for an instant, then leans back into her leather seat. You feel a humming in your knee, in your thigh where the wound is. 'Please excuse the circumstances, I'm sure you must be tired.'

'No,' you say, 'I was just... was just... somewhere else until a moment ago.'

'Yes,' says the old woman and smiles. 'Hai. You've had a long journey.'

The door behind you is closed. You're not on the street. A hall in semi-darkness.

People as tall as your chest dancing in the semi-darkness. Dancing directly in front of you. Then moving more slowly. You gaze into their fixed faces, at their angular jaws. Only then do you realize they're puppets. Do you see the long, thin strings. And men in black robes, with no faces, standing barely visible behind the puppets. You slide down against the door. Singing and words reach you. You recognize figures on a long platform, in front of it a lattice of pale bamboo sticks, some sitting, some standing, that's where the singing is coming from, the words you don't understand, you see them moving their arms behind the lattice, or are they the arms of the giant puppets? You see the shadows moving on the ground, between the puppets whose protruding eyes look at you, and the black faceless men with the strings move away from you with their puppets.

'I wish I could have brought you to a better theatre.'

'What theatre?'

'An old, very old tradition, Kraushaar-San. You were on the edge of Shinjuku, on the edge of Kabukichō, Kraushaar-San.'

'I don't know where I was.'

And you feel your way along the wall, sitting on the floor, but it doesn't bother you because you've seen that they often sit on the floor here, in this faraway country where they sent you to recover. You can't remember that but the man in Hakone said so.

And you watch out of the shadows, 'Kage', says one of the men without looking up, while you lean over the chopsticks stuck in your rice. You watch the puppets out of the shadows and can still barely make out the puppet-masters dressed in black, their faces concealed

425

beneath the black cloaks that you might call kimonos, but you know that's not the right word. The singing and the voices coming from the platform on the opposite wall get louder and louder, sound more and more dramatic, and you try to grasp how the voices and the movements of the puppets fit together, belong together. And you realize you don't have to see them, ought not to see them, the men pulling the strings.

A woman puppet in a blue kimono laments loudly and sings loudly, bends over, takes a bow. Puts her hands to her chest, puts her hands to her hair. Some kind of disaster must have happened, you think. And then you think that you haven't called your wife yet since you've been here, been in this country, but then you realize you don't care. Then you think of your son, but that too is far away and doesn't touch you. And wasn't with you in all the days you spent wandering lost in this city. And the longer you stare into the semi-darkness of the hall, the more you spot other spectators crouching on mats, the longer you stare at the puppets playing, the more you understand of the story. A father and a son. The son's lover. The father wants him to leave her. The father seems to be a respected samurai. The father of the son's lover belongs to another clan. A war, a feud. The old story, you think. The story of the world. Each of the giant puppets has several puppet-masters, who move the puppets' limbs in perfect co-ordination. And only the faces of those pulling the strings for the heads are visible. Pale faces amid the dark fabric. You feel great fatigue. Just rest for a moment, just lie down for a moment. The loud singing, the choir of voices from the other side of the room. You can't see the lattice any more. Your head descends slowly onto your chest. You feel an ache in your legs, an ache in your arms, how many days and nights did you spend wandering lost without sleep? You remember Hakone, that strange swathe of land somewhere on the island, somewhere near this gigantic city, you remember your fear of the darkness of sleep whenever you lay in the house made of paper and wood. The quiet sounds of a strange forest where you went walking some nights, trees like great ferns, sometimes it snowed and you wondered why the ferns kept their leaves in winter, perhaps a kind of Far Eastern fir trees, *How are thy leaves so verdant*, the moon sometimes above the woods when the sky was clear, the stars in an arrangement you weren't familiar with, you stood sometimes by the shore of the lake, in your city, by your house, with an old revolving star chart you used to use years ago in astronomy lessons, looking for the charioteer and Perseus and the Great Whale, and in the little woods you lean your head back and think that the world is a different place now, you're wearing a white kimono as if covered in snow but you're not cold, you take a few steps between the trees, look into the shadows when the moon is there, look into the darkness when the moon's not there, the snow always gives a little light as though it stored up the day, you lean on your stick, sometimes you hear quiet voices between the trees but you know there's no one there, you walk on into the woods and you know you only have to follow your tracks to get back, even if it's snowing, it's not far, *a rhyme, a rhyme, my kingdom for a rhyme*, Matthias Reim, 'Goddamn I Love You', and you laugh out loud at the cheesy hit in your brain and you wouldn't be surprised by an echo, but your laughter disappears into the snow and between the trees.

Once you saw a rabbit or a hare, a grey and white speckled rabbit, and you see that rabbit again in a cage at the 24-Hours Pet Shop, it was perched in the middle of a circular clearing, barely visible against the snow, the moon was there and the moon was not there, it seemed large to you, the rabbit, had only one and a half ears, frozen off, bitten off, and that's why you recognize it in the cage at the 24-Hours Pet Shop, what is it with you and the animals in this country, on this island, you think, a trip to the Japanese zoo and you can't find the exit.

The father shuns his son and laments and weeps and then sings of his suffering. While the son stands in the shadows and holds a sword in both hands. And then disappears into the darkness. Where does he go? You touch the leaves of the great ferns. The mother, at least you think it's the mother, runs to and fro between father and son, sings high, almost screeching, and you hear a laugh from the audience while the warriors march on stage. A hill in the middle of the woods. Only two or three stunted trees up there. Your breath steams white in the night while you stride, leaning on your stick, across the crunching snow, stopping at the three trees. The hill is not particularly high but you can make out the contours of your house, the guesthouse. Far behind the trees. And the slightly taller houses of the estate where the man from Hakone welcomed you as his guest. Guest of honour. Such an easy word in your language: *Ehrengast*. Once, you saw him as you looked out through one of the windows, saw him leaning over a table full of tiny glinting stones with a magnifying glass over his eye. You squat down and press your hands into the snow, hold a few tiny flakes against the moonlight between your fingers. Two conifers and a half-parched fern.

The large fan-shaped branches and leaves are yellow, branches or leaves with smaller leaves like the broad blade of a knife. You remember that you once (or more than once, your memory's not that precise) went to the botanical gardens in your city. When you were a child. Didn't you look for some kind of fruits there, from plants, exotic plants you'd dreamed about? Or read about. You gathered up hard, woody tubers in your backpack. And a couple of soft, overripe fruits you didn't know? But what did you know anyway in that past under the bygone stars? And you laugh again and you see the rabbit with the one and a half ears at the foot of the ferns. Green and earthy like a giant frog. And it's soon gone again because your loud laughter in the silent woods scared it. You think. And didn't you stand by ferns, your red or blue camping knapsack on your back, ferns that reminded you of huge stinging nettles so you didn't dare to touch them? And now you're here and you lean against the dead tree, between the stunted conifers. You've never thought much of great explanations. By night in these woods your memories are strangely clear. Your friend Steffen always had some quote or other at hand. From his *Hagakure* or the chinwags of Buddha, you've almost forgotten all his books, even though it's not long ago yet. And didn't he give you one as a parting gift? And then he did want to make progress in his career, just like all the others. When it came to business. Used to bang on about the path of the samurai and then he did leave, left the city, left you, the path of the Angels more like, but you did like him.

There were few people you could talk to at the time. But he knew you've got to get off the streets. 'Yeah, yeah,' you say loudly, you say quietly and you think that the old fern hasn't quite died yet, because the stunted conifers at least gave it a little protection up here. A few green leaves here and there on the fern's large yellow fans. Does your old friend Steffen know you're here? But how would he know? You don't even know it really yourself. You climb down the hill, slipping a few times, and land on your arse. Bloody kimono. Not much fabric covering your body. You grab at the snow on either side.

Your arms spring up in the air. You're squatting on ground level and something drives you up. Rips you upwards by your limbs. And you turn around and look for the dark figures that you ought to be able to make out in the sudden, blazing light. And music reaches your ears, reaches your head. Women ahead of you. A large group of women dancing in strange patterns through the middle of the large room. The enormous room where you were just sitting against the wall. Or are you in a different room? The women's faces are painted white. They're wearing leather collars in various colours. You dance with them and you don't know why, and you don't know anything. You hear the calls from the audience, no thoughts in your head. And the women's panties disappear synchronously, and you see their cocks, small ones, big ones, dark-skinned, pale-skinned, swinging to and fro between the women's legs (*Wait a minute, they're not that big!*). And as if a vacuum pump (market crier 1: *Coooocks, great big cocks!*) were sucking you across the room, you tumble under someone else's control through this crazy dance troupe.

You crouch, you stand. Limbs and cocks in your face.

Two tiny women cling to your sore legs. Dwarves, their heads hitting your belt. You yank open a door and you're standing on the street, searching for your sunglasses in the pockets of your coat, in the folds of your kimono. Because rays are burning your retinas, the layers of your eyes. You lean your head back and see a multi-coloured sun above the buildings, you stumble into the alley, a hand touches your shoulder, you don't want to turn around, sleet settles on your reading glasses, *but you haven't got glasses yet, for fuck's sake.* 'Stay with us in the shadows, tall man.' And you run.

'So how do you like our Disneyland?'

You're holding a glass, looking out of the tinted windows of the big black limousine, nothing new to be seen on these streets.

You're tired and strangely awake at the same time and you no longer register all the lights and movements around the limousine, you've long since become part of the stream. 'Why do you speak such good...?'

'My grandfather loved the German language,' says the white-haired lady, 'he worked for the German embassy, sixty years ago. The old axis, you understand.'

'The old axis,' you say, 'Berlin, Tokyo...'

'Berlin, Rome, Tokyo,' says the white-haired lady. 'Grandfather sent me to a German school. I've always been interested in German culture. Hölderlin, Brecht..., "Ode to Joy". Mozart. My grandfather was a highly educated man. I've read many German books. I was head of a German-Japanese club for many years. We met once a week. We still meet up now to talk and read.'

'A German-Japanese club,' you say.

'Sweet May hath come to love us, / Flowers, trees, their blossoms don; / And through the blue heavens above us / The rosy clouds move on.' She moves her arms, hands in front of her chest, as she recites, and her voice sounds much higher, almost like a flowing song, so that it seems for a moment as if a different old white-haired lady were sitting before you. 'The nightingales are singing / On leafy perch aloft; / The snowy lambs are springing / In clover green and soft.'

'Beautiful,' you say, but she's not finished.

'I cannot be singing and springing, / Ill in the grass I lie; / I hear a distant ringing, / And dream of days gone by.' She inclines her head and smiles.

'Really, beautiful,' you say again.

'Heinrich Heine. My grandfather loved that poem. In your city, Kraushaar-San... how do you work there?'

'How do we work there...?' you say and you raise your glass slowly until it touches your lip, cold, but you don't drink. Her voice still in your head. *The snowy lambs are springing.*

'Kabukichō,' says the white-haired lady. 'We live in a land full of whores.'

'We live in a land full of whores,' you say.

'Have you ever been to Japan before?'

'No,' you say.

'A long time ago there was a theatre here. Hence the name, Kraushaar-San. Kabuki. The building really did exist, over fifty years ago, though we've forgotten it now. Later the yakuza came here. But I don't like that name.'

'The yakuza,' you say.

'No,' says the white-haired lady with a smile, 'I'm not a yakuza. And I prefer to call them *gokudo*. Not many streets away is where McDonald's begins. Kabukichō is dying, slowly. The boundaries are shifting. Our own young people have no respect for the old business ways.'

'Your German is excellent,' you say.

'You're very friendly, Kraushaar-San.'

'*You're* very friendly,' you say. 'What may I call you?'

'My name is Sansori,' says the white-haired lady, 'that's how you'd say it, in Europe.'

'How did you find me, Mrs Sansori?' you ask.

'What does that matter?' says the white-haired lady with a smile. You look at her little teeth, almost as white as her hair. 'I wanted to make your acquaintance, Kraushaar-San. We work in the same trade. You were having problems with your business?'

432

'There were some differences of opinion,' you say.

'Differences of opinion: *Meinungsverschiedenheiten*. A beautiful German word. Someone came out of the darkness with a sword? And you were between the worlds?'

'I don't know where I was,' you say.

'It's all very simple,' says Lady Sansori, 'You were a guest in Hakone, now you're a guest in Tokyo. So that you can then return to your city. *Willkommen*, Kraushaar-San.' She inclines her head. And you incline your head too.

'You said *gokudo*...'

'That is someone who is seeking his path, Kraushaar-San.'

'You're welcome to call me Arnold.'

'Did you not like it in Hakone, Arnold-San?'

You don't answer. Lady Sansori tops up your whisky and takes ice cubes out of a compartment of the bar with a pair of silver tongs, drops them into your glass. 'Help yourself, Kraushaar-San. This is the best Japanese whisky. Deplorable that the young people only drink American or Scottish whisky in Japan. Do you drink Japanese whisky in Germany?'

'I didn't know...'

'... that we have very good whisky in Japan?' Is it her deep, gentle and yet rough-sounding voice that makes you feel so calm and utterly relaxed? As if you'd been driving through the night in this limousine with her for hours. And could simply sit here for hours to come. When Lady Sansori pronounces the word 'Japan' she elongates the last A, one long, seconds-long A after the first short one. Japaaan.

'Our world is different. A different star. A loud "yes" means no. "Perhaps" means never. I'm sure you have many questions, Kraushaar-San.'

433

'I don't know. Maybe just one.' You hear yourself speaking and suddenly you don't know how much you've told her already and how much you've asked already and how much she's asked already and how much she's told you. The stream of her words.

'It is an old tradition,' says Lady Sansori, 'like in your country. It was my path to tend that tradition.'

And once again you're surprised at how almost perfect her German is. The old axis. Who would have thought it? Grandfather Adolf. And out there, outside the tinted windows, the streets are getting darker now, you make out tower blocks at the edges of the broad pavements, sparsely lit towers, broad vacant spaces between them, then stone and glass again in strange conglomerations, the lights of an elevated street, green and red traffic lights, then silent streets again, broad paths, the night seems to be night here now. Is there a second man next to the driver? You can't tell behind the dividing wall, in the middle of which is a small window, also tinted.

'The laws, I must explain, Kraushaar-San, ban intercourse. Excuse my plain words, but that's how one says it... for money, Kraushaar-San. Here in Japan.'

'You want to know more, about our... my business.'

'You're very cultivated for a *gaijin*, Kraushaar-San. I'm joking with you. I'm an old woman.'

'In my country, these things you speak of aren't so simple either. But there are also ways there for this old tradition.' It seems to have grown darker inside the car as well, but the yellow lamps directly above the doors are still on.

'*Gokudo*,' says Lady Sansori and nods. 'The people in your country wouldn't like it if they heard us talking.'

'No,' you say, 'they wouldn't. And your business, Mrs Sansori?'

'We're a land full of whores.'

Didn't she say that before, you wonder. Her lips are very thin now, her dark eyes scrutinizing you. She takes a cigarette with a long white filter, lights it, and you think it looks very elegant, the way she smokes. 'Excuse my words, Kraushaar-San. I'm a tough old woman.'

'I can't really judge,' you say after a while, because you don't know what to say.

'Oh yes, you can, because you know who I am. What I am. You understand these things, Kraushaar-San. That's why you're here. And that's why I'm speaking to you. And that's why you're speaking to me.'

You look out of the window and see that the car is driving along an elevated road, along one of the elevated highways, you see the dull lights of the city as if through fog, far away a bright flickering, but your eyes are tired, the car is in a tunnel, leaves it an instant later, you see another elevated highway crossing the carriageway above you, then the car changes lanes several times and it seems to you as though you were driving back, back the way you came – isn't that the pale snow-capped cone of Mount Fuji on the horizon? But how would you know that, and your eyes are tired.

'We always say the young generation has lost respect. The old laws no longer apply. But we ourselves have grown greedy, Kraushaar-San. There was a time when I ordered my goods from Thailand. The great trade route of the Thais. I did business with the triads. I did business with the big new syndicates. Bought my goods at McDonald's. But why?'

'Did it give you an advantage?' you say, 'Goods... at McDonald's...'

'Things aren't that simple, Kraushaar-San. Once there were the women we called *asobi*. They were talented entertainers. In Kabukichō there are now... schoolgirls. Like a thousand years ago, the *ukareme*, the simple whores. And the triads bring the Thais across the water. We've forgotten the old values. Business has made us cold, Kraushaar-San. Cold and greedy. How do you work in your city?'

She extinguishes her cigarette in the silver ashtray, drinks a sip of her whisky.

'It's not always easy to do business with the right people,' you say, 'it's better to stick to your own business. Go your own way.'

'You are a *gokudō*, Kraushaar-San. But someone will destroy you one day. Perhaps.'

She smiles. Her lips are still thin, wrinkles up to her forehead, wrinkles on the forehead beneath her white hair, but her lips look very young when she smiles. 'We don't know how to continue, Arnold-San. You, I. Go honourably when the time comes.'

'So as not to lose everything?' you ask.

'You understand, Kraushaar-San. Even long ago, we honoured the *asobi*. And the *jokagu* were the ladies at court, the ladies of the aristocracy. They were well trained for the aristocracy. They lived in big castles and palaces, they were often aristocratic themselves. You love the aristocracy in Europe, don't you?'

'It still exists,' you say, 'but we tried to get rid of it.' You want to tell her about the Bielefelder, who's supposed to be blue-blooded, but then you don't.

'The Queen,' says Lady Sansori, 'the Prince of Denmark. But this world, our world, is different, Kraushaar-San. Many years ago I was the mother of the *asobi*. The syndicate of the women entertainers. But things changed. Greed, Kraushaar-San. Business. I saw goods and profit. We had to go new ways so as not to perish. And in the end we're disappearing nonetheless.'

'Goods,' you say and you look at her as the streets outside get brighter and more colourful. Is it morning beginning, or night?

'*Gokudō*,' says Lady Sansori, 'they were destined for nothing else in their lives.'

'The Thais?' you ask.

'Them and us. It's not easy to go new ways and honour the old ways. We're destroying ourselves so as to keep in business.'

'I don't mean to criticize, Mrs Sansori,' you say, 'but I'd never talk about goods in my business...'

And she laughs. You drink. The whisky burns in your mouth. Lady Sansori takes a deep breath.

'You really are a very insolent *gaijin*. Dealing in the same goods. Without your stick, Kabukichō would have beaten you to death long ago.'

And as you walk along the glass walls, hundreds of feet above the city... And as you stride through the large room, hundreds of feet above the city... And as you hold your hand above one of the candles to grasp that you still exist, hundreds of feet above the city... And as you find her deep voice again in your head... hundreds of words and hundreds of sentences...

'I told you that fucking's forbidden, *gaijin*. For money. As a business. You saw the blow job salons, *gaijin*. Where the wooden head of your stick saved your head. You saw the massage salons, where the *gaijin* money and the *gaijin* dicks are welcome. Where the little Thais sit on your back. Where fucking's forbidden, *gaijin*. And where they'll fuck you anyway, *gaijin*. You man from outside. Don't you know your own business? Behind the curtain, behind the dark glass? Do you want to know how I've been watching over these things for almost fifty years? Don't you tell me about your Angels, about your innocence, *gaijin*.'

And you walk the three glass walls, yard for yard. You see the big key with the 27 stamped into it on a table. But you're not in a hotel. You touch the bottles in the bar. See the candles on the low tables by the bed. A silver ashtray, a cigarette smoking in it. You put your head against the glass. The cigarette between your lips, and the glowing tip touches the window, and ash and embers fall on the carpet, and you crouch down and dust them off carefully with both hands.

And below you the city. The morning is grey. And no mountain behind the clouds. Where would it be, when you only saw it once, thought you saw it, looking out of the window of the train. The city lies quiet and nothing moves down there. You see small white spaces between the streets and the paths. It must have snowed. And you stand upright and go over to the bed. Throw your cigarette in the ashtray. You're naked. When you lie down on the old woman she wakes up. She's tied a blue scarf around her head. You see the tips of her pale hair at the sides. You hold her by the shoulders. Her pubic hair is grey. A long scar runs from there to the ribs beneath her small, pendulous breasts. She's perfectly silent, and then she sits astride you and you feel her hands around your neck, on your neck. You walk slowly through the portal of the small temple. 'A demon, a possessed bull, once went on the rampage there. They collected up its hair and put it in a shrine. Sacred. Stay down, you damn *gaijin*, Arnold-San.'

And you stride through the doors between the walls made of paper. Walk through the yellow light as if through a tunnel. You see two children sitting at a table. They're wearing hair robes, you can see their white

438

skin between the furs. They're busy with paper in front of them on the table. They reach their hands out to each other across the table. They look at you, and you recognize yourself in the round mirrors of their eyes.

EARLY EVENING IN EDEN CITY

I.

Jerry's crossing the Naschmarkt square. The Dead Railwayman is exactly 0.9 kilometres' distance from the Naschmarkt. Says so on ye olde tourist sign, done up in curly writing, although it doesn't say the Dead Railwayman is 0.9 kilometres away, it says the central station is. Jerry's going to the central station, and not just because that's where the Dead Railwayman is – he wants to get some cash out as well. 'Cash and dash?' No, that's not my style! *Prefer doggy style?* I don't care. As long as she's a spermophile. *Not without protection!* Pass the pitcher over! ('Cash and dash' in the sense of: 'Upselling, a fairly common practice not long ago. First the client was >solicited. Had he then agreed on a service, for instance >French, it was possible that the woman, having received payment for her services in advance, merely spoke French to him.' *German Encyclopaedia of Prostitution*, 2003. Jerry reels and rustles through the pages and the decades.)

Jerry's sitting in the Dead Railwayman, above the staircase leading to the platforms. Take the register: Frank's here, *flash the cash!* No, Reiner's the one with the cash! (Except after a game of cards.) You gotta laugh, eh! Reiner's sitting right at the back at the bar, drinking schnapps. My first, he says, it's past five. *Excuse me, sir, the hairdresser's is across the way.* Bernd is here, Mr Stoneface is here, no one knows the guy, he's just been sitting here for the past ten years. *Stasi, or what, an old agent?* (Whispered – Frank, Reiner and Bernd are discreet. Jerry is too.) Or was he in the Rock? Alcatraz, in jail, in the slammer. Back in the day, that is. Stone makes you silent. And the Stasi makes you meshuga? *You from Berlin, or what?* Behind bars, in the bunker, black Mariah. What's that got to do with it? A pitcher of beer in the Dead Railwayman holds two litres.

If we don't find out today why old Stoneface never says a word...

Don't you have somewhere you've got to go, Jerry?

Somewhere over the rainbow. *The only place I've got to go is to my grave.*

Jerry's crossing the Naschmarkt square and laughing. Because he doesn't know exactly why the Naschmarkt is called Naschmarkt, and because *naschen* means nibbling and because there's a Neumarkt as well, and because he's thinking about getting cash out and about the Dead Railwayman. And because he sees giant ferns growing in the little side streets. Breaking through the ground and growing up the stone. Thursday. He thinks about thumping. Humping. And the underground trains rumbling beneath his feet. Right behind the Naschmarkt is the marketplace. What's the real name of the Dead Railwayman? 'Platform 8 Bar'? Or 'Station Bar Platform 8'? Funny you never look at the sign any more, even though it shines out all day long; it's always kind of dark at the central station. Even though they gave it a complete overhaul ten years ago, loads of glass. No, must have been longer ago than that. Flying lizards perched in the arches. Bad luck that Jerry's change of life started when they rebuilt the central station. He had other things to worry about. *What the fuck are you talking about?* Jerry pulls himself together as he walks through the town hall arcades, past the tobacconist's. He's given up smoking; it's not a laughing matter. It can't be an underground train 'cause the underground line's not finished yet. Under construction. Quiz question: *Who in here's done time?* If you lie you pay for the next pitcher.

And how are you going to know that, Director Detector?

Not me! (Frank, Bernd, Jerry). Reiner says: You know I've done time, twenty-eight years ago, 'cause of the Stasi.

No, I never knew that, you never told me that, or am I going meshuga?! (Come on, tell us!) Jerry notes down the question for later, whether Mr Orpheus or the Man behind the Mirrors have ever been inside. No, probably not. They're businessmen, stupid prejudice, you might as well ask the same of big Mr A. from the big bank.

Ring a ring o' roses, we all fall down. The ferns are getting bigger and bigger beneath the glass dome.

Platform 8 is where the trains for Berlin depart. International Congress of Eros Centres. You gotta laugh, eh? Wasn't much of a joke though. He must have drifted off in the canteen. As he nods off for a second, the abbreviations flicker behind his eyelids. Jerry works for an insurance company, that big one, *the RSB's tied up with it*, no, not health insurance, or not directly. A serious matter. *You can't be a jailbird there.* OS, OS / is just as good as FS! / FS, FS / now everyone wants AS! Arsenic, or what?

You can hear the tannoy announcements clearly if you're not too noisy. They like to imagine all the places they could go. Paris. Only eight hours away. Moulin Rouge. Thursday's a good day. The other day that girl, the one who always stands over by the side entrance where it goes down into the dark, she goes running to the train to Paris and nearly knocks me over when I was coming out of the Railwayman, just for a look. *It's not a direct train, though.* Change at FFM. They all do three-somes, nowadays.

Thursday's a good day. The weekend humpers come

442

on Fridays. Everyone in the Railwayman knows exactly where he goes, every Thursday, but he still doesn't say where, even though they're very discreet in the Dead Railwayman, *red lips are sealed*, Moni with the cherry-red lips, protruding down below, apt. number 3 on the left. Over in House X. Where they write the services provided on the front doors in felt-tip pen. And old Stoneface hasn't said a word for ten years. The RSB is almost bankrupt. Regional State Bank.

No, he did say something once, 2.3 years ago, Jerry remembers it now, it's my fifth, it's only just gone one. And Reiner yelled at old Stoneface, *...ready to depart on platform 8...* that he'd seen him personally, in the jug, Jerry'd never heard that expression before, as a description, place and circumstance, and he had to think about it for a moment, even though he thought he knew all the slang, from the former butcher who runs the club he liked going to, where he'll go on going to until the butcher or he gives up the... because the butcher handed him the *Encyclopaedia of Prison Language* across the bar, the butcher's never been inside either of course, thinks Jerry, and almost knows it for a fact and dashes from the Naschmarkt to the station and onwards, ever onwards. And usually on foot because he does have to have a drink and wants to check that the ferns are still there, that they're still breaking through from the layers beneath the asphalt, mycosis was stamped out several decades ago, no one pees mucus and blood any more, India rubber drips from the hollow stems of the ferns into the cans tied tightly to them.

Did you read there's this one who offers EWO now, what's that stand for, everything without or what? Yeah. She must be crazy. The women's eyes glint like diamonds. Fresh air freshens the blood. He sucks on a Fisherman's Friend.

'Girlfriend Sex', says the ad. *The delayed Intercity continuing to Hamburg...* Only my friends call me Jerry! *Just a bit of period blood.*

And Reiner wanted to beat a mining tunnel into old Stoneface's face, because all of a sudden he was Major Stoneface, and if someone doesn't say a word for ten years and only raises a finger to order a beer then you can't blame him for wanting to take a look, behind the granite. *Oh, go and get a haircut across the way.*

Jerome, what a lovely name and what a lovely man

Cash and dash? No, not with me. Anyway, they're just old legends from the distant past. But I'm generous anyway, more of a gentleman, that's how I see myself, yeah, I'd call myself a gentleman, the generous type in my way, old-school perhaps, I'd say. *Cash and splash.*

II.

There's a rumbling beneath Jerry's feet. And it's still Thursday, Thursday again. Naschmarkt. Nought point nine BAC. Suddenly he's all alone. For a while now he hasn't understood what's going on in the black city. Nothing surprises him though. He sees the giant body of protesters moving, first behind the building and then along the boulevard. Oh, right. That's where they've all buggered off to. To get a good gander. And he remembers them announcing it on the radio that morning. *You're listening to ninety-two point...* The women were tied to each other using a complicated bondage system forming a single body, closer and closer, higher and higher, hundreds of women, more than five hundred to be approximately precise, and more and even more, because visiting demonstrators from all over Germany are getting tied into the knot, *People of the world, look upon this city!* He probably knows most of the local women incorporated into this giant corpus. And that body's marching now. If they haven't got anything better to do. The Christmas market was dismantled weeks ago.

And then he remembers he has to get some cash out. He'll have to wait until the big protest march is over, though, if he wants to blow it on a woman. Before he can go ringing at the doors of the properties, apartments and clubs, that is. KNOCK, KNOCK. Anyone at home? What crazy ideas the whores' union has sometimes. *We have to show society we're in their midst!* He feels around in his pockets. He sees the queue of taxis below the market. He sees the huge, swaying figure behind the buildings, then on the boulevard, then back behind the buildings. *Where are you going?* And then he's suddenly at the little stall with the wooden figures. Because it's market day today. Naschmarkt, Neumarkt, central market. As he nods off for a second the pictures rotate behind his eyelids, before his very eyes. And then he's back, standing to attention. What a stupid invention, the taxi drivers call out to him, the city'll sink beyond redemption!

They must mean the thumping and rumbling beneath his feet, the drill-bit digging. Jerry wants to get cash out, the cash machine is always right. And more and more holes in the Swiss cheese beneath the city. *There's the night train to Zurich.* Maybe we'll drink another pitcher and then all climb aboard.

And on Wednesdays they do shots and fruit brandy for half price at the Dead Railwayman. It's not a Wednesday though. Good thing too, because bodies need their spirits. (*Jan* Brandy, says Bernd, who used to be a German teacher, Pear Brandt. Not much of a joke. No one gets it, not even Reiner.)

Our Jerry knows all about huge bodies and halved

shots, because he's forty-eight and the RSB is financing the quaking beneath his feet (*partly* at least), and Human Resources keeps Accounting on their toes, and everyone's running on the spot, and Field Service is running round in circles, and the bosses are discussing the ferns and the properties in which the women are flat on their backs exhausted because the weekend is over and because the whores' union is demonstrating for a modification of the prostitution law, *And what's that got to do with us?* And Jerry runs and runs up and down the levels where the latest art's on show, stopping in front of the pictures for a moment before he runs on and runs off, giant ferns stroking his shoulders, he stares into the embers and into the evening, and then he runs on and runs off along the corridors, like a wounded deer. At home he has to shower his cheesy feet clean, especially on Thursdays. *Electrons are cast at a molecule, leading to oxidation.* If only it wasn't so hot, the molecule, neutrinos reaching into bodies, reaching into bricks and mortar, rock and stone. Jerry flicks through the new *Geo* magazine in the canteen. He's sold off his porn mag collection – who's he got to bequeath it to anyway?

So I'll be turning... forty-six this year. I work for an insurance company. I haven't got children and that's nothing to do with my wife, actually. Yes, I'm divorced, no, I wouldn't call it office work directly. Yes, I've had a few different jobs since the Wall, because... well, everyone seems to know my girlfriend and I aren't married. In the canteen and in the Dead Railwayman. Not that I care what they say about me behind my back. I've always been open in that respect, even if she doesn't know that. In theory it'd be possible, seeing as I'm divorced. I used to work in a big chemicals plant, yes, here in the city, galvanizing and that, bad for your lungs. That's why I gave up smoking. There's a brothel now where the old plant used to be. What's left of the old works, I mean. There's only one building. Mind you, I wouldn't call it a brothel exactly, it's actually a great club. I always get my usual drink as soon as I sit down at the bar there. And then the boss comes along and we have a chat about this and that. If he's got time. Usually he's really busy. Me too, when I'm there. That's just what you say, *the wife*, *my wife*, *your wife*, even if you're not married. And children, or maybe just the one kid, wouldn't be a problem for me, actually. That's no big deal at thirty-eight nowadays. For a woman. Anthony Quinn did it at almost eighty, I read a while back. Is he still alive? And yeah, of course she wants to. You do still have dreams after all the years. The thing is, though...

Why am I telling you all this?

Jerry's standing in the slush on the Naschmarkt and talking to himself. One seven three zero on the digital display. Why are they still drilling down there? Must be even colder down there. And Mr Orpheus rams the drill deeper and deeper into the stone. At some point they hit black granite, someone told him once. That's why it's taking so long. And apparently they're reaching further and further down into deeper and deeper layers. Hence the ferns. It's funny, isn't it, in the middle of winter. And apparently they've come across old streets and alleyways and neighbourhoods down there. Because it was good *fertile soil*. Still is. Kupfergässchen, Ulrichsgasse, Münzgasse – Copper Lane, Ulrich's Lane, Mint Lane. They found an almost fossilized wooden sign down there in the underground. 'Corpse board'. What a stupid name for a brothel. *How d'you know that, Jerry?*

Wouldn't you like to know!

The boss of the old place, where the new place is

now, the boss of the nightclub, that is, he told him about it because he bought the sign, on the quiet. Knows the right people. And then he gave it to the Old Man of the Mountain, so they say. No guarantee of accuracy. So shoot me. Mind you, at the moment all sorts of faces are appearing in between the big round and triangular leaves of the ferns winding their way up the façades. *Get back to your jungle!* There are two royal ferns, people say, *osmunda regalis*, growing high above the roofs of the city. One out by the lake, next to a villa by the shore where you can see all the way to the mountains, and the other north of the central station. Where the women wait in the mirrors.

There's an echo in his ears from the market, MEAT, CHEESE, CHEESE, bouncing off the portals of the central station, SO FRESH IT'S STILL ALIVE, direct from the heart of the seven seas, even though the central station's about a thousand metres away from the market. Jerry wants to measure the distance, step by step, because it can't be true. Hopscotch, crotch by crotch. *Further, much further.* And Jerry buys one of the figurines at the wooden figurine stall, for his wife you see, who isn't his proper wife yet, not before the law, as they say. That's not down to him. Or down to her either – Jerry lives alone.

The city imposes itself on him with a time lag. Grey, pink, *give me pink!* He hears music from far, far off... somewhere, sex canteen, he sees his own death in a shop window, *no, that's too cheap, really now*, a glass building, Fashion – Reduced Books – Delicious Pizza – Baker Boy – Boyzone – Fashion –Modern Kitchens – Kitchen Club – Sven's Super Kebabs – Sweet & Sour – Glassware – Carpets Mecca – Crossover Shop – Mäc-Geiz – Burger King – Talstraße Administrative Office

– King Kong – Men's Hats. Jerry reads 'Men's Nuts'. Ding Dong. Yeees? It's blowtime!

What I mean is that sexually, pretty much, I'm actually at full capacity. I mean, at forty-six, you've had this and that... nothing of inhuman concern is common to my interests. No. There's some guys tell the whores they're single, and I tell them I've got a wife at home. Well, she's not actually my wife yet, it's just an engagement ring. From Galeria Kaufhof. And he's drawn away from the dice game at the Dead Railwayman to the MECCA OF PORNOGRAPHY, *I can feel a one coming*, and further, much further, Frank's taking notes, who's going first? Pass the pitcher over. Jerry creeps through the sludge. Wood holds tight to hands. Jerry strokes the little figurine. Jerry doesn't know what's drawing him on, it's cold and empty at home, or he doesn't want to know, *what she don't know won't hurt her*, standing round the back of the central station outside 'Sex World', later known as 'Angels Club', he sees the women waiting in the mirrors, the giant fern casting shadows because the moon has arisen, when suddenly everything moves differently in the white mists, he thinks, he feels like he's standing at the precise geometric centre of *something*, reduction, deceleration, decelerated insemination, testicular galvanization, *wonderful!* Jerry rummages through his pockets, *playing pocket pool?* He's given up smoking. That's not a laughing matter.

III.
And there's the little wooden elk, not a stag, perched on the beer pump, with huge lips pursed in a kiss. The night imposes itself on him with a time lag. Grey, pink, *give me pink!* Because Karin takes him upstairs to a room. *He was*

so lonely, poor little guy! Shrapnel raining down from the clouds; they didn't predict that. Puts a real damper on things! Outside, the big black chariots glide by. Inside, the music's turned up louder. First pop of the night. Half an hour's budget session. *OS, OS / now they all want OS / FS, OS / I never offer AS!* Top hits of the eighties.

And the trains from Berlin arrive on platform 8, and soldiers alight onto the platform. Reiner and Frank and the others with the bit-parts look out through the fogged-up windows of the Dead Railwayman.

And they stride past them down the stairs, Adidas shoes, gold, *oh gold*, round their necks, oh necks, *impossible ain't nothing*, Puma socks *forever long lasters*, great big guys, Arnie on the beach, looking pale brown, jungle, Turkish delights, the dark chariots waiting outside to collect the soldiers. 'Berlin, Berlin, we shit on your Berlin!' That's old Stoneface, leapt to his feet and yelling beer and brandy, the air full of liquid and full of fear, and everyone ducks down behind the bar. And then later it turns out, in the whispering bar, in the Dead Railwayman, that old Stoneface used to be a driver nearly twenty years ago, the driver drives a hard bargain after eight brandies, and he was with the Stasi as it turns out, formerly, and then that job went out the window and before you can say Jack Robinson he's driving the girls, the old unemployed major, back then, *we always knew it, he went and blew it!* And now he's yelling till his lungs hurt, those lips ain't sealed, and the little wooden elk is vibrating on a different beer pump elsewhere, red lips, and then up in the room, *where's Jerry gone?* And the Nubian soldiers cross the city on foot and in the dark chariots. Wounded deer. No, still only just past GO, Old Kent Road, Electric Company. Some are clever and ride in snow-white coaches. Put your foot down, put your foot down, it's time for some fun in this town! Bollocks, it's time for cash, white gold, it's time to join the dance, ice-cold gangsters on a runaway train, trouble's brewing, what's new about that, do you think Jerry's with his pussy cat? *Pocket pussy or what?* What's that when it's at home? You know, a rubber dolly, 'I've heard a lot of girls do without rubber these days,' oh you know all about it, do you, 'I doubt it,' I'm not crazy! And Jerry's left his little wooden elk behind as he unlocks the steel door in the subway connecting all the platforms, right under platform 10a, using a square key he wears around his neck like a talisman. *Into the deep valley of the super-witches.* The moisture on the walls has frozen. The trains rumble above him. One-way streets and railway tracks. They talk on and on in the Dead Railwayman like there's no tomorrow, like they haven't a care in the world. 'As long as the beer's good!' 'Yeah, the beer's good.' Far away, he hears the drill. It has hit black granite. That's what he read in the paper. He worked for the city construction department for a while and he knows almost all the entrances to the catacombs. That was after the galvanizing plant and before the RSB. 'Have you heard the Old Man's sending his son to some military school?' 'What old man?' 'To Afghanistan or what?' Reiner, lighten up! They'll give him a good stoking. Like Wolfgang the stoker or what? The Old Man's son, Afghanistan? (Didn't he have a gang? Gang bang, more like!) No, the Old Man. Adidas. Gold, oh gold... *Like father, like son, knocked off the throne!*

And the little wooden elk is back on the edge of the table, in the mirrored room at 'Sex World', later known as 'Angels Club', bobbing along to the big humping session. It can't be just that nine-stone weakling, it must come from... hark, what sound through yonder window breaks! FS, FS... the great quake in Eden City. The lube tube rolls across the table. Dildo 1 tips over. *Get a move on, you old ram, and next time take your socks off.* Actually no, I don't want to see what's underneath them. 'Respect, that won't buy you anything these days. Values decreasing, everything's getting cheaper and cheaper.' And Jerry's elk watches with eyes wide as Karin turns ten, fifteen, twenty years older underneath the ram in the mirrored room, as the ram suddenly hits black granite, top bargains – bottom prices. And then twenty, fifteen, ten years younger. Young girl, old woman. And outside, shrapnel rains down from the clouds.

And *Jerry lui-même* (Hold on, hold on, school's out forever and I only learned Russian!) wanders through the catacombs to the westernmost edge of the city, where the big new nudist club is. The legendary 'Fortress of Love' is in the other direction and is nothing but a ruin now, most rooms abandoned, most whores abandoned ship, most abandon banished elsewhere. Time to take a look at what's new.

And in the west there's the harbour and in between the industrial canals are the apartments let out by the Old Man's firm, *if only Agony Auntie knew, her loving heart would break in two.* Jerry always liked reading fairy tales. And now he hears a trampling of hoofs in the distance. *That can't be right! Appearances are deceptive. Appearances are always right.* And not far from the empty warehouses of the old harbour is the big new club. I never thought much of bargain bangs. Good job it's Thursday. The guest punters come on Fridays. And on Sundays the leftover rest of the punters. The deers are drained and wounded by then. On rest days there's no punting allowed, and the perverted thought-criminals come out to play. *Leftover layabouts.* We seek the maximum. And today? The early bird gets caught in the storm.

And Jerry hears the echo of his trampling, onwards and ever onwards, further and further, and he hears a voice singing. *With the hoofs of his horses shall he tread down all thy streets*, he thinks.

IV.

Sing, nightingale, sing... What an ugly voice you've got! And the naked man gets a slap on his bare flesh. Jerry's sure he heard a woman singing.

The song you sang in May time... A fine firm smack that'll leave a mark, and the man sings on all out of tune. Boom, boom. (No, that comes later.)

Sing, nightingale, sing, bring the honeymoon... He gets the spanking of his lifetime and crawls whimpering and singing in front of the little Vietnamese woman walking him on a leash. 'Do I hear: please? Please? Do I hear: please?' And she stands legs apart and only naked *down below* (you're too slow!) above him, and he tips his head back. Heads back, drinks down, that's what they say in the Railwayman. So the leash hangs loose onto the floor. Pleasepleaseplease. My pot-bellied pig. A nice golden pitcher on me! *Reiner, come on!*

And Jerry stands by the open steel door, water dripping on his head but he's still staring. Getting all sentimental. There's a lot going on down in the catacombs. And up above, the chariots stuffed full of strangers drive through the evening city. *If only you knew, friends of the sun...*

And at 10 p.m. an attack is launched on the door of the Eden luxury strip club. And on the disco two streets away as well. Both owned by the R. brothers. Some say S. has a share in the ventures too. But people say a lot of things when the day is long. A sudden evacuation of the streets. The fever dreams stay at home. *This, my boys, is reality*. The Real supermarket is open until 10 p.m. as well. Netto. Lidl. Spar's not there any more.

And Jerry, who's only come for some bargain humping, *nude! nude! pay once on the door, drinks are free, food is free, and every fuck's at Aldi prices...* My boy, my boy, it's time to start out on your travels. Standing by the half-open steel door. 'Mistress? Do I hear: mistress?'

Another smack. Great echo. Great arse. Hers, that is. (Although the man stretches his up too, but it's not quite as interesting, his corrugated old flesh.) He's got the best view of her magnificent back. *An arse, an arse, my kingdom for an arse!* Like his little elk up in the mirrored room. Watching in amazement as the thin man disappears into the body of the alternatingly young / old Lady K. as she sits astride him. Only the socks left on the sheet. That's the way to do it, someone's turned the tables and really buried that hatchet. And tiny blossoms growing out of her white shoulders (sunbeds are out, they only turn your skin to leather), and the elk's head over heels in love. Oh, let me abide here 'til the end of my days. Shut up, blockhead!

Mistress. The man's face not visible behind the black mask. And then the light refracts, red, gold, and he drinks.

And Jerry's mouth goes dry because he's all drooled out. Such a big mouth, I'm ashamed of myself. Because he suddenly recognized that little Vietnamese girl. 'Have a feel of that lump, Jerry, do you think it's cancer? Oh God, it must be cancer, it's been there for months and it's getting bigger and bigger.' She presses his hand to her ribs, directly below her left breast. How does he know she's just about to tell him about her little dog? She had to give it away because she had no time, and the poor thing was always on his own and then he'd always crap on the carpet. She doesn't, though. Tell him about the dog. Here we have the stretching rack. The gynaecologist's chair.

And before 'Sex World', later known as 'Angels Club', gets hot, the wrecking crews have their first clash. And up in the office sits a man, thinking and planning and knowing that it'll all go his way in the end. Dildo 2 tips over, there's so much shaking going on.

And if it is cancer? *Strip, bitch.* The way it comes over you suddenly sometimes. *Three-hole pony.* Haven't you got a dog that always shits on the carpet? And then she says: 'I'd like to get a horse, one day.'

And Jerry strides through the mud of the catacombs, the deeper he reaches the damper its gets, thinking only of the big new nudist club where Polish and Czech and Hungarian girls make up more than eighty per cent of the staff, so he's heard. Indians for a night, foreigner quotas, diversity management on the road. Vitamin bombs. 'I always say, never mind night, night, night, manager of the night and all that crap they say. It's rubbish. The girls in my properties do most of their business during the day. Right, during the day. OK, the nudist club is in the evenings, usually at night. That's an exception though. "Sex World" and Co. and House X and so on, Club Hans, yeah, that's at night, that's why we have a division of labour, me and my esteemed colleague, the one who'll soon be up at the top in the "Angels Club". One has the majority of the apartment business, the other the majority of the clubs, the brothels, to put it bluntly, although there is a difference, of course, between brothels and clubs etc. of the night, and there we are again. Sure, some of the sex workers in my properties work until two or three in the morning. But only very few of them. The bourgeois punter, to put it bluntly, goes out creeping by day.'

And Jerry creeps away from the door, which is also half open, bumps against the wall and feels his sore bum, *Johnson's Nappy Cream, soothes big babies' bums after crèche*, Bepanthen's not bad either, and then there's this blue tube from good old England, Savlon, that does him gooood. Product placement. And Jerry saw and heard men behind that door. They raised their glasses and forged their pact. He knew a few of them, knew their faces, to put it bluntly, in the year when he's out and about in the catacombs, so right now, *kapow, kapow*, they have bars and discos and restaurants, and by now they've withdrawn their investments from the red-light sector, years ago, it's just easier to run a restaurant, isn't it? Don't talk crap, it's just as hard, *watch out or you're in for a clip* (clip round the ear vulg.: slap in the face, medium-strength blow to the face). Ouch, no, my bum's still hurting. That's enough of that dumb bum word, enough flora and fauna, wasn't he wondering earlier about the giant ferns, whether the chariots stuffed full of strangers (who aren't all that strange, in some cases, because of course they already have a base here in the city... the syndicates pay the mercenaries, fetch the brothers...) would stop and stare at the exotic plants and forget the next attack on the next door is due for 22.22 hours?

And Jerry wonders at the report sheet in his hand. A real fine form sheet. The lamps on the ceiling of the corridor, behind barred frosted glass, and only the odd one still intact, in other words working, give off barely any light to read it by. I'll stick the dildo in you while I fuck you. OK? Says man, says woman? That hatchet's getting buried, the tables getting turned. Creeping and crawling: C, Squatting: B, Tolerating pain: C, Obedience: C+, Singing: E, Drinking: B.

I mean, you can't be both, can you? The torturer and the tortured. *Reiner, give us a laugh!*

Old Stoneface has been talking for three hours flat. Live and let lie. *Where d'you get that crap?* Porn Queen, Jungle Camp. Sure, there are people who are only specialized in one thing. Sado maids or maso me, maso you, yeah. But if I think of myself, no, I can still do all the old-school stuff, at the end of the day... *It doesn't always have to be a pearl necklace.* And I'm a gentleman then, I'd say. Take your socks off! (Actually no, we don't want to know... but they stink! And the little elk's down on the floor, half under the bed, and moaning quietly to himself and surprised by the Armani suit, its soft fabric almost touching his antlers, because the pants next to it have skid marks on them.) I reckon a good few of my regular girls see it that way too. I reckon, definitely. Indefinitely.

And the drill hits black granite and the city's inner belt vibrates. The great quake in... One day later there's an attack on the gym where a few of the door crews go to train. Few months later it burns down. None of that 'only strangers' crap. We've got connections and we're looking for connections, and we don't yet know that we're soon to go. The great comedy. The great stage play. A rift opens up in the stone. And Jerry's missed his cue, the bar stool is empty at the Dead Railwayman, and the gang goes on banging away anyway, and he tips his head back and spies through the thin gaps into the grey sky at night. Might be daytime, mind you. Clouds drifting by. Not far from him, in the dock, a yacht sails past. Champagne on deck. The Man behind the Mirrors has left his office and is planning the new deals. *Smog from Berlin, let's hurry on in.* New guests, naturally. The others who came by train

457

are tiring themselves out on the streets, and onward, ever onward, Free German Youth, strive on! Ouch, says Jerry, five minutes early. And knows nothing yet of the new order soon to come, M&Ms, glass beads ready to change hands, a snack between meals, Mr Machiavelli, it'll be months yet, and Jerry climbs up the rusty iron ladder because the big new nudist club is up above him, *good job I've got a refreshing wipe on me*, the walls of the corridor feel warm. Liquids seep through the stone.

V.

Boom, boom. And Jerry falls. Accidentally, so to speak. A red railwayman. Outside on the boulevard... submarines diving in the canal. The Old Man sits on his veranda and looks out at the lake, let them plan what they like on their yacht, first of all this takeover has to be averted, perhaps too big a word, *attacks, Turks and Arabs, attacks*, men from the city, men coming into the city, no boats, no sails, even though spring's coming, summer's coming, or is he dreaming of the wrong time of year again? A blanket over his knees, *as long as it's cashmere*, and Jerry nestles his head on the asphalt.

A man with a little silver pistol gets back in the limousine. The car disappears on the empty boulevard. Behind the harbour and behind the industrial estates, the headlights criss-cross on the motorway. Distant service stations. Divorce lawyers in neon light. Blondes on the Naschmarkt. Gibberish in dark chariots. *The façade was the target, the glass was the target, mirrors included.* Collateral damage creeps across the central reservation. A train station in the menopause. Long time ago now. New modern art on the walls of the RSB head offices. If you go out the back way you see the columns of houses.

Joy, you beautiful spark. A night-time angler by the dock. The canal ends in the middle of nowhere. *A million is the target.* I said: silently. Raise the pitchers. The body creeps out of the chalk drawing. Ferns from primeval times. They find caves, deep beneath the granite. *The hairdresser's across the way!*

My leg, my leg... a cramp in my flesh. Bye bye, my Saxonland. There are more important things at stake. Business. Resilience. Reshuffling. Afghanistan. Half-full money pipelines. The angler crying by the dock. *Reiner, give us a laugh.* It's a miracle the computers survived, more than ten years ago now. *A round of Jan brandy!* Wild geese flying in a V beneath the clouds. South, south, which way is south? We're all friends here, aren't we, my dear? A boy in uniform sitting on the veranda and looking out at the lake. Young man / what have you done?

Firing lines are re-routed. Passenger trains stop at the job centre and continue empty. The line ends in the mountains. *The only place I've got to go is to my grave.* As long as you're happy.

Jerry in flashes of lightning. It's dazzling me, you dirty bastards! Jerry in cold storage. It's cold, you dirty bastards. Sees a diamond under his new buddy's skin, right next door. Maybe the wrong time of year. Gates crash, gates stand resilient. And the little elk perched back on the bedside table, sometimes in the mirror room, sometimes in the cheap room, sometimes on the bar. Market struggles, power scales. Discreet...

The drill goes on drilling. The underground trains pass beneath the city. Dildo 3 tips over. Jerry's crossing the Naschmarkt.

THE GREAT COUP
(THE LONG DISTANCES BETWEEN
THE STATIONS)

In the spring of '09, on the train to the small town of G. where he was to meet the man from the capital, Hans read various newspapers. He was on one of those regional trains that stop at every village, it was morning, and he watched the few people getting on over the top of his newspaper.

He flicked through the racing newspaper because he'd been thinking of buying a racehorse for a while. An old acquaintance from Berlin had a couple of horses in training out at Hoppegarten, they even won the odd race now and then, and he'd called him a month or so ago and told him all about one of his horses' most recent success. It had won what's called a listed race, apparently, with more than twelve thousand prize money for the winner. Hans had only been to the races a couple of times, back in Berlin, out to the track at Hoppegarten or the harness races in Karlshorst, a bit of a bet, a bit of a drink, and in recent years only to the city racetrack on the first of May. There was always plenty to see on International Workers' Day at the racetrack, on the terrace with bubbly and finger food. He'd never understood much about the subject but his old acquaintance from the capital had infected him with his enthusiasm. The guy had told him how he regularly visited the stables, watched the training sessions, planned the races with the trainer. You've got to do something when you get old. *Quiet! Who's whispering that nonsense inside my bonce?* It's more something for the future, he thought, when I start slowing down. *A bonce is a head.* He put the racing paper aside, picked up the city daily and flicked through and folded and rustled

460

the pages.

He had put a cup of coffee on the vacant seat next to him. He'd intended to get it from the new Starbucks they'd opened up in the old waiting room just before the train left, then he'd gone to the little coffee place a few yards away before he remembered there was a chain in there now too. The little coffee place with the dark corner where he'd often sat with a good large americano and a few newspapers and magazines (football, boxing, chess, *Der Spiegel*, Donald Duck) over the last ten years had been taken over some time in the past few months (later he found out the chain operated numerous branches all over Germany and a couple in Austria), but at least it was better than the American syndicate. Unfortunately they'd remodelled the place and his dark corner had disappeared. He'd seen that little ex-jockey there a couple of times, the one they told all the stories about. He'd come creeping in in the evening hours, wrinkled trench coat, order an americano as well, but usually a medium one, *he went doolally, looking for his wife, no, his girl, his daughter.* That was a few years ago now. Leave him alone, AK had said a couple of times, for some reason. *Free ticket.* Probably dead by now, poor guy.

Everything's getting syndicalized, he thought. He flicked on through the paper, looked out of the window, the line tracing a wide curve around the lake. He saw the houses and villas of the city's suburbs and even though it seemed to him like they'd been moving at least half an hour already, when he looked at his Glashütte he saw it had only been twenty minutes. He checked his phone again because his Glashütte had started getting slow, only one or two minutes but still he had to correct the time every morning. He saw the lake beyond the trees, beyond the houses. AK lived somewhere out there, somewhere near the famous painter whose pictures were worth so much money, he'd been to his exhibition at the big museum with AK, when was that, two years ago? He'd often thought about moving to that suburb as well, where the rich and famous and the bourgeoisie and the politicians lived, the former top cop too, not far from AK. But Hans had other options. And as the lake disappeared from view and the flat land grew ever more hilly, he tried to remember the cartel theory AK had explained to him once, or was it the old Count? Because the thing was, and this was the only thing he could remember now as he drifted off, the newspaper on his knees, the thing was it didn't really deserve its negative meaning, the word 'cartel', because all it was was an agreement on rules, in the Middle Ages, the old knights, *the last of the independents*, the negative effects of lack of competition on the market...

He looked out of the window, saw wide fields still bare in the nascent spring, dabs of green between them, woods, little houses and farmyards, like in Brandenburg, he thought, the area around the steel town along the border, the sky clouded over and a twilight above the land as though rain were coming, and then he saw the dark blue horizon in the other window opposite. There was a young girl sitting there, headphones over her blonde hair, moving her lips and taking no notice of him as he looked her up and down. The conductor must have checked his ticket already because he walked straight past him, looking down at him with a brief nod. The man from Berlin didn't know he'd lost his driving licence, for one small dent and nought point nine BAC. It was the least conspicuous for both of them to take the train, no one tailing them, no licence plates, and no one would ever suspect that negotiations were held at the station in the small town of G. and in the small town of G. at the end of the world, home to Germany's longest station platform, a fact known to only trainspotters and passionate commuters, a town where Hans had had his eye on a property for a while now, an old villa, he had the keys on him, an ancient second cousin or third cousin of his wanted to sell the place. The first time, he'd taken the car to G. to meet the old man. He wasn't even certain they were related but he did know his father and had fallen out with him and told all sorts of stories about his great-grandmother, whom he remembered. When he was a child, in the steel town, they visited them in a neighbouring village a couple of times. On the way back from G. he slid into that cunt in his Skoda, a very slippery December, no chance to sort it out between gentlemen, Call the cops, then, you arsehole! He should have floored the cunt and fucked off, sold the car straight to Poland... but he couldn't be arsed with all the hassle. So now he was sitting on a train, drinking his coffee, looking out the window or reading his papers. It couldn't be much further. *Witness makes serious accusations.*

He had read the sports pages first – Red Bull, Bundesliga, a very interesting article about snooker, a game he'd always wanted to try out even though it was pretty exotic in Germany, and he'd always been a fairly good pool player – and then when he flicked through the front pages of politics and the latest news from the big state of Saxony the little article caught his eye. It said 'dpa' in brackets underneath the headline. 'The main witness in the so-called files affair yesterday made severe accusations against her superiors from the State Office for the Protection of the Constitution. After the allegations became public, so the witness claimed, key files on the case had disappeared.'

463

He'd heard about it. Pretty nasty story. And it was boiling over now while things came to a head in the city, the invaders advancing slowly, April 2009. A few people had asked him what he knew about it. *Nothing! What have I go to do with that dirty business?* He knew AK had once got a couple of Russian women busted because they'd been doing dodgy business with underage girls from Russia, not far from a few properties AK was renting out. There was no insurance against dirty business, sadly. But what he read now was a whole different kind of dirt. The mires can be bottomless. 'Specifically, witness XXX listed reports on meetings with secret service sources and statements from seven different information providers. The files allegedly contained indications that children from Eastern Europe were to be brought to XXX for the purpose of sexual abuse. The source reports were also said to have included information on corrupt police officers and sexual inclinations of court officials.'

Sometimes he couldn't quite believe all that crap. Like some kind of nasty movie: conspiracies, 8 millimetres. But he'd known it was true fifteen years ago, when he'd just moved to the city, when similarly dirty business was spilling through the underground. Judges, public prosecutors, cops who were hot for young flesh. The businessmen who believed in the red-light-sector share had presumably helped make sure the bastards disappeared. And legend whispered that AK had somehow got his hands on photos of the dirty bastards... He shook himself. *Shut up, old man.* He knew enough people from the street brigade, guys who wore T-shirts printed 'Death penalty for child abusers' now and then, and they'd have given anything to get their hands on guys like them. That was the problem with people.

They were passing through idyllic countryside. Had he come in his old BMW (people were already taking the piss out of him for still driving the old banger, almost a vintage car), he wouldn't have been able to savour the view of the Saxon forests, which must be Thuringian forests by now, the view of the fields lined with mist on the horizon, steeped in light, wouldn't have had time for the view of the small lakes suddenly appearing in clearings, the rivers, the hillsides rising on either side of the line and falling again, all that would have gone unnoticed. What peace. He'd always liked travelling by train. He crumpled up the newspaper and remembered how he'd once had the idea, only a few years ago, to see the country, the whole country, by train.

He'd been standing by the door with his coat buttoned for five minutes by the time the train finally halted with a screech. No, it had stopped silently and slowly. The long screech was only in his memory, from the trains in the Zone, dirty trains at the border town station, green artificial leather upholstery on arrival at the station, Eastern Station, *we put our hands over our ears...*

'Welcome to Germany's longest station platform.' He looked at the sign, that sentence, that greeting beneath the name of the little town of G., heard the doors closing behind him with several beeps and then a slam, heard the train picking up speed again, felt the breeze at his back, against his coat, and then looked around. Only three or four passengers had alighted with him and they'd all walked some distance already, so that must be where the tunnel was towards the town. Another train was on the opposite side of the platform. Jesus, the platform really was long. He'd always come by car before, or that one time when he came to view the old villa.

The platform had a roof over it and stretched

apparently endlessly in both directions. It must be at least half a mile. His back to the vanished train, Hans looked over at an embankment beyond the tracks. The platform was so long that the other train was a good distance away. Hans looked at the last carriage and then back at the embankment, saw the blue bridge with its blue arch curving high above the tracks. The platform didn't seem to end until underneath the bridge. In one direction. In the other direction, the one he'd come from... he'd always known he was starting to need glasses.

'Mr Pieszek?'

'Yes?'

In front of him was a man wearing a grey army parka and underneath the parka a suit, no tie. And glasses, frameless.

'Excuse me, you are Mr Pieszek, aren't you?'

'Yes, I am, sorry.'

'No need to apologize. You must be speechless from the view, eh?'

'You could put it like that. Welcome to Germany's longest station platform.'

The man gave a brief smile and looked around, and then they shook hands. They both clutched their leather gloves in their left hands.

'Respect for the choice of opera house, Mr Pieszek.'

'What...?'

'Just a little joke.' They were still shaking hands, scrutinizing each other. The man looked around sixty.

Grey, almost white hair; he pulled on a wool hat.

'A fresh wind blowing in the east.'

'Although this is more like the south,' said Hans. He let go of the man's hand and pulled on his gloves. 'Shall we get straight to work?' the man asked.

'All in good time,' said Hans, 'all in good time.' The

train the man must have arrived on was departing.

'Sorry,' said the man, 'the name's Fischer.'

'Nice to meet you, Mr Fischer. We ought to stop apologizing for today. Direct from Berlin?'

'Via Göttingen.' He gestured towards the departing train.

'Was it a long journey?' They walked a few paces, the platform was empty now. Hans ran his leather glove over his head and didn't know what else to say for the moment.

'No problem,' said the man called Mr Fischer. 'Time to think. Did you have a good journey?'

'Only a stone's throw in comparison,' said Hans.

'Yes,' said Mr Fischer, '*we've* taken the longer journey, if I may say so. Out here. To you. To this small town...'

'Which is irrelevant,' Hans said. They were standing next to a low brown wooden building. The windows boarded up. The wood weather-beaten. Stairs down to the subway, heading underground. On the other side of the hole in the platform – it was nothing more than that – into which the stairs led, a broad, almost identical pale brown structure, boarded up like the first building. They stood directly in front of the hole and the stairs, between the two wooden huts. On the platform. Which had space for thousands of people.

'Do you want us to talk here?' asked Mr Fischer, pointing his still ungloved right hand at a group of benches far beyond the second wooden building. In front of the benches was a pane of glass with black birds fluttering motionlessly on it.

'I'm sure we want to talk about everything in style,' said Hans and gestured at the stairs leading down to the depths ahead of them.

'We do indeed,' said Mr Fischer. He removed his

frameless glasses, held them away from his face and looked through the lenses at the welcome sign. 'You were right about one thing – we're certainly undisturbed here.'

'And everything else,' Hans said and walked down the steps, 'everything else we can work out, I'm sure of that.' And he heard Mr Fischer descending the stone steps behind him.

Then they were standing on the blue bridge, with the big blue arch high above the railing, looking down at the platform where they'd just stood and said hello.

'A small, quiet town,' said Hans. 'Over there,' he pointed at the buildings of a derelict factory perched in front of a small hillside, 'that used to be a thriving operation. Old tradition.' One of the buildings resembled a cupola hall, with two small chimneys protruding from the dome; on a high brick-red and black-weathered oblong rested a green triangular pointed roof that seemed to be stabbing at the low-hanging clouds; systems of rusted pipes connected the cluster of rubble and collapsed towers.

Hans thought of how he'd imagined that morning that they'd do the deal right there on the platform, walking to and fro, falling silent when people got out of trains, or walking to another part of the endless platform when people were waiting for trains and potentially eavesdropping... But neither he nor this Fischer were going to rush into anything. There was too much at stake. But everything was actually quite simple.

'And what did they do there, I mean, produce?' Mr Fischer fumbled a crumpled bag of Krügerol throat sweets out of the chest pocket of his military jacket. He took one out, put it in his mouth and held the packet out to Hans. 'Oh, don't mind if I do, a good old East German product.' He took a sweet and sucked on it for a while before he said:

'Malt.'

'Malt? A malt factory. A thriving business, eh?'

'They used to need malt everywhere. The freight trains left from here for all over the country. We had a planned economy, Mr Lawyer.'

'Mr Lawyer?'

'The left-wing lawyer who once wanted to change the world...'

'You're the one with the utopias.'

'Utopias. I used to like reading about them as a child.'

'The important thing is that we write new stories.' The lawyer spat his half-sucked sweet onto the footpath, turned to Hans and smiled. '*The Route to Japan.*'

'The route to Japan,' Hans nodded. 'We ought to have a coffee somewhere in peace before we discuss itineraries and tariffs.'

And as they left the bridge, walking into town past the villa for which Hans possessed the key, past a little shop for model railway equipment, the lawyer began to get on Hans's nerves, to seriously annoy him, making him turn to him several times, 'Yeah, yeah, the famous Hans...' He looked him up and down and tried to understand what the bloody hell was going on, here in the town with the longest station platform in the country, leading them on and on to the centre of town, to the heart, to the source, to the target, and Hans smoked two cigarettes to calm down on the way to the market square where there was a bakery and café. Maybe some kind of test, he thought. Scraps of cloud drifted grey above.

'So you're a real tough guy, are you?'

'What's all this crap about?'

'Formerly active in Berlin, football brigade, bone-cracker brigade...'

'And you, have you always been on the take?'

'Business, my dear Hans, business...'

'I didn't know we were on first-name terms.'

'I thought that was standard in your circles. Especially in the old days. Everyone first names only in the night and among comrades...'

'Stop playing bloody games!' Hans stopped short, pointed his cigarette at the lawyer's face, moved the burning tip so close to his mouth, his nose, that a thin thread of smoke rose to lick at the lawyer's grey hair. They stared at each other in silence. Hans opened his mouth several times, taking a breath, starting to speak and then shaking his head. He thought he saw a brief smile moving the corners of the lawyer's mouth, he saw that smile in the eyes of Advocate Fischer, if that was his real name, but that was irrelevant.

'Don't take it personally, Pieszek...'

'You're the one talking crap, not me. What's up all of a sudden? You can talk crap all day long if that's what you're used to, in your circles. I can wait till you get to the point.' He flicked the cigarette, still in his out-stretched hand, past the lawyer's head. And the lawyer smiled, really smiled. He opened his mouth and gave a laugh. 'How vulgar. Are you our man?'

'No. I've just got the passage to Japan. Safe and discreet and with clean money. How vulgar.'

They were on another bridge now, a far smaller one this time, looking down at the foaming water of a thin river. 'Doesn't look like I'll ever get a coffee today,' said the lawyer.

'Coffee,' said Hans. He looked at the water and wondered how AK would have dealt with the situation.

470

Chucked him in the river and watched him floundering. 'Oh, stop it...'

'What?'

'Nothing. I think I'm in urgent need of a coffee as well.'

And Hans looked down at the foaming water of the thin River P., which snaked back between the hills and the mountains, crossed rivers and small towns, flowed into a dam where the water lay black, left the dam on the other side, flowed past the big lakes of the big city. For so many years the river had vanished beneath the bricks and mortar, beneath the stone, in the catacombs below the city, flowed through pipes and underground channels where the rats lived, dark, stinking mud, only breaking up out of the underground again between the buildings in the north of the city. Now it shows itself, like a canal, beneath bridges, at terraces outside restaurants, in front of the big old courthouse in the centre, then descends again and loses itself somewhere between the mires on which the city was built almost eight hundred years ago, before the rest of the narrow trickle, thin as a stream, enters another river, the channels densely interwoven above and below ground, the drips seeping through the stone, flooding the tunnel they're building for the underground line beneath the centre of the city, mini submarines inspecting the damage, pipelines mounted on masts in crazed patterns above the city out to the great lakes, from which the water seeps back into the ground, flows into the rivers and canals and pipes, AK's been thinking of buying a yacht but he hasn't got time, the voices seep through his business and he senses and knows that times are getting worse, that it's time to don his armour again, while the first strangers are prowling the night, *Can I count on you, Hans? You*

471

can always count on me, you know that! The stories circle the central station and on and on around the whole city, AK's Makarov is safe in the safe in the villa, *The Angels are coming to town? Do we really want them to come?* It's still peaceful now but the first strangers are already prowling the night, in the W. brothers' strip club a group of them tries to disturb the peace at the bar, *We're just the advance party*, voices seep out of the capital, troops come out of the capital, reinforce the strangers in the two cities that have almost grown into one, the mires have as good as dried up over the centuries, reinforce the terrorists (*because they are terrorists, they want to take the market away from us by means of terror...*), investing via Armenian Pierre (*Why's a Turk called Pierre?*) in heroine and coke and crystal for the past few years, although coke still puts the big money in the pockets of Marshall Tito and the Albanians (*Why haven't the Yugos wiped each other out like in the Balkans back in the day?*), the rumours circle the central station like a whipping wind, *Just whip your trousers down so I can see what's up!* the security crews on the doors of the clubs and discos are arming themselves, Friday night to Sunday morning, AK drives around the city and checks up on his properties, visits old friends and old foes, *On your knees, you piece of shit, and look at me so I can tell from your eyes if you're lying*, the Count's holed up in the fortress and sees in the books he flicks through that the lights are going out, one way or another, time for a couple of chess moves, time to prepare for retreat, it's time... and the streets glitter wet with rain, Eliot Ness leans back and calls the capital and feels the silver strings swinging, vibrating, and waits for the domino effect and waits for the great falling, while the Man behind the Mirrors strokes the cool wings of a green-tarnished metal angel, the girls go home after work or

472

out to a nightclub on the weekend... it's time... or out to the cinema, where the real, big-time gangsters live, quiet and dark and almost black, before the light reaches across the room, *An invasion will take place*, says the old fortune teller in her caravan on the fairground, the screams waft over from the big rollercoaster with the Olympic rings, she's in town for the first and last time, *Why are you just saying that and not talking your usual hieroglyphics? – And then I see a great shining in the darkness, diamond eyes*, and Hans stares into the foaming water, throws a cigarette down into it, a sweet stuck to the filter, 'Malt, it was carted everywhere from here.'

'A flourishing operation, then?'

'Yes, a long time ago. As I said before.' They look at the green pointed roof on the tower of the old malt factory, still visible behind the buildings.

'Yes, so you said. You really do know your way around thriving businesses.'

'I don't like the way you say that.'

'No, seriously. Why do you think we trust you, what do you think?'

'I'm not sure you really do trust me...'

They'd walked on and were now outside the café on the marketplace of the small town of G.

'I wouldn't be here otherwise,' said the lawyer, taking off his leather gloves and brightly coloured woollen hat. He put his gloves and hat in the pockets of his military jacket and opened the door to the bakery. A bell rang, Hans walked in behind him, and while the lawyer spoke to the woman behind the counter, he closed the door with a last glance at the empty marketplace. The brick building with the small portal was presumably the town hall. The round basin of a waterless fountain in front of it. Winter had only ended two weeks ago.

'What exactly is *smetana*?' he heard the lawyer asking and he stepped up to him at the counter.

The saleswoman, a short, blonde, rather buxom lady in her mid-forties, the perfect Mrs Bun the Baker's Wife, thought Hans, was about to answer but the lawyer went on talking. Jesus, he's annoying, thought Hans.

'Well,' said the woman and took a deep breath, 'our *smetana* cake is made of shortcrust pastry filled with a mixture of egg custard and, well, *smetana*.'

'Traditional recipe,' she added.

'Sounds good. We'll both have a piece with our coffee, won't we, Mr Pieszek?'

'Very good,' said the saleswoman, 'Go ahead and take a seat.'

They went to the rear part of the shop while the woman rattled crockery.

'Wonderful,' said the lawyer, 'no latte, no extra foamed milk, no frozen this and shaken that, no decaffeinated extravagance with vanilla, just a nice cup of coffee.'

He took off his military jacket and draped it over the back of a plastic chair, Hans put his coat aside too. They sat down. The saleswoman brought the coffee and cake on a tray, put the cups and plates on the plastic table. 'Here you are.'

'Much obliged,' the lawyer nodded and smiled after her. Hans picked up his cup and drank.

'Ah, you drink it black.' The lawyer took one of the tiny pots of UHT milk balanced on the saucer, shook it for a moment, ripped the lid off and poured the milk in his cup. He took the half-full sugar dispenser from the middle of the table, shook it for a moment like he had with the milk, held it up to the light as if there might be foreign bodies inside it and then carefully shook a little sugar into his coffee. Hans drank in small sips and watched him over the top of his cup. He put the cup down and watched the lawyer stirring his coffee with the tinkling little spoon for what felt like five minutes.

'So.' He put the spoon down on the saucer and then drank a sip. 'Wonderful.' Hans shook his head.

The lawyer balanced a piece of the *smetana* cake to his mouth on his cake fork. Hans picked up the firm looking piece of cake with both hands and bit into it.

'Ah, yes, that's the way to do it,' said the lawyer, chewing, 'with wonderful cake like this the best thing is just to bite right in.'

Hans wiped his mouth. 'It's cake. I've had better, I've had worse.'

'Well, I'm sure you're right about that. But it's the situation, the atmosphere, the details that make a good coffee and cake experience.'

'I'm glad sitting here with me seems to be good for your appetite. Atmosphere, eh?'

'Well now, we've both got plenty to be getting on with. Business, Hans. Important business.'

'Significant business, yes. You know what I've got to offer. The jewellery dealer is a good friend of mine.'

'Let's put it like this: my clients are certainly interested in the opportunity.'

'It would be a route no one would suspect. To the other end of the world.'

'Ever been to Japan, Mr Pieszek?'

'You can call me Hans if you like.'

'Emil. Pleased to meet you.' He held his hand out across the table to Hans. 'You might think the deal was perfect, Emil,' said Hans, pressing the lawyer's hand, which felt moist and warm.

'It's the details, as always, Hans,' said the lawyer, 'but there are standard market guidelines. Seven point five per cent for storage and placement.'

'My man from Tokyo is coming to town in the second half of the year. I don't know about your itinerary, timing-wise...'

'We've got time, my dear Hans. My clients want part of the goods to take different routes. Routes no one would expect. My clients have no interest in rushing things, don't want any stress at the moment.'

'You've already had some stress, so I've heard.'

'Mmm. My clients are criminals.'

'If you say so...' Hans looked over at the saleswoman behind the till. The bell on the door rang and an old woman entered the shop. She shuffled to the counter, ignoring them or seeming not to see them at their table. 'Hello, Marlene,' said the sales assistant.

'Don't get me wrong, Hans. I mean perfectly normal thieves. Burglars. Professionals. Criminals. Mr Pieszek... I mean Hans... I'm sure you've met plenty of professional criminals in your time.'

'Huh, that's how you lawyers think. Red-light sector, whores, night clubs and lots of bad-guy criminals.'

'No, Hans. Quite the opposite. And that's what I'm getting at – you're an honest entrepreneur. You haven't had any stress with the authorities for years, you run your place as best you can... you're transparent, as far as you can be, you pay your taxes, pay your staff, you keep your club clean, as far as possible. You've got a good reputation, you offer fair working conditions, you make your cut.'

'Emil and the Detectives. And if my cut was that great I probably wouldn't be sitting here now.' (*Bloody hell*, he thought, AK would say you're a total idiot, a total negotiation loser.)

'Oh, Hans, who can say no to a lucrative deal on the

476

side? And you know just as well as I do that we did our due diligence before we...'

'The big international consortium, eh? You sound almost like the Count...'

'The Count?'

'Oh, forget it. And no, I've never been to Japan.'

'Interesting culture. Great culture. Honour. Strength. What I meant when I said, Mr Pieszek... Hans... that you've no doubt met plenty of professional criminals...'

'Don't get your knickers in a twist. Of course, back in Berlin, just after the Wall, everyone wanted to make a quick buck, but I wouldn't necessarily call it professional. Adventurers who came from the other side as well, bank jobs were pretty popular, early, mid-nineties, everyone wanted to make a quick buck... there were a couple of specialists, of course, but it was all peanuts. The real money was in property and the Trust Agency. How did *you* make your contacts?'

'I was never in the bone-cracking trade, Hans.'

'You don't understand bugger all, Emil. It was a kind of freedom, back then. Trying things out. Not giving a shit about conventions. Having a laugh. Back in the Zone, I mean. And later. We had our own rules. A bit of fun at the matches, extra time on the streets. Sticking together, forming a strong unit. And we were young. The end of the eighties. And later old enough to join in the big games. I bet you were sitting in some nice chambers in nice West Berlin...'

'It way a mangy old dump, Hans. West Berlin. A dump. But it was good. And then along came the East and it all turned into even more of a dump.'

'We threw all our welcome money at you.'

'And now we're giving a few crumbs back. The percentages are right if the price is right. If Tokyo says yes, we'll all make a mint.'

'Tokyo will give you a good price, Emil. I can guarantee you that.'

The old woman shuffled to the door, not looking at them this time either, holding a brightly patterned cloth bag with loaves or bread rolls bulging out the fabric.

They looked out of the big windows of the villa at the bright stalls and carousels of the little spring fun fair set up on a field behind the houses. Only a few people ambled between the stalls and rides, it was early afternoon and still rather cool. The sky was hidden behind clouds; there'd probably be rain soon.

They each had a glass of whisky in front of them, having toasted the deal. Only a table and three chairs in the empty room, the wallpaper dangling from the walls in strips, the plaster visible in places, and the wooden floor wasn't in the best condition any more either.

'You really want to invest in this house? Your dream of a home to retire to?'

'Ach, who said anything about retiring? But I do want to get out of the city some day, I mean to live. And it's not all that far by car.'

'By car to the town with Germany's longest station platform...' They laughed. Hans picked up the bottle of Johnnie Walker Black Label and filled the two glasses again.

'You saw the pavilion earlier, the little old station concourse?'

'Yes. What a wonderful building. The magic of the old railway...' They had stood in the small hall and listened to the echo of their voices and footsteps. From the tunnel they'd come out of, a breeze blew the smell of old railway subway through the stone to them. Hans thought of the

478

trips to away games in the mid to late eighties, the droning chorus of the horde. A few of the guys from the old days had joined the Angels, others had settled down, but what did that mean...?

'Around 1860. They're pulling it down soon. They want to build a car park.'

'Is there so much coming and going that they need a car park here?'

'No. They're idiots. It used to be the Party members, then the Trust Agency...'

'Worried about the homeland's cultural assets, are you, Hans?'

'Actually I need something in the proper countryside. I've got another option, not far from the city either, just in the other direction. A real castle.'

'You want to buy a castle, Hans? You're kidding. That'll take more than our little deal.'

'No, not the whole castle. There's this outbuilding, right by the water, on the water, like a little island. It's a water castle. In the middle of the woods. Like in a fairy tale.'

'Are you that keen on solitude?'

Hans takes a cigarette out of his case and then holds it out to the lawyer. 'Why not, thanks.' Hans gives him a light and then lights his own.

'How do you want to deliver the goods to me?'

'DHL. Registered letter with return receipt.'

'You're kidding?'

'We'll be in touch beforehand.'

'I've just had enough,' says Hans, 'all the noise. Turning round and round all day long, the big windmill. It's getting too noisy for me, you know? Something solid in the countryside. Always been my dream.'

'And that's why you contacted us? So you could leave

the city? Start capital?'

'Is that how it went? Did I come to you? My man in Tokyo knows quite a lot. Of course I could afford this dump here anyway. But as you said: it's hard to say no to a lucrative deal on the side.'

'I always say, Hans, a good tax advisor is the most important thing. Nothing better than that. Helps you sleep at night.' He takes a sip of his whisky and presses the half-smoked cigarette out in the ashtray. 'Not bad, this Johnnie Black.'

'My favourite. For more than twenty years now.'

'I've switched to single malts, Hans.'

'Hmm. I've got Glenfiddich at my bar.'

'Get yourself one or two more, it's the latest trend. Talisker. Lagavulin.'

'Maybe in Berlin it is. Hardly anyone even drinks the Glenfiddich. I used to have a good Japanese whisky in the office. Never knew before that they make top whiskies as well. My friend from Tokyo brought it one time.'

'Your mysterious friend from Tokyo...'

'There's nothing mysterious about him. That's why you think he's the right man for the little transaction, just like I do. He sells to the nouveau riches in China. The enterprising communists have to catch up on prosperity.'

'True, Hans – the world as we knew it, one bloc here, one bloc there, it doesn't exist any more.'

'I'm glad of it. In the Zone we wouldn't be sitting here drinking Johnnie Black.'

'That's not what I meant...'

'Never mind. It's late.'

'It's late.'

They looked out of the big windows in silence. Hans lit another cigarette. Outside it got gradually darker, the

480

grey clouds hanging low, drizzling rain, tiny drops on the glass; the lights of the carousel began to glow. He remembered the fairgrounds of the steel town where he grew up. The fairgrounds in the villages around the steel town, the tents for dancing, brass bands, the shooting ranges, the old men who'd been in the war winning prize after prize, little carousels with their paint peeling off, wooden horses, fire engines, double-deckers, giraffes... his father had often taken him to the fair...

'My train leaves soon,' said the lawyer.

'Mine too,' said Hans and looked at his Glashütte.

'Time for one last drink?'

'Time for one last drink,' said Hans. The lawyer picked up the bottle and poured. 'It's not bad at all here,' he said.

'Yes,' said Hans, 'here or at the castle. I'm not sure yet.' *Don't tell him so much, you idiot.*

'My clients...'

'No,' said Hans, 'I don't want to know.'

The lawyer laughed. 'Only what it says in the newspapers. If I was too... how shall I put it... forceful earlier...'

'That's alright. Part of the game. Part of the job.'

They drank. Then they stood up.

The tracks branch out, lead over bridges, through tunnels, through stations small and large, suburbs, main roads, last trains of the night, passengers going home tired, the concrete sarcophagus of Südkreuz station, the rumble of the underground trains beneath the tracks, two men on the mangy boulevard of West Berlin, a late-night minimart closing, Zoo station beer bar, two men in a car outside the big Kaufhaus des Westens, security at the department store changing the usual paths, diamond saw on glass, dark clothing for the night,

481

cable cutters, alarm-free zones, two Lebanese brothers, gentle motions on the front of the Kaufhaus des Westens, constellations far above the clouds, façades in the yellow light of the night, ropes on the façade, glass is put aside, leather gloves, hairnets underneath hats, masks, the light of the stones in the light of compact torches, the cool sharpness of the karats, stopwatches ticking backwards, time slot, the goods sliding into the pouches, glass display cases, capped electricity seeping into the earth, the careful placing of the evidence next to the cases, cheap quartz watches set to the second by the atomic clock, the light of a torch refracts in a silent explosion in a heap of incredible beauty, in Tokyo a man sits with a magnifying glass in one eye, and in the small town of G. in Thuringia two trains stop at Germany's longest station platform.

Pimp? Yeah, yeah.

I mean, I'm part of a dying race. An endangered species. In theory – I'm not active any more, not for a few years now. So I ought to talk in the past tense. But when I think back to the years, you know, it's all right there. Sure, I imagined the whole retirement thing differently. And Claudi did keep saying, must have been around 2005, she did say, 'Randy, keep your paws off of shares.'

Yeah, but Randy had his own ideas, as usual, when it came to business. Come 2008, all my stocks and shares weren't worth zilch. All gone. I mean, if I'd at least blown it all on the high life. And now I'm sitting here in my little house in Bottrop and having problems paying the mortgage. Good job Claudi creamed off a bit on the side. She'd have had something coming to her for that if the thing with the shares had worked out. I'll say that again. But come 2008, even in the years before that, I wasn't the old bulldozer any more – watch out, Randy'll flatten you! Yeah, I got my due respect back then. I mean, back in the day, cleaning up, wiping the floor with someone, that was more like an exception. Mind you, Claudi didn't take it literally... But of course that's what Coppenrath & Wiese... by the way, that's my creation, that term... it's going round now and a whole lot of people, especially those beasts from the East, you know, they keep claiming they've got a monopoly on it, but no! They stole it from me when I was over there back in '91. So whose line is it? Old Randy's, alright.

Anyway, what I was saying was, Claudi put a bit aside for safekeeping back then and went in on a friend of hers' boutique, and it's doing OK, so that's what we live

483

on now. Round where we used to run around with a girl on every finger, you know, Dortmund, Essen, the whole Ruhr Valley, it's all run by the Turks and Arabs now or the Russians or the Angels, or they have these giant brothels put up by young investment stags, the red-light sector share always seems to be on the up. But the old school like us, the old guard – forget it.

And you mustn't underestimate how many girls work for themselves these days, in big places, nudist clubs, posh bordellos, brothels, where no one can just come along and paw them.

I used to divide my girls up back in the day, two in an apartment, two on the street. If I had four chicks on the go, I mean. I never had a huge great harem, then I could have opened up a brothel, but no, far too much work, that's a real back-breaker of a job, that is. Couple of my old mates went in on a place or opened one up, some of them even have proper bars or restaurants. I did think about a bar or a restaurant for a while, but see above. I mean, I really did earn a lot, the girls worked their arses off in the nineties, Claudi most of all. We had this classy apartment in Dortmund where we all lived, and then I had a flat in Essen as well, I put Melanie in there 'cause she didn't get on with the others, and later on Grit, and then swapped them over, it's not like I didn't have any work to do. Not at all. You try keeping a whole handful of girls keen. Most of them always came of their own accord. And that's how it all started, back in the golden eighties.

I wasn't a great big hulk or a karate champ like U., who I knew pretty well. He started off working the doors in the Ruhr, like so many others. In the famous discos in those days. Sure, sport was always on the agenda – you've got to look good, physically. Some guy who looks like Quasimodo's not gonna attract any chicks, is he? Neither is a nine-stone weakling. Mind you, there was that F. from Schwerte, he had a face like a car accident, like he'd had a run-in with a lawnmower, but dangerous. Mind you, he was a great hulk of a guy. I'm more the wiry coyote type. Minus the coyote. Used to be a hotshot at athletics, but I was always nice and smooth when it came to fisticuffs. Used to train with U., the karate champ, now and then, but I was never one for joining a club. Claudi's always complaining or taking the piss these days when I start in on the old stories. Quasimodos and nine-stone weaklings. I've put on a good bit of weight. But back in the day... well, I could hardly keep her hands off me, that must have been '88. Not that I wanted to.

I was always out at discos since my school days, since I was fifteen, sixteen or so, I did OK in my exams, though. I looked about twenty even then. One of my best friends had a bar, he was much older than me and he came from the same estate in Bottrop, this old working-men's estate where I grew up. The whole pimp scene used to hang out there. And I often helped him out alongside my apprenticeship. I trained as an interior decorator, don't even know if you can do that any more, and I helped out in the storeroom and fetched and carried this and that for the boys, for the pimp scene that used to hang out there, and once I had my licence later on I used to do a bit of driving for him and the others, picked up the girls when the boys had had one too many, that kind of thing. My boss, the guy I did my apprenticeship with, he used to get a bit funny when I got us a commission, for a club or an apartment.

I always admired them, to be honest, from the very beginning. They drove the hottest cars – sure, you used to say, I want to drive a dream machine like that one day.

And they always had plenty of free time, those boys. Got to go to the best bars and discos every night, the best there were back then round our way. They had the priciest leather jackets, leather coats, Hugo Boss was at the cheap end of the range, let me tell you. Really pricey watches, big fat rings, chains and all that. And not just the hottest cars, the hottest chicks as well. Well, no wonder little Randy's eyes went googly. Only total babes. Yeah, let me tell you, it was like something out of Arabian Nights. And they didn't give a shit about anything. They lived in their own world. And when my mate, the guy with the bar, when he pulled the blinds down things really hotted up. White gold and all that, if you get my meaning. And then in the morning, so some time around three or four, they went on to the discos. And their girls really stuck to them like glue. Sure, little Randy did sometimes notice there was the odd clip round the ear, between colleagues or between competitors, and for the girls sometimes. But never anything really bad. I have to add right away that I was more of a Don Juan later, myself, a real charmer of a guy, so it was really rare for me to ever raise my hand... against my girls, that is. And the first one came entirely of her own accord. I'd just turned twenty. I was really only dabbling at the time and it took me a couple of years to work out how to do it properly, how to keep a girl like that keen. And even though Claudi doesn't like to hear about it, the girls from the pimp brigade, they really gave me a good seeing to, a little lad like me, and their men used to laugh about it 'cause they all had a lot of time for me. You give the lad a bit of a treat. But when push came to shove because some guy started an argument or whatever, I was always right on hand. They all underestimated me, all of them. Not for long, though. U., the karate champ, and he really was German champion some time in the early or mid-eighties, I knew him pretty well by then. Mind you, they went a bit over the top back then, with the karate names. There was Karate Andy, Karate Mike, Karate Theo (alias 'Handsome Theo'), Karate Werner, and then the guy we called the Karate Granddad, Karate Schwärtner, Karate Manfred from Essen, Karate Horst, Karate Mike, Karate Steffen, no, that was some Easterner years later, Karate Karl, Karate Bernd, Karate Cock... although hardly anyone knew him outside of Bottrop. Plenty of them were tough guys but there was the odd one who was more of a karate film fan. Bruce Lee and all that. No, that was kung fu.

I wasn't all that into the whole karate boom but the thing was, I knew a couple of the karate guys pretty well. And when it came down to it I could fight my corner just fine without karate. The estate in Bottrop where I grew up, it was real Ruhr Valley-style. Tough place to live. I bought my little house somewhere else, or we did I mean, Bottrop-West, with a nice view of the countryside.

Sure, we have countryside here.

And my first girl, I must have been about twenty-two, she pretty much fell from the heavens right onto my lap. Well, not quite. But I think the boys wanted to test me out a wee bit. That disco's long gone now. Like I said, a dying race. She pretty much threw herself at me, as they say. And there was this other scruffy bastard, actually the only scruffy bastard because most of what I earned in my job, just after my apprenticeship, I spent on nice clothes. I couldn't afford my little red Corvette and all that yet, I was a back-seat driver in those days, but I used to spend hours at the best hairdresser's in town, I had naturally curly hair and that took a good bit of time.

Anyway this scruffy bastard was kicking up a fuss

because the girl was with me at the bar and then on the dance floor. And when he starts getting fresh with us I had to stand up to him. Stand up and run into him. It all went pretty quickly though 'cause he'd underestimated me, the athlete. And then I had a reputation to protect. Stupid thing was I was still secretly living with my mum at the time, more or less. But G., one of the boys, sublet one of his flats to me right off. And then it all started. Sure, first it went great, then stops and starts again, the way it always is. And she was a lovely girl, Grit from Bochum, no two ways about it. A lovely young woman. She stayed with me till the mid-nineties, almost ten years that was. Then she met some guy who wanted to start a family with her, or she wanted to with him, 'cause at some point there's no resisting the nesting instinct, although the two of us, on our own to start with and then with the other girls, we had a nice little nest of our own. The guy, and Grit wanted it that way as well, he put down a bit of money 'cause he knew what was up, of course, 'cause that was how he met her in the first place. That's how it always went when a girl wanted to leave me. I mean, you had your hardcore pimps, I can say this looking back, they never missed a trick and they took every single mark off the girls, but in return the girls had a really nice life, so it depends how you look at it, discos, clothes, rings, champers and highlife, but I always gave my girls a little something, I wasn't stingy about it when I had the cash in hand, those gorgeous old deutschmark notes, gets me all sentimental thinking about them. Claudi was happy enough once Grit left because she was always a bit jealous of my first girl.

Anyway, that's how one thing gave way to another. I chucked in my job at some point, can't tell you exactly when. '86, '87 maybe. Sure, we used to keep an eye out

488

for talent in the discos as well. Have a good look round. What's up, who's up, which girl might. Where can you get a foothold. I mean, back then I was a real hunk, always fit, body and mind, always had a smart car, 'cause I bought the Corvette right off as soon as the money started coming in through Grit. And so on. I mean, it wasn't all that hard if you were one of the boys, in those days. Sure, now and then you had to work harder to persuade a girl. You know the line, I'm at my wits' end, baby, if you don't do me a favour with some guy or other, that's it, I'm gone. But before that you'd take her out in the Corvette, a big fat gold necklace and then a weekend on Sylt, I mean, it was the eighties, girls like that who didn't have much cash, or much of anything else either, you could spot them a mile off. I was always in the inner circle, with the boys I mean, the ones I knew from my mate's bar... you were somebody in those days... I was somebody, yeah, and I had the reputation I needed, that Randy's not afraid to get in a fight... and the girls usually had friends who were easy to get hold of... and if Karla had a job on the till at Karstadt and had been hanging around my disco for months with her gorgeous big eyes, yeah, gorgeous eyes, I was right onto her, of course I was, if the boys gave me the green light. What can I say, it took a bit of persuasion sometimes, but it wasn't like I had to slap the chicks about or anything, no, not at all. Maybe later, every now and then. But as I said, that was never my style.

I'd say they were all pretty much up for it, back then. True love to begin with, champers, sex, champers... and over and over. Over and over. Then we used to stage things. Oh dear, baby, is someone giving you trouble, don't worry, it's Randy to the rescue. Come to help you. But as I said, when you hang out at the bar with the kings they practically... yeah, believe it or not, they practically came of their own accord.

Baby, d'you know how much money we'll make, forget everything else. And then out of the council estates and straight into the high life. Parties, champers, coke, money. And hunky Randy – who loves ya, baby?

It went on and on like that. And we had money coming out of our ears. Me and the girls, the girls and me. Claudi, she was my real true love, she did her bit. She preferred street work, sure, we knew all the brigades by then, sometimes she preferred one of the brothels in Bochum... and Claudi herself worked the street in Essen, but not any old street, she was the queen. Everyone knew her, everyone respected her. Because she was a classy woman, still is, and Randy right behind her. And then came what they called the Wall...

We didn't really notice to begin with. We were always partying, the girls were out earning, so the nights often didn't end till the next morning, disco, disco and the champers flowing, I managed the girls well in them days, Claudi kept things ticking over as well, she always knew when one of the girls had a bee in her bonnet or needed a holiday or whatever, we were like a big family, or more like a big marriage community, back then I had Rosie as well, she was from Bavaria, from the countryside, you could tell her anything, and she'd done a couple of days on the mile in Dortmund for me. A good pimp – and I say this with a certain professional pride even though I've been retired a good while now – a good pimp has to understand a lot about psychology. But the girls had a good life with old Randy, no two ways about it. Everything in excess, who'd say no to that? Well, anyway, then the Wall came down. It was all a long way off for us. But it wasn't until early '90 that we started thinking about it. The business side of things. There was suddenly this huge market open to us, all at once. There was this mass migration, in both directions. We suddenly had the Easterners over here, creeping and kerb-crawling and looking for a real whore for the first time in their lives, because they didn't have any of that over there for all those years. But it wasn't like it filled up our pockets overnight. I mean, it did a bit. We were clever enough, we introduced special rates for the price of that welcome money they got on their first trip over. There was more than one ended up at the railway mission because he was all cleaned out after one or two sessions and didn't even have a ticket home. Or they'd send their old lady to Karstadt and then stand around in the station quarter or on the mile with their mouths and their wallets gaping.

But I'd already realized it might work better in the other direction. The mass migration, the mass copulation. You wouldn't believe all the crap that flowed into the East then, early '90. What a load of cheap trinkets and junk food we lugged over there. Not us directly, the good old Pimps & Co., no, I mean adventurers and wheelers and dealers and all kinds of rip-off merchants. This guy I knew used to buy up yogurts by the ton once the best-before date was nearly expired. They never even looked at the date anyway they were so mad for the stuff. Right, me and my mates thought right off, we had to get our girls over there too, at least they were fresh, and I don't mean that disrespectfully or nothing. Klaus the Baker, this friend of mine, an old-school pimp from Bielefeld, he got himself a little snack van, burgers, hot-dogs, chips, he knew a bit about all that 'cause he used to work in a bakery in the seventies, and he was looking for a second man, and that's when I first went over

491

to the East. I took Claudi and Rosie along and the rest of the company stayed at home, which was a mistake, looking back, 'cause without Claudi there the girls just got out of hand and one of them was gone by the time I got back. Klaus had two of his girls with him. So then we went tootling round all those small-time Saxon dumps. Zwickau, Karl-Marx-Stadt, Mutzschen. People went crazy for the food, chips with ketchup and mayonnaise was a total hit in the Zone, and the news soon got around that we had the girls with us on the special menu. That was before monetary union in June '90. So we had all these bundles of East German money that we changed back at one to two, Klaus knew someone at the bank in Bielefeld, or at least that was the plan, to put the money in the bank. Sometimes a couple of thousand went missing. But things really took off later in the summer. The whole burger van thing was too much hard work in the end, the girls only used to stink of grease 'cause they were way better at frying and chips and all that than Klaus and me. So we sold the van, can't even tell you who bought it and for how much, it was in some pub in a dump by the name of Altenburg, but by that time there was suddenly a chips van on every corner in the East, no quick bucks to be made there any more, and anyway it was only really an idea to camouflage our real business.

So me and Klaus headed back home to the Ruhr Valley, or Klaus back to Bielefeld. And when I think of my first tour of the East, I have to say the Zone Joans, the babes from the East, were really something, I actually liked them a lot better than our Ruhr Valley Sallys 'cause they were just natural in the way they used to talk, the way they used to hold their bodies, really confident, all firm and relaxed at the same time... and always totally calm. Never put on airs or anything. Now they've been having all these anniversaries for years, all the whole celebrations and commiserations about the fall of the Wall and the new Germany, I often think about what kind of a world it was over there, back in the day. I mean, the Ruhr Valley's crumbling away for good over here, brick by kick, and in the East they've got all those shiny investment palaces, but back then we were the only ones shining. Some of the buildings there were such dumps that I used to say, when we had a room somewhere where the girls could give the customers a quick seeing to: 'Don't go over the top or you'll end up breaking through the floorboards.' Yeah, that's how it was. I mean, the really big deals back then were with the Trust Agency, buying up old East German factories and houses for a pittance. We were more like a manual operation. This mate of Klaus's, Klaus the Baker from Bielefeld, he really got in on the game later, in the big city down in the East. A hundred and twenty miles before Dresden – the whole city was really pissed off they didn't get made state capital even though they were expanding big time, the big city practically swallowed up the next town, they're always saying 'A million is the target,' some arsehole came up with it and got it registered as a slogan, that's what I heard anyway. It's a good target, used to be mine and all, although they mean population, not money. The mass migration really emptied out the East, 'let's be lonely together,' as they say, but there in the big city things worked out, funnily enough. From the mid-nineties, anyway. And then Klaus's mate – he had the necessary means though, he was part of this red-light consortium kind of thing – he went over and opened up a big club, a real fortress. Like an Eros Centre.

But back in '90, yeah, it was all still a wasteland. The big chaos after the big bang. So we were sitting in Bottrop in my old mate's bar, the freelance pimps' association I mean, the maps spread out on the bar. And we weren't the only ones, let me tell you. They thought exactly the same way in Hamburg and Munich. That we had to get over there, that we had to get our girls over there, not just a foot in the door, better the whole door. Emerging East. It all sounded good, all sounded easy. And old Randy had been over before, early '90. But the second wave was supposed to be a bit better thought-out. No chip-shop capitalism this time. I still think we'd still be in charge of the new/old states if we'd all got together properly. None of that small-time stuff. But even a guy like Karate Cock from Bottrop started getting big ideas of his own all of a sudden. They gave him a pretty quick bollocking over in Zwickau, though. There are even people who say he got stuck down in Hof with his one Sally, he never had more than one, at a truck stop, 'cause he thought that was where the big money was. Transit, transit, import/export. Never heard anything of him again.

Anyway, it was a real gold-rush feeling at the time. Me and U., Karate U., and Klaus agreed pretty quickly we'd all go over to the big city. Where they were still pissed off they hadn't been made state capital. You can say what you like but the Saxons, they're just funny in the head. Must have something to do with their history. That's what Klaus the Baker used to say, anyway. The history thing. And I think, but I've said this already, if we'd have gone over all together, gathered the troops and done a Napoleon on them, we'd easily have won our Battle of the Nations. But OK, old Randy was more the smart kind. And so the three of us went over. Klaus, U. and me.

That must have been in autumn '90, round about.

The other day Claudi tried to tell me it was in '91. She's usually right about that kind of thing, she's got a good head for numbers, did our taxes for years, or what came in above board and not below board. They put Karate U. away good and proper a few years later for tax evasion – couldn't prove anything on aiding and abetting prostitution in the end. Like he was Al Capone, they only got him for tax stuff and all. I only really started on the bookkeeping, transferring some of the monies, in the mid-nineties, or what Claudi used to do for me. She had this regular, you see, he was a tax adviser, and they used to have a kind of training session after the usual session. He was a pretty big cheese, actually, used to work for Inland Revenue. He had this little flat that came with the job and Claudi spent a good few weekends there with him. Judging by the money that came in, he was pretty much hooked on her. And she was hooked on me. Although Claudi gives me a good piece of her mind now if she hears that. It wasn't all cloud cuckoo land but it worked fine. For her, for the girls and me. Sure, for me most of all. I'm the first to admit it – I was never into hard graft, never one for donkeywork.

But then I had a registered company, mid-nineties, and everything went through the company. Everything that was supposed to. The rest was cash in hand, business as usual.

And then came our big trip. Klaus had done a bit of asking around. We were in Erfurt for reunification. Claudi's right about what she says. Because it was all a whole lot of commuting to and fro back then. Big city, Ruhr Valley, small town, Ruhr Valley, big city. Then over to Dresden for a bit, where two mates of mine had opened up a place. Officially a bar, hospitality business, but it was a brothel plain and simple. And it wasn't like they gave my girls good rent rates, either, no. Those two were pimps plain and simple. Mike and Samuel G. from Gelsenkirchen. Nowadays I'd call them Dumb and Dumber. Mind you, their place over in the state capital did really well for a while. And I only had my girls there a couple of times. It all went belly-up later, for Schalke Sammy and Mike. Bloody Ruhr Valley connection.

The first time I went to the big city... it was a bit of a shock, to be honest. But in a way I thought, yeah, it looks good. In my memory, there was always fog drifting along the streets of an evening. Grey fog, grey façades. The central station like a collapsed black sandcastle. They only had coal heating everywhere and in the autumn when we got there – spring '91, Claudi always says, but that's rubbish – anyway it was all covered in like a layer of ash. Like after the eruption of Vesuvius. That's what Klaus the Baker used to say, but he was the first one to bugger off. Did his baking somewhere else after that.

On the way to the big city, we'd already stopped at a couple of caravan alleys. In Thuringia, for example. Near Weimar. Yeah, the classic set-up. You could get caravan licences in the Ruhr Valley as well. Wasn't my thing, though. I mean, we knew the score and we had two nice models with us. I had to get myself a Mercedes 'cause it wouldn't hitch up to the Corvette. But round that way I thought the caravaners must have taken over the entire red-light trade. There was one whores' campsite after another. We got a foot in the door OK in Thuringia, we had Karate U. with us and we had our artillery under the seats. If anyone gave us stress they'd get it on the East German skull. 'Bonce', that's what they say over there. I mean, I come from an athletics background but there was a lot at stake, big money and big business, so I didn't hold back, let's say, and a couple of people got a good stewing, if you know what I mean, but Claudi always says it was all pretty harmless on the way to the big city. Because the whores' and pimps' trailer parks were relatively international, and by that I mean East and West German. They were stood there and parked there from all the provinces and city-states of our new/old Germany.

And Claudi says there were even mornings of the days and nights when they'd sit together and have a good natter, set up the barbecue, exchange tips, how do you run your business and how does it work with you and your girls. I always say that's her holiday-camp idealism, but on the way to the big city, she's right about one thing, we did make more than enough to cover our expenses, if you get my meaning.

Now the Italians are in on the game in Erfurt, Thuringia, I hear, and they want to open up a big place à la Pascha, maybe they already have, not that I'd care, but it's obvious the pizza connection wanted to get a hold on things and still does... They were always in Duisburg and Bochum but they never really bothered us much, they were more interested in property and restaurants and business like that, they were more the calibre of Klaus the Baker's oh, so legendary Bielefeld buddy.

And when we rocked up in the big city with our caravans and our girls on board, '90 or '91, yeah, yeah, alright Claudi...

I need a bit of time out now, gimme fifteen, as they used to say in the Zone, I might as well crack open a bottle of that Springer Urvater I've got down in the cellar for nostalgic reasons. I've got a whole crate of the stuff. No one drinks it these days. I tried it in the mid-nineties when I went back to the big city with my little company, tried to deal the stuff to the crazy beasts from the

East. I had a whole wagonload of it. My old schoolmate got hold of it for me. Sixty wagons eastward. No, that's a film, a western, I used to love that one as a kid. *Sixty Wagons Westward*. Or was it *Westward Ho, the Wagons?* It was about this huge load of whisky on its way through Injun land because the saloons west of St. Louis had run dry.

And I knew they must be all crazy, over in the East, I knew it the moment I heard they suddenly got into our old Winnetou westerns in the Zone in the mid-eighties. Bloody hell! Old Shatterhand and Winnetou. That tall blonde Lex Barker and handsome Pierre Brice. It was twenty years after we'd watched them, some time in the early to mid-sixties, I remember the repeats in the seventies, and they were queueing up outside the cinemas in the Zone for them. They went mad for that old crap. Can't nobody tell me that's normal.

And in the big city, anyway... first of all we took a couple of nice rooms in a nice hotel. Right in the centre. View of the centre. A long way up. Twenty-seventh floor – no point doing things by halves. Right by the central station. And not far away was the meeting point for the caravans, Pretty Peepers Alley, it was a kind of de facto free-trade zone for the city. According to the city's official policy, let's say. Hard to imagine it now. And old Randy, me that is, stood there wide-eyed at that low-rise Disneyland. I could have imagined a big wheel in there. A big wheel full of whores. Glittering above the roofs of the city, glittering and brightly coloured above the roofs of the caravans. And that's when we saw, Klaus from Bielefeld, Karate U. and me, that there was already a big market cooking away there. A meat market, I'd say now. Like how they cook up methamphetamine or whatever there now, these days, but that's a different story, a

498

different market. I'm well out of it, thank God.

So anyway, we soon hooked into it to get started off. With our classy caravans, with our classy girls. We met a few friends and acquaintances right off as well. But the atmosphere was already jumping. Pimp 12 to Pimp 23: 'Time you thought about buggering off home.'

Karate U. got a migraine after three days. His girl and then my Claudi had to massage his neck to calm him down. My Claudi was better at that than his girl, that's why. I told him right away, hey, that'll cost you for loss of earnings. And then we emptied a couple of bottles of champers and made up again. We always had our artillery on us there, all of us. Most of them had a couple of pieces at hand. But they did pull themselves together so as not to scare off the clientele. Still, things often exploded. Boom, boom. Yeah, exactly the way it sounds. Couple of shoot-outs. I'll never forget the hole in the caravan. We were all there and no one wanted to leave right then. I still remember how the people, the clients I mean, came in there, how they strolled around the corral. Wide-eyed. And the girls lining either side of the path. And the caravans wobbling and the cash flowing.

What can I say – we'd underestimated the East. There was this one guy, he used to do the doors of the Zone discos before the Wall, he had his crew, old bone-breakers from the days before '90, and you had them on your case as soon as you wanted a permanent parking spot on Pretty Peepers Alley. So OK, you'd make an arrangement. A note here, a note there.

And we were negotiating eye to eye. OK or KO. It's normal for a bit of cash to flow. But don't get fresh with us. Us old Ruhr Valley pros did try to stick together.

So this AK, this MBA man who later went his own way in the big city, did his own thing, the one you hear so much about these days, he had this football crew behind him back then but he was clever enough to keep out of the chaos. Invested in amusement arcades and it seems like he knew the city would ban all the crazy shit on Pretty Peepers Alley, which we hadn't seen coming. Off the streets and into bricks and mortar. Apartments, properties. The future.

For a while it all went fine on the streets – the East loved our girls. And we had the artillery. And the business experience. The beasts from the East had the street crews. And the Yugos coming pouring out of their collapsing state where they had all those wars then and later. They had no inhibitions, none whatsoever. Yeah, and old Randy playing piggy in the middle. My real name's actually Reinhold but everyone's always called me Randy.

The East chewed us up and spat us out. And it wasn't like we didn't try to get into the property game. Klaus and U. and me, we'd pooled our funds. There was this old mill on the edge of the big city where we wanted to put a brothel. Our East German branch. But just when we were in the middle of the negotiations the cops come running into our hotel and they knew exactly where to find our artillery. Bloody communist connections. One gun in the minibar. One gun in my spare cowboy boot.

And Bob's your uncle, that was us out of the war zone.

I knew this one guy vaguely, friend of a friend of a friend, he stuck it out for a while in the big city. In among the Yugos and the Eastern crews. He had this little club. Put a bit of money into it. And one day, must have been around '93, I'd been back in Happy Valley for a while by then, my girls on the street like they should be, the Eastern Bloc – so the Russians, Romanians and all the other pick-n-mixes – and the Turks and the Arabs on

500

their way to absolute domination, Klaus the Baker used to say: 'How we love our foreigners; if only they'd stay abroad,' anyway what I was saying was, back in '93 I met this guy, he was up to his neck in plans gone pear-shaped, it was in Bottrop in my old mate's bar, and he was such a nervous wreck he'd given up his nice little club over in the big city. He was ripe for a shrink, the good fellow. But I still had a bit of a chat with him at the bar. And I have to admit I had a hard time back then when the shots were fired on Pretty Peepers Alley, remembering my athletics days. Run Randy run.

And I told the guy who ran away from the big city a nervous wreck about Sammy and Mike, who I knew pretty well from the good old days in Happy Valley. The days when we ruled the discos and stuck gemstones on the girls' bare skin. So we could rinse them off again with champers. Randy's off on one again, says Claudi.

Those two had their brothel in the state capital, their club. Yeah, says the guy, I had a club in the East too.

In the big city?

In the big city.

His hands twitched on the bar like my hands used to twitch on Pretty Peepers Alley. The trick is to make sure no one notices. If only your hands would twitch again like that on me, says Claudi. Enough of that! Yes, I know you're the one bringing home the bucks, baby! Bloody retirement.

But back then, '93 or '94, I'm telling the guy the story about Samuel and Mike. How they suddenly came up against a whole lot of pressure down in the state capital.

Some guys put on pressure, others have a shotgun.

Looking back now, I know the two of them were let off for self-defence. We uncorked a few bottles for that. Although the old days were well and truly over. But it

501

was one last little victory over the East. Oh no, Randy's not running! Or rather: OH YEAH.

I just wanted to explain to the guy how lightly he got off. Of course you can see it either way, as always. But the Nazi wrecking crews in the state capital were a force to be reckoned with. It wasn't the bone-breaker brigade, it was the ideological bone-breaker brigade. Oh boy, I'm still the same old Randy! But what kind of dirty bastards are they if they think our traditional trade, our centuries-old business ain't German enough for them? They want to get the streets of the state capital all clean and German again.

Hello?

So I'm telling the guy with his bad case of post-East-matic stress syndrome about how Mike and Sammy's club got smashed up by the neo-Nazi crew a couple of times over. But the two of them had a shotgun. As I said. And then when Mr Topdog Nazi, funnily enough not from the East, he was from the Ruhr Valley, this guy who did ideological training with the crews there in the East... anyway the next time he came in to make a complaint the two of them shot him down. Boom, boom.

Yeah, says the guy, we all badly overestimated ourselves over there.

We did, says I, we did.

Back then there was a rumour going round that this investor from the West, from Hessen somewhere, got pushed out of the market pretty radically up on the coast in Rostock. It was true and all. The whole rumour.

Signed his own death warrant. The armies mustered on the beach promenade. How can you ever win in a foreign country? What I always say to Claudi when we're talking about all that old stuff and we need a laugh: Who was the longest-standing mayor of Rostock?

How do I know?

Heinz Kochs! Geddit? Cocks, Kochs, longstanding?

And they had these container brothels, back then, run by the Mecklenburg crew. The ones who shot each other dead and stabbed each other and beat each other into a coma. Not a big pie to divide up. Just a little pie. There was a rough wind up there on the coast. A rough wind blowing in the East. Not the right place for Randy. Never mind Heinz Kochs. Bollocks to that!

So we stayed put after that, stuck to doing our business here in Happy Valley. Pimp? Yeah.

Yeah.

I went back to the big city again in '96. I had my registered company, for the Inland Revenue.

Old Randy, me that is, we had this idea for settling down. By that time I only had Rosie and Claudi.

True love was over and done with, but I don't let Claudi hear that kind of thing.

I met the Karate Granddad again one time, by the way, when I went to visit my old mum in her retirement home in Hagen. It always used to look like the East over there. In Hagen, I mean, not in the retirement home. That place was classy. I was still making good money in those days.

I even had two employees. In the decorating company. That acquaintance of Klaus the Baker's got me the order. For a club in the East. Let's not even talk about how much of a cut Klaus got out of it. Anyway, I was back over there with the crazies. There was money to be made.

My lads were supposed to set up three mirrored rooms there. In the Bielefelder's fortress, that guy Klaus knew, then in some little club, and then there was this other guy, he was pretty well known even then and he had one or two places in the city or wanted to open up one or two places, don't ask me after all this time. He's a big deal now, at any rate, a good businessman, so I hear. In with the Angels as well. Anyway, his order went belly-up. '97! says Claudi. Yeah, yeah, you could be right.

We were supposed to meet up in some twenty-four-hour bar there. They were all hanging out there. AK, who was making big waves at the time in apartment letting, the Bielefelder came in sometimes, a couple of property arseholes as well. You know how it is, these things always end up taking days. All I wanted was to get the deal sorted. A couple of guys came in who used to run round on Pretty Peepers Alley, members of the various crews, signed up to security firms in the meantime. They didn't recognize me. I had shorter hair and a moustache. The girls always used to complain about that moustache.

There was peace in the big city. They'd sat down together at a round table. They're not so dumb, those beasts from the East. The red-light-sector round table. They must have suddenly got the whole democracy thing. Forged a pact. Shared out the pie crumbs. All for all, and every man for himself.

And they certainly knew how to throw a party there, playing darts for a couple of hundred marks, free munchies on the bar, bubbly and beer, and from around four or five the girls turned up as well. Just like our old place back in the day, just a size smaller.

And one time when I was there the guy I was supposed to fit the mirrored room for in his club, he jumps up on the bar and starts singing the Internationale. *Arise, ye workers from your slumber...* And the beasts from the East all joined in like a choir and then went back to playing darts.

Then on the second night I was there they were all on about some old Stasi stuff – not a lot I can say about that... it was about some file or other, I think maybe AK's, the guy who got a business degree and is such a big deal these days, and they gave this one guy a real seeing to, one of the security guys, 'cause apparently he told the Stasi something about AK at the end of the Zone days. But the next night he was back at the bar again. With his eye all swollen. No one seemed angry any more. I joined in for a round of darts and lost two hundred marks. Fuck it. I got shot of my little company at the end of the nineties. I got those two rooms done in the big city. Things went on for a while with the girls. But that was it then. Too much pressure. Too much competition. Tough times.

When I look out the window I see the Ruhr Valley. I'm happy enough. Don't get fresh with me. I'm Randy!

FACES

He was facing a wall. Ivy-covered, bushes in front of it,
low trees. Grave slabs on top of the brickwork or embedded in the stone. Weathered letters, names, inscriptions.
He couldn't make out any way through to the other side.
He had come up against other walls before, blocking
his way. They ran all over the plot of land in apparently random order. Now and then he found a gate, a way
through, once even a kind of small tunnel, an empty
mausoleum open on both sides. A burial building. Like
a tiny temple on the inside. He could see the impressions
left by the broken grave slabs and plaques. A sill along
both walls, a slim ledge presumably meant for sitting on.
He had strode quickly through the open crypt, hearing the loud echo of his footsteps, fallen leaves on both
thresholds, then he was on the other side. The same plot
of land behind the wall, behind this gateway. What was
he doing here? And how had he got here? All he knew
was that he'd suddenly found himself outside the main
entrance to the big cemetery, car keys in his hand. The
car parked on the other side of this narrow, silent street,
outside a café, plastic tables on the pavement, no guests
in sight and no passers-by.

He walked up the slope. The path led through groups
of pines, firs, deciduous trees, the land rising, a hill ahead
of him. He couldn't tell how far the little wood went on
– the further he got from the entrance gate the denser it
grew, bushes, trees, ornamental plants, hedges; and the
stones, the graves, large, small, medium stones, graves
surrounded by low iron fences, grave figures, statues,
rocks with names carved into them with the appearance
of boulders, then small pale stones above new pale urn
graves, huge family graves lined by trees like islands

or by walls, which still divided the cemeteries that had grown together over the decades but were linked by several gates and passages. He turned around and could see the very pointed and very black tower of a church downhill in the distance behind and between the trees, stabbing into the sky like a thin, bare and branchless plant, presumably somewhere outside the graveyard. He couldn't remember ever seeing that church, that tower before. There was a slim, high window below the tall steeple, a black-framed blue, a couple of ragged white-grey clouds behind and beside the tower. He had to think briefly what time he was in at that moment. Even the month wasn't quite clear to him and it took a few seconds for him to locate himself in this October 2010. Afternoon. He had taken off his watch a few hours ago when he went for a swim, it must still be on the veranda. He hadn't swum in the pool; he'd walked down to the lake instead. The water was cold and clear and he could see the brightly coloured squares and triangles of sails far out. It was a gorgeous October but the wind was fresh, blowing in from the hills on the opposite bank that were hard to make out with the naked eye, curved silhouettes that got rockier the farther they were from the city, wooded hill country interrupted by steep cliffs and ridges. An express road led through the hill country, widened and newly surfaced only a few years ago, and sometimes he drove there around the great lakes to the hills, to the forests.

He looked for his phone. Then he remembered he'd left it in the car. He tried to make out the clock on the church tower, squinting against the light of the low sun at the church he couldn't remember. That tower must be visible for miles, stabbing up so long and thin between the buildings. Was it four?

He could only guess at where the hands were pointing. He'd probably need glasses for distances soon as well – he carried his reading glasses in a leather case in the inside pocket of his coat. He took them out, held them away from him and looked through one of the lenses like through a magnifying glass at the tower and the clock and saw through the blur that it really was ten to four. He noticed the silence. No birds singing. The city was not to be heard here. He had driven around aimlessly. He'd often done that in the old days when he needed to think, when he had to consider business matters, when there were problems. Usually he'd drive around at night, listening to the radio, a classical music station – it relaxed him. Investments, properties, what are the Yugos up to? Should he pass on the information about the Russian madam? The one doing her dirty little deals with her daughter, but all that was more than ten years ago. And a stream of colours, memories, trips, women, banknotes, deals, houses, shares, calculations, birthdays, crises, profits, attacks, Christmas parties, lights, women, short circuits, *Son, my son, what have you done*, in the meantime. In the meantime. How many years? When he drives aimlessly around the city, through the centre, through the suburbs, over to the other, smaller town where he has properties too, Eden City 2, but the villages are becoming suburbs, the neighbouring cities are moving and shifting closer, the connecting roads getting shorter and shorter, the passenger train runs through a tunnel beneath the city, when he drives that route he sees the construction machines and ditches and the tall thin arms of the cranes, he sees the German flag fluttering in the wind on the roof of Madame Gourdan's club, as he sometimes calls her in jest, he drives past the old stadium on the edge of the city where he spent so much time back then, over twenty years ago, more than that, drives past the new stadium, alongside the river and the flood basin where the children once drowned as he stood by the window, drives over the bridges of the small rivers and canals, 1999 and some place and some time in 2010. He hears the church clock chiming. The sound of the strikes touches his back, spreads out around him, passes through him and dissipates between stones and trees. He's standing in front of the wall that borders the cemetery up on the hill, waste ground beyond it, dilapidated empty allotments, barren land, a declining hillside, rubble and scrubs, and then the grey houses of the suburbs, the margins, the peripheries, arterial roads, and the evening edges closer, red and pink. He walks along the wall, there in front of him a wide gap, a way through as large as a gateway with no gates, he comes up against a construction fence, perhaps they want to extend the cemetery here, put in a new field of graves, he sees three figures a few hundred yards away on the wasteland. They're moving around inside a large square made of red-and-white barrier tape. They seem to be digging something into the ground of the long patch of land behind the graveyard. Doing something he can't make out with crates and apparatus. He holds his glasses up like a magnifying glass again. But before he can narrow his eyes he hears a dull bang. Narrows his eyes and sees the three men in orange suits standing behind the tape, a thin white cloud of smoke rising from the middle of the marked-out square. Another bang, very dull as if it were coming from deep beneath the earth, another small thin flag of smoke alongside the first, almost dispersed by now. He remembers someone once telling him about the old method of loosening ground using explosives. He turns around and walks back, keeping to the wall.

He stares at the stone face. It was growing out of the wall directly in front of him. Empty eyes, the mouth open as if lamenting. Writing above it, a plaque, the letters and words so weather-beaten he could hardly read them. Some kind of lieutenant, died young before the first war, as he gathered from the only partially legible dates. Some time before, maybe twenty or thirty minutes ago, he'd found himself in a kind of small court-yard, sectioned off by walls, and in the middle of the courtyard rose a pillar with a round stone emblem resting on the top, a hammer and sickle, behind the pillar a row of gravestones. He remembered he'd been there once as a child, with his class, with other school classes, some kind of memorial day, perhaps 8 May, Liberation Day, pioneers and blue-shirts, teachers and Party secretaries, officers, and gradually the picture came back to him of standing there and looking at those graves. Russian soldiers. Soviet soldiers – that was what they used to say at the time. It must have been in the mid-seventies. Speeches were given. Or did he only remember the memorial site but hadn't set foot in it since then, *now*, that strange stone face in front of him. Another soldier. But he'd died during peacetime. Heart, cancer, booze, suicide. An accident. A duel. He turned around a few times, looking across the paths, between the trees, where was that young warriors' copse? Was it perhaps his memory of the great silence between the great speeches that had brought him here, to this grave-yard on the edge of the city? Voices, faces. *Why are you here?* He wanted to walk back to the street, to his car, drive back to his office, drive home, go down to the lake, but he'd been there that morning. It was all right so far. He thought of Tokyo, that neon-lit metropolis at the other end of the world, robots and humans on the island soon to be flooded by radiation. That was where he'd disappeared the first time. In the year zero. He had flown back home. Carried on. Year after year. He had survived all the attacks and the offers. Yugos, Turks, Arabs, Angels, politicians, friends, Russians, allies... He had acted as if everything were perfectly normal. Inside him. With him. He had driven through unfamiliar neighbourhoods by night. Found himself in repetitions. Found changes. Letters he had never written, documents he ought not to have, information, contacts that surprised him. He went to a therapist. Got his brain checked out. Got his soul aired out. Absolutely normal. Made business progress. Sold his shares before they went down the pan. Invested in properties. Negotiated in Berlin and Hannover. Bought art. Drank with the Count, that semi-impostor who still impressed him. And who introduced him to the Austrian who used to be a lawyer and now ran an exclusive club that had earned him a fortune, a showpiece for Austria's bureaucrats, a clean house that made the authorities and the Austrians happy.

Dreamed with them of the red-light-sector share. Champagne. No, he hadn't looked at these graves earlier, the fallen heroes of the Great Patriotic War. But he heard the music played back then, sung back then, the choir of soldiers, when he'd stood there in his pioneer uniform, red neckerchief, blue cap. Soft at first and then louder and louder, the dead heroes, hearts shot to pieces, lungs ripped apart, from whom this last great song... He'd even sat out that crazy cop, as if he was a thoroughbred politician, that gaunt old man who lived not far from him and hadn't been a cop for a long time now and had wanted to press his nose in the dirt, his whole face in the mud. He should go rummaging round the town hall, that crazy old man caught up in his own net, light

511

burning every night in his window, he saw him pacing up and down his conservatory, restless for hours and for years, he should go digging the dirt on the fat cats who now owned whole streets. With whom he did business, nothing more. All clean. Bloody good clean business. He'd got goose pimples when they'd played and sung the anthem of the great Soviet Union. His Russian was still not bad. He could read the plaques and the inscriptions on the graves. '...fallen in the Great Patriotic War.' The end of the utopias. 'Glory and honour to the Soviet Union.' The end of the insanity. The beginning of the other insanity. '90. A real insanity, at least. He was still staring at the face in the stone. Young man, *what have you done?*

He heard the birds. He'd been surprised all along that he hadn't heard any birds. Here in this green, this forest. Where there must be thousands of them. But perhaps it was the approaching evening that made them grow active. A chirruping and singing from the trees that suddenly died down, though. Then it began again, then it died down again. Him staring at the face of the young lieutenant all the while. *For peace and socialism: be prepared!* He looked at the girl in the row in front of him, he liked her a lot, down by the canal, two days ago they'd been to the old harbour warehouses together, he'd told her about the book about the utopian town of Eden City before he kissed her, he's twelve years old, there's so much he wishes he knew, and he dreams of the ports for ships and spaceships, and he feels and he sees the beat of her heart, his hand on her breast, and he's ashamed and wants to be alone with her again and then he looks at the stone emblem, hammer and sickle, thinks of the big hydraulic hammer he sees and he hears through the open works gate, the heat pressing out to the pavement

512

and the street through that open gate, the constant blows of the giant hammer working the metal with sparks flying, the steel or whatever it is, they chase him away when he gets too close, he squats on the pavement and watches the workers in the foundry, the big forge, they squat there together on the kerbstone, their shoulders touching, before they walk to the old dilapidated harbour, he sees her face in this silence, the choir of the Soviet soldiers, there must be a hundred of them or more, he doesn't want to count, he's almost forgotten Thor's hammer by now, the teachers didn't like it one bit; utopian literature – now that's something different, it's socialism and utopias amid the stars, oh yes, what do you want to be when you grow up? I want to be a salesman, I want to be a businessman, I want to build houses, for me and for others, I want to build big harbours, and then they walk away, *always prepared!* They walk hand in hand between the graves, deeper and deeper into the little woods, the groups of trees, bushes and ornamental plants gone wild, come up against walls, sit on stone benches, see the evening coming and then touch, somewhere in among it all, the angel's wings, the angel's beard, he too sitting on a stone bench at the foot of a grave site, his head lowered, his eyes closed beneath his furrowed brow, they knock at his skin and hear, TOCK tock, DONG dong, that the statue is made of iron, they think, some kind of metal that has gone green in the course of unfamiliar decades.

He was still staring at the grey face in the stone. Perhaps that was why he was at this cemetery. *Where are you going?* A place he hadn't been since that year, he couldn't say exactly what year it was, mind you... if he was twelve or thirteen, then... He counted, using his hands and fingers to help him, which made him laugh. What did it matter? The evening came slowly over the wall. Quiet, dull bangs. They ran, holding hands, saw the three men in orange on the other side of the wall...

He had found the book again a few months ago. *Eden City*. He had bought it in one of the second-hand bookshops in the city centre. A very tall, very haggard man with a bald head had looked for it for a while in the back room, he had heard him murmuring and whispering, perhaps he was flicking through a register or index of utopian books, of socialist utopian literature, and while the thin man rummaged around his storeroom he walked up and down the shelves, studying a few titles with his head cocked to one side. He didn't read much fiction, only the odd crime novel, he was interested in history, Machiavelli, the decline of the Roman Empire, the history of prostitution, *Das Kapital*, its fat leather volumes now directly in front of him on the shelf, he'd never worked his way all the way through, only read larger extracts that interested him, he had exactly the same edition, brown artificial leather. He pulled one of the volumes off the shelf, 'Dietz Verlag Berlin 1951', he flipped the pages and saw that the former owner had underlined entire passages in red, page after page, here one or two sentences, there whole sections, here single words, he flipped on, took the second volume off the shelf as well, and found the red underlinings in this one too... *The tendential fall in the rate of profit is linked with a tendential rise in the rate of surplus-value, i.e. in the level of exploitation of labour... The rate of profit does not fall because labour becomes less productive, but because it becomes more productive... The market must, therefore, be continually extended, so that its interrelations and the conditions regulating them assume more and more the form of a natural law working independently of the producer, and become ever more uncontrollable...* Holy shit! He laughed, put the books back on the

514

shelf, yes, and then he remembered, he'd read it a few years ago for his degree. When he'd done his apprenticeship, in the late seventies, early eighties, he doesn't want to add it all up now, he'd steered well clear of old Master Marx, like most people. He stared at the face of the thin man that popped up in the gap left by *Das Kapital*, on the other side of the double shelf. He might have been watching him for a while now, but then he saw that it wasn't the bookseller at all, on the other side of the shelf, it was some customer, some other visitor standing there and studying a title through a big pair of brown-tinted glasses with his head cocked at an angle and apparently not even seeing him. He put the two volumes of *Das Kapital* back on the shelf. Later, the thin bookseller had brought him the book he was looking for at last, dug it up out of some box, he'd bought up a large collection of GDR utopian literature a few days ago, he said, 'You've come at the right time,' and later, over coffee at the office between two appointments – someone was interested in an apartment near the old harbour, an upcoming location because they were planning to put it back into operation in a few years' time – when he finally flicked through *Eden City, Metropolis of Oblivion*, smelled the pages, he saw that the book had been published in 1985. But he'd read it as a kid. Over and over again, he'd wandered through the bunker worlds in his imagination and sometimes in his dreams at night, had stood up against the hierarchies, united the clone people and led them out of their cold, grey world, conquered the luxury beings... he must have been twelve or thirteen, or even if he'd been fourteen or fifteen... No. Later, when the football and the insanity came into his life, he'd hardly read anything, and the utopian literature gathered dust on his shelves. '1st edition, 1985'. But he'd stopped finding such apparent unclarities surprising.

He walked slowly away from the lieutenant and the stone face in the wall. The paths were covered in fallen leaves. He put his hands in his coat pockets; it was getting cool. He took two ginkgo tablets every day, the Count had recommended them once, 'Good for your circulation, good for your brain, even old Goethe used to take them!' He tried to find the path he'd come on. But he kept coming up against a wall, he had the feeling he was going in circles, he was sweating. Yellow and red leaves on the trees, on the ground. He realized he hadn't seen anyone since he was here, during this time. Why was nobody visiting the dead on a day as beautiful as this? No, he had come across a woman when he'd been walking up the hill, earlier. She'd been singing something, he couldn't quite make it out, and she'd fallen silent when she saw him. An older woman but not ancient, perhaps sixty or seventy, hard to say. Short hair, or was she wearing a dark wool hat? A woollen hat, yes. Perhaps a funeral hymn or something. She had looked down as they passed each other as though ashamed of her singing but shortly later he'd heard her voice again, very quietly as if from far away; he hadn't turned around again. He scanned a few of the names on the gravestones, left the main path and got lost in the small branches between the graves. *Schuster Family, Jochen Krien, H. and F. Gehrleben, Leer Family, Our Dear Mother, 1908-1989, love springs eternal.*

He rarely thought about death. Was that true? The landlord of love. For love springs eternal. He laughed. The older woman could have been a man. She was wearing a pale, perhaps grey coat. Or a ladyboy grown old gracefully, but older examples of that particular peculiarity were probably rare, it would be a few decades before the young trannies got old, indistinguishable from men or women, depending on direction. Medical progress made it possible – he'd seen several gorgeous women who'd previously been men and now welcomed in the lovers of that transformation in return for good money. It was only a question of time before some of them contacted him to work in his apartments. But maybe he'd have got out of the business by then. In that future that wasn't far off. *Old as a tree, that's how I'd like to be...* Maybe that's why I've come walking here, he thought, to plan things, to look into the years to come. And so he walked on, rustling the leaves at his feet, thought of this, thought of that, felt very far removed from the city, walked with his grandmother through her little village, carried the watering can on the way to God's field, as she called the village graveyard, tried to remember the name of that tiny village close to the small industrial town, its factories and refineries casting their glow far across the crops at night so that they could see them, flames above the chimneys, his grandmother and him when they sat by the attic window where the little TV was. Black and white. He'd like to tell someone about it. His wife? His son? His son was going through the insanity of other games. Like he had once. Perhaps that was a good thing, perhaps it had to be that way. If he wanted to hand everything over to him one day. The properties, the company, the fitness studio. No one could take that away from him. No one would take that away from him. Too many years. After all the years. Too much energy and time. Was that all? he thought sometimes. And he thought it again.

He stood at the foot of a broad staircase. Only a few steps up to a large door, pillars on either side of it. He turned around. Behind him a pond, a square one, a lake encased in stone. It was still fairly bright. The light of a late October afternoon. The building to which the staircase led, a strange geometric form, was reflected on the water, a high front with a dome-shaped roof, like a large entrance portal. The doors between the pillars, closed. He saw the evening sky on the water. Where was he? He couldn't see the church tower anywhere; he craned his head in all directions. Two ducks on the water. He had to go back to his car, drive back into the city that was somewhere far away, back to his office. Make some phone calls. He reached into the inside pocket of his coat and felt the packet of ginkgo tablets. No ducks on the water.

'I never thought it would be you.'

He didn't turn around straight away, the sudden voice behind his back. He looked across the water, across the graves and the walls, across this ever-extending stretch of graveyard he had been wandering. So now he was here. 'And who are you?'

He turned slowly to the building. A man was sitting there, on the top step, directly outside the still-closed door. He wore a blue work coat and a kind of flat cap resting directly above his eyes, concealing his forehead. 'Although I never really thought,' said the man, his head resting on both hands, elbows on his knees, 'that your lot would come here.'

'Here? My lot? I'm on my own.' AK took a few steps until his shoes touched the bottom of the staircase.

'Are you?' The man on the stairs took his hands away from his chin, slowly, leaned back and surveyed AK. 'Did they send you all on your own?'

'And who, who sent me?'

'The Angels.'

AK went down on his knees. He laid both palms briefly on the stone slabs of the floor, which felt warm, and looked the man directly in the face from down there before he stood up again, recognized nothing, saw nothing, which might have been because the lower part of his face was concealed by a short dark blond beard. 'No Angels,' he said. 'I'm just taking a walk.'

'Aha. Taking a walk, the big man. And comes here to me.'

'And where am I? And who exactly am I looking at?'

'You don't know, big man? You're standing in front of my front door and telling me you don't know where you are?'

'I just said I was taking a walk. But now I'm here. Come down and tell me your story. I'm all ears.' He put one palm against his right ear. Or perhaps it was the left one, because he wanted to keep his right hand free by his hip. He was too old for this shite.

'You come up here, Arnold Kraushaar, and tell me your story.' The man was still sitting at the top of the stairs, his body leaned back, palms on his knees.

'Seeing as you seem to know me, I presume you already know my story.'

'More than the legends, big man. I watched you a long time along your paths.'

'So why the game? Who are you? What do you want?'

'The game, the game, Master Kraushaar. You're the one, the Angels are the ones playing a game. Always the same sandpit games, eh? This is my castle and you're not allowed to... and so on. We make the market and the world the way we want it.'

AK walked slowly up the stairs. Step by step. To look the other man in the eye. To recognize what he was starting to think he remembered. 'And,' said the man with the beard, standing up, also very slowly, and they stood directly opposite each other, separated by a single stair, 'who's behind the mirrors?'

'I never thought I'd see you again. After all these years.'

'And I never thought you'd buy your way in like this, the great Arnold Kraushaar, to the Angels, behind the mirrors... I never thought my head would be your entrance fee. Your insurance policy, your gift to your new business partners.'

'You're wrong. I go my own way. No Angels. No mirrors. Call it a coincidence that I'm here.'

'A coincidence, aha. How did you track me down? How did they track me down?' The bearded man took a few steps back, leaned his back against the closed door between the two pillars.

'No one tracked you down. You ought to know me. Even though it's a long time ago. I always thought you were sitting somewhere in the lap of state-funded luxury. House, wife, kids and a new name. Or are you telling me they put you here?'

The bearded man laughed. 'No. Although it wouldn't have been the worst idea. Who'd look for the traitor outside the walls? In the funeral business. In the great flamarium.'

'Betrayal,' said AK and thought for a while to recall the exact phrasing, '...like beauty, is in the eye of the beholder.' He cocked his head, *that surprised you, old friend, didn't it?* and saw that the lake was turning pink under the evening sky. It really was, as they say, a golden autumn evening in October, even though the colours were getting confused.

'Beauty... you know all about that, my friend, don't you? But while we're on the subject... there's no need to put a gloss on anything. Nothing at all. Not you. And not me anyway. I always thought things would go differently, would end differently.'

'Who knows when anything's finally over? I even understood what you'd done when I heard about it. No more, no less. Maybe you should have stayed here, stayed with me...'

'Maybe I should have done. Back then. But the Angels, the big trip, the big business, the power of the...' he laughed again and moved his arms up and down, 'winged horde. That was always my dream. That's what I believed back then, thought back then. And now I've come back by tram.'

'No one knows you're here.'

'*You* know.'

'Yes. Now I know. And that's all. How?'

'... did I end up here, is that what you want to know? It's not a long story. The cops made me some offers but I knew they weren't safe. Even though I wanted out and I got out, I still heard this and that. And then I cleared out of my own accord.'

'You did a lot of talking first...'

'Do you want a drink? It's time for me to knock off work, if you like.'

'Suddenly so tame and trusting? You don't think they'll launch themselves at you at any moment, pop up from behind the trees and graves?'

'It would be over already if you'd wanted it to be, if that was why you came. Why not believe in coincidence for once? Have you got relatives buried here?'

'No.'

'You see? A yes would have made me doubt your story.'

'Maybe I'm too clever for you.'

'Could be. Come on in, bring good luck with you.' He pulled a large bunch of keys out of the pocket of his work coat and opened the door.

521

They crossed a large room lit only by a few small lamps on the walls, rows of chairs, pale, plain, almost bare walls, and again the bearded man opened a door that led to a kind of domed hall, pictures on and in the large blue dome that was so blue that he thought at first he was gazing at the sky, if it hadn't been for the pictures and frescoes he couldn't quite make out, the bearded man's voice ahead of him, Steffen, that was his name, that used to be his name, 'This rotunda is a depiction of the cosmos, they built it like a temple back then, 1915, to all the gods, but that won't interest you much...' AK didn't answer. He wasn't sure what wouldn't interest him exactly. It was strange enough just being here. Meeting Steffen. He knew he had the obligatory price on his head. The green, green grass stands out a mile, he thought. And wasn't it possible that he'd got a tip-off and that was why he was here? But from whom? He was certain no one knew Steffen was here. As a guide and a worker in the 'great flamarium', that was what he'd called this place of the dead, this building that seemed to be a crematorium. He'd thought a lot of him, always imagined he could be his second or third man one day.

A man who wasn't so easy to get rid of. Who knew how to control his strength and his work. He'd come from one of the villages around the city back then, a young man, martial arts, judo, wrestling, kung fu, but a man who didn't just use his head for breaking noses in battle. Who was also interested in the philosophy behind it all. Who knew that their market sector was a very sensitive one. Who read *Hagakure* as if it were the bible. And Sun Tzu. The book about the art of war. Steffen had showed it to him once. AK remembered that now, even though it must have been fifteen years ago, and he was surprised that he hadn't recognized that past straight away in the

522

bearded face. A different person. This man ahead of him. *The greatest victory is that which requires no battle.* It said so on the cover of the worn notebook. But it wasn't like Steffen had taken that quote to heart, because he knew how to fight. When it was necessary. The bearded man, who hadn't hidden his face behind a beard back then. *Standing on the defensive indicates insufficient strength; attacking, a superabundance of strength.* AK had read the book when Steffen had disappeared. It wasn't like he'd simply gone away, he had taken his leave, if you like, wanted to go to Hannover, or did he want to go to Kiel first and end up in Hannover later? The pictures and conversations, the memories of those past years were gradually returning. *The general who is skilled in defence hides in the most secret recesses of the earth; he who is skilled in attack flashes forth from the topmost heights of heaven. Thus on the one hand we have ability to protect ourselves; on the other, a victory that is complete.*

He never knew what to think about it. Steffen wanted to join the Angels. Long before they came to the city. And he'd entered into their web, Steffen, vanished between the threads (the *silver strings*, who had said that?), in the structures, bought his way in, worked his way up, Kiel, Hannover City, got lost, back then. Like his loyal Alex now. Should he cash in the bounty? For what price? What could *they* offer him that he hadn't already worked for himself? In all the years. Him, the general, the Old Man, the man with the companies and the deals.

And as the bearded Steffen, the man he wouldn't have recognized if he hadn't given him a clue, as he unlocked another room... no, as he said, 'We'll just sit down here on the frame and take the lift down,' he began to get suspicious. What if it was the other way around? Who was waiting here for whom? And where did the turncoat,

523

the former Angel who was now a former crown witness, want to take him? Who else was down there? Were the stories even true? Was he really a former member? But AK sat down next to him on the long iron frame in the plain mourning hall, a framework constructed on a platform, presumably for holding the coffin in front of the mourners; he had taken the paths and he wouldn't stop here. *No red-light stop on the freight ring* (who had said that, years ago?).

It wasn't so much a ride, not a fall either, more of a slow, almost soundless sinking, rods on the walls of the brick shaft, 'Last stop on the line,' said Steffen, 'all passengers alight here.' A corridor with the light of a room falling into it, into which the short corridor led, only a few yards away. AK ducked down slightly as he walked, although he could just about stand upright – his head would only have touched the ceiling if he'd stood on tiptoe. The small room was illuminated by several conical lamps that seemed to grow straight out of the stone of the ceiling and were surrounded by circular grids, two slim rectangular pillars, and then AK saw the two openings in the red-brick wall, at floor level. 'Why are we here?' he asked, his voice sounding dull, muffled, subterranean. Steffen's explanations had echoed upstairs beneath the big dome and even in the plain hall, what was what here, mourning hall, chapel, 'Encircled by flames, an also winged genius holds aloft a bowl, a focal point as it were, which emits collimated light,' no, he hadn't seen that in the frescoes inside the dome. His guide's words and phrases echoed and doubled and bounced back on themselves.

'Why we're here? To talk?' A steel girder, a rail, ran towards the openings at a height of about six foot, held by steel or iron ceiling struts, a kind of movable pulley

524

system with chains and hooks, presumably for lifting the coffins and taking them to the openings, which also had rails leading into them, on ground level; strangely, they were patterned in black and yellow.

'To talk. Yes. Maybe we should.' Three small two-wheeled carts stood directly against the wall, below the pulley system. He sat down on one of them, feeling fatigue or rather a kind of dullness, *Oh, how still I feel by evening*, he thought, is that a nursery song? The two-wheeled cart tipped onto the floor and he stood up again.

'Can I get you a chair?'

'I'm fine, thanks.'

'Do you want a drink?'

'What a good host. What have you got?'

'Cognac. For a good guest.'

'A glass of cognac. Why not?'

AK watched Steffen walking to a brown metal locker, which reminded him of the lockers at his fitness studio. Then he saw another door, in the wall opposite the dark openings, which didn't seem to be locked, the flamarium or whatever was behind them, the burners, the grills, whatever was in there. Next to the door was a small table; AK took a few steps towards it and saw that it was covered in strange brochures, small and larger leaflets, a few of them open, he saw plants, flowers, trees, herbs, in other booklets pictures of birds, *the common snipe's beak is yellow and very long*. He leaned against one of the pillars, heard the locker door opening and closing, what genius did he mean up there, as though he was reading his sentences from somewhere. Steffen handed him a plastic cup, 'I'm afraid I can't offer you cut-crystal glasses,' 'Doesn't matter,' 'To your health, Arnold,' 'Perhaps to yours too,' and then they drank. It seemed to be a really good cognac, no cheap rubbish. They drank, breathed in the heavy scent, breathed out the aroma through nose and mouth, enjoyed the subtle finish, before Steffen said: 'Did you know the fire's not allowed to touch the bodies directly? It's a law from 1933.' And as they drank, Hans was sitting in the cellar of his club, at the other end of the city, which must be somewhere out there, sitting in his room, and he stared at the little safe in the wall with the stones inside it, and he felt his heavy face, his swollen eyes, the now full, pendulous cheeks, felt too the bodies humping above him, the dull, apparently distant grumble of music, wondered whether he'd messed everything up now that his dead man had turned up, but he still believed in his luck (raids and shit like that never happened to him, not to them, everything was secured, agreed, and no one knew... and only Inland Revenue was on his case and popped in, and the whores' trade union, the whores' association, but they were easy to deal with, often former working girls, and they could see everything was above board in his club), the chimes of the two hammer-wielding men on the roof of the very old and not very high high-rise in the centre of the city, a white cloud like a slow, contorting mushroom cloud of steam ('So not a mushroom cloud then!') rises into this sky behind the central station, the planes flashing red between it like the wind turbines that grow out of the fields outside the city, the headquarters of the municipal utilities company, that cube of glass and stone, lets off pressure, old people who can't sleep lean out of the windows of the retirement homes and think war's broken out, taxis drive the last guests home or go home empty because there's not been much going on these past few years, the autumn storm whips the water of the great lake with the old digging machines resting on the bottom... *The moon has arisen*, in the Angels' Club too, the last guests are leaving and the girls are trying to come down a little, shooting stars drop into the lakes, how the water hisses, a woman (30?) leans her hands on the big glass window and looks out over the dark city and feels the cock in her body big and strange and still laughs to herself, what an idiot, what an idiotic gentleman to pay so much for a hotel visit, laughs silently because sometimes everything seems so simple, the clocks are adjusted, the hands rotate... *the last starlets glisten*... through the fortress, near the motorway exit, the shadows wander, the turnstiles are locked, empty taxis draw tails of light in the night, Turks and Arabs dream in the capital of taking over, *we take what we can get*, the foehn wind blows like the Gulf Stream all the way to Austria, where the former lawyer sits in his modern club and makes the taxman happy, *why hide anything when you've got plenty to show... and the white fog wonderful...* and the Count investing somewhere else and sitting in his fortress in Frankfurt/Main, *what the hell's going on here*, good morning, Germany, the October evening settles over the small woods on the edge of the city.

'The flames... it's cold down here.'

'Will you have another?'

'You're good to your guests. All of a sudden.'

'Can't put the fires on right now.'

'And do you plan to sit down here all the time in the future and poke at the embers and collect up the ash? Or up between the stones? A gardener and undertaker?' He held the plastic cup out to Steffen, who filled it again.

'Not an undertaker. That's a different industry.'

'Come on, cut the crap. That's not what I mean.'

'If you lot let me.'

'We've already cleared that up, that there is no *you lot*.'

'Have we, Arnold? But it doesn't matter where I turn around, here or somewhere else, the shadows are always

527

there. I could have gone to France. And do you think I'd be safe there?'

'I don't know. You're the grass. Grass so green it stands out a mile.'

'We've had that already. You probably want to know why...?'

'Why you went for a chat with the cops?'

'Do you still smoke?' Steffen produced a pack of tobacco from his pocket.

'Gave up long ago.'

Steffen placed a wad of tobacco on a cigarette paper and fiddled and rolled.

'Didn't the cops promise you something, a lot? Wasn't there more in it for you than this here?'

He nudged Steffen's arm and the tobacco fell down, fell off the paper onto the floor. 'The advantages of tobacco, my friend, my stone guest,' Steffen didn't let it bother him, put new tobacco on a new paper while the old, crumpled one he'd thrown away sailed very slowly down to the floor between them, 'have been known for centuries. Pipes, cigars, cigarettes that enhance wellbeing. The minor poisons that accompany us on the path between these gateways.' He pointed his rolled cigarette at the pulley system and the rails below the ceiling. And at the two rails painted black and yellow on the ground before the two openings he'd been speaking of.

'I don't want to be cremated,' said AK, 'I want a nice big coffin.'

'I'd lost the faith, Arnold.'

'The faith? Did you join the church? That's news to me.'

'No. Spare us the jokes. The faith in my religion of power. I always thought we... the Angels, I mean, were the spearhead, the ordering force.' He smoked, spitting out a few crumbs of tobacco.

'And that's why you go to the feds and tell your story, go and betray *your* firm, betray all the years you invested and sacrificed, and reaped the rewards, I assume.'

'It's not that simple.'

'Of course it's not. Was it ever simple? Have you ever read Marx?'

'What?'

'No. You never have. You got stuck on your *Hagakure* and Sun Tzu and all that far eastern claptrap. What did you imagine when you went to the Angels, the great adventure, Great Freedom No. 7? I mean, you were here, four or five years, you were with me, you knew how things work, how the market runs.'

'What would you do if someone pulled one over on you? If someone wanted to take your place? If they blamed things on you that you had nothing to do with, nothing at all. If they wanted to push you out, take everything away from you because they believed some random arsehole who wanted a quick leg-up to the top...'

'The top? You were a foot soldier, a private, maybe a lieutenant but still a soldier. In the service of... Wallenstein's Camp. Everything you just listed like my secretary has happened here and to me. There's nothing new in the East or the West.'

'You're not on bad terms with the cops in your city, either. Arnold Kraushaar, friend of the feds.' He dropped his smoked cigarette on the floor and put it out with the tip of his shoe. AK was still leaning against the pillar, looking at him. How long had he been down here now? Twenty minutes, an hour? Their conversation seemed never-ending, seemed to have begun long ago. Two players, their sights set on each other, but what were they playing for? On the rear wall of the room, he spotted a system of pipes and cylinders from which the pipes came that led into them, valves, dials, meters and below the ceiling two larger pipes alongside one another, running from wall to wall, that seemed to deliver something to the two openings and *what lay behind them*, extracted fire, gas, smoke or fed them in, he didn't understand these things, what normal person knows the workings and the functions of a crematorium, a flamarium, the room was in semi-darkness, *reverent*, he thought, hadn't there been more light before? He felt that he was sweating. He was too old for this shite. He'd turned forty-nine a bit more than a month ago. He was still gazing at the venous system of pipes. Then suddenly he felt the plastic cup in his hand, which he'd almost squashed; as he drank he felt cognac on his skin, a tiny crack in the thin, crackling plastic.

'Where were we?' Had they really both said that at the same time? No. Presumably not.

'I heard they want to get shot of you, Arnold. That the Angels aren't behind you any more. That *he* wants to pull the strings. Alone. No sharing the market any more.'

'You don't just talk a lot. You hear a lot too, a lot of crap, so it seems. Holed up in here. I ought to go. And you, lock the doors tight, bury yourself down here, stay under the ground. It's better for you.' He threw his empty cup in front of the openings in the wall, wishing for a moment he could squat down and look into that darkness, to see whether there was a gate somewhere behind the entrances or whether the path, the rails led directly into the chamber.

'The great AK, losing his nerve? Are they getting to you so badly, old friend?'

'Friend? Those days are gone. Long gone. It's not so

much that you're a traitor...' He had calmed down again but still walked slowly towards the door they'd come out of.

'Traitor? Maybe. Neither of us are the men we used to be, I guess.'

AK stopped by the door. Steffen was leaning on the pillar, not looking at him, looking at the opposite wall, holding his plastic cup close to his chest. AK didn't respond, waiting. He knew the other man would say something at any moment. Knew he wanted to tell his story, wanted to justify himself. Later, in the evening when he was sitting out on the veranda looking onto the lake again, drinking a glass of red wine and gazing at the silhouette of the mountains, he tried to remember his escape through the catacombs, his return to the room with the openings resembling stove doors. As a child he'd once peered into a bakery, in his grandma's village, had seen the giant loaves (in his memory they're as large as his body) being pushed into the semicircular openings on metal trays, the ovens glowing red inside, he tried to remember whether... and did he really stumble along those subterranean passages, only hours ago, the voice of his former employee Steffen behind him, not pursuing him though, and why had he run? Or did he simply want to get out of there, disappear, head home, back into the autumn afternoon that had long since turned to evening? Scurrying ducked down, the air now cold, now stuffy, doors made of iron, tunnels branching off, and over and over a tangle of pipes, tubes along the walls, cylinders, taps with measuring gauges, grey zinc pipes, reddish copper pipes, the air now hot, now cool, he didn't see any ventilation shafts, every few yards the matte glow of a small light bulb behind barred frosted glass, then suddenly light from above, moving in waves on the floor ahead of him, a large rectangular glass window in the ceiling, AK looked up into the pond, the long water basin outside the crematorium, because he can't have got further than that, saw the evening sky through the clouded green water, the sky moving too, streaked reddish, are they fish or birds circling above the water surface, or planes further up, zeppelins brought to him by the pool, the water in a strange refraction, as if through several lenses... he hears the crunch of the pane of glass above him, 'Come inside, it's getting cold. And it's supposed to rain.'

'In a minute, Katrin. I'll just finish my wine.'

'Katrin?'

'Sorry.'

'Don't drink so much!'

'I've had a long hard day.'

'Yeah, yeah, you always have long hard days. And you'd better tell me who Katrin is, and all.'

He runs through the passage, ducking down, bumps his head a few times, hears laughter from somewhere but perhaps he only imagines it, perhaps he has to go by the pipes, has to follow the venous system on the walls that doesn't lead into all the branches off the passageway, which divides again, he shakes at an iron door, 'System III' it says on it, flaking black paint, someone knocks from inside, who's locked in there? Does he hear voices? But he goes on, he has to find the way out, then he hears the roaring behind him, louder and louder, the water breaks over him, he holds his breath, he falls, dragged along by the current, he floats with open eyes, swirls of water all around him, the lights behind barred frosted glass, he purses his lips, sees the room with the two openings ahead of him, he tries to hold onto the walls, fights against the current dragging him there, he used to be a good swimmer, still is... yard for yard... and there they are, looking at him, the faces... staring out of cave-like entrances or exits.

'Ever heard of the Chinese mile?'

'What?'

They're both sitting against the wall, right next to the rails leading into the two openings. Between them a bottle of brandy. He picks it up and looks at the label. His hands are moist. Trembling slightly.

'What did you expect? Remy?'

'Looks like the cops didn't pay all that well. What were your pieces of silver?'

'Safety. For me, my wife...'

'Your wife.'

'You can't take your drink any more, old man. I told you about my wife and my kid...'

'Where...?'

'Even if I trust you, I don't trust anyone that much. That's my price, that I...'

'You left them?'

'Yes. She didn't want me to. It all went wrong.'

'I'm sorry. But you didn't have to...'

'What other option did I have? My post was highly sought-after... and when I showed weakness...'

'You knew you couldn't just turn around. Just walk away. Or: It's no fun any more. I've lost all my ideals...'

'Ideals. As if we ever had ideals. A clean market. Yeah, yeah. Power. Money. Brothers. And if you believe it or not, I would have gone on. Honesty – reliability – respect – freedom. But not much of all that was left. My Angels flew away. But still I wanted to go on. Probably. Most probably. Let's call it a mid-life crisis.'

'I'm having one of those too. But I can decide for myself how far to go, when to stop where, who to do business

533

with...'

'You think so, do you? The Angels are greedy, don't forget that.'

'So? I could leave. At any time. I've got my company, my agency. Got my fitness studio...'

'Monopoly, Monopoly. And at the beginning there were two amusement arcades. Old Kent Road.'

'If you believe in the old legends...' He picks up the bottle and drinks. Passes it over to Steffen, then he wants to look at his watch but his wrist is still bare.

'They pulled one over on me,' says Steffen. 'Have you heard about the Turks in the capital?' He moves the bottle to and fro in front of his face.

'Heard the odd thing.'

'Of course you have. Turncoats suddenly becoming big bosses. Business, deals. And no sense of honour any more. Sounds stupid, I know. Capitalism, I know. The old rules don't apply any more. Maybe I'm too nostalgic. I never wanted to grass. No, I never wanted to.'

AK holds his tongue. He's heard a different story. Two or three years ago. But he knows how it is with stories. Variation A, Variation B, System III – it would be too simple to blame it on perspective.

And the cops wait and make their offers. When they know that Person X is weak, having difficulties. But he'd heard a completely different story. That Steffen went of his own accord. To the cops. A few years ago now. But he didn't want to believe all those things, couldn't believe them just like that. In the old days, photos were photos. That's different now. Insider informer Steffen at his meeting with the Organized Crime inspector. Oh, see, OC! Anyone can glue that together, virtually. He himself hasn't been on any better or worse terms with the cops than any normal person, for twelve or thirteen years now. No Organized Crime inspector investigating him. He has a business to run. Since January 2002, since the Prostitution Act came into effect, it's all been much simpler. That's what he thought to begin with, at least, in that now almost mythical year when they changed the old laws, when the civil servants discovered they had to get the money under their control, the women's rights and the oh, so important moral issues came along for the ride, collateral if you like but better than nothing, that's what he thought back then, a beginning, and that was what Mr B. thought too, someone he remembers now and then, remembers often, his esteemed colleague in the capital, whose apartment brothels had been tolerated all the years and run with no major problems and who had made his profit and let the women make their profit on his property, the peace and the prices and the working conditions in his places were almost legendary (like with AK; they met in the late nineties at a conference of landlords and operators of model apartments and brothel-like operations), and suddenly, after 2002, his colleague Mr B., someone he remembers now and then, remembers often, came into the focus of the authorities, got their sights set on him, got regulated, legally registered, the Planning Department torpedoed Inland Revenue's profit intentions, 'those dual-headed snakes,' who had said that back then...? The administrative appeals court stuck its oar in, the land utilization ordinance, Inland Revenue sent out agents, supposed to encourage the administrative courts, the land utilization people and all the others tangled up in the mess not to prevent the appointment apartments, apartment prostitution, the brothel-like operations from making money, the land utilization people contradicted each other various times, the courts contradicted each other various times, everything got more complicated than before, appointment apartments, brothel-like operations or was it apartment prostitution, but then the individual, in other words the prostitute, has to live in the apartment, brothel-like operations are not permissible in residential areas, or are they, because on 9/8/1996 the Mannheim Administrative Court (my God, what a long time ago it was, thinks A K and strokes the stone face on the lieutenant's grave and asks himself when he's seen this eyeless smile before, wasn't that strange man they called Moon-Eye at the conference as well?)... subsequently, however, on 9/4/2003, the Berlin Administrative Court ruled: 'Brothel-like operations are principally not permissible in general residential areas; in particular, they cannot be permitted as other non-disruptive commercial areas in accordance with § 4 No. 2 Land Utilization Ordinance...' and then they afflicted them with the term 'sector-related disruption', 'Oh Coppenrath & Wiese!' he'd have said back in the day, maybe he'd still say it now, although he knew that the pimp from Arabian Nights or Dortmund or some other Ruhr Valley city had started claiming copyright on it, that witticism, and he went to Berlin in 2002, or was it '03, to support his friend and esteemed colleague Mr B., because he'd helped him out with a property matter on one occasion, thanks for asking, Mr A., Mr B., we have to stick together when it comes to beating the authorities, *noise in the stairwell due to unsatisfied and/or inebriated customers, ringing at incorrect apartment doors, approaches and harassment of women and girls living in the same building, additional traffic and violent concomitant phenomena of the red-light sector,* the Federal Administrative Court left the question or the answer open under NVwZ-RR 1998, p. 540, as to whether brothels were to be classified as entertainment facilities or commercial enterprises, the problem of distinguishing the brothel-like operation is thereby not sufficiently explored, the Osnabrück Administrative Court, in turn, contradicted, in its ruling of 7/4/2005 (April seems to be a good month for rulings), the as yet unpublished legal document of the Rhineland-Palatinate Administrative Court (Jesus, is this a matter for the federal states?) MWRE 101080400, yet was the general classification of prostitution in brothel-like operations and elsewhere not ruled indecent back in month twelve of the year 2000 by the 35th chamber of the Berliner Administrative Court, as it had been all the years previously to the introduction of the Prost. Act...? If the citizens' initiatives 'Contra Major Brothel in Dülmen' and 'Front against Major Brothel in Heidenau' hadn't succeeded, a case brought to the Hessen Administrative Court... What other option did AK have but to buy property, even in the nineties they virtually forced him into the property game, no kindergartens nearby, no churches, no municipal authorities, no OAPs' homes, so that he could let the properties on a purely commercial basis, so that no one was bothered, only whores were permitted as tenants, but somebody was always bothered by his plans, his presence, his necessity. And all he wanted was to go about his business here in the city, perfectly normal, like in any other sector. Even in the early nineties he dreamed of buildings where only whores worked, his buildings, brightly lit windows or lights behind the curtains and hearts like diamonds. And he had kept up the right ties over the years, cops, politicians, officials – that was easier than in Berlin where his esteemed colleague Mr B. had to file for bankruptcy in 2004 (years later he heard who was allegedly behind that).

'Everyone's screwing everyone, Arnold. Greed – they all want to take the fast track to the top.' Steffen raises the bottle to his lips again.

'Wasn't that always the way?'

'No. Not like this. Sometimes I think it's to do with the internet. With the speed, the disappearance of... Do you know the Chinese mile, Arnold?'

'Do you remember that strange man they called Moon-Eye?'

'From Berlin?'

'Yeah.'

'No.'

'Fast track to the top,' AK looks around the room, barrows, a coffin, a small table covered in papers and magazines. 'That's what you wanted too. You wanted to fly far and high with the Angels. Even back then. And you forgot everything, forgot all about insurance, you let them dump you and you went running to the cops instead of fighting.'

'Like you?' Steffen laughs. Hands him the bottle. 'You had your insurance policy. AK's big cock insurance. Everyone knew that.'

'What are you getting at?'

'Nothing. Nothing at all. But weren't photos still photos back then?' He takes his tobacco out of the chest pocket of his work coat. Rolls a cigarette, very slowly, his fingers trembling. 'Sure you don't want one? To celebrate our meeting.'

'You've got a nerve, Steffen, I'll give you that. Making your big speeches about my cock and... like we were back in Ivonne's bar or something...'

'Ivonne's bar. Karate Steffen with the nerves of iron.' He laughs again. 'That was then. Didn't I tell you about the Chinese mile back then?'

538

'They say you chose to get out years ago. Offered your services. Served two masters for years.'

'They say, they say... you know yourself how much *they say* is worth. It's bollocks.'

'Not all information is bollocks.'

'Information? Gossip, Arnold, that was always a factor in our line of work.'

'Could be. But the sector you chose back then when you left town was never my line of work... motorized syndicates.'

'You've got one behind you yourself. As of lately. So I've heard.'

'Gossip, Steffen.'

'Touché, touché. I can understand your decisions. Preventative measures. Insurance. As I said, the Angels are greedy.'

'Then we don't need to say any more about them.'

'No, we don't. That's why I'm here. With the dead.'

'I'm alive. You should have come to me, back then, you should have come back to town. Either way. We would have found a way.'

'Don't lie to yourself. Don't lie to me. How would I have worked for you? The Angels were on the approach. And that was the best thing for you, at the time. Turkish and Arab attacks, Los Locos. The big bad takeover. There's no need to pretend otherwise. And the spirits that you conjured...'

'Let's leave Shakespeare out of it. And I wasn't the only one who conjured them.'

'Goethe. And what does it matter now that they're here and expanding, ever expanding...'

'I'm far from finished, just so you know.' AK reaches for the bottle. He feels that he's talking much too much, opening up the way he doesn't want to open up. He wants

539

to press his lips together, hears the rushing behind the wall they're leaning against. He's unbuttoned his coat; it's warm down here. Unbuttoned his shirt.

'Who says you're finished? You're the one bringing it up. But two years ago, or when was it exactly, you thought they'd steamroller you, am I right? The Turks and Arabs, the Los Locos. And you all send for help, from the faraway kingdom...'

'All we did was make offers. All we did was bring things to a head – the allied troops were on standby already. Hannover, Berlin.'

'Loosely based on Wallenstein, right, General? And it was happy ever after with the new guardians of the night.'

'Clausewitz. Business went on. As usual. A few new contracts, agreements... as usual.'

'Business as usual.'

And then they stop talking and sit, leaning heavy against the wall. Passing the bottle to and fro. The bottle now so moist that the label's beginning to come off.

'I didn't see any other way out. At the time.' Steffen draws up his knees, rests his arms on them and turns slowly to AK. 'For the first time in my life, I felt fear.'

'Fear's not always the worst thing,' says AK.

'Sure. You don't get too careless. But it depends on the dosage. Remember how you sent me in to see those Yugos that time, to their place...?'

'You weren't alone. Alex was with you.'

'Yeah, yeah, your Alex the Great... It's the dosage that counts. It was all small stuff back then. And then I hear you're dead. And then I hear you're alive.'

'I could have made good use of you back then. The Yugos had respect for you.'

'For you as well. Otherwise they wouldn't have

kneecapped you.'

'Let's leave the old stories be...' AK stands up, walks slowly to the table, looks at the opened magazines and books, runs a hand over the illustrations of plants, trees and birds. *Snowdrop anemone, globeflower, red helleborine*, two books with notes and photos inserted between the pages, *Botany Manual, Zoology Manual*. He pulls a photo out of the animal book. Steffen in front of a Harley, next to him the Godfather from Hannover, almost two heads taller, both in leather waistcoats, the glowing-red, shining-white Angels. He puts the photo back in the book. Takes out another one: Steffen on the veranda of a garden house next to a woman; he has his hands around her protruding belly and he's laughing.

'... and when the Angels said I'd done this and that behind their backs. And when they said I'd also done this and that... deals, on my own account, withholding money from the brothers is the worst crime, first commandment: Thou shalt not screw thy brothers...'

'And, did you?'

'No.'

And when AK is sitting by the lake later on, on his veranda, his coat buttoned up to the top, the wind coming cool from the hills on the opposite bank, as he fills his wine glass again although his wife is nagging again, even though she drinks one prosecco after another, those little cans they're all drinking all of a sudden, his cleaning crew's already complained that some properties are chock-full of the things, 'Yes, Arnold, could be, but we only ever have one or two cans after we knock off work!' 'Sure, sure, Sleeping Beauty,' and when he looks out at the water, no moon, no stars, neither there nor up above, he only hears the occasional slight grumble of a plane somewhere behind the clouds that began to cover the sky a few hours ago, there's a scent of autumn, the wind growing stronger, the flashing of the navigation lights between the scraps of cloud, 'You've been sitting here staring at the water all day,' he hears the TV far too loud, one of those stupid talent shows, *Sing Yourself to Millions* or something, how many bodies or coffins has Steffen burned since he's been working down there, out there? And he sees him in the firelight, pushing coffin after coffin into the glowing-red opening of the huge oven, 'It's like wood, when I burn them, nothing, just long dead logs,' yellow smoke above the trees, the water like a dull, blind mirror in the rectangular basin, who's behind the mirrors? He left the protection programme because there was a leak, that's what he says, right? They knew where he was, he left his wife and child to protect them, he said the system had leaks on both sides, and not just because of him, things would change, he said, and reorganize but still stay the same, he had talk-ed about the inside man whose fairy tales kept the whole Federal Criminal Police Force on its toes, 'And you're sure you're not talking about yourself?' *Mirror, mirror in the dark, who'll come and save me from the sharks*, the inside man who even brought the boneheads from the National Socialist Underground into it to make himself important, to get as much as possible out of the game, 'You mean those crazy Nazi terrorists? What have they got to do with the Angels?' 'Nothing. On princi-ple,' arms deals, the meat markets in faraway Kosovo, 'I don't have any scruples, you know that, but I always thought the Angels structured the market and kept it halfway clean,' oh, you fool, in the end banknotes don't ask questions, pieces of silver, we always loved those biscuits they call pigs' ears as kids, no, they're pastries, and the ones they call Americans, it's bloody hot down

542

here, bloody cold down here, and now he remembers the thing about the Chinese mile, and Steffen meets this half-dead guy in Kiel jail, who tells him: incriminate the big guys, the Godfather from Hannover and all the important ones, and the unimportant ones while you're at it, that's the only way to get onto a witness protection programme, south of France would be lovely, wouldn't it? And they're sitting in 'Ivonne's Eck', AK, Steffen, Alex, Hans, the man from House X, now under new management, the Wöhler Brothers and a few of the other usual suspects, important ones, unimportant ones, five in the morning, a twenty-three-hour bar with hot food twenty-three hours a day, banknotes on the bar, darts approaching the board in slow motion, triple seven, the bull's eye in the middle of the circle, the girls drinking bubbly or white-wine spritzers, or coffee with or without Irish, 'Did you know the Chinese don't measure distances by exact measurements?' 'What d'you mean?' the bottle's been empty for ages, it must be night outside by now, he slept in a coffin once, he says, 'Don't believe you!' darts boring into the triple seven, the bull's eye in the middle of the circle missed again, one dart bounces off and clinks into the small glasses, 'What's this stupid internet, what is it exactly anyway?' 1997, 'Science fiction or what, a case for Lem!' Hans laughs and snatches up the banknotes because he shot his points neatly down to zero round after round, 'Herbert Lem?' someone asks, 'Rubbish,' says Hans and stuffs the money in his jacket pocket, 'You mean Herbert Lom, that's the baddie out of *The Treasure in the Silver Lake*,' 'If you don't know the great Lem there's no helping you,' says AK and puts out his cigarette, not even half-smoked, he wants to give it up for fuck's sake, but it's not easy when they all smoke like the chimneys of good old Bitterfeld, not that anything's smoking there nowadays, thank God, in the winter it all used to waft over to the city, smog alarms at the end of the eighties, *Live Is Life*, and they all bawl out the song, Gabi's eating beef olive, she'll end up looking like that Molly Luft from Berlin, that big fat working girl, does someone say that? And that idiotic Chinese mile? 'You don't have the necessary understanding, Arnold. The Chinese, the old wise men and philosophers...' and he walks along the bank, still holding his empty wine glass, and then hurls it out into the darkness, hears it hitting the water, sees first the shadows and then the faces between the bushes (his son? Mary? ... Alex? The almost forgotten face of Lübbke, the one they called the 'Bricks and Mortar Man'? Bärbel? But they're not your business! Who are you?), '...the difficulties of the path, you see, so the miles were always different lengths. Depending on what lay between them, how impassable the way was, rocks or mountain passes or rivers with no bridge. They could never say: the distance is this many units. The Chinese mile can be a mile long or a mile and a half. Two thousand metres, fifteen hundred metres...'

'And what's that supposed to tell me? Am I supposed to understand the world differently now?'

'No. Nothing. I just remember telling you it one time.'

Smoke above the building. He stumbles along the paths. Why does he think his son is running around out here somewhere? Might be running around out here in the dark. But that's a different chapter. Stones as far as his eye could see, ahead of him in the dark. The outlines of trees, bushes, he came up against walls as he tried to find his way out. The hills on the opposite bank of the lake.

He looks and stares and doesn't know what he's seeing. An angel between the bushes, on a stone bench.

Head down, brow furrowed, a long beard descending to his chest. The wings arching above his shoulders. His eyes are closed, one hand supporting the lowered head. He's weathering with time. A telephone rings somewhere. AK turns around, sees the light on the veranda and walks back to the house. Two drones with night vision cameras circle silently beneath the clouds.

BEHIND THE MIRRORS

Veeery elegant! With a touch of Alice.

'What do you mean?'

   'Oh, sorry, I must have been thinking out loud.'

   'Alice, Alice, who the fuck is... Or do you mean Alice down at the bar?'

   'Yes, probably.'

   'Well then, let's call her Alice from now on. A nice-sounding name for our guests.'

   'OK. Right, we can start now if you like, sir.'

   'So you've come to me and you think you can just start off willy-nilly.'

   'I've heard you're not the chairman of the Angels any more, I mean Angels GmbH here in the city.'

   'That's a big question, my friend. I think we ought to postpone our conversation for a while.'

Waiting. Days and nights. And staying silent. Days and nights. And listening. And watching. In a room made of mirrors.

'So how are you today, young man?'

   'Fine. And yourself, sir?'

   'Fine. I'm sure you've prepared a lot of questions this time.'

   'Your press spokesman was very helpful on that front, sir, on the selection front.'

   'The press spokesman. Why aren't you talking to our press spokesman? You know how far you'll get there...'

   'Not far?'

   'As far as everyone else. Are you like everyone else?'

   'I don't know, sir.'

'Yes, you don't know anything. Of course you know nothing. You can drop the "sir", we don't stand on ceremony here. Would you like that?'

'Yes.'

'Forget all that Alice crap. Did you talk to her?'

'Yes, sir. Briefly.'

'And what do you think our ladies tell you?'

'I try not to ask too many questions.'

'There wouldn't be much point. Do you like music?'

'Yes, sir, but I wouldn't say I...'

'Slowly, slowly, lad. Do you like the music in our bars, in our rooms?'

'I don't know. It's just music, sir. I'm relatively open in that respect.'

'So you don't mind what kind of music you hear?'

'There's not much that would bother me...'

'You're not trying to tell me you don't have an opinion on music. You must have a favourite band, a favourite composer...'

'I used to like going to jazz concerts.'

'There we are then!'

'Well, I try, I mean, with regard to our conversation, I'm trying to avoid clichés...'

'You're trying. How do you like this room, my office?'

'It's... very impressive.'

'The mirrors don't bother you then?'

'No.'

'Can you remember your last question, ten days ago?'

'Yes. But it's more than ten days ago.'

'Are you keeping tabs?'

'No. Not on the details we talk about here.'

'And do you still want to hear details about the changes in our management structure, young man?'

'The word on the street is a certain P. is apparently

about to take over the management.'

'Aha. The word on the street. Not in the city's parlours? You hear a lot, young man, seems to me.'

'In this case that's not very difficult.'

'Hearing is one thing. Seeing and knowing's another matter.'

'So you're not denying it, sir?'

'Our press spokesman's responsible for denying things. This isn't an official conversation. So I can tell you all sorts of things. For example that a certain P., as you put it, has already taken over the official management of the Angels here in the city.'

'But I'm still meeting *you* here in this room, in this office...'

'I've been sitting here for many years now. You know the business was going before all the changes, you know I've been doing my business for years, decades you could almost say.'

'In the city.'

'In the city. I was born here.'

'And how...'

'How does it work now? In principle, the same as before. What did you expect? The great coup, the great revolution?'

'Didn't that already happen when the GmbH opened a branch office here three years ago? And wasn't it you who pushed things forward, sir, at the time?'

'Forget the sir, my friend. It's an unofficial conversation. Let's try again... what was your question?'

'Didn't you play a decisive role at the time in the GmbH opening its branch office here, and didn't the status quo, didn't the circumstances in the, in the...'

'You want to say "milieu", don't you? What's that supposed to be? A "moist milieu" as my old business friend

A. always used to say? "Coppenrath & Wiese" was another one of his admittedly stupid phrases. He didn't
invent that one, though. An old pimp from the Ruhr
Valley coined it. A few people from the West tried their
luck in the city back then, long ago, the big gold rush
days. Like it was San Francisco, 1848-49. While the
barricades were burning here and in Europe they were
panning for gold in the New World. West Coast. The
wild nineteenth century. Status Quo. An old rock band.
Great rock band. Do you know your way around history, young man? Sorry, my mistake.'

'What do you mean, sir?'

'We were supposed to be on an equal footing, my curious friend, none of the patronising "young man" stuff.
Let's start again.'

'I don't understand...'

'Slowly. Very slowly. Staying silent. Listening.
Waiting. Days and nights. And correcting or admitting
to mistakes calmly and without fear. We weren't going to
stand on ceremony.'

'That was your suggestion.'

'And we'll stick to it. So, my mistake. Bear that in
mind. That it's not a man sitting here – how do you all
say, behind the mirrors? – who's not capable of taking
responsibility for things. So, do you know a bit about
history? And I don't mean old rock bands like Status
Quo.'

'I wouldn't say I was an expert.'

'Well, I wouldn't go that far myself, either. But I'm
interested and I try to educate myself on the subject.
Milieu. The word seems to me to be a sign of ignorance
on the part of those who like to use it for all the inexpli-
cable and unsavoury things beyond the realm of their
imagination. Let's take Alice...'

'Alice?'

'Yes, Alice for example. Look, there she is, sitting over there in mirror number 3, now don't act so shocked, you have to keep informed of what's happening when you run a business like this. If you're running any business. Two weeks ago she was still called Caro, but I thought your suggestion for a stage name was rather acceptable. Especially because there was an Alice working here three or four years ago and I must say, she was a good girl. In my business that's the only kind of girl you want, girls like Alice back then. She had that special something. That spark. And she was clever enough to take the money and run, off to a new start. Caro, who's now called Alice because of you, my friend, is a wonderful woman too. Go ahead and make a note of that. A wonderful woman.'

A young black-haired girl at the bar. She nods her head to the music. Other girls, other women, next to her at the bar, in the booths, on the dark leather sofas. Alice strokes her hair off her forehead, smokes a cigarette. A man sits down next to her. Not much up yet, it looks like. Early evening in Eden City.

'It's nice for me, seeing these moments of calm from up here. The evening's beginning. The girls are still alone together. It's not like I watch them. I just cast the occasional glance at the mirrors. It's part of the job, going down now and then, greeting a few regulars, chatting to the men on the door, a bit of small talk with the girls... You know, we have a big bonus here...'

'Security?'

'You've done your homework. Angels GmbH provides security.'

'And the rivalry with Los Locos GmbH? A while ago

there wasn't a trace of security, here in the city I mean...'

'Los Locos... let's just let that name speak for itself.'

'Does that mean that the Angels GmbH are a rationally behaving organization by comparison, a company that runs the market, the markets, including part of the so-called red-light sector, with rational, controlled business practices...?'

'Hold on, hold on. Don't get too bold on me. Just kidding – I know what you're getting at, of course. Firstly: I don't want to bear a grudge. The playground games in our city are long since over now. And between you and me, although it's no secret either, most of the business in the red-light sector of the city of M. on the beautiful Elbe is run via Los Locos GmbH.'

'Yes, I'm aware of that. Will the Angels GmbH try to get a foot in the market there?'

'You're too fast, my friend, far too fast. And you do think in the old clichés. Patience is one of the most underestimated virtues in my business. What I was getting at is not the well-known fact that Los Locos in the city of M. operate and control part of the business, but that their chairman is an old friend of mine. I respect him, he respects me. It's just that we work for competing companies. Or do you think that Merkel and, let's say, Steinbrück or Steinmeier don't sit down for a glass of wine together every now and then too...'

'But a grand coalition between the Locos and the Angels just isn't possible. De facto.'

'And de jure. Bravo. You've spotted an unfitting comparison. But let's say the CEOs of two large companies. Ruling out a fusion, of course...'

'And a hostile takeover only when it comes to territories and markets, correct me later if I'm wrong. But while we're on the subject of fusions and takeovers and coalitions and...'

'Yes?'

'... then I'd like to come to the touchy subject of Berlin.'

'The good old capital city of the German Democratic Republic. A touchy subject, you say...'

'Just out of curiosity, how old were you when the Wall came down?'

'I was twenty-four. The best age, if you ask me. But I'm with the Beatles on the subject of age, now. It was the Beatles, wasn't it?'

'Stayin' Alive? Just kidding. When I'm Sixty-Four.'

'Right. I've still got eighteen years to go. But it all goes very quickly now, the years, the constant changes. The Angels try to be a constant. But where were we...?'

'Berlin. Among other things.'

'Yes.'

'I mean, there's been a lot about it in the press...'

'And that's precisely the problem.'

'But there are facts that can't be denied...'

'No one's arguing. No one's denying. I just told you there are plenty of relationships, friendships, acquaintances and respect when it comes to relations between the Locos and the Angels.'

'But a whole section of the Locos going over to the Angels, as I heard happened in Berlin, that's still a remarkable occurrence, and highly contentious within your organization.'

'Firstly: I stand for the Angels. Always for the Angels. That's our motto...'

'Honesty, reliability, respect, freedom.'

'Of course. That too. But what I mean to say: I'm part of the organization. A worldwide organization...'

'Isn't the mafia a worldwide organization too?'

'The mafia. Firstly: which one? The Italians? Which

552

ones? The Russians? The triads? What kind of crap are you talking?'

'Sorry. I didn't want to compare Angels GmbH & Co. with a mafia, but...'

'Then don't. You're insulting the Angels, you're insulting me. And you're sitting here in my office and thinking I'll let you get away with it.'

'Would you like us to continue our conversation another time?'

'You're a clever little bastard. Sorry. Now we're on a par. Who do you think you're dealing with, a stubborn child?'

'The ex-head of the Angels, Eden City branch?'

'A science fiction fan, I see. No, let's both take a deep breath. Lack of respect is something I find hard to deal with, I can't help reacting. I'll admit to that. Mafia – good grief.'

'I didn't mean to be disrespectful, I just wanted to add a little spice to our conversation.'

'I must admit I understand that and I do respect you asking certain questions, drawing certain lines, and thinking you'll get away with it. Because hardly anyone has the balls for that.'

'Thank you.'

'Save your gratitude. It wasn't a compliment. But on principle you can ask anything, of course. And when it comes to Berlin...'

'Since one of their most important and strongest sections crossed over, Los Locos are now de facto non-existent in Berlin.'

'I won't contradict you on that. But look at it like this, when we were talking about fusions earlier, although this fusion, you're right about that, leaves the name and the company out of it, it's just a question of a transfer, the takeover of qualified personnel. Wouldn't we – the Angels branch in Berlin – wouldn't we be stupid to turn down the offer, the opportunity? I'd even talk about a pacification of the market as a consequence. Things have really calmed down in the capital.'

'The market we're talking about here is the red-light sector.'

'Good thing you've brought us back to that point. "Red light" is a similar monstrosity for me to "milieu". What's it supposed to be? We read the headlines, we watch the films on TV, like that crime show the other Sunday...'

'The episode about the Angels and their business partners in the city of H...'

'Their alleged business partners. Exactly. And it portrayed the Angels as human traffickers, libelled them as a permanently violent, absolutely unscrupulous organization. Staring grimly at the horizon, zooming around town on their mopeds like the riders of the apocalypse, chucking girls in the rubbish.'

'At least when it comes to staring grimly, I do have to say...'

'What do you expect? Mummy's boys with middle-partings on Vespas and Schwalbes?'

'Mr & Mrs K... Seeing as you mentioned it, I've got a Schwalbe in my cellar. '78 model, tip-top condition, waxed and polished. It's a real cult scooter.'

'I'll give you that. My granddad gave me a Schwalbe when I turned fifteen. A year after my youth initiation ceremony. A blue one. I loved that thing. Tinkered away at it with my mates until it did almost sixty. Then later I was stupid enough to swap it for an S51.'

'And then when you were eighteen an ETZE, hundred and fifty or two hundred and fifty, right?'

554

'MZ. 125.'

'Now a Harley?'

'Right. Are you a bike freak?'

'Not really. All I've got now is the Schwalbe. Sometimes I take it for a spin down to the lake in summer.'

'You should have turned up here on your old Schwalbe. Would have made a real impression.'

'The Angels as a club for motorbike freaks?'

'Of course. That too. Excuse me for a few minutes, I have to pop downstairs. If you want anything to drink, beer, whisky, vodka or water, just help yourself.'

Alone between the mirrors. The pictures in the glass. Harleys parked in a row down on the street outside the Angels Club. A police car over at the crossroads. The Angels logo above the desk at the other end of the room. The winged heads staring silver out of the mirrors. Music and voices, small speakers above the glass. Alice in conversation with a guest, down at the bar. *Well, this is grand! I never expected I should be a queen so soon. If you only spoke when you were spoken to, and the other person always waited for you to begin, you see nobody would ever say anything, so that...*

The club fills up gradually. Alice drinks a mini-bottle of bubbly. The man has a beer. They both smoke. On a black leather sofa, an elderly gentleman sits between two ladies. He's wearing a cord jacket. In the entrance area stands a man in a white tracksuit, a white baseball cap printed with 'Angels' on his head, talking to the two dark-clad security men, greeting a man who enters the club in a leather coat with a handshake. The man on the sofa gets up and walks past the bar with one of the girls, heading for the rooms. Cigarette smoke passes through the mirrors into the room. Two foxes in the middle of the little road outside the club, slinking briefly around the Harleys and then disappearing between the buildings. They have made their winter quarters in an old carriage on a siding at the central station, disused for years.

'Good old Reynard the ever-hard fox.'

'So where were we?'

'Red-light sector, perhaps? Hence my first line of dialogue when I looked in the mirror. Just kidding.'

'Er, yes. We don't have any particular agenda we have to follow.'

'No. We can just chat away, about God knows...'

'Are you religious? Stupid question, maybe.'

'There are worse questions. No. Not in the strict sense. Back in the Zone I met a few Christians. Anyone who took a critical view of the state back then had my sympathies. It was an absolutely different world, though. The Christians' world, I mean. But some of them had balls. Had courage. *Swords to ploughshares*, I understood that, that made sense back then. Maybe even now. But it was never my thing. An ideal that human beings simply don't match up to. It's more the old philosophers who interested me. Even the greatest ass asks himself at some point why he is.'

'Plato GmbH & Co.'

'All the way to good old Heidegger. I'm glad I can talk to you about philosophy.'

'I wouldn't call myself an expert. But seeing as you mentioned the ass, it always interested me a bit too.'

'Never mind the ass, my friend, it was an exaggerated comparison.'

'No, I mean it without the slightest irony.'

'Irony is for know-it-alls and bullshitters. But I've got

nothing against a good joke. And I'm always coming up against the big and maybe even little questions. Plato GmbH is a good way to put it, especially when someone like you is interrogating me about the Angels and the red-light sector... I meant to say something about that, but we've got plenty of time...'

'If you've got the time. I don't want to keep you from your business. Or interrogate you.'

'The night is long. And I can rely on my people. But anyone who gets kept from business and distracted ends up out of the game sooner or later, out of the business. Discipline.'

'Has your sporting experience, let's call it that, has it helped you with that? You used to box and you worked in boxing coaching for a while.'

'That's a long time ago. It's a really long time ago. And it matches up with one of your clichés again. But that's the kind of thing you have to just ride above. Because I really did have my heart in it. It doesn't matter. No, it does matter, of course it matters. The boxer, the ex-box-er whose path led... and so on. But it was a great sport. A sport I still love to this day. And I met some wonderful people. Later on as well, as a coach, that was by the late eighties, early nineties. My back went on strike early on, I couldn't be active in the ring for as long as I wanted, I'd have liked to go on with it much longer. But we had a great amateur boxing scene here in the city. It's not like that any more, sadly, although there's still a few crazy types who won't let anything get them down, in the pro-fessional world as well.'

'Philosophy and boxing and the red-light sector. Is philosophy the unusual element in this triptych?'

'You're trying to test me, are you? You think I must be going blind and deaf and dumb behind the mirrors?'

'No, that's not how I meant it.'

'And speaking of the red-light sector, that's where we were.'

'You mentioned a possible pacification of the scene in Berlin earlier on, you implied the conflicts over the market might come to an end. How do you explain the assassination attempt on the new so-called Godfather of Berlin, who came from the Locos and now has a high-ranking position with the Angels, to put it mildly. Or the shots at the Germanenhof, the well-known rockers' bar.'

'I'm not the great oracle or old Uncle Albert Einstein who can explain everything and knows everything every member of the Angels is up to. Yeah, yeah, crisis in Berlin, crisis everywhere. And the European crisis is still going on, some say it's a war, they're broke and the others are bankrupt and others are entering the arena... and then there's someone going astray... we're all trying our best, aren't we?'

'Better to go astray than catch a ricochet.'

'What the hell's that supposed to mean? Are you referring to the poor bugger who got killed on the streets here a few years ago? We were already trying to curb the invasion at that point. It would be cynical to talk about collateral damage. And I can't recall us Angels causing similar damage to persons here in the city or even in H. or the capital. We expressed our honest sympathy in a newspaper ad at the time. Which was only printed by the press hacks because it was under a pseudonym. So what are you getting at?'

'All I mean is, the much-invoked peace between the two major competing firms doesn't seem to be working. In our neighbouring city, which has been a de facto part of our city for years now, the Locos still seem to be active after withdrawing from here, from the centre of the big stone. Next door is getting closer. The margins are getting closer. For a while the motorized syndicate the Outsiders was here, but they were dissolved, as I've heard, under a certain amount of pressure, because the business of a certain A...'

'A certain P., a certain pressure... I told you before that you know nothing.'

'Which brings us back to Plato.'

'At least you admit it.'

'What? The universal validity of the great philosophers?'

'No. Also that we all know less than we think. What do you think my role is here? We're here. The others are there. And we're the others too. And yet we're not. Riddle me that.'

'If Deutsche Bank, excuse the comparison, makes an investment somewhere in the world or makes a bad investment, it's still Deutsche Bank, isn't it?'

'My friend, you're using knockout arguments. The Angels aren't centrally organized by a works council or a global president. Hegel says, with reference to Aristotle and others, or quoting them: in metaphysics, and if you ask me that means necessarily in our so-called reality, we have a contradiction between substantiality and individuality. Essentially, we're chemistry. Chemistry that moves around in space. I as an individual am not responsible for the things that happen in the Angels Club worldwide.'

'I'm impressed...'

'Nothing can be determined. Existence, what's that supposed to be? Are we nothing outside of our time? Who the hell is knocking at our door?'

'Is it possible that I saw someone down at the door

earlier, your old, and as far as I've heard former business friend A.?'

'Aha, did the mirrors speak to you?'

'How can anyone be without them here?'

'You must have been seeing things. He's been here a couple of times, of course, and we've known each other for many years, of course. Done business, exchanged ideas, made agreements, old AK and me. But the mirrors were fooling you today. That was a different leather coat you saw.'

'What's your position on your old pact?'

'What pact? Have you been listening to whispers on the street again?'

'How can I put it... one man: the rooms, the clubs. One man: the apartments. Correct me if I'm completely wrong again.'

'It's been a long day. The night is long. And the explanations are endless...'

'I...'

'Come back in a week.'

Alice has disappeared. The bar is almost empty. The two foxes are crouched in the old railway car on the disused siding behind the central station. They're still looking out into the night through the open door of the freight car. They'd like a vixen. But the other foxes are elsewhere. They die when they cross the motorways and major roads. There's plenty of space in the parks. Rubbish and leftovers underneath the bridges. Three Harleys still parked outside the Angels Club. In the police vehicle at the crossroads, a minibus known colloquially as a six-pack, two uniformed men are asleep. A woman in the driving seat is reading a glossy magazine she's rested on the steering wheel. Prince Charles is dead. No. The obituary of a dead lady by the name of Sexy Cora. She's been dead for a while though. Got her tits fixed and fell asleep on the operating table. Bad anaesthetic. The uniformed woman extracts a packet of cigarettes out of her sleeping colleague's pocket. I've given them up. The man who had his club in the west of the city, southwest actually to be precise, has disappeared. The woman splays the magazine carefully across the wide double passenger seat next to her colleagues. She lights a cigarette from the cigarette lighter. Six-packs don't have a cigarette lighter. The last tram screeches into the terminus loop two streets away.

At the Angels Club, Alice comes out of the shower. *Queen Alice.* Fuck it, I'm done for the night. Here comes one last regular. Who always wanted her a lot. So she does sit down again. Drops of water on her brow. On the beer taps, a little wooden elk nods its head. Lips poised for a kiss. No one knows where it comes from. The late guest sits down with Magda on the now-cold leather of the sofa, after all. Ah, fuck it. Fine by me. I'm done for the night. We're asleep standing up and sitting down.

The next moment soldiers came running through the wood, at first in twos and threes, then ten or twenty together, and at last in such crowds that they seemed to fill the whole forest. Alice got behind a tree, for fear of being run over, and watched them go by.

'Are you on Facebook?'

'No. I think it's a dangerous medium. It destroys our social structures. It's beginning to control society. Maybe I'm a bit old-fashioned about it. Mind you, some people from our industry laughed about the internet itself when it was new, in the mid-nineties. And now every grungy little brothel's got its own site. The

561

advertising possibilities are huge, of course, everything used to go via the print media, *Bild*, red-light guides... whereby we shouldn't underestimate *Bild* & Co., we still have our small ads in there. But they link to our website as well. I won't see the end of print advertising in my lifetime, that's for sure.'

'So you do think there'll be something like an end to print culture. What do you think of sex-cams, is that a market you can imagine becoming active in?'

'Who says I'm not already active in it? We've been evolving our website, the club website, for years. There's a client forum, you can pay a virtual visit to the ladies, there are short films, but not with speaking or chatting to them, there's a guest forum where clients can exchange views, post criticism, at the moment we're fitting a few special rooms here in the building with sex-cams so that one or two girls can sit there and strip if online clients want that or do a live dildo show or a lesbian performance, you wouldn't believe how many people sit there with their credit cards and... for hours on end. Do this, do that, put that in there.'

'Let's get back to Facebook. They have a so-called hump button there now. Are these diverse opportunities to find sexual partners, "My Dirty Hobby" and so on, are they bad for the sexual services business?'

'I think they are. Webcams, pornos, YouPorn and all the masturbation machines tend to get men turned on. And then they used to come to our clubs in droves. But now there are so many ways to find a sexual partner on diverse sites. Although I'm convinced there'll always be enough clients for whom it's still too much work. And in the end no one can tell me these forms of sexual measures don't come with hidden costs. In the old days you'd hear, oh boy, I take a woman out to dinner, get her a few drinks, then the taxi... I might as well go straight to a brothel. That was just one of those stupid sayings, of course, but that's the thing with sayings, the truth is...'

'I'm sorry to interrupt but you're talking about the old days. You could mean only a period back to the early nineties or the market mechanisms prevalent in the old West Germany, which we're familiar with too, of course, at least to some extent. Or you are, I think. Brothels and brothel-like operations didn't exist in the GDR, de facto.'

'More like de jure. If we're on the subject again. There were a few possibilities, and I don't mean the famous trade-fair prostitution or the venerable "Stork Bar" up in Rostock. That was more for the customers with West German currency or dollars. There were a couple of pubs where people knew they could ask some geezer or other, and he'd give you an address... but it was very isolated. That was down to the political system, of course.'

'Was it not due to a certain openness, a certain relaxed attitude to making sexual contact? Nudist culture, marrying young to get a flat, a quick one with someone from work, and so on...'

'That was also down to the system. I think if there had been state-run brothel-like operations, as you call them, then... Jesus, we're talking like Doctor Ruth here...'

'There were a couple of points we only touched on last time, that I wanted to...'

'No need to be so formal. Go ahead, shoot. I've got another appointment at around one.'

'Trafficking.'

'What's that about? What's it got to do with me?'

'I know I'm picking up on things that your Average Joe, let's say, is constantly reading about in the press. But when it comes to the globally operating Angels GmbH...'

'Some guy goes to the import/export shop and says,

I'd like a couple of women from the Ukraine, or what? You're very welcome to go through the club, my friend, and talk to any of the women working here, you're welcome to ask them, and in the other places...'

'You said yourself I wouldn't get very far that way...'

'Amazon, temping agencies, cleaning companies from the Eastern Bloc, trousers and shoes from Singapore. Isn't that trafficking?'

'There have been various figures about the red-light sector...'

'The red-light sector. The famous red-light sector. Are we the only people working in the sector? You're better off going to the Russians, the Albanians, if you want to ask about trafficking. And figures? Oh, we do our figures, we keep our books up to date. We have to pay our taxes to the good old Nanny State. You've seen there's always a six-pack over at the crossroads. And you don't want to know how often we get checked here, how transparent our business is. Do you think I could afford to have any kind of illegal or semi-legal crap going on here? We stick clearly within the bounds of our laws, have done for years'

'The German laws?'

'Of course. What else?'

'The laws of the Angels?'

'What would they be, in your opinion?'

'Perhaps power first of all? Domination on the street, in the red-light sector – sorry, I said it again.'

'Very many of our members have perfectly normal jobs. Some, like me, work in the service industry. That's all. Some work for security companies. Power interests me in philosophical discourse, perhaps. What it is, and who has it, and how it takes effect. And when does it corrupt... And when does power lead to the exercise of a certain monopoly on the use of force? We're not talking about power here, we're talking about making money, plain and simple. And about certain values that no longer exist as such in bourgeois society. I've got a couple of clubs. I want to do my business, along with the Angels. And the Angels and I guarantee a certain invulnerability for our business.'

'You've got two children, you're married.'

'Yes. No further comment.'

'Is it true that your companies, including your clubs, are registered in your wife's name?'

'Once more for the record: I don't reveal details about my family or my private life – just imagine: I have one too – on principle.'

'I understand that you want to protect your private sphere. And I didn't mean in the slightest to claim you have anything to do with trafficking or the like. But the Angels network goes around the globe, as we all know. And terms like "trafficking" or "arms dealing" or "drug trading" keep coming up. And in the case of branches in Canada or the USA, the motherland of the Angels, the link has been proved.'

'You seem to be watching all those *documentaries* on NTV, or what channel is it again...?'

'Well, I mean they are documentaries...'

'The world keeps on turning...'

'Yes, it does.'

'No reason to start splitting hairs, my friend. What I'm getting at is that since the beginning of human history, I'm formulating this deliberately vaguely, there have been wars and violence, I'm saying that's an elementary part of our existence. That doesn't mean I condone it. But that's how it is. There doesn't have to be an Angels GmbH for there to be weapons. All over the world, people are dying pointlessly as we speak in some war or other...'

'But the accusations that branches or members of the Angels have been involved in trafficking people or women...'

'The branch in our city is clean. I can only speak on our behalf. And I'd give the shirt off my back, as we say, that the branches in all of Germany are clean. Trafficking? No. Our members hold certain values and we're also the most closely monitored people in Germany.'

'A few months ago there was a spectacular police operation in the city of H. against the chairman of the local branch, who is said to have been one of the most influential Angels in Germany.'

'Spectacular, is that what you call it when militarily organized special forces abseil out of helicopters onto private property, shoot dogs, trespass, kick down doors, threaten the man with rapid-fire weapons...?'

'There must have been certain suspicions against him.'

'Suspicions, aha. Other people are asked to help with enquiries. And what did they find? Nothing. Was he imprisoned? No. In the end he could be glad, and I mean this without a trace of irony, that all he had to bury was his dogs. It seems to me that members of the Angels GmbH lack fundamental rights in this country.'

'He's since resigned or given up his chairmanship of the branch. Was that a tactical move to take the GmbH and himself out of the firing line, to carry on business elsewhere? He has or he had, like you, several businesses in the red-light district of the city of H.'

'Do you play chess?'

'Not very well.'

'Then I might even beat you, because I don't play particularly well either. Started too late. I got myself a chess programme a while ago though. Learn, learn, and once again learn...'

'Lenin?'

'I never liked the Reds, as you can imagine. Dogmatic and narrow-minded. Halfway to being fascists. Chess and boxing have a few remarkable things in common.'

'So your own resignation isn't... how can I put this... it's not a move to carry on your business in peace, that P. character isn't just a straw man while you carry on behind the mirrors...?'

'You watch too many films, my friend. And I don't mean the documentaries on NTV. Do you know that motto of the Angels...?'

'Once an Angel, always an Angel?'

'Almost. Angel forever, forever Angel.'

'Is it easier for you to do a big deal with the former fortress as the ex-president?'

'What big deal? And what fortress? I don't do business in the Middle Ages.'

'So it's only a rumour that you want to open up a kind of first-class brothel in the vacant premises of the "Love Fortress" that the Bielefelder and the consortium opened up, I can't remember the name of the organization, it's almost twenty years ago. And that the Bielefelder is bizarrely one of your business partners for the project?'

'I certainly wouldn't do business with him. He let the place go to rack and ruin over the years. The fortress, the "Love Fortress", what an idiotic name...'

'I can't tempt a yes or no out of you?'

'You can't tempt anything out of me. We're just talking, having a bit of a chat.'

'Then let's chat a bit more about the current situation

here in the city...'

'I much preferred talking to you about the old philosophers. Boxing, chess, music, virtual worlds...'

'Football, maybe? You used to have good contacts with the scene in Berlin...'

'Berlin's a big place. Let's get away from all these old stories. Back then, in the Zone I mean, it was an act of rebellion against the state...'

'A., who covers the apartment prostitution sector here in the city, but we've talked about that already...'

'No. Not that I know of.'

'We touched on the old division of the market, briefly.'

'Touched it up, or what? What are you getting at?'

'Well... it's conspicuous that he, A K I mean, that there are certain similarities in your biographies.'

'I don't see it that way.'

'At least concerning football, the hooligan scene...'

'That word didn't even exist at the time. Your lot always see things in black and white, you never differentiate enough. And you think a man spends years studying law or economics and then takes over or opens up a brothel or a club or lets properties to service providers?'

'It seems to happen now and then. A. got a degree in business administration, as far as I'm informed.'

'Yes, later. But he didn't come out of university and then decide to pursue this line of business. Of course there are exceptions. Like that ex-lawyer in Austria. And there aren't any out-and-out rules for how to work successfully in this market sector. But it does call for certain leadership qualities, of course, things you don't learn at university, a certain assertiveness, business contacts... but you need at least a basic knowledge of how to run a business or a partner who has it, and don't imagine

568

that wasn't a simple or a long path...'

'A double negative? Do you know a man named Steffen?'

'What? No. Of course I do, more than one. I've worked hard for my position over the years. It was our little economic miracle, back then, while insanity reigned all around us. In the nineties. But I don't want to pat myself on the back here, it's up to others to judge. Ask a manager or a banker or an entrepreneur what accounts for their success. We didn't invent the red-light sector, to use that term again. We just try our best for it to become a perfectly normal trade, which it is, in our opinion...'

'We? You and AK? There are rumours that his position here in the city is no longer particularly stable. That the market has become too inflated, that there are people for whom his monopoly in the apartment prostitution sector has long been a thorn in the side... The old saying about the pie being big enough to go round doesn't seem to hold true any more?'

'I keep being surprised by how much credence you give to random gossip. Keep away from those vicious rumours, if you ask me. That kind of thing only ends up poisoning you. And on the subject of thorns, in the end maybe he's putting on the crown of thorns, even though that's a drastic comparison, seeking the blame in others because business in this day and age just isn't as good as a few years ago. The financial crisis hasn't passed us by and sometimes we have to make certain concessions. I don't want to say any more than that – we've always respected each other over the years.'

'Perhaps it's time to make active investments, for example in an exclusive night club, a kind of king-size brothel with style, like the Pascha in Cologne, but then

569

wouldn't you have to, let's say, wind things down a little elsewhere? Or close them outright?'

'Competition has always stimulated business. Even you ought to know that. The market will regulate it all on its own.'

'You just mentioned the much-cited financial crisis... and we've already talked about the possible effects of the exploding virtual opportunities, the sex-net.'

'Of course it's not good for us if everyone has to watch every penny. If the country's rocked by uncertainty. There mustn't be price reductions in our industry, even for simple moral reasons.'

'Moral reasons?'

'Of course. No need to act so surprised. For a while there was a risk that all the whole flat-rate crap would spread to the sexual services market. If I want to spend an hour with a lady, that hour has its price and it ought to have its price. There are too many stingy bastards, and I know what I'm talking about, I don't just sit behind the mirrors, I've been talking to the girls who work here all these years, Alice for example could tell you stories, the old Alice and the new one, although we're lucky to have a certain standard of regulars here at our club. What I was getting at is that all this cheap-as-chips crap leads to a decline in mutual respect.'

'The famous moral decline?'

'I wouldn't go that far. When I talk about morals I don't want to be all holier-than-thou about it. But the idea that you get more and more for less money is counterproductive, and I mean that literally. I told you that I respect AK and his business here in the city, and I'll stand by that, but I don't think much of the Nudist Club model.'

'The Nudist Club that he's been operating for a while

alongside the apartments?'

'The business model in itself. Pay a flat fee and then have as much sex as you want for as little as possible. I really would prefer the Pascha model.'

'But the market regulates itself, according to you. And seeing as there seems to be demand on the part of the consumers for the Nudist Club model...'

'The much-cited financial crisis caused mass migration from the Eastern Bloc in particular. The women come from Hungary, Czechoslovakia, Poland, the Russian federate states, or the former Soviet Union, and of course working in the Nudist Club, just as an example, still brings good earnings, for them. I don't want to get locked in on it because the model's been around for a long time now. And don't let's misunderstand each other, women from all nations work in my clubs, from the Eastern Bloc as well, and there's nothing wrong with that, quite the opposite, as long as the mix is right. There are guests who prefer German girls and others love a bit of exoticism or the deep Russian soul. What about you?'

'Oh, I don't have any special preferences.'

'Take a seat downstairs later and soak up the atmosphere.'

'What would you say if I came to you and said: Hey, I've got my eye on a little property on the edge of town, I'd like to open up a little night club. Four or five rooms, a bar, four or five girls...'

'If you can find them.'

'Hungary, Czech Republic, Poland, you said...'

'Have fun with the authorities, I'd say, and don't be surprised if you get a few visitors.'

'How do you mean?'

'Don't imagine it's all that simple – I'm not the only man in the industry in our little big city.'

'It was just a *what if*.'

'Who wants to be a millionaire? The market would spit you out without anyone having to lift a finger. You'd need contacts, security, you wouldn't find anything off the bat like that. It wouldn't be possible. I won't say any more than that.'

'It's nearly one o'clock.'

'You should be my agent. Have you got a lot more questions?'

In the mirrors, the flickering pictures of the night. Do you know where the term 'red light' actually comes from? It's Alice's day off. She's going to visit her mother. With her daughter. She'll be five soon. It's the summer party at the Angels Club in four days' time, they're putting up a mobile swimming pool out the back. The cops are getting ready to frisk all the guests. Angels from Holland have said they're coming. Angels from Berlin. The Outsiders, who don't have a branch in the centre of the big city any more, are coming on a friendly visit. In the neighbouring town that's growing more and more into the city, the situation is tense. Madame Gourdan is up on the roof, raising the big flag. I'm glad to hear you like classical music as well. We ought to meet up for a game of chess now and then. Alice wants to have a baby one day. It can wait until my early thirties, mid-thirties, though, that's normal these days. My mother was twenty-three when she had me. I'm doing fine with the cat. Cats can cope on their own. Sometimes I see foxes out in the backyard. *There can be only one.* The old cop is sitting downstairs at the bar, still dreaming of his mahogany boat, the long trip to the lagoon. The diamond in his breast pocket. What do I care about my colleagues, I'll go where I like. Eliot Ness is asleep in the conservatory.

His head resting on the tangle of papers. Who the fuck is the layer-cake equator? Five hundred yards from the six-pack, a crystal freak kicks an old man's tooth out. He's only got ten euros on him, though. Must have been on his way to the 24-hour garage. The Angels Club is busy. In the entrance area, they're talking about Hans's disappearance. Is it a full moon tonight? Alice is asleep up in a room. Her last guest calls a taxi. Everything goes strange in your sleep. The moon distorts into a big yellow egg. Alice is lying on the bed but her bare feet are touching the floor. Just a quick lie-down to rest her eyes. The Man behind the Mirrors is wearing a silver necklace with a small silver boxing glove pendant. You guys take care of the real scum instead. He keeps it at home in a drawer of his old antique bureau, a wonderful piece of Biedermeier-era furniture. The drawers are full. Memories of the old days. I wear a different chain at work. It's practically a twenty-four-hour shop. No, job. *Like it was part of me.* Where is Alice? She's dreaming. I'm riding on a sailboat bed, like Little John, through the night sky. *However, the egg only got larger and larger, and more and more human: when she had come within a few yards of it, she saw that it had eyes and a nose and mouth.* Someone orders champagne. AK drives his last tour and then sits on the veranda and looks out at the dark lake. His telephone is lit up in his coat pocket. I'll be with you again soon. I wish I could play Mahler in the club but they'd say I was crazy. When Cora comes into the room there's a little black-haired girl in a white dress perched on the edge of the bed. No one would believe a word of it – that smile.

'Doesn't it seem absurd to you that sex rules the world, the media, the internet, advertising, everywhere, but the ancient trade of prostitution is still frowned upon by society? Or is that not the case, am I getting the wrong impression?'

'No, you're getting the right impression, that's the way it is. A few weeks or months ago, I think we talked about it last time, there was that Sunday-night crime show, *Tatort*.'

'Do you watch every episode?'

'If I can, yes.'

'I'm sorry to interrupt your train of thought, or ours, we'll come right back to it, but have you got a favourite detective, a team or an investigator you particularly like watching?'

'Oh, I don't have any special preference. My wife likes the Munich episodes best.'

'Batic and Leitmeier?'

'Yeah, that's them. I used to like Axel Prahl with that Boerne guy, the pathologist, but that's got a bit tired now. And in the old days, yeah, you could say I was a real Schimanski fan.'

'You liked the whole Duisburg Schimanski thing?'

'Yeah, he was a great character. Him and his workmate, the uptight one, they were really good together. I've got a hard disk recorder, you know, it records *Tatort* for me when I can't watch it because of work, and that's often enough. You should get one. Or have you got one already?'

'No. But it does make sense.'

'The team here in this city, though, they're really crap.'

'The two detectives, the short dark one and the other guy.'

'Yeah, he's got like a ridiculous mini-moustache.'

'The last episode was alright, mind you.'

'The one with the kids fighting on the tram?'

'Yeah.'

'Yeah, that one was OK.'

'But you were just talking about a particular episode of *Tatort* that got you rather angry... Was that the one set in H., the one about the motorbike gang?'

'That's the one. Something along those lines. I have to say, you couldn't top that episode for stupidity and ignorance.'

'They were trying to act authentic but in principle it was nothing but cheap clichés. Is that what you're getting at?'

'Of course. I'm not sure if we didn't talk about it in one of our last conversations, though.'

'I'm not sure either. There was the evil boss of the gang modelled on the Angels. The ones who traded with throwaway girls and then really did dispose of them in the rubbish.'

'It's a film, of course. So of course it has to have some kind of narrative arc. Like the ridiculous ties to politics. But there was this one scene where the woman detective, that blonde one, asked her boyfriend if he'd ever been to a whore.'

'I can't remember that scene specifically.'

'Anyway, he ums and ahs and she's totally shocked. That's the kind of soft-focus hypocrisy that makes me sick. And of course the image of the Angels, the way that test-tube club modelled on the GmbH was presented. And the dark red-light sector that only exists under compulsion. And right afterwards on that Günther Jauch's chat show, right after that episode, they only go and claim that ninety per cent of prostitutes are in forced prostitution. Like the Prostitution Act was never invented, never mind that it needs improving. And the knowledge of this ancient business, the history, the myths, that's also the story of our history, our centuries.'

'What do you mean by that?'

'For instance, we've got our German pope now, right? Not that I care, but the fact that there was a Pope Pius the Fourth who had a giant brothel built in the fourteenth century to channel the takings, part of the takings, into the church, that's... that never comes up when they're talking about the unspeakable milieu.'

'Unspeakable?'

'Just the word, just the word. Because I can't stand all the hypocritical crap any more.'

'So you've studied the history of the red-light sector?'

'Or at least I know where it all comes from, where it all started. And that it's always been part of society. Whether people acknowledge it or not.'

'What would you say to Meryl Streep or the German feminist Alice Schwarzer, for example, a determined enemy of...'

'Enemy, opponent.'

'Yes.'

'Nothing. Nothing at all. There's no point in even starting a discussion.'

'How do you get to be an Angel, actually?'

'I've always been fascinated by the legend. I always thought, couldn't that be a special path? Even in the mid-nineties. A path of your own, because society wasn't laying out paths any more, a union that stands for something.'

'I could ask what for...'

'We've been there already.'

'Was it the fascination of an all-male club as well, a kind of secret society?'

'Rubbish. I was in contact with members of the Angels even in the nineties. I read the old founder B.'s biography. *Born to Be Wild*. Met a good few Angels who are still friends now.'

'Including the big man from H.?'

'Yes, of course. Otherwise I wouldn't be so upset about that stupid *Tatort* episode. He's someone I found very impressive. A consistent man. He always stuck to his path, never lost his way. And he stuck to the path of the Angels. Reconciling those two things, perhaps that's one of our big... ideals.'

'There was a branch of a smaller motorbike club here in the city for many years, regarded as an offshoot or a supporter of the Angels. It can't be a coincidence that the Angels only came and you took over as chairman at a point when the market was under threat of a hostile takeover by the Locos...'

'Listen, my friend, spare me the theories. Just because I'm tired doesn't mean you should overstep the mark.'

'And now you've stepped down as chairman of the branch. For whatever reason...'

'Do you know where the term 'red light' actually comes from?'

'No.'

'In the Middle Ages the women had to wear red hoods as a sign of the trade.'

'So Red Riding Hood was a whore?'

'You'd better go now. I've got a lot to do.'

Night. Morning. The club is empty. The city is empty. The moon is a yellow egg. Cats creep across the yard. A little girl stands by the window. A man sits behind the mirrors.

DEAD PIGEON ON FLUGHAFENSTRASSE

Hans blinks at the sun, quite high in the sky directly above the low building in front of him. No clouds, no wind; he wipes his sweaty neck. The smell of decay again and he glances at the overflowing bins next to him against the wall.

It seems to him that it's much hotter and more humid in this small backyard than outside on the street. He can hear the traffic, just after four, Friday, three days ago was the longest day of the year, rush hour, commuter hour, home time, footsteps in the driveway behind him, he turns around but no one's there. He looks at the windows of the low building, the sloping tarred roof shining liquid in the sun. Apart from the traffic noise, louder or quieter, there's nothing to hear in the courtyard, as if all the buildings were vacant. Hans looks up at the façades of the houses. Some of the windows are open and the curtains are moving slightly, although he can't feel a wind.

Hans reaches into the inside pocket of his jacket but puts his cigarette case back again. Far too hot to smoke and he's still a bit dizzy from the bubbly he had earlier. He could have done without all that. Am I too old for this shit? he thinks and shifts his jacket collars aside. Once again, it seems to him something is moving in one of the windows of the low building and he touches his belt, where he wears his phone in a small leather pouch. A few months ago he dug out his old handbag, he'd heard these man-bag things were back in fashion. Phones, sun cream, cigarettes, sunglasses, pepper spray, everything a gentleman needs, but now he laughs when he pictures himself strolling along Flughafenstraße with his hand in the loop of the little brown leather bag. His father gave it to him for his seventeenth birthday and he hadn't found out that some people took the mickey out of these wrist-bags and called them 'Stasi bags' until a few years later, in Berlin. A few people from the *firm* really did carry those bags, back in the day when they tried to recruit him, two years before the Wall fell. *Onwards, and no forgetting... Neither stubborn ox nor ass shall stop socialism in its path.* To the very end. Steadfast to the very end. Me too, he thought and he blinked in the sunlight and took a few steps towards the low building. He knew a couple of people who'd gone straight from the firm to the business. Or ex-cops, from the Zone. They had good contacts and they were experts on security. From the Stasi to the brothels. He gave another low laugh, and as if his laughter had echoed in the muggy backyard and rent the sluggish silence, the door of the building opened and a man stepped out onto the small wooden platform, like a veranda, from which a few steps led down into the yard.

Hans put his hand to his forehead, above his eyes, saw white towers, concrete slab prefabs behind the low building, blurred in the flickering light above the asphalt of the many streets, saw the city and the neighbourhood and the buildings moving in the light, grey walls, red bricks, high silos, thousands of windows casting their glassy rays fan-like through the shortening day, vapour trails from planes above them in the pale blue, and Hans looked into the face of the lawyer Emil Fischer, with whom he ate layer-cake in the small town of G. in Thuringia more than two years ago, or was it a local speciality by the name of king's *smetana*, with a subtle note of malt? The lawyer stood on the bottom step and held out his hand to shake. In the other hand he held a briefcase with his jacket draped over it. 'Glad to see you, Hans, the others are coming in a moment. No offence, but I've got to dash off. In a rush. Business, business.'

He was wearing loose brown pleat-fronted trousers and a short-sleeved white shirt. A dark red tie adhered to the sweat-soaked fabric. 'And *our* business?' Hans let go of the limp, damp hand that was already wresting itself away because the lawyer Emil Fischer had already half-turned to go. 'Our business,' he said and put his hand briefly on Hans's shoulder, and Hans could feel it was suddenly no longer limp but pressing firmly, 'everything's sorted, everything's sorted out, my friend, the goods are on the way to the land of the rising sun, the rest of the commission's waiting, it's all tied up as neat as a pin.'

'I thought you'd be here to complete the... hmm... *formalities*. It's a big sum of money. That's what we...'

'Discussed. I know, I know. But now I do have to... pop off... somewhere else.' He reached rather fussily into his pocket and pulled out a pocket watch; Hans was surprised by the sudden silvery sparks in the lawyer's hand. 'But I think,' the lid of the silver watch sprang open and Emil Fischer looked at the face, and for a moment Hans thought he heard a faint melody, 'I think we'll see each other later. Maybe we could go out to eat. There's a very good restaurant not far from here.'

'On Flughafenstraße,' said Hans.

The lawyer laughed. 'No, not on Flughafenstraße. It'll be a big surprise...'

'Baby, what a big surprise,' said Hans.

'Chicago,' said the lawyer. 'I could spend hours going over old relics with you. Glad to hear you knew what good music was in the Zone.'

'What do you think we... where we...? On the dark side of the moon?'

'Hans, the others will be here any minute, rush hour, business, you know the deal, so I'll see you later...' He gave a brief wave and disappeared into the dark corridor to the street; Hans heard his footsteps fading. He sat down on the steps leading up to the wooden platform and the door. 'It's a good meeting place,' the lawyer had said on the phone, 'a discreet little oasis, my clients have a kind of little office there, import/export.'

Hans had left for Berlin early in the morning. The city was quiet at the moment. The backdrops didn't seem to be moving. A woman stood by one of the windows on the fourth floor and looked down at him. She closed the window and he saw her drawing the curtains. On the drive over he'd thought about whether to put some of the money into the properties the lawyer had recommended so highly. But he'd still have that option later on. He'd always kept out of the bricks and mortar business. His friend AK had invested in the sector years ago (what does that sound like, like a past century, but shit, it's true!). But everything had changed in such a short time, the last two or three years since the invasion, although you couldn't see it directly and people were still talking about the great peace. 'Take a step or two back, Arnold, you don't have to prove anything... Let them fuck each other over. The Angels, the strangers, who's got the biggest danger...'

'No, don't say I... we're too old for this shit.'

'No, no, that's not what I meant. But over all the years... all those years you were... you sorted things. Everyone knows that. We were, and we are.'

'Absolutely right, Hans. We were, and we are. I heard that you...'

'What did you hear?'

'That you're getting wanderlust, you want to go away,

my friend.'

'A bit of a holiday's never done anyone any harm, Arnold.'

'As long as you come back stronger. I'm counting on you. I need you here.'

'The last of the independents. Plural.'

The backdrops don't seem to be moving, he thought as he changed lanes and approached the capital, but... *The silver strings are turning into trip wires.* Shut up! But he'd have put it pretty much the same way. The Angels were working with the Turks and Arabs now. Absolute syndicalization is the goal. That's how he'd put it. Turn the radio on and listen to music. Why not, *mon général*, whoever you... whoever's chatting away in my head. But his radio sticks between two stations and tootles out mixed songs and voices, news, the super-hits of the eighties, *Ba-da-da-dum buy on ninety-nine point nine.*

It's only ten when he hits the ring road. He breakfasted at a service station. At McDonald's. But that was pretty crap and he went over to the petrol station and got a cold schnitzel in a bread roll. The long queue of trucks. He remembered it used to be a trend, *house&hotel&truck*, squashed up tight in the ads, space is money, but he'd never offered anything like that for his freelancers, his employees. The security of the club and outcalls only by arrangement with the girls. Because then they'd have to negotiate certain conditions, a room price even out there where the moon shines. No loneliness in the little cabs. Although it was certainly a way to make earnings, a business opportunity, for them. If they'd wanted to... Elsewhere, AK, the apartments operated by S., who managed to serve a small market segment for a while by arrangement with AK... Hans had always kept to agreements, to the contracts once sacred, long ago (*We raised*

582

our cups and forged our pact. Shut up!). But if anyone gets too close to me I'll break his neck. That's enough of this crap. At last he gets a radio station, Berlin, Berlin, we're going to Berlin. The smoky little oasis of his nightclub. He sees the TV Tower, its tip poking at the clouds.

Hans looks again at the blue, absolutely cloudless sky, which dazzles him, a pale blue mirror, so that he puts his hand above his eyes although the sun is behind him, sinking slowly, very slowly.

He hears noises in the driveway, 'Looks like an heirloom, your big fat silver dollar,' he can't remember the lawyer having that pocket watch in the little town of G., 'Memories, Hans, pure sentimentality, an old present,' footsteps fade, curtains move, someone opens the entrance gate to the driveway, low voices, he doesn't get up. Do the bin men come on Fridays in Berlin? He left his BMW a couple of streets away. He doesn't know his way around Neukölln, the last time he came this way was nigh on twenty years ago. In the morning he drove through Prenzlauer Berg and Mitte. Made his way gradually towards the Wall, towards the stadium, wanted to pop in and see Biene on Prenzlauer Allee but then he didn't bother. The bar was still there, he hadn't been sure, but then he switched on his hazard lights and looked at the door and the big window front. He couldn't tell whether they were open yet but then he saw an old man and an old woman, hand in hand, stopping outside the bar; the old man said something and she gave him a slap on the cheek, they laughed and then they went in.

'Give us another beer, Biene.'

'Sure, Hans.' And she put her hand on his hand, and he moved their two hands around the counter and hummed a tune, because the tune was playing on the radio, and Biene joined in: 'If I had a hammer, I'd hammer in the morning, I'd hammer in the evening...'

'Hans has a hammer, he hammers in the morning, he hammers in the evening, he hammers all night long...' They laughed. They drank. A night at Biene's place. Some night in '89, in '88.

He stops outside a few other buildings too, remembers standing on scaffolding, standing on roofs, painting walls, *up and down with never a frown*, paint in his hair, remembers digging in dark, damp cellars, lugging bricks, mixing cement, Hans the helpmate, Hans the builder's mate, Hans the bricklayer's mate, and sometimes he worked in the discos at the weekend or at dances out in the villages. When he didn't go to the stadium, when he wasn't at an away match somewhere in the provinces. He never went along when they played in the steel town. He wasn't as crazy as the others either, the ones who went every weekend, yelled the craziness out at every match, but he was glad he'd met people he could count on, back then when he'd come to the big capital city of the GDR. After the Wall, things really took off on the building sites. The cranes grew up to the sky, *that's how he'd put it*. Shut up. He drives through the suburbs, the high-rise estates, Schöneweide's not such a pretty meadow as the name suggests, he stopped at some building site, got out of the car and took a few steps towards the scaffolding, breathed in the smell of dust, earth and damp, breathed deeply. Sometimes he wishes he could stand on roofs again, walk along scaffolds, gut flats, make the mixture, breathe in that smell.

They were good times. 'Hey, no trespassing.' Shut up, I'll trespass you in a minute.

'Hansi?' No one's called him that for nigh on twenty years. He stops by the car, keys in hand, and turns around. A man in dusty blue dungarees walks towards him. He takes off his helmet, his hair also dusty and grey beneath the dust.

'Who wants to know?' No, he didn't say anything and he waited in silence until the builder was standing right in front of him, the helmet pressed to his chest.

'You are Hansi, aren't you, I recognize you, don't tell me you're not Hansi.'

The builder smiles, nearly laughing, laughs and smiles with his whole dirt-encrusted face, eyes, nose, mouth, forehead. 'Achim?'

'Yes, Hans, Achim.'

Hans drives slowly down Brunnenstraße. No traffic behind him. His shoulders are still a bit dusty. They hugged for a long time. He'd aged, had Achim. He'd taught him a lot back then. On the sites. His bricks-and-mortar business. Used to take him out for a bit of cash-in-hand work on the weekends, to the countryside and the suburbs. Make a bit on the side. Tiles, walls, floors, roof repairs. Cash and payment in kind. Once, they'd got twenty crates of Radeberger from a pub landlord in some little dump near Neubrandenburg. Then they flogged them off in the capital. Or that was the plan, at least. Wasn't much left to flog in the end. He gave three crates to Biene.

Achim knew how to get hold of material, he knew nearly every foreman in Berlin, siphon off a bit here, shift something a bit there, ten crates of beer, a thousand cash, swap plasterboard for tiles, forward deliveries, snowball system, Sly Achim, that's what they used to call him. They'd lost touch around '90. Hans was only working in the discos and bars by then, new doors to work everywhere, and he already had a certain reputation. Hans the Man. Hans the Hatchet. 'What did you just call me, you arsehole?'

585

'Achim. You're still on the roofs, still swinging your hammer. Once bricks and mortar, always bricks and mortar, eh?'

'Ach...' He breathes out audibly; they're sitting on the kerb by Hans's BMW and smoking. 'Mustn't grumble...'

'You are grumbling, Achim...'

And Hans drives towards the Wall, through the Wall, drives around the patch of ground they now call the Wall Park, drives too far and doesn't know for a moment if he's already on the other side of the Wall. A railway embankment stops him from going any further and he drives along parallel to the tracks for a while, turns underneath a bridge and heads back eastwards, then he sees the floodlight masts of the stadium above and behind the buildings. He's wound the windows down and he's sweating – perhaps he should have brought his Mercedes estate, it's got air conditioning, as it bloody well should nowadays, but it's full of crates and bottles and other crap and he was too lazy to unload it all the evening before, the morning before. He was in his office until three, a bottle of lemonade in front of him, he has to be clear and fresh in the capital, sugar-free because he's having problems with his right molar, been dabbing it with clove oil for weeks and the girls say he smells like a dentist. He treats himself to a glass of Talisker, he's had it on the menu for a few months now, twelve euros for four cl, that's a moderate price when he compares with what it costs elsewhere and what the bubbly and champers cost at his bar. In the old days he'd have popped a few pills or done a line in the morning or whenever, before he left, but since he'd been seeing the shining stones before his eyes and deep in his dreams, where they float in the murky water alongside the bodies and shoot rays through the endless tides... yes, for fuck's sake, they're mires, subterranean, slow-moving, black, no light and no oxygen and no nothing... A mire, and empty, he thinks and sits sweating, his head leaned back, in his BMW, which he parked before the roundabout, and he looks up at the rusted, almost black railway bridge under which the roundabout leads. Little woods on either side of the street. He winds the window up even though he's sweating so much. The dull detonations of a motorbike. Sounds like a Harley. Two Harleys, three Harleys. Get the hell out of here, Angels. The Turk's the godfather now, new alliances, old pacts cancelled, new ones forged, thrown away, freshened up, parcels dispatched. Above and below, the channels change direction... dark limousines drive from Mitte along Kurfürstenstraße, Kurfürstendamm, Charlottenburg, winged motorbikes, get the hell out of here, Angels, a toast to the new prince... the king is dead, long live... king-size beds, folding deckchairs... Hans stood outside KaDeWe, didn't go inside the department store, a whole lot of bricks and mortar, a whole lot of stones inside and all. He leans back and sees that the railway line leading to the bridge no longer exists. No railway embankments any more, just this black iron bridge, forgotten, in the middle of the trees above the road, above the roundabout. He moves, lowers his head, seeking the sun, the metal of his car glowing hot but they're in the shade, and the tips of the trees close in above him and his BMW like a big dark roof.

Hans watches the car bonnet moving slowly, slowly out of the covered driveway into the backyard. He's still sitting on the steps of the wooden staircase. The silver-metallic Mercedes stops in the shade, the sun's migrating strangely, then it's back in the light, clouds or zeppelins in the sky. Hans puts his hand above his eyes, takes it away again, shades his eyes again, decides to stand up but then stays where he is. Time for a smoke he thinks, and reaches for the case in his inside pocket. He inserts the cigarette between his lips and looks for his lighter. The rear windows of the car are tinted and all he can see is the driver and the man in the passenger's seat, blurred as if the car was resting on liquid asphalt. Hans stands up, the cigarette in the corner of his mouth, still looking for the lighter in his jacket pockets with his left hand.

'Herr Pieszek?' The window on the passenger side glides down.

'Yes,' says Hans. *Who wants to know?*

'Good to see you,' says the man and leans out of the window. Turkish, thinks Hans. Or something along those lines. The man is wearing a grey suit jacket over a black T-shirt, his dark hair combed back into a parting.

'Good to see you,' says Hans and takes two or three steps towards the car, the back of it still in the shade of the driveway.

'Sorry we're late,' says the man in the grey suit jacket, his arm dangling out of the window and his hand touching the silver metal of the car door, 'but the city kept us waiting a bit.'

'That's alright,' says Hans, 'I've only been waiting here for two hours.'

'You're kidding,' says the man and smiles, or at least it seems that way to Hans. 'I hope you'll accept my apology. May I give you a light?'

'You may,' says Hans and walks past the silver star to the passenger door.

'It's about zero hour in Tokyo right now,' says the man in the grey suit jacket, and he moves his arm slowly between his lapels and holds out a lighter to Hans. It's a green disposable lighter and it takes Hans a few seconds

588

to see in the bright light of the sun that the little flame is burning. He leans down to touch his cigarette to the flame. 'Not exactly good weather for smokers, is it?' says the man.

'No, not really.' Hans puts one hand on the warm roof of the car, looks over the shoulder of the man in the grey suit jacket, whose head is still stuck out of the window, looks at the back seat where two men are sitting, leaning back, relaxed, it looks like. *Two in the back, two in the front, and the deal's as good as done.* Well tied up, then. A done deal. Shut up.

'On the subject of our deal, Hans...'

'I'm listening.' Hans leans forward again, blowing the smoke past the man into the car interior.

'In principle, everything's sorted,' says the man and turns briefly to the one on the driver's seat, a short fat Turk, *or something along those lines*, staring apparently indifferently through the front window with barely a movement, looking at the low building and into the sun. Hans throws his cigarette away, he's only taken a few drags, moves his arm so that he can see his Glashütte and says: 'It's now precisely thirty minutes past midnight in Tokyo.'

'Great, then we can go straight to the office.'

Hans fancied a shag. Shit, he thought, what's up with me now? He patted the dust off his shoulders and walked around Neukölln. The doors to the amusement arcades were closed and he saw his reflection in the tinted windows; gamblers don't want any light to disturb them, he thought.

Neukölln Town Hall, and on the opposite side of the road a glass shopping mall. He walked into the entrance area for a moment, stood still among all the people walking past him, coming and going, saw an ad for a jeweller's on the top floor. Next to it an ad for a bookshop on the basement level. It wasn't far to Pannierstraße. When he'd noticed he fancied a shag he'd gone into a newsagent's and bought himself the *Bild*. And another Berlin paper but he didn't need that one, he'd already found something in the small ads that was just round the corner. He'd actually been intending to go over to Moon-Eye's place for a drink but then he remembered the bar wasn't there any more.

Someone had told him so not long ago. Wasn't it AK, even? But AK couldn't have known he'd be coming to the capital, no one knew he had business here. And the backdrops were moving here and the silver strings were shifting. And the Angels had taken over nearly every-thing here. Now the man behind the big capital's mirror was a Turk. That was what they'd heard, far away in the little big city, and yet close enough. But what did all that crap have to do with him? Hans fancied a shag. Damn, he thought, what's up with me now?

He walked passed countless amusement arcades and gambling dens, the sun at his back, the sun in his face, just after twelve thirty by his watch. The Glashütte was always a couple of minutes fast. And he always adjusted it back slightly, every two or three days. He'd put it in for an overhaul twice now. 'That's normal,' said the old master watchmaker, who'd learned his trade hundreds of years ago in Glashütte, 'that's the old Spezimatic mechanism...'

'But it was Erich Honecker's personal...'

'Are you sure about that?' said the old master watch-maker, the magnifier over his left eye, leaning over the opened casing.

'Absolutely certain,' said Hans, 'take a look at the little stones on either side of... of the brackets for the wristband, and you can see the initials as well.'

'Oh yes, it's a nice piece.'

'Like I said.'

Hans held the watch to his right ear. He moved his arm to and fro and heard the faint rustle of the Spezimatic mechanism, which registered every motion, captured it and converted it to energy. *That's how he'd put it.* And with the constant quiet ticking of the Glashütte in his ear he looked out across Pannierstraße.

Trees grew at regular intervals on either side of the road. He couldn't spot any gaming parlours like on Flughafenstraße. He used to do a bit of gambling and gaming now and then. Nothing special, just to calm his nerves. Fruit machines, roulette, poker. Nothing special, and he'd lost interest after a few years. It only ate up time. Hadn't AK started out with two amusement arcades, back in the day, in the first few years after the Wall? The sunlight frayed in the tops of the trees, the street looked quiet and calm and he checked the ad he'd torn out of the newspaper again, compared it to the house numbers. Well, let's get going he thought, and off he set.

At Sweet Life he chose a Russian blonde. The place was on the ground floor, the door right off the pavement. He had rung the bell, the door had buzzed, and the madam, a woman in her mid-fifties who'd greeted him with a 'Hello, young man' (*What's that all about?*), led him into a small room of the converted basement flat where he took a seat on a sofa, a coffee table in front of it with a bunch of flowers on it (*Yeah, yeah, Hans the Hatchet, Hans the Man...*). Then the girls did their parade while the madam introduced them, five girls. The Russian blonde came third, 'This is our Tanja, a pearl of a girl.' Tanja, in knickers and bra, beach weather, stopped in front of him with a smile, turned around once, turned around twice, put her hands on her hips, sought eye contact, and he nodded at her and she went away again.

Later, he tried to remember the other four girls. And how the madam had introduced them. A feminine, slightly chubby Turkish one. *Aisha*? Didn't most Turkish girls in the industry call themselves Aisha? A thin German blonde, a Croatian brunette with pouty lips... He'd known straight off it would be Tanja, or whatever her name was. When did I last come to a club privately, he wondered while he took a shower. He'd picked the mirrored room. Tanja had shown him around the rooms. Yes, the mirrored room wasn't bad, a bit like the mirrored room at his place. A mirrored room's a mirrored room, as long as it's not too small or too grotty. The mirrors need constant cleaning and care. They mustn't get streaks and the stuff mustn't be too acidic either, and the ceiling mirrors are real hard work – he often stood by when his cleaning crew was dealing with his mirrored room. What was the guy's name who put it in for him again? He'd done all or nearly all the mirrored rooms in the city, in the neighbouring town and the whole region. The guy had a mirror monopoly. Not that there were that many mirrored rooms. Buggered off after a while. Moved on with his company, changed trades or went into retirement. But actually he didn't know anyone who'd gone into retirement. You need to have put a whole lot aside for that, and you need a good reason and all. The cash flows and flows, usually in both directions, in and out, the old game, and we were, and we are, and as long as you've got your place in the big game it goes on... and on and on. What else was there to do – lounge on a beach? A slice of cake every afternoon? He leaned against the tiles and let the water run over his body. *We're thinking around a lot of corners today.*

Did he have a good reason? The little castle? Or the little outbuilding of the big water castle. Wasn't that too close to everything? And what would he do there, sitting round on his own? It wasn't like he didn't have any other options. In all the years since his divorce came through he'd always had women, relationships, semi-relationships, sometimes even options. He'd been in his mirrored room a couple of times with Mandy, Mandy 1 that is. That was one of the options. But then she left. That kind of mousey brunette wasn't bad either. Around forty. Bit uncertain of herself. Those words he doesn't speak. But Tanja had mojo, her very pretty round face had strength. Yes, that was how he'd put it.

He turned off the shower, dried his hair, wasn't that much left to dry, he put on the flip-flops Tanja had given him, dried himself properly and then picked up the bathrobe. Then he realized he needed a shit and sat down on the toilet, flushed beforehand to cover up the sound – it was quiet in the property, perhaps he was the only customer (*guest! Comprende?*) so early in the day. He wiped his arse and then took another shower. A quick one. His place didn't open until nine in the evening. It was a nightclub though. With a bar. Sweet Life opened at noon, he'd read in the ad. Capital city, Neukölln, lots of people, lots of places, lots of men, hot meals twenty-three hours a day, sweet life, and first come first... *Affordable solutions for better f...ing*, he'd read above another ad. That place didn't open till the evening though. 'Would you like something to drink?' asked Tanja when he came into the mirrored room.

Where are you? Dust in the sunshine.
    'Sometimes, Hans, I think: this can't be all there is.'

'Who doesn't think that sometimes? The usual.'

'And then I think it can't just be gone.'

'What? What's gone?'

'You know, the time. Our time.'

'Was it so good for you back then?'

'Better than now, Hans. Don't you sometimes think the same?'

'About back then?'

'No. In general. I'm going to retire one day. My back's still OK. Funny. And Berlin's still OK. Funny. Maxi left home ages ago... You do remember Maxi?'

'She was only so high back then.'

'I don't know how to say it, how to... Sometimes you go a bit doolally, don't you feel that way as well?'

'No. Well, yeah. But life always goes on.'

'What a load of bollocks we're talking here.'

'I don't know, Achim.'

'... sometimes I think you can go back. You know, like with an old pulley. No one believes a word of it these days. How we used to lift sacks and stuff with a pulley... Like a line, kind of. That was sometimes here and sometimes there. On the scaffolding. First, second, third. And sometimes I think I'm still holding the rope in my hand. Ach, forget it.'

'The rope, Achim.'

'Like a line, Hansi. Where it was, that was where it was. It can't be gone. Actually. Do you get what I'm trying to say?'

'I think so.'

Where are you? How long have you been looking at yourself, stretched out naked? Looking at yourself and yet still asleep.

'What time is it, Tanja?'

'Hang on, I'll get you your watch.'

She rolls onto her side and reaches for the chair where his things are. Hans cocks his head and looks to the side into another mirror. Sees her putting the watch on his chest. Feels the watch cool on his skin.

'Two o'clock,' she says, 'we've still got time.'

'Good,' he says and he wants to speak Russian with her but he can't find the threads and strings in his head.

She's sitting astride him and he sees her arse in the mirrors. Puts his hands on her back.

Sees himself alone on the big bed. A sheet over his legs.

Where are you?

She reaches for his balls and he pulls himself together. Looks here, looks there and closes his eyes. Flughafenstraße is all lit up, the sun high in the sky. On Pannierstraße, the trees fracture the light.

'Plenty of time,' says the Croatian brunette, says the Turkish one with the huge breasts, says the thin German blonde, and they tap their fingers on his watch, which is back on his left arm. *As if it were part of me. Shut up.*

They drink Söhnlein and the Russian one tells her stories. Daughter, sister, making money, little village. An hour and a half tick away on the Glashütte.

What was the name of the place, you think later, the place she told you about? Where she lives. You paid for another hour because your appointment's just round the corner. Maybe you'll take a taxi anyway though. Somewhere out near Schwerin. Hans listens because she's talking about her daughter. And saying she only works here three days a week. Tuesdays, Wednesdays and Fridays. Why not Thursdays? Hans thinks. 'And it's going alright?' he asks.

'Yes,' she says and smiles, 'it's going fine.' He digs up his rusty Russian; it's not easy.

'Meenya zavut Gans,' he says when she's sitting astride him and he's looking at her arse in all the mirrors.

She laughs and almost chokes and leans back and then she does roll off him.

He sees his dick in the condom, hanging like a hat from the bell end, what a stupid word, ring my bell, because there's no H in Russian and they use a G instead or some other funny letter that sounds like a hoarse cough, as far as he remembers anyway, that's what they learned at school, 'Meenya zavut Gans,' and the Söhnlein bottle's almost empty and she only drank one glass, and he remembers all the Russian words, *morozhenoe s fruktami*, 'Yes, you're a real fruity ice cream, my Gans,' 'No, you're a fruity ice cream, ochen krasivoe fruity ice cream,' and he doesn't know how many times they shagged in the three hours, hold on, how can that be, he must have got something muddled up with the time, the long rope of the pulley, three hundred euros, or was it four hundred because of the mirrored room? And as he walks in the end, along Flughafenstraße, she was a right chatterbox, that one, wouldn't shut up, and she told him her child, her daughter, stays with her sister when she's working because her sister works in a takeaway but it's not so full that she hasn't got time all the time... and so on, you know all these stories but you still listen to them because this blonde, very nice Russian Tanja tells you them after an hour and a half, and you bite your lips to keep yourself from telling her about your club, as if it would make any difference, but maybe it would, and Hans takes forty winks that take twenty minutes, and comes round and reaches to the side and she says: 'Hey, my Gans, I'm not Liv,' and he rolls onto her so she says: 'Hang on,' and goes out again because there are no condoms left, but he just wanted to press up against her, 'Come on, love, don't

596

be like that,' *Hey, you can tell those lies to yourself*, no, not a word of a lie, and the sun migrates quickly, and he gives her an extra note that she doesn't want to take to begin with, 'Come on, love, now...' but then they have another glass, her second, a new bottle, who gives a shit, it stays behind at the head end, half-full, half-empty, and Hans blinks at the sun, feels weak, feels strong, doesn't know for a moment which direction to take, tries to remember the landmarks and... and wakes up gasping for air, strokes the leathery skin, *Hold on a mo, Tanja*, her hair lying damp on his chest after the shower, he inserts coins into the stupid fruit machine in an amusement arcade on Flughafenstraße, the girls used to complain sometimes behind his back, what was it again, at school? *Learn, learn, and once again learn*, Lenin, it's not easy running a club, Tanja sits astride him and he feels the mirrors in the semi-darkness on his body, his face, and Hans is standing under the trees on Pannierstraße and looking at his watch.

There's still time and he's got change making lumps in his trouser pockets. *The way we still keep on trying to be private. Or get private. Because sometimes you can't avoid it. It comes the way it comes, no matter if you want it or not.*

'So, you had some good winnings already today?' said the man in the grey suit jacket, still not getting out. 'Out on the street. We all ought to be investing in those machines.'

'During the great time of waiting,' said Hans, surprised because he wouldn't usually put it like that, 'I just took a look around at how you live here, if that's what you mean.'

'It's not about how anyone lives,' said the man in the grey suit jacket and opened the door. 'We did a good deal. You were the right man. German-German relations and the old Tokyo axis.' He got out of the Mercedes and Hans stepped back so the door wouldn't touch him. 'Let's go up to the office and get everything tied up. I think we can all be happy.'

He held his hand out for Hans to shake. 'I think so too,' said Hans and took the hand and turned his head, only a little, while he was holding the hand, towards the low building and he blinked at the sun and blinked at the city. Motions.

It's still hot in the afternoon and he's sweating. He wipes his hands on his trousers and inserts a few more coins and waits for the diamonds. It's an old machine, he remembers playing on one like it years ago. To calm his nerves. Where was that? And he sees his sweaty forehead on the machine, sees the other players beside him, behind him, the quiet tunes, the electronic twirling noises of the virtual cylinders, wipes his sleeve over the glass, thinks of the grotty mirrored room in Hildesheim, because he'd been wondering before where it was when he thought about the mirrors. *On the wall, on the wall...* He'd stumbled into the place drunk. Then they go and make stupid comments. He can't stand that, when someone makes stupid comments for no reason. 'Shut your mouth or I'll break your neck.' He had his hand on the neck already, the neck in his hand already, the dumb doorman, but he still had himself under control, pretty much. *That's one way to put it, Hans, isn't it?*

They shut up then and he fell asleep in the grotty, much too small, mirrored room. He can't remember a woman. Hildesheim, Ruhr Valley and so on, midlife crisis, that's how he'd put it. When he thought he needed to get to know the whole country, drive all the way round it. He always wondered why they didn't give him a good beating in that dump near the station in the city of H., didn't give him a good seeing to. Maybe because he handed out money all round the place and because he was wearing an expensive coat, and it wasn't the kind of place that looked like people handed out a lot of money there. No diamonds coming up. They get you extra games, that's when the numbers go up. Why is he playing it? Maybe a kind of superstition. Tokyo, year zero. The man at the other end of the world. The man he helped out, years ago in the city. Not every Jap can do kung fu. And there's Hans standing in the shadows and seeing them giving the man a good seeing to. For whatever reason. And he thinks for a moment and then intervenes. Young lads, he's rid of them in no time.

Well, it did cost him a tooth. At the front – he's had a gold one there for nigh on fifteen years now.

And the tunes twirl in his ears, *I'd like to get a horse, one day*, and then he's back on Flughafenstraße, or is it still Pannierstraße? And he doesn't know where he parked his car, then he remembers and he knows where he has to go, checked out the terrain by the driveway entrance hours ago, *But we all ought to be happy with this commissioning deal*, he's annoyed that he only went and stood at the old stadium for a minute or two, the four floodlight masts like crooked steel fingers, and he couldn't find most of the old pubs and bars even though he left home so early, and he looks at his watch and thinks: Let's get going then.

And as the doors of the silver-metallic Mercedes open and he's on the steps to the low building...

'Shit,' he says, 'get your hands off me.' The guy's wearing a bobble hat and it moves behind his back, sways to and fro, that big bright bobble, because the guy's moving his torso up and down. He's not talking, he's babbling. And he grabs at Hans and grabs Hans by the shoulders.

'I get it, you want money, well, I can help you out with a little donation. But no touching, mate.'

He shakes himself, back again and looks at the man with the woolly hat standing there in front of him and laughing and opening his mouth so wide that Hans can see the brown and black stumps. A smell of rot wafts his way. Hans takes a few steps back and looks into the little barrow, a handcart, which the guy is dragging after him. Plastic bags, empty bottles and cans, newspapers, and in amongst all the rubbish he sees grey feathers on a small grey body, a beak poking through the paper that barely covers the body. Black eyes, moving, not moving. A dead bird lying on its side, its talons closed.

The guy babbles something and leans over almost to the pavement and takes a few steps and pulls the cart with the rubbish and the dead pigeon after him.

Hans sweats and searches his pockets for money; suddenly there are children running around the man and his cart. They pat at the man, push at him, speaking Turkish or whatever it is, and Hans stands there, his hands in his pockets, and doesn't know what to do.

He stands in amongst the band of kids and wants to chase them away, the whole of Flughafenstraße seems to be full of kids, dancing screaming and laughing around him and the bobble-hatted man and his barrow.

And Hans sees his left leg getting longer and longer. Sees his foot gliding across the ground. A step almost like doing the splits. Something cracks in his back. DONG, and the sun flames up dark red, behind the houses, in front of his face. He turns around and falls into the barrow, the great grey hole in which the feathers glint. 'You watch what you're doing, you little brats!'

'Gans, hey, Gans, it's nearly three, you wanted to leave.'

600

'No, Achim, you mustn't look at it like that.'

'Go ahead and answer, it seems to be important.'

A phone's ringing, Hans reaches for his, someone steps on his hand, briefly at first and then heavily, the bone breaks, a man jumps on his head, a phone rings, old and shrill.

Breathing into the ground... 'Yes? Don't you lot know what time it is?'

'Eight thirty. You interested in a club?'

'A what? A swinger club?'

'No, a nightclub. Just gone on the market. Not in Berlin though.'

'So?'

'You wanted to go independent.'

'Who...?'

'You did. We'll give you a loan, you take over, the boys in the city are fine with it. You've got a good reputation, worked hard for it.'

'What's all this crap... Let me just wake up a minute. Who is it, anyway? Markus?'

'Who do you think, the former Bonebreakers GmbH. It's about time for a bit of serious business. We'll give you a loan, and you give us information from the city, now and then...'

'Are we with the Stasi, or what? Come round if you want something.' He slams the receiver down on the hook; his skull fractures. His nasal bone penetrates his skull. Someone's standing on his pelvis.

His eyes moving, not moving. Silver-metallic reflecting. The blocks behind the low building move, faster and faster. His spine bends and he tries to roll away. You've got to get back on your feet. The world is bright and red and something's not right with it.

Roll away, just keep rolling away, the sunlight hits

him silently, his larynx getting kicked into his wind-pipe. *And he's still moving.* 'Different dreams,' says Liv, says Sonja, says Mandy, says... 1993. The phone sounds like a fax connection. The first blow. Plural. He sits there and inserts more money and waits for the diamonds. But only the bloody birds come fluttering across the screen. Wood hits his head when he tries to turn around. In the pub next to the driveway they're chatting about the best meatball recipes, homemade. 'No, listen, you have to get the ratio right... more breadcrumbs...'

When he falls onto the staircase he manages to get his arm underneath his jaw. A foot on his throat and he feels his front teeth breaking.

It's quiet in the castle outhouse at this time of year. The light falls through the treetops and sprinkles the road, the pavement. 'We've never given a fuck about rumours, Arnold.'

'If you listen to this, Hans, I'll try again later, get the fuck out of there, wherever you are, Berlin, doesn't matter, I... someone wants to buy his way in to your place, call me back as soon as you can...'

Eight feet working on the body. Skin bursts, eardrums tear, blood vessels traumatized. Blood in the lungs. One eye is open, white. One eye is closed. The hand that belonged to Hans moves.

He walks along the river. In the sand on the bank he finds a black-and-white stone with a hole through it. He waves at a ship disappearing beneath the iron bridge. And the sun migrates quickly.

'And until those... stones suddenly turned up in your life, I mean, your business was going well...'

'Depends how you define well. And what's your actual question? What I did without all the fancy stuff?'

'Yes. Before the...'

'Go ahead, say it. Before the diamonds came up...'

'Yes.'

'The usual, of course. And dreamed of them.'

'I can't tell you everything but there's this little spa town not far from the city. I mean, I can tell you *that*. I've been going there regularly for a few years now. They have wonderful mud baths and sulphur baths. For my back. Yeah, my back, you've picked up on that already, Liv. It's probably because of my days on the building sites. No, don't keep harping on about my age. Trying to annoy me, aren't you. A friend of mine, Arnold, I've known him for nigh on twenty years, he tipped me off about it. He goes there sometimes for his leg, both legs actually. He had an accident. That's twelve years ago though. No, rubbish, let's just be honest. They knee-capped him, shot him in the legs. Supposed to be some kind of warning but it went wrong. Some say the Yugo was too stupid but I think he just overreacted, lost it. I mean, we'd just had this terrible war just before that. And that same year, must have been '99 all of it, with the leg and the... NATO and our German planes were bombing Belgrade. So he was an ex-Yugo, to be precise. Serbian. Serbians. They were still doing good business in the city back then. Arnold, my friend Arnold I mean, is in the letting business. Apartments. For women. Yes. Whores. They rent apartments from him, and he's got a nudist club as well. I've got a nightclub. With women as well. It's a great bar and everything's legal, basically. I mean, Liv, I'm nothing more than a perfectly normal businessman. Basically. How did I get into it? Oh, it's a long story. No, a nudist club's not a fun paradise for na-ked sunbathers. You're sweet, you are.

My place is a normal nightclub. Like a brothel com-mune with a bar. Well, I'm kidding you a bit. But not some grotty old dive, we've got the best drinks and cocktails and wine and champers... you know, everything.

And we always make sure we're not in the little spa town at the same time. Me and Arnold. No one's supposed to know we're curing our aching bones either. People only start talking and you know how it is with gossip. Two old granddads sitting in the mud bath talking about the old days. It's pretty run down, the whole place, used to be a really flourishing health spa. Famous, I'd say. Wonderful station, the old spa train used to stop there because there's another spa town nearby. It's out of service now, the station, and I don't know if the spa's still going in the other town. Probably be a bit stupid, sitting next to each other in a mud bath. Everyone wants a bit of peace and quiet in their time off. Yeah, yeah, my age, don't start teasing me again. And why I'm telling you all this before I tell you my dream, although I do wonder how... how something like this comes together, how dreams like this come about. I mean, I don't really understand why I'm dreaming it now because it's months ago that I was there. In the autumn. And just before, I... I shot someone, killed him. It kind of went badly. You could say I only wanted to warn him, actually, some people will say I lost it. Huge calibre, stupidly enough. Not the man, I mean, the gun.

And when you come out of the baths there, get out again, it's a real joy, let me tell you. We have to go there one time... I feel so right there. I'm cool there and relaxed, yeah, like now, but really deep down, no, that's not what I mean, it just gets right into every tense muscle, yeah, you can spare me the jokes, it gets in between every crooked backbone. And when I come out of the baths there, the guy I killed was a real arsehole, Liv, believe me! Anyway I fancy taking a bit of a hike. There are woods right nearby, there's a huge heath, almost all the way to our city, no, not the steel town, it's not that big a fairy tale forest, I mean up to *my* city.

So I drive a little way across the villages until I see this nice path and a nice patch of woods, and then off I set along the edge of a field. It's a nice autumn day even though it's almost November. Beginning of November it was, I think. I like the woods, Liv. I used to go for a lot of walks in the woods on my own as a kid. Yeah, I like the woods. When the evening comes or early in the morning. My old man always told me off when I came home late or buggered off in the morning. Mind you, he was always telling me off anyway. And later, many years later and up to his death, he didn't say a word. Yeah, yeah, I'm just getting to my dream. I just have to tell you how I found the castle. Reinharz. Funny name. Sounds kind of familiar but I'd never heard of the place before, 'cause the whole village, a pretty tiny village where the castle is, is called that.

So I'm marching through the forest, it's afternoon but it's still quite light. Early afternoon. I usually go to the baths in the morning. I leave home really early so I can start my programme at nine when they open up. Sulphur, mud... you know. And then suddenly I see a signpost. Next to a little field, right by a very narrow path branching off the main route. There were these marshy fields between the trees. I don't like mires, they're spooky. But I've always been fascinated by them. There was this mire right by a lake, I think it was called the Blue Lake. Do you know it, Liv? Can't be far from here. It's getting more and more marshy. All these mires around it. And narrow paths in between. One time, I took a long wooden stick, it was really long, it was. And I dipped it in the mire, right next to the path, and... it was gone. Yeah, yeah, I'm getting to the point. The signpost, right. "Castle Café" it said. And I think, shit where's there a castle here or a café, I mean, I was in the middle of the woods. And nothing to be seen between the trees. So I walk along the little sunken path, you do say sunken path, right? There were trees on one side and marshy fields on the other. And then the path has a crook in it and leads into a kind of park, a kind of garden. But it was all a bit overgrown. This huge horse chestnut. Smaller decorative trees. Flowerbeds, but the flowers all brown because it was autumn. And a couple of weathered stone statues between the paths and lawns and trees. I could see a little brick wall on the other side of the park. And these big empty stone flower pots. Yeah, and all as old as the hills. And this incredible silence. Only the rustling of the trees. The birds don't make so much noise in autumn, do they, but there wasn't one dickie bird to be heard there, like they were in awe or something. And me, I tell you, I was pretty impressed and all. It was like an enchanted garden, like in a storybook. So there's me walking round the park, surrounded by trees, big deciduous trees. The woods were more mixed. Partly conifers, evergreens. And water shimmering through the trees. At first I think it's the sky but then I see a swan, right between the branches, the trees weren't quite bare, the opposite actually when I think back, they were brightly coloured, golden, the way it is in autumn, but in my dream I saw them bare later, and all these ravens or crows on the branches, but that was only at the end of my dream, mind you, can't say there was a real chronology... I don't know, it was all pretty mixed up, and I don't know exactly what was the end, the beginning or the middle, yeah, yeah, Liv, I'm getting to the point, have a bit of patience, sweetie, I have to watch out it doesn't all slip away. Anyway the swan. And I walk towards the trees surrounding the park and see a big lake. Actually several lakes linked together. There were two of them, I think. One of them full of water lilies, covered in water lilies, so at first I thought it was a lawn or something like that. Dark-green water lily leaves, in my dream the water lilies were flowering, at some point anyway, it feels like I dreamed it years ago but it was only just now, yeah, Liv.

And ahead of me a little bridge, the trees open up like a gateway, a little stone bridge over a ditch that leads into the lake, two swans swimming on it, just a couple of water lilies dark green on the water. What happened to all the water lilies, you want to know?

A bit further after the lake with the swans, next to the path I came along, the sunken path, by the edge of the woods, a narrow dam between the two lakes.

But none of that interested me any more, Liv. 'Cause that's when I saw the castle for the first time. I was standing on the bridge and it was right in front of me. Whitish-grey walls, a high red tiled roof, the outer walls directly on the water of the lake with the swans, and in the middle of the long building stood a tower so high I could barely make out the top, I had to lean my head back. It was almost twice as tall as the building and right at the top it tapered off into a green, onion-shaped dome. I don't know how to describe the castle to you properly, we really have to... yeah, yeah, calm down. The thing was like a giant U, I can't think of any other way to describe it, except the outer... what shall I call them... bars... were shorter, pointed into the courtyard, I mean the two outer wings of the building. And the bottom bar, if you imagine a U shape except a bit longer, and the tower between the two wings, it wasn't exactly round, more octagonal, not that I counted... oh, Jesus, it's hard to describe, I'm just a nightclub-owner who trained as a slaughterer, I mean gardener of course. Anyway the tower was built to... yeah, to jut out from the building, the back part of it in the building... oh, bugger it, Liv, it's a beautiful castle, nearly brought tears to my eyes, I've never seen such a, you know, such a beautiful enchanted castle. It just lay there like on a big plate, in the middle of the water. And no one around, far and wide. And that's where my dream starts. With me standing in that courtyard. And back then, I mean it's not all that long ago, I thought for a moment, you know the way you think things, believe it or not, that I'd ended up in a different time somehow. Even when I first set foot in the castle grounds, which I didn't yet know were castle grounds because I couldn't see the water castle behind the trees yet. Maybe it was because of October. Because everything was so quiet and so... golden. Fallen leaves on the lawns, fallen leaves on the stone slabs of the castle courtyard. You could lean over the low walls and look at the water. And later, maybe that's why I dreamed it, I discovered an outhouse, another bridge led to it across a water ditch, it must have been a servants' house or a farm serving the castle, what do I know what they call these things, and anyway it was up for sale. Had a sign on it. With a phone number. So I wrote it down right there and then, of course. And later I called the number and all. A beautiful little yellow house, two floors, baroque, well, you could tell that without knowing much about anything, baroque. Like the whole castle. I knew straight off it was for me.

I knew I'd retire there one day.

And maybe that's why I had that dream here with you. In the steel town where I was born. I've never dreamed of that castle before. So I'm standing back in that courtyard but the castle looks slightly different. It was a bit run-down, you see. The roof was new but the walls, I mean the plaster, was a bit crumbly. I mean, of course, it's on the water, right above the water. And at first I thought, in my dream I mean, shit, now you really have gone back in time, no, seriously. You haven't killed anyone yet – mind you, the guy was the worst kind of arsehole, I'm telling you, he wanted to mess something up for me, mess me up, but... that doesn't matter now. And then I see two servants, right by the entrance gate down at the foot of the tower. They had these wigs on, baroque wigs, with a little pigtail. I used to like reading *Mosaik*, you know that comic, yeah, the one from the Zone, and some time at the end of the seventies those three pixies ended up in the early eighteenth century, in the baroque era. No, I wasn't a kid any more by then, but it wasn't just for kids. They were in Vienna, imperial times, and then even in Paris where that Sun King was on the throne. And that's exactly what the guys looked like, the servants. In like livery. And then I see that I'm dressed like that and all. Well, a bit different, posher, like a duke or something. And this coach comes up over the bridge behind me. And I turn around and there's this road going across the grounds and then through the middle of the woods. Two white horses and a guy on the coachman's seat. All baroque. Hm, yeah. And this guy I know gets out. And he says something to me but I can't understand him properly. Sounded like French. Or Italian. And he really is a count in real life. Of noble birth, as they say. Or that's what people say about him, anyway.

He runs a big brothel. It's not going too well at the moment, though. Yeah, there are all these rooms, lots of them, and women in them. He makes his money out of the rent they pay him. They don't have a bar there, see. Yeah, he owns it. Or at least he owns a share in it. In our city and elsewhere.

610

Dressed up in the full Monty. Like me. Knicker-bockers. High-heeled shoes. Gigantic wig. Coat-tails down to his knees. And then we're suddenly inside the castle, walking down the long corridors, doors everywhere and servants everywhere. And candelabras on the walls everywhere. Candles. And tapestries in between and old oil paintings. Maybe I saw something like that in *Mosaik*, 'cause I never actually went inside the castle. And then I feel like I've always been in there, always lived there. In the dream, I mean. Reinharz. It's all in my memory, in my head.

And at some point we're sitting in this huge room, more like a hall, the finest crystal chandeliers dangling from the ceiling, and the light, 'cause there's hundreds of candles on them, you've never seen such radiant light. And candelabras on the table we're sitting at, then. Up at the top end my old friend Arnold, the one I told you about, the letting king, no, not red-light sector, he doesn't like that word, and at the other end of the long table is... no, there's no one sitting there, just an empty chair, magnificently decorated, like a throne. And me and the Count sitting on either side of the table. It's laid, of course. Hundreds of carafes, bottles, glasses, platters of roast meat and platters of fruit and grapes, like you imagine they must have dined back then, the rich, the aristos.

And on one side there's this cembalo piano, some-one's tinkling away at it, and a couple of guys next to it fiddling Bach or Handel, I don't know much about music. Beautiful music, anyway. And the walls are hung with muskets and sabres and swords and all kinds of weapons.

And I look at Arnold, sitting there in his big white wig, his hands folded, just sitting there, a silver chalice in front of him, lofty like a king. Or a count, duke, but either way like the boss of our little group. But he doesn't even look at us, just gazes at the empty throne-like chair at the other end of the table.

And you know how it is when you suddenly see everything, not just what you can see through your own eyes, usually. But it was still real, every single moment felt so real. No, not a dream. Down in the courtyard, the coaches pull up. Coach after coach. Must be ten or twelve, at least. The whole castle courtyard full of aristocrats. And then they're all sitting at the table with us, just the one chair stays empty. And I can't stop looking over at it and I don't know why. And I knew some of the people dining with us. Our mayor for example, no, he's never been to my nightclub. But a couple of other guys from the town hall, from the state capital, and they all looked like August the Strong or someone.

And people like the W. Brothers were there as well, they've got a strip club and a couple of bars. And people like Alex, well, that'd be going too far. And real-estate arseholes or wankers from BMW or Audi. No, I've got nothing against them. Not really. Can't turn down good customers. AK and the others do the odd deal with them. Property, I mean. I never wanted to expand and I didn't want to invest my money either, probably would have been better, thinking about it. Bricks and mortar are lasting values if you get it right.

And then later I wake up, must have nodded off for a bit. The drinking and eating was a great big party. All I know is that I laughed a lot, a whole lot. During the meal, I mean. And only AK sat unmoving at the head of the table and drank occasionally from his big silver chalice. And I'm all alone at the long table. Place is a total mess by now. Broken bottles, everything on the floor, tablecloth stained, don't even ask. You wouldn't want to clean that up, Liv.

And no one there any more, the musicians gone as well. And I go over to one of the big windows. And outside the evening's coming, very strange reddish light behind the trees on the horizon. Far away, you sometimes see everything blurry. In dreams, I mean.

And there's people floating in the lake. Bodies, I mean. They seem to be dead but I'm not quite sure. All these brightly coloured clothes. And the two swans in among them. And I can't tell you if I'm surprised or scared. Because I can't quite make it out from up there.

And I wander along the corridors and look for the others. It's only then I notice I've got a dagger or a sabre in my belt.

I look into every room. Candelabra in one hand. The candles flickering. Big four-poster beds. Like through fog, I see that they're humping. Yeah, sorry. I can't help it, can I? Not even if it's my castle, or probably a share of it is. Everything's screwing into itself, I can't make out any faces. And I don't know where the women come from.

But I do hear laughter. From far off, somehow. Women's laughter. And I tell you, it was a real men's club before that. And the Count's sitting in one room, the one who's supposed to be a count in real life, by birth, his father was an aristocrat, that's what they say anyway, he's sitting there talking to the mayor, who I only know by sight, and other men with him at the table, real-estate types, in the corner there's this negro holding a tray, and when I look in they all go silent. And I can't make out whether AK is sitting in there with them. All these gold coins on the table. And papers, loads of papers, with sealing wax on them. Like candlewax. And a couple of shiny stones.

And somehow I'm suddenly in the castle dungeon, don't know how I got there, sometimes you're totally weightless in your dreams.

And there are the women, and funnily enough a lot of black women. And I was that negro at the same time as myself, and I saw myself and looked into the room, 'cause I wanted to see if AK or anyone else was sitting in one of the dark corners, I could make out a pair of reading glasses, see, or an old-fashioned monocle, but no more than that, probably 'cause I forgot my glasses on your bedside table, Liv, and me as a negro and me as Hans, neither of us had a good feeling in that room, what they were getting down to and negotiating in there. But I've always been good at minding my own business.

The dungeons are full of women. They're standing there all squashed together, all naked. It's cold down there. Water seeping through the walls. 'Nubian pearls,' says someone behind me, but when I turn round there's no one there, of course. Ha, ha, should have seen that coming. Yeah, stark naked. And the servants keep coming out of different doors and fetching a few of the women at a time. I mean, when I think about it now, I mean I'm not Freud and my conscience is absolutely clear, for fuck's sake. Absolutely. And what's all the crap about, I don't have anyone down in my cellar, not any women anyway. And I don't have S&M dungeons or anything either. I've often thought about it, though. I mean, it must be such a shit dream because people always think exactly that. Yeah, Liv. Like it's all a criminal network and that. In every stupid crime show. All forced, all in the dungeons, the evil, evil pimps who really aren't pimps at all. You can fuck right off. Sorry, sweetie. Sure, things go wrong here and there. Like in all walks of life, like in every business. I know enough people who make me sick. I could tell you stories, we'd be here all night. And maybe I'm just too stupid and too old to notice everything that goes on behind closed doors with the big, big world of politics. And we're not in the breakfast cereal industry. And the women, the ones in the water castle dungeon, they're laughing. Laughing and laughing. Like I was laughing at the table, upstairs at the party. It sounds kind of spooky. All these voices laughing, never-ending...

And then I'm somewhere else in the castle, the laughter and music accompany me and I'm holding a dagger in my hand. The candelabra's disappeared. And I walk and walk, into this room and that room, then I'm in the grounds and then suddenly in the courtyard and then somewhere else. And I think it must come to an end at some point. Because I haven't felt for a moment like I was dreaming.

In one room, Arnold is whipping his son. And shit, they're naked, both of them. And papers next to them on an ornate little table, and I want to take a look at them but I can't make anything out, just a big black seal, and I break it to open the letter, it's a big envelope, and you know those pressed flowers you used to find in old books, well in the envelope there's a little pressed hand, like a child's hand. People say, I don't want to tell you this, Liv, and I'm not telling you it, they say Arnold has photos and documents, there was this... in the early nineties, no, I'm not telling you, I wasn't even in the city back then, on my way there at the most. And Jesus, in another room Arnold's kneeling on the floor and his son's whipping him and wearing his old man's clothes and a white wig with a big black three-cornered hat. And I don't get any of it. His son, you see, he went to the military 'cause his old man wanted him to. He's back now, though. And I want to say something and Arnold turns around with his back bleeding, whip in hand, and he says something like: "If you want to join in..." And then I stabbed him. It was easy. But the blade went through both of them, father and son I mean. I left the dagger in their corpses and walked away. But later, up on the tower, I saw Arnold again. He was back again like nothing had happened. Nicely dressed, baroque, of course, wig on his head. He was busy with these huge telescopes. They were screwed down up there. Right at the top of the tower. We stood behind a little wall right underneath the tip of the onion, on a kind of viewing platform. A pair of old-fashioned crutches leaning against the wall next to him. "I've been waiting for you so long, Hans." Jesus, that's exactly what my father said. But I can't know that yet. And then we look out over the land. And all these riders in the distance. Two hordes. One a lot further off than the other. But both still on the other side of the woods. And all the trees are bare. "We have to burn down everything, everything, if we want to keep our castle." Yeah, that's what he said. And he swung the telescope round somewhere else, up to the stars. It was evening by then. And when I was back, hours later, hours and hours later it seemed like, when I was back in our ceremonial hall, only a few candles left burning, there's a man sitting on the chair that was empty all evening, all through the party. Like he'd always been sitting there. Yeah, and of course I know him. We'd always made our engagements, no, arrangements, over the years. *We raised our cups and forged our pact...* Ach, forget it, Liv. But I'm still pretty sick that he's sitting here in our castle. With the wild hordes of riders at the gates. My dagger is gone, must still be in one of the Arnolds, and I notice I'm hobbling on crutches. And all these mirrors on the walls and I don't know whether they're just our reflections, some are fixed and don't move, as if the originals had left the hall long, long ago, others are pressing their noses up to the glass from inside. And then I have to admit I'm scared, for the first time in my dream. Horribly scared, like a little kid. Because the hands and feet and faces start coming through the mirrors. Yeah, and that's it. Then I woke up. And I was so glad to be here with you. Oh wait, I forgot about the desk, the old bureau, it was in the room that must have been my study in our castle, and when I open the drawer there's a tiny little man inside it, telling me off, and he's got a big wig on as well, baroque, to scale with his size of course, and because he's naked I see that he's a woman. I've got a daughter, I don't need Freud to work that one out, I haven't seen her since she was little. And I used to have a dwarf, she worked in my club, I mean... well, she wasn't totally tiny but she was like a semi-midget, and she only worked at my place for a little while, she was a sensation at the time, just the one season, she wanted to fund something, wanted to start something up with the money and then she buggered off again, no, never mind, I just made that up, that little truth, and I forgot the bit with the little semicircular stone bench by the edge of the woods, when the women were suddenly all over the castle wearing huge crinolines with taut waists, the hordes of riders had disappeared and there were only women left, like the castle suddenly belonged to them, and we sat there like we'd been expelled, on that silent bench... but I don't know if...'

'Hans, hey, Hans!'

'Yeah?'

'Anyone at home?'

'What?'

'You've been sitting here talking to yourself for an hour. Everything OK?'

'Yeah, Liv. Yeah, Arnold.'

'Who? I thought you were going to steer clear of the white gold, my friend.'

'I'm only drinking, Arnold.'

'You need a holiday.'

'That's what I'm planning.'

'But don't get stuck somewhere where the sun shines.'

'What do you mean?'

'I've heard you want to go for good. Got some deal going somewhere.'

'Crap.'

'I need you here in the city, my friend.'

'No worries, *hakuna matata*.'

'Come, I'll call you a taxi.'

'Did you use to love *Mosaik* as a kid, as well? It's still going but it's shit now.'

'*Mosaik*, Hans? I wish I had your dreams.'

'No, you don't.'

TRANSFER (BYE-BYE, MY LADYBOY)

Drinking champagne. That's something I came to late in life. Sparkling wine, that was normal. You'd have the odd glass of it with the ladies. But it gave me a headache, later. Got my heart racing. Practically tore my head in two, my heart going like a machine gun. AK. I haven't been able to drink sparkling wine since that year, since that night in the big year before the zeroes.

Drinking champagne. That was something I used to smile about, never knew what I was missing, and I smiled as well when the Bielefeld Count who impressed us all with his blue-blooded swindle decapitated the bottles with a sabre. No headache, no racing heart from champagne. It must be to do with the storage and the production. Classy. And dark. And brut.

Decapitating the bottle with a sabre. That's something I imagine on and off, now. When I look out at the lake and think of the days when I'll have so much time I'll be able to spend winter evenings by the fire, drinking champagne. I didn't know that an upper part of the bottleneck gets cut off as well, split off by the force of the blow from diagonally below to the top, not until the con-man Count showed me. The old boy will have impressed one or two gatherings with his tricks over the years, in his business. Travelled far and wide. Got to give him that. And now, after fifteen years, round about, he has to leave the fortress. Now I'm sure he'll have covered his back and I know about his shares in other companies, know about the other locations in his chain. The Schlecker drugstores have gone bust. He's just exhausted, burnt out in this city. His dream of shares. How we laughed. The red-light-sector share. And him assuring us it would turn out that way one day in the future. We'd just have to be *one* company. We wouldn't have to set up anything new, just come together, form a syndicate, nationwide. The laws had changed, he said. For us. And he said – how else could it be – he had enough contacts in business and politics. If you believe that, you'll believe... *Plop. Let's drink. Return from our thoughts.* The soul, I feel like I can see your soul, girl. I'm ashamed. Emotional impulses. And I look you in the eye, your pupil as far and wide and shiny as a nebula of stars, a nebula of planets, the blueish-pink shimmering 'cat's eye', that nebula in the dragon constellation, so far, far... How do I know all that, you ask? The ring nebula of Lyra. When I look into your eyes, the colours and the spectrums are different, left and right.

Well, I believed in his contacts to begin with, for a long time. Business, politics. I had and still have enough contacts of my own, but him, the great man of the world, the traveller of all Germany, the Count, the bottle beheader, the champagne connoisseur. How long ago it all is now. And his dream? Was he right? Not long ago, one or two years ago maybe, I met the man from Austria, the man who started out as a lawyer and then found his way into the business with the pretty peepers, the luminous stellar nebulae, I silently whisper the comparison into your ear, silently lay it on your eyes with my fingertips, ashamed of my emotional outbursts. The red-light sector share, yes, he said, that was his dream too. The expanding Austrian. I remembered the theorems about the principle of the share, how long ago that is. The founding of a joint-stock company. The Austrian had visions. Like the Count, that semi-swindler we used to smile about. But we did respect him to begin with. Unite forces? Everyman's in it for himself. Chains. Drugstores? No, thanks. Bigger. Was it the Count or the

620

Austrian who said that? Austro-Hungarian. Imperial and royal. Or the other way around.

Drinking champagne. Not losing myself. Impossible. And possible. Dreaming. It's got lonely, at the top. And here. It's always the dual perspective. I know. Where we come from, and where we are. Much more. And further. The capital is there, the turnover is there. Impressive, yes.

You tell me, suddenly, in your confusing voice, that you've had to pay every day since 2006, how long ago that is and yet just the other day. I know that and I hold you tight. Of course I know it – you're part of the share. I'd like to tell you about the dual perspective I've read about. You mean the twenty-five euro flat-rate tax. I know, my girl, peanuts, I know, forget it. You are, I say. And you? you ask. I'm ashamed. Empty phrases. *Value exists only in articles of utility, in objects: we leave out of consideration its purely symbolical representation by tokens. … the commodity becomes a social product. Do bats eat cats?*

And we're going to the concert. And we certainly don't think what is generally thought. About things, objects. I'm just as much an *object* as you are. We speak the word tenderly. I've never forgotten that that is *that*.

You don't understand me? You do understand me, you say then. Because we're sitting in a restaurant together, before we go to the concert. Because we're drinking champagne. And because we're eating and because we're sitting up there, sitting by the glass and looking out over the city, and because I don't care if anyone knows me or recognizes me. Because I'm cutting off all these thoughts at this moment. In this time when I'm vulnerable. When someone could stab at my soft sides. When you stroke my soft sides. When you're almost naked in the room, up there, that I've rented for us.

621

Cork projectiles. And you really want to go to the concert with me? you ask. I touch your arse, run my hand along the long string of fabric disappearing *between*. You're almost naked. Over the river and into the woods. I can't be tired. Not like this. I'm ashamed, I'm fighting my mouth, my brain, which bring out all the stupid things and thoughts and ideas and dreams, bring them to you. What's a man to do? I sit on the edge of the bed, the angular edge, square glass in front of me, lights, planes, city, cities, family and friends? I say it doesn't matter to me. Now. And time stretches out. And I don't know whether I'm lying.

My forehead's on yours. We fall and fall into our tunnel. I kiss you and I want you to kiss me. And you tell stories although we're silent. NO, Jesus, we're not silent. Empty phrases. The two of us. We disappear in our stories. You're almost naked and I strip off the rest.

You say, 'No, no,' although I make time flow into one and the light falls only through the big rectangular, four-cornered glass. So where there's little light. Outside. Where the ceiling lamp inside only glimmers, the light trembling barely perceptibly in the wire, dim the light, dim it, because we're still strangers to one another. But then we're not. Because for a few months now you've been sitting and lying and waiting in a west-end apartment that belongs to me. You've come a long way, my exotic girl.

And I've travelled a long way to you too, my exotic girl. Is this the new age? Are we already in the eleventh year of the new millennium? I put together your set card but I didn't dictate it. Back then, it's not long ago but it seems past, so long past (how we exaggerate in our confusion), I asked you back then how and what and what numbers. People wanted more and unusual options.

You came from the western border of the country. And I asked myself, what do you want here? In this strange city.

And I thought, what a beautiful girl. When the media and the net were spreading horror about our city. BOOM, BOOM. The wars on the borders. When the Bielefelder struck the conical cork from the bottle and the length of glass went with it, using his old sabre that was allegedly an heirloom from his forefathers, but he probably or possibly bought somewhere, some time at a flea market, back then I thought... that dry plop in my ear, I didn't think...

He sits by the window and smokes. I sit behind him. Put my arms around his body. Put my hands on his chest. He feels cold. But when I press my hands, my skin, my body to his skin there's no cold any more. His hair, his head, shimmer grey. The clocks change in a few days. It's still dark in the early evening. But warm now. No one's ever told me so much about the stars and the universe, the all.

All that. And about my eyes. In which he sees all that. Sees that I'm getting scared. And then I'm not. It's the fear in which I feel that I still am the way I don't want to be any more. The childhood fear. The boy's fear. Fear that goes between your legs. Between my legs. So that I feel what I don't want to feel. Burning fear. So that I remember the time when I was a child. And that it's so long ago for me. That it seems endlessly past, but then it's suddenly there again. As I press my legs together so my knees touch. X. Almost an X. I press my knees together, take them back again, press them apart, both legs, and together again. A fit of knee shivers. It sounds muffled, quite quiet actually on the trouser fabric, and I press and pull and beat both legs together as though I weren't quite right, over and over. I rub my knees against each other, my upper body leaning forwards, cramping up, my whole body cramping up and I sway my upper body back and forth. I don't know, I don't know, I don't know. And I don't want to. Don't want it. I clamp the thin, wet... dick between my legs. It gets smaller and smaller in my fear. My whole body goes crooked. And I think like a child. As much as one can think, as a child. And later it gets worse and worse. Puberty. What a stupid word, no stellar nebula – black holes. Me coming out of the cinema. Me wanting to be someone else. *But it's my capital... and I do so much sport. I don't think I'd earn much if I was overweight.* I get the feeling he's scared too. I... but it's funny that I'm not actually scared when I'm behind him and leaning on him, when he's behind me and leaning on me. When I think about it, I mustn't think about it. I'd never ask him how old he is. I only know approximately. I'm so glad he's not old enough to be my father, otherwise it would be... I don't know. Almost not. Father. Old enough. Though it would be possible. Only in theory. I'm thirty-one now, a Leo a Leo a Leo, totally stupid, and he must be about fifty, more likely younger. I don't know exactly, though. His short silvery hair.

He's so grey. And he's scared. Not of me. Or maybe of me. And yet of so many. Much. Scared they want to take everything away from him, his business, but what do I know about that? It's fine that way. There are his hands on the nape of my neck. On my nape. There he runs his hands over my breasts. There he gives me his cigarette. And even though I rarely smoke, because it's not compatible with my tablets and no good anyway, I smoke along with him and breathe the smoke out, his silvery head, his back, to which I press my breasts, push them up. Our arms tangled. Me coming out of the cinema.

I'm always thinking I ought to let my hair grow. Is this what they call a pageboy cut? His hands on my shaved nape. And then the fear between my legs again. Me coming out of the cinema. Me running away. Me wearing trousers, a pair of leggings, but a long T-shirt over the top. Like a dress. Almost down to my knees. Me choosing it beforehand. Pale blue. And my hair in a pageboy cut. Although it was still boyish; my mum cut it for me. And lipstick from Mum. Yes, secretly. Which I never dared to. And never knew if I should. If I was allowed to do it. And knew I couldn't. And I stood in front of the mirror and looked to see whether my teeny-tiny breasts mightn't be growing like a girl's. Shoved my top half out so hard it almost hurt above by backside, my poor back. And extra-tight pants. So that it's pressed right up to my leg, gone. And I especially went a long way to the cinema, in our little town, to a small cinema on the edge of town. You could see the factories there, the pits, almost all of them closed down by then. Early or mid-nineties, I don't want to think about it. I started working at twenty. Because I thought I could be a woman that way, the way I am, thought I could finally be a woman in public. What nonsense, I think now. *What a sweet little ladyboy!*

I was a nail designer. There are lots of things I can't remember. Because I'm supressing it, because I cut off those memories because they're torments and because I want to be now, and here.

I feel his dick inside me. With him, every time is like it's all new and full of longing. I've granted myself the right to a bit of kitsch, saved up so long for a bit of feeling. *Fuck me, fuck me!* That's how I fire on the guests so they fire off faster, so I can tick them off and just get the money. It's stupid how often people say they feel secure, I don't understand how to feel something like that. But now I do. A little. The grey man, I think I was scared of him. To begin with. Or it was deference, respect, I wanted to keep a distance to this man who seemed cold, who seemed a stranger. And far away. Even when he spoke to you. Perhaps that was the menacing thing, the feeling of fear. Because I wasn't scared, of course. I've been in Freiburg, in Cologne, in Bremen, in Bochum, big brothels, massage salons, clubs, apartments, hotels... drinking champagne. *What a sexy little ladyboy!*

My dick is very small and doesn't matter to me, if you can say it that way. Two girlfriends of mine who I met in Cologne, they've got rid of them now. I feel like a woman and I am one too. Either way. And I don't like it very much when they touch me there. My breasts are very good, from the hormones and two small implants. I've always been a woman, I was always a girl. We can't understand why it was made so difficult for us to be the way we are. My father's Italian, from a guest-worker family. Catholic. Strict, as they say. I can't understand why he doesn't want to see me any more. I can understand why he doesn't want to see me any more. I always think I'd love my child, no matter what they're like and no matter whether their mind, their soul or whatever you want to call it, and their body are the way they are. I didn't say I could do this now *and or but* that. Because you don't have a choice. Or you mess *yourself* up because you lie to yourself your whole life. Mess yourself up. I think everything's right the way it is, even if there is a god or something like a god, who'd have to be a kind of hybrid if you ask me, a WoMan or whatever you want to call it, so if there's someone up there who makes you what you are, the way you are, and I think then you have to find your own harmony, or you're allowed to, whatever. It all sounds esoteric, maybe that's the remains of

626

my Catholic-infested childhood but in all the years that make you hard I've earned myself something soft. At last. Just once.

Why are you laughing, you ask. And I say it's just because I feel very good right now. And that you're here now, with me, that we're up here lying together, sitting, drinking, fucking and talking, that that's something special. I say I've never felt like this before, we're not kids any more, but that for me it's...

He pulls me close, my head resting on his chest. Drinking champagne, lying together in peace... And I run out of the cinema, hear the laughter behind me, how do they know I'd come here to this little cinema, no one from my school or my class comes here otherwise, no *Dirty Dancing*, no *Rocky 5* or any of that crap, I'm thirteen and I want to watch Audrey Hepburn. I'm wearing leggings and a long T-shirt over the top and I've put on lipstick and done my eyes and I'm wearing a bra with little foam pads, and I want to be alone. In the dark of the cinema, in the light of the film.

I've brought you something, you say. Your phone buzzes somewhere in the room but you don't pick up, you don't look for it, and it will buzz a few more times until you turn it off in the end, checking the numbers and messages beforehand. Just quickly.

I know you've got a lot to do. I know your firm, your company is in a tricky situation. I know that the recent difficulties – the fighting, the unrest that was in the newspapers so often in the past months, almost years – are over now. That your business was going well again, undisturbed, for a while, and that now the next unrest is beginning, these waves, these movements through which you have to navigate. I've heard a lot, the kind of thing you hear, where only half of it is ever true, or

half of it is half-true, and since we've been up here, lying here, drinking, fucking, pressing into one another,
you've been talking. Sometimes you lie here as if asleep,
like in a dream, on your back, on your side, your eyes
closed, dark shadows under your eyes, your stubble
shimmering grey, your voice quiet and moving on me
and in me, the Angels in the city, the Outsiders around
the city, this city that's been moving slowly into the
nearest, smaller town for years and migrating strangely
across the maps, that's how you explained it to me, planes
flashing on the flight path. And you see that too or you
hear it, because your eyes are closed in the twilight of
our room, and you talk about going away, and you tell
me you once went to Tokyo, that shining metropolis on
and between the islands at the other end of the world,
through which the radiation is now slowly creeping, I'm
so glad the TV up here is silent because it's always on
during my work and between my work and reporting
on things that shouldn't interest me and don't actually
interest me, but that offer distraction, that show pictures
that help me, even if they're none of my business, I read
the news in the newspaper and it's not like I need help,
and you say it and said it and say it again and again, or
it echoes again and again in my head, that I'm so strong,
that you admire how strong I am, that you admire many
of the women who work for you, work in your firm, in
your company, admire how strong they are, and that
it's part of the business, letting strong women into your
company and not just any old Joan Bull, I don't know
where I got that name from, from you, from our silent
conversations, from the cut-up memories of my childhood? 'Coppenrath & Wiese,' you said once, and I know
exactly what you mean, that every Joan Bull would act
like a fussy bitch, all: 'What have those stupid tarts got

628

to do with me?' She'd get het up about this and that, about the way you talk, about who you talk about. But *that* is *that*. Because we're different. And we're opening up to each other. But still holding tight and embracing.

Can there be only one? you ask. And you mean the unrest in your business, in your firm. You mention the Man behind the Mirrors, getting more and more powerful since the hostile takeover was blocked, the chief of the Angels. I like the way you stroke my dick as if unconsciously. I don't usually like that.

Like feathers. While you fuck me and then clasp my breasts with both hands.

I run and run and don't stop running, although there's no one behind me any more. But the laughter wafts through the streets, echoes between the houses. I've climbed up one of the old pit-head frames, in the wasteland outside town. They begin right behind the houses, the old pits, the rusting steel skeletons of the old factories and frames. Steel doesn't rust? I sit up there and look out over the land and look out over the town when I turn around. Somewhere back there, the river flows. Somewhere back there, the sun's about to set. Somewhere back there, it already has set, almost, pale pink in the cloud haze. Like a nebula back there above the river. Late summer, end of September. I wipe my face and my hands are wet, and my eyelashes are running and my make-up is smeared across my palms. I'm ashamed. I don't want to be a poof. Just a woman, just a girl, just Audrey Hepburn. I laugh, because that's not a *just*. And I liked *Dirty Dancing* too, although it was on at the cinema years ago and is only showing again now because there's a second part, and everyone pretends Patrick Swayze was the star of the nineties now but all they want to do is get the eighties back, when we were kids and much too small for all that, and then I remember that *Dirty Dancing 2* only came out years later, 2004, or will come out then, and I'm sitting up on the old pithead frame and laughing. I go to the hairdresser's and get my hair cut how girls and young women wore their hair in the eighties. I dye it black as well. It holds fine, even in the rain. I can't go home like this or my old man will flip out. I'm grateful to him now, that I speak Italian. Taken a couple of holidays in Tuscany. I like the sea. And I went to the sea. The guys, the boys around me like a pack of young dogs. My black hair tousled at the front and a bit longer at the back and sides, but still fairly short, like the women and girls had in the eighties.

My dad used to hit me. That's not true.

Only the once. He must have seen early on that I wasn't the boy he wished for. When it came to development. But father, my father, I was always this way. And the boys around me, Tuscany, the sea, and me proud and drinking champagne, no, it must have been prosecco, proud and unapproachable but joking with them, among them, in the cafés, on the beach, on the Tuscan plain.

Why are you laughing, you ask, what are you laughing at? And you wake like from the depths of a dream. Eyes open now. Your stubble shimmering grey in the dimmed light beneath the ceiling. I lie close to you and on top of you. You push me away, but only to press up to me again. With your strength, with your impatience, with your patience. I admire you, that you're lying up here with me. You admire me, you say, or you said it in the minutes and hours beforehand. For what? My cold man, whose coldness and strangeness keep drawing me close. As though it were part of me. As though it weren't part of all that outside.

As though all that's important were only in here, up

here, here with us. The short days and hours of the lie. Why that? Why a lie? Because we are, after all, and because we're here, after all. Isn't that everything, and is that *everything* for us?

Drinking champagne... Like Audrey Hepburn. And he tells stories. He talks about his son. How can I be angry with him, he says, when he's just like I used to be?

I stroke the scars on his legs. First left, then right. He never talks about them. It must have been eleven years ago, that, but I don't want to know. I was in Cologne at the time. I'd met up with my girlfriends, still working as a nail designer, and we had our little meeting place, coffee, prosecco, Cathedral Café, trans club, we were all waiting for the year with all the zeroes. We laughed about that later. We were still exotic extravagancies on the big red market then. And we laughed about the men, the zeroes who brought us the money because they were wild for us to, for them to... *Bend over, my little ladyboy.*

Father?

Yes, my son?

You're seeing homos?

My boy, you know how much harm gossip can do.

You're seeing a tranny, father! *Oh son, my son, what have you done?*

I wake up. And I say we have to leave, the concert's beginning, and then I feel that I'm still not quite there, my hand weak on her shoulder, and that I can sink right back into my dream, my son, the sheets covered in blood, the pillow covered in blood, what am I doing? Does it matter what I do? *Leave her alone, son!* In these times. To disappear, after all the years. Or: now's the perfect time to disappear. The disputes are increasing but I'm still here. The Old Man won't leave, *oh no*, the Old Man will fight. Taking a stand as he knocks out one

631

of the new-born Angels, a man he's known for years who refuses to accept the territories and the division of labour, with the new strong power behind him, as a new-born member-in-waiting, *The Angels are coming to town! Hurrah, they're here now!* whom he, the Old Man, the manager ('Manager? I'm an entrepreneur, there's a difference. I plan, I run my business, invest, expand. But I don't dig out the ground beneath our feet in the long run, we only take money where there's money to be had, a simple enough deal.'), the Angels he himself once and not long ago invited to the city, Eden City, market of dreams. The Old Man has his own people, what does he want with you? And he knocks him out. When he gets fresh. A kick to the head, a foot to the temple. And he goes down. I'm standing, the Old Man, the man who wishes he could disappear but goes on fighting. The man too tired to go on fighting much longer. The man who thought the business would run and run and he'd have his peace, with a boat, a little yacht for sailing on the lake. Travelling and coming back. Collecting art. And steering the flow of cash, like in all the years. He was almost shocked at how fast he brought the new-born Angel to the ground. As if he were fifteen years younger. Like before that night in that year, in the autumn of that year. *Dreaming? No, I'm cold.* But then why *her?*

And his back's still aching from that unexpected kick, the thin skin over the right-hand scar split open, only a little blood, the man on the floor not bleeding at all and trying to get back on his feet, his back hurts for weeks, and she sits astride him while he lies on his front, massages his aching back, and he feels her little dick gentle on his skin.

Drinking champagne, taking hormones, being a woman. And he talks in his dream, his hand on my

632

shoulder. It feels cold and it moves, and I see by his watch that it's ten past seven. The concert starts in fifty minutes. My father took me to a concert once and once to the opera. Something Italian, of course. He wants to listen to Mahler. A man's never invited me to a concert before. Some kind of festival in the city. I don't know Mahler very well. Maybe I've heard the odd thing but I can't remember anything specific. I used to listen to classical radio or the local culture stations. Because classical music always calms me down. I've always liked the film music to the old weepies. It's like classical music, Audrey Hepburn, *Giant* with gorgeous Liz, I always liked those two best, the others never understood why I was so into the women and men in the old movies. But they never understood me anyway. Understood that I was the way I was. It was hell, actually, thinking back. Maybe that's why I love *him*. Do I love? I don't know. I wanted to be like those slim, dark-haired, almost black-haired girls with dark eyes, and I admired the handsome men like Rock Hudson and James Dean and Marlon Brando and fell in love with them, like... my father was a painter, painter and decorator, started at the very bottom as he liked to tell us over and over, worked his arse off on building sites in Duisburg and then in Bochum and started his own company in his mid-forties. *Why haven't you gone under the earth, Father? Like the others.*

The heart, boy, my heart, girl. Look lively, look sharp, here comes the foreman. Father used to take tablets, right to the end. He was always an old father. What did your father do, I ask him. When we're lying together again in our room after the concert, at the very top of the rectangular tower, drinking champagne again as if there were nothing else in the world or as if the variety of exquisite drinks confused us, only a few freight planes in the sky at night. They're yellow like the post office vans, I've often seen them taking off and landing next to the motorway. *Strong. Determined.* He tells me he rarely listens to classical music but a friend of his recommended the composer. Though he wasn't a real friend, actually. We saw the mayor. With his wife. We walked right past him. I recognized him from the paper. And he nodded at us, at him. Politely, bending over slightly, and he, my landlord of the night, nodded back, 'Good evening, good evening,' no, in silence, my broker of might, his wife gave a short smile, a middle-aged blonde in a white dress, fitting for her position, her middle age, 'I have properties all over the city,' you say suddenly as you stroke my breasts, 'more than that. First me, then no one else for a long time. There was this children's book, you won't know it, it's from the Zone, I gave my son a copy even though the Zone was long gone by then...' You laugh. 'Cheerful in tempo and cheeky in expression.' That's what I read in the programme. There really was one jolly, cheerful part. Towards the end. This festival. We've attended two concerts now. *O Mensch. O Mensch.* That touched me. The way the singing started in so suddenly, I hadn't expected it. Eyes closed. *Ich schlief, ich schlief.* Asleep deep in the past. My father on a ladder, in white painter's overalls. He worked even long after he had his own firm, couldn't let it go. *O Mensch. Gib Acht.* Take heed.

Over and over the cinema, me coming out of it, in the summer, me a girl for the first time, absolutely and not at all. The laughter. And me running. The pit towers on the horizon. Did I want to jump down? No, I didn't. I can't remember wanting to. But when it fills you up from inside, so full you could vomit, you could puke because the bitter spit presses into your mouth, you cling to details no one can know yet, the finale in the roar of the drums, but I'm still thinking of the lamenting *O Mensch*, wasn't it Herbert Grönemeyer who sang something like that a few years ago, yes, death became part of his life... he was from Bochum, my childhood city, that I left, went back and back to see the doctors, for the body, for the mind, my work, peace sometimes. I thought for a long time about getting rid of my dick as well, my new name in my passport and on my ID card, the Transsexual Act (*in order to adjust the official sex, up to 2011 the individual additionally had to be permanently incapable of propagation*), and I still think about getting myself opened up, further and without a dick, once and for all, and to begin with I was surprised when he never said I should stop working in his property and stop working at all, not once, surprised when he began drinking champagne with me and fucking and talking and going out with me, as though everything else were far away and didn't matter at all. The fading voices in the concert house, the cube opposite the opera, the long rows of lit-up taxi signs, *when did I decide to become a whore, and when did I decide to stay one*, hundreds of people in evening gowns and suits strolling around and inside the illuminated glass cube, later the sea of white-haired listeners below us, before us, we feel young in comparison. No one knows I'm carrying a little dick in my panties, between my legs, I'm wearing a lilac evening dress from Dolce, finest lace, how handsome my breasts look in the mirrors in the cloakroom, how handsome we are, he radiates such dignity and toughness at the same time that they're sure to respect him, even if they don't know who he is, the good citizens, Coppenrath & Wiese as he once said. For a moment I'm scared I might meet a client, and I really do think for a minute that the old gent... that the salt-and-pepper gentleman in the grey suit fucked me in the arse a few days ago, a big cheese from the bank, but it's only *us* that counts, and I can still feel *him* inside me, no condom because that's my protection from *them*, like I can't feel the big cheese from the bank inside me and never did, not in my mouth, he paid very well indeed and I have to admit that I do have pleasant clients and not just wankers like him. If *he* wanted, I'd stop working. But I'm not a dreamer. Never have been. Maybe back then in the cinema, and by that I mean the time when I was eleven, twelve, thirteen. And mayl e still when I changed my name and trained as a nail designer. I don't know how it might go on.

I don't know how it'll go on. Business is booming. The city's going places. Should I stay or go? Where could I go? I'm sitting by the window and she's asleep behind me. I hear her breathing, sometimes fast, sometimes slow, as if she were having unsettling dreams. An hour and a half in that cube, as if we were somewhere else entirely, as if we were someone else entirely. What touching music. Am I getting old? Am I going mad? What am I doing here? We survived the invasion. Fetched the Angels as devils. Depends on your standpoint, Alex would say. My people are drifting away. Betrayal's doing the rounds. I could disappear right now, hand over the business. Even more money? That's not what it's about. Even more of the market? Control? Power? I look out at the night sky. Three thousand eight hundred million years have passed since the big bang. The most distant galaxies shine ten billion times weaker than the human eye can see. The year 1999 is out there somewhere. Just like the other years. Time is accelerating, boundaries are disappearing. Where am I? I saw the ladyboys in Tokyo once. Full of disgust and fascination.

The great dance of the *kathoeys* from Thailand. *Futunari*, as the Japanese called them. Beautiful women with little dicks. Some of them had big dicks. By comparison. They showed them to the enthusiastic crowd. A few of the *kathoeys* had pre-installed pussies. What dirty bitches, I thought at the time, almost meant it as a rough kind of compliment, and yet I did feel a sense of fascination too, a premonition, the change to space. And beauties among them and sex bombs among them and beauties among them, like you'd seldom see in my apartments. Or seldom saw at the time. In the year zero. When I thought the nineties were over. Trannies were rare. There weren't any in our city. There were a couple of tranny whores in Berlin, in Hamburg... I wouldn't say tranny to her, now. How gorgeous she is. And her eyes, far and deep and like stellar nebulae, the blurring of the colours, memories, worlds.

Enough science fiction. I know it could be the end of me, I know it will be the end of me if I keep on running round town with her, lying up here with her. Or wherever. Do I love her? I miss you, old Count of Bielefeld, you were more cultivated and educated than the others, although *he*, the Man behind the Mirrors behind the central station in the north of the city, would surely say otherwise. Yeah, yeah, we're part of society, collect art, go to the opera, read books... and soon we'll be writing our own, will we? The mayor only nods his head, or perhaps he'll shake hands? No, not that. We're the landlords of the night, have we got blood on our hands? No need to get too dramatic. *Dirt?* No. No more or less than anyone else on the move through any market. No more or less than the mayor himself. The top cop wants to challenge him at the next election, so I hear. How's he going to govern the city if he can't even control the streets?

I look out at the few lights in the centre of the city. Most of my girls are asleep by now.

My's the wrong word. I've always taken a pragmatic view, strictly business. In exchange for the money you pay me you're independent, safe, well managed, well brokered, well represented. Independent. Management and ménage, do they come from the same word? No, probably not. Over there by the industrial estates, where the night sky shimmers blue, are they the night refineries? The factories, as large as small towns and always illuminated and always in smoke and flames, no, they're further away, thousands once worked there, some of my friends and acquaintances too, some thirty years ago now, hardly any flames or smoke or toxins in the air now, of course, but a modern glistening and glowing that hurts your eyes when you pass by the steel glass installations by night, I used to do a lot of driving alone at night when I needed to think. What is it that draws me to her? Over there near the industrial estate where I once had an office and my construction company's containers and machinery, where I sat back then and studied by night, in the evenings, business administration, over there three properties run a night shift, for the restless, the wanderers, the desperate, the men with desire provoked by drink – the poor girls will wank them till their muscles ache, blow them till their jaws lock – the posh gents who want to get out of the house. The hagglers. The perverts. The regulars, the lonely hearts, the tenderness-seekers. The hardcore fuckers. The strokers. The rough and ready. The flatterers. The crazies. My phone's always on and my people can be reached first and always, but the nights are quiet. The Turks and Arabs have gone. What's coming next? Do my people know I'm here? She'll be working again the day after tomorrow. Not for a second do I think she's a man. Was a man. It's her soul and almost her whole body that's woman. Even without a pussy, without a cunt. I penetrate her. There has to be an end to it. Before I lose myself entirely. In her. What did the Count say once, or was it me, back when I came back from Tokyo? 'We have to totally reinvent this whole myth.'

Janine – hot sex bunny! Hi there honey, do you want to escape everyday life? Are you looking for a kick in bed? Do you have unfulfilled wishes or dreams of something special? Then I'm the right girl. Discreet, private and with no time pressure, let me be your temporary lover...

Over there where only isolated yellow dots are on the move on the motorways and highways, there's hard-working Janine, until two in the morning. We didn't reinvent anything. We're all too poor. Not in terms of money.

My God, how young you look, you really don't look thirty. Your dark hair, your slim face, your breasts, OK, you do have the advantage that they've only been there for ten years or so. Just a joke after midnight. To show myself how cold I am, still capable of being cool. Back there, slightly further to the right, the moon's not very full above the dark city, there's you in my apartment, my property, working. You pay your daily rent like all the others. *Hi, my name is Bella, I'm a young transsexual with a very slim, feminine body. Sweet Snow White with a little secret. Be my lover and I'll abandon myself to you.*

What season is it, even? Sometimes I think about just disappearing, dissolving into nowhere. But no, you'd like that! Sitting over in the north of the city, not far from here, behind the central station, sitting there behind your mirrors and waiting for me to disappear. *There can be only one*. But it was never like that. And weren't we friends? Business partners? Comrades? Colleagues?

'The best way to win a fight is to avoid it.' I've never said any such crap. It's true now and then, of course it is. But I've been on the side of the great Machiavelli for many years. I could discuss it with the old Count. And I hear your tinkling laugh behind the mirrors. How cultured we are today, aren't we?

'We heard you met the traitor, S.?'

'How can I have, he's dead.'

No champagne left and I take a 5-cl bottle of cognac out of the minibar. I'll drink to the Outsiders, who'll be shutting down because the competition's shooting and the cops are getting tougher, the Los Locos are in the next town and looking over at us. Farewell, Outsiders, who stood behind me now and then and also stood close to the Angels. Ach, Machiavelli. A blood-smeared car by the tracks. The phone buzzes again. A text message. The light of the fridge dazzles me. They should never put cognac in the minibar. We didn't use to give a shit about that kind of thing. I pour the liquid, VSOP, Veronica Swallows One Pint (who used to say that crap? Was it Hans?), Very Superior Old Pale, into the bulbous glass and warm it from below with my lighter. Letters and words on the screen. Property 11 closing for the night. *Evelyn – a vivacious, voluptuous vixen.* I hear you breathing behind me. Keep calm now, keep calm. As though you could sense my movements in the room and on the edge of the bed. And as though that sent your dreams somewhere else. What do I even know about you? Although you've told me so much. And I've told you too. We walk around silent for years and decades. I warm the little glass with my lighter until I almost drop it, it's got so hot. I put it on the bedside table to cool for a while. I smell the cognac.

If only everything were as simple as warming a good cognac. I've been to France on holiday with my wife, two or three times now. Biarritz. I don't want to start counting... *When princes have thought more of ease than of arms they have lost their states... For among other evils which being unarmed brings you, it causes you to be despised, and this is one of those ignominies against which a prince ought to guard himself...*

The drone of a last late or early plane reaches us. It almost seems as though the window were vibrating. The piece we listened to in our days together, over in the cube of music, wasn't it his unfinished symphony? Or that's what I read in the programme. I don't know his work well, like she thought. Or like I thought she thinks. It was just this festival, a couple of people recommended it. Had tickets. International orchestras, world-famous conductors and this old composer, almost a hundred years dead. Too much meaning in all things. *Disney World.* I must be dreaming already. What touching music. I want to lie down by your side. Am I lying down already? What's this long feather doing on the bedside table? Did *she* bring it along? I run the feather along the chained bones of her spine, up to her nape, the start of her hair, short black hair, pageboy. Innocence, little-girl-lost, deep former wounds... or whatever you'd call it. Maybe that's it. What I see in her eyes, her face. I run the feather, which seems larger and larger and wider and wider in the semi-darkness, along her back, over her arse. I gave her a book, an old rare edition. Beautiful illustrations, old copperplates. I went by myself to the antiquarian bookseller by the big city church, where I'd never been before. A children's book because she told me about it, how she wanted to be like the little girl in the book. No, not Snow White, for fuck's sake!

When we sleep: *The nasty crow won't get me here, she*

thought. It's much too big to squeeze between the trees. But I hope it stops beating its wings so hard, it's causing a storm in the forest. I throw the feather out into the darkness; it hits the floor with a tinkle.

At some point he wakes up and the door to the room is open. He can tell straight away. Before he sees it. The corridor outside in the twilight. He can't make out the numbers on his watch. He listens but all is silent. He sees the phone flashing on the bedside table. *No memory space for new messages.*

No, she's still here. She's lying on her back and he sees her open eyes. She's staring at the ceiling, so it seems. He wants to get up and go to the door. Where the shadows are. Something is warm underneath him and around him. That's when he wakes up. *Son, my son, what have you done?*

Drinking champagne. Lying beside her. He looks at the flashing of the streets, the red glow of the high chimneys on the edge of the city. He lies beside her. Strokes her face. Yes. Yes. Yes.

I'D LIKE TO GET A HORSE, ONE DAY

I don't do kissing.

In all the years I haven't done it once, not with tongues. Not without tongues either, at least not on the mouth. No, I don't do it. I let them kiss me goodbye, but only on each cheek. If they want to, but when I think about it it's only the regulars who do that. Most of them just disappear without a word.

I've got a friend, she's in the escort business, accompanying them out and that, first dinner then sex, sometimes first sex and then dinner. Posh restaurants and hotels, she says. Four stars, five stars. Sometimes just the sex. But there's always champagne, she says. I don't give a shit about champagne. Anyway, she does kissing. Even likes kissing. It's not like I don't like kissing. In private. I haven't got a boyfriend right now. So I don't do any kissing. No wait, I did have a snog at a party the other day. But with a woman. It was nice. Maybe it was the coke. I've done it a couple of times with women but that was a long time ago. She was a sweet young thing, crazy for my coke. And for me, of course. Oh yeah, for me especially. Hans said it was cradle-snatching. Hans the Hatchet, we call him, but not because he's violent or anything, just because he used to be a butcher. He's got giant hands, as big as plates. I went to bed with him a couple of times, years ago now, and he can be really gentle with his giant hands. I started out in his club back then. Or was he a slaughterer? Didn't he come from a village? It's funny I can't remember, it's a long time ago but... The thing with the party where I met him and got off with that young girl, that must be a few months ago now, maybe even six months, because his club's been closed for a while now and no one knows exactly why. Couple of girls who know him say he's buggered off down south, Mallorca, Rio or somewhere, gone into retirement. That'd do me good as well. In a couple of years. I can't remember anything, I'm always forgetting all sorts of things, whole chunks of memory are suddenly gone, I feel really funny-peculiar when I think about how much has gone missing recently. I keep meaning to go to the doctor's about it but what should I say, hello, I'm thirty-three and I'm getting Alzheimer's? It's pretty funny that Hans of all people was a butcher or a slaughterer, we used to joke about it back in the day but when someone he didn't know came along and asked him about it then Hans the Hatchet's giant hands weren't gentle at all. I saw him in action two or three times when he had to chuck a guest out or someone was kicking up a ruckus. That wasn't funny-ha-ha at all. Sometimes when I wake up I feel like I've gone back in time and it's suddenly 2002 or 2010 or 1999 again, that's when I started working – I was nineteen. A lot of nines in that year.

I told you I don't do kissing. No, you can do what you like, I'll just turn my head away. Yeah, yeah, I'll give you a blow job but only covered, I told you that as well. I'm an old-school whore! And what do I care what the others do? You're with me now, kid, and let me tell you, I'll give you a good blow, even covered. I can get it in really deep and I don't want you spilling your load down my throat. Yeah, yeah, you can put your cock really deep in my mouth, yeah, right to the hilt, don't you worry, I can deal with your cock. Yeah, yeah, even if it's gigantic, course it is. Want to know where it is on my personal cock scale? No, better not. It's fine by me that it's not such a monster. No, no BJTC and no BBBJ. Man, the kid's annoying. Wet behind the ears, a little pup of a boy – most are around thirty-five/forty upwards. Mind you, I wouldn't swear by that. I'd have to compile some statistics. Maybe I can get funding for it. The other day I had an eighty-four-year-old, or at least that's how old he said he was. Looked younger though. I'd have guessed eighty. But he had no problems getting it up, probably Viagra, used to be a soldier, he said, probably for the Führer, he fucked me standing up, from behind, he took an hour to finish and I was finished, I tell you, my legs ached for days, but I'll show this little pup how quickly he gets his bag full. Bareback blow job and blow job to completion. I don't do that. 'If I suck them off,' says my little escort babe, sometimes I think she might be just right for me, she's got lovely white skin, black hair and classy pale skin tone, I spend so much time on the sunbed you'd almost think I was black, sometimes I think of that when we meet up for a glass or two, white on brown, and how nice that must smell, 'I mean, if I suck them off I can't catch anything...'

Yeah, yeah, you clever little thing, you just suck them off and let them splash the cash in your mouth, but me...

Can he come on me, asks the greenhorn and he whimpers as he says it, like his mum's giving him a good spanking, and he twitches and fidgets in my mouth so I have to watch out I don't bite through the condom, I used to have strawberry flavour but only for a few months because it was shit, it was in summer, strawberry season, and whenever I passed a fruit stall, one of those strawberry stalls... no, it was no good. Now it's unflavoured all the way and I like the taste of strawberries again. What's the difference between a strawberry and a slut? A strawberry isn't as messy when you eat it.

Ha ha, how we laughed, me and Babsy, I mean Petra. She always tells such stupid jokes. It's crazy, I know this other girl, she calls herself Petra and her real name's Barbara, and we all call her Babsy, like the opposite of

Babsy, I mean Petra.

From the neck down, but only down to my belly, obviously, they can splash all over me if they insist, classic Cum On Body, COB, come on, boy! And I take a hygienic wipe out of the dispenser and pull off the condom and hold his cock and make sure he doesn't give me a facial.

'On your breasts, please, on your breasts!' Sure, kid, the collarbone doesn't do it for you, or what?

I wank his cock and aim it at my tits like a gun. Funny, I call them tits and he says, no, whimpers, all polite and well-mannered: 'Breasts, on your breasts please!'

I do have nice breasts. Nice tits? Tits yeah, but *nice* breasts. They're really into ejaculating on them, I'm so lovely and tanned, Copacabana, you know.

Hallelujah, kid, you must have had a lemon squeezer implanted. And another glug. You think it's all over and then you get another load. Career profile: sperm donor.

'Can you... can you rub it in?' Been watching too much porn, have we? No way, Jose. Piece of kitchen paper. One sheet does plenty.

'You're beautiful.'

Yeah, yeah, kid, I know that myself and I'm always hearing it. But a compliment in the workplace improves the working atmosphere. 'You're beautiful.' And now I do smile. He puts his head on my tits, where his cum just was, and I get the feeling he's having a sneaky sniff. Most cum smells grey.

I stroke his hair, I guess I get maternal feelings for a moment, and he tells me again how beautiful he thinks I am, and I feel the vibration of his voice between my tits. Alright, that's enough now, the little cock's crowed three times over. And do you mean me or my pussy? Because that's where the train's heading, and judging by the way he presses his hand first to my belly and then moves it down and then to my pussy, it looks like it's a one-way ticket. And he seems to like my landing strip. I had it all smooth until a while ago and it said 'smooth shaven' in my ad. I liked it actually when I was so soft and smooth.

At eleven or twelve I had this fluff, it was never as soft as that again, but it still bothered me, I wanted my smooth pussy back again, so I took my dad's razor and cut myself really badly, because my labia are pretty big and they stick out a bit, which most of them like but it's also a bit of a problem because they do so much fumbling around and I don't like that one bit, and I tell them, too, if they start doing too much fumbling.

I had to show my mother, what with all the blood. And my dad put me over his knee, once the blood had stopped flowing anyway. I didn't have my periods yet and I was already bleeding down there, and it hurt so much, not so much the smacks on the arse, OK, they did hurt a bit. Why did the old man have to put me over his knee, anyway, see, Dad, a mutilated pussy and spanks on the arse, what does that do for your career profile...?

I can still feel the tiny scar when I stroke my left labia. I wonder if the guys feel it when they lick me out? At least my private lickers. This guy Alex I was with for a while, I told him about it. The razor story. More of an affair, actually. He was a good guy, Alex was. Shame he doesn't work for the boss any more. He's with the Angels now, I've heard. I used to know this girl, she worked as a slave for a dominatrix, she had them sewn up, yeah, her labia. No one believes me when I tell them. She had all these scars, on her back and all over. I don't get it. But she was really into it, apparently. Right, that's enough, we're not in the petting zoo. I get up and go to the bathroom. Wonder how old he is – early twenties? When I was in my early twenties...

I wipe the flannel over my tits and smile at the mirror. Tall and blonde and Nordic. Hello, Miss Valkyrie. You've come a long way from Schwerin.

And I wipe the cold cloth over my face. And I look in the mirror and wipe and wipe, my shoulders and neck... and I've only gone and forgotten what I was just thinking about, hello, I'm thirty-three and my brain's sprung a leak. There was something, some stupid joke of Petra's, I mean Babsy, no, the other way round, the other one never tells jokes. I've got it now. When the boy was unloading his pint just now I remembered this stupid stoner joke. I can always spot a stoner, at the latest when he comes on me. Or let's say when he *wants* to come on me. It's not like I get hordes of stoners coming to me but there's been a few over the years. I don't mind a joint now and then, just to relax. This crazy German teacher who was a regular until a year or two ago, when he started coming he'd always want to smoke a joint. Are you crazy – not in the apartment. I don't go into his classroom and roll a giant doobie, do I? Bad enough that the geezer always started reciting poems when he wound down after his first go. It's like a dripping tap with them. The stoners. Pitter, patter, and another drop. It always spills over my hand and if they wank themselves off, some of them want to wank themselves off before they come on me, yeah baby, yeah baby, I'll give it you good, well go on then, get a move on, and pitter, patter on the sheets, although I've already got my kitchen paper at the ready. Right bloody mess. Hello, I'm a stoner and my cock's sprung a leak.

Yeah, exactly, I've got the joke now. And I won't let go of it. Three stoners, no, two stoners, sitting around at home and smoking a nice pipe or a bong if you like, anyway they're really smoking it up. And they're chatting away, you know what stoners are like. Chatting a pile of crap. But that's not important for the joke. And then the doorbell rings. And they smoke their stuff, and five minutes later the one guy goes: 'Hey, the doorbell just rang.'

'Hmm, yeah,' says the other one, 'guess you'll have to open the door then.'

'Nah,' he doesn't want to, right, 'you go.'

'OK,' says the guy, 'just a sec.' And then they go on smoking, and another five minutes pass and they look at each other. 'Didn't the doorbell just ring?'

'Right. Weren't you going to go?'

'No, you.'

'Right. OK.' And then they smoke a bit more and another five minutes go by, and then one of them gets up and goes and opens the door. And there's their stoner buddy and he's really happy. 'Wow, I only just rang the bell and the door's open already.'

I really did remember the whole joke. Usually I forget jokes instantly. Doctor, doctor, I'm thirty-three and my Alzheimer's is cured.

I go back into the treatment room and the greenhorn's only got another hard-on. You must have had a sneaky wank, you cheeky chappy, to get your money's worth out of the hourly service. 'Would you blow it again for me, please.'

Oh my! A little gentleman who knows the magic word. Nice behaviour in the workplace improves the working atmosphere. 'Sure thing,' I say and roll on a condom. He starts moaning before I even take him in my hand properly. Then I kiss him, I mean his wrapped-up cock, and then he fucks me, he lies on top of me and he's all excited and practically trembling. 'Is is good like this,' he asks, 'is it good like this?'

'Yes,' I say, 'you're doing great. Give it to me, baby.'

And he wants to kiss me again and I turn my head away, and he strokes his face over my shoulders and my neck. Then he's suddenly finished, although it wasn't such a surprise for me because I reached over his back for his balls and he goes as stiff as a board, and there's only half an hour gone by of the hour he paid for.

I stroke my pussy, it's a bit swollen because the pup's number 5. Been a good day today. And the evening's only just starting. I need to use more lube. Yesterday I was on my own almost all day. Just one after-work punter at four. He stayed for a hundred and fifty so my balance for the week's OK. Working nine to five, what a way to make a living. GS-Jürgen was supposed to come yesterday. Such an unreliable arsehole. GS-Jürgen, that's the name I've got in my work phone, and if I told anyone, which I don't do of course, discretion comes first, one way and the other, they'd probably say, 'What, Goldman Sachs Jürgen?'

No, not Goldman Sachs. Golden shower. He lies down in the bathtub and I piss on him. Then Jürgen wanks off. I make a fast buck but I have to drink pints of tea because I've got a pretty good bladder, and after that I have to give the bath a good scrub. Vinegar's the best thing. And I only ever take a bath at home.

The kid rolls off and snuggles up to me. I get up after a while and he curls up in a ball. Just like a puppy. And I tear off some of the Plenty kitchen paper, I should do adverts for them, 'One sheet for every shot! Not a drop gets lost!' And then I pull off the condom and clean his cock for him. I take a hygienic wipe out of the dispenser. 'You're...'

'Yeah, yeah,' I want to say, but then I don't. Best to

treat guests well. And I give him a slap on the arse and he's back to playing around with his limp dick again. Take your time, Rambo.

I screw up the paper with the condom in it and throw it in the little bin. The lid opens when I put my foot on the pedal. I go into the bathroom and wash my hands again. And then I lie down next to him again and smoke a cigarette. I offer him one. I never do that, usually. 'Thanks,' he says and takes the lighter. He coughs a bit when he exhales the smoke. You keep coming back to mummy, my boy, we'll soon get that sorted out. We lie around for a bit, not talking. Some of them start chatting like there's no tomorrow when they're finished and there's still a bit of time on the clock. Others can't get their clothes back on quickly enough once the condom's full. A lot of them only pay for one go. It all has its pros and cons. Endless loop in my head.

The boy's not been gone ten minutes and I've already almost forgotten what he looked like. Blond? No. Never mind. Did he give me a kiss on each cheek before he left? Yes, he did.

Maybe he'll come back again. He'd make a nice regular. But nice or naughty... I go home at night. If they were all like that it'd be easy. It is, though, pretty much. If the boss goes into retirement one day, and I've been hearing all sorts, there'd be a lot in motion again, the Angels and that, and then I could work somewhere else. Until I go into retirement as well. But I'll keep going for now. Doesn't matter where, doesn't matter who I pay my rent to. Mind you, the Old Man, the boss is a nice enough boss and I always feel safe. I'll keep going. Keep on keeping on.

He was low-maintenance, that kid. No major hatchet

job. Which reminds me of Hans the Hatchet. Wonder what he's doing these days? I wouldn't work in clubs any more. Too much booze, too much bad air. I light one up. All has its pros and... I have many stories, tales for both the young and old. I have many voices to describe many places... I hum it to myself. This cartoon guy with a guitar used to sing it on TV when I was a kid. And then there'd be a story. Some of the guests are really into prostate massage. It's the latest trend. I put my rubber gloves on. But it's better than when they go off ramming you like Black & Decker Black & Decker Black & Decker... endless loop in my head. Once I went to this twenty-four-hour bar after work with Hans, this place where they all hung out. He used to eat beef olive with red cabbage and dumplings, right at the bar. And he bought us bubbly and wine. The boss, I mean my boss now, he used to go there sometimes too. It's all got much calmer these days. The boss too, since he got out of hospital back then, but I was still working for Hans then. And once Hans buggered off, even left his beef and red cabbage, wanted to go to America. Sometimes chunks of memory open up again suddenly. But you can't forget something like that. No one ever believes the story when I tell it. Because he said it said on the toilet roll in America how often you can take a crap with it. Three hundred shits per roll, he said, but maybe it was another number.

That was *the* subject for us for a couple of months. Hans in America. Was it 2001? Such a long time ago now. And they all laughed at him, come on, three hundred shits. Because everyone craps differently, don't they? But Hans the Hatchet wouldn't let it go. It's America, isn't it, he said, it's a whole different world. And a week later he was back and he'd brought a roll with him and he plonked it down on the counter in the twenty-four-hour bar. And it really did say something about three hundred or a thousand, a pretty big number. But nothing about shits, my dear Hans. What it said was 'sheets'. As in squares of toilet paper, like on my kitchen roll. I've always been good at English. And Hans lost a whole lot of money because of course he'd bet on it, was it still deutschmarks or did we have the euro by then? He'd been to New York after the Wall fell, you know. Package trip. He often used to talk about it. Back when I started working at his place.

The phone rings. It doesn't actually ring, it's next to me in the charger and the screen just flashes like a tiny lighthouse. I turned the ringer off. I always have an eye on it. I don't answer it if I'm in the middle of working.

I pick up the remote and turn the TV down. I turned the sound up loud when the pup left, even though it was just some stupid show, with subtitles, where they match up ugly boys with ugly birds, who knows where in the world.

Current and forthcoming books by Fitzcarraldo Editions

Zone by Mathias Enard (Fiction)
Translated from French by Charlotte Mandell
'A modern masterpiece.'
— David Collard, *Times Literary Supplement*

Memory Theatre by Simon Critchley (Essay)
'A brilliant one-of-a-kind mind-game occupying
a strange frontier between philosophy, memoir
and fiction.'
— David Mitchell, author of *The Bone Clocks*

On Immunity by Eula Biss (Essay)
'A vaccine against vague and incoherent thinking.'
— Rebecca Solnit, author of *Wanderlust*

My Documents by Alejandro Zambra (Fiction)
Translated from Spanish by Megan McDowell
'Strikingly original.'
— James Wood, *New Yorker*

It's No Good by Kirill Medvedev (Essay)
Introduced by Keith Gessen
Translated by Keith Gessen, Mark Krotov,
Cory Merrill and Bela Shayevich
'Russia's first authentic post-Soviet writer.'
— Keith Gessen, co-founder of *n+1*

Street of Thieves by Mathias Enard (Fiction)
Translated from French by Charlotte Mandell
'This is what the great contemporary French novel
should be. ... Enard fuses the traditions of Camus
and Céline, but he is his own man.'
— Patrick McGuinness, author of *The Last Hundred Days*

Pond by Claire-Louise Bennett (Fiction)
'An extraordinary collection of short stories – profoundly original though not eccentric, sharp and tender, funny and deeply engaging. A very new sort of writing...'
— Sara Maitland, author of *A Book of Silence*

Nicotine by Gregor Hens (Essay)
Introduced by Will Self
Translated from German by Jen Calleja
'A luminous and nuanced exploration of how we're constituted by our obsessions, how our memories arrange themselves inside of us, and how – or if – we control our own lives.'
— Leslie Jamison, author of *The Empathy Exams*

Nocilla Dream by Agustín Fernández Mallo (Fiction)
Translated from Spanish by Thomas Bunstead
'There is something deeply strange and finally unknowable to this book, in the very best way a testament to the brilliance of Fernández Mallo.'
— Ben Marcus, author of *The Flame Alphabet*

Pretentiousness: Why It Matters by Dan Fox (Essay)
'Dan Fox makes a very good case for a re-evaluation of the word "pretentious". The desire to be more than we are shouldn't be belittled. Meticulously researched, persuasively argued – where would we be as a culture if no one was prepared to risk coming across as pretentious? Absolument nowhere, darling – that's where.'
— Jarvis Cocker

Counternarratives by John Keene (Fiction)
'Keene's collection of short and longer historical
fictions are formally varied, mould-breaking and
deeply political. He's a radical artist working in
the most conservative genres, and any search for
innovation in this year's US fiction should start here.'
— Christian Lorentzen, *Vulture*

Football by Jean-Philippe Toussaint (Essay)
Translated from French by Shaun Whiteside
'For any serious French writer who has come of age
during the last thirty years, one question imposes
itself above all others: what do you do after the
nouveau roman? ... Foremost among this group,
and bearing that quintessentially French distinction
of being Belgian, is Jean-Philippe Toussaint.'
— Tom McCarthy, author of *Satin Island*

Second-hand Time by Svetlana Alexievich (Essay)
Winner of the Nobel Prize in Literature 2015
Translated from Russian by Bela Shayevich
'In this spellbinding book, Svetlana Alexievich
orchestrates a rich symphony of Russian voices
telling their stories of love and death, joy and sorrow,
as they try to make sense of the twentieth century,
so tragic for their country.'
— J. M. Coetzee, winner of the Nobel Prize in
Literature 2003

The Hatred of Poetry by Ben Lerner (Essay)
'Reading Ben Lerner gives me the tingle at the base
of my spine that happens whenever I encounter a writer
of true originality. He is a courageous, immensely
intelligent artist who panders to no one and yet is
a delight to read.'
— Jeffrey Eugenides, author of *The Marriage Plot*

A Primer for Cadavers by Ed Atkins (Fiction)
'Discomfited by being a seer as much as an elective mute, Ed Atkins, with his mind on our crotch, careens between plainsong and unrequited romantic muttering. Alert to galactic signals from some unfathomable pre-human history, vexed by a potentially inhuman future, all the while tracking our desperate right now, he do masculinity in different voices – and everything in the vicinity shimmers, ominously.'
—— Bruce Hainley, author of *Under the Sign of [sic]*

Nocilla Experience by Agustín Fernández Mallo (Fiction)
Translated from Spanish by Thomas Bunstead
'With this bitter-sweet, violently poetic dream, Agustín Fernández Mallo establishes himself as the most original and powerful author of his generation in Spain.'
—— Mathias Enard, author of *Zone*

The Doll's Alphabet by Camilla Grudova (Fiction)
'Imagine a world in which the Brothers Grimm were two exquisite, black-eyed twin sisters in torn stockings and hand-stitched velvet dresses. Knowing, baroque, perfect, daring, clever, fastidious, Camilla Grudova is Angela Carter's natural inheritor. Her style is effortlessly spare and wonderfully seductive. Read her! Love her! She is sincerely strange – a glittering literary gem in a landscape awash with paste and glue and artificial settings.'
—— Nicola Barker, author of *Darkmans*

This book has been selected to receive financial assistance from English PEN's 'PEN Translates' programme, supported by Arts Council England. English PEN exists to promote literature and our understanding of it, to uphold writers' freedoms around the world, to campaign against the persecution and imprisonment of writers for stating their views, and to promote the friendly co-operation of writers and the free exchange of ideas.

www.englishpen.org

Fitzcarraldo Editions
243 Knightsbridge
London, SW7 1DN
United Kingdom

ISBN 978-1-910695-19-7

Design by Ray O'Meara
Typeset in Fitzcarraldo
Printed and bound by Nørhaven, Denmark

The translation of this work was supported by
a grant from the Goethe-Institut London

Fitzcarraldo Editions